Indigo Dusk

By Kristy Nicolle

Queens of Fantasy Saga
The Aetherial Embrace- Book 7

Trigger Warning:

Chapter Fourteen's concluding scene contains graphic sexual assault which may be distressing for some readers.

First published by Kristy Nicolle, United Kingdom, April 2020

QUEENS OF FANTASY EDITION (1st EDITION)

Published April 2020 by Kristy Nicolle

Edited By- Jaimie Cordall

Adult Paranormal/Fantasy Romance

The right of Kristy Nicolle to be identified as author of this Work has been asserted by her in accordance with sections 77 and 78 of the Copyright, Designs and Patents Act 1988.

ISBN: 978-1-911395-21-8

www.kristynicolle.com

HIGH LORDS & LADIES CHARACTER GUIDE

FAE

FAE OF NIGHT- KINDRED OF APOLLO
HIGH LADY HYPNOS
HIGH LORD MORPHEUS
HIGH LADY KODIAK NGUYEN
HIGH LORD ALISTAIR SOL

FAE OF LIGHT- KINDRED OF APHRODITE
HIGH LORD PHINEAS BECKETT (FALL)
HIGH LORD QUINN ARLET (SPRING)
HIGH LADY NEVE EIRWEN (WINTER)
HIGH LADY EMBER CYRUS (SUMMER)

DRACONIANS

DRACONIAN- KINDRED OF HECATE
HIGH LADY GENEVIEVE THOMAS
HIGH LORD LUCIEN DELAURENT

DRACONIANS- KINDRED OF NEMESIS
HIGH LADY ANASTASIA DRAGOS
HIGH LORD GAGE LEE

EQUINIANS

ARESIAN EQUINIANS- Kindred of Ares
High Lord/Chieftain Asher Oswald
High Lord/Chieftain Landon John Archard

ARTEMISIAN EQUINIANS- Kindred of Artemis
High Lady Aliandara Montgomery
High Lady Evangeline Senft

SEPHILIM AND NEPHILIM

SEPHILIM- Kindred of Zeus
High Lord Aro Black
High Lord Caleb Abara

NEPHILIM- Kindred of Hera
High Lady Storm Shaw (Deceased)
High Lady Harmony Baker (Deceased)

This one is for all the chronic pain and invisible illness warriors.

Never forget who you are.

PROLOGUE

HERA'S DEFIANCE

THIS STORY, YOU WILL be surprised to discover, does not start with Hera.

Not at all.

No, this story, in fact, begins with Prometheus.

Prometheus had always been close to Zeus. Perhaps closer than either of the god's brothers could claim to be. The two were thick as thieves, best friends, and yet still, Prometheus found himself coveting Zeus' devoted worshippers.

It was nothing personal against the King of the Gods, but Prometheus longed to be unconditionally adored too. He longed to leave his mark and to make sure he was remembered.

Zeus was world-renowned, made so through art, literature and poetry as inspired by the muses, as well as being the chosen God of the people of the Lower Plains.

In fact, he was so well known that even though the ancient Greeks had long since fallen to the Romans, there were still many who adored him among mortals.

Despite the stellar reputation of his best friend, Prometheus was still virtually a stranger to the religious canon of the Lower Plains; a fact he felt like a consistent weight upon his shoulders.

He found his solution, or what he believed to be, not in one individual but in many. He looked over to one of Olympus' bordering nations, The Eternal Kingdom, and observed a force of divine beings that were not jealous, nor envious, but simply pure, devoted, and yet full of power. They worked well together and served one known only as Him without thought or question. They were called the Seraphim, and as winged beings of total divinity, he was in awe of their diligence to their master.

Prometheus knew that these creatures were not High Born. Oh no, they had come from the earth, from Gaia's lands, made immortal by their master after a lifetime of servitude in His name.

Prometheus was decided then — he would raise his own force of these Seraphim, their immortality his blessing, sourced from his spirit, and they would spread his message, worship, and serve him. The Seraphim, he dreamed, would elevate him so he might be revered just as much as, if not more than, Zeus.

In order to bless mortals with some of his power, he needed the Immortal Flame, a gift given to Zeus after the fall of Cronus. The flame would allow him to segment some of his innate power, to bless his chosen mortals. And so, he took his plans to Zeus, hoping his best friend would sympathise with his plight and aid in his quest for notoriety.

This, of course, was naïve folly.

Zeus laughed at Prometheus, sure that giving mortals immortal life was insane. He claimed sharing his power would allow them to rise and challenge the gods and that no diligent follower or believer could be made from this method. Humans, said Zeus, are too unstable to have access to such power. They will only destroy themselves in the end.

At these words, Prometheus' covetous heart, a thing which had plagued his soul with consequent guilt for many years, mutated into an unstoppable force, no longer held at bay by the god's moral compass, but set wild and free by his rage instead.

And so, that night, Prometheus made his choice and stole the flame from Zeus' secret vault by force.

Then, he fled and did as he had proposed, creating the very first Kindred, the Seraphim of Prometheus. He took the chosen men from across the globe, picking them for their devotion to servitude. They rose with the sun upon the dawn of a new Earth day, transformed but in a world that remained the same as it had always been.

Upon discovering what Prometheus had done and what had been stolen from him, Zeus flew into one of his infamous wild rages. Though, it was not like any Olympus had felt before because Prometheus had been Zeus' friend.

Determined to make an example of him, he sentenced Prometheus to torment down in The Underworld and sent Nemesis' daughter, Thanatos, to carry out this interim sentence until he could decide how to rid the universe of Prometheus' treacherous soul forever.

Next, Zeus turned to the abominations Prometheus had unleashed upon Gaia's Kingdom. He knew he could not leave the Seraphim to walk the mortal plains, for it put magic too close to the average man and gave them power to rebel against the Gods, just as he had warned Prometheus it would.

Zeus now looked to the final gift his mother had given him. Her final gift of protection to her sons in death.

It was called Aetheria.

After the fall of her husband Cronus, Rhea and her sister Aether had decided their time among The Higher Plains was done. They used their life energy and created a barrier between The Lower and Higher Plains as a final act of protection to keep Cronus from further troubling his sons. Their magic was pure, great, and created a pocket dimension called Aetheria that was rich in magic.

Zeus, placing the Seraphim of Prometheus here, forgot about them for nearly ten years until one day he received word that they were trying to free their creator from his torturous prison down in the underworld.

Outraged, Zeus knew he must rid himself of both Prometheus and his Kindred once and for all. He took Prometheus and decided to end his existence altogether, placing his ashes and soul across two different dimensions so that they might never find one another.

To guard his ashes, and to rid him of the Seraphim, Zeus created his own Kindred, the Sephilim. This race of dark angels shared his power to wield the lightning of the skies and rose in a force unlike anything the Seraphim of Prometheus could have ever imagined.

Hera, meanwhile, watched the Sephilim and Seraphim go to battle, knowing that while the Sephilim would surely triumph, creating Kindred of such strength and power-hungry personalities, Zeus would surely lose control of them from afar.

She was, of course, correct.

The Sephilim did indeed triumph, dethroning the Seraphim and leaving them little more than extinct.

Then, Brutus, the very first of Zeus' Kindred, took the throne for himself without pause. Hera watched on as over the following days the men beneath him split into sects, devising ways to usurp the king and take the throne for themselves.

Civil wars erupted between the Sephilim with many being killed in the most brutal of ways, leaving Zeus' army upon Aetheria floundering as each day brought the spilling of more blessed blood.

This, thought Hera, *needs a woman's touch.*

She asked Zeus if he might allow her to create her own Kindred, so as she mellowed her husband, they might mellow the violent and ambitious Sephilim. Perhaps by gaining lovers, they might feel they had more to lose, and the fighting would cease or at least be saved as a last-resort solution. Perhaps the women in their lives might even inspire more civilised politics.

Zeus, of course, laughed at his wife.

She knew nothing of such matters, being merely a goddess.

This vexed her, and so being Hera, Queen of Olympus, she naturally defied her husband and took the Immortal Flame to hand, creating the very first of her own Kindred. Harmonia, the first Nephilim, and the winged female equivalent to her husband's Sephilim was born.

Despite his anger at the stubborn woman, Zeus wanted more than anything to prove her wrong, so he decided to forgive his wife and let them watch how the situation developed together.

Harmonia predictably enraptured Brutus, who was hanging on to the throne of Aetheria at this time through mere stubborn will alone.

She did as Hera had expected, placating him, melting his heart and making him take a moment before crying out decrees that would lead to more precious Kindred being lost.

Years passed, and all seemed peaceful as Brutus had seemingly gained the respect of his people at last. Zeus could not deny his wife's triumph, and so the Nephilim continued to increase in number.

All was well.

This was, until one day Brutus finally met his end at the hand of none other than his beloved Harmonia. She, it seemed, had grown tired of constantly trying to talk him down from the ledge of decreeing the decimation and destruction of his own people behind the closed doors of their bedchamber, knowing now that he could not be changed at his core. She felt her failure to Hera like lead in her heart and saw no other way to carry out her duty to the Goddess.

Zeus took the news to his wife, smug as ever, but as he relayed Brutus' obituary, Hera heard the cries of Harmonia, all the way from Aetheria.

Hurrying to the looking-glass chamber, she gazed down upon Aetheria and found Harmonia, sobbing, in a puddle of her lover's blood.

It seemed from the dagger clutched in her palm that she had, indeed, murdered him.

"Hera, Queen of Olympus, why have you forsaken me so? For no woman could truly love, nor change a King of death crowned by violence and baptised as monarch in blood. All he ever had to do to prove himself worthy of the crown was the cold-blooded murder of another— how can this be your will? No immortal king championing the agenda of peace can ever be birthed from war. Don't you see what folly such a task is as mine?"

Hera thought on this, running her long languid fingers down the ample curve of her defiant jawline. She looked next to the Aetherial crown, tinged scarlet in a pool of Brutus' cold blood where it had fallen from his head.

She knew what she had to do.

That night, long after Zeus had retired to bed, no doubt to dream of another, Hera went about cursing the Crown of Aetheria.

No King would be crowned unless coronated willingly by a marked Nephilim of her choosing.

In order to be worthy of the throne, the heir would have to win the heart of her chosen Nephilim, one which would be known this day forth as Heirbound.

The crown could not be taken by force any longer, nor could it be stolen by manipulative cunning. Now, it could only be laid upon the King's head by a Nephilim, chosen by Hera for her gentility, grace, and value of immortal life.

Hera smiled, as ever defiant, thinking next upon the joy she would gather from her Husband's undoubted and inevitable fury.

I

THE GREEN FAIRY BOOK

KAIRI

THE SCALES SHEEN LIKE rain slick whetstone, refracting the intense light of the surrounding cavern. My palms sweat, slipping against the heavy crystals inlaid into the metal handle of my sword, biceps aching.

Whirling, the world tilts on its axis as the dragon before me allows its jaws to spread wide in time with my pupils, a sound of primal beastly fury shattering several stained-glass windows. Kaleidoscopic glass explodes from where it was just moments before filling gaps in the crystal walls, which throw my trembling reflection back at me a million times over. Adrenaline hits my bloodstream, curdling with my fear, heart pounding harder against the inside of my ribcage, and yet my legs remain steadfast beneath me.

I duck, feeling shards of glass pepper my face and snag in my hair, shielding my eyes as I move on pure instinct.

It rears while the enormous talons attached to its onyx front feet flash violet, catching the moonlight pouring unfiltered through the glassless windows behind me.

I step back, a sign of weakness, breath coming in and shallow wisps. The air around me chills and I brace myself against the vibration of the very rock beneath my feet as the beast lands back on all fours with a deafening crash. The scent of wintergreen fills my nostrils, causing my mind to sharpen as I realise that attempting to face the dragon is futile. Its sinuous wings spread wide, veins illuminated as though the entire wingspan is made from charred leaves by the hematite chandelier that dangles, glinting gold overhead.

I take another step back as the beast tosses its head from left to right in anger, talons digging deep into the single cerulean plane of the floor, holding me captive then with its gaze.

Blackness consumes me, the pupil of the dragon a starless void, a chasm fractured from all light that causes the last of my courage to evaporate as though it were never more tangible than smoke. In that split second, I feel all bravery slip through my fingers before rising fast into the atmosphere above, never to be seen again.

My sword falls from my grasp, fingers succumbing to fear-induced atrophy as they drop slack against the cold gold of my armoured thigh. The blade sings on impact, lamenting its own uselessness and reflecting a slice of my reflection up at me, capturing only my terrified stare, the epitome of my paralysed expression.

I turn, hair flying out around me in dark tangled tresses, as I give one final glance back at the nightmarish scene behind me, finally finding the strength to push myself into forward motion.

Mid-pivot, something catches my attention, a figure barely visible in the shadow of a far corner. His hair boasts a dim viridian sheen in the half-light, eyes contemplative and surreal as I take him in for only a moment.

If I had longer, his strangeness would surely stop me in my tracks, but I don't have time to wonder who he is or why he's here.

Fight or flight had always seemed like a choice, a decision one makes that determines who you really are.

Now though, I know it's primal inevitability, an urge that runs so deep we cannot break free from it any more easily than a hummingbird trapped in a gilded Victorian cage.

And so, with that thought in the back of my mind and my blood pounding fast in my ears, I run.

"Kairi, medication!"

I startle awake at the sound of my Pa's voice, an old leather-bound copy of *The Green Fairy Book* by Andrew Lang propped open and heavy against my aching ribcage.

"Okay—" I hear myself speak, cottonmouth making the words sloppy and inarticulate.

Buttery sunlight falls across my chest, warming the lavender tartan blanket covering my now stiff limbs, joints full of broken glass. I sit up, shoulders creaking, neck twinging and causing an electric shock, no doubt due to a trapped nerve, to fizzle down my spine without mercy. My eyes, still heavy with sleep, fall closed again as the ache I'm so used to comes back to me fully.

I shouldn't have slept in the window seat, should have known better than to head into one of my old favourites for easy night-time reading under the moonlight. I had wanted respite from the pain of yesterday, but my carelessness will most likely cost me today's comfort as well.

You know better. I scold myself, stretching and hearing my elbows click, a rush of pain sparking down each of my forearms in turn.

Most twenty-three-year-olds don't have to think about making this kind of bargain with their body. But I am not like most twenty-three-year-olds.

I'm a Zebra, suffering from Ehlers Danlos Syndrome, a connective tissue disorder that has reduced my life to exactly this. Bargaining, pacing, compromising, never quite knowing how I will feel five minutes from now or if I'll feel the same even five minutes after that.

The diagnosis had changed everything, and I'm still too devastated to hide it or hope that I'll come out the other side.

Even if I do, I know I won't be the same woman I was going in.

I push the thoughts of my painful evolution down deep, ignoring the shame that comes with admitting how weak I've become, how much my body is failing me for someone so young.

Catticus Finch, my stocky ginger tomcat, eyes me from the floral violet cotton of my bedspread, not impressed by his lack of a human heater for the night. His eyes are startlingly lime, watching my hunched frame with superior reproach as his fat tail swishes left and right, disturbing dust that catches like glitter in the early morning Tennessee sun.

I sigh out, pushing from the padded baby blue window seat that looks out over the balcony, which wraps fully around the outside of the attic of the converted barn. The scent of coffee climbs the stairs, creeping beneath the heavy oak of the door and rising until it settles just beneath the wide beams supporting the steep apex of the ceiling. The beams are wrapped in fairy-lights, my attempt to bring the night sky I love so much indoors when I can't leave my bed, the floor scattered with piles of books that don't fit into my multiple and overflowing bookshelves.

I'm wearing only a pair of boy shorts and a baggy t-shirt, so quickly tug on some soft navy yoga pants and my oversized UCLA sweatshirt. Glancing in the mirror as I pass, I find the grey tone of my skin and my glassy periwinkle gaze staring back. My hip is agony as the floorboards creak underfoot, my heart plummeting as I take in what I barely recognise as my own face anymore.

I look like crap, the same as yesterday and the day before, and so yank my long caramel hair up into a messy bun and turn my back on the disappointment in my expression as I yawn and walk with painful slowness toward the door.

9

I take the stairs down to the main floor with excruciating care, the place still not feeling quite like home despite the fact I've been living here for the last six months. My knees complain right along with my ankles, but I ignore it, choosing instead to focus on the twirling wooden ceiling fan that hangs over the great room, blanketed gold by the light of the early hour.

"Morning, sleepyhead," my dad, Michael, calls with familiar gruffness from the kitchen as he hears my slow amble down the creaking wooden stairs.

My hand clings to the railing as I fight my crappy lack of balance, brain still foggy from sleep and eyes burning against the too-bright glare of sun-drenched wood.

"Hey—" My voice cracks, and I know I should say something more, but I can't find the energy just yet.

Even breathing in and out is effort, my mind becoming once again used to pacing the crumbling cage in which it's trapped, rattling angrily on the bars.

Catticus overtakes me as I reach the fourth stair from the bottom, trotting onto the plush bohemian rugs that are piled haphazardly across the floor of the open-plan living room, his orange butt wiggling with natural feline sass.

As I hit the ground floor, I make a half-turn to face the kitchen, finding my dad making breakfast and Matthew, my pa, sitting at the table reading the news on his iPad.

The entire space is carved from gleaming rich oak, carrying the scent of sawdust as it mingles with the coffee that Pa is drinking while he gazes at me with contemplative attentiveness. The expression is familiar and expects a status report as I step fully into the kitchen, but all I can do is give him a small smile.

I slip into my usual seat beside his, tired of standing already. Here, a barrage of luminous orange pill bottles, caps off, are lined up next to a glass of water atop the chunky farmhouse table, waiting.

"Sleep well?" he enquires at my lack of greeting, covering my hand gently with his and looking up as his eyes cloud with familiar care and sympathy. I plaster a smile on my face, slipping my hand quickly from beneath his, not wanting to worry him.

"I did, thanks."

Across the table, my dad pulls a bowl with a peach floral pattern around the rim from the microwave within seconds of it eliciting a high-pitched ping that rattles around my skull. It's too early for my body to process any kind of intense sensory input, and it causes goosebumps to rise on my arms, leaving my stomach churning like a storm-tossed sea.

I wrap one fist in my sleeve, gritting my teeth as I pick up the glass in front of me and take a sip as distraction. The cold water rushes down my throat, making my eyes water and teeth tingle before settling in my stomach, icy and foreign.

As I set the glass back down, dad places a bowl of oatmeal topped with blueberries and honey in front of me, steaming.

"Pills—" Pa reminds me in a pretend offhanded tone, looking up from the screen he's holding in his dextrous hands and gesturing to the luminous bottles with his eyes.

I feel my jaw tense against the ache it constantly provides.

It's impossible not to feel infantilised with a condition like this because often I need help doing things that even a child could manage. Frustration seeps into my subconscious, causing an icy clarity to fall over everything, rage waking me with more effectiveness than any pill.

I want to say something, to scream that after a year of dealing with this day in and day out that I know the drill, but I also know that he cares and that he's doing everything he can.

So, I take the pills.

Swallowing all seven with water, I watch as my dad circles behind his husband, delivering a swift kiss to his stubbled cheek before sitting down to join us with his breakfast.

"Got any clients today?" I ask as he lifts a glass of freshly squeezed orange juice to his lips. He swallows, almond-hued eyes widening substantially and nodding with enthusiasm.

"Yes, I have! A veteran actually. I think we are going to work with Archie for a bit. He's the most laid back of the lot, so I figured we'd start there," he explains, voice thick with pulp, and I smile for the first time this morning with genuine pleasure. My body finally relaxes as I slump back against my seat. I pop a blueberry into my mouth, savouring the cool juices as they burst over my tongue in a tart torrent, thoughtful as usual.

I don't know why, but I spend my waking hours either lost in the past, trying to make sense of the narrative that has brought me to where I am today, or the narrative created by authors I've never met. Indulging the present and practising mindfulness as so many of my therapists have preached seems impossible, and what's more, unimaginably painful.

11

I have enough of that already.

I lean forward again, twirling my spoon slowly in my palm and taking in the faces of the two men who raised me as their own. My dad, Mike, is well groomed, dark hair slicked and divided by a clean side-parting. He can usually be found wearing any number of obnoxiously loud band t-shirts paired with tight-fitting jeans. Matthew, however, is almost the polar opposite. I guess what you'd expect from a successful PhD in media and journalism. Hair wild and caramel coloured like my own, his green eyes always pop from his face, contrasted by the crisp button-ups he wears, collar sharp enough to cut you.

Both my parents had been screenwriters back in LA, but since the move, Mike, the younger of the two, has set himself up as an independent trauma counsellor, specialising in Equine therapy. We have six horses in the stables around back and miles of land on every side that are home to four separate paddocks for use by clients. It still amazes me the insane difference in property value as you move farther from the west coast. I mean, our house in LA hadn't been small, but it was nowhere near this big and probably worth at least twice the amount if not more.

I observe their tired smiles, thinking about everything they've sacrificed, and popping a half spoonful of oatmeal into my mouth, stomach grumbling in anticipation.

When I was diagnosed, they sold the house I grew up in, and we moved across the country so I could be close to Nashville and the best doctor in the country for my condition.

They had left their lives, friends, jobs, everything— to help me live a better life.

This is not the first time I have felt guilty, and I know it won't be the last.

It has been such a long road to this place as getting diagnosed alone took twelve months. I mean, being adopted hadn't helped as I have no known medical history, and the genetics of my biological parents remain an inconvenient mystery. My reality was reduced to hospital visit after hospital visit for a year while dealing with multiple dislocations, excruciating pain, and fatigue every single day. I was exhausted from it all, and I still am.

Nobody had answers for the pain until one day, the three words I try not to think about came into my life, changing how I perceive everything.

Ehlers Danlos Syndrome.

I didn't expect the answer to come with no cure either. I didn't expect to have to give up everything I'd worked for at UCLA in securing funding for a master's degree because my new reality meant that making it to lectures and staying awake was impossible without being bedridden the next day.

Everything changed, just like that, and yet the one thing that stayed the same was my parents' unconditional love for me.

My heart becomes leaden as my mind whirs back into the anxious, self-loathing cycle it seems to occupy all too often these days. Staring at them now as we eat breakfast like any other family across America, I know I don't deserve them because of the burden I've become.

They didn't ask for this when they found me on that beach, an abandoned baby squalling on an incoming tide in a handwoven basket made from palm leaves and cane.

It was a miracle I'd even been found alive and not washed up dead, let alone that the couple who just so happened to run across me decided to adopt me as their daughter.

Stirring the honey deeper into my oatmeal, I chew my bottom lip and feel my leg beginning to jiggle beneath the table.

I'm such a mess, and yet the two men sitting in front of me haven't ever given up on me, not once. My eyes tear up, and I wonder if I've reached the point in my life now where I just start randomly bawling into my breakfast.

My Pa notices my sudden drop in mood, an all-too-common occurrence, and clears his throat.

"You know what day it is?" he asks me, a coy smile upturning the left corner of his mouth.

"Warehouse Wednesday? Already?" I ask, perking up immediately. I lose track of the days so easily I hadn't even realised.

"That it is!" he grins, taking a sip of coffee from his cliché I heart L.A. mug.

The world seems to right itself suddenly, my mind flooding with those feel-good chemicals I'm always desperate for.

"Wheelchair or braces?" he asks me, not making eye contact as the question comes tumbling out into the air. My breath catches in my throat as I eye the wheelchair I hate so much, propped innocuously by the back door behind him.

I don't want to need it, but I don't know if after last night I'll be able to make it around the enormous used bookstore in my knee braces.

"Wheelchair," I bite out, not catching his gaze as I heap another spoon full of oatmeal and blow on it, dispelling the heat.

"I thought so. You look— exhausted. Are you really okay, did you sleep okay?" Pa asks me, mouth thinning as he holds his breath.

He knows I hate it when he asks.

My dad looks between us both, spoon frozen halfway to his lips as the air thickens with discomfort.

"I'm fine, just tired. Really. Please, don't worry," I reply, the answer not even truly meant but just default.

Tired just doesn't even cover it.

It takes just over an hour before I'm finally sitting in the driver's seat of my trusty orange pickup truck also known as The Tangerine Terror, Pa loading my wheelchair into the back. My fingers caress the curve of the steering wheel as I eye myself in the rear-view mirror. My cheeks have finally coloured up a little, thanks to the food and medication, not to mention the fact that I look forward to this exact trip every single week.

The ranch sprawls out on all sides beyond the windshield heather, lavender, and wildflowers swaying gently beneath the golden sun as the silhouettes of horses, just fed and released from their stables, gallop free against the horizon.

"Okay, all loaded up! Let's go." Pa smiles at me as he clambers into the passenger seat, yanking on his seatbelt. I tear my eyes from the easy grace of the horses, dark tails streaming behind them like inky ribbons in the distance, focusing on the task at hand.

Hearing the click of pa's belt engaging, I start the ignition and lean back into my seat, enjoying the familiar low rumble of the engine. Then, after a deep breath and a few last-minute checks, I begin the drive down the long stone road that winds between Hickory Oaks' surrounding fields.

Driving feels foreign at first seeing as I only really get behind the wheel on Wednesdays now, but eventually, I relax my tense posture, the tall oaks on either side of the path coming at increasingly sparse intervals the closer toward the main road I crawl, listening to the gravel crunching beneath the freshly pumped tyres.

"So how do you like Old Hickory?" Pa asks, making conversation as I check both up and down the road for oncoming traffic, neck twingeing.

"It's fine— The ranch, I mean. Hickory Oaks, it's beautiful." I stick out my tongue, concentrating as I straighten onto the highway.

"I fucking hate it here," he confesses, and I feel my head snap sideways, a shooting pain zipping down my left trapezius. My Pa never swears.

He catches my startled expression and sighs.

"Sorry, I shouldn't have— I just, I had to say it to someone," he admits, and I feel my mouth turn up at one side.

"Don't worry. I fucking hate it here too—" I admit, and he smiles, mirroring my expression with twinkling eyes.

"I know. It's just so—" he begins, and I nod in agreement before finishing his sentence.

"Rural?" I ask him, eyebrow arching.

"Exactly. I miss— the noise and the bustle of L.A. There was so much going on, and now I'm just stuck searching for a new job, with my own thoughts, surrounded by grass on all sides."

I smile, remembering walking L.A.'s perfectly angular concrete jungle with a latte in hand and shades shielding me from the unending sun. I just know the smell of gasoline, the sea intermingled with expensive perfume, and the constant honking of angry drivers in the clutches of road rage will be something that will always be an intrinsic part of me, no matter where I sleep at night.

I miss the city— the sense that just by living there you were in the centre of everything important in the world— but it's more than that.

"I miss it— I just, those last few months— the noise— it was too much for me sensory-wise. I was constantly overloaded when I was out. It made even going out to grab a coffee painful," I remind him, realising that perhaps I don't miss L.A. quite as much as I thought.

Perhaps, in fact, I miss the person I was when I grew up there, before the chronic pain, before the medication, when it was just me and my books, future sprawled out in front of me like flawless raw silk. Sensuous and alluring.

Now when I think about my future, it looks like a tangle of thorny vines, shredding what I had once thought was coming into delicate smithereens instead.

"I know, honey. This isn't your fault. When me and your dad became your parents, we knew we would always put your needs first, and faced with the same choice I'd do exactly what we did again in a heartbeat. I just wish I could find a damn job is all. I'm not great at sitting around playing house." He smirks, and I roll my eyes, knowing the utter truth of this sentiment only too well.

My Pa is a great writer, an amazing dancer, is fantastic at chess, and has a knack for being able to predict who will win America's Next Top Model, but a man of leisure he is not. He gets restless so easily, and where dad is far more laid back and spontaneous, Pa has always been a strenuous planner.

"I'm sorry—" I admit. He shakes his head, eyes becoming fierce.

"Don't you dare. I love you more than anything, sweetheart. You know I'd do anything for you." He places a hand on my shoulder as we devour tarmac beneath the tyres, and I smile at him, though I can't quite make my eyes sparkle like they should.

We pass the rest of the journey in thoughtful silence, a father and his daughter lost in a nostalgic sea of what had been and everything we've left behind.

After around a forty-five-minute drive, I pull The Tangerine Terror into the parking lot of my favourite place in Tennessee; *The Book Lover's Warehouse.*

The building is nothing special to look at from the outside, a simple, squat, one-story, metal-framed warehouse that sprawls the entire width of the parking lot with a corrugated roof, but inside lies buried treasure for people like me.

Wasting no time, I pull into a parking spot close to the double glass doors, turn off the ignition, and wait for Pa to unclick his seatbelt before opening the passenger side door and stepping out into the midday heat of summer.

Lines of hot air waver above the tarmac in my rear-view mirror as his door slams, filling the truck with the scent of baking dust, which I inhale deeply. Knowing then I've been cooped up in the ranch far too long, I proceed to watch my father haul the wheelchair from the back of the truck.

I take the moment he's setting it up to slump back in my seat, ankles and wrists stiff from over-use during the drive. My neck aches too, so I do a few simple stretches to try and alleviate the pain. They don't work, not that I expected them to, but at least I tried, and even the illusion of control over my body and condition is better than giving up altogether.

Pa wheels the chair round, and I yank the keys from the ignition, my bookworm keychain - that actually looks like a little glow-worm with glasses – tinkling as my palm closes around it. He opens my door for me, and I step out slowly, the heat sticking to me like cling film as my feet hit the ground and my knees protest with a loud creak.

I don't waste much time, not thinking about the connotations of the wheelchair as Pa closes my door for me and I take a seat.

It confused people at first, before we moved here, when I first started using the chair because I don't need it all the time. Most people think that wheelchairs are only for the immobile elderly or the permanently paralysed, and that caused me problems when it came to my friends.

They didn't understand why some days I needed it, and others I could walk. I look fine, just like anyone else, and it wasn't long before I started to see their impatient, not-so-secretly exchanged glances. What was worse was catching the ends of comments like:

'Why can't she just walk?'

'Must be nice to have someone else to push you—'

The memory of their ignorance is painful, and though I'd had a thriving social life once, I try not to think about that anymore. Everyone I'd been so sure would be in my life forever turned out to be not quite as permanent as I'd thought, not that I really blame them.

I mean, who wants to be friends with someone whose pastimes include mandatory afternoon naps and repeatedly cancelling plans at the last minute?

It's easier for me to ignore the pain of their betrayal if I place the blame on myself rather than their lack of empathy.

Pa wheels me forward, taking a gentle left curve as we move to a part of the sidewalk with a low curb where he tilts me back and then pushes forward. I hear his breath catch at the exertion, causing a pang of guilt to resonate through my already tired body.

Soon we are through the glass double doors and inside what I'd like to think of as my haven.

We pass from the squeaky linoleum of the entryway plastered with posters advertising local book groups, self-published authors, and charity coffee mornings, and onto the soft padding of worn crimson carpet, the building hotter than I remember with only a few free-standing fans dotted around the interior and no air conditioning.

"Kairi, I was wondering when you'd show up!" The familiar voice of Mr Chaikowsky brings an unintended smile to my face, causing my left cheek to dimple in the way it has for as long as I can remember.

"Hi," I blush, feeling a little embarrassed by the chair. I haven't used it the last four or five Wednesdays we've visited, opting for braces instead, and making me wonder if I'll have to justify why I'm sitting in it now.

Pa turns me right, toward the checkout where Mr. Chaikowsky is leaning forward on weathered elbows, sheathed in skin that maintains the appearance of age-crumpled pages. His cloudy blue eyes fall beneath the lower rim of his half-moon spectacles, taking me in with a relaxed smile.

To my relief, he doesn't comment on the chair.

"Looking for anything in particular today?" he asks, face genuinely intrigued, and I shrug.

"Who knows, I like being surprised—" I admit, my shyness rearing its head as I bite down hard on my bottom lip.

My neck twinges as I continue to stare up at him beyond the sharp ninety-degree edge of the cashier's counter.

"I wish I had a hundred more customers who love paperbacks as much as you do. E-readers are just not the same, I tell you— nothing compares to that old book smell. Let me know if you need anything, alright?" He gives me a firm nod, and I return the gesture, inhaling the scent of the warehouse.

After a moment of silence, the chair turns to face the maze of freestanding shelves that are quite literally packed to bursting with books of every size and shape, I hear the owner pick up his current read behind me, returning to whatever story he was lost in before I arrived.

The smell of books is otherworldly to me and has been for as long as I can remember, especially in places like these where all the volumes are second-hand. Dust from the places a volume has seen, the acidity of eager fingers left behind on pages long since turned, paper, ink— the spine glue. There's nothing else like it, and it calms me completely.

"Where to? Independent authors first?" Pa enquires and I nod, silent, my eyes skimming over the thousands of spines as we glide through the maze of shelves, wheels muted on the carpet.

We are the only people in the entire store, not surprising as the parking lot was empty, and I revel in the simple quiet, the calm that only comes from being surrounded by stories, by the physical portals to worlds waiting to be discovered.

Reaching the back of the store where the independently published books are kept, Pa slows his step, allowing me to examine the first shelf as I run a finger along a multitude of fantasy romance novels.

"Ooh, this looks good, what do you think?" My Pa hands me a thick paperback with a dragon climbing a pentagram, surrounded by a jade and ominous sky. The cover reads; *Rise of The Realms: Reborn* by D. Fischer. I turn it over in my palms, skimming the blurb.

"Looks like a good complex storyline," I give my assessment, and Pa laughs, finding me predictable.

"You always have loved the fairy-tale-esque—" he comments, and I shrug, trying not to think on the girl who used to wear floaty dresses and heels, the girl who enjoyed putting on makeup and didn't come out in a rash from any and all synthetic chemicals and fabric. I mean, I can't even wear jeans anymore, and I feel like the person he's remembering has been replaced by an alien.

"I forgot to pick up a basket at the door— Hang on, I'll be right back. You'll be okay for a second?" He bends down, looking me in the face, expression fixed with anxiety.

"You kidding? You could drive off and commit a murder, and I wouldn't notice until they closed," I joke, mouth curving a little in the corners, and he emits an unrestrained chuckle.

"I miss your smile, Kairi." His eyes grow wide and emotional, something so unlike him I find myself momentarily breathless. He places a single kiss on my cheek as we stare at one another in the shadows of the towering oak bookshelves, causing my face to flush and my chest to swell with unexpected emotion.

"I'll be right back," he promises in a whisper.

I hear his familiar soft pad disappear into the distance of the vast warehouse space, turning back to check the shelf on my left.

I'm looking over a poetry book by Julie Anne Addicott when something catches my eye just as it disappears around the corner of the aisle.

A flicker of viridian.

My ears are suddenly teased by a faint melodious laugh.

The book falls from my fingers to the floor as something shrouded in the thick woven fog of dream and memory spurs me into motion.

I'm immediately on my feet without conscious thought, knees groaning at the sudden motion as I storm forward toward the edge of the row of bookshelves I've been browsing, heart pounding.

Maybe I'm going crazy.

I catch the heel of what seems to be an indigo slipper disappearing as I round the end of the aisle moments too late, vision blurring as my blood roars in my ears, ankles screaming as my soles pound hard into the carpet underfoot.

With a desperate curiosity to discover the source of the vivid colours in my otherwise sepia world, I ignore the fact that my ankle joints are betraying me entirely, threatening to twist and leave me splayed out on the floor.

My chest constricts as I skid around the next corner, weaving haphazardly as blackness threatens to consume my vision.

Staring now down the lengthy stacks of Philosophy and Ancient History, I find him waiting, standing stone still, observing me with a wickedly impish grin plastered across his surreal face. Clad in a violet, tailored jacket that is embroidered with silver wildflowers and teal velvet leggings, which highlight the spindled endlessness of his legs, he cocks one hip and gives a cheeky wave.

I just manage to glimpse a single dreamcatcher earring dangling amongst his blueish-green locks as he spins, disappearing into thin air right before my eyes.

I open my mouth to scream, protest, or maybe even call after him. Whichever it is though, I'll never know, because before I so much as draw breath into my heaving lungs, the blackness framing my vision takes over entirely, and I'm plunged, helpless, into a warm darkness.

2

THE STRANGER

<u>ARO</u>

THE AIR TAKES ON a kind of metallic viscosity as the moonlight bathes the aether, floating with calm elegance, sparkling through the night. Charcoal stains my fingertips as I lean forward, elbows propped on the golden vines that creep up like organic matter from the dark amethyst underfoot, sketching the lines that made up her coy smile. The page is lit, highlighting my poor rendition of her face as golden moonlight defines the thick cloud that surrounds Soleus, turning the indigo dusk splendid with gilded edges and fairy-tale elegance.

"Good evening, Lord Black." The familiar voice startles me, causing my wings to spread defensively. The night light causes the gold-en-plated tips of every feather to become inflamed and glorious as I refuse to turn.

I had not heard the Fae High Lord of Night enter, nor expected him at this late hour.

"Don't you knock?" I snap, fiddling with the cuff of my black jacket; it's threaded through with the same pale gold that tips my feathers, each embroidered vine curling and encasing my wrists with a masterful intricacy that could only have been produced by Fae hands.

"It's a little hard to knock when you're incorporeal," Morpheus replies, causing my eyebrows to rise.

If he's astral projecting here, then he must have something important to say.

Letting my wings tuck gracefully against my spine, I set down the stick of charcoal with which I've been sketching for many hours, inhaling deeply the scent of fresh water and lilacs from the muted roar of the Oblivion Falls nearby.

21

"What is it?" I abandon my position on the balcony, pivoting on the spot before striding with purpose betwixt the two golden drapes that frame the glass back doors of my suite, made art by the indigo threads that form climbing amethyst lilacs and splendid suns.

"Something— unusual—" Morpheus reveals with a flourish of his long fingers, eyes twinkling in the golden light from nearby crystal sconces that trap an undying electric current. His viridian hair looks neon against the dark violet amethyst of the walls, chameleonic irises reflecting that same purple hue back at me as he shifts, though uncomfortable or excited I can't discern.

"Well, spit it out. I'm a busy man." Folding my arms across the solid gold buttons of my double-breasted jacket, I stare at him intently.

"I think— dear friend, I think I've found her. Storm, I mean."

At the sound of her name, my heart simultaneously turns to lead and heats with desire.

"Impossible," I reply with venom, refusing to let myself hope.

"Perhaps. Or perhaps not. It looks just like her. She even had a dream featuring what I believe to be The Astrid Keep at Drakos Vale. That can't be coincidence. I think she recognised me too, though maybe I alarmed her more than anything." He shrugs, the velvet of his shirt rising and falling artfully over his scrawny frame. The scent of wisteria and jasmine seeps through the air, poisonously sweet as I stand stone still, trying to work out how I should respond to this insane supposition.

"What have you been smoking, Morpheus?" I ask him, cocking one eyebrow and taking several steps across his shadow toward the wine jug and goblet sitting atop the quartz coffee table. "Wine?" I offer him, bending to rest against the chaise longue, which is upholstered in onyx velvet and studded through with precious metal adornments, reaching for the Baroque curve of the solid gold pitcher. It's cool upon my fingers as I listen to Morpheus exhale an exasperated breath.

"Nothing more potent than usual. And again, incorporeal, so unless you want to cause more work for your maid, it's a no on the wine."

"Right—" I dismiss the technicality with a half-hearted roll of my dark eyes, pouring myself a generous goblet of Soleus-sourced merlot before setting the jug back onto the golden service tray.

Leaning back so I'm lounging comfortably, I stare up at the Fae High Lord, waiting for him to convince me his claim is worth taking seriously.

22

"I'm just saying I think this girl deserves your attention. Especially after everything we've been through lately with breaches in The Nether because of that situation with Haedes performing unwarranted resurrections. You never know, maybe some of her memories escaped and mingled in with this woman's dreams— or maybe—"

I raise a hand, stopping him mid-sentence. The only sound that can be heard for a full minute is the rose-hued flames crackling in the hearth and my Adam's apple bobbing as I take a large swig of wine. The flavours explode across my tongue, rich, sensuous, yet potent with hints of last summer's wild storms, traces of its memorable and plentiful hot rainfall arousing my taste buds effortlessly.

"Maybe— that's the key word here, isn't it? We don't *know*. This is all guesswork. What if it's simply some look-alike?" I demand, and his eyes become steel silver as his chest inflates with an exaggerated intake of breath.

"She recognised me, Aro. Something *is* going on here. You can't tell me that her dreaming about dragons, looking as she does, with Storm's history with the Draconians is a coincidence. Not even you can deny it's highly improbable such events would coincide."

I watch him fidget, withholding my reply, as his irritated gaze rises to the hearth that glows a warm baby pink, silhouetting me before it. His eyes narrow in on the portrait of myself in the throes of battle with a large white dragon hanging above the mantle. "Fae artist?" he enquires, semi-curious as he takes a spritely step across the crystal floor, tread indiscernible from the silence.

"But of course," I reply, taking in the expert layering of oil paints that brings the bulge of my biceps and the uncompromising edge of my sword to life against the stormy backdrop of the battle scene.

"Funny that you might fantasise about fighting a dragon such as Algoric, the very beast that slayed Queen Pandora, to the point that you had this painting commissioned, and yet you're reluctant to even go and check on the possibility that the woman you claim to love, who was stolen from you by that same enemy, might still exist in one form or another." He ponders, and I read his intent immediately, also succumbing to his bait shamelessly as I feel my status questioned.

I think on the Draconians, blood boiling close to the surface of my skin, Storm's devastated face shedding tears at the horrendously painful consequences of their mutinous betrayal came to pass. Those very same consequences that led to her death and to us being parted after two lifetimes of encircling one another, two souls destined to gravitate only toward the orbit of our potent affection.

"And where exactly would one find this mortal girl if one *was* so inclined?" I take another sip from my goblet, ignoring Morpheus' smug and impish smile.

"Tennessee, a converted barn on a ranch situated on the outskirts of a town called Old Hickory, the ranch itself is named Hickory Oaks." The location, the fact that it is in America, surprises me immensely. If I had thought to find her anywhere, it would have been in London where we first locked eyes all those years ago.

I open my mouth to dismiss him, but a knock sounds at the heavy gold-veined mahogany of the suite's double doors.

"Enter!" I call, leaning back and staring into the pink of the flames whilst swilling the remaining red wine around my goblet in concentric circles.

"I have come to turn down your bed for the night, High Lord," Dawn calls, her familiar thick accent causing me to exhale a tension I hadn't realised I was courting.

After all, my days have been long recently, dealing with updating the trade bargains with The Blazen Plains and Artemis' High Lady, Aliandara, is nothing short of exhausting. Still, their fabrics, exquisitely light in jewel tones, are a must for the high heat here in Soleus and cannot be ignored.

As the door creaks open, heavy wood protesting its hinges, I glance to where Morpheus had been standing only moments before, all traces of him simply vanished.

Dawn shuffles into the room, her ivory and periwinkle-tipped wings rustling behind her. The lengthy silk of her skirt brushes the flawless amethyst floor underfoot, the tight sky blue of the gown slimming her figure and making her elegance known, her presence only describable as demure and delicate in its consistent gentility. I watch her, the golden blonde of her hair piled up onto her head in a crown of braiding catching the pink of the flames, turning each interwoven lock rose gold and shimmering.

She crosses the threshold of the double glass doors, stepping out into the aether-rich air and bringing her dextrous and well-worn fingertips to her lips. A loud whistle emits from her and into the sky only a few moments later, followed by the routine beating of wings as my companion returns home for the night. Ariah, the enormous black-winged lion, known more colloquially as a Kensari, appears among the dark clouds of the night sky, his wingspan larger than any other of his kind in Soleus.

The repetitive drum of his wings as he slows in descent toward the balcony, followed by the gentle thud of paw pads on crystal, let me know he has landed. Dawn makes a kissing noise with her lips, herding him in through the open balcony doors before shutting them behind her and pulling the drapes closed.

Now, the only light that permeates the room is that from the fireplace and the dimming amethyst crystals which glow within their wall-mounted sconces. I hear Ariah approach, his gait all too familiar to me as I swing around, sitting upright to greet him.

Evening. I acknowledge him cordially, though I know not to expect the psychic response of which he is fully capable. The creature has the personality of an incredibly angry old man, his only true joys being food, sleep, and complaining about everything which occupies the time between.

His golden eyes are piercing in the half-light, his dark mane and slick onyx fur making him into mere shadow as he tucks his wings against the flanks of his torso. I reach out a hand, running it through the tangles of his fur, feeling him stiffen beneath my touch as I get to my feet, taking the rest of the wine into my mouth in a single swig.

"Long day, my Lord?" Dawn queries, moving to extinguish the rosy flames which flicker still within the crystal hearth.

"Aren't they always?" I ask her, my mouth tilting up at the corner as I try to remember how many years she's been attending me.

"Don't I know that to be true, though it's easier amongst good friends, don't you agree?" she asks, and I wonder now who I would consider for this role.

Since everything happened with Storm, I've been cut off, isolated, and swept up in my duties as High Lord.

I falter in my reply, unable to force the words past the soft flesh of my sculpted lips. Placing the empty goblet down on the service tray from which it came, I stride across the room in place of a response, taking up the sword lying across the end of my bed instead. It's heavy in my palms, a suitable weight considering the intent with which it is wielded. Drawing it slightly from the ornate Equinian-made sheath, I catch a flash of my indigo irises in the scuffed slice of reflective metal. The loneliness in the dark depths of my pupils startles me, so I snap the sword back into its holster and pass it off to Dawn as she rounds the chaise longue and approaches the bed.

25

I slide off my jacket, the slits in the spine providing adequate escape for my wings, to reveal the pure unblemished white of the shirt underneath. Pulling the silver cravat from around my throat, I throw it carelessly onto the floor beside where Ariah is pacing now in a circle, his mental space silent as ever.

As the enormous lion settles down, curling his tail around himself, Dawn moves to fold down the many layers of velvet atop my mattress as I loosen the collar that clasps my throat in the crisp, unforgiving cotton of its grasp.

Once the pillows and comforter have been pulled back, the drapes around the mahogany four-poster drawn, and the last of the lights dimmed with a touch of Dawn's blessed fingers, she turns to me.

"Will that be all?" she asks, dipping slightly in a curtsey. I smile at her obedience.

"Thank you, have a good evening."

After dismissing her with this sentiment, she quickly grabs the tray from my low hearthside table, the cherrywood logs smouldering even still, and gathers up some discarded clothes on the floor before exiting silently, leaving me alone with my thoughts.

I strip off, shirt first followed by my breeches until I'm standing nude in the dark, black feathers tickling the alabaster skin blanketing my spine.

My wings ruffle as I climb into bed, the darkness comforting after the intense pace of the day. Tomorrow, it will begin again. Deals to be made, correspondence to keep up with, events to attend, complaints to hear with an open heart. It's enough to make most people recoil, the responsibility, but not me. I know I was made for this, to lead, and to bring my people to a new level of liberty despite our role in this place.

As the mattress cups my back, my wingspan becomes a cocoon of sorts and I feel my body relax, my mind clearing in that way I always relish before sleep. Then, though, I see it, her face.

A memory long since forgotten, the pain that comes with it almost too bitter to bear.

Her hair tumbles in a cascade of soft caramel over one shoulder as she descends the stairs, her blue eyes quaint as any clear brook, winding its way, unstoppable, through the meadow of her loveliness.

"This is Briar," her father's voice has not dated in my mind, not a day. I still hear it, the low rumble as if he was the preceding build to the crescendo of her own delicate symphony.

Her waist is made tiny in a duck-egg blue corset, collarbones protruding provocatively above the square cut of her neckline. The many layering skirts that she wears with demure confidence crinkle, heavy against the spotless cream runner that falls the length of the solid oak stairs. Her fingers brush the balustrade, a caress, as I stand at the foot of the staircase inside the London townhouse, entirely enraptured.

Arranged marriage had always been a dread of mine, a thorn in my side, but now I see that I was dwelling on the dangers of the stem and not the rose it boasts instead.

"My Lady," I bend, my finery stiff across my narrow back, cumberbund cutting into my waist.

She brings a delicate gloved hand to the rosy silk of her lips, blushing, eyes sparkling in the pure light from the candle-studded chandelier overhead.

"Call me Briar, after all— I am to be your wife," She holds out her hand, clad in white Chantilly lace, as she descends the final step, the drop in her height causing her to have to look up to keep my gaze. The scent of roses and vanilla creeps around me, intoxicating me and lulling my doubts into memory.

I thought I would die right there, having found heaven in this fragile blushing body, and so we stared, each lost to the fascination of discovering the other.

I stare up at the ceiling, lost in the memory of her, even the moment of meeting still holding a certain inescapable gravity.

What if Morpheus truly has found her?

After all, stranger things have happened.

Who can claim to know the will of the gods?

I wonder if this is a sign that everything I have ever wanted is in fact destiny, and so floats, like a drifting ship lost at sea in the past, finally, toward the shore of my present.

I lie there, letting my fingers trace over my ribcage, remembering the gentler stroke of her tiny delicate hands, the unassuming innocence of her eyes, the pucker of her hungry lips as I held her flush against me.

We have drifted apart and together again over two lifetimes already— so why not a third?

Could she really be waiting for me in the 21st century— after all these years?

I realise as my usual descent into untroubled sleep is stunted that I must know unequivocally and without a doubt or I might never rest peacefully again.

But first, a makeover is required.

3

LES MISÉRABLES

KAIRI

STIRRING FROM SLEEP FEELS like wading through neck-high concrete, my limbs heavy as lead, joints cracking and popping like rice cereal. My eyelids flutter open, weighed down only by the extent to which my body fights its own existence. The only sounds that can be heard are my own heavy breathing beneath the warm, furry bulk of the ginger tom lying across my chest and the rain slashing mercilessly against the windowpanes.

I struggle to sit up, causing Catticus to emit a disgruntled yowl as he stalks off to the far end of the mattress.

Beneath the sheets, I know I need to stand, my joints locked into place after what feels like an eternity sleeping, and so place my bare feet onto the worn wooden floorboards, shuddering unwillingly at the cold.

The room is illuminated after a moment by a sudden fork of lightning splitting the sky outside. Catticus hisses, and I grunt at the ache in my bones as I stand, both sounds diminished by a roll of thunder.

How long have I been asleep?

On the oak bedside table, an icy thermos full of fresh water stands, left by one of my parents, beside which is the old cell phone I barely use nowadays. When I pick up the device, it feels alien and chill as the metal presses against my palm in a way that used to be so habitual. Before, in L.A., I had been just as plugged in as anyone else—but then, social media had become more of a highlights reel for everything I could no longer have, including my friends, and my ex.

I press the *On* button and wait for the Android handset to power up, knees throbbing. I'm curvy now, heavier than I had been before the diagnosis, but with my crappy joints, I might as well have put on one hundred and forty pounds.

The screen is blinding, flooding my irises with stark blue light, burning my own image into the back of my eyelids. My screensaver is of me at the very last figure skating competition I had entered before leaving for college, holding a bunch of flowers with a gold medal hanging around my neck. It was taken by my dad in the foyer after the event, and my trusty skates are slung over one shoulder by their laces.

I stroke the screen, the face of the girl I used to be, letting out a heavy and emotionally charged sigh before getting back to checking the date.

Friday.

I've been asleep for a day and a half.

Crap.

The device in my palm begins to vibrate and for some reason, against my better judgement, my heart leaps as the notifications flash up on the screen.

I want so badly for it to be them.

Or him.

It isn't.

It's a message from my network provider.

My heart fissures a little deeper, worsening the existing crack where Holly and Andrea's abrupt absence in my life had caused a kind of damage that I'm still not sure how to repair.

As I slump down on the side of the bed, staring gormlessly at the phone, the memories of those I've left behind in L.A surface, threatening to drown me in unwanted nostalgia.

We'd been friends since Kindergarten. Holly and I had skated to-gether, and Andrea and I both loved books more than any of the currently popular television series that seemed to obsess every single other girl our age. They had felt like the family I chose rather than my parents who chose me, but since my diagnosis, everything had changed. I couldn't go out any longer, couldn't drink, couldn't go running with them, or skating, or go-karting. Couldn't even stay out for longer than a few hours without needing several days to recover.

I was no longer fun, and what's worse is that they couldn't see any-thing wrong with me so assumed I was being dramatic or anti-social, that I'd grown tired of them.

It sounds harsh like perhaps they're bad people.

They aren't.

I know that. They just didn't adjust to my circumstances as quickly as I had to, and maybe it was my fault too for pushing them away because I felt like nobody could possibly understand what I was, and still am, going through.

It was the same story with Oli, the boy who had stolen my heart at nineteen and kept hold of it until twelve months ago. It started along with the pain, my resignation to romance and the idea of a relationship. I hadn't wanted to have sex, hadn't wanted to date, and talking about what was happening to me just made me feel sick. Some days I couldn't even find the strength to shower, let alone make myself look halfway decent. He quickly went from being my escape to a fellow prisoner in the situation neither of us had asked for, and I watched, horrified, knowing it was my responsibility to fix things.

I broke it off with him, telling him I no longer loved him, but that wasn't true. I just couldn't bear to watch him suffer alongside me. It was too much.

It wasn't until I discovered he was dating Andrea behind my back, not three weeks after we had split up, that I started to wonder if he'd ever really loved me at all, or if he was only in it for fear of being alone.

Now, I'm just numb.

I'm sitting on the edge of my comforter, pondering who changed me into the fleece pyjamas I'm currently wearing, when another lightning fork illuminates the room. It floods the space, highlighting the shadows in the high beamed ceiling and the old floorboards, bouncing off the spines of hundreds of books that are stacked, haphazardly against the walls.

A few seconds after the light diminishes as quickly as it came, thunder rumbles out from the Tennessee sky, the pitter-patter of raindrops upon the roof a small comfort as I wrap the blanket on the end of the bed around my shoulders.

Shivering, I attempt to get my bearings, trying to reacquaint myself with inhabiting the body that's failing me all over again after such a long period of unconsciousness. It's like meeting a very rickety, old, and unwelcome friend you can't get rid of.

Turning off my cell phone, which is still vibrating with pointless notifications from news apps and Twitter, I place it back on the bedside table, crossing my legs beneath me and trying to relax. Unfortunately, another hiss from Catticus makes me jump; causing my heart to race despite the fact I'm sitting down.

As I feel the hunk of muscle thundering inside my ribcage, I wonder how long it's been since I took my last dose of heart medication, knowing that I'll be feeling the consequences of skipping them for the next few days at least. I'm about to reach for the top drawer in my nightstand, looking for some extra pills, when Catticus yowls, heightening my pulse even further.

I turn, craning my neck and squinting into the dark, the lime flash of his terrified irises catching me by surprise. His silhouette is curved, tail erect and puffed up, trying to be intimidating.

That's when I hear it.

A creak from overhead, too loud to be from a bird, too deliberately solitary to be the shifting of old wooden beams in the storm.

"What is it, boy?" I reach out gingerly, offering my fingers as he slinks forward toward me, skittish. He curls into my side, eyes wild and whiskers twitching as he gazes toward the window, the heavy rain beyond forming a greyish haze that obscures the full sprawl of the ranch.

I wait, stroking the animal at my side, listening intently in the middle of a storm for anything else that might explain why Catticus is acting so weird.

Nothing.

After a few moments, the ginger tom relaxes, curling up in my lap amidst my fleece blanket before beginning to purr.

I don't know what time it is, but I do know that after sleeping for the last 36 hours I won't be finding any deep rest soon.

I wrap Catticus tighter in the blanket, sliding out from beneath it and getting back into my double bed, stacking pillows behind me and snuggling down into the warmth of my thick comforter.

Then, I light a lavender and daisy-scented candle on my nightstand, pick up the copy of *Les Misérables* I've been rereading for the fiftieth time, and lose myself in it the predictable tragedy of its tale as the storm continues to rage on outside.

I read on until the earliest hints of dawn creep onto the horizon, transported from my body and into 19th-century Paris, the slow but consistent vibration of Catticus' purr calming my nerves as the language soothes my soul.

As the sun tiptoes closer to being visible, I decide a change of scenery and some fresh air would be nice, and so, placing the novel under my arm and grabbing the lilac tartan blanket from the window seat, I make for the door, careful to keep my tread as quiet as possible.

The early morning air is full of the scent of citrus from where the wide bannister has recently been polished, specks of dust dancing in the half-light of five a.m. I descend, Catticus following curiously at my heels, taking the stairs with my usual careful slowness while trying to avoid the boards that squeak.

I stride past the cream leather corner couches that form the centrepiece of the family room, creeping beneath the high eaves of the ceiling that remain blanketed in the night's shrinking shadows.

The entire barn is encapsulated by a full wrap-around porch that folds into the silhouette of the house's foundations, mirroring the continuous balcony overhead.

Pulling open a glass, sliding door, I step out onto it barefoot. Sighing, I feel loose strands of my hair catch in a chill but gentle breeze, my nose filled with the scent of the nearby free-waving heather that sprawls to the farthest easterly point of the ranch. Hay and the familiar waft of horse manure mingle with the freshness of the passing night, but I don't linger to take it in, my arms aching from the weight of the blanket and book. Instead, I step down off the porch and relish the cool damp earth on my heels, inhaling the scent of last night's passing storm as I make my way to my favourite place in all of Hickory Oaks.

The ranch is divided by high wooden fences, dividing the golden-emerald land into sections of both paddocks and free space where crops had probably once grown. It seems to expand endlessly on all sides the farther I get from the house, and if I didn't know any better, I could almost trick myself into believing it spreads to the end of the earth.

The horizon tinges lemon as the sun prepares to make its grand entrance.

I walk for a good five minutes toward a cluster of willow trees that rim a tiny pond, the water level high and reflecting the sky overhead flawlessly. There's a wooden gazebo here, and inside, a swinging circular chair padded with white fleece blankets and chocolate-coloured pillows, perfect for reading. My dad hooked it up the first week we moved here when he noticed I had no desire to explore my new surroundings.

I climb up the damp wood of the shallow steps, Catticus overtaking me at a sprint as he flies into view, an orange blur against the shadow cast by the rain-darkened roof. I place my novel into the hold of the cushioned seat, watching it dangle from the single chain that's hooked around the wooden beams overhead.

Then, wrapping myself in the blanket in my arms, I bunch the fleece into my fist to secure the warmth of the tartan cocoon, grabbing my book once more and lowering myself into the blissful, free-floating hold of the hanging seat.

I let my head rest back against the chocolate suede puff of a pillow, listening to the sound of my breathing.

Catticus leaps from the floor and up into my lap, causing the swing to waver slightly in its position. I open up my book, taking a final look at the horizon, which is now bruising pink, before plunging back into the story I've read more times than I can count.

I get through about three pages of the luxurious prose before something pulls my attention back to the early morning sky, now a mixed palette of pastels. It isn't the changing warmth of the light that draws my attention though, but the rigidity of the cat in my lap and the sudden rustle of nearby leaves.

"Hello?" I call out, eyes darting left and right.

I wait, listening intently, glancing beneath the weep of surrounding willow trees for anything unusual, my breath caught in my throat as paranoid anticipation builds.

After a few moments, a figure appears from between the curtains of leaves on the opposite side of the water, brushing them aside with a pale hand and causing the surface of the pond to ripple.

"Who are you? What do you want? This is private land!" I stutter, unprepared for a random stranger's appearance and realising with a sense of vulnerable horror that I'm still wearing my pyjamas.

Catticus leaps down onto the deck as I adjust to a more upright position, hissing as his paws thud on impact, tail puffed like a feather duster.

The figure on the other side of the pond steps forward, the sun rising from behind me illuminating his face as he sheds his hood.

I inhale, heart beginning to race within my aching ribcage.

His dark, thick locks are tousled atop his head, gleaming gold beneath fresh sunlight. His skin is pale as bone, the architecture of his skull statuesque, and his body tall and extraordinarily broad at the shoulder from what I can see beneath his cloak. He pulls it around himself, placing one hand up in the air, a clear surrender, but I'm unsure of him even still.

Pushing the blanket aside, I rise to my feet as he closes the distance between us, his reflection skirting the left side of the pond as he approaches, black velvet cloak billowing behind him.

Weird. I muse, wondering who the hell walks around wearing something that looks like it belongs at a Dungeons and Dragons meeting.

I stand, folding my arms across my bra-less chest, not sure whether to run or scream.

Somehow though, neither materialises.

Instead, I remain on the spot, hyperventilating and with my book clutched in my sweating palm as blood roars, a sudden and terrible tsunami in my ears.

Catticus emits another hiss, curling around my ankles as the man's tread grows louder, his shadow closer.

As he reaches the far side of the gazebo, however, he stops, staring at me standing there in my lilac and lemon fleece pyjamas with hair unruly from sleep.

"Storm?" He whispers the word, almost like it's a name and not a natural event, the enormity of his shoulders becoming only more obvious as I examine him up close.

"Excuse— Excuse me?" I blurt, not in control of my mouth, let alone what comes out of it.

"I'm sorry. My name is Aro. I didn't mean to intrude—" He gives a small bow pulling the left edge of his thick cloak across his torso. His lustrous dark hair falls forward across his forehead, rising to mine as he straightens.

A wave of something like nostalgia ripples through me, my heart skipping a beat against my consent as our eyes finally lock.

I take a step forward, finding extraordinary irises within that gaze and unable to help myself as I move to get a better look. Beneath thick, dark lashes, indigo irises specked with the lightest lilac shine out into the world, a galaxy trapped within a man.

"What are you doing here? This is private property." I repeat my previous assertion, but this time, the confrontational tone behind the sentiment has dissipated as though it held no more weight upon first expression than smoke.

"I'm sorry. I mean no harm. I came looking for someone— she looks just like you, but— I guess I was mistaken." He looks crestfallen, the definite line of his strong jaw tilting down as his gaze drops, and he moves to turn.

"Wait—" I say the word before I know why I'm saying it.

"Yes?" he asks, turning back, and I shift on the balls of my feet, a little uncomfortable despite the fact I haven't been standing more than a few moments.

"Maybe I can help, I mean— I just moved here but maybe I could give you directions or something?" I offer, feeling bad about the rude way I'd greeted him. "I'm Kairi." I extend a hand, not sure how else to act other than formally.

He glances down at my hand, something catching his eye as he tilts his head, brows knitting together.

"That's a very unusual— uh— mark," he comments, and I feel my eyes sweep to the three-pronged that blemishes the inside of my left wrist, a kind of tentacled star. I have had it as long as I can remember to the point where I forget it's even there.

"Yeah, I guess. Birthmark." I shrug, taking back my hand before he can reach out to grab it.

As I let my gaze rise back to his, his expression has changed, taking on a new intensity as he examines the planes of my face. "So, uh— who are you looking for?" I ask him, self-conscious beneath his scrutiny as I rub my bare shoulder and try to dispel the goosebumps there.

"A girl I knew a long time ago. Someone told me she moved to this town recently— guess I got kind of lost."

"It's not hard to do that around here— I'm from L.A. originally so I'm not used to all this empty space either." I relinquish this, the tiniest piece of personal information, and move to sit down on the step as I feel my body wavering on the spot.

"Are you alright? You just went a little pale—" Aro reaches out, his long, elegant fingers rising to my cheek and then to my forehead, appraising my temperature. His fingertips are beyond gentle, leaving my face tingling a little in the wake of his caress.

"Yeah, I'm fine. I have this thing. It makes me tired sometimes," I explain myself, immediately minimising the extent of my pain out of habit.

"You're sick?" Aro takes a seat beside me, his long legs spreading out in front of him, exposing the sheen of his dress shoes beneath matching black pants.

"Yeah. For a while now. I get tired, and I hurt—well, all the time. It's a problem with my joints, but it affects pretty much my entire body," I explain further, my shoulder giving an audible crunch as I lean back, letting the sunrise bathe me in welcome heat.

"And there's no cure?" He looks concerned, and I shrug, closing my eyes against the new light.

"No. There isn't. It's okay though. I'm fine, really." It's a lie, a huge one. One I've gotten so used to telling everyone around me, to make them comfortable and to deflect their sympathy, that I don't even hear the words anymore as they fly out of my mouth.

"No, you're not." Aro's response startles me, my eyes opening as I turn to him, angry despite the fact I know he's only saying what's true.

"You don't even know me." I deflect, shrugging off his directness and trying not to sound as annoyed as I am.

"No, I don't. But maybe I should." His forwardness broaches the inappropriate as his words die, their sharp, assured sound echoing for a few moments in my ears.

He reminds me a little of Mr Darcy. Brash, and honest without apology. "Sorry, that came out— wrong. I just, you seem lonely to me. Am I wrong?" he asks, making yet another assumption as he takes in my face.

I wonder momentarily what it is he's seeing in my expression because honestly, even I don't know what my face is betraying or concealing.

I want to get up and walk away, want to be angry that a total stranger is reading me like an open book, and yet, something in me is left vulnerable and raw at his unfiltered honesty. Maybe, beyond all of my placating, I want someone to notice how deeply I'm drowning in my own pain. Perhaps then, my suffering is making me weak and needy for someone who really understands.

I don't deny his claim; in fact, I don't say anything at all. I don't want to need anybody; I'm burden enough to those around me already.

"That's what I thought," he says in a low tone, his voice deep and pained as though he really cares. "I'm sorry. I'm lonely too. Ever since I lost her— the girl I'm looking for, I mean."

"I'm sorry," I say it automatically without real sympathy. Men like him, with faces that look like they belong on knights dressed in shining white armour, very rarely stay lonely for long. I'll bet that this girl he's looking for is searching frantically for him, too.

After all, he seems genuinely thoughtful, something I view as a rare commodity in males outside of fiction or my fathers these days. If it was me, I would want to hang onto a man like that.

"So, you want me to ask around town for this girl you're looking for?" I suggest, feeling Catticus curl into my left side as dappled sunlight falls in thick buttery rays over the gazebo, the sunrise glorious as it sets the land alight in a sepia shimmer.

"That would be helpful. I guess I could come back tonight if I don't find her today? Would that be alright?" he asks me, gentle as he covers my hand with his.

I flinch back, feeling unexpected sparks of electricity twining up my arm as his skin brushes mine.

My heart races a little as he looks down at where I've pulled away.

"I'm sorry. I—" I begin, but he shakes his head as he jumps to his feet.

"No, the fault is mine. I was just trying to get better traction so I could stand. I didn't mean to—" he begins, but I shake my head, feeling ridiculous. After all, what kind of tall, dark, and handsome man would ever be interested in a sick girl with no prospects and a serious bout of depression?

"It's fine. I overreacted. Really. So, what's her name again?" I demand, trying to move the conversation away from the unintentionally intimate and toward a more productive subject.

"Briar Shaw," Aro says the words like they're magic, taking a few measured steps toward the edge of the small pond.

"Okay, I'll ask around, see what I can find out."

"Thank you, Kairi. I'll return at dusk," Aro promises, his vernacular far too proper to be local.

In fact, he sounds undeniably British.

As he turns, striding away from me with only a momentary glance back, I wonder why I'm offering to help him, especially seeing as I did only just move here, and my only social connections lie with Mr Chaikowsky.

Perhaps it's the old romantic in me, the lover of happily ever after and swooning Victorian ladies that's pushing me to help two Kindred souls come together.

Or— maybe I'm just bored.

4

ONE HUNDRED YEARS OF SOLITUDE

LUCIEN

THE HEMATITE COLUMN GROANS underfoot as it rises from the depths of the mountain. Tucking my wings in close to my spine, I observe Genevieve's pale skin turn blue, the cerulean topaz of the throne room floor closing in on all sides as we rise through the earth. The column rotates as it ascends, lifting us in a clockwise corkscrewing motion until finally jerking to a stop. I step off the platform, the symbol etched upon it the same as the design inked in above my heart and identical to the tattoo that winks out from the nape of Genevieve's neck as she runs her fingers through her albino braids.

We're both relaxed, far more so than we had been upon descending into the pit a few hours ago, and she stares at me for a moment, eyes kind, before scanning the surrounding throne room.

Silence echoes out on all sides as we both pivot slowly, eyes falling appreciatively over the grandiose structure and feeling no need to speak. The walls are carved from moonstone that shimmers in the light of many candles that line the walls, each sconce made from labradorite and carved into a reptilian claw sporting inch-long talons. Wax drips in fat globules, sliding down the sides of the candles' once generous lengths, the only motion in the empty room other than our own.

Genevieve sighs, and I glance at her, nervous in her presence as usual. It's true she's my best friend, but she can put me on edge faster than anyone. Not surprising, considering the amount of power being held within the seemingly fragile white flesh that coats her equally pale bones.

"He seems good, don't you think?" she asks, and I know then she's feeling the same guilt that eats at me after every single one of these little visits.

It's inevitable, and despite my best effort, staring at the stunning architecture isn't going to make a shred of difference. It's a necessary cruelty but a cruelty nonetheless. That fact cannot be denied.

"I think they all do, considering we're keeping them captive—" I admit, letting the knee-high, supple, brown leather of my boots trace the flawless sheen of the topaz underfoot. Taking a step closer to her, I skirt around the seal in the floor.

Her white hair is braided tightly against her skull, the work intricate and by a hand not her own. Her body is wrapped in jade leather, silver buckles tying the corset close to her tiny ribcage and making her slight height even more obvious. Her skirt is made from a matching jade cut of leather, two slits running up either side of the fabric's scaled imprint to give her free range of motion while still protecting her modesty. She's, as usual, barefoot beneath it all, and her emerald eyes are sharp when contrasted against the pallor of her entire body. She could be mistaken for a ghost except for the fact that her hair is tinged ever so slightly rosy at the root, as though it's bleeding from her skull instead of growing. I reach up to put a finger against her bare shoulder, comforting her and trying to dispel the misery that clings to both of us.

She steps back, shaking her head.

"Don't—" she whispers.

Her wings suddenly spread wide from her, pure snowy white made reptilian by intricate creases that carve between each and every scale. They're slightly translucent despite the fleshy armour, candles sheening through only just and highlighting the enormous thick red veins that run through the delicate limbs like rivers.

I hear what it is that's caused her stance to change, turning to meet the encroaching heels that ring out too loudly, against the crystalline silence that has surrounded us, their click a bullet abruptly shattering the fragility of the emotionally charged air between us.

"Anastasia." The name of the approaching High Priestess spills from me like a habit. Her silver-speckled raven locks flow out from her head, liquid chocolate laced with starlight. As a smile forms on her voluptuous lips, her eyes meet mine, the sea frost hue haunting as it's always been.

41

"Lucien. I thought I might find you here. Genevieve," she curtsies out of respect for the pale silhouette at my spine, the liquid galaxy of her thin cloak pooling in a puddle of constellations at her ankles as her wings flare out from her on either side. The diamonds studded among the navy scales of her wingspan catch the firelight from the candles lighting the throne room, setting them ablaze like tiny asteroids burning as they shoot through the night sky.

"You're looking for me?" I enquire of her, and she nods, loose raven locks falling around her face and causing her scent to plume. The rich aroma of ink and ripe plums swell through the air on a tide of their own, unmistakable as belonging to her. She is one of the few Draconians who doesn't braid her hair, her position as High Priestess of the Observatory as well as being a Draconian High Lady of Nemesis giving her an otherworldly and undeniable strength that comes not from the line of her jaw or hunch of her shoulders but from something else less tangible entirely.

"Indeed. I have received a vision, and I was wondering if you could help me discern its meaning," she reveals, cocking her head.

As she speaks, I feel Genevieve slink back to the pale throne at the head of the room, watching us.

I look back at her; worried I've caused offence as her emerald eyes sharpen against the rigid set of my spine.

"Isn't that your job?" I ask Anastasia, looking between the two High Ladies and wondering what on earth she could need my help with. I'm a High Lord, true, but I cannot claim to have half the connection to the Goddesses that these two possess. After all, according to literature, Genevieve and Anastasia are practically physical embodiments of Hecate and Nemesis in appearance, despite the fact they hold no real love for one another. Not that Genevieve holds love for anyone mortal, even me. She's my best friend, and even I feel the chill of the walls she's erected around herself on a daily basis. If it weren't for my own directness of tongue, my refusal to coddle, and the blunt edge of my indomitable strength, we never would have been more than equals politically.

"Well, the vision involves you, so I thought it would be better to hear what I want to know from the mouth of the beast himself." Anastasia is no fool. Her pale eyes are startling as they focus on me with the intensity of the Aetherial Sun.

"Fine." I bite out the response, bored of the conversation already and wishing I was back at home by the fire.

"Have you ever seen this woman before?" she pulls a rolled piece of parchment from the inside of her cloak, unravelling it as the paper crumples against her smooth palms.

Adjusting my position to get a better look as she reveals the contents to me, I squint, taking in the face sketched in fine pencil.

Her eyes are wide, innocent, hair curling gently around her shoulders. I feel my eyes widen, my heart thudding for no reason, unable to catch my breath.

"So, you do know her—" Anastasia assesses my response, inhaling quickly, but I shake my head, brow furrowing as I force my eyes to burrow deeply into the image, trying to figure out why I've had such a visceral reaction.

"No— I don't know her. Sorry." I reply, letting my face relax as I take a step back, distancing myself from whatever nonsense it is that's causing me to gawp at a simple sketch.

"You're sure?" she asks me, and I roll my eyes.

"I told you, not a clue. Sorry." I'm brash; irritated that she doesn't believe me. After all, why ask for my help if you're not going to listen to my answer?

"Odd. Very odd indeed. I had a vision this morning of you two together, and it looked like you were running from something—" she informs me, rolling up the parchment and placing it in the innermost pocket of her bedazzled cloak once more.

"Impossible. I have no idea who that is. Also, I don't run." I growl, brows pinching together yet again. Anastasia stares at me, her face unmoving, eyes turning white as she calls the vision back to her right in front of me.

I brush a strand of my poker-straight, ice-blond hair behind one ear, feeling heat crawl up my back, uncomfortable at the way she simply checks out of the conversation and in with her higher calling as though it's no more than popping into the local post office. Back in Paris, when I was mortal, that was called bad etiquette, but I suppose we're past all that trivial nonsense now.

I flex and ball my fists, tensing as I wait for her to return and trying to distract myself from the absent dreamy look on her possessed features.

Glancing back over the black scales of my wingspan, I find Genevieve looking equally as bored as she yawns without even trying to hide it, crossing her legs and tilting her chin at me.

Returning my attention to her then, I find Anastasia has returned.

43

"The vision remains. It could be the future, I suppose." She shrugs, giving me a hesitant look as she turns to leave.

"Sorry for the wasted trip." I bite the skin of my bottom lip, an urge I can only describe as completely unexplainable, causing me to add, "If you have any more visions like this, will you let me know?"

She looks back over one shoulder, eyebrows raised in surprise.

"Curious," is all she says, tread effortless and measured as she leaves the hall behind her, bat-like wings tucking themselves in close to her spine.

"I never did have her faith. Sometimes I'm jealous," Genevieve calls as I watch Anastasia's glistening cloak disappear around the corner of the corridor beyond the throne room doors.

"Getting visions you can't understand and don't want? I can't think of anything worse." I reply and look back at her once again. The weak golden light of the waxing moon falls through the monochrome stained glass of the window at her spine, turning her skin a jaundiced and sickly hue.

"I can think of a certain comfort in seeing the fact that everything is laid out, that we're all just pieces being moved around a board." She twizzles the end of one of her braids around a pale finger, green eyes watching me carefully.

"I can't think like that or I'd go mad. I have to believe that we shape our own destinies. Without that— well, it's just hopelessness and an inevitable death. Don't you think?" I ask her, unable to mince my words as ever, and she smiles, the expression not touching the cruel joy behind her eyes.

"Exactly. And now you see why I haven't been hopeful for years," she admits, voice lacklustre as usual as she gets to her feet. She walks up to me, giving a low and ironic curtsey before striding toward the small passage on the left, which leads toward her chambers.

"Goodnight, my Lord. Dream of me," she giggles, the noise too girlish to be genuine, and I roll my eyes.

She can't help but poke fun that I haven't yet married, or at the fact that I conceive such a notion with anything but disgust, or constantly berate the way women throw themselves at my feet, willingly, but I cannot spare them a second thought.

Then again, if I'd been treated as she has at the hands of men, I'd probably find even the whisper of such a ritualistic notion barbaric and the women who are pining pathetic.

She hates the fact I desire strong women, thinking it a lie I tell myself just because I know of her past. She claims that the day I find a woman who is a worthy opponent for my volatile temper and quick, uncompromisingly honest wit, I'll run in the opposite direction. She says that men know exactly what it is they want, but those of us with moral standards refuse to accept it. Refuse to accept that we are little more than slavers looking for slaves to kneel before us and weep.

I aim to prove her wrong— one day.

Standing alone in the hall quickly loses its appeal, a chill running rampant through the room as I head off towards the exit of the Astrid Keep, ready to be home.

The Astrid Keep wraps around and tunnels deep within the tallest peak in Drakos Vale, the sprawling regal structure weaving in and out of the mountain as it wills. Despite this closeness to the earth, I have always found the place oddly removed from any sense of homeliness.

I pass more clawed sconces; some of their candles extinguished by what I fear will be awful weather outside though I shouldn't be surprised. It's always cold here with few fireplaces and even fewer fires, not that Genevieve has ever had any problem keeping herself warm at night.

Making my way through the maze of moonstone walls and icy blue floors, I wonder how it must be to actually live in this place. There's no warmth in these outermost corridors, and not a soul to be seen except a few solitary and frozen-looking guards in black metal armour adorned with scales and stone-still wings. The scent is sterile yet comforting to me as it reminds me of flying and the way the sharp wintergreen of cold air stings the inside of my nose, making my eyes water and waking me up to all five of my senses.

Finally, after navigating the labyrinth of twisting staircases that fall continuously down the side of the mountain, surrounded by seemingly endless icy corridors, I reach the outermost hall. I pass through the space in four long strides, my legs long and powerful as they carry me soundlessly across the entryway and toward the veil of night that blankets the outside world.

I find my sleigh where I had left it as I leave through an enormous moonstone archway and listen to my tread crunch against new snowfall as I head toward the gleaming chocolate wood of the vehicle. Hauling a thick, white, fur cloak out from the driver's bench, which is carved from rich mahogany, I wrap it around my shoulders in an effort to dispel the stiff but welcome chill from my bones. The sky overhead is endless, and I take a moment to breathe, missing the rush of its endless dark against my wings. I cannot dwell on the clearness of the night, so instead, turn my attention to the five spectral mountain dogs that will be in charge of getting me where I need to go. Phantom, Ecto, Spirit, Shadow, and Wraith get to their feet, the ashen scent of my scales alerting them that it's time to move as they shake snow off their luscious white coats.

I walk down the line, checking the harnesses and ensuring they're ready to run as they pant, looking into wide golden eyes and those of glowing glacial blue with a kind smile and a ruffle of the fur between their ears.

Once the dogs are prepared, I walk back to the sleigh, looking up at the blackened sky and the sliver of golden moon, which seems too far away to truly illuminate anything at this point. The stars twinkle, powerful by comparison, and I wonder if Anastasia is looking at them right now.

And what of the girl? The one with the round innocent eyes and lustrous flowing hair who caused my heart to skip a beat. Is she looking at these same stars right now?

I want to hope, to think on it, but then I remember Genevieve and how she will remind me, at every opportunity, we might be supposedly blessed by the goddess Hecate, but that means we serve her and any benefit to us in this life is merely coincidental.

Perhaps she is right.

The arctic white of tree trunks and their canopies that weep heavy with snow and ice rise around me, as I suddenly feel very small standing on my sledge and staring up into the bitter clarity of the night.

Inhaling the scent of Drakos Vale and banishing what might have been from my mind, I yank hard on the reigns, and the barking of dogs rises around me as we pull off into the icy darkness.

ARO

I arrive in a flash of static electricity, conducting back into my suite, heart pounding.

How is this possible? I ask myself, stunned by the seemingly odd sense of humour belonging to the universe.

"Hello, stranger—" A sickly-sweet purr creeps through the air toward me, causing me to turn on the spot as I unfasten the cloak that's been hiding my wings.

My eyes fall upon her, drenching her naked body in too obvious disdain.

"Does nobody in this place have any sense of my personal space, of privacy?" I ask, beyond irritated.

Her steely eyes glisten, pale skin dressed in a thick blanket of fragrant bubbles from beyond the open bathroom door as she lounges in my Amethyst claw foot tub, the entire bath crafted from one enormous geode and lit from beneath. The gold fixtures of the bathroom and the white fluffy linens contrast against the rich indigo of the walls, ceiling, and floor as fresh cobalt sunlight pours in through the periwinkle-stained glass of the enormous arched windows. The intruding Nephilim's profile is silhouetted stark; skin flushed a cool cyan and her expression not the least bit apologetic.

"What can I say? If you wanted to be left alone, you shouldn't have taken the best tub in this place—" She raises an arm from the bubbles, letting perfumed steam rise from her skin as her long-nailed fingertips drip generously.

After a moment of silence between us, she beats her wings slightly, causing bubbles to spray up into the air, a playful, coy smile twisting at her bold lips. Her feathers are pure arctic white, spattered with silver as if she's stood in the way of an abstract artist at work. "Oh, for Goddess' sake, lighten up—" She rolls her eyes, unamused by my lack of good humour as she raises a leg from the tub and into the blue light, examining the cold glow profiling her long limb with a defiant flutter of her dark lashes.

I take a step forward, cocking my head to one side as I bite down on the soft flesh inside of my cheek.

"Get out. I'm busy," I snap, grabbing a towel from the rail on the wall and tossing it to her with force before turning to walk away.

"What on earth happened to your hair?" she calls after me, voice high-pitched and rife with intrigue. I don't turn back, shedding the cloak onto the now-made bedclothes beside Silver's discarded white gown, elbow-length silver silk gloves, and lingerie.

Unfortunately for me, this particular Nephilim has never been known for her ability to let things go, and so she follows me through from the bathroom, wrapping herself in the towel as she drips rose-scented suds over the floor, glare tenacious. Pulling a large silver clip from her hair allows the whiteness of her lustrous mane to fall around her shoulders, a deceptive halo.

"If you must know, I've just been to the mortal world. I think I've found her. Storm, I mean." I watch her reaction unfold just as I knew it would, eyes widening but then narrowing just as quickly.

"That's ridiculous. Did you hit your head when you lopped off your hair?" Silver asks, her feathers rustling, dispelling water as she strides past me, clearly irritated at the mention of another woman.

"I'm serious. Morpheus located her. She looks just like Storm. Not only that but she has the heirbound mark on the inside of her wrist." I turn from her as she drops the towel at the foot of the bed, picking up her lacy underthings and beginning by pulling sheer stockings up her legs.

"That's impossible. She's dead. You know that. I know that— Goddess, even Hera knows it!"

Heading toward my vanity in the farthest corner of the room, I yank open the top drawer and bend to sit on the upholstered velvet stool, noting the scissors still lying on the table from where I'd hacked off my waist-length black locks. I do a slight double-take as I glimpse myself in the oval mirror, unused to my cropped hair.

Rummaging through the depths of the drawer, I toss out several antique cufflinks and a few pieces of Storm's jewellery I hadn't found myself able to part with.

"Exactly. Don't you think it's possible that Hera might have intervened after the way Storm was lost to us?" I ask, hearing her clipping the sheer stockings onto a garter belt with quick fingers.

"I think you put too much stock in Hera and Zeus. Aren't you the one who's always saying they don't give a shit about us? What's different? Having a change of heart now you believe they've saved the soul of your lost beloved?" She practically spits the sentiment, and I roll my eyes, reaching further into the depths of the drawer, frustrated. "What are you looking for?" she adds with impatience, closing her corset over her breasts as I glance at her at last, bored of her intrusion.

"Ah! There it is!"

I feel the smooth, silver filigree of the locket and clasp it in my fist, the metal cool to touch. Pulling it out of the vanity, I hold it up to the light streaming in through the glass double doors that lead out to the balcony. Silver rolls her eyes, stepping into her skirt and pulling it up high so it cinches around her waist.

"You think that will convince her? She probably thinks you're insane." Her words don't deter me as I slide a fingernail underneath the locket's clasp. It falls apart as I lay it in my palm, the face of the woman I'd lost staring back at me from the oil miniature within the silver frame.

"Perhaps. But perhaps I can convince her to believe me; after all, Morpheus said he thought she was dreaming using images from one Storm's memories. Maybe she's in there— or maybe it's my chance to start fresh. To save her this time." I feel the weight of these words, hope blooming inside of me like a sun in supernova, desire running thick and hot in my veins.

Too many years I've been alone, been waiting for— something beyond logic, beyond my actual comprehension. Call it destiny, or fate, or maybe even karma.

Perhaps this is it.

I snap the locket closed as Silver pulls her hair up out of her high collar, regal looking but far too decadent for my tastes. She reeks of a kind of desperation for attention, everything about her purposeful in drawing the eye. Storm— or rather, Kairi as perhaps she is now, has never needed to try to draw the eye, for when she is in the room, I can't tear my eyes away. Even in her pyjamas, hair messy and eyes blackened from fatigue, she was more beautiful than Silver could ever hope to be, her innocence and delicate features, as ever, beguiling.

"I don't want to catch you in here again. Are we clear?" I warn her, and she shrugs, a playful mischief dancing across her face. "I'm serious." I bite out, annoyed by her blatant disregard for my authority. She isn't a High Lady, nor my superior, and her behaviour is unacceptable.

"Sure thing, my Lord—" She winks, causing me to clench my jaw, still sitting as she gives a low curtsey, mocking my title.

"Very well then, seeing as how you seem to be doing nothing of importance, you can run some errands for me. I need a bouquet of crystal roses, long-stemmed and the freshest you can find." I order her, eyes cold. Her face visibly ices over, mouth becoming a thin and steely line within the softness of her heat-flushed cheeks.

"I'm not a maid," she snaps, turning on one heel and making for the door.

"Are you disobeying your High Lord, Silver? Is that what I'm hearing from you?" I ask her, standing now, locket clutched in my angry palm.

My tone drips with noxious intent as I tilt my jaw upward, looking down my nose at her spine. Her shockingly white wings stiffen as she turns, eyes dead in her skull, the beauty she had forced upon me unapologetically deceased.

"Of course not, My Lord." This time she gives a meek curtsey, and I nod, dismissing her. She wrenches the door open with a faux calm about her now as I stand stone still, watching her go.

"You know, bringing her back here will be dangerous for all of us. Don't forget that." Her voice travels through the air, laced with what sounds like fear but I know to be envy. The door slams behind her as she leaves, and finally, I am alone.

Once her furious footfall has vanished into nothing, I sigh, letting my shoulders relax and my fist unclench. That girl needs to learn her place.

For without it, not only she but all of us are lost.

I place the chain of the locket over my head, wrist tickled by the short locks of my hair that stick up, defying gravity without the weight that had held them poker straight for centuries. The weight of it reminds me of the day I'd received it, causing me to once more relinquish myself to memory.

The rain falls, covering the London streets and washing them clean of their usual mortal dirt. She stands perfectly upright beneath an umbrella that shrouds her delicate paleness in shadow. The sound of every droplet is crystallised and tinny as we linger at the gate of her father's London residence. A merchant, his grounds are kept lush by hired help, the windows cleaned from the inside by maids that wear black and white modest cut frocks and disinterested expressions.

I cannot help but ask myself if I will prove so fortunate in business as her father but then remind myself that the course of my destiny has been changed as that of so many other men this day by a call to war for the Empire that cannot be ignored.

"How long will you be gone?" she asks, her eyes watering with tears. I find the image of her walking toward me in a delicate white gown and floor-length veil shattering and falling from her eyes, indistinguishable from the weep of the skies.

"As long as it takes. I have been called to protect Her Majesty's empire against the French, and I can imagine that being no small feat." I'm honest, refusing to make any promises as I lift her chill knuckles to my lips, adorning her porcelain flesh with a single kiss. She blushes, brushing the cascade of caramel honey-coloured locks from her shoulder, a single tear falling and drying on her cheek.

"You will return to me, won't you?" she asks the question as if I can possibly answer her with any kind of certainty.

"With everything that I am, I will try. I will have you for my wife, Briar Shaw." I vow this, chest filling with imaginary icy water.

"I have something for you, here—" She reaches into the pocket of her double-breasted navy dress coat, pulling out something that glimmers dull silver in the shadow of her umbrella.

She drops it into my palm, the weight of it telling me immediately that it is worth some small sum.

"Open it," she requests, eyeing the locket excitedly and shifting on the balls of her feet. Rainwater drips from the tips of the umbrella, creating a damp and intermittent veil between us, the bride and groom who are forced to postpone for the sake of yet another war.

Slipping a fingernail under the catch, I pop open the face of the locket, finding a miniature rendering of Briar staring up at me from within.

I sigh, the gaze of her painted face almost too real to be merely art as I glance between the real thing in front of me and the locket in my palm.

"I'll wear it always," I promise her this, slipping the pendant over my neck and tucking it beneath my cravat so it might lie close to my heart.

"Don't forget me, Samuel." Her lip trembles as I lift a finger to the angelic curve of her jaw.

"Impossible," I whisper.

Tucking that very same locket beneath the t-shirt I had borrowed from Leo, I wonder how I should approach revealing my true nature to Kairi.

She seems shy, reserved, just like Briar had always been, but perhaps behind that façade is the heart of someone who would willingly believe in the magic that permeates my existence but is missing from her own. She's sick, and I wonder also if her condition would be improved by the Aetherial sun.

If this is the case, I may not have as much trouble convincing her to stay.

51

I think on her face, stunningly youthful despite the pain she clearly bears. It's refreshing, reminding me of the day we had first met before things became so very complicated.

Perhaps this really is a second chance, but even if she isn't Storm reborn by some divine magic, I know I cannot stay away, not when she so perfectly recaptures that which I've lost.

So then, it lies on my shoulders to woo her. To court and infatuate her, to show her how her life could be with me.

I know it could be risky, especially after everything I've done to ensure that the other Kindred races stayed onside after I lost her, after everything I've sacrificed to prevent war. Yet, I can't think about that for too long, not really, because I know that no matter what the risk, I would do anything if I could have her truly by my side once again. I will do whatever it takes to capture her heart and protect it as my own, just as I had gone to great lengths to retrieve the locket after my death.

So now, the only question is how do I get such a modern, exquisite damsel to fall?

5

PERSUASION

KAIRI

I'M SPRAWLED OUT ON one of the long, cream, leather sectionals that form the square of the room's focal point, listening to the sound of some blonde girl with enormous blood-spattered breasts screaming her head off on the TV. I'm not actually watching the 80's horror flick like my dads, who never miss out on this odd Friday night tradition but am instead searching online for anything I can find on one Miss Briar Shaw.

I've tried all the social media outlets I can think of but come up empty, not on the name but on anyone of the right age or physical description. There's no-one by that name in the area, the closest individual located somewhere in Ohio called Middlefield.

Internet search results haven't proven much better, but at least I tried.

"You working on that book blog you were going to start?" My dad asks me, his arm slung over Pa's shoulder as the two of them turn away from the onscreen carnage and toward me instead.

"No. I guess I just can't find the time. Every single time I manage to get posting reviews regularly, I suddenly flare up and have to stop. It's a nightmare, and people hate it when you're unreliable," I explain, watching the two of them go from excited to concerned in two seconds flat.

"What?" I ask, knowing exactly what it is they're going to say.

"You were so ambitious before. It's just sad, and we're worried— All you do is read books. Is that enough for you?" my dad asks, and I shrug, licking my bottom lip and sighing deeply.

Nobody knows that I've fallen far from who I once was better than me, and while I know they mean well, the tide of my guilt rises, threatening to wash my positivity clean.

"It'll have to be—" I shrug yet again, but it doesn't placate their concern, and I can no longer stand the uncomfortable silence between us.

Closing my laptop, I get to my feet, observing as the sun lowering outside the enormous windows creates an intricate silhouette of weeping willows, swaying heather, and grazing horses.

"Are you alright? I didn't mean to upset you—" My dad reaches out and grabs my hand before I can move to leave, staring up at me with unconditional care.

"I'm okay. I guess I'm just trying to find out where I fit in the world now— you are right. I was ambitious. And sitting around doing nothing after working so hard for so many years is killing me." He squeezes my fingers as both men sit upright, giving me their full attention and putting the TV on mute. I continue, wondering if they've been waiting for this kind of confession from me. "Unfortunately, my body doesn't want to cooperate, and reading is the only thing I can think of to keep my mind distracted. But no— it's not enough. I don't know if anything short of better health ever will be. I don't know how to do this, to be this weak, sick person. It isn't me. In fact, I hate her. This pathetic sick girl." I'm blunt, unable to summon the strength to be anything else. My back aches as I stand, hand caught in his, eyelids heavy with fatigue.

"What can we do? Tell us." My Pa pleads, looking up at me from the couch.

"Just— love her, and don't give up on her, that sick girl. I don't think I'm strong enough to do this without you," I implore, my throat thick with the pain of acknowledging the truth of all this. I'm weak, and what's worse it's becoming increasingly obvious to me that the failure of my physical self has caused my mental health to fragment. I see it now as a clear fissure between what I had been and what I am now. I want to bridge the two, but can find no way; because there is simply no way back to the person I had been before the pain.

It isn't fair, but it's my reality, and I can't escape it.

Letting my hand fall gently from his grasp, my dad watches as I pad across the room in bare feet and move toward the stairs, laptop under my arm.

"Where are you going, to bed?" he guesses, but I shake my head as I look back over one shoulder.

"No, I'm going to get dressed and go and read a little out at the pond," I explain, and the two of them nod, eyes concerned but undeniably steely against their sympathy.

I run my fingers back through my thick tangled locks, beginning my climb up the stairs in silence and waiting for the sounds of a blonde being slaughtered to rise from the main room before releasing the breath I'm holding.

My eyes water with tears, body pulsing with errant shocks as I climb each step as though it were a mountain. Finally, I reach the landing and dive into my room.

This is something no one can fix and watching the two people I love most in this world clambering to do everything they can is making me feel a little helpless. They've always been my heroes, my knights in shimmering white armour who saved me all those years ago from the sea, and yet now, there's nothing they can do. The grief of their inability to come to my aid is deep in my chest, melding with the guilt that I cannot escape.

I close the door and lean back against the thick honeyed oak, before slumping to the floor, and bringing my palms to rest against my cheeks as tears threaten to spill and sobs fight to wrack my body.

My laptop falls from under my arm, making a clunk on the floor, but I can't bring myself to care.

I feel so alone.

Like I'm trapped in a hell I can't escape, watching everyone else around me go about their lives, oblivious.

But he hadn't been.

A small voice, something like the hope that I've long thought had abandoned ship, whispers inside me.

He'd seen me, seen the bars behind my irises, the cage my body has become, the way my heart beats now only to hear the echo of its own lone thrum.

My eyes dart to the window, to beyond, where the sun is sinking toward the horizon fast, rays of dappled butterscotch light pooling on the mattress where Catticus is puddled, more furry fluid than feline.

I'm supposed to be meeting him soon, and though I know he'll be disappointed I haven't found Briar, maybe he might consider staying around and hanging out with me instead.

I allow myself to sit on the floor for a few minutes, letting my racing heart calm and my tears dry salty on my cheeks. I rest my head against the thick wood, thinking about his face and the way he'd stripped me of all my defences without a second thought. It's true I've been fighting pain all day from the incident at the bookstore and the flare that followed, but I've also been unable to completely forget his extraordinary eyes, the curve of his jaw, and the way in which I can't shake the feeling that I've met him before.

In another life perhaps?

The thought is ridiculous, perhaps a testament to how desperate I am to want my story to change course, for this illness to be only a chapter, and yet I cannot help but wonder.

Maybe reading so much has addled my brain.

Getting to my feet, I take a deep breath, ignoring the ache in my knees and spine, and try to pull myself together. I'm meeting Aro at dusk, and the sun is fast falling toward the horizon.

Striding across the breadth of my bedroom, I open my closet and try to figure out what I should wear. It's not like I particularly want to impress Aro, only that last time I hadn't even been wearing a bra, and I don't want him to think I'm a total slob.

I pick out a sundress I haven't worn in years, the vintage silhouette coming to mid-calf, in white cotton with heather contoured in deep aubergine embroidery around the hem. Selecting a white lace bralette and simple nude cotton panties, I unwrap the fluffy white robe that's cocooning my battered body, letting it drop to the floor in a puddle of fuzz and shedding my tropical, floral pyjamas underneath.

Closing the closet door, I gaze at myself in the mirror that hangs on the outside of the door, staring at my naked body. It looks perfectly normal with flawless flesh coating my skeleton and muscles roping themselves beneath a thin layer of fat softening my curves. The stretch marks on my inner thighs make me pause as I reconsider the dress, not wanting to have the crude and jagged red lines on show. They're everywhere though, including on the backs of my shoulder blades and my buttocks, making me feel uncomfortable by highlighting the weight I've put on since I had to stop exercising so intensively. In fact, it's almost as though they're claw marks from the inside, and because I have so many, hiding them isn't easy.

Running a finger over the edge of my hip, I find more of the same but cannot deny how my fingers tingle as they trace over my skin. I haven't wanted the touch of a man in so long, feeling unattractive and unsettled in my own skin, but I can't deny that pleasure would make a nice change from the pain.

I turn my back on my reflection, pulling on the panties and then the bralette before shoving the sundress over my head and pulling it down over my curves. The bust is a little tighter than I remember, but otherwise, it fits nicely. Grabbing a hairbrush, I pull my long, caramel tangles out of the messy bun that I usually shove them into, careful not to dislocate my shoulder as I set about brushing the dark, honeyed locks, scalp prickling at the slightest snag.

I hadn't realised how long my hair had gotten, and it now hangs way past my breasts.

Assessing myself, I decide the length makes me look too childish, and so pull the silken tresses into a high ponytail, leaving only two short strands hanging down in front of my ears.

I look myself in the face as I apply Chapstick and dab organic white musk oil behind my ears, along my collarbone, and on the inside of my wrists, seeing myself approaching who I had been before if only slightly. My eyes are still ringed with dark circles, my skin pale and sickly looking even in the rich glow of sunset that pours in through the window, but the dress and having my hair detangled has made a real difference.

Slipping on a pair of nude ballet flats with memory foam insoles, I grab a vintage copy of *Persuasion* by Jane Austen, having finished *Les Misérables* just after lunch. The edges of the pages are finished in gold leaf, the cover embossed with swirling font, and the spine well-weathered against my palm. I love the weight of it as if the story itself has a real presence.

Leaving the room, I return downstairs, getting a whiff of the lemon chicken with rice and collard greens we had enjoyed for dinner, feeling content and more like myself than I have in a while.

"You look lovely." My Pa inhales sharply as he speaks from the kitchen, clearly surprised as he drops a plate full of suds into the sink with a plop. His shock speaks to exactly how crappy I look daily.

"Thanks, I was sick of wearing pyjamas."

Both my parents look at one another, the pride on their faces hard to swallow. I don't wait around to give any further explanation, wary of time passing, and so head past the television where credits are now rolling and out the double glass doors onto the porch.

The early summer evening air is rich with the sound of the very first waking cicadas, their bodies acting as bowstring and cello as they orchestrate their natural symphony with innate, natural mastery.

Stepping down from the reddish wood of the porch, I feel long grasses rub gently against my ankles and bring up a hand to shield my eyes from the intense orange glow of the sun.

The horses have been put away in their stables for the night, and a peace settles over me that I simply can't explain as I stroll through the fields toward my gazebo, my limbs swinging along with the high ponytail that tickles my spine.

Inhaling the sticky smell of a Tennessee summer that comes with strong connotations of sweet iced tea and warm peach pie, I make my way to the pond.

Here, weeping willows plume lime and gold drapes that fall gracefully into the water, reflections eerily still and perfectly symmetrical.

Looking around, I find Aro isn't here yet. I guess it isn't quite dusk, so I move instead to wait. As I begin to tread around the edge of the pond, brushing willow branches aside, I feel myself becoming nervous, stomach twisting in anticipation as my pulse heightens and my mouth becomes suddenly dry.

I have no need to be nervous or excited, and yet the thought of seeing him again is causing my senses to run rampant, making colours brighter and sounds louder.

A blinding flash breaks the still scene, the crack of it like a tree cleaved by lightning or a hard whip splitting the surface of a frozen lake.

My head snaps to the source.

Out of thin air, he's there.

Standing, enormous wings outstretched from his spine, every single inky feather blazing with the dying light of the sun.

Wings.

He pivots to face the gazebo and finds me there, his beautiful mouth curving into a smile as I crumple to the floor, losing myself once more to the endless dark.

I awaken to softness caressing my cheek.

My eyes flutter open, finding the sky a soft velveteen periwinkle overhead, the sun long gone as stars start to wink down on the world with a bashful coyness. I'm splayed out on the dusty ground, my head resting against something hard and warm.

"Oh, thank goodness—" his voice comes as a rapid series of exhales as my pupils dart up to his face.

I'm lying, cradled in Aro's arms, his wings blanketing me from the fast-cooling air. His velvet jacket is wrapped tight around my trembling shoulders, the fabric deepest black and scented like violets, a heady combination.

Shaking my head and trying to clear the chaos within, I scramble, trying to crawl away from him, my entire body weak but alert with panic.

"Hey! Hey! It's okay. It's okay. I'm not going to hurt you!" he pleads as I lose the last of my strength and slump face down in the dirt. Looking back over my shoulder with great effort, I find him, muscular shoulders narrower than they had appeared to me before but silhouetted against two enormous black wings, every feather tipped gold.

"You're— a— a—" I stutter, tongue tripping over the word *angel* as my mind implodes with questions.

"I'm a Sephilim actually, and I didn't mean you to find out this way. For that, I apologise. I thought I was early so I'd have a chance to talk to you before I showed you my full wingspan," he explains, holding out a hand to me.

"Please, you're in shock. Let me hold you," he pleads with those galaxy eyes, the lilac in them almost silver beneath the rising half-moon.

I shiver, blood racing around my body but refusing to warm me.

Blinking, I take several seconds, absorbing the image of him – wings and all – before I let my shoulders visibly slacken. I don't move to take his hand, simply letting it hang between us, eyes narrowing.

"What is this? Why are you here?" is the only thing I can think to say as I tuck my knees under myself and pull his jacket closed around my chest.

"I'm sorry. Please, don't be afraid, I can explain. Just come here. You're cold and shivering. I'm worried. I promise you I won't hurt you. If I was going to do that, I would have acted while you were unconscious." His words are surprisingly calm and even, his wings staying perfectly still as they hover behind him. I can't take my eyes off them, pupils darting from one to the other and then fixing on his face over and over again. He remains on his knees in front of me, looking at me as though he's afraid that one wrong move might cause me to bolt.

I breathe out a second, and that second is all it takes for my body to betray me and relax entirely. My form hunches, slumping, and in the second it takes me to realise I don't have the strength to run from this strange, winged man, he's already swept me back up into his arms. While carrying me toward the gazebo, his wings tuck themselves in at his spine, and I am left with nothing to do but gaze up at him, painfully aware of the unmistakable brute strength within his tightly packed chest and arms. He handles me as though I'm no more than a ragdoll.

Sitting down on the wooden deck, he places me in his lap, curling his wings around me to stave off the slight breeze, grabbing a blanket from the chair and tucking it around me over the top of his jacket. I take a moment to examine him while he does this, finding him to be wearing a loose white shirt with the collar open and simple black pants.

On the edge of the gazebo, something catches my eye, glistening ever so slightly in the light, and before I can turn back, he's followed my gaze and is smiling down at me.

"Those are for you, but I had to put them down so I could catch you. It seemed more important at the time," he explains with a boyish grin.

Reaching over with a long arm, without letting my body so much as slip, he presents a bouquet to me, but I soon realise that this is no ordinary bunch of flowers.

"What—" I begin, but the question becomes lost as he places the heavy stems in my palm. I tilt my head, eyes widening as I allow my fingertips to come up and trace the exquisite flawless curve of the amethyst roses, the crystal cool against my skin.

"I know you must have questions, and I want to answer them, but first I have to ask - are you alright? Can I get you anything?" His face is sincere, eyes catching mine and refusing to let them go. My mouth hangs open, heart suddenly sprinting as I feel his body encapsulating mine at such intimate proximity for perhaps the first time.

"No, I'm fine, just overwhelmed— as you can imagine—" I glance at his wings again; examining the delicate curve of each feather and feeling their soft plumes tickle my bare legs.

"Of course. I really am sorry about how I arrived; I didn't think you'd be here already. Interdimensional travel is— tricky—" he gives a heartbreakingly boyish smile as his eyes become apologetic.

"Interdimensional travel— so— you're from another dimension?" I ask, feeling completely stupid.

"Yes. A dimension that lies between this one and the one of myths and legends. A border dimension called Aetheria," he explains, not dropping my gaze for a second. The silver stems of the roses warm in my palms as I become further aware of our closeness but still am unable to find the energy or will to move.

"And you're— a Sephilim?" I recall the name he had uttered before with difficulty, the word feeling odd and foreign on my tongue.

"Yes, and a High Lord to boot. Chosen and blessed by Zeus himself."

"Zeus? As in lightning bolts and giant pecs?" I cock an eyebrow, wondering if I am dreaming or at least still unconscious.

"That's the one. We share Aetheria with other Kindred, chosen by other gods and goddesses, but Zeus is kind of the boss of them if you like—" He's watching me intently, face tight with concern as I blink slowly, trying to absorb the information and make sense of how this impacts me.

"So— you're looking for Briar Shaw to take her back with you?" I guess, sitting up a little in his arms and chewing the inside of my lip, body stiff with exhaustion and shock. "I did look. I couldn't find her though—" I add, eyes dropping to the flowers in my lap and wondering why he's presented them to me.

"Yes, about that. It's the reason I'm here." He takes something from around his neck, reaching into the crumpled open collar of his shirt and lifting the pendant from beneath. He offers it to me, dropping it in my immediately open palm. It's heavy and still warm from his skin.

"Open it," he commands, all authority even though the volume of his voice has barely risen above a whisper.

I look up at him with curiosity then back down to the oval, silver locket, opening it with slow, shaking fingers. When my eyes absorb what I'm looking at, I inhale sharply.

"But— that's *me*." I squint down at the tiny miniature portrait, finding myself in every gliding line, stroke, and dab of the artist's tiny brush.

"I know—" Aro's hand glides beneath his jacket and rises to the top of my spine, palm warming my skin as we stare at each other.

I relax into him as he helps me support myself while remaining upright. "But I don't understand how it can be— she died a long time ago." His words bring a sadness down around me like heavy fog, one that I have no right to indulge. I never knew this girl, and even though she looks like me, it's no reason for me to mourn her.

"So— if she died, then why did you ask me to find her?" I demand, narrowing my eyes, suddenly suspicious. He only laughs though, looking up through devastatingly long lashes and closing my fingers around the locket in my palm before bringing them up to his lips. They brush the back of my hand; causing me to flush despite everything telling me this is completely insane. "The truth?" he asks me, and I nod vigorously, lips parted as I breathe deeply through my mouth, tasting the night and the scent of him intermingling upon my tongue in a haze of violets and moonbeams, starlight and lavender.

"Because by some magic, I think you *are* her. I wanted an excuse to see you again if only because when I first laid eyes on you, I thought you were the most beautiful creature I've seen since I lost her. I felt this draw to you— almost like we've met before on a deeper level— but it could have just been me." He shrugs, and I find my heart pounding at his confession.

This must be a dream.

"I felt it too," I admit, voice barely audible, face growing hot beneath his scrutiny.

"You did?" he asks, cocking his head, and I nod.

"I want to say no, to tell you that you're mad, but you made my heart skip a beat." I'm bold in this statement, finding my shyness at sudden war with my desire to split open and spill my secrets.

"But you don't remember me? Not at all?"

"No. I don't. It's more like— I don't know, some kind of instinct, I guess." I feel inarticulate as I fiddle with the roses in my lap, dropping my gaze and looking out over the pond beyond the gazebo, the moon reflected flawlessly in its mirror-esque surface.

"I know what you mean—" He tilts my head so I'm forced to meet his gaze, a single finger caressing the line of my jaw.

His every action is commanding in a way that leaves me unable to pull away but also in a way that would stop me from ever wanting to. His eyes glisten, dropping to my lips as we hang in a moment that's halfway between a nightmare of hope that will never be fulfilled, and a fantasy whereby everything I've ever wanted is firmly within my grasp.

He drops his fingers from my skin, and we enter a moment of heavy silence as I hand the locket back to him and he replaces it around his neck.

I turn from him, resting my head against the warmth of his chest and letting myself relax. I enjoy the moment, for I suddenly realise that there is no way that anything can grow between us.

If everything he's saying is the truth, then we're two entirely different species living in two entirely different worlds.

"You should go." I hear myself say the words and wonder why I'm pushing him away. Then realise that perhaps it's because this stranger is fast growing the ability to hurt me, and I already hurt enough.

"You want me to leave?" he asks, sounding more wounded than I'd expected.

"Don't you have to be getting back to Aetheria— or whatever it's called?" I ask him, shuffling to get some distance as I leave his coat in his lap, shivering against the cold. I grit my teeth, feeling stupid for letting myself get caught up in his compliments and lingering gazes.

I know better.

"Look, I don't know why you think I'm here Kairi, but I wanted to invite you to come back with me. To see if it causes any kind of memories to return. But I can leave if that's what you need." I hear him getting to his feet, leaving his jacket crumpled on the floor, and I turn, brows furrowing.

"You want to take me to Aetheria with you?" I'm acutely aware, in this moment of the insanity, of my desperate desire to hear him say yes.

I am pining to leave for a dimension that probably doesn't exist with a man who is quite possibly crazy and has somehow managed to create realistic-looking fake wings.

Perhaps I should have taken my parents up on their offer to pay for a therapist—

Have I really become so desperate for change that I'm willing to succumb to hoping that fairy tales exist? That a winged knight might save me from everything I'm currently going through?

He gives me a look of utter surprise as he walks past me and down the stairs of the gazebo as though he's actually seeing through my expression and gazing right at my low levels of self-esteem. His wings flutter as a chuckle spills from his lips and his tread against the wood echoes in my ears.

As I watch his extraordinary silhouette, something else occurs to me.

"It was you— wasn't it? On the roof during that storm—" I accuse him, thinking back to that night, to how Catticus wouldn't stop hissing.

"I won't lie to you. Yes, it was." He's earnest as he strides a few paces away, making me think momentarily that he's going to leave. But instead, he merely bends down, retrieving something from the dirt.

As he turns and strides back, I see he's holding my copy of *Persuasion* in one hand.

He offers it to me, and I take it, not reaching his gaze as my fingers close around the spine.

"How long have you been watching me?" I demand, feeling intruded upon yet unafraid against all sense.

"Ever since Morpheus told me he thought he had found my long-dead lover in her dreams." Again, it isn't the answer I expect, but the face of the man with surreal, viridian hair comes to the forefront of my mind, the image of him right before I had collapsed branded into my memory.

"So, I wasn't going crazy. I really had seen him before? He was in the bookstore!" I blurt, cocking my eyebrow and scratching my forehead, temples beginning to throb.

"No, you're not crazy. And I never intended to do anything that might seem untoward. But you have to understand that I needed to know if Briar really had come back somehow. My intentions were innocent." He's so formal in his explanation, so in control of himself, his words, and his expression as I scan him, searching for a flicker of malice, of false promise anywhere.

I come back with nothing.

"Was she like you? I mean, with the wings—" I point to his wingspan, and he nods slowly, straightening. His eyes harden noticeably, steeling against his memory.

"Yes. She was chosen by Hera as a Nephilim, the female equivalent of my race, before she was lost to me." His porcelain skin crumples a little, a small crack in the façade of his seamless personal control becoming apparent.

He obviously really loved this girl, whoever she was— or I was.

Can it really be possible?

I want to believe it can because, if I do, then every story I've ever read about magic has the potential to be real. I'm a dreamer who walks through worlds built from words and the imaginings of fantastical minds— but what if the imaginary could become tangible?

What if it always has been?

It sounds like a dream come true, all of it, right down to the face of the man standing before me, but still, I won't let myself hope.

I cannot, however, deny my curiosity.

"So, if I did come to Aetheria with you— what would we do there? Where would I go?" I ask him, and the corner of his sculpted mouth tremors with the beginnings of a smile.

"I would take you back to my palace, the Solis Castra in the city of Soleus, and show you my world. I'd also like to get to know you a little better, obviously." At these words, I decide to finally stand, grasping the crystal roses in one hand and my book in the other.

"Bit extravagant for a first date, don't you think?" I ask him, keeping my expression neutral even though the very walls of my reality are shifting, my eyes opening to possibilities I have been blind to for twenty-three years.

"Who said it was a date?" His eyes sparkle with mischief, causing me to flush deeply as I consider how to respond.

"You whisk a girl off to your palace in another dimension, and it's *not* a date?" I ask, but he doesn't reply, simply stepping forward and placing his open palms on my hips.

I'm painfully aware of his touch, not because it hurts but simply because I feel like despite his gentleness, my skin is burning deliciously wherever his fingers make even featherlight contact.

"If I say it's a date, will you accept my proposal?" he asks, moving close to me.

My breathing becomes shallow as the scent of violets intensifies.

It takes me a few moments to decide how to reply, torn between terror and ecstasy at the thought of such a seemingly romantic fantasy adventure.

"Can I have a day to decide?" I request, my entire body humming at his proximity.

He nods, stepping back and placing both hands behind his waist with unfaltering restraint.

"Of course. Meet me here tomorrow if you wish to take me up on my offer. If you don't come, then I'll leave you alone, and you won't have to worry about seeing me again." He lunges past me, moving faster than I'd thought possible, grabbing his coat from the floor.

I watch on with fascination as he dresses, wings pushing themselves through convenient yet discreet slits in the back of his jacket. I wonder now if I can live with having seen such a creature, and not follow my curiosity to learn everything about him and where he comes from.

Buttoning the coat, he straightens his collar, leaving the chain of the silver locket peeking out against his pale throat beneath.

"Goodbye, Kairi." He gives a small bow, wings spreading wide as I've ever seen them, and I find his face beaming as he stares at me with adoring eyes as if he's committing my face to memory.

Then, there's a flash of lightning that almost blinds me, and he's gone. Leaving me with far too many questions, a choice to make, and a bouquet of crystal roses.

6

GREAT EXPECTATIONS

ARO

THE SECOND MY FEET touch down on the pale amethyst floors of the Solis Castra's extraordinarily large main room, a sense of urgency that I cannot ignore clutches at me, knotting my stomach. She was easier to convince than I had expected, perhaps because she feels our connection just as I do, a relief in itself.

I look up at the enormous octagonal ballroom that soars skyward, surrounded by cobalt stained glass on every side. It's glorious in the moonlight, but nowhere near what I need it to be.

Not yet.

A guard stands at the door, his golden armour made luminous and cold by the night light pouring in and drenching the floor in its sublime chill. Striding over to him, I square my shoulders and allow my wings to spread from my spine a little, widening my shadow.

"I need your captain. Go and find him for me," I order the Sephilim guard, whose name I do not know and can't say I care for, before watching him take off into the air in search of his commander. His hand rests sturdily on the hilt of his sword as his dove-grey wings beat a quick rhythm, and he rises, posture otherwise unchanged.

I let myself wander the room, thinking on her face, on the lack of resistance she had put up against my courting, about the way she'd leaned against my chest, so trusting, so pure.

I forget how unguarded mortals can be, how young they are, and how their souls have not yet been tarnished by the doubt and cynicism that comes with years of immortal life and the Kindred politics of the senate.

I have lived only two hundred and twenty-six years, and yet I feel my ability to hope, to wish, and to dream have diminished with every one.

Still, though, her new optimism, the untainted spark behind her eyes, has begun to awaken a sense of belief in the universe and its divine mechanics I thought was long since lost to me.

I spin on the spot, gazing up to the spired ceiling that pierces the thick blanket of cloud surrounding Soleus over one hundred and fifty feet above. A rose quartz chandelier is strung from the very peak, each crystal glowing as the design sweeps through blooming roses and twining vines, otherworldly, beautiful.

I bet Kairi will love it.

As I continue to turn on the spot, picturing the possibilities for how I might transform the ballroom for tomorrow night, I hear the pulsating rhythm of beating wings approaching, the rustle of feathers a familiar prickle echoing against the surrounding walls.

After only moments, Captain Bond and the soldier I had tasked to find him return, shadows growing smaller as they fall through the torrent of golden moonlight-tinged duck-egg blue.

Their feet touch down without sound, the landing elegant on both their parts.

Leo ruffles his deep red hair, which looks unkempt despite being cropped short, leaving me wondering if I've woken him.

He straightens to greet me, his broad chest and biceps tensing visibly.

"My Lord?" he queries, bending his head in respect.

I nod back, bored with formalities and ready to get to work.

"I need this place transformed in the next twelve hours. I want security tightened, and I'll need you to get the kitchen's chief Nephilim, a carriage driver and— Miss Silver, and quickly. I don't have time to waste," I explain, pausing on Silver's name with a smugness I can't restrain as I clap my hands together with impatient enthusiasm.

The captain nods, hazel eyes growing wider with curiosity.

"Might I ask why?" He crosses his hands in front of him, and I take him in, finding that he's wearing chocolate brown leather pants and a loose, cream tank top, his chocolate-coloured wings stained burgundy at the tips.

"I'm having a guest. A mortal girl. She'll need protection while she's here." I announce, watching his freckled nose bunch in surprise and his ruddy eyebrows rise on his forehead.

68

"I see." He does not ask any further questions, but I can sense his concern. No mortals are allowed here; it is the law. For if we allowed it, then everyone with living relatives would be bringing them here and offering eternal life under the Aetherial sun.

However, this is a special case, and I will defend my decision with blade and fury to anyone who tries to suggest the situation otherwise.

He turns, curtly ordering his inferior to locate a carriage driver as he moves to find the two women I seek.

Taking off without sound, I marvel at his speed in the air. I am a High Lord and far older than he, and yet the captain can fly circles around me any day, hence why I chose him to lead my best unit of aerial troops.

I wait only minutes before Silver and Dawn conduct into the room, both wearing extravagant gowns that flutter just off the crystal floor in shades of arctic white and shimmering pearl.

"You rang?" Silver sounds bored, flicking a lock of hair from her neck with a gentle and intentionally flirtatious stroke of one finger.

"I did. Dawn— why are you here?" I ask, knowing full well that she isn't who I requested.

"The captain said you wanted to speak with Susie, the head of the Kitchen, so I thought I could take the message and relay it as they are in the middle of preparing late supper. I was headed there for some milk and honey anyway," she explains.

"As always, your thoughtfulness knows no bounds." I smile at Dawn with affection, eliciting a cough from Silver that grates on my nerves like a fraying bow upon out-of-tune violin strings.

"Silver, I need you to go to the dressmakers in town and ask them to come to the palace in the morning. I will need a few things custom-made for Kairi to wear so she fits in, and I'll also need you to get Vail on your way back so I can discuss music choices with her, please," I inform her, observing with satisfaction as her eyes grow wide.

"Wait, you're bringing her here?" she looks incredulous, and I smile, unable to hide my victory against her.

"Yes, she's agreed to join me for the evening tomorrow." I know she's done no such thing, but seeing Silver's rage stirring just beneath the surface of her otherwise pristine, cold beauty is more than worth the small lie.

"I'll also need you to get me some maids for decorating this space for dancing, and I would like to talk to some gardeners about ensuring everything is flawless outside as well." I pile up the responsibilities, watching her fingers curl into a small yet furious fist at her side.

"All this for a mortal? I'm not a servant either unless you've forgotten, Aro," she snaps, throwing her side fringe slightly away from her furrowed brow, lips pinching into a scowl.

"I am your High Lord, and you felt fit to impose yourself on me yesterday, so I have no doubt you'll be overjoyed to do this with me today. After all, who else can I trust with such a special event?" I ask her, mixing in my authority with half-compliments.

I watch her tense, lips pushing hard together as the blood leaves them.

"Fine." She exhales a huff, slim frame sagging within the embroidered pearlescent confines of her bodice.

"Good, see you when you're done." I dismiss her without courtesy, hearing the sound of paws thudding against crystal. My eyes rise from Dawn's face to find Leo returning from above, accompanied by his golden Kensari, Phyllis. The winged lioness is running vertically down the gargantuan height of one of the eight surrounding walls, dark hazel eyes glinting as he catches my glance, glimmering golden feathers tremoring with every step.

The captain touches down once more beside Dawn, my eyes as the small smile he always gets when he flies tugs at his lips insistently.

"So, what exactly did you have in mind with regard to tightening security?" he asks, not wasting time. Dawn smiles at him, taking in his young and determined face with motherly affection.

"I'm thinking of doubling troop presence around the Solis Castra. I'll want some guards to accompany the carriage here, and I expect you to stand guard at her door personally." Folding my arms across my chest, I allow my index finger to tap against the velvet of my sleeve as the captain becomes thoughtful.

"Then I should consult with Lord Abara?" he suggests, suddenly unsure of my intent, but I stiffen and narrow my eyes.

"You will not. He has nothing to do with this, and I don't want him involved." I allow my tone to hang low, a warning growl barely audible to those without Kindred hearing. Phyllis sure hears it though and looks up at me, her deep brown eyes flashing a warning as she stiffens at her master's side.

"Then I'll probably have to pull some men from the eastern border of Nirvana—"

"I don't relish the idea of that either. I'm trying to be discreet." My tongue flicks out to wet my bottom lip as I straighten my spine, imposing my shadow on the commander in front of me.

"Why not just conduct her here if you're trying to be discreet? You don't think a carriage and guard will pull attention?" he asks, placing a hand on his hip and relaxing his shoulders, a stance of inevitable surrender to my request.

"I want her to see Aetheria, but I also want her identity protected. You know our history with the Draconians—" I trail off, tired of explaining myself as I gesture for Dawn to take a step forward.

"I'll want to run through what I'm thinking regarding tonight's dinner menu." She moves gracefully toward me, and I turn my back on Captain Bond, listening as his quick, hard footsteps fade into the distance.

"So, four courses?" she asks, tilting her head so she's looking up at me, intent to listen and serve as always.

"Five, I think— I want to wow her, Dawn. I want her to fall in love with this place, with me— I don't know how long I can wait patiently, knowing she's back and not at my side." I sigh, feeling the impossibly high expectations I have for this one night.

The thing is, we've only just met one another, but for me, I've been waiting hundreds of years to make this woman my wife, and after finding her soul housed in new and innocent porcelain, I am desperate to keep her with me, to keep her safe.

I lost her once, and it almost broke me and shattered every dream I had for the future.

I won't squander this second chance to earn her heart, to convince her of my worthiness.

If nothing else, I owe it to Briar to uphold the vow I made all those years ago, in the rain, among the bustle of a London Street to which I never returned.

KAIRI

I'm sitting in bed, staring at the same page of *Great Expectations* as I have been for the last two hours, eyes darting to the window where beyond, the sun has long since risen. I barely slept last night, tossing and turning both physically and mentally as my mind tries to make some kind of logical narrative out of the events of the last few days.

He was a— a *Sephilim*.

An *angel*.

He had *wings*.

A part of me wants to shake it off, to pretend it isn't real because denial is safe. It's choosing to see only the world in which I'm at the very top of the food chain as a mortal and in charge of my own destiny. I've lost so much power over my body, over my life, that perhaps it would be easier to be purely terrified of the prospect of a Higher Power, of winged men and far-off realms.

And yet—

The thought of somewhere so distant, of a world governed by other rules where the residents can fly, where magic could exist— it's too tempting to ignore.

I find myself sighing, the weight of indecision pressing heavy on my chest in the late morning hours, my body tired from lack of rest.

He says that my soul is her soul.

Briar.

He says that I've been rehomed in this body but that we've met in another life.

I want to deny the claim, to forget about him as merely insane and move on, but I cannot deny how my heart skipped a beat at the sight of him, at how I feel calm when cradled within his wingspan, by the way, I feel like a part of me knows him despite the fact we only met two days ago.

We barely know each other— and yet, there's something— something that feels like coming home.

A knock disrupts the series of thoughts that have been going round and round inside my skull, flying between the bony walls and through the chasm of fog in between like ping-pong balls.

"Kairi?" My dad's voice comes from behind the solid wood of the door before it opens a crack and he pokes his head inside. "Oh good, you're awake." I nod, sitting up a little from where I'm propped up in bed, attempting and dismally failing to read.

"Hey, Dad, what's up?" I ask, my voice raw and unused. I watch as he, and then my pa, both enter the room, walking across the squeaking floorboards before slumping down on the side of the bed.

"We just wanted to check on you. We heard you pacing all night—" My dad gives me a concerned glance, and I sigh yet again, unable to push them away but frustrated with their constant need to look at me with faces full of sympathy.

"I'm okay. Just haven't been able to get comfortable," I reply, shrugging inside the thin cotton of my plum nightshirt.

"We were thinking last night, well, talking— you know, trying to come up with ways to help you," my Pa begins, and my heart becomes leaden. I don't want to listen to what they have to say because I honestly feel so helpless already that in even suggesting asking or looking for help, I feel as though I'm letting the disease win, like I really am a sick person.

"Have you thought about support groups?" My dad chimes in, and I shrug. We've had this conversation before, and my answer remains the same.

"I told you they're so depressing. It's just people complaining, and honestly, I moan enough to myself as it is," I snap, my blood heating in my veins.

"Okay, well, what about online dating? Have you thought about trying to find someone special— you know, romantically? Someone who isn't sick?" Pa asks, face so calm, so wise and measured that it makes me even angrier.

"I don't want a boyfriend, and let's be honest. Who the hell would want to date me? I'm basically an anxiety attack waiting to happen for anyone who cares," I mumble, my words stinging as they hit the air like a wound that's opening wider and wider with every syllable.

"Kairi, you can't think like that." Pa scowls and I scowl right back.

"Why? It's true, isn't it? I'm not going to lie to myself about this. I can't even get dressed some days or function without a million freaking pills— and even they don't take away the pain!" I feel my eyes begin to water, frustration coming in waves like nausea.

"Well then, we need to go back to the doctors—" Dad insists, and I explode.

"No! I'm done with the hospital! I am done with needles and tests! I am done! Nothing they ever suggest helps, and I'm tired of it. I just want to be left alone!" I cry out, balling my fists into the duvet.

"You're just so angry—" Pa whispers, reaching out to touch my leg, but I flinch away, throwing off the covers and leaping onto my feet, rage allowing my pain to become momentarily unimportant. My heartbeat roars in my ears from the sudden exertion.

"Really, Pa? Well, I wonder why that is? Could it possibly be because I've had my entire goddamn life taken from me? Could it be because I worked my ass off for years, didn't party, didn't do anything except what I was supposed to do like a good girl, and then none of it made a freaking damn bit of difference anyway?! I had a boyfriend and friends, and now they're gone. I had a future, and that's gone too. Even my ability to walk down the street and function like an adult person is gone! Just like that with no warning and nothing I can do about it and nothing anyone else can do either. But I'm sorry if I'm angry! I guess I'm just a little pissed off at the fact my entire life has been destroyed—" I'm left gasping, my heart pounding, fists balled and warm at my sides, legs shaking beneath the hem of my nightshirt.

The two men who have stood by me my whole life stare up at me, faces shocked. I'm a shy girl, a quiet girl— and this is perhaps the first time I've ever seriously yelled at either of them.

But I can't take it back, can't rewind time and remind myself that this isn't their fault either.

My dad stands, holding my pa's hand firmly in his and pulling him behind.

"We're sorry, Kairi. We were only trying to help." His tone is deflated, a little angry but overwhelmingly sad as well.

The two of them trail out of the door, closing it behind them and leaving me standing there, tears rolling down my cheeks.

Rage explodes inside me as the silence blankets the room, and before I know what I'm doing, I have snatched my phone off the nightstand and am hurling it across the room with as much fury as I can manage. It hits the window beyond the nook where I usually read, leaving a crack spiderwebbing across the pane and fragmenting my view of the beautiful Tennessee morning.

I fall to my knees, sobbing, and for a moment, I let myself truly wallow in what I've lost. I haven't cried like this since before my diagnosis, not since my grandmother died, and I wonder if this is something that's been a long time coming.

I've tried to be strong, to stay positive, to cope and not complain, to make the best of things, but I just— I'm too tired to keep pretending like everything isn't falling apart. Because that's the truth of things.

Things are falling apart, and it's not just my body but my mind as well.

The water is tepid as I lie beneath the surface, looking at the distorted image of my body. My limbs feel boneless, my skin pruning as I soak in the Epsom salt-water bath, my eyes red and raw from crying. I feel the isolation from pushing my parents away on all sides, the chill fingers of loneliness grabbing for me, trying to drag me down into the darkness of yet another depression from which I'm unsure I'll recover.

The clawfoot white tub cradles my spine, and I lift a hand from beneath the surface, watching the evening light catch in the droplets as they fall from my fingertips.

The light caught in the prism of the water reminds me of the dying daylight setting Aro's feather tips ablaze.

What am I doing? Sitting here, dwelling in self-pity and despair.

This isn't who I was, isn't who I've ever been, so why now?

Is it just the pain, or is it something else, something inside of me that's intrinsically broken after losing so much of what I had loved in my old life?

Life has become mundane, I won't deny it, my only escape being between bound pages.

So why is it I'm still undecided about jumping into the unknown with Aro?

After all, what more have I got to lose?

Surely death would be less painful, more peaceful than my current existence.

Have I become so sheltered that I've forgotten how to live? To take risks despite the fact it might hurt— Am I now the one who recoils in the face of change, who turns from their chance at adventure?

As a reader, I've always thought that I'd grab the chance for romance, fantasy, and adventure with both hands. Have I come so far from the core of what makes me who I am that I'm saying no to what could be the opportunity of a lifetime?

These questions float around in the lavender steam that's still hanging around in the air, and suddenly, I'm angry again.

This time though, I'm angry with myself.

I can't miss out on the chance to lift the veil on what I perceive as reality, to learn about the secrets of the universe.

If I miss this opportunity, I'm going to spend the rest of my days regretting that decision and wallowing in what I am not instead of what I am.

With that thought, a fire ignites inside my blood, and suddenly I'm pulling myself up out of the tub, my listless limbs not aiding me as they should while my shoulders pop under the strain.

Once I'm standing, I pull the plug and step out onto a butter-coloured bathmat that covers the wooden floor, listening to the water drain from the tub as I reach for the large lemon-coloured towel hanging from the wooden ring on my left. The ceiling is sloped, my bathroom occupying the other end of the attic space in the converted barn, and the entire room suddenly drips golden as the clouds beyond the window part, the lazy afternoon sun drenching everything including me in heat and light.

I close my eyes, turning on the spot, my skin flush from the heat of both the bath and the window beyond the thin gauzy curtains, and for a moment, I can focus, not on the pain but on the absence of it. My skin continues to warm, and my jellied muscles seem to sigh out in relief, my lips upturning at the corners. The world beyond my eyelids remains a pure daffodil hue as I bask, letting myself breathe and leaving my anguish behind.

After a few moments, I bring the towel to my face, blinking away water droplets and beginning to dry myself from head to toe. Wrapping it around myself, I leave the bathroom, sun warming my back as I head toward the door, and then make my way across the landing and back to my room.

Once I'm inside, I close the door behind me and let out a deep breath, wondering what exactly I should pack, or wear even, to a different dimension. My eyes catch on the amethyst roses that are lying flat on my desk as I don't own a vase, but the flora gives no clue as to anything about Aetheria at all. I mean, I don't even know if they grow there or were made—

It takes me a few minutes of pacing to get the strength back into my legs from where the Epsom salts have drained away my tension, but eventually, I stop, staring at myself in the mirror.

My hair is wet and ratty, falling long and heavy around my shoulders in wild tangles, and my blue eyes are startlingly wide almost like I've woken up after being asleep for years.

Careful not to pull my shoulder out of joint, I set about brushing my hair, sectioning the locks off and focusing on one at a time. Then, I yank open my wardrobe doors, once again stumped for what to wear.

I hadn't asked about the weather or the terrain— or well, anything.

The magnitude of just how much is unknown hits me, and though my throat tightens in fear, my heart flutters with excitement. Letting my fingers drag across the hanging fabrics, I try to ignore my instinct to appear as attractive as possible and move instead to thinking about what garments would be sensible.

My first thought is that I don't do well in the cold. My joints lock up, and my muscles ache terribly, so layering is probably the way to go. After all, if I get too hot, I can always take a layer off.

I pick out a pair of thick, soft, aubergine leggings, the most slimming thing I own that doesn't cause me to come out in a rash, and throw them onto the bed. Picking out a ribbed grey vest and a fluffy grey jumper that hangs baggily off one of my shoulders, I settle on my choices, selecting seamless underwear and a white lace bralette plus some thin socks before throwing the pile of clothes to join my leggings and then closing the doors with a thick bang.

I pull on the underwear and my leggings, and then my mind jumps to packing other essentials. I grab a lilac leather backpack that's silky soft to touch, still wearing only leggings and my bralette, and begin to pace some more, thinking about everything I'll need.

It feels like when I first started to learn how to deal with my conditions, having to wrack my brain for everything that could possibly go wrong and what I'd need to handle it when out in the streets of L.A.

I dart around the confines of my bedroom, more energised than I have been in days, grabbing my spare pill bottles from the nightstand, tampons, moisturiser, ibuprofen gel, my sensitive toothpaste, TENs machine, ankle supports, wrist supports, and compression gloves. It seems like a lot as the bag begins to grow fuller and fuller, but I don't want to risk getting hurt and being unable to take care of myself.

My hair is almost dry thanks to the heat from the falling sun that pools on every surface below the window, and so I pull it into a thick braid that falls down my spine. Once that's sorted, I pull the jumper over my head, and grab *Great Expectations* from the nightstand, squashing it into the backpack as a last thought. I try never to go anywhere without a book unless it's a bookstore.

White musk oil applied, I debate throwing on some mascara but eventually decide against it and apply Chapstick to my lips, unsure about the casual comfort of my clothes but unable to justify wearing anything showier due to my lack of information about Aetheria.

Aetheria.

The word itself tastes like magic, like the first bite of your dream wedding cake or maybe the cookies you always eat right before bed on Christmas Eve. It feels like promises, like new beginnings and unlimited potential.

I try to picture it in my head, thinking of something similar to Tolkien's Middle Earth, and can't help myself as excitement causes me to hum, and a smile warps my face into an unfamiliar expression. I stare in the mirror, realising that it's one I haven't seen on myself in a really long time.

Joy.

Slipping on a pair of lace-up grey leather boots with great ankle support and grabbing my braces from where they sit next to the dresser, I slump down on the edge of the bed.

Pulling the carbon fibre cages up to surround each leg in turn, I line them up correctly with the knee joints before messing with the many Velcro straps, getting them stuck to myself and then each other as I wrangle them into submission.

Finally, I stand, struggling at first to get my balance with the braces adjusting the position of my knees, and therefore how I stand, but rushing against the discomfort as I grab my knapsack and throw it over one shoulder.

Looking back, I take one last glance around the room, my towel still discarded messily on the floor and Catticus asleep at the foot of the bed, before closing the door behind me.

Descending the stairs, I notice the house is quiet, and I find a note on the coffee table as I pass, which reads-

'Gone to visit the city for the weekend. Thought you could use the space.

We love you millions. So sorry if we are clingy and overbearing, but we just worry. Anyway, relax this weekend and enjoy the house without the old fogeys in it. Remember, no wild parties!

We'll see you soon.

P and D x'

I'm winded for a moment, remembering their faces as they left the room after I'd screamed at them.

But maybe— maybe it's what I needed.

They don't seem mad, only supportive as always, so I guess I should just be grateful that I won't have to make up an excuse for my whereabouts.

Still, I can't help but wish I could give them both a hug, to apologise for making them the target of so much pent-up rage. I mean, they haven't done anything wrong.

Grabbing the house keys off the hook, I lock up the front and back doors from inside before slipping out through the family room's sliding glass doors and onto the porch.

A quick twist of the keys and a reassuring wiggle of the handle and I head out across the ranch, looking up at the sky and wondering if the dimension I'm heading to will have a blue sky— or if it will be something entirely alien instead.

My braces rub as I walk, and as much as I want to be terrified and should probably slow down, I can't keep the rush out of my step or the smile off my face.

I pass by endless emerald fields patchy with long gold grasses and swaying heather until I finally reach the weeping willows surrounding the pond, heart racing so loudly I'm surprised I haven't scared off the birds that nest in the trees, unblinking.

There he stands, waiting in the gazebo with a smile on his face, almost giddy with smugness.

"I knew you'd come." He grins, taking a few hurried steps toward me and holding out a hand. His indigo velvet coat turns pinkish in the dying light of sunset as the gold buttons of the double-breasted fit gleam like fiery stars, and I stand self-conscious as I become excruciatingly aware of the braces holding me upright.

Taking his hand, I feel shivers run up my arm and bite down on my bottom lip to stop my breath from catching audibly in my throat, hauling my backpack higher on my shoulder.

He pulls me close, his black wings glistening as they cocoon both of us, eclipsing the sun and blanketing me in feathers of jet and precious metals.

"Ready?" he asks, tightening his grip on me with a provocative Hollywood smile.

7

BRAVE NEW WORLD

KAIRI

I'M AFRAID TO TURN around at first, afraid to open my eyes as a breeze catches the baby curls of hair on the nape of my neck, causing an involuntarily tingle to run up my spine. I inhale, the air thick and humid, tasting like cold vanilla cream upon my tongue. A tinkle, like glass on delicate silver, hits my ears.

"Kairi, open your eyes. Look—" Aro's voice is a whisper against my cheek as I hear his wings unfurl at my spine, his hands moving up to my shoulders to turn me away from him.

I open my eyes, obeying him, and my breath comes in an inhale so sharp, so awed that I blink repeatedly, unable to believe what I'm seeing.

"Is this— heaven?" I tear my eyes from the explosion of colour and magic around me, staring up at his face shining pure in the light of the setting cobalt sun.

"Welcome to Aetheria." He places his hands around my waist, and I don't stop him as he drops a kiss on the crown of my head, pulling my spine against the rigid heat of his abdominals. I feel his heart beating fast beneath his shirt, my stomach erupting in a flurry of butterflies at his closeness and the ease with which we fit together.

The sun is a bright and otherworldly blue as it kisses the horizon, the sky overhead an explosion of indigo scattered with diamond-esque stars. The air is thicker here, the light purer, and when I focus on the air in front of me, I see shimmering particles like the finest glitter you can imagine, swirling in discrete clouds.

The sound I had heard becomes obvious when I take a step forward on the earth, my boot crunching against powdered white crystal, maybe quartz, underfoot.

Spanning from me on all sides, silver and gold stems sway, their delicacy exquisite and alien as I find every one topped with a crystal bloom. The flowers, both earthen and not, reach endlessly for miles, petals tinkling gently against one another, the macrocosm of faceted light and colour like something out of a dream.

I gasp as the full force of the beauty hits me, wanting to reach out and touch only one petal, wanting to feel the weight of the amethyst lavender, rose quartz peonies, and sapphire blue hydrangeas cool against my skin.

I turn on the spot, spinning beneath the indigo dusk as I realise that the truth of this is that I've stepped into a fairy tale. My breathing comes easy as I finally let myself exhale, the scent and taste of the air sweet and intoxicating as it drenches my skin and lies as heavy perfection on my tongue.

I look back over my shoulder as I move to brush my fingers along the citrine petals of a daffodil, the meadow of crystal wildflowers glistening like a sea of multi-coloured glass as the light of the day fades slowly with the sinking sun.

Aro is staring at me, his wings exposed and glorious as a smile contorts his features, eyes utterly adoring.

"I never thought I'd see you here again—" he steps forward and holds out a hand.

I take it, and suddenly, something else hits me.

Nothing hurts.

I look down at myself but find my braces exactly where I put them, caging my knees.

"I— I don't—" I begin, and he smiles, stroking the side of my face with a finger before cupping my cheek.

"Hurt?" he asks, and my eyes widen.

"How did you know?" My voice is a whisper, my eyes watering as my heart pounds even harder within my ribcage. And yet, where before my skin was alight with a million live wires, where before my bones ached and screamed, now there is only silence.

"You walk differently now you aren't in pain." He brings his free hand up to squeeze the top of my arm as we stand among the flowers, the dusk thick and charged around us.

"You knew this would happen?" I ask him, voice still struggling to rise above a wisp.

"I had a hunch. The Sun Of Second Life takes away pain in mortals— or so the stories say."

I throw myself at him, wrapping my arms around his neck. He lifts me off my feet, twirling me around among the tinkling crystal of petals.

Laughing as he sets me down, I offer him my hand this time, a wicked smile dancing across my lips as the world around us grows dark.

He laces his fingers with mine, and I take off, running through the flowers beneath the stars as a bulbous golden moon rises in place of the disappearing blue sun.

"This way!" Aro speeds up, overtaking me as I relish the feel of my lungs burning, my legs moving, feet pounding against the earth and kicking up glitter with each and every step, my body stable beneath me. The air feels rich, my skin flushed beneath my sweater, suddenly being pulled along to a destination of which I'm not certain and don't care to worry about.

My soul spreads itself the width and breadth of my heart, stretching as though reawakened and resurrected.

It takes a while as we make our way through what seems to be an endless crystal meadow, but eventually, a road comes into view in the distance, defined solely by rows of amethyst clusters springing right up out of the ground beneath. I can't help but continue to stare at Aro's wings as we approach, now tucked tightly behind him to stop them getting in the way, wondering what it must be like to fly.

Eventually, we make it to the edge of the field, and what stands in the middle of the glistening powdered crystal of the road causes me to stare, mouth slack in awe.

A carriage, arctic white and encased in a cage of solid gold filigree that swirls and curves as if it's organic, stands behind two brilliant, alabaster stags. Their coats shimmer with the same glitter that dances through the air, silver antlers catching the light of the moon and tinting gold as well. On the front of the carriage sits a driver dressed in violet velvet breeches and a black long-tailed coat embroidered with golden vines of ivy. Tilting his head to me in greeting, he tucks his simple black wings behind him while fingering the reins that connect with the stags in front of him, their tails twitching like heart-shaped pom-poms on their behinds as they shift from one silver hoof to the other.

"Is this for us?" I pant, bringing a hand to rest above my racing heart.

"Of course, My Lady." Aro gives a small bow, and I smile, an unstoppable laugh escaping from my breathless lips as I reach down to adjust my braces, which slipped during our dash across the meadow.

"Do you really still need those? They don't look very comfortable—" Aro asks, gesturing to the metal cages, and I feel my face heat beneath the scrutiny of his inquisitive dark stare.

"Um— I guess not." I move to bend down and begin unstrapping them in the middle of the road, but Aro places a hand on my shoulder to get my attention, striding forward and pushing down heavily on a gilded gold door handle.

"Come, sit." He gestures to the white leather of the padded seat within the carriage, and I watch as a small ladder falls and expands so it reaches the ground. My eyebrows rise on my forehead and I blink slowly as he waits for me.

Is this guy for real?

I walk slowly forward, climbing the tiny white steps and sitting sideways on the edge of the bench so my legs hang out of the door. Aro then gets down on one knee and begins to unstrap my braces like the disabled Cinderella equivalent of fitting the glass slipper. His hands are gentle on my calves as they rip the Velcro free from itself, his long fingers dextrous and quick. He's focused, and in this moment where he isn't staring at me, I take the opportunity to stare at him instead.

His skin is flawless. Not a wrinkle or blemish, almost as though it's made from ceramic. His eyelashes are stunningly long, his mouth elegantly sculpted and plush as it purses in concentration.

"Lift—" He requests, glancing up at me. I see my intrigue reflected in his glassy pupils; the way they dilate to dark as he takes in my face.

I do as he commands, and he gives the brace on my left leg a tug, pulling it off over my boot. "And again—" He taps the right leg, and I do the same, watching him as he removes the remaining carbon fibre scaffolding and places it on the ground with the first. He runs his hands up the undersides of my leggings, causing my stomach to knot with a delicious tension I've been missing for a long time.

"How does that feel?" he asks me, a wicked glint kissing the galaxies in his irises like a shooting star winking in and out of view. I flush crimson, cheeks burning.

"Well, it doesn't hurt—" I smirk, a laugh bubbling at the back of my throat that I have to struggle to stifle. I can't believe this is really happening. It's like something out of every little girl's fantasy— a magical kingdom, a handsome and righteous white knight with gilded carriages, real manners, and actual respect for his princess. I'm overwhelmed, wanting to express just how amazing I think all of this is, how grateful I am to him for bringing me here, and yet I can't think of any words to do justice to how I'm feeling.

Instead, then, I pull my legs up into the carriage, taking my braces as he hands them to me from the sparkling crystal dust coating the road, shuffling across the bench and making room for him to join me. He folds himself elegantly inside, his wings tucking themselves into his spine as he's careful not to sit on the very bottom tips of each one.

"Are they awkward?" I ask him, tilting my chin toward his black feathers, and he smiles.

"I'm used to it, but at first, yes. I would find myself tripping over them and learning to sleep with them was a pain too. Now though, I think I'd miss not having them to keep me warm at night—" He smoulders at me as the reply hangs in the air between us as though his shyness has been left behind in the world from which I've come.

Giving a knock on the roof of the carriage interior has the entire vehicle lurching into motion, the sound of stag hooves on crushed crystal echoing around us.

"So how exactly do you keep yourself warm at night with these—" I ask him, reaching out tentatively but then recoiling as I wonder if I might be considered rude. After all, I know no etiquette about dealing with wings, seeing as he's the first person I've ever met with them.

"Go on— you can touch them," he encourages me, allowing one of his wings to stretch toward me a little. I blush again, my heart beating heavy as I reach out and bring my fingers to gently brush against the feather closest to me at the tip of the wide span.

It's softer than I expect, not rough like it belongs to a bird but instead silken and slick between my fingers as I stroke it gently. Aro watches me closely even still, a shudder rippling through him as I reach out to run my hand along the topmost edge of the enormous limb.

"Careful of the terminal phalanx. It's sensitive," Aro warns, his cheeks reddening as he reaches forward as if to distract himself, picking an amethyst crystal from a small holder in the wall. He wraps his fingers around the acutely angled facets, and after a few moments, I find a glow illuminating the space between us.

"How— what did you do?" I ask him as he places the now glowing bulb of amethyst back where it came from. The inside of the carriage is cast into visibility by the light, exposing the undeniable luxury of the interior.

"As a Kindred of Zeus, I can manipulate electricity. The amethyst stores the current in a kind of infinite loop. We use them to light most stuff around here," he explains, shifting on the bench beside me and propping one foot on his knee as we jostle along the road at speed.

I take this opportunity to glance out of the window on my left, finding the world beyond moving by in a blur of exquisite silver-twined tree trunks, crystal leaves, and swirling glitter.

"How— I know this must sound an odd question, but how do the crystals grow on the flowers and the trees?" I ask him, feeling my curiosity grow as my awe recedes. The more scenery I absorb as we fly through Aetheria, the more questions that present.

"The water here is full of that glitter you're seeing everywhere. Aether. It's part of what is left from one of the Goddesses who created this place— again, Aether was her name, hence the name of this world. It's taken up by the trees, the flowers, in the water from the rain and the rivers. Then, they grow crystals instead of leaves or flowers. When the leaves fall, the aether is returned to the air as the crystals disintegrate, and the cycle begins again." The explanation makes sense in a crazy, magical kind of way, but instead of letting my mind toss it around and rip it apart, looking for comprehension, I simply nod, letting myself float on the surface of the concept, enjoying the view rather than fighting my way down into the mystery of its depths.

I spend the next ten or so minutes in silence, leaning forward so I can get a look at everything there is to see beneath the rich gold of the moon's glow.

"We should be approaching the outskirts of The City of the Sephilim. It's the capital of the floating continent, Soleus," Aro explains, leaning close to my ear to speak and causing me to shiver slightly as I feel the cool musk of his breath on my neck.

"I see, and where do you live in the city?" I ask, turning back over my shoulder so our noses are almost touching.

"If you wait until we're closer, I'll point it out." He smiles at me, looking down into my eyes as I grin back at him. I'm enjoying the fact his proximity isn't making me anxious for fear of pain at a mere touch, that my spine isn't screaming every time the stags pull us over a rough patch of road. It's remarkable how quickly I'm beginning to revert to my old self, back to Kairi before the pain.

He has helped me remember who I was, and I don't know how I'll ever repay him for that.

All I know now is that I never want to leave, and I only just got here.

My belief that I will struggle to return to the real world is confirmed as Aro points out of my window, and I turn from him, finding the city upon us.

Every house is formed from a combination of crystal and precious metals, the entire settlement ringed by a thick river that's passed over by delicate silver bridges and lined with hundreds of amethyst trees that glow, lighting up the perimeter.

I gape, finding the centrepiece of the city to be an enormous crystal cluster rising from the earth and forming itself into the most intricately stunning castle I could ever imagine.

"That's where I live. Solis Castra," Aro whispers as my eyes settle on the delicate silhouette. I turn, my head snapping quickly back so I can gawp at him.

"You live in a palace?" I snap, eyebrows drawing together fast.

"I told you I do." He smiles, smug at my shocked and impressed tone.

"I thought you were kidding! What are you, King?" I ask him, confused. I thought he was a High Lord.

"Maybe one day if the Gods decide that is to be my fate," he sighs, leaning back from me, his face turning weary as he moves to look out of his window instead.

I don't press any further, the subject obviously one he finds either tedious, irritating, or both. We pass more minutes in silence, the only sound the bustle of early evening city life. I spot people walking the quartz sidewalks, carrying baskets full of what seem to be rich fruits or fine fabrics, their wings pressed against them as they rush from one Quarter to the next, packing up their wares for the day.

"There are so many—" I whisper to myself, awed, letting my chin rest in my palm as the world outside the window passes by, turning my eyes wide and excited.

The women are dressed in gowns, not dresses but gowns. The embroidery on each one, even the simpler ones, looks heavy and intricately organic in design, the range of textures and colours from their billowing skirts bringing the streets to life in a flurry of ruffled petticoats and swaying hems.

The men hold their own with tailored jackets and breeches of fine silk or thick crushed velvet, long socks, shoes shined to perfection, delicate cotton shirts, and cravats that hug their thick muscular necks as biceps quite obviously bulge beneath the civilised mask of their finery.

"We are many. As the oldest of the Kindred races, we are the most advanced, the most well-populated too." Aro throws the information in, and suddenly a question burns inside my chest.

"Where are all the children?" I ask him, peering through the pulsating crowds, attempting to spot a sticky hand pulling on a mother's skirt or the small head of an overwhelmed infant.

"We don't reproduce. We are chosen. So, when a human who is destined for this life dies, they are greeted by Zeus or Hera in a personal vision, kind of like an invitation you could say, and then physically remade to live as immortals, as Kindred in Aetheria. We are immortal but infertile." His face doesn't betray sorrow at this sentiment, only fact, and I wonder what it must be like to live forever.

"Living forever— isn't that lonely?" I ask him, frown marring my expression, which had only moments before been slack with awe.

"It can be. Why do you think I've been so desperate to have you here with me?" he asks, taking my hand in his and raising it to his lips. I turn my body to face him fully, watching as he kisses my knuckles and observes my small smile.

"So, Briar— she was a— Sephilim?" I ask him, thinking about how easily I could call the place flying by outside the windows home.

"The female Sephilim is called a Nephilim, chosen by Hera. But yes, she became a Nephilim, and we met again here after being betrothed in our mortal lives. Her name was Storm when she awoke—" He looks wistfully into my face as if he's recalling everything he shared with the girl who isn't me.

"So, if she was immortal, what happened? I thought immortals couldn't die, so—" I swallow, wondering if I want to know the answer as I fidget in my seat.

"She was stolen from me by another Kindred race, the Draconians. Immortals can't die of old age, but they can be killed. The Draconians— they took her, broke her wings, and murdered her." His eyes become almost hollow, a single blazing ember alight somewhere in the dark depths as his entire expression hardens into stone.

"So, the Draconians, they are chosen by whom?" I feel hairs rise on my arms at the very sound of their names, an irrational fear but one that's seemingly ingrained nonetheless.

"Hecate and Nemesis." The two goddesses sound formidable in name alone as well, and I shudder visibly as Aro places a hand on my thigh and squeezes.

"Kairi, it's alright. I won't let anything happen to you. I would die to protect you. The Draconians will not take you from me again. I could not bear it." His confession elicits a warmth that blooms deep in my stomach, my mind enraptured by the sincerity of the vow by someone I've only just met and barely know.

"You don't even know me—" I whisper, not wanting his claim to be true. Not wanting to be in so deep after only days have passed. I swore I'd never drag someone down with my own burdens again, not after Oli— and yet, here I am.

"I know your soul. I have for hundreds of years, and you know mine. There is no way you would have trusted me to bring you here otherwise. You cannot deny that this place feels like home. I can see it in your face." He cocks his head, dark inky locks falling across his forehead as his expression morphs serious in the glow of the amethyst on the wall beside him. He's so direct, so intense, but for some reason, I find this wildly attractive. Perhaps, coming from a world where men seem to revel in mixed signals has made me crave this kind of romantic openness, where the male in question is not afraid or even unsure of his feelings but pursues them with the virile certainty of a predator closing in on his prey.

Aro knows how he feels, and I know unequivocally that he'll spend the rest of his days proving it to me if I let him.

I open my lips to protest as I think about this new world, but he's not wrong. I can't deny that this place feels more like home than anywhere ever has, even L.A.

And what about how I was found as a child? I seemingly have no parents, appearing from nowhere as a baby in a basket on the shore.

Is this why?

"We're pulling up now," Aro informs me, and I look out the window again to find us approaching a quartz path that is flanked on both sides by a lusciously thick row of trees, the canopy of its leaves casting the moonlight violet as it falls and hits the glittering quartz gravel of the path.

The Solis Castra rises high above with intricate turrets, stained glass windows, elegantly twining metal balconies, and flawlessly smooth amethyst walls glimmering beneath the majesty of this otherworldly night sky. I inhale, the sight of it approaching touching something deep within me in an unexplainable and very real way. I glance back to find Aro staring at me once again, examining my face.

"I can't believe this is real," I confess, smiling without hindrance as I take a deep breath, filling my lungs with the sweet cool air.

"Believe it, Kairi. You're home." He moves to take my hand, sitting erect in his seat with a look of complete contentment on his face as the carriage comes slowly to a stop. I grab my backpack and braces, preparing to step out into the surreal amethyst entryway.

A footman in a velvet violet suit with gold embroidery steps forward and opens the door of the carriage, his top hat tilted at a surreal angle among the luscious crop of his golden curls.

"My Lord." He nods to Aro in greeting, eyes brimming with respect as Aro pulls me out of the carriage behind him. Aro nods back without a word, ushering me forward as he places a warm hand on the small of my back. With that same palm, he moves to take my backpack from my shoulder and the braces from my hand, relieving me of the weight of both despite the fact I'm no longer feeling it as I would in the mortal world.

"Come, let me show you to your suite." He strides forward, and I trail behind, staring up at the cavernously high ceiling carved from solid crystal. The entryway is an open-aired space, the crystal of the place forming an awning permeated on both sides by large archways that stand, supported by enormous golden columns. I spin on the spot as I try to take it all in, the sweet night air warm against my cheeks, caressing my skin with all the gentleness of a lover.

I can feel my eyes watering as I refuse to blink, trying to etch each and every curving facet into my memory so I never forget. I don't want to miss anything, so find myself craning my neck into odd positions to try to observe the architecture from every possible angle.

"Kairi?" Aro's voice breaks my awed silence as he smiles back over one shoulder at me.

"Sorry, I was just—" I begin, but he shakes his head, smirking.

"Take your time. I forget sometimes just how incredible this is. Sadly, I suppose the years I've spent in residence have kind of put blinders on me when it comes to the uniqueness of the place." He halts, waiting for me in the middle of the walkway and watching as I dart toward the archway closest to my left.

The gardens of the palace sprawl, the light of the night reflected in its crystal majesty. Enormous emerald pines become viridian pools of starlight beneath the night sky, the ruby roses bloody caves filled with fiery moonglow. Crystal paths sweep across the well-kept haven, and suddenly I hear it, the rumble of something naturally magnificent.

"Is that a waterfall?" I ask as Aro steps close, staring out across the gardens that shimmer with both reflected and artificial light from the amethyst fountains which spill glittering water from exquisitely complex functional sculptures.

"Yes. Oblivion Falls is what you are hearing. The Solis Castra sits right on the edge. It's where the river water falls and evaporates, the aether condensing to form new clouds. There's a good view from your suite, seeing as it's right at the top of the main tower." He takes my hand, leading me down the rest of the entryway with determined focus.

Once inside, I find the hallways strung with exquisite works of art, intricate tapestries, and littered with Grecian pedestals in different coloured crystal displaying one-of-a-kind sculptures, pots, and vases.

I could spend forever examining every inch of the place, but I feel Aro is growing impatient and so let him lead me through the labyrinth of corridors that spider intricately through the innards of this enormous crystal cluster made palace.

Finally, after what feels like forever, we emerge into a central octagonal room where the floor is so clean that my reflection stares flawlessly back up at me. I see my hand locked within Aro's, the way we fit together, and can't help but smile.

"Ready?" Aro draws his arms around my waist.

"For what?" I ask him, and he glances upward. I follow his pupils, finding the room becomes a towering central column, with railed balconies poking out into the airspace and leading off to other parts of the place.

"Of course, you don't need stairs—" I murmur, and he chuckles.

"No. Stand on my toes, and I'll fly us," he commands, and I feel my stomach stir in a flurry of excitement like cherry blossom leaves set free from their branches by the first soft breeze of spring.

"Don't drop me, okay?" I say, feeling nervous at the amount of trust I'm putting in this man who was a stranger only days ago. He smirks, tilting his head and giving me a look that reads, never.

When I step onto the toecaps of his shoes with my boots, he gives a small grunt under his breath, looking down at me and then up to the ceiling with a grin, wings unfurling on either side of him.

He bends his knees and gives an elegant jump upwards, his wings beating a frenzied rhythm in the air as we begin to rise. I cling onto

91

him, palms sweating as they clasp together at the back of his neck, watching as cobalt stained glass that's fragmented into mosaic design passes by. We ascend faster than I think possible, and soon, we are touching down on the topmost balcony with my gaze catching on the rose quartz chandelier which comes in and out of view beyond Aro's rhythmic flight.

"Here." He sets me down, ruffling his feathers slightly before pulling his wings back so they rest neatly against his jacket once more. He passes me my backpack and then the braces, gesturing to the hallway behind me.

I turn, finding this corridor paler, being situated at the top of the crystal shards, the walls the palest lilac as I pass them and head toward a cloudy set of double doors at the end. A man stands beside my door, auburn hair shocking against the pallor.

"This is Leo, Captain of my best Aerial Unit. He will be stationed outside should you need anything. Dawn, your handmaid is also waiting for you inside, to help you get ready. Dinner will be served in two hours, followed by a night of dancing. I hope that's alright?" he queries, bowing slightly and taking his index finger to lift my chin so I'm staring directly at him.

"Alright? Are you crazy? This is like— like every dream I never knew I had," I stutter, and he smiles, teeth gloriously white and eyes brimming with hope for the night ahead.

"Very well, I will collect you in two hours. Be well, Kairi." He bows again, picking up my knuckles and kissing them gently as he examines my face with intense desire.

He turns with that sentiment, letting my fingers slip through his and leaving me standing there, watching as he builds into a run and launches himself off the end of the balcony with a loud whooping sound. I laugh at his boyish behaviour, the man who is seemingly so contained clearly just as excited as I am as his wings stretch wide right before he disappears from view, catching him mid-fall.

I turn, grinning unabashedly, and Leo opens the door in front of me.

"I hope you'll enjoy your stay—" he smiles at me, the freckles across the bridge of his nose wrinkling as he examines my wonderstruck face.

I don't reply, simply giving him a shy smile.

Stepping through the door, I find the suite is carved from rose quartz and pale amethyst, the place sprawling luxuriously in front of me as I inhale the scent of jasmine and rosewater.

I drop my backpack on the floor, my braces too, taking a few steps forward as my heart rises like a helium balloon in my chest, my lips unable to contain the laughter that comes exploding from me before proceeding to bounce around the spacious chamber.

My steps quicken as I spy it, an enormous silver four-poster bed covered in crushed white velvet sheets. Throwing my arms out from me like I'm on the bow of the Titanic, I launch myself onto the mattress, laughing so hard my ribs ache and breath comes in gasps as I'm caught by the cloud of sheets and pillows. Flopping onto my back, I stare up at the turret of crystal overhead and sigh, biting my bottom lip and shaking my head.

This has to be a dream—
It can't be real.
Can it?

8

BELOVED

KAIRI

"UM— HELLO—" THE VOICE comes as a shock as I continue to smile up at the ceiling from the hold of the super-king four-poster, causing me to bolt upright.

In the amethyst archway, which leads to what I assume is the bathroom, a winged woman stands, her blonde hair twisted up on her head in a multitude of braids, her hands folded in front of her minimalist blue gown.

"Oh— you must be—" I search for her name, knowing that Aro mentioned it but unable to find the word as I shuffle off the end of the mattress and stand before her soft gaze.

"Dawn, Miss." She gives a small curtsey, and I find myself immediately uncomfortable.

"Oh, uh, please— you don't have to curtsey, and you can call me Kairi." I extend a hand, which she looks at for a few moments with wide eyes before taking it in her own.

"As you wish. You're just as lovely as he said you were. Though, I can think of a few ways to polish you up for this evening. How does an aromatherapy bath sound?" she asks me, and I flush, remembering my tepid Epsom salt soak from what feels like a few hours before. I open my mouth to protest, to tell her I'm already clean, but then I glance at the bathtub behind her slim silhouette and find myself nodding instead.

"Okay, fantastic. I can also give you a manicure, pedicure, and I'll be doing your hair and make-up for dinner this evening." She's rushed as she speaks, turning on one heel and heading back into a bathroom that leaves me gaping.

Enormous, it is carved entirely from rose quartz. A sumptuously round bathtub rimmed in gold with matching faucets that twist into the shapes of lilies leaves me breathless as I watch Dawn kneel by the side of the tub, her skirts pluming around her like a puddle on the dusky pink crystal of the floor. I stare as she winds her fingers through the weeping lily petals of the tap and turns, and there's an immediate and pungent hot steam billowing into the room as it fills.

As I take in the grandeur of her ivory wings where every feather looks as though the tip has been dip-dyed the exact blue of the early morning sky, something occurs to me.

"If I'd have expected this kind of formal grandeur, I would have packed my ball gown instead of leggings," I say this as a warning, wondering if there's any point going to the effort of transforming my face and hair if I'm going to dinner in a sweater.

"Oh, don't worry about that. Lord Black had that all taken care of. There're dresses for you to choose from in the wardrobe on the far side of the bedroom. They were delivered by the seamstress a few hours ago." She gets to her feet, saying this as if it's nothing out of the ordinary.

A seamstress?

So, if Aro had these dresses custom-made— how did he know my size?

"May I?" I point back over one shoulder as Dawn moves to the countertop on my far left and begins selecting tiny crystal vials from a gold wicker basket by the sink.

"Of course, this is your room. You don't need my permission." Dawn smiles as though my lack of formality is somewhat a relief, and so I excuse myself from leaning in the archway and turn to face the bedroom, spotting the wardrobe she spoke of immediately.

I take painless and excited strides across the floor toward the antique of porcelain and silver, but as I reach the doors and stretch out a hand to stroke the handle, which is shaped like an orchid, I find myself transfixed by something else entirely.

Beside the wardrobe is a set of double glass doors, and what lies beyond captures my attention and refuses to let it go. I step sideways, pushing down on the handle without a second thought and stepping out into the warm night air, gaping at the view.

The room I'm staying in is situated, as Aro had said, at the very crux of the tallest tower in the place, and as I lean over the crystal balcony, I find the falls he had spoken of as well.

The entire palace sits on a curved crescent of land where the ground suddenly ends and the world of Aetheria is carried on as nothing but air and cloud. The roar of the falls is deafening, but I can't help but stare, unperturbed, as gallons of sparkling water tumbles in a mess of shimmering froth from the highest peak of the curved ridge, transforming itself into dense cotton candy clouds as it descends in freefall. The newly made clouds shimmer golden beneath the moonlight, and the indigo hue of the night sky makes the scene entirely otherworldly. I continue to stare, unable to believe that this isn't all a dream – and sure that I'll wake up in agony at any moment.

I lean over the balcony for longer than I realise, savouring the lack of burning friction in my hips and the absent crunching of my knees protesting beneath my weight. Breathing feels easy, my mind clear among the thick vanilla cream of the night air as it coats the inside of my nose and slicks the back of my throat, the feeling so liberating it's as though this world is beckoning me to sing.

Maybe then, I muse, *this is why Disney princesses can't seem to help but spontaneously burst into song.*

"Miss, your bath is ready." I hear Dawn's voice float over my shoulder as I turn to find her in the open doorway, her face made tranquil and lovely with a gentle smile.

I take a step toward her, my excitement obvious as I grip her hands in mine as though she were an old friend.

"Now Dawn, what did I say about calling me Kairi?"

The next couple of hours are pure bliss. I soak for an obscenely indulgent length of time in the rose quartz tub, the scent of rose and jasmine oil making the air rich and hazy as I relax, sinking among the bubbles. Once I'm fully cleaned and my limbs have reached Jell-O status, I climb from the tub, wrap a towelling bathrobe around myself and relish the blood rising to the surface of my skin as I dry.

While I was soaking in the tub, and with her eyes politely averted, Dawn set up a kind of beauty station in the main room, pulling out tools, powders, polishes, and scrubs from an enormous carpetbag she's procured from seemingly nowhere. She leads me toward the table, which I believe she's pulled from the entryway of the suite, and sits me down on one side and herself on the other.

Then, it's to my nails, which she buffs, files, and shapes before applying a glittering nude coat of polish that shimmers just enough to be noticeable but not enough to draw the eye. As she's doing my nails, my hair dries, and once she's applied a topcoat, moves me to sit at the vanity in the far corner.

Picking up heavy brushes backed with precious metals and set with shimmering pink sapphires, she runs the bristles through my damp locks, asking me about the mortal world and chattering excitedly. I sit quietly in a world of my own, giving her simple answers and instead, thinking about Aro and the night ahead.

What is he expecting of me?

Will I seem so terribly crude and uneducated in comparison to his years of wisdom and refined etiquette?

What about dancing? I can imagine the kind of dancing he's talking about, and I don't think my nightclubbing days are going to cut it for experience.

The longer I sit, the more the doubts and worries pile up inside my chest like a stack of heavy stones crushing my lungs and making it hard to relax.

"What do you think?" Dawn asks me, pushing a final pin into the back of my hair which she's been dutifully styling while I've been stewing. I look at myself in the mirror, really paying attention now, and find not Kairi but Briar— or perhaps even a bland version of the immortal Storm staring back.

"I look—" I twist my head one way and then the next, staring at the relaxed updo with awe as my hair becomes lustrously thick and shining all at once as it twists and curls around the back of my skull. "I love it, thank you." I turn to Dawn, place a hand on hers, and smile.

"You don't have to thank me. It's my job." She dismisses the compliment, flurrying back to the carpetbag and pulling out make-up stored in prized and perfectly kept crystal pots and jars, the containers alone more exquisite than anything I've ever seen.

"But you do it so well. So, I will thank you anyway." I am determined not to let this kind of treatment get to me. I'm feeling more alive, more beautiful than I have in years, but it does not and will not ever escape me how much work has gone into all this on Dawn's part.

Dawn gives me another smile and then sets about unravelling a purple suede wrap filled with make-up brushes adorned with gold handles and white bristles. I reach out to touch one with my fingers, the bristles softer than any makeup brush I've ever used.

"What are these brushes made from?" I ask her as she begins to layer concealer onto my skin with a sponge.

97

"The bristles are unicorn hair, and the handles are nine-carat gold, I think. They're Equinian made," she explains as she starts to contour around my cheekbones. I nod, not understanding anything she's just said apart from the word *unicorn*.

I'll have to remember to ask Aro about the Equinians later.

She applies the only wings a mortal like me can ever dream of, brushing the dark eyeliner atop my lids in a single flawless sweep, before applying featherlight mascara, shading my brows, and then glossing my lips with yet more nude shimmer to match my nails. She looks to me for approval as she steps back, admiring her handiwork, and I smile at her, the face staring back at me both a princess and a stranger.

"Wow." It's all I can say, and she smiles, moving from me without pause and heading across the room toward the wardrobe I had abandoned earlier. She pulls open the doors; releasing layers of rich-coloured fabric hung in uniform transparent garment bags.

I get to my feet, giving the face in the mirror one last appraisal and trying to etch the image into my memory because, in all honesty, I'm aware I may never get the chance to look like this ever again.

"Well, you won't be short on choices—" Dawn smiles, pulling out a few dresses and showing them to me from the hangers. I gaze with hungry eyes at each one; the lavish jewel tones heavy with embroidery on the bodices, skirts layered many times over with either silk or tulle.

"I don't know how to decide, they're all so beautiful— Which one do you think Aro would like?" I ask her, cocking my head and sitting down on the edge of the mattress and allowing my legs to dangle.

"You want my honest opinion?" Dawn asks with a surprised expression, and I nod vigorously.

"Well, all these dresses are nice, but they're a little much for his tastes. Silver picked the fabrics, you see— but there is one— hold on, let me find it." She rustles around in the wardrobe for a moment, narrowing her eyes before they widen with satisfaction.

"Here, this one would be perfect. It's his favourite colour as well," Dawn announces, pulling a flurry of concord purple tulle from the wardrobe. She holds it out to me, and I reach out, letting my fingers graze the bag.

It's perfect.

I nod, and she grins, closing the wardrobe doors and hanging the gown on the top of the four-poster's railing before getting onto her knees and pulling out a corset and panties from the drawer near her feet.

"Here, put these on. I can help you with the back of the dress when you're ready. I'm going through to the other closet to find you some shoes," she informs me, pushing the plum lace and silk into my hands and walking past me without another word.

"So—" I call after her, something suddenly occurring to me. "Did you dress Storm; you know, before she was killed by the Draconians?" I ask her but hear no reply, only rummaging.

Pulling the panties up under my robe, I look next at the boned corset that lies on the bed, contrasted rich in colour against the white of the sheets. I've never worn a corset, so god knows how this is going to feel. All I know is that this kind of boning would most certainly have brought me out in a rash before, so I can only hope that it doesn't now.

I unlace the front and wrap it around myself, and after several minutes of fiddling with the thin silver cord that tightens the bodice fast around my ribs, I find myself staring down at a cleavage I hardly recognise as my own.

Well, if he wasn't interested before, he will be now—

I blush.

Turning my attention away from my busting chest and to the gown, I pull it down from the railing where it's hung, unlacing the hand-stitched garment and letting my fingers caress the thick velvet of the bodice. The sleeves look like petals made from tulle, delicate and intricately sewn together, and the skirt is truly fairy-tale worthy, made of layer after layer of matching concord tulle that bursts from the narrow waistline like a weeping willow's plume.

I unlace the back of the gown, placing it over my head with enormous difficulty as I try to remain balanced, and let out a sigh of relief as the fabric hangs loosely around my lower body, the unfastened bodice falling past my breasts.

I pull the gown up, adjusting the sleeves, and Dawn returns, quickly turning me to face the window and lacing the back of the gown so tight I can barely breathe.

"I used to dress Storm, yes. And what was that you were saying about the Draconians?" she asks me, biting down hard on her bottom lip in concentration.

"Only that Aro said she was kidnapped by the Draconians and killed— I just wondered—" her head snaps up, and her eyes widen, a look of confusion marring her face.

"I'm sorry, dear, but we don't talk about that. It was a terrible thing. A terrible, terrible thing." She shakes her head, and I scowl a little, confused by her lack of willingness to tell me about my potential past.

"Do I really look like her?" I ask, cocking my head at her.

"Yes. I'd even go so far as to say you could be her. She even had this same mark." She points to my wrist at the three tentacled birthmark.

Following my gaze, she adorns my wrist with a simple yellow gold bracelet, a minimalist chain with a T-bar clasp, and then my lobes with a pair of chandelier earrings that weep amethysts, which fall to just above my jawline. Then, getting down on her knees once more, she places one high-heeled, purple, silk stiletto on each foot as I hang onto the bedframe for balance before fluffing the tulle of my skirt and standing up to appraise me.

"A vision," she compliments, drawing me around toward the entryway where a floor-length mirror I hadn't noticed on arrival hangs on the left-hand wall. "See," she gestures, bringing out a bottle of something from one of the pockets in her skirt and spraying me with it. It smells like lavender and jasmine, and I cough slightly as the fine mist settles over my skin.

I stare at myself in the gown, my waist tiny and silhouette made soft as a blossoming rose within the tight velvet and pluming tulle that flares out from my hips. My skin glows, my eyes sheening milky periwinkle from the contoured angles of my face, hair falling flawlessly in tamed silken curls over one shoulder. I look for the girl I know but don't find her, this one practically unrecognisable from the girl who lives life in pyjamas with her hair thrown up in a messy bun.

As I'm gawping, Dawn checks a pendant around her neck, flicking it open and scrutinising a dainty clock face within before snapping it shut and herding me toward the door.

"He'll be expecting you in a few minutes," she explains, and I gape. It's been two hours already?

It feels like moments, like I've been whisked into a dream, into the story of someone else, and each and every second leaves me more awed than the last.

I step out into the hallway beyond the confines of my suite, heels clicking loudly against the crystal floors, my balance questionable after so long out of practice in heels.

He stands silhouetted by the moonlight pouring in through the central column, body rigid and shapely as he turns at the sound of my approach. His pupils dilate, lips slightly parting as he inhales a sharp breath.

"Hi," I blush, letting a hand rise to rest over where my heart pounds beneath the shimmering porcelain of my skin.

He closes the distance between us in several quick strides, whisking me off my feet and into his arms without a word, my skirts thick in his tight grasp as one of his arms latches behind my knees and the other around my shoulders. He turns, smiling down at me, adoration in his eyes as his wings flare out behind him. Carrying on his brisk pace, he runs through the corridor, and we plummet, my stomach falling like a heap of bricks as a scream escapes my lips. He laughs in a deep bellowing exhale, his wings beating suddenly as he banks left, spiralling down the tower with me clutched tightly in his arms and stopping our freefall. His eyes glisten like those of a young boy running through endless fields, unhindered as the air around us whips around my ears and I throw my head back in a laugh too, my spirit lifting with the curve of our path through the air of the cylindrical ballroom.

We touch down after two more passes around the room with practised finesse, me still in his arms.

"You look beautiful," he compliments me, setting me on my feet and then reaching into his jacket pocket. He pulls out a key, passing it to me. "The key for the door to your suite." He nods, pushing me to take it. I smile, looking at the object, a stunning gold sculpture rather than a functional item as it drops, the metal cool against my palm.

"Will you, uh, hang onto that for me, this dress doesn't exactly come with pockets," I ask, passing the key back to him and letting my fingers linger on his as our eyes catch, as though the icy blue comets of my eyes have become caught in the orbit of his deep galaxies.

"Of course. Are you hungry?" he asks me, slipping the key back into the inside pocket of his jacket. I take a moment as he fumbles, to note what he's wearing.

He's changed into a jacket that matches my gown perfectly, a black shirt beneath and a plum cravat knotted around his throat to compliment the black crystals that are threaded into the embroidery around the collar and cuffs. Black dress pants end in shoes so shiny I can see my reflection staring back at me from below, and as I look at both of us, I realise that we look like a pair.

"Yes, I'm starving." I smile at him as he takes my hand in his, leading me with a gentleman's elegance across the vast octagonal dance floor and through several grandiose amethyst archways leading off to labyrinthine corridors that are yet again peppered with art, antiques, and treasure.

Eventually, he turns left, opening a pair of arched double doors carved from a dark wood that is veined through with gold, revealing a long banquet table central to the dining room beyond.

An enormous gold chandelier dangles above it, holding crystals that light the space. A fireplace with flickering rosy pink flames that dance lazily lies on the left, warming one side of my body as I follow the High Lord with wide eyes.

However, I realise we are not alone as I stop, still mid-step, only a few paces later, finding an enormous, sleeping, winged cat curled in front of the hearth. I say cat as though it and Catticus could be cousins, but in fact, it's a freaking *lion*. I falter to a standstill, and Aro looks back over his shoulder, smiling at me and then at the winged lion.

"Oh, don't mind Ariah. He's a grumpy old thing. A Kensari— well, I say *a*, but he's actually mine. He found me shortly after I turned. Lots of Sephilim and Nephilim have Kensari partners," he explains, and I glance down at the cat with a wariness that's been ingrained inescapably into me since I was a small child.

Lions you run from.

You don't keep them as pets.

As I give a nervous glance back over my shoulder, Aro steers me forward, placing an insistent hand at the base of my spine and leading me towards the other end of the room.

Allowing my attention to finally stray from the winged feline guest behind me, I find the table is, unsurprisingly, solid amethyst veined through with gold. Adorned with precious metal place settings, goblets, and crystal vases overflowing with long-stemmed roses that bloom faceted ruby petals, it couldn't be more perfect. Candles also litter the space, for atmosphere I suppose, flickering in the breeze that carries from the garden beyond the head of the table. The French doors leading out to the veranda are thrown open, and gauzy gold drapes blow in the night air, bringing with them the subtle scent of vanilla and jasmine.

"Sit." Aro gestures to a chair at the foot of the table, but I shake my head, choosing my seat closest to the head of the table instead. "Very well." He seems surprised as though he's unused to anyone disobeying him, let alone a mortal.

Regardless though, he comes to join me, taking his place at the head of the table.

"I thought this would be better for talking," I explain, and he smiles, resting a hand upon my own.

"Of course, it was silly of me to arrange such a formal seating arrangement," he admits his mistake without ego or annoyance, simply shrugging it off.

A waiter with the wings of a magpie, dressed in a formal top and tails adorned with a golden broach depicting a sun, enters the room with a bottle of wine in his palms.

"Wine?" Aro asks me as the waiter takes the length of the table in a few strides of his abnormally long legs.

"Please."

I watch as the waiter uncorks and then passes the bottle to Aro for him to decant.

As he's pouring the wine, a white-gloved hand reaches over my shoulder from seemingly nowhere, delivering a delicately woven basket full of herbed bread. I take a piece, bringing it to my lips and inhaling the aroma of rosemary and thyme before I take an enormous bite, the fluffiness unparalleled to any other baguette I've ever tried.

"Try not to fill up on the bread." Aro winks, taking a piece for himself.

"You can't give me this bread and then tell me not to fill up on the bread, that is just plain cruel. I didn't take you for cruel." I grin at him, giving him a bold wink in return that causes my skin to flush. I'm never this forward, especially not with men, usually being so shy I can't get a word out. With Aro, however, it seems I can't help but tease and flirt.

Perhaps then, it isn't me being shy at all but that I haven't been breaking bread with the right men.

"We have five courses to come, so leave room," he warns with casual sweetness.

"If I'd have known that, I wouldn't have worn a corset." I shake my head, suddenly anxious as I tuck a loose ringlet behind my ear.

"They will be small portions. Don't worry," he assures me, sitting back in his chair and letting his fingers rest on the edge of the table.

"So, tell me about yourself—" He smiles, and I feel my eyebrows rise on my forehead.

"You want to know about me? Why? When you have— all this—" I gesture to the room as more waiters pile in through the doors, this time carrying silver trays and steaming plates.

"Because you fascinate me," he replies, placing an elbow on the table and resting his chin in his palm.

"I could say the same thing about you. Obviously." I gesture to his wings which are tucked neatly behind him against the back of the dining chair.

The waiters place bowls of soup down in front of both of us, the scent of pumpkin and thyme wafting before my face. I grab another piece of bread, dipping it into the thick soup and bringing it to my lips without hesitation. Aro doesn't take another piece of bread, instead brandishing his spoon with elegant fingers and letting it hover above his bowl as he considers my face.

"Well, why don't we take it in turns? You ask me a question, and then I will ask one of you," he suggests, and I nod, caught up in a whirlwind of spices and vegetables as it slicks my gullet and pools warm in my belly.

"That seems fair. May I go first?" I ask him, and he nods, plunging his spoon into his soup and bringing it slowly to his lips.

"Very well."

At his reply, I take a few moments to think about what my first question should be.

"Dawn didn't want to talk about the Draconians, but I still want to know what happened to Storm," I say decidedly, taking more soup into my mouth and swallowing slowly as his gaze takes a downward turn.

"I can see why. It is not spoken about very often. Things concerning the Draconians have always been— difficult, and to avoid war we rarely speak of the events. They stole her away on the night of our wedding, hacked off her wings, and threw her from the highest peak of Drakos Vale, their kingdom. That is all I know and perhaps all I've ever wanted to know."

"That's abhorrent!" I feel my mouth twist into a grimace, eyes leaping to the beautiful onyx and gold feathers behind Aro and imagining them bleeding scarlet instead.

I shudder.

"Yes, well, the Draconians are— I don't want to say monsters, but when you are blessed by Hecate and Nemesis it's hard to think they'd be anything else. They seek war and have never offered the help of their kind to the others here in Aetheria. A few years ago, their High Lady Genevieve secluded them to Drakos Vale after our previous King Midas bested them during the war, built an enormous wall around the entire floating island, and we haven't visited since. We see their High Lords or Ladies at formal occasions sometimes, but they are cagey— almost like they're there purely to assess us for weaknesses. I don't trust them, and I don't know anyone else among the Fae or the Equinians that does either," Aro explains, spooning the last of the soup from the shallow bowl and into his mouth before setting his cutlery down with a clang.

"I see." I nod, and he looks deeply into my eyes as both our empty bowls are removed briskly and silently by more waiters, their presence unnoticed as if they were no more than formally dressed ghosts.

"If you ever see one, you run. You will promise me this?" He grips my fingers in his so tightly that I fear he might break them.

"I promise." Aro visibly exhales, shoulders slumping at my vow. "So— now it's your question," I prompt him as plates of steaming venison and asparagus are laid before us.

"I don't suppose any of this is bringing back anything, memories? Does it feel familiar, The Solis Castra?" he asks, looking desperately hopeful.

I sink my knife into the thick Venison, watching as steam rises and a little blood pools upon the gold.

"No, I can't say it does. I wish it did. I wish I could tell you what you want to hear—" I feel suddenly guilty as though Aro deserves more than just me but the woman he waited so many centuries to find as well. I wish so badly I could give him that after all the kindness he's shown me, but when I try to feel for a memory or any kind of past life, there's simply nothing to be found.

"It is alright, Kairi. I do not expect anything. I just had to ask. I'm sure you understand why," Aro explains with a sigh before digging into his own Venison with vigour.

"Of course, you loved her. Still do, it seems to me." My words come out sounding more entitled than I intend, as though I'm almost bitter at the fact there was someone in his life before me, even if we do look exactly alike.

"I always will, but I am sure she would understand if I expressed my feelings for another, especially one who embodies her so completely." He puts down his knife and fork, reaching once more into the interior of his jacket and pulling out a large, flat, velvet box, handing it to me. "I was going to wait until later, but I feel now I must make my intentions clear." He nods, picking up his cutlery once more as my fingers caress the purple velvet, pulling open the lid and gaping at what lies inside.

A gold chain from which hangs a small chunk of amethyst.

"For me?" I ask, swallowing hard.

"So you will always have a part of Aetheria with you— no matter how far from it you may be." His words sting like a slap across the face as I nod, trying not to allow tears to form in the corners of my eyes.

Minutes pass in silence after his comment fades into nothingness between us, the only sounds the clatter of cutlery and the moving of mouths. When Aro is finished with this course, he clears his throat, asking me another question.

"So, what about your mortal life? You have a family I assume?" he asks, and I feel my eyebrows rise, the change in subject sudden. I clear my throat, licking my lips thoroughly before answering.

"Yes, I have two fathers actually. They adopted me when I was a baby," I say, finishing off my plate. Before I have even put the cutlery back down though, more winged servants are bringing our next course in the form of peppermint sorbet adorned with dark chocolate set in the shapes of mint leaves.

"A palette cleanser," Aro informs me, picking up a spoon from directly in front of him. I nod, placing down my knife and fork before reaching for my own. I wonder as I carry out these simple motions if he's not reacting to the fact I have two fathers because he comes from a period where such things were thought unnatural. However, before I can remind him that it's accepted now, he speaks again.

"So, you have two fathers. They are a couple I presume?" he asks, looking sideways at me as he pops some of the pale green ice into his mouth. I nod.

"Yes, they got married a few years ago. I was the bridesmaid." I smile, remembering the rainbow theme and how I had gotten to choose the loudest and most colourful dress I could find for the event. I had walked my Pa down the aisle, and my aunt had walked her brother, my dad, down right after. It had been such fun, from what I recall anyway, I spent a large part of the reception tipsy on rainbow-coloured slushie cocktails from the bar.

"You know— I'm amazed you're so relaxed about it," I say cautiously. "You just seem so old-fashioned to me; I would have thought—" I elaborate as his eyebrows rise suddenly, and he smirks.

"That I'd be bigoted? On the contrary. I saw the suffering of those who lived unrequited love lives for years. One of the very last friends I made before my death was in love with another soldier in our squadron. They both died never having known how the other felt. It was— harrowing." Aro's face softens. "Age is no excuse for small-mindedness or ignorance, Kairi. You'll find many of the Kindred here have found new freedom in their blessed lives, and they make the most of it as a second chance."

"That's— well, it's exactly what I hoped you'd say," I admit, finishing off the sorbet from the cut crystal goblet, and licking my bottom lip.

I relax then, realising that perhaps we aren't as different as I'd originally thought. It's true, Aro comes from the past, but he's also lived all the years between then and now.

I guess I underestimated his knowledge of the mortal world despite it no longer being his own.

"So, do you go down to the mortal world much?" I ask him, placing my spoon down and sitting back in my chair, breathing easier despite the fact he's watching me with the same scrutiny.

The necklace he gave me lies between us, untouched. The connotations of it being a parting gift make it too painful to wear.

I take a sip of the wine, lifting the heavy goblet in front of me and letting the taste explode across my tongue. As he ponders my face, not answering my question and seemingly stuck in a kind of daydream, our plates are cleared and replaced again, this time with dessert.

A honeycomb cheesecake topped with edible gold and dripping in rich dark honey is set down before me, and despite everything I've already eaten, my mouth waters at the sight and scent of it. I love honeycomb.

Throughout the rest of the meal, Aro tells me about the few times he's visited the mortal world. It's always been at night, and he is clearly put off by how women's morals have considerably shifted from his time. He's a traditional man, which doesn't surprise me. I'm just grateful he isn't bigoted and hateful about how others choose to live even if he knows it isn't how he himself would be happy.

The open-mindedness and intellectual speed of the conversation carry us from dessert, through cheese and crackers, and then finally to coffee and mints as we empty our wine goblets and clear our plates amid fleeting glances and explanations of the past.

It's funny because I hadn't realised how much I missed talking about myself in a way that has nothing to do with my pain until now. It's as if I'm empty, and with each question asked and answered, my soul is becoming more contented to live in the present moment and cease worrying about the next.

Aro makes me forget about everything that's been weighing on me as we dine on fine food and sip gloriously rich wine, and I can't stop myself from smiling.

Finally, I sit back in my seat, the coffee sweetened with honey but dregs in the bottom of the gold-gilded cup and saucer before me.

"Ready for dancing?" Aro enquires, reaching out across the table and helping me to my feet as he stands.

"Well, I need to do something to help burn off the endless courses you've just fed me—" I sigh, giving him a small smile, acting as if his request is a chore rather than pleasure.

"You do not enjoy dancing?" He looks surprised as he pushes my seat back against the table with his hip, rounding the corner and placing a hand against the small of my back as he releases the other. I watch as he swipes the necklace from the table before placing it quickly and discreetly back inside his jacket.

I think about saying something, perhaps apologising for my reluctance to wear it and accepting that it means all of this is somehow more temporary than I'd wanted to admit. Instead, though, he presses me for an answer to his prior question as we sweep the length of the room in quick synchronised strides, the tulle of my skirt floating behind me.

"Well?"

"I suppose if I had wings, dancing would be the last of my concerns. What's it like to fly?" I ask, eyes sparkling with curiosity in the dim candlelight of the passing candelabra. My face is made warm, as is his, by the rose-coloured flames of the hearths as we make our way to the corridor beyond the double doors of the dining suite.

"I suppose— one could say it is like finding the perfect partner to waltz with—" He turns the corner, taking my hand in his again without pause, the act so natural I can't help but feel butterflies, or maybe tiny Sephilim, fluttering madly in my gut.

"How so?" I ask, lips twisting into a thin line as we make our way down the length of the corridor, steps still perfectly in time.

"Well, once one has practised, the wings become kind of like the perfect partner. They move with you as if they can tell exactly how you're feeling without you having to actively think about it or make any kind of indicatory gesture." He's thoughtful as we reach the octagonal ballroom once again, and I listen intently, fascinated. "Flying is— it's like dancing without music where your emotions can run wild and there's no physical boundaries or forces to halt them. If you're angry, you fly wild and fast, barrel-rolling and corkscrewing through cloud and aether until you can no longer breathe from exhaustion— and if you're happy— well, it's like gliding. Effortless and free."

"That sounds— incredible." I think on how much of a prison I often perceive my own body to be, imagine how glorious it would be to have utter control over myself and soar over and above everything holding me down.

He doesn't reply, simply watching my expression as I notice the band set up on a multi-level stage made from white marble at the far end of the room.

"Live music?" I smile, and he nods.

"Of course. The Fae and Nephilim combined make up some of the most talented musicians in the universe. It would be a shame not to make use of their blessings. Especially on a night like this." He gestures to the high walls which are draped with torrents of gold silk so perfect it looks fluid as it moves, molten and effortless in the breeze. The golden moonlight only exaggerates the precious hue, and the purples of the walls turn luscious as the golden light mixes with the cobalt panes of stained glass. The band itself is dressed in metallics too; simple sheath dresses with asymmetric silhouettes that fall over their bodies in seamless waterfalls before pooling upon the white marble.

Aro leads me into the centre of the room, placing a hand on my waist and taking my palm in his before setting the frame for waltzing between us. I smile up at him, unable to stop myself from nervously warning him.

"I've never danced like this before—" I mumble, feeling inadequate despite the ornate skirts of my dress and elegant coif of my caramel tresses. Aro only smiles, taking his hand from mine and using it to tilt my chin up further.

"Worry not. I'll lead."

Retaking my hand in his sure grip, he nods to the blonde Nephilim who is standing front and centre on the highest part of the makeshift stage. She gives a small bow as her white feathered wings, tipped baby pink, rustle, drawing an alabaster violin to her chin. The bow is gold, and as she raises it to the strings, I notice other strange things about her fellow musicians. Barely visible, their wings flash with glassy iridescence as they each ready themselves to play, insect-like and fragile. Their pointed ears are noticeable from beneath complex but natural-looking up-dos and ruffled boyish locks, eyes glinting bright jewel shades that glow unnaturally.

So, these must be the Fae?

I don't have any more time to stare though as the music begins, almost biblical in its purity, and the sound rises through the immense height of the room, lifting my spirits with it.

Aro takes the first step, and I follow his lead, feeling frail and porcelain in his arms as he leads me around the dancefloor.

We spin and twirl, our steps forming an ever-growing mandala of motion as my skirt blooms and recoils around my waist.

I look into his eyes, those galaxies that have me caught in their gravity so completely and know I could easily dance like this forever. There is no pain, no twinging in my knees or aching of my spine. There is only the heating of my skin as he adores every inch of me, both of us moving together in time to this divine endless melody.

Eventually, though, the song does come to an end, and he moves closer. Looking down at me as if I'm his entire world, he presses me against his chest.

"Stand on my toes," he whispers in my ear, and for a second, I think he might linger as he pulls back, might kiss me. I hold my breath, but the move never comes, the scent of violets leaving my head swimming.

I do as he asks without question, placing my hands behind his neck and locking my fingers in a tight weave as I step gently on the toecaps of his polished dress shoes. His wings expand sideways, their breadth astounding as they begin to beat, and we rise into the air.

I think he might begin dancing with me, guiding my feet atop his own, but instead, we rise quickly and with purpose.

We touch down at the end of a corridor much like the one to my suite, but this one isn't nearly as high up.

"Come on, I want to show you something—" He looks boyish, grabbing my hand as soon as my arms have fallen from around his neck and breaking into a run down the length of the corridor. I struggle to keep up as he pulls me behind him, my shoes rubbing against my heels as the sounds of our footsteps grow faster and louder.

He looks back at me, finding me struggling before dropping to his knees in the middle of the corridor and putting his hands under my skirt. My breath hitches intensely, but I should know better and soon find that he's doing nothing more than removing my shoes.

"Leave them," he shrugs, tossing them aside and pulling me after him once again, my soles cool against the indigo crystal of the floor.

The corridor seems to go on forever until suddenly, it doesn't. It stops, just like that, and I'm left skidding to slow down and smacking into Aro's wings as he abruptly halts in front of me.

He turns, looking at me, and places his arms around my waist.

"Do you trust me?" he asks, and I try to get a peek over his shoulder at what lies beyond.

Is it a balcony?

"I— I do," I relinquish, suddenly nervous as a chill breeze blows my skirts back against my ankles.

"Hold on tight." This is all the warning he gives me as he locks his fingers around my hips and careens backwards.

He falls straight back from the glassless arch in the side of the Solis Castra's main tower, clutching me to his chest, eyes reflecting the crisp starlight from above in a flawless mirror image.

I try to scream, but the world is moving by too fast, and the air is ripped from my lungs. I squeeze my eyes shut, immediately sure and terrified I'm falling to my death.

Moments pass, the world of Aetheria tilting around us as we plummet toward Oblivion Falls, the scent of vanilla and violets overpowering in its growing intensity.

Then, in a single moment, I hear Aro's wings stretch wide, and we're no longer falling.

I open my eyes.

We're *flying*.

He laughs, the sound deep and true as I release a breath, and my whole body goes limp on top of him.

"I thought you trusted me," he teases, and I glare up at him.

"There's trust, and then there's this!" I call over the sound of rushing wind, looking around as my fingers dig into him even harder.

The world is stars, aether, and frothing cloud on all sides, making it almost impossible for me to tell which way is up and which is down.

Aro straightens, somehow lifting me so I'm in his arms like a baby instead of lying on top of him. I don't want to even think about the logistics of how he manages this because, in all honesty, I'm still terrified of him dropping me.

We fly through the night, the world suddenly quiet and small beneath us for a while, my eyes growing wide as I attempt to take in the beauty of the endless glittering skyscape.

Then, Aro does something I don't expect, coming to land on a large shimmering cloud bathed gold in moonlight. He places me on my feet, and I grip on tightly to his hands, not quite able to believe that the cloud underfoot will support my weight.

"This is—" I begin, feeling the cool mist tickle my ankles beneath my skirt. Loose strands of hair stick to the sides of my face, having come loose from my updo in the fall.

"The aether, in places it makes the clouds dense enough to stand or sit on. I thought you might like to get a better view of Aetheria." He smiles down at me, head tilted as though no one in the world may be more perfect, and my heart races as his hand curls around my waist again.

"May I request another dance?" he asks me, this time not waiting for a reply as I straighten in his arms, staring out over a whole new world below. Just like that, beneath the stars and the endless sky, we are dancing atop a cloud, and I cannot help but wonder if I am dreaming.

How can anything this wonderful be real?

As I ponder on how no book could ever compare, islands float peacefully beneath us and palaces of rich metals and flawless crystals slumber on, unaware.

Overhead, we dance on, kicking up constellations that will one day tell our story, stars forming in the wake of each synchronised and lovestruck waltzing step.

After what feels like hours of dancing among the stars, Aro finally convinces me to plant my bare feet back on solid ground. We land atop a stone veranda that leads out into the luscious sprawl of the Solis Castra gardens behind where we had dined, the roar of the falls audible even from this far side of the property. Aro ushers me to the left after setting me down on bare feet, to where an enormous quartz fountain weeps glittering fluid from a Grecian urn that's been carved to look as if it's tipped over, its contents spilling abundantly into the lit pool below.

He sits, and I match his posture, smoothing my skirts and lowering myself onto the cloudy crystal rim of the fountain.

As I do so, he reaches into his jacket, retrieving and popping open the velvet box from dinner. He removes the necklace from its cushioned clutch, undoing it and indicating I should lean forward so he may fasten it behind my neck. I feel the clasp catch and the weight of the amethyst pendant as it falls to rest just above my newly ample cleavage, the scent of violets clustering in the air as Aro's free hand comes to trace the line of my jaw.

The weight of the pendant feels too much like a goodbye, and after everything, I worry I might burst into tears.

I shudder as he pulls back a little, his face so close to mine I can feel the warmth of his breath and smell the red sweetness of the wine we had drunk with dinner. Then, slowly but surely, he places his free arm around my waist.

I don't resist, merely a malleable damsel in his arms as he cups my cheek and pulls me closer.

He kisses me, and although it's the very first time, it feels like the very last time I'll ever have a first kiss. What's even crazier is that I want it to be, because I can't imagine anything will ever compare.

His lips are passionately soft against my own, the taste of him rich and intoxicating as I mould into the shape of his chest, placing my arms around the back of his neck and pulling him closer. The only sounds that can be heard are our mingled breaths, the trickle of the fountain behind us, and the racing of both our hearts as I feel his pounding beneath the breast of his velvet jacket and mine punishing the inside of my ribs. My hands explore him as our tongues twine and a deep passion trickles down into my stomach as though the urn of my long-dormant desire has tipped over too.

He ends the kiss slowly, tracing his fingers down my jaw, then my neckline and eventually lacing them with mine as we sit under the stars, gazing at each other with pupils scorched black and wide at the sight of the other.

"Kairi, listen to me. That necklace— When I said that I don't want you to ever forget this place, to forget me, that's true. But— I also never want to say goodbye to you again... I don't know if I can," he confesses, placing a hand on the back of his neck and rubbing nervously, his gaze falling.

"What are you saying?" I ask, heart suddenly pounding, and this time it's not from his kiss but from the expectation and the hope I'm hanging on his words.

"I'm saying I want to invite you to stay here with me— forever."

His words echo around me as I continue to stare at him in a state of frozen disbelief, my lips still hot and plump with rushing blood from our first kiss, the taste of him lingering on my tongue.

"Wait— you want *what*?"

9

THE AGE OF INNOCENCE

KAIRI

LEANING OVER THE BALCONY, I'm ed in the purest sunlight I've ever seen, and will ever see again. It falls, dappled, onto the pristine white silk of the floor-length nightgown that shrouds my well-rested muscles, as I sip on a cup of tea infused with rosewater from thin bone-white china adorned with a silver rim.

I want you to stay with me— forever.

The confession echoes around in my head on repeat, the prospect both so exhilarating and terrifying that I cannot wrap my mind around it.

Our date had intensified after those words, my lips spilling questions about how such a thing could possibly work and trying to make sense of the proposal he was laying out in front of me.

I don't want you to live in pain, Kairi.

I don't want to lose you again, Kairi.

I can't imagine my life without you in it.

Please, just think about it, for me.

I know it's sudden, but I've been waiting centuries. For me— you are my future. You're what I've been waiting for.

His words, his arguments, his biases aside, I cannot deny that I feel myself pulled beyond all logical reasoning to accept.

We had returned to dance in the ballroom as Fae with pointed ears sang, and the blonde woman who was enchantingly adept played her violin for hours. Then, lost in one another's gaze, we waltzed on thin air, my skirt weightless around me as though it were no more than a concord-coloured cloud.

His arms had been so sure as they wrapped around my waist, his eyes so wanton and adoring. I'm beginning to wonder if I'll be able to say no.

How can I walk away from the only man I've ever met who seems to say everything he is and is everything he says?

I know that I will never find another like him because men of his breed went extinct with the passing of the Victorian era.

The date had ended with us both breathless, pressed against the wall of the corridor outside my suite, tangled in one another's arms, lips red and sore from kissing for what felt like days, and yet still was not long enough.

I reach up to touch them now as I let my teacup sit on the balcony's intricate crystal railing, feeling them soft and tender beneath my fingertips, the same fingertips that had roamed his skin like a lioness prowling the savannah.

That kind of desire has been absent for so long in my life I had been wondering if I'd forgotten how to give over to it, to trust my body once again and just *feel*, but what I'd experienced with Aro was more than that. It was more than anything I ever experienced with Oli— or anyone. It feels like coming home, and while there's still the excitement of our newness and the adrenaline spike of lust whenever he touches me, from the moment we first kissed, I have become enraptured in a kind of contented calm, a kind of freedom from anxiety, from fear.

If I'm with him, I know everything will be alright.

I don't want to give that up, and yet, I can't quiet those two voices I know so well that continue to haunt me from the back of my mind, from my twenty-three years as Kairi Freemont.

I can't leave my parents, not after everything. I can't abandon my mortal life just because I've been offered something so insanely fantastical— it isn't fair.

I would be depriving my parents of their daughter— and myself of everything I've ever known, even if a large part of that is pain.

My heart falls through my chest, wingless and destined to crash through the clouds of this fantasy as the ghosts of their familiar company, the nostalgic pain of missing their smiles and voices, possess me, causing my heart to ache.

I know then that as much as I like Aro, as much as I could maybe even come to love him, there's no substitute for my family. For the two men who chose to make me theirs when they had no obligation, who have raised me and loved me through the terrible teen years and my gawky childhood obsession with Barbies.

They've held me through my tears and they've hugged me when I've triumphed.

There's nothing on earth or even beyond worth trading that kind of unconditional love for.

Not even Aro.

Tears prickle behind my lashes as I continue to stare out over Oblivion Falls. Fragments of rainbows are thrown by the frothing water as it hits the light, brightening layer upon layer until the entire crescent of the natural drop-off is glittering and multihued.

It's beautiful, but this isn't my world.

My world is something far less extraordinary, far less magical.

And yet, it's still mine, and nothing will change that.

Home is home, and family is family.

No matter how much you wish you had wings.

A knock at the door startles me as I sit in my nightgown, popping perfectly ripe grapes into my mouth. I sit among the dishevelled field of arctic white sheets, enjoying the luxury while I still can. I can't deny that I slept better last night than I have maybe ever, even before Ehlers Danlos Syndrome. I can't be sure if it was the dream of remaining here that made me sleep so soundly or the cloudlike mattress and weightless fluffy bedclothes that did the trick.

Either way, this will all soon be over.

"Come in!" I call, and the door opens as Aro lets himself in.

"Good morning, Sunshine." He beams, eyes boring into my face so hard I could swear he's trying to read my mind. His eyes drop momentarily to the low plunging neckline of the nightgown I'm wearing, eyes glistening with wicked intent as they roam the plains of my bare skin.

"Hey—" I crawl forward through the tangle of sheets so I'm sitting on my heels at the end of the bed, skirt tucked tight under my knees.

"Have you given my proposal any more thought?" he asks, cutting right to the chase. I shouldn't be surprised by his directness considering how open he's been about everything else, but still, I feel the air leave my lungs, fleeing at the thought of announcing my decision.

"I have— and—" He sits on the end of the bed, picking up my hand and raising it to his lips, brushing a chaste kiss on the back of my knuckles that sends a wave of tantalisation running rogue up the length of my arm.

"And?" His tone is too hopeful, too optimistic, and my heart feels like it might spasm knowing how disappointed he's going to be.

"I can't stay here with you, Aro." The words come out in a torrent of slightly angry emotion, not how I want them to at all. He drops my hand, mouth sagging at the corners.

"I see. Why?" he asks, brushing invisible lint from his trousers with both hands and stiffening noticeably in the shoulders.

"It's not you. Or Aetheria. I just can't leave my family. I love them, and I couldn't bear leaving them thinking I just up and disappeared. You understand that, don't you?" I implore him to empathize, and he nods slowly.

"I suppose I do. Still, are you sure you won't reconsider? I don't like the idea of you suffering—" he mumbles, perhaps the first time his speech has not sounded eloquent and self-assured.

I nod.

"It's my cross to bear, not your problem to solve," I remind him, giving him a quick kiss on the cheek.

He pulls away, and my heart fractures slightly at the distance he puts between us, getting to his feet fast.

"I just— If it wasn't so temporary, if it was just visiting, then of course. But I can't just move here— I'm sorry." My shoulders sag, and he shakes his head as though I've broken him, face turning stony and sharp.

"I can make a case for you to live here permanently with High Lord Abara because of your condition and your link to Storm, and because of your feelings for me— but I cannot simply let you come and go as you please. I must lead by example; I hope you understand. If I let you hop between dimensions on a whim, then soon this place will be filled with mortals wanting to live forever. We cannot sustain it." His words come out with a stony authority; any sense of uncertainty instantly gone.

Biting down hard on my still sore bottom lip, I sigh.

"I understand. It isn't your fault. We just— we belong in different worlds, I guess." I reach out for him, but he takes another step away, not meeting my gaze.

"Indeed. I think then it is time you pack your things. I'll take you home." I open my mouth to speak, but before I can utter another word, he's out the door and dropped off the end of the corridor beyond into nothing but air.

It doesn't take me very long to pack my things. After all, everything I've worn since arriving has been provided. In fact, my braces and backpack are still exactly where I left them upon first entering the suite.

I get back into my soft purple leggings, deciding to keep the underwear that I find in the bottom drawer of the dresser, as I'm pretty sure no Nephilim would be caught dead in second-hand silk panties. Pulling on my socks, vest, and sweater, and then looking around the room to check I haven't left anything behind, I'm left with an uneasy feeling that whatever business I have here is strangely unfinished. And yet, still, I cannot change my mind about leaving.

I don't belong here among winged immortals, unicorns, and Fae. I'm a broken mortal girl with two fathers who love her, and for whatever reason, that has always been enough for me—

Is it still?

Fingering the amethyst pendant, which I still haven't taken off since Aro and I first kissed, the coldness of the stone leaves me wondering about what it takes to sustain love for an immortal.

I'm too young to make that kind of a serious commitment, and Aro had to know that— didn't he?

He had given me this, said he wanted me to have a part of Aetheria with me always— so then why did he seem so broken when I had told him I couldn't possibly stay? Did he really expect me to give up my whole life to fly away to a magical castle with a winged man I've known only days?

Is it crazy that a part of me wants so badly for it to be my destiny, that I feel physically sick at the thought of walking out of this place and never looking back?

I can't allow myself to wallow, to dream, or doubt my decision, because deep in my heart, I know it's the right thing. Even if it does royally suck in too many ways to count.

Turning my back on the glittering sheen of the crystal walls and the opulent view beyond the open glass doors, I make my exit. Leaving the key on the unit closest to the door that holds a vase of quartz lilies, my backpack heavy on both shoulders and braces in one hand, I step outside, closing the door quietly behind me.

I expect to find Aro in the corridor outside, but instead, I come face to face with the pale-skinned Sephilim with chocolate-coloured feathers and freckles dancing across the bridge of his nose. He has been the one guarding my door, but I can't seem to remember his name.

"Uh— hi, are you here to take me home?" I ask him in a small voice, searching even still for his name.

I feel my chest deflate as I flail, wondering why the man who had taken me away from everything I'd ever known on a personal whim couldn't be bothered to take the time to return me.

Is this it?

Am I worthless as a human being now he knows he can't possess me?

"Yes, and it's Leo." He doesn't call me 'Miss' as Dawn had done, and his uniform suggests him as far superior to a mere mortal— I think Aro had mentioned he was some kind of lieutenant—

As I'm trying to remember, I become lost in the sheen of his armour, which is layered to look as though vines hold the metal plates together. It's polished to within an inch of blinding perfection, and unmistakably Aetherial from head to toe.

"Sorry, I'm forgetful," I say as resolution, not wanting to tell him that I've just not been paying that much attention because I've been too wrapped up in Aro.

He takes me by the hand without asking, and I tighten my grip on the braces in my palm as I gaze around the four walls of the corridor, sad. Of all the views I could have as my last, the hall is completely underwhelming by any kind of comparison.

"Hold on tightly," Leo instructs, and before I can even flinch, his grasp on my hand has become vicelike and the world has disappeared in a blade of pure white light that slices through the Aetherial scene and clean into the mortal dimension from where I've come.

We reappear just outside the gazebo, exactly where I had stood with Aro what seems like a lifetime ago.

The sun even looks to be in the same place—

"Has any time passed?" I enquire, and Leo looks at me with an odd curiosity, this expression the first I have seen from him that doesn't stem from a formal and duty-bound detachment.

"Of course. Sunrise—" he replies, and I'm not sure I'd believe him if it were not for the way that it is morning birdsong and not the evening serenade of Cicadas that fills the air.

"Thank you for bringing me home." I try to seem gracious, though honestly, I'm close to tears. I'll never see Aro again or the world which has enraptured me so completely. Instead, I must now continue to live as though nothing is different even though everything has changed.

"Goodbye, Kairi." Leo nods, and in a blinding flash that passes so fast I could have blinked and missed it, he's gone.

I'm left alone amongst the willow trees beneath the scorching heat of the new sun, by the edge of the lazily rippling pond.

That's when it hits me.

The pain returns, and all I can do is sink to my knees, lying down, broken once more among the reeds.

ARO

I stand in the garden under the moonlight, sword clutched between shaking palms. The gilded handle drips heavy with rubies, like droplets of blood have crystallised there over the years. So much death, so much destruction, and yet this feeling of— emptiness, of the plunging of my once soaring hopes, is far worse than any battle I've ever fought.

I can't sleep.

It's been three days, and I still can't find comfort in unconsciousness, so here I am, hacking at the trunk of a perfectly innocent tree instead.

The cloud hangs low in the sky overhead, a heavy blanket bathed golden in the moonlight as I raise the sword once more, readying myself for another blow.

"Be careful Trinity doesn't see you. Your stance is more crooked than the nose on a witch-doctor." The southern drawl startles me, so I spin fast on the spot, sword still raised high above my shoulder.

"Woah, easy there—" Vail lifts a pale hand as a sign of surrender, her blonde hair blowing freely around her shoulders. The baby pink silk of her floor-length nightgown matches the tips of each white feather that graces the wings tucked against her spine, her baby blue eyes wide with uncertainty.

"Sorry—" I mumble, turning back to the tree to try my hand at another swing.

"Y'all torn up over that girl, huh?" Vail continues to pry, papers in her hand crumpling. I don't know what she's holding, but if I had to guess, I'd say sheet music. She's the most incredible violinist I've ever had the pleasure of hearing, though what she's doing wandering the gardens this late I couldn't tell you.

Then again, I'm hacking up a tree, so I can't exactly say anything.

"Do none of you Nephilim have any notion of a man's sacred private space?" I ask her with an exaggerated sigh, the conviction fading out of my words as I let the sword drop to the floor amongst scattered wooden splinters.

"I grew up in a house with 12 siblin's, darlin'. Ain't no such thing." She smirks, sitting down on a crystal bench at the back of the quartz-lined clearing, crossing her legs. A flash of pale thigh is made gloriously pearlescent by the light coming from nearby amethyst torches, her mouth puckering as she cocks an artfully sculpted blonde eyebrow.

"I just— I don't know what I did wrong. I couldn't convince her to stay here even after we had such a wonderful evening." I slump onto the floor, propping myself against what remains of the tree trunk, resting my wrists on my knees so my hands hang down loosely between them.

"Wrong? Ain't nothing wrong with what you did, honey. But—" she begins but then thinks better of it, sitting up straighter and pulling her robe closed tighter around her torso.

"But?" I press her for the truth, but she just shakes her head.

"Well, that ain't my place to say, Your Lordship."

It's as though she's just remembered who I am, but this doesn't stop my frustration or my curiosity.

"As your High Lord, I demand you to tell me what you were just going to say." I scowl and she smirks, brushing her fringe from her forehead with quick fingers before shrugging.

"Well, it's only that you two seem to hardly know each other. I guess things were changin' even while I was alive. I can't imagine how loose women have become by now, must be like taffy left out in the sun if you understand my meanin'." She flushes slightly, porcelain cheeks reddening to the colour of almost ripe raspberries. "I heard rumours you don't even have to marry to climb into bed with any young fella. Now ain't that just ghastly?" Her cheeks continue to flush, her silken lips making the words fluid and entrancing as the southern twang of her mortal self runs rife with her vernacular.

"So, you're saying you think I was too hard on her?" I snap, eyes blazing with challenge.

"I think young ladies need time to commit. It's not like it was way back when. They ain't bought and sold after a single meetin' anymore." Her face is so innocent, and suddenly I see something in her features that I had tried to deny seeing in Kairi.

Kairi hadn't swooned at our first kiss because it wasn't her first. She hadn't become nervous as I wrapped her in my arms and let my fingers wander across the plains of her skin because it wasn't fresh or new.

She has been with men before— men who aren't me.

She might look like Briar, like Storm, but the reality of the fact she is neither suddenly hits me full force.

The thought stops my heart cold, turning my blood icy, and my fists curl at my sides. The thought of any other man touching her is enough to make me consider picking up the sword once again and felling the tree at my spine in a single swing.

I can't let that happen.

"So, what is it that you suggest?" I ask.

Vail only shrugs, the motion of her slender shoulders causing her feathers to ruffle.

"Court her over a longer period, milord. She was more smitten with you than a starving man with a cob of butter-slathered corn the other night. I saw it. But— you gotta give her time to adjust. Time to choose you without forcin' her hand. Women are stubborn creatures. Like studs, they take time to break, patience— finesse. You see what I'm sayin'?" She gets to her feet, and I look up at her immense shadow as she blocks out the moon behind her.

"Lord Abara would never agree for her to come and go as she pleases, convincing him to allow a mortal girl to visit like a tourist will be near enough impossible," I look to her for answers, feeling low and useless.

"Didn't Dawn tell me she has the mark?" Vail enquires, and I feel my eyes widen.

"So what?"

Vail moves to walk away down the garden path, leaving me sitting amongst broken wood and shattered stone.

"Well, it's only that if that mortal girl you wanted to visit was responsible for choosing the next King of Aetheria, I might reconsider— if I were also a High Lord—" She smiles, not waiting for me to reply as she walks away silently into the night.

I sit there listening to tinkling crystal leaves and the trickle of water, left with nothing but curiosity and a rekindled ember of hope that had not been there before.

The meeting is quick to arrange, seeing as there are no High Ladies to consult since the loss of Storm. Now, it is only Lord Caleb Abara and I can claim the title of High Born among the Kindred of Zeus and Hera.

As I stroll around the solid gold circular table, in what had long ago been the war room, I think of the day I realised I was different from all the other Sephilim.

I had electrocuted and subsequently melted an entire row of solid silver trees into shimmering, bubbling puddles topped with piles of amethyst leaves after getting into a fight with someone who I was on watch with. He was asking me inappropriate questions about women, and with each crude remark, I recall only too clearly how my blood had boiled closer and closer to the surface, my temper fraying ragged with the raging tide of my pulse.

It's funny— I was young, and I don't even remember the name of the man who had vexed me so. I was so enraged by mere words back then, volatile—

Anyway, the incident and my clear superior skill at manipulating electricity had brought me to the attention of Midas, the man who held the title of King of Aetheria when I was reborn into my Sephilim wings. I miss him sometimes, the lazy habits that made him easy to bend when I wanted something special for Storm, the way he had known without question that the Sephilim were the rightful summit of the Kindred pyramid. He knew and understood our greatness, and yet he had been foolish enough to try and bargain with the Draconians, a move which had led to first the death of his Queen, and then ultimately his unexpected demise.

I myself had been foolish in that regard also, inviting their High Lords and Ladies to the celebration of my betrothal to Storm. I had hoped to make political allies, and it had been the biggest mistake of my immortal life.

My fists clench at my sides, manicured nails biting into my palm as a blinding flash of light alerts me to my fellow High Lord's expected arrival.

"Aro, what is the meaning of this? It's far too early for formal meetings. I haven't even broken fast yet." The enormous black Sephilim grumbles, voice deep and visceral. His wings spread wider before shrinking to rest against his spine, their pure silver feathers, tipped onyx, shimmering in the early hour sunlight that seeps in through the faceted cloudy crystal of the spire ceiling.

"You know you don't actually need to sleep," I remind him, pulling out one of the high-backed golden chairs from around the circular table and moving to sit upon the thick purple upholstery.

"Doesn't mean I don't enjoy it." He shakes his head, running his hand back over his thick cornrows. His violet irises are hazy with unnecessary sleep as he slumps into the seat next to mine, the tailored black silk of his jacket straining around his enormous muscles. His huge hands rest on the table for a moment, fingers drumming as he stares forward blankly without even acknowledging me. Then, in the time it takes me to blink, he's facing me with a stare more potent than any Fae drug. It makes me uneasy, hairs rising on the back of my neck as nerves cause my heart to beat erratically despite its continued slowness within my chest.

"Well? I don't have all day." He shakes his head a little, bringing his arms so they're folded across his wide pectorals, the pure white of the crisp white shirt beneath his dark jacket a startling contrast.

"I have a request—" I begin, but as I draw breath to continue, he laughs, the sound thunderous as it bounces from the faceted walls.

"This wouldn't just so happen to be about the mortal girl you brought here without consulting me, would it?" I blink as he corners me without thought for gentleness or subtlety, the heady cologne of his skin - the scent of dirt that's been thoroughly pummelled by early fall rain - causing my nostrils to flare.

"Actually yes. I want to allow her visitation." I continue.

Lord Abara slumps back in his seat, contemplating the golden ivy forming the body of the chandelier overhead before answering.

"Huh, that I did not expect. Why, Aro? You know that's a big ask—You also know the reason why." Caleb looks curiously at me, the silence between us thickening as I consider my answer, straightening in my seat.

Still, the other High Lord does not meet my gaze, making him hard to read despite the fact I've known him for years.

"I do. But she is no ordinary mortal. She has the Heirbound mark just as Storm did. She looks just like her." I confess my theory, un-blinking as my feathers ruffle against the warm metal at my spine.

125

"So, what? You believe she is Storm resurrected?" he sounds incredulous, glancing at me at last with what is clearly curiosity mixed with subtle disbelief in the back of his now misty eyes.

"Reborn perhaps. In a different body. She said, Kairi— the girl I mean, that the mark was one she has had since birth. She doesn't remember me. Or Aetheria. She just says I feel familiar—" Caleb's face contorts with something on the verge of being a smile as his strong nose flares, his intake of breath deep.

"Why Aro, I do believe you're blushing— You can't tell me you're in love with a mortal," he teases, but I don't deny it, every muscle in my body tensing at the vulnerability this fact might suggest.

"I'm not here for your blessing, Caleb. I'm here because as my fellow High Lord, I need your permission before allowing a mortal to come and go as she pleases." I bite out, features sharpening under the stark blue sunrise that filters through the crystal walls and casts the room in a frosty hue.

"You'll need a lot more than that. This isn't mere Sephilim law. It applies to all the Kindred races. You will have to attain majority permission from the senate." He reminds me, and I realise I have been simplifying this problem. Of course, this isn't purely a Sephilim issue. It's an Aetherial issue, affecting all of us, even the Draconians.

"Do I really need to take this so far up the bureaucratic chain?" I ask him, and he cocks an eyebrow.

"You and I have sat in this room through how many battles? Planning the slaughter of other blessed beings how many times? What do you think?" He asks me, the answer obvious despite my wishing it were otherwise.

"So, what? I don't have your agreement?" I spit, wondering if I should just go ahead without informing any of the others regardless.

"I'll tell you what. If you can convince the Equinians, Fae, and the Draconians to give her their blessing to visit as she pleases, then you have mine as well," he announces, and I narrow my eyes.

"How can I possibly ask them to allow a mortal access they've never met? Especially the Draconians— you know how they feel about the prospect of a new Sephilim King. We've been at this standstill ever since we lost Storm. And you know as well as I that this democracy is hanging by a thread. The second we bring in anyone who gives any kind of hint of being the next Heirbound here— well, it could result in all-out war." I gesticulate wildly, but Lord Abara is unmoved as he gets to his feet.

"I would suggest you practice your dancing and small talk in that case. Bring Kairi here, to meet the others at a formal ball. If they decline her access, even after seeing what you claim to be Hera's divine mark and her likeness to Storm, then it would seem to me that you're a lonely fool, desperate to see things where they are not."

"You trust that they'll not try to sabotage any symbol that it is time for a new king to rise?" I spit at him.

"Perhaps. Though, you have both the Fae and Equinians onside already by our trade leverage over them. And besides, anyone worthy of becoming King of Aetheria would be able to handle such a situation with the Draconians with grace and poise. Don't you agree?" Caleb asks, and I can't deny he's right.

The Draconians caused the fall of our last King, and anyone who plans to take up the crown must be able to prove themselves formidable enough to keep them at bay if they want the respect of not just the Nephilim and Sephilim, but all the Aetherial people.

"Is that all?" he asks, looking down at me as I continue to sit.

"Well, I suppose all that's left to ask now is fish or chicken?" I spit at him, voice cold and irritated by his old-fashioned obsession with protocol and rules.

He laughs, shrugging before his wings flare out from him like two metallic blades and he disappears in an instantaneous forked flash.

Sitting for a long moment, I sigh loudly into the cavernous space, overwhelmed.

After all, what could possibly go wrong inviting together four species of Kindred who desperately hate each other?

This is going to be a disaster.

Especially when they discover that I'm trying to get them to agree on an illegal action that benefits not them, but me.

THE AWAKENING

KAIRI

MY DAD PLACES A tile onto the Scrabble board.

"Your turn—" he prompts me as I stare at my letters, the game board resting on the couch between us as the room darkens and sunset fades into early night.

The tiles float and rearrange themselves in front of my eyes, and I try to focus but know it's hopeless. I haven't been able to concentrate in a week, and the cause is no mystery. I know why.

I had walked slowly and in agony back to the house after waking up beside the pond where I'd fallen unconscious. The pain that I should have experienced during the activity I had undertaken in Aetheria unleashed as a high wave rushing straight for me with no warning. The impact had hurt in the worst way possible, not just because my bones felt like they were made of fine china, fragile, breakable, and ready to shatter – but because I knew I was actively choosing to live with this pain for the rest of my life.

I can't even claim that it's out of my control any longer because I chose this. I chose to stay here with my fathers, to give up a life in Aetheria with the sun that magically evaporated my pain and discomfort as though it had been imaginary all along.

I dream of Aetheria still, every night. The rustle of leaves reminding me of feathered wings ruffling against velvet, the starry sky overhead underwhelming in almost every regard. In my dreams I remain firmly in Aro's arms, twirling an endless waltz on the air of the Solis Castra ballroom for the rest of my days, but then I wake, cold and alone in the darkness of my ever-so-ordinary bedroom.

I sigh.

"Kairi?" My dad prompts, reaching out and placing a hand on my shoulder.

"Sorry, I'm just tired I guess—" I admit, smiling sleepily as I take in his face. I have never appreciated him and my Pa more than I do now. After leaving the familiar behind me in my journey to another world, returning to them feels like coming home more than ever.

We have spent more time together since they returned from their Nashville trip, my dad reading aloud to me as he had when I was a child every night as the sun sets and bathes us in lazy buttered light, or playing board games and taking drives with Pa through the endless rolling fields during the early afternoon.

If truth be told, I feel like Pa is enjoying getting out of the house more often just as much as I am, if not more.

It feels different like perhaps I've turned a corner, taken control of my condition and agreed to bear it for the sake of the life I don't want to give up here. I made this choice, and while that's terrible, I've found it to be some kind of relief, an act of acceptance too.

I've been sleeping more soundly, enjoying the books I've been reading more, and feeling generally less depressed all around. My head has hit the pillow each night, my body weary from more exertion than it's used to in an attempt to get back to some form of thriving, not merely surviving, and I've slept deeper than I imagined I ever would again.

Perhaps having been given a get-out-of-jail-free card from all this has made me realise that despite the pain, despite the symptoms and the difficulties I face every day, it's worth it for my family. That even if I had the choice to live another life pain-free, I wouldn't give them up for anything.

I chose to be here, and so now, I choose to be happy.

After all, there's no cure for this, so why fight against it?

Why waste energy being miserable about something I can't change when I have so many things to be grateful for?

I've been so focused on what I've lost, I've become blind to what I still possess.

I ponder on this small miracle of changed perception as my dad's face creases empathetically.

"It's okay. You're doing more than usual, so it's expected you'll be tired. Why don't you go up to bed, get an early night? I can pack this up." He gestures to the board scattered with lettered tiles between us, and I give a small tired smile in gratitude, stretching and feeling the burn of my joints as I get to my feet, steeling my mind against paying the ache too much attention.

I won't let this pain control me, or dictate what I can and can't do, any longer.

"Night, Dad. Love ya." I lean down, kissing his stubbled cheek and ruffling his tousled hair as he grins.

"Night, Kairi. I love you too," he calls after me, and I feel my heart warm, the fact he's so close in comparison with only a few days ago a comfort in more ways than he'll ever know.

I climb the stairs, opening the door to my room and finding Catticus staring up at me from the floorboards near the foot of the bed.

Meowing, he trots over to me as I enter the room, curling around my thick fuzzy socks and tickling my knees with his tail. My eyes are drawn to where he was sitting when I entered, an envelope I don't recognise revealed by the absence of his fuzzy behind.

Curious, I step over him, careful not to trip, and make my way over to the envelope.

Swiping it up off the floor, I hold the thick sparkling parchment between my fingers, continuing to pace until I sit on the edge of the window seat. Staring down at my name in elegant quill-formed scrawl. Turning it over, I find the back is sealed with silver wax, a sun debossed firmly in the middle.

I look at where the envelope had landed, then at the glass doors. It's clearly been pushed beneath them from the balcony outside.

An audible creak from overhead has my heart instantly in my throat, fingers rising from where they're lingering over the silver wax seal and to the amethyst pendant that I haven't been able to bring myself to take off.

Setting the envelope down to one side, I get to my feet and stride over to the doors, yanking one open and stepping out onto the wrap-around balcony, the night air refreshingly cool against my flushed cheeks.

I look up, finding him perched atop the highest eave of the barn's sturdy roof, silhouette majestic against the dusk.

"Some people might consider this stalking," I announce, unable to think of anything wittier or more intelligent to say.

He stills at the sound of my voice, clearly not having noticed me until now.

"Kairi—" Aro's eyes are sadder than I've ever seen them, his mouth falling slack as he leaps upward from his crouch. Spreading his wings and slowing his fall, he descends toward the balcony, landing upon the wooden boards with a seamless grace that could only ever have been inhuman.

I chew on my bottom lip, annoyed at how much he affects me after everything.

Obviously, I'm still hurt from how he left so suddenly before as my guts twist uncomfortably like someone has grabbed a fistful of intestines and is squeezing mercilessly.

"Hello, Aro." I sigh, sounding as though his presence is the world's biggest imposition.

A part of me wants to be thrilled I'm seeing him again, something I doubted would ever happen, but the other part of me wants to tell him to leave me the hell alone.

"You don't seem very happy to see me," he observes, leaning over the wooden railing and pulling his wings in behind him so they lie flat. I turn so I'm leaning over the balcony as well, staring out over the ranch left a deep blue by the fast-fading sun.

"I can't say I am. I was under the impression you wanted nothing to do with me." I glare at him, feeling more confident than I have in a while.

"I suppose I deserve that—" he shrugs, voice not as sad as it is irritated. He doesn't look at me but continues to stare out toward the horizon instead. I wonder if he's ashamed.

"You do." I acknowledge, stretching my neck out from left to right.

"You don't want to know why I came back?" he asks me, expression surprised as though the bindings keeping his features stony have been cut away, allowing them to meld into something more artful, more beauteous than the mere statue he becomes when enraged.

"I assume you're going to tell me. Or you were going to let your letter do it for you?" I retort, shifting my weight from one foot to the other.

"After you left, I was beside myself. I kept thinking there must be some way to allow you to visit. I understand now that asking you to give up your life here was too much and far too soon. We need more time to court. Need more time to get to know one another." He brings a hand up to stroke a strand of loose hair behind the shell of my ear as he closes the three-foot gap between us.

"Figured that out all on your own, did you?" I ask him, still not ready to fully forgive him.

131

I had fallen so hard and found him such a fairy tale. The realisation that he was perhaps just like any other man, petulant once he didn't get what he wanted, was more painful than I ever want to admit. I have been left feeling naïve, feeling like a fool, and as much as I'd love to fall into his arms, I'm wary this time.

"Actually no, a young Nephilim reminded me times have changed," he laughs as though he is surprised by this.

"Oh really?" I ask, and he nods, mouth twisting into a crooked smile.

"Really. I called a meeting with the other High Lord of the Sephilim. He reminded me we need the approval of the senate to allow your suggested visitation. So, I'm arranging a ball." He announces this, causing me to blink once, then twice as a wisp of his violet musk catches in my nostrils and causes my heart to unwillingly squeeze.

"That's rather presumptuous. What if I don't want to dress up in a magnificent gown and schmooze mystical creatures all night long?" I smirk, and he shakes his head, thoroughly missing my attempt at sarcasm.

"Forgive me. You're right— I shouldn't have assumed—" He drops his head, cropped inky locks falling across his forehead.

"You're really holding a ball for me? You went to all that trouble?" I ask him, pressing my fingertips to his chin this time and lifting his face so his eyes meet mine.

"I want you by my side. Even if only a few days a month. I haven't wanted anything this much in centuries," he confesses, leaning in and staring into my wide eyes with those galaxy-riddled pools that spill the secrets of endless possibility, promising all the magic and adventure I've ever dreamed could be real.

I attempt to answer, but my answer is lost as he leans in and presses his lips to mine, twisting so he's facing me fully and pulling me into his body. His wings wrap around my shoulders, cocooning me as he caresses the side of my face.

"I'm sorry, Kairi—" he whispers into my ear as he pulls me into a tight embrace against the silk of his double-breasted jacket.

I inhale him, tears springing to my eyes.

I feel ridiculous, but I can't help it. I guess what he did hurt me more deeply than I truly realised. Have I really gotten in so deep with this angelic creature so utterly fast?

"It's alright. And yes, I'll come to your ball— if what's in the envelope inside is an invitation?" I cock an eyebrow as he plays with a strand of my caramel hair, twizzling it idly between two gentle fingers.

"Of course." He gazes at me, taking in my face and tracing his finger across my lips, then my cheekbones, cupping the side of my face. I lean into him, a happy glow spreading through my entire body beneath the fleece of my pyjamas.

"Alright then, when is it?" I ask him as he unfolds his silken feathers from my shoulders and tucks them behind him.

"Tomorrow night. I can pick you up in the late afternoon so you have time to get ready and then mingle with the other Nephilim. You should meet them," he suggests, and I nod, simultaneously nervous and energised all at once.

"Okay," I breathe, trying not to give away how incredibly excited I am.

"One more thing, the Draconians may be present. I had to invite them as we need their approval," he reveals, and I frown.

"But— you hate them—" I say, not understanding why he would want to break bread with people he abhors.

"I do, but our laws are ancient and created by the Gods who made us. I must abide by what they decree, or I will be stripped of my position," he explains, and I'm immediately thoughtful.

Fear creeps across the forefront of my subconscious, and Aro observes my body as it stiffens, bringing my hands so they're held within his tight grasp.

"Kairi, I will never let anything happen to you. You're safe with me, I promise," he vows, kissing my knuckles as if it's habit, and allowing his gaze to drill into mine, assuring me.

I feel my body relax at his certainty, slumping into him and wrapping my arms around his waist. The feathers of his wings tickle my forearms.

"I missed you," I admit, inhaling the scent of him one last time before I take a step back.

"And I, you. I regret that I must go. I have much to prepare before tomorrow," I feel my heart sink a little, believing the pristine planes of his face unreal even still.

"I understand," I reply, though I don't.

How can I?

He's a High Lord, a man of breeding and politics, and I am a twenty-three-year-old unemployed, disabled bibliophile who loves her own company far too much. We are as I have said before, worlds apart. Though, when I'm in his arms, it suddenly doesn't seem to matter as much as I'm certain it does while I'm tossing and turning all night long.

"Until tomorrow, my love." He bows before me, kissing me on the cheek. His fingers leave a lingering electrical charge along my collarbone as his eyes turn into adoring vacuums of velveteen black, and I shudder unwillingly.

I flush, embarrassed by my brazen lack of restraint around him and my body's autonomous betrayal, but before I can reply with anything awkward or unintelligent, he's gone.

The silence of the night falls around my shoulders like a glittering shawl, and I stare out over the Tennessee skyline. To me, the newborn stars are once again alive and shimmering, as though they'd never been anything else.

LUCIEN

The knock sounds as I'm scooping the last dregs of honey from a jar and into the depths of my tea, a copy of *Draconian Sword Making- A History*, placed on the countertop, pages splayed open as I peruse its contents.

I pad across the thick cream rugs that cover the mahogany floor; silk slippers almost soundless as I peer curiously through the stained glass of the dark wooden front door.

"Yes?" I call, balling my fist at my side.

It's too late for visitors or, at least, anyone who claims to be civilised.

"Lucien open up! It's Kaiden. I'm freezing my balls off out here!" His modern vernacular never fails to illicit a laugh from me and, more often than not, an eye-roll as well.

"Some might say you're a little late for a nightcap—" I remind him, grabbing the thick metal keyring from the ring beside the door, unlocking it, and allowing him inside.

The draconian that greets me has a thicket of dark curly hair topping a skull made undeniably recognisable by one-of-a-kind broad cheekbones and an equally distinctive and broad forehead. His dark eyes sheen as he exhales, rubbing his hands together, breath condensing in front of him as a gale of cold air sweeps across the threshold and teases the hem of my robe.

"Some might say you're becoming an old man; what is this, slippers and a robe? Don't tell me you've got a cup of tea steeping in the kitchen?" he smirks, and I roll my eyes.

"Yes, and it's getting cold. What do you want?" I cut to the chase, closing the door behind him and leading him down the long, high-ceilinged, hallway with midnight blue walls, and into the muted grey slate of the kitchen.

"You want?" I ask, gesturing to the cup of tea on the counter, but he shakes his head from the opposite side of the granite-topped island.

"No, I can't stay. I just came to deliver a message from Lady Thomas. There's an invitation for you up at the Astrid Keep. Delivered by one of those Kensari from Soleus."

As he finishes, I'm already back behind the counter, eyeing the book again as I listen with half an ear. However, as his words pass through the sweet steam of my tea and reach my ears, I slam the volume shut, eyes widening.

"What?!" I ask him, and he shrugs.

"Don't shoot the messenger."

I take a long drag of tea, burning my mouth in the process as I eye him with scrutiny over the porcelain rim of the silver cup.

"You realise we haven't had correspondence from Soleus for over one hundred years. You're sure she said it was from there?" I ask him and he nods, the deep navy blue of his wings shaking a little as they shed slurry over the floor.

My lips pucker, fingers drumming rhythmically upon the cool granite as we stand in total silence, the steam of my tea continuing to rise between us as the moonlight bounds off the copper saucepans strung overhead.

"Anyway, I had better be going. It's late," Kaiden relinquishes, breaking the tense cloud of thoughtfulness that's formed above my head. I wonder momentarily as I stare at him, hopping from foot to foot, if the cold bothers him so much.

"Right, well uh, thanks for stopping by." I dismiss him, and he smiles.

"Goodnight, my Lord."

Bowing his head slightly, he turns and leaves without another word, his footsteps crunching on the snow outside just seconds before I hear the door slam shut in his wake.

Picking up the cup of tea and the saucer it's resting upon, I place the thick leather-bound volume under my arm and adjourn to my study down the long adjoining hallway.

The study has high ceilings, and all walls except one are crowded with shelves that climb the entire height of the room and are brimming with books. Thick, chocolate, leather armchairs litter the space in front of the only free wall, which is opposite the door, where a ceiling-high leaded window lets moonlight illuminate the space in rich tones of both coffee and navy blue.

The entire place holds the musk of caramel and dust from finger-worn pages clasped between aged leather covers, and I inhale it fondly as I sit in my favourite armchair.

Facing the window, I gaze up at the stars, taking another sip of my tea, the now cool brew running warm and slick down my throat with the caress of honey mixing in seamlessly with the Drakos Vale-grown tea leaves.

Out there, somewhere, the Sephilim High Lords are planning something big. They must be, or they would not have gone to the trouble of sending an invitation here.

The book in my palms weighs heavy with the wisdom inside, but I find myself unreceptive to its secrets as I ponder instead of what it all means.

By the time I've reached the bottom of the teacup, still unable to focus on the relaxing evening I had planned, I've made up my mind.

Leaving the cup resting on the arm of the chair and the book abandoned atop the cushion, I prepare to leave immediately.

The night air whips against my face like the lash of a steel chain, my wings rippling loudly as the breeze catches beneath them.

I could have taken the sledge, and I'm damn sure that would have been far more comfortable, but as it is, I don't want to waste any time. Snow peppers my face in enormous wet flakes as I rise above the thick canopy of mist that hangs around the base of the highest peak in Drakos Vale, and though I'm unreceptive to the cold, the turbulence is making my stomach churn.

As I approach, I find the lights of the Astrid Keep twinkling like beacons in the night, informing my flight path.

The palace twines around the base of the mountain and up through the endless hematite ore, winding within it and playing with its many levels as the architecture turns it into something liveable. The scent of wintergreen and peppermint is thick in the sharp night air, the weak light of the moon barely enough to see by as it is absorbed by aether thick cloud both above and below.

Banking left then right as I approach, I try to focus on making a successful landing on the tiny balcony of Genevieve's suite.

I can see from afar that the glass doors are flung open, leaving the interior of her room at a low temperature, just the way she likes it.

Diving through the air, I narrow my eyes like a hawk, the talons at the edges of my wings making my shadow familiar as I near the edge of the mountain. It comes into sharper focus as I fall, foot by foot, through the night.

Stretching my wingspan as wide as it will go to slow my descent to a stop, I manage to touch down on the white marble of the balcony without much sound, jumping down onto the stone and feeling smug at my precision.

Not bad for an old man.

I hear it then, coming from within the open glass doors, white gauzy curtains flying out, phantasmal in the raging storm outside.

Genevieve is screaming.

Taking a deep breath, I stride through the open doors and into the chill interior of her suite.

She has an enormous four-poster bed, the frame carved from white marble to match the bedclothes, and I find her splayed out among the arctic silken wasteland of the sheets, her white gauzy nightgown heavy with sweat as I approach, clinging to her every curve. The solid jade crystal of the walls and floor make the white of her skin even more startling, corpse-like even.

I stand over her, finding her mouth slack, white hair spread out around her in a tangled mess of curls, desperate cries emitting from her lips as her eyeballs swivel wild behind the thin veils of her eyelids.

"Genevieve!" I call, bending over her and trying to determine her temperature from afar.

I can't discern how hot her skin is with the cold rushing in from outside, and as I stare at her, the white drapes of the bed hanging around the doors fly around the room wildly in the fast-circulating air. The fireplace, long since diminished, smoulders in the corner and fills the room with the smell of woody smoke.

I reach out with as much tentativeness as I can manage, touching her shoulder.

Flinching back immediately with a hiss, my fingertips are scalded raw, the sweat slathering her paleness near boiling point.

"Shit!" I yell, despite knowing better, turning around and hopping from one foot to the other before biting down too hard on my tongue and smashing my fist into the deep jade wall; an attempt at distracting myself from the pain.

The sound of my knuckles impacting crystal wakes her at last, and she bolts upright in bed, the scorching white ghost of a star shining angrily in the dark.

"Lucien?" She says my name, and though the tone is furious, the volume is no more than a hoarse wisp. I turn around to find her wings flaring out behind her, the tips reaching far beyond either side of the mattress.

"Sorry, you were having a nightmare," I explain, feeling dumb as I bend down so I'm looking up into her wide and tired expression from the edge of the bed.

"Did you burn yourself?" she asks, staring down at my hands, aggravation marring her features.

Then, she wraps her arms around herself as though she's cold. Her tone deflates as she takes a deep shaky breath, the power of her fury gone as though the cold wind has extinguished it entirely.

"Only a little," I sigh, scrunching my throbbing fingertips into a ball so she can't see the damage. The tattered nerve endings scream in protest, but I work hard at keeping my facial expression neutral.

"What are you doing here anyway?" She turns from me, almost swatting the side of my face with one of her polar white wings as she kicks the sheets from her legs and gets out of bed.

Once she's standing, the gauzy white of her nightgown pools around her ankles from where it has been ruched up around her crotch. Her nipples are steel as her silhouette is cast against the dark green of the walls, the paleness of her skin almost invisible beneath the fabric.

Almost.

I try not to stare, withdrawing my eyes from her pallor as she strides across the room, pouring herself a glass of ice water.

"Well?" she asks again, running her fingers through her scarlet roots, a gasp of relief escaping her lips as she sets down the glass on the table in front of the smouldering hearth. Her fingers continue to caress the cool glass of the pitcher before her, eyes not meeting mine.

"Kaiden told me you had an invitation for me, from Soleus? It sounded important, so I thought I better come and see for myself," I say, straightening from where I'm still crouched and folding my hands behind my back.

"You know it's not urgent. There's no need for you to fly here in the early hours of the morning. You can write a polite decline after a good night's sleep, I have no doubt," she announces without missing a beat.

I observe her carefully before replying, the lace that clings to her leaving so little to the imagination that it's impossible for her to hide the fact she's still physically shaken from her nightmare.

"What do you mean, a decline? I haven't even opened the invitation yet." I remind her, confused.

Perhaps she is still muddled from her night terror.

"Well, what else would you possibly respond with? You can't break bread with the Sephilim, Lucien. They hate us, and we hate them. That's a precedent that they chose to set long ago." She dismisses any reply before I make one with a wave of her long fingers.

"You don't even want to know why they're sending an invitation?" I ask her, but she only shrugs.

"Doesn't matter. They're *Sephilim*. We don't make nice with *Sephilim*. We kill them, and that in itself, after everything, I consider kind," her tone is icy as the blood running through my veins as my fingers continue to throb from the heat of her skin.

"That isn't your call to make. I want to at least know what I'm turning down before I decline. It could be important." I cock an eyebrow, eyes steeling over as I tilt my chin. I love Genevieve as a sister, but I too am a High Lord, and I can make my own choices.

She turns to me, affronted.

"You will listen to me in this matter, Lucien. You might be too young to remember what vileness accompanies Zeus' dark angels, but I am not." She is facing me head-on now, white hair wild around her face, which is flush with blood for the first time I can remember in years.

"Give me the invitation. I will make up my own mind. You will not make it up for me," I warn her, tone lowering so it's halfway between a snarl and a roar.

"I don't need to tell you what you risk by getting involved with them. What will happen if we are exposed?" She uses this as a final threat, but I ignore her as my curiosity burns bright within the skies of my consciousness, a guiding star.

"Fine!" she snaps, nodding to the pale wooden writing desk that sits in the corner. I take the room in several brisk strides, finding the familiar glistening parchment of Soleus sealed with silver wax. I tear it open, unimpressed by the pomposity of the stationary and more concerned with the implications of any request made by Zeus' Kindred.

I find a thick parchment folded inside, and as Genevieve takes another mouthful of water, her skin utterly free of goosebumps despite the cold, I begin to read.

"Well?" Genevieve asks, and I consider keeping the information from her.

"They're holding a ball for a mortal girl—" I feel my brow furrow deeply, confused.

Mortals aren't permitted in Aetheria.

So, what the hell is High Lord Aro Black playing at?

"What?!" Genevieve almost spits the water she's just taken into her mouth all over the jade floor.

"It says High Born guests will be invited to meet her before a formal conference to explain more about the *situation at hand*." I scan the letter, trying to decipher the overly complicated formal vernacular.

Genevieve's eyebrows rise on her forehead, emerald eyes incredulous as the glass in her hand shatters.

"It's a trick," she snaps immediately, no more questions asked as glass tinkles to the floor. She doesn't flinch, merely remains stone still, blood slowly dripping down from her palm and staining her nightgown in the moments that follow.

"But, hang on. Didn't Anastasia say that there was a mortal girl in her vision? What if she's in trouble?" I ask, and Genevieve shakes her head adamantly against the idea in all forms.

"No mortal is worth the risk you'd be taking by attending, Lucien. It's a dirty trick put together to lure you from Drakos Vale after centuries of dis-communication with the rest of Aetheria. For all we know, they might be setting up an ambush to kill you," she guesses, and I cock my head.

"I'm not exactly helpless Genevieve, I'll take Ebonara," I add.

She opens her mouth, horrified.

"Don't be so utterly absurd! You can't go there— with her!" She is on her feet now, and though I can't quite discern why, I have the strong gut instinct to oppose her on this where normally I might relinquish.

"The Sephilim hate us as much as we hate them. If they're sending a formal invitation, then something important is at the root of this," I retort, and she snorts loudly.

"So, some fancy calligraphy is enough to get you to forget years of bloodshed and death? After everything they've taken from us?" She's angry. Even her toes tense as they curl beneath the skirt of her nightgown.

More shattered glass falls from her fingertips followed by quickening droplets of blood.

I pocket the invitation, walking past her.

I'm done arguing, mainly because I know that I've made up my mind and there's no changing hers.

I'm going, and that's it.

I'm too curious to do anything else. Especially after Anastasia's vision has implied that there's something important on the horizon and that it involves a mortal girl.

Perhaps *this* mortal girl.

"Lucien, don't you dare—" I hear her voice, but soon it's whipped away as I break into a run, darting across her suite, through the wide double doors, and launching from her balcony on the side of the mountain and into the snowy night.

The cold is a relief as I soar higher and higher.

Becoming lost against the endless dark filled with mist, cloud, and frost, my heart hammers, fingers still throbbing from Genevieve's scorn.

II

WOMEN IN LOVE

GENEVIEVE

I STARE AFTER LUCIEN from the velvet of the chaise longue, watching his edgy silhouette disappear into the night beyond the thick blanket of sleet-filled cloud. Stepping over shattered glass, I stride through the open balcony doors and out into the raging wind, relishing the pain in my slashed and bleeding palm.

The air whips around my body but fails to cool me as much as it should. The fire isn't merely crawling over my skin; it's far deeper than that, far deeper than anyone could reach and quell.

The embers will forever be stoked by my sense of injustice, the climbing flames spitting memories – abhorrent, fractured, and dissonant – from the scorching heat of my past.

My white hair flies out around my face, made damp by the slow onslaught of falling snow. I narrow my eyes against the contrasting dry icy cold of the air, pursing my lips and banishing the nightmare to the recesses of memory.

Lucien's dissent is troubling, but not as troubling as the fact the invitation had arrived in the first place. Arriving not even by Sephilim but by Kensari as if they couldn't be bothered to travel this far in person.

So if we are not worth such courtesy, why send the invitation at all?

Staring out across Drakos Vale, I find the pinpoints of firelight flickering at steady intervals along the spectacularly high hematite wall that rings my lands, the surface of the rising rock slick and slippery with metallic moonlight and sleet.

Draconian guards walk the length of the very top, their ionised black steel armour flashing momentarily and caught only just by my supernatural sight, hawk-like and pristine as any other immortal predator. My gaze lifts, imagining the rest of the military force who are on duty tonight scattered amongst the clouds, creating a dome formation atop the floating island. I shiver at the thought of spending the night among the clouds in this snowstorm, not for one moment taking their diligence for granted.

If the Sephilim were more discreet when they arrive, our smaller number might be a concern, but seeing as conducting is far from subtle, and their feathered wings make it difficult for them to navigate the turbulent skies overhead, I've always been cautious, but never too worried about a breach.

They know that we're heavily fortified as both a defensive landmark and a people. If they didn't, I fear we would have been wiped out, or greatly reduced even further in number, long ago.

My heart aches when I think about what they've done to us, what they've taken.

In banishing us here, they've left our kind struggling to survive against the cold, a fact which they were well aware of when they made the decree. Many of those most precious to us have died, and if it weren't for the vent-heated underground caverns, I fear it would have been an extinction-level punishment.

I am fortunate, the heat that burns inside of me a gift from Hecate, though some would call it a curse. Her blessing has kept me strong, kept me untouchable and wild amongst the oppression of those who would try to tame us.

I remember the day that we were banished as though it were yesterday, the rage still as hungry for revenge as it was then.

After the death of his Queen, Pandora, at my hand— or rather Algoric's, Midas had banished us, the war that had raged for the latter part of the seventeenth century and the first half of the eighteenth finally coming to an end with this decree. He wanted me to bend to him, to use the powers that my people and I had been gifted by the Goddesses who blessed us to further his agenda in the name of Zeus.

I declined.

I will *always* decline.

I simply could not allow him to use me and my people for bloodshed, for violence, and to inflict terror on his opponents.

It had cost me so much, cost all of us, and yet, given the same chance again I would not change my decision.

I would not bend to him.

I will *never* bend to a man again.

143

Turning my back on the night, I stride back into the jade confines of my chill suite, closing the balcony doors behind me with a click and then quickening my pace as I move across the moss stone of the floor and toward the arched doorway.

Letting the thick mahogany door fly behind me as I exit, I hear it bang against the wall and then close, rebounding with a loud slam.

Stalking through the corridors, I find guards stationed every few metres, their jet armour scaled and fierce, making them shadow-like and invisible against the jade walls.

My bare feet cool against the stone, and I watch their lingering gazes trace my form beneath the near-absolute transparency of my nightdress.

I wear my nakedness as armour, knowing it weakens them, knowing that it is my power alone to wield.

My nipples sharpen like knives against flint in the corridors with torches extinguished, and my curves hold more weight than any defensive shield as I pass their wandering eyes, head held high, superior and regal in both body and mind.

The paths twine like veins filled with the poisonous clutch of the cold, the walls fading from jade through to aqua tourmaline, and then to the iridescent glory of moonstone on all sides the closer I get to the heart of the Keep.

The throne room opens up, ceiling a lofty crystal dome made grandiose with stained glass astrological maps, as I descend a final steep set of stairs that hugs the steep declining curves of the mountain.

I speed my step; anxious to get where I'm going as quickly as possible.

I reach the centre of the room, standing over the hematite seal bearing the multi-spoked and archaic pinwheel, symbol of Hecate, the same symbol that adorns our copper coin.

I bring my fingers to my palm, reopening the new and slow clotting slash caused by the glass I'd broken. The gash meanders across the lines of my palm like a river, as in a single quick slice of my pointed nail, the red mist of my temper is made cold, fluid and real.

It stains my pale fingers as it runs fast and wild.

Holding my palm out in front of me, I observe the scarlet droplets falling upon the metal below in a quick torrent.

I step onto the symbol as I hear the column begin to grind while the blood is absorbed, rotating in a corkscrew as it descends beneath the thick crystal of the floor, a mystical lift leading to where the real treasures and most guarded secrets of the Draconians are kept.

Access remains strictly granted only to those with our blessed blood.

Urgency clutches at me as the column descends through the solid crystal, my ghostly reflection visible in the mirror-sheen of the stone that surrounds me on all sides.

Finally, after a whole minute, the shuddering rotation ceases, the polished floor of the throne room ceasing abruptly just above the cavern's bare rock ceiling begins. Stalactites drip aether-thick snow run-off down onto the floor where it lands in shimmering pools and causes them to ripple. My nostrils fill with the smell of molten metal, burning flesh, and the stale air of underground as I step down from the column, my bare feet met by the warm stickiness of slightly damp soil, the natural underfoot heating evident as ever.

My soul's vast heat quells from scalding to warm as I walk past several handlers who are preparing meals, armour, and other supplies around the entrance with calloused palms and dirt-peppered faces. Their eyes light with respect and reverence as I pass with only a curt nod, focused on only my destination.

The caverns sprawl beneath the entirety of Drakos Vale and have been kept secret for centuries, ever since the banishment and their fortuitous discovery the following summer. We have grown far more than any foreign reconnaissance might assume, our nursery and The Academy of Arcane Arts having been founded among the security of this rock and darkness.

From where there was nothing, we have carved out a life despite the back-breaking effort and slow determination it has taken, despite the other Kindred who had wanted so badly for us to rely on them and forgo our independence.

We are survivors, and we have done exactly that.

Several of the handlers bow, their leathery wingspans pulling in tight against their spines as they do so, eyes pinned on my face so as not to wander across the valleys and peaks of my all-but-naked silhouette.

I give a small and painful smile and then almost bump into Gage, the other Draconian High Lord, blessed by Nemesis.

"Sorry," I breathe out in a sharp exhale as he sidesteps me, his cheeky boyish grin and handsome face relaxed where mine is knotted with tension beneath the smooth façade of my expression.

"If you're looking for Lucien, he's already gone, took Ebonara and left in a hurry too," he informs me, and I nod, rolling my eyes and pressing my lips together hard.

The young High Lord is dressed informally and is wearing a sooty white shirt that's rolled up to his elbows and is tucked into loose dress pants. He is chewing some kind of toothpick- as usual- flashing several of his silver teeth in the process as his opaline white and aqua wings quiver slightly at his spine.

"Yes, foolish thing thinks he can break bread with the Sephilim and live to tell about it." I brush off Lucien's blatant opposition with a relaxed hand, but my eyes steel with rage at the thought of his callous disrespect of my greater wealth of experience with the dark angels.

"Well, won't that be an interesting tale for him to tell on his re-turn—" Gage runs his fingers through his caramel faux hawk, and I shake my head at his youthful naivety as his eyes skim over the surface of my body with half-interest.

"Or one for me to tell at his funeral. Should make for a good eulogy!" My voice turns grim in tone at the thought, lowering the previously shrill pitch.

Anxiety pools, solidifying icy in my gut at the idea of my sentiment becoming reality.

I don't know why. After all, it's not like I didn't warn the fool.

"Ye of little faith!" he calls back, continuing to walk as he turns from me with a jump in his step, his shadow stretched long by the sconces spitting intense red sparks at regular intervals along the jagged cavern walls.

I shouldn't be surprised at his faith in Lucien. I just so happen to think he idolises him a little. After all, Lucien is the one who has been showing him the ropes of his place in our aristocracy, not to mention he has taught more than a few classes at The Academy in the last several centuries. The students seem to like him, which is more than I can say for myself. Whenever I give a lecture, they stare at me with such silent and terrified intensity that you could hear a pin drop.

Turning a corner, I come finally to the destination I've been think-ing about since the last time I left. The subject of my affections is waiting, as usual, manacles chaining him loosely to the wall; he lies curled up like a sleeping cat.

I approach, admiring the way his white scales are polar matte at one angle and turn into glistening opals flecked through with mint shimmer at another.

Genevieve. My name echoes around my skull in a throaty rumble as Algoric's eyes slowly open to reveal the pale mint oceans of his irises.

Hello dear friend, I respond, feeling for our bond through the telepathic walkways within which we have leisurely strolled together for centuries. *How are you feeling today?*

He gets to his feet, the white talons dragging up dust as the sound of falling chains hitting the floor rings loudly in my ears, paining me more than any single sound ever should. He is enormous, around twenty feet tall, with an elongated scaled neck, the underside of which glows. He's a fire-breather, his skin never feeling hot to me but brutal and scorching to another. His skull is that of an oversized Elk with horns that curve and jut in two spiralling ivory protrusions from the top of his head, and he has a lithe body like a Komodo dragon mixed with a prize stallion stud. Despite his might, his extreme weight, and intimidating shadow, he has a kind face for those who take the time to look, and his soft curved nostrils flare as he inhales the scent of me, his rider. Eyes sparkling with joy as our gazes join like lock and key, both our minds splay open for the other to read.

Sticking his hindquarters high in the air, he leans back slightly, stretching his claws wide and sprawling his two front legs before him like a cat just waking from a nap. His jaws spread wide in a yawn, forked tongue lying like limp roadkill within the cavernous moist pinkness of his gums. I feel the heat coming off him in waves as he blinks, eyes watering from sleep, my hair blown back ever so slightly from my face.

You know. Cramped. Bored. The usual. How was your day? he asks me, curling his front legs beneath his broad chest and sitting once more. His long white tail flicks idly behind him though the speed and power of the limb could quite easily crush a full-grown man to death, and the scent of his intense, almost fiery, spearmint odour wraps around me like a blanket.

I should be scared.

According to every fairy tale ever written, and every lie spread by those who want the dragon's power for themselves, I should run. Instead, I feel the safest I ever have anywhere, in all my five hundred years breathing in and out.

Algoric was the true blessing I received from Hecate; not immortal life, nor the power to scold any man who thinks to lay so much as a finger on me, but instead, a creature with whom I share an irreplaceable and sacred bond.

I know and have always known since the day the very first egg containing his babyish body fell from the skies and hatched right in front of me, since the very first time our eyes met and the imprint bond was formed between us, that given the choice, I would give up my own life, my own power for the magnificent alabaster creature before me in a heartbeat.

It is the privilege of a Draconian to form such a bond with a dragon, but it is also a curse.

For years, the Sephilim tried to weaponise them, to turn them bitter and cruel, without knowing what beautiful souls lie within the harness of their armoured bodies.

I had risked everything to keep Algoric and the rest of them safe, away from war and violence, but it has come at a cost.

The rest of Aetheria thinks they're dead, and many of them wish they were. Where once they took freely to the skies, spread their wings and breathed fresh air, they're now hidden away in the underground heated caves, the cold bad for their unregulated body temperature.

I had told Midas that banishing us here would kill them, but he didn't care.

As they say though, life finds a way, and it had.

We had.

They live on, only stretching their wings now under the cover of heavy storms, restrained by chains mounted deep in the earth, wasting away as shells of what they once had been.

I take a few steps forward, reaching out and placing a gentle hand on the scaly pallor of Algoric's beautiful face, my one true love, my sanctuary.

He nuzzles me, eyes twinkling kind and adoring from familiar depths of cool verdant intensity.

That bad, huh? he asks me with a sigh, and I nod, closing my eyes and leaning into the warmth of his cheek, tears falling fast from my eyes and trailing down my own.

He brings his front leg from beneath his chest, cupping my body and pushing me close to him, the warmth and solidity of his scales becoming yet another layer of armour for me to wrap myself in.

I love you, Algoric, I whisper down the bond between us, the thick rope of it woven from years of suffering and the grit it took to keep moving forward despite overwhelming odds.

They think he's the monster, but he's not.

He's the thing that makes them monsters, that shows their true colours and exposes their ugliness to the world.

And I love you, Gen, he replies, his voice cutting my thoughts short.

As I stroke his cheekbone, a low purr comes from the glowing portion of his throat as his large reptilian eyes fill with oceans of salt and water.

Have you ever seen a dragon cry?

It's like looking into the face of your God and knowing you have failed.

We stand there in the cavern where he's held captive by the hate of others, chained by their destructive urges, holding each other close and crying out of desperation for a different world.

ARO

The kitchens of the Solis Castra lie in what were once assumed to be catacombs for the fallen Sephilim aristocrats.

As it is though, at the point of death, a Sephilim returns to the clouds as aether, and so the space has been largely redundant.

The entire basement level of crystal architecture has long since been renovated, the low sweeping eaves opened up and the shadow-filled tombs used as cold storage or pantry space. The thick, partially-opaque quartz making up the walls has been punched through and glass windows set to let light into the chill underground caverns. Oblivion falls roars just beyond the thin leaded panes, spattering them with a thick crust of glittering aether that requires an entire team to clean off.

The whole lower floor is devoted to housing maids, waiters, kitchen staff and the castle laundrette, and it sprawls for more miles than I want to admit with underground service tunnels allowing for discreet deliveries as well as staff comings and goings.

The scale of the place speaks not only to the size of our household staff but also to the estimated numbers of dead aristocrats expected by the gods when they formed this place, a fact which lies in my stomach, putrefying and cold like a dead rat.

The scent of fresh bread rises against the ceiling as I descend a spiral staircase carved of slick grey slate, the haze of its herb-infused aroma a moist warm cloud that fogs my mind with thyme and rosemary, lulling me calm despite the fact there's still so much to do.

"Ah, my Lord." Alicia's familiar voice pierces the haze of my consciousness with its undeniably shrill pitch.

"Alicia, how are things progressing?" I ask, a quick and courteous smile marring my face out of habit.

"Other than the fact the first batch of sugar-jellied violets aren't setting right, and one of my moronic apprentices overboiled the third batch of devilled eggs—" She gives me a stern look, wiping her long, dough-covered fingers on the apron that lies creaseless in fine white cotton against the jersey of her blue floor-length gown.

"I see—" I say, not sympathetic at all as I watch two women with dirty pots and pans crash into one another. The stacks of pans they're taking over to the enormous sinks, which are set into the gleaming white granite countertops, scatter on the floor, the noise causing everyone to stop and stare.

Both women go bright red in the face, wings rescinding behind them as they try to make themselves small and invisible.

"Well, I suppose it's to be expected. Give a kitchen this small an event the size of Aetheria itself to cater, and you're bound to have slip-ups. It isn't my staff's fault you act with spontaneity and no thought for others." The quip is supposed to be biting, her gaze piercing mine as she turns her back from the two women who are now scrambling to reassemble their stacks of dirty copper cookware.

I pause a moment, deciding whether I should cause a scene and make an example of her sharp tongue.

"Do you have the wine I asked about?" I enquire, not looking her in the eyes as I scan the room with cold reserve. The sounds and blur of diligently working kitchen hands, sous chefs, bakers, and cake decorators hard at work rise and fall in a cacophony of boiling, stirring, kneading, and chopping. The domestic symphony is, in a way, enchanting to watch like a well-choreographed if not slightly chaotic dance.

"I have been busy putting out fires all morning and haven't found the time. I'll just go down to the cellar now, my lord." The formal address at the end of her sentence sounds stiff as if she's grinding her teeth behind the thin veil of her lips. Freckles scatter her nose as she looks down it, wiping her hands yet again as though it's an anxious habit more than necessity.

I watch as the dark raven braids crowning her head bob in time with the sound of her heels on the quartz as she moves through the labyrinthine kitchen before she disappears around the corner.

Standing there, I take this moment to wander slowly around the islands of granite speckled through with rose gold flecks, taking in the rich scents of floral desserts and the hot crackle of sugar caramelising in scalding hot pans.

I spy one of my favourites, mirror-glazed orchid tarts that are topped with spirals of edible gold and sprinkled with white chocolate petals.

Side-stepping the counter, I make my way to the tray where the rows of shiny indigo tartlets have been left unattended, the smooth reflective pools of glaze setting slowly.

Reaching out, I look left and then right, cocking my head and inhaling the scent of the rich jam, before a voice I absolutely don't want to hear startles me.

I turn, looking into Silver's ambivalent eyes with alarm.

"I wouldn't do that. She already threatened to cut my hands off for trying to touch one of those chocolate rose and wild-berry meringues."

"What are you doing here?" I breathe out between gritted teeth. Even the floral talcum scent of her is irritating among the sweet delicacies of the room.

Silver isn't sweet despite smelling so. She's bitter.

"Annoying you, what else?" she asks rhetorically, her pearlescent gown wavering around her ankles as she sidesteps me and hops up onto the counter so she's looking down at me.

"I'm busy." I move to turn away, but she calls out, stopping me cold.

"Do you really think the other Kindred lords and ladies are going to let you play house with a mortal?" she sneers, and I whip back around to face her.

"You call the Solis Castra a house? You wound Zeus deeply—" I roll my eyes, not rising to her bait, but hers only widen.

"What, you want her to live *here*?" She sounds as incredulous as she looks.

"But of course. I can't protect her if she's not in residence," I say.

The words are sharp as steel and twice as cold, but I smile at her even still.

"I won't live here if you move her in. I won't be made a fool of, Aro." Her voice becomes high-pitched and girlish. I laugh, unable to help myself.

"And how does me moving in my beloved make a fool of *you?*" I cock an eyebrow, painfully confused as some of the kitchen staff raise their eyes subtly to watch the two of us bicker.

"A high lord courting a mortal so blatantly when you have beautiful Nephilim surrounding him looks pathetic, don't you think?" she retorts, and I snort.

"What makes you think she won't be a Nephilim like you someday?" I spit back and she narrows her eyes a moment before shrugging.

"She's nothing special. Certainly not blessed, despite her likeness to Storm." She doesn't meet my gaze, examining her long nails and swinging her feet carelessly.

"She's more special than you ever will be," I hiss, turning away from her once again and coming almost nose-to-nose with Alicia. She's clutching a bottle of dark violet glass, the cork coated in rich gold.

"The vintage you asked about..." She passes it to me, and I hear the ruffle of Silver's skirts as she dismounts the counter behind me.

Her breath tickles the back of my neck, causing me to clench my jaw and increase my grip on the bottle as I pull it close to me.

Onyx grape and Jet Iris Merlot, bottled 1790.

"You can't be serious. Why would you want to serve that?" Silver looks at me like I've gone insane.

"Because I'm hoping it might help her remember. Besides, it's time. I haven't served this since 30, and we have cases of it." I recall the night I had last drunk this wine, the way I had felt like I was on top of the world. Like nothing could touch me because she was well and truly mine forever.

It had been the night of our rehearsal dinner, the night everything had changed.

Then, as I nod to Alicia and hand back the bottle, I'm reminded of another memory, this one faded and far more sepia than anything I have experienced in Kindred life.

It's Briar's nose, wrinkling delicately as she sniffed her very first glass of wine.

I grin but then remember how many times in my mortal life I had found myself picking up after my spirit and wine merchant father.

About how alcohol and its vices had been what kept him in ruin after the sinking of a fleet full of expensive wine and bourbon just off the coast of Greece.

Many men would have moved on, would have taken back their power, but not my father. My father took to his remaining stock, finding more value in oblivion than the ability to put food on the table for his own family. He had burned up, but rather than rising again, he simply stayed wallowing in the city of his own ashes.

Not that I should be surprised. Nobody was ever good enough for him, least of all me. A man like that, a man who holds everyone else to such impeccable standards cannot help but be a hypocrite when it comes to his inevitable failure.

A tyrant, a drunk, a perfectionist, the only thing that was ever good enough for my father was the bottle.

I wonder now what he would make of the Aetherial wine, of what became of his disappointment of a son.

I had wanted his approval so badly, but it wasn't until I met Briar that I realised I was seeking pleasure and validation in the wrong place.

Coming back to myself, I find the two women staring at me and so shake my head, clearing my throat.

"This is fine. Thank you. See that it's reserved for the toasts after dinner," I order Alicia, and she nods obediently, turning with the bottle in hand and not saying another word.

"Where are you going?" I hear Silver calling after me, but I merely call back over one shoulder, not gracing her with any more of my precious time.

"Not that it's any of your business, but I have to place another custom order with Morpheus for some party favours of sorts," I reveal, waiting for her reaction.

I hear Silver swallow despite being almost on the opposite side of the room from her at this point. Her expression, I'm sure, is pinched with anxiety, but I can't stop and revel in her discomfort.

Heading past lines of women kneading dough and icing webs of sugar onto small butterscotch and daffodil crumbles, I retreat up into my crystal fortress overhead.

After all, there is still so much to do.

A TALE OF TWO CITIES

KAIRI

AS I SIT WITH Dawn piling my hair up onto my head in intricate braids, it occurs to me just how radically different life in Aetheria is from the mortal world.

Everything here is beautiful and seems irreplaceable in its perfection. Where in the mortal world, everything has that air of disposability, that air of rushed lack of care, a kind of 'oh, this will do' mentality.

Here, every piece of furniture is lovingly crafted with great technical and artistic effort being put into all aspects of the design. Even the palette, from which Dawn begins to powder my face with another of her many unicorn make-up brushes, is exquisitely detailed. The silver of its shell casing drips with emeralds that hang along the metal vines decorating the small but beautiful piece. Here, everything is resplendent, and even the benign manages to become art, become precious and intrinsically important.

Perhaps that's why I've always loved beautiful leather-bound hardbacks, I wonder as Dawn paints natural hues and subtle shimmer onto the blank canvas of my face. There's something about a book that seems so forever, as though you know that no matter what happens, it will witness far more than you can ever hope to in your single mortal lifespan. Books hold stories, not just in ink but in the places they have been and the people that have fallen in love with them.

The ritual of beautifying me is much the same as it was before, though this time Dawn seems far more deliberate in her work, not asking my opinion and instead, working on autopilot. I'm nervous as she layers shimmering white eyeshadow onto my eyelids before lacquering my lashes in a pale lavender mascara that smells strongly of a flower I can't quite place.

"Done. Now, put on the undergarments I've set out for you on the bed while I go and get your dress." She gestures to the alabaster lace lingerie, almost invisible atop the pale sheets. I walk in bare feet across the room so I'm standing in front of the wardrobe, the silken white robe gliding over my skin like cool lake water as I undress.

Pulling on the pure white bralette that plumps my cleavage and then stepping into the matching thong, I notice something I hadn't the last time I was here sitting by the ball of my left foot.

Dropping to my knees, I allow my fingers to splay across the facet of rose quartz. The pads of each one catch in the fissure, this once invisible crack the only thing marring the entire room. I inspect it, finding spidering webs of split crystal radiating from the centre of the main gash, my brow furrowing as I bite down hard on my bottom lip.

"What are you doing?" Dawn's voice makes me jump as though I've been caught chewing gum by a strict math teacher.

"Oh, nothing. I just never noticed this crack before. It's kind of sharp on bare feet—" I mutter, standing upright as quickly as I can. Savouring the lack of pain such a sudden movement doesn't cause, my eyes are drawn to the masses of cream tulle draped over Dawn's outstretched arms.

"A crack? How strange— I'll have to talk to maintenance about getting that fixed." She smiles at me, cocking her head as she examines the crack too, tracing over it with the very tip of her shoe.

"Hmm, how odd— anyway— let's get you into this dress. You're due to wait in The Nest with the other Nephilim while the foreign guests arrive. We wouldn't want to be late."

She sets about unbuttoning the back of the gown, which resembles the purple dress I had worn to dinner a few nights ago. Only this time the skirt is not quite as full, the sleeves more ruffled and the neckline far more demure.

Holding it open, I let her slide the garment over my head and then turn so she can button it closed.

As she's fastening the amethyst necklace from Aro around my throat, I realise the implications of what she's said and the nerves I had been feeling before triple in ferocity. I haven't had much of a social life lately, and even before, I'd always had a baseline level of social anxiety.

As I stand here, clad in perhaps the most elaborate dress I'll ever wear, even the thought of making small talk with the immortal Kindred of Hera is enough to make me want to curl into a ball in the back of the wardrobe.

I wonder as Dawn sets flat ballet pumps on my feet how I will seem to them.

Do they see mortals as so awfully temporary?

Like a bluebottle to their splendiferous butterflies?

I wonder if they'll think me stupid, or if, in fact, they're just curious about the dimension I've come from. I mean, times have changed so much since most of these people were alive and walking the same world as I have been for the last twenty-three years— perhaps I seem strange and alien then?

"Beautiful!" Dawn claps her hands together, startling me as her periwinkle blue eyes sparkle with anticipation.

"Are you coming too?" I ask her, hopeful, as she leads me toward the door.

"I will accompany you to The Nest, but then I am to attend to other duties. We can't all be High Born." She looks sad for a moment, and I want to tell her that I think she's one of the most beautiful, the most radiant women I've ever seen. To me, she is the epitome of High Born not because of her face but because of the way she cares so attentively to those who can be described in no other way than to call them relative strangers. She catches the sadness in my eyes, her silken skin crinkling around the edges of her lips as she turns a kind smile.

"You have fun. That's what is important, alright? Don't worry about anyone except yourself." She raises a hand to my cheek, a gesture that I imagine I would expect had I known the mother who abandoned me.

"Thank you for making me beautiful." I kiss her on the cheek, affection for this immortal handmaiden swelling in my chest like a helium balloon as if I've been missing this maternal connection more than I ever realised.

As she leads me out the door, her eyes turn sad, reflecting my expression back at me in those same coloured irises.

Then, she simply says.

"Oh, sweet girl, I didn't make you that. You already were."

Conducting with Dawn is less smooth than with Aro, though I couldn't possibly tell you why that is. All I know is that upon arriving at the lofty heights of what she calls The Nest, it takes me a few moments longer than usual to get my bearings.

When I do, all I can do is gawp.

My ears pop with the height, my ankles tickled beneath my skirt by the thin layer of cloud spilling through the arches that lead to open sky on all sides. Pillars of glass climb like liquorice twists high into the air before curving to make up the many gaping archways that meet overhead in a towering spire topped with a cube of angel quartz balanced on one tip.

The floor underfoot is, from what I can see, angel quartz too, the iridescent pastel tones within made bold and bright beneath the setting cobalt sun that is gleaming in front of me. The tower itself is little more than a crystal pedestal with a spiralling glass gazebo attached, and yet it's been transformed into the most incredibly beautiful bar I've ever seen.

The scent of vanilla and something else I can't place fills my head as I stand there letting the breeze from the surrounding sky cool my warm and nervous blood. That's when I realise, as I stop gaping up at the incredible square-shaped spire overhead, that the room around me is silent.

I drop my gaze immediately to my hands, finding a multitude of purple eyes staring at me. It's something I'd never noticed before, how all these winged immortals have some shade of purple in their irises, but now I can feel them boring into my human pallor, it's all I can think about.

Dawn places a hand on my shoulder, giving me a small nudge as I take a step forward.

"Why, you're all gawping like she's some kind of steaming cow turd in the middle of a snowstorm! Where are your manners, ladies?" The southern drawl startles me as a winged woman with pale lavender eyes and a baby pink gown, more magnificently detailed than anything I've ever seen, singles herself out from the mass of curious faces. Her waist is made tiny within the constriction of the magnolia-edged corset, the skirt flying out from her hips in a rich plumage that makes her seem like some sort of pastel swan. Her neck is long, blonde hair swept up from it and knotted at the back of her skull. Two tresses hang, tightly curled, in front of her ears as she gathers her skirts and turns her back on the watching Nephilim, holding out a white-gloved hand to me without a second thought.

"Vail, it's a pleasure." Her voice is as sweet as her face, eyes twinkling with what I can only describe as genuine excitement. I take her hand in mine and watch as she pulls my wrist up to her eye line so she can examine it.

158

"Oh, my. It is true—" she gasps, placing a hand dramatically over two perfectly painted pink lips, her cheeks filling with blood as my eyes widen. "Oh, I'm sorry. Don't mind me— it's just— it's been so long since I've seen the Heirbound mark. I didn't expect to see it on a mortal, no ma'am." She reaches forward and pulls me toward her, letting my hand fall between us as she plants a firm kiss on each of my cheeks.

"What—" I begin, but before I can finish my question, she's fluttered a few feet away and is calling several women over to the solid gold bar situated at the farthest end of the platform.

"Can we get this young thing a drink, pretty please?" she hollers.

Swallowing, I take a moment to meet several gazes of other Nephilim, unable to take in the utter onslaught of their supernaturally pretty features.

Despite their allure, their faces are pinched at the sight of me, bodies wrapped in dresses just as grand as Vail's, if not more so, with crystals and jewels embroidered heavily along almost every single panel of fabric. Their skin is collectively radiant like they've been baptised in starlight, their wings luminous and pure with different coloured tips, made glorious and divine by the unfiltered sunlight streaming in on all sides.

I must look like a complete mess by comparison.

No wonder they're staring.

Not knowing what to do, I twine my fingers together, turning my inner wrist toward my body and chewing the inside of my cheek.

I turn to ask Dawn for guidance, for any kind of instruction on how to act or what to say, but upon glancing back over my shoulder, I realise she's gone.

Nerves fizz around like angry bees in my stomach, causing me to hop from foot to foot, inhaling deeply.

"Señorita." A woman with a luscious mane of black hair, displaying white wings that look like they've been dip-dyed in blood, steps forward to save me as I hear Vail's distinctive voice berating whoever is in charge of making drinks.

"Um, hi." I brush a strand of hair that's come loose in the breeze behind one ear. She's wearing a scarlet sheath of rubies, nails lacquered crimson, her beautiful tanned skin glowing slightly as one of her extremely long legs protrudes, exposed through the slit in the side of her skirt.

"Call me Trinity." She turns back to look over her shoulder and calls, "Aaylah! Serenity! Get over here and say hi!"

Two more Nephilim make their way toward us, and I'm grateful to see the rest of the crowd of feather-toting females returning to their prior conversations. Turning, I can't help but feel their eyes continuing to dart across my skin in judgemental figure eights, but I suppose I can't blame them.

A stunning woman with the most flawless dark skin I've ever seen catches my eye first, her gown the colour of limes and ornately jewelled with peridots in luscious floral clusters. Her hair is braided thick against her head in heavy cornrows intertwined with lime ribbons, and her eyes are startlingly light, a similar lavender to Vail's.

"Serenity." The girl in the lime offers me her hand, which I note is also gloved in lime silk. In fact, now I check, all the women here are wearing gloves—

Everyone except me that is.

"Aaylah." A girl with generous curves, caramel honeyed locks, and peachy skin introduces herself from beyond the circumference of her enormous cream and pale coral skirts. She's beautiful, her violet irises glinting bright beneath her thick chocolate lashes. She, too, holds out a hand to me, her delicate forearms gloved in cream lace and tied at her elbow with peach ribbons.

I shake their hands, one after the other, and catch them both glancing at my wrist, but as I'm about to ask why everyone seems to be so focused on me, Vail returns with a cut crystal tumbler in hand.

Ice clinks against the rim as she passes it to me and simply says, "Mint julep," with an enthusiastic nod.

I bring it to my lips, throat parched from nerves, the circle of women staring at me seeming increasingly claustrophobic as their feathered wings make a kind of makeshift enclosure for our conversation. The burn of the bourbon tickles the back of my throat with icy fire, the hint of mint sharpening my mind as I realise that I have questions to ask.

"So, it's true. She really does have the mark," Aaylah relinquishes, turning to Vail who raises an enthused hand to her throat which is wrapped in thick chokers of pearl.

"It would seem so, honey," Vail replies, and I frown in response.

"What are you talking about— what is air bound? What does that mean?" I enquire, and Veil blinks slowly, the glass in her hand sweating and slowly dripping cool water onto the floor as she stares at me.

"What, you mean Lord Black didn't tell you?" Trinity asks, breaking the spell of Vail's confusion as I shake my head.

"Aro?" I ask, and Trinity nods. I purse my lips, taking another sip of my julep as I prepare to admit my lack of knowledge.

"He didn't tell me. What is it?"

"It's *Heir*bound, you know, like heir to the throne? Anyone with the mark is bound to their crown, it's their responsibility to choose the next Sephilim King of Aetheria," Serenity says, her voice melodic but clipped as she adjusts the strap of her gown.

My mind stutters, almost like a circuit somewhere is overloading and threatening to burst into flame.

"What? And this— this is the mark? But I'm—" I begin, but Vail interrupts me.

"Mortal? Yes, honey. That's why you've got Lord Black in a royal tailspin. He thought he lost his chance at the crown when those Draconians kidnapped you on the night of the rehearsal dinner— or so the story goes. Was before my time— that's right, isn't it, Trinity?" Vail asks her, taking a sip of her drink and raising her eyes expectantly over the gilded rim to query the Spanish beauty beside me.

"Yes. That's right. He was betrothed to the last Heirbound. Her name was Storm— and she was a High Lady. In fact—" Her Spanish words twist together like smoke, dangerous but alluring, as she cocks her head, examining my face.

I finish her sentence for her.

"I look just like her—" I breathe, and Trinity nods.

"Ah, so Señor told you this much? Interesting." She considers this, but right as she looks like she's about to say something more, her eyes dart to the ceiling overhead.

I hear a stir and so turn, watching the Nephilim crowd dart to one side of the glass arches in a flurry of swept skirts. They flock to the archways, teetering on the edge of oblivion as the sound of something remarkable reaches my ears, and my eyes widen.

"Come on, Kairi. You'll want a front seat for this!" Aaylah takes my hand in hers, pulling me through the crowd and using her wide peaches and cream lace skirt as a buffer to help us slip closer to the edge of the room.

Reaching the point where the floor ends and thin air begins, I cling to the glass of a nearby column for balance, knuckles turning white.

Though, what I see next as it breaks through the clouds causes my grip to slacken, my breath catching in my throat.

There, amid the dusk, the sound of horses can be heard, though not their hooves. Instead, it is their snorting breaths and whinnying that catches in my ears as familiar, only seconds before the very first bursts through the cloud.

Enormous wings spread, white and pure, dripping with glittering diamond chains that continue around its body and then its nose in a shimmering bridle. Between its eyes, a horn of iridescent ivory protrudes from the centre of its forehead, magic made reality.

The alicorn gallops through the cloud soundlessly, leaping into the air like it's going to jump a paddock fence and spreading its wings further as it swoops close to The Nest.

I feel the breeze tickle my face as the creature passes close. Its hooves shimmer solid silver, eyes glistening aquamarine like tropical waters beneath the setting cobalt sun. I watch as several gold-armoured Sephilim escort the horse, struggling to keep up with its epic speed, but then realise it's not the horse they're protecting at all but a woman draped in rich jewel-coloured silks, riding side-saddle upon the back of the magnificent creature as though she's no more than waiting for a manicure at her local salon.

From this distance, I can't see her face in detail, but what I can see is the regality with which she holds herself, with which she commands the stunning elysian creature beneath her. Her blonde hair trails out behind her in cold icy tresses, gaze not so much as giving a single fleeting glance to the onlooking Nephilim.

Goosebumps ripple into existence up the lengths of my bare arms, and my heart races in my chest, the entire spectacle making me breathless as more alicorns follow in the wake of their leader.

Ranging in colours from the jet-black abyss of a demon's gaping jaws to the pure white of a star, they come in a stampede of agility and speed, each one donning a female rider who appears to be completely in control of both themselves and the animal supporting them.

They dance in and out of the skyscape, hooves touching down on individual clouds for but a second before galloping back into oblivion, coats sheening so reflective that they turn momentarily to the purples and pinks of the dusky sky.

I watch them in awe, wishing I could even begin to feel as strong as they look.

Hanging there, I observe the fleet of winged unicorns until they're but a speck in the distance, lowering into their landing formation, long after the rest of the Nephilim have returned to chatting over drinks.

Aaylah sighs beside me, smiling wistfully.

"They are beautiful, aren't they? Almost the fastest winged creatures by far," she adds in this information, taking my hand in hers without a second thought and leading me back through to where Vail, Serenity, and Trinity are now sitting upon spindled golden chairs, legs crossed beneath their flowing skirts.

The glass table between them is small but holds the drink of each woman and a pitcher of iced water with floating twizzles of too-green apple peel bobbing on the top.

"Almost?" I ask Aaylah as she takes her place on one of the free chairs and gestures for me to do the same. "So, you're saying there is something faster than those— horses?" I don't want to say the word unicorn, as if muttering the word will break some kind of spell, causing the fantasy around me to dissolve.

"Well, Dragons are faster— but—" she begins, but I cut her off, slumping down into my seat and exhaling heavily.

"Dragons!?" I ask, eyes wide with shock, though why I'm surprised I couldn't tell you.

I've seen winged men and unicorns this week alone, so why are dragons such a surprise?

My stomach churns a little, images of the dream in which I'd run screaming from such a scaled monster looping on repeat inside my skull.

"Don't worry, Kairi. There haven't been dragons in centuries. Not since the Draconians were banished to Drakos Vale. The climate there is too cold, and the dragon population died off. Luckily for us all, anyway," Vail comforts me, pressing a hand to the knee that's shrouded by the many tulle layers of my skirt.

My chest deflates, though out of relief or disappointment, I couldn't tell you.

"If the dragons couldn't survive there, why were they banished to Drakos Vale?" I ask, and Trinity places the glass from which she's sipping down on the table.

"A long time ago, hundreds of years ago, in fact, there was a great war between one of the Draconian High Ladies, Genevieve, and the Sephilim King at the time, Midas. He wanted to utilise the dragons for Aetheria's military, but Genevieve wouldn't allow anyone but Draconians to ride the creatures and would not take orders from anyone, not even the King. She said dragons were the gifts of Hecate and Nemesis and were only to live beside the Draconians as they had been chosen for their ability to remain unbiased and to provide justice above all else." She rolls her eyes a little at my awed expression. "It's all a bunch of rubbish if you ask me, an excuse because dragons threatened Aetheria in a very serious way during the war, and there's no justice in that. The Draconians just wouldn't step into line with the rest of us. I guess Midas didn't want to leave such an enemy with so much power. So, they were banished, and the dragons died out. If the Draconians hadn't been so stubborn about working together with everyone else, they'd probably still be around." Her Spanish accent fails to make the words pretty, their connotations horrifying.

"Yes, banished alright, but not before we went to war, and Genevieve herself slaughtered the Nephilim Queen- Pandora. I've heard that she even makes her people call her Queen now. Who does that?" Serenity says before taking a sip of her drink with pinched lips and narrow eyes.

I can tell the subject is not one that's brought up often, as so many of these immortals lived through it, and don't want to remember. I can tell it pains them, so much that their reaction to the topic is teetering on defensive boredom.

"I see. Uh, thanks for filling me in. Aro already warned me about the Draconians, but that makes why a little clearer—" I express, realising that his warning had not come only from personal vendetta but also from well-known historical feuds. The air between the five of us goes suddenly quiet, and for a few minutes, none of us says anything as the lowering sun begins to disappear entirely and the glittering shroud of night is pulled overhead.

"So, will the Draconians be here tonight?" I ask, finishing the final dregs of my drink and feeling the bourbon make me brave. Aro had already said they'd been invited but also that they might not turn up, and I wonder if the women here might have any further insight.

Aaylah snorts.

"Pfft, I doubt it. I mean, I guess they had to be invited. But they never actually turn up for these things, so their vote is voided. Makes things easier, I guess, because it's one less person to convince when it comes to decision making. They relinquish the right to any input if they decline the invitation."

Her words remind me of the fact that I'm here to be judged. Here to be deemed worthy or discarded as merely mortal. My stomach churns harder, the bourbon suddenly seeming more enemy than friend.

Sitting here, surrounded by winged beauty, I realise that I want nothing more than to hear Aro's reassurance that everything will be alright. That I will be allowed to return.

After all, there is so much still to learn about this place, and it's clearer with each passing event that I have only scratched the very surface.

I watch as Vail pulls a lace fan from a pocket made invisible by the pleats of her skirt, face reddening slightly as she brings it to shield her mouth.

"Kairi." The voice is familiar, and I turn to find Leo standing in masculine shadow amongst the feminine light of the surrounding Nephilim.

Eyes dart toward him, and so he straightens, wings flaring out as his red hair catches starlight from overhead and sets it ablaze.

"Ladies, festivities are about to begin, you should all adjourn to the ballroom immediately," he announces, and a flutter of excitement ripples through the feathers of the crowd.

One by one, I watch them depart. Vail is the last to go as she squeezes my hand and lets her eyes linger on Leo's face for just a moment, something like shy affection blossoming right there beneath the lavender stained glass of her irises.

"Good luck," she whispers, and then in a flash that leaves my skin tingling with static, she's gone.

Leo and I stand among the thin layer of swirling cloud in the now-empty Nest, the sky breathlessly regal overhead.

"Ready?" he asks, his gold armour shining as though it's never once seen a scratch from the sword of another. In this moment as I stare, it's as though Leo is untouchable.

"Yes," I mumble, my word coming out small and frightened as I rise to my feet and take the hand he's holding out to me.

With my heart thundering in my ears, a flash of lightning carries us away from the starlight and down into the dragon's den beneath.

LUCIEN

I pull at my cravat, loosening the silver silk from where it clutches my throat, adorned with a sapphire that cinches the fabric tightly around my pulsing carotid.

It's warm here, warmer than I remember, even with the sun having long since set, and so I sweat lightly beneath the grey cut of my double-breasted jacket, the buttons gleaming silver and cold in the golden moonlight that showers the land.

Ebonara is hidden away in one of the caves behind the falls, her ability to camouflage yet again beyond useful in ensuring her continued freedom and survival.

I'm flying low, nostrils filled with the pungent sweetness of Soleus as the amethyst towers of the Solis Castra soar overhead, casting me small in their shadows. The night overhead is a spattering of glitter upon a canvas of indigo velvet, a beauty that is lost at the lower altitude of Drakos Vale being revealed and leaving me breathless.

As I touch down just outside the winding crystal roads that lead forward into the extraordinarily large double gates, my eyes rise, pinpointing Sephilim defences.

Guards float in solid gold armour that is jaundiced further by the gilded moonlight, hanging like lanterns in the night and floating almost effortlessly on all sides of the building.

Ebonara would make short work of them, a mockery even, but that's not why I am here.

As I ponder the face of the girl that I'm half-expecting to see, I try to recall the last time I was here.

It has been centuries, and despite the fact my memory is usually pretty good, reaching out through the mist of the past comes back with nothing but fragmented images. The recollection is a mere whiff of the vanilla that laces the air, a flash of how the Aetherial sun catches the water tumbling down over the edges of the enormous floating continent, but nothing useful.

Following the crystal path like liquid light, I continue forward without a falter in step as I draw closer to the enormous golden curves of the intricate baroque-style gate.

In front of the twining metal vines, two guards stand in that same solid gold armour, the height of pomposity if you ask me.

"Draconian. What are you doing here?" One of them spits at me, grey-speckled wings flaring out from his spine as he takes in my silhouette. I take a step closer, unafraid, boasting my wingspan as my talons glint maliciously in silent warning.

Reaching into my jacket, I present the invitation and shove it into his hand.

"I was invited, crow." I spit the insult, narrowing my eyes and feeling ice harden the blood in my veins to scarlet steel, fists balling at my sides.

The guard blinks once then twice, clearly unaware of the fact such an invitation had been extended, either that or nobody had expected an answering Draconian High Lord to turn up unannounced.

I want to smile, the power of my anonymity rife in the air around me like static electricity as the second guard watches me, eyes widening and taking in my silhouette as though assessing the edges of a blade.

He's not wrong. I could very well be considered a weapon in stature alone, and that's without the other magical tricks I'm hiding up my sleeves like a pair of wicked aces.

"Seems legit. Though, I will insist that one of us escorts you inside, just in case." The guard holding my invitation in his hand crumples the paper like some kind of heathen, and I wonder if he believes he could subdue me. Even if he wanted to, even if it was warranted, I'd have him sprawled out and bleeding before he could blink.

Instead of giving him an answer, I merely stand there, shoulders squared, wings raised so that the talons at the peak of each one are pointed as high as they go. My shadow becomes mountainous as both men's gleaming breastplates are cast mustard and dank.

Continuing to look forward without wavering in posture, the guard directly in front of me grows increasingly uncomfortable as I refuse to break eye contact with him.

"Well, take him inside!" he barks at his inferior, rolling his eyes at me as if he might elicit some kind of sympathy or common ground. Proving he'll try anything to prevent the icy shards of my gaze from piercing ever so slowly into his soul.

"Very well, follow me." The guard who's been charged with escorting me doesn't move to open the gate as I guess I'm not worth the effort, instead, glancing upward and bending his knees before leaping into the air.

I give the remaining guard an unfeeling expression, hoping that goosebumps have rolled up his spine in a sickening wave so he will not forget who he's dealing with. Then, springing upward from only slightly bent knees, I rise the twenty or so feet to meet with the very top of the gate before letting myself drop to the path on the other side, my suit tails flaring out around me in two smoky points as I straighten.

"Lead on," I command the guard who is waiting for me, his eyes examining my wingspan with nervous half glances as he turns on the ball of his boot.

Moving forward, his chocolate wings tuck themselves in neatly behind him as his armour rattles with every step.

I follow him, though not too closely, as I examine the increasingly luxurious surroundings.

We pass the gardens of crystal flowers and flowing fountains, the scent of it all too pungent to be intoxicating and too sweet to be even slightly pleasant.

Alright for some, I think to myself as we stride quickly through the entrance hall and past pillars displaying fine art, antiques, and relics from the Sephilims' violent history.

I breathe deep as we move through the labyrinth of the place, trying to recall my last visit more definitively now, my mind mapping escape routes and possible makeshift exits as we delve deeper into the crystal cage.

Finally, we come to a grand set of double doors, which the guard opens with one swift push and no pause. The doors swing open, revealing me to a room of Kindred who immediately cease all sound.

Female Equinians with their blood-hungry faces and lustrous manes of hair glare at me, the raw muscles of their hunter's bodies made soft by outfits of jewel-coloured silks hanging from accentuated curves in fabric waterfalls, pooling like cold blood upon the floor. Their male counterparts stare, enormous tanned biceps that are marred by tattoos depicting battles won pulsating as their eyes lock on my form and they identify me as other.

As the enemy.

Sephilim stand before their female counterparts, posture stiff despite the fact they still hold champagne flutes between dextrous fingers, free palms wandering toward weapons holstered at the thigh or hip. The blades lie in bright metal sheaths that look as if they've never actually seen battle.

The Fae of Light and The Fae of Night are perhaps the most neutral of all the Kindred, but even they say nothing to break apart the scrutiny, their exquisite features merely surprised or disgusted rather than hateful.

Wings rustle, the air thickening with prejudice as I step through the doorway, sucking in a deep breath and wondering if I should say something.

As I am about to open my mouth in a snarl of warning, another lone voice breaks the silence, and the crowd collectively turns to face the grand staircase at the other end of one of the Solis Castra's many ballrooms.

"Presenting, for your pleasure, Miss Kairi Freemont." The Sephilim with red hair and earthy brown eyes steps aside from the top of the staircase, moving out of sight just after he opens both doors that lie at the top of the staircase, facing the room.

She steps through, clutching Lord Black's hand in her delicate grasp, the caramel brown of her hair swept up from her face. Her blue eyes lock with mine, and something inside of me snaps. I don't know whether it's the delicate curve of her jaw, the petite rising and falling of her chest, the way her tiny waist twists and moves inside the Sephilim Lords clutch, but I see red.

Red is everywhere, a curtain of blood falling over this staged tragedy.

Rage curdles in my gut, though why I couldn't tell you.

I should be intrigued, not angry. She's the girl from Anastasia's visions. I'm sure of it, the one I haven't been able to stop thinking about.

Gritting my teeth as she smiles up at Lord Black, his statuesque features angelic beneath the black sweep of his newly cropped inky locks, my fingers ball into fists.

Anger rises in me so violently I have to stop myself from rushing headfirst into the crowd and smashing my fist into the closest face.

It is clear as our eyes suddenly lock and I am frozen to the spot, paralysed by un-dilated fury, that she is not only the girl from Anastasia's vision but something far more as well.

THE GRAPES OF WRATH

KAIRI

THE DOUBLE DOORS ARE pulled forward, and Aro tugs me into the light that shines down from half a dozen scattered chandeliers. Eyes turn from a mystery focal point at the opposite end of the room, where another pair of double doors have been drawn open, falling instead to me in a wave of sudden scrutiny.

Aro's gloved hand tightens on the pale skin of my delicate fingers, his hand then rising quickly to cup my waist. He ushers me forward toward the first step of the grand amethyst staircase that sweeps in a luxurious violet curve down into the wide circular breadth of the main room.

I let my fingers tickle the golden balustrade as we descend when a fleet of harps suddenly strikes up as the crowd clears the dancefloor. The rhythm is heavenly, exquisite, and mesmerising as my feet struggle to keep up with my mind, the forms of my subconscious already waltzing.

Aro smiles at the crowd and then down at me with unfaltering confidence as I raise my chin to meet his gaze with my own. His eyes sparkle deeply, my face reflected in the sky-made-liquid pools of his irises.

He presents me to the room, more confident than I, and I find jewelled irises and pastel-gilded pupils scavenging my form, some resting on the birthmark on my wrist. I blush, heart racing as I realise, *I'm going to have to dance in front of all these people.*

Swallowing, I try to remind myself that I have danced with Aro before, but then go further and note that it was privately, and I was only able to follow his steps as his lead is so undeniably strong. I can only hope for the same direction now, saying a silent prayer to whatever gods are watching.

Aro seems unphased, unaware of my raging pulse and clammy palms as he tugs on my elbow, indicating I should take my place in his arms. I circle him, an anchor of pristine masculine stature, grounding me in the centre of the dancefloor.

The harps continue to pluck a whimsical tune, but as I move in close to the Sephilim, who has seemingly captured my heart and is playing a tune of his very own on its delicate strings, they fade to silence.

The lights overhead dim considerably as Aro waves a gloved hand with more elegance than any man should possess, and I wonder how he does it.

I hear the rustle of feathers and the crystalline tinkling flutter of those insect-esque wings that spread from the spine of each watching Fae.

Closing my eyes and swallowing deeply, I turn my attention fully to Aro, looking up into his face and letting the galaxies in his eyes ground me in their orbit, simultaneously turning me weightless with a sense of being home, with being safe.

For a moment, the only thing I can hear is his breath against my ear as he pulls me flush to the velvet padding of his torso, the thud of our hearts banging on the thin glistening fabric veils between us.

"Ready, beautiful?" Aro's whisper is just audible as suddenly a single soulful voice breaks through the fragile silence like a diamond arrow of both clarity and inflection.

Harps join the solo vocalist, who I can't see through the crowd, but it is too late to search for the source of the angelic tenor as Aro spreads my arms so we form a frame of limbs in which to dance.

The music grows louder, and I'm painfully aware of the eyes drilling into me as I begin to trace the steps of Aro's certain lead, terrified of falling over my skirt. My skin becomes clammy, my palm damper with increasingly apparent sweat in the grasp of his white glove. My stomach tightens, tying itself into an intricate maze of knots as I try to maintain simply breathing.

"Just look at me," Aro commands, smiling down at me with gloriously arctic teeth.

I do as he asks, obeying without question, and allow myself to recover that sense of weightless freedom I felt in the moments just before the music began to build.

172

We twirl around the crystal floor, choreographed and beautiful as the harps continue to enrapture both us and the crowd of surrounding Kindred in a web of sophisticated yet nostalgically romantic notes. I want to get a better look at the people who I'll be trying to impress, but instead, I'm unable to tear my eyes from Aro's statuesque face.

The dance after we lock eyes this time passes in a melodic blur, and I remember little more than Aro's adoring expression and the firmness with which his hands grasp both my fingers and waist as we waltz for what could be hours or minutes. My skin heats in the rush of the dance, my heart slower now, counting beats with the musicians that are cast ever still in the shadows of the room's wide corners.

As the harps fade into silence, Aro presents me, and I give a curtsey like he had instructed as we stood waiting to be introduced to the room.

Aro gives a bow, and the lights once again brighten substantially, revealing the crowd as a kaleidoscopic cacophony of colours, textures, and wings.

"Lord Black." His official title takes me by surprise, and he pulls me closer to his side as a woman far taller than me, not to mention more stunningly beautiful, makes a beeline for us both.

She comes into the light as the crowd floods toward the space they had cleared for our first dance, dark hair tinging midnight blue as she stops directly beneath one of the many chandeliers.

"Lady Montgomery," Aro nods curtly, almost as if they are old adversaries who cannot quite bear to be kind, and the woman's eyes dart without subtlety to me. I stare up into the golden tan of her face, her eyes wide as moons and twice as luminous. Quicksilver slithers beneath the mirrors of her pupils as her gaze narrows, awaiting my introduction.

Aro saves me as I notice her feathered silver wings widening from her spine, growing her shadow substantially, and I shrink a little.

"This is Miss Kairi Freemont," Aro remarks, and I nod, still lost for words as my eyes leisurely stroll across the silver paintings etched into the golden canvas of her skin. Tattoos climb her limbs like intricate vines, and as I'm trying to decipher the story they're telling, she snaps her long fingers in front of my face.

"You know it's rude to stare, even for a mortal!" she barks, and I blanche at the harsh tone of her voice, the pitch like metal striking metal.

"I'm sorry. Your— Ladyship," I stutter, flushing crimson as my face heats. Glancing around, I check to see if her outburst has caused any attention to fall on our exchange, but it seems that the crowd is unsurprised if not used to her voice being raised.

She takes a single, long stride toward me, looking down her perfectly straight nose and grabbing my wrist as she promptly closes any distance between us. While she examines it, cocking her head, her dark berry-stained lips purse as she looks between my face and birthmark.

"Interesting," she spits, shoving my limb back at me. I step back, feeling the heat coming off her body like she's housing a small sun inside.

"Don't torture the poor girl, . You can be pretty intimidating even to us immortals." The blonde-haired woman I had witnessed leading the flock of Equinians through the clouds props her angular chin on Aliandara's shoulder. She smiles kindly at me as I gaze at her. Aliandara shrugs her from the curvaceous arc of her shoulder, from which a deep midnight blue silk made thick with sapphires falls in torrents across the muscle-clad lines of her willowy form.

"And you, Rohana, should mind your own business," Lady Montgomery, or Aliandara as she had been called, cautions her as the blonde takes two tactical and practised strides around the disapproving High Lady.

"I'm Rohana, pleasure." She holds out a hand, and I wonder if that's because she's clearly not a High Lady. She's beautiful, and she had knocked me back in awe when I had seen her arrival, but up close, there's just something— *different* about Aliandara. It's like she shines.

"I saw you—" I stutter, struck dumb by the way her golden feathers glimmer with her motion.

"Ah, you saw our arrival. I always lead the charge. It's safer that way—" she explains, and Aliandara's eyes widen, her entire body tightening and becoming erect as a lightning rod, as though the girl has let slip some great secret.

"Rohana, enough. You need not explain our ways to a mortal." She dismisses her, and Rohana merely shrugs and gives me a small unperturbed wave before turning and disappearing into the crowd.

"Excuse my head of security. She is young. She has much to learn." She looks at me, brow relaxing as though in apology, though the sincerity doesn't reach those luminous orbs fixed inside the cage of her sharp skull. Thick black lashes flutter as she blinks, turning from me and regarding Aro once more with increased intensity.

"So, this is why you called us here? For a mortal girl? You really think she's the next Heirbound?" She shakes her head slightly, disbelieving, and Aro nods.

"Absolutely. You cannot deny the likeness between Lady Shaw and this lovely young lady—" He smiles at me, though his eyes warn with a sudden chill that I should mind what I say.

I'm grateful for his guidance, but as of yet saying far too much isn't a problem.

I can barely form words.

"Well, yes. There is that I suppose." She waves a hand, dismissing the theory as utter nonsense.

As we stand there and my grip tightens on Aro's hand, a laugh that causes goosepimples to rise on my arms travels over one of my shoulders, snaking through the air like a drug.

"Oh, Lady Montgomery, do relax. It's a party, for Apollo's sake. You look like you've had a spiked toadstool inserted into your rectal cavity." The words make me laugh without meaning to, the burst of sound escaping my lips as I turn to find the source, his viridian hair just as vivid as I recall.

"And you must be Kairi, I do believe we've met. I'm a big fan. Your dreams are just as vivid as your beauty. A reader I presume?"

"Uh—yes." My shyness rears, mouth drying up as the elegantly long fingers of the Fae I'd chased through the bookshelves takes my hand and raises it to his velveteen lips. Planting a kiss upon my knuckles, he bows low with a seductive glance up through thick cobalt lashes, the scent of wisteria thick and pungent like some kind of noxious gas in the air surrounding him.

"I can always tell you know; there's just a certain— *texture* to the dreams of a reader—" He straightens, the familiar dreamcatcher earring glimmering gold with silver thread and lilac feathers as he raises his eyebrows and gives me a cheeky grin, his lips feline and his features alive with colour.

His chameleonic irises change shades from blue through to violet and back again as he takes me in, and I give a small curtsey as his eyes rise to find Aliandara's beyond me. His irises darken to a shade not far from obsidian as he catches her gaze, and I imagine the look on her face is one of utter distaste as if she's sipped milk far past its sell-by date.

175

"Well, you can thank Morpheus for this little soiree, Aliandara. He found Kairi and recognised Storm in her," Aro explains as we turn back to face the Amazonian huntress glaring pointedly at the Fae, who rounds my shoulder with a spritely skip.

"Indeed. I should be unsurprised the Fae are involved in such nonsense. And where is Hypnos?" Aliandara asks him, chin cocked with superiority as the current song ends and another takes its place with seamless continuity.

"She had business in The Nether preparing for her classes in Polytechnic Pastures tomorrow," Morpheus explains, sipping generously from the golden fizzing liquid within the flute he grabs from a passing waiter's tray.

"Would you like a drink, Kairi?" he enquires, holding up an elegant hand and stopping the waiter before he can move on. I stare into his eyes for a moment, transfixed yet simultaneously awkward. He's been inside my dreams, so despite the fact we're relative strangers, it's as though he knows me in a way more intimate than anyone in the room, as though he sees through my skin and right into my mind.

"Please," I nod, hoping a distraction from the conversation will help loosen the knots in my stomach.

Grabbing another glass, he passes it to me before downing the remnants of his own. Promptly taking another, he places his empty flute back upon the highly polished tray and sends the waiter on his way.

"So kind of you to offer myself and Lord Black a drink—" Aliandara rolls her eyes, folding her arms across the unfaltering sapphire glisten of her gown.

"I assumed you weren't drinking, considering the obviously tiny and ever-unaltering circumference of your asshole." Morpheus cocks his head, giving a smug smile and then kissing my knuckles again in a motion faster than what my mortal eyes can visibly see.

"Toodaloo—" he sighs dreamily in my ear, gallivanting off into the crowd. I can't help but smile after him, only to find Aro and Aliandara staring at me strangely.

"She's an odd one, Aro. I hope for your sake and mine, she is not the next Heirbound. Making nice with the Fae is far from a good political move, my dear. The namby-pamby, wishy-washy, hippie-dippie. That's what you can expect from the Fae. If you want to understand the true calling of the Kindred here in Aetheria, you might ask Lord Black here to show you some of the military forces." I raise my eyebrows, shocked at the invitation. "I personally would be thrilled to show you the extent to which the Artemisian forces can crush such nonsense as Morpheus with a single soldier." With that final sentiment, she spins on the spot, the skirt and cape of her gown flaring out around her before she takes her leave and wades back into the crowd.

Bringing the flute of fizzing golden liquid to my lips, I take a deep drink, my taste buds exploding. I had expected champagne, but this is something else entirely.

"What is this?" I ask, licking a stray drop from my bottom lip as the fizz tickles my gums.

"Buttercup and dandelion cordial with fizzing elderflower infusion. I thought you'd like it." He smiles, clearly happy with himself.

"I do, it's the most delicious drink I've ever tasted," I admit, swallowing the thick buttery fluid and quickly taking another sip.

"Just be careful, I have a very special vintage of wine for dinner. You don't want to end up ," he explains, and I scowl slightly, confused.

"So, it's alcoholic then?" I ask him, wondering how exactly that works. It certainly doesn't taste like any alcohol I've ever had and, if he hadn't mentioned it, I would never have guessed.

"If Morpheus is drinking it you can mostly assume so. If he's downing it like it's the last drink he'll ever enjoy you can say it with absolute certainty," he explains, chewing the inside of his lip with an odd smile, almost as if he's fond of Morpheus but doesn't want to admit it.

I look at him as I finish the glass in another large gulp, finding the taste more addictive than any alcohol I've ever experienced.

"I think that's enough for now. I'm serious when I say it's strong stuff. It has to be. Kindred don't just get drunk off any old paint thinner," he cautions and takes the glass flute from me, passing it off to another waiter and not offering me a replacement.

We stand in the centre of the room for a moment, and while I'm busy making polite smiles at immortals who seem to glow and move as if they're floating on air, the room starts to tilt. I grab Aro's forearm tightly, preparing for my body to fail me.

"Are you alright?" he asks with urgency, bending slightly and looking into my face as I try to take deep breaths. Flushed, my skin grows warmer beneath his scrutiny as he frowns.

"You need a glass of water. That drink has gone right to your head. Probably Morpheus' intention all along." I giggle a little but then raise my hand to cover my lips as he rolls his eyes. I wonder, as the world spins and turns, exactly why all these Kindred are so suspicious of one another.

Surely, after so much time, they must be able to read each other like well-known books?

"I'll be right back," he murmurs, allowing his fingers to wander listlessly down the length of my forearm before he disappears into the crowd, leaving me standing alone. I notice as disgusted expressions linger on my face, or what I think is my face until I realise that the glances aren't targeted at me at all, but rather just over the top of my head.

"You must be her, then." The voice is sharp but deep, half rumble, half furious bird song, and it causes terror to ripple through me as I spin on the spot, the world still happily moving of its own accord.

His scent is what hits me first, causing my nostrils to flare at the intense mix of wintergreen and peppermint. Those eyes catch me next, piercing me so I can't so much as think about moving. His face is broad and undeniably unmissable in a crowd, his bone structure thick and immovable to match the rest of him that sprawls broadly and with definite bulges beneath the fine cut of his tailored three-piece suit. White blonde hair falls in poker straight sheets from a centre parting at the top of his skull, cutting the air as it tumbles far past his shoulders with knife-like precision. His lips are perhaps the palest I have ever seen, and as they move, I am unable to hear what it is he's saying.

Instead, I simply stare. Despite being scolded only minutes before by Aliandara, I can't seem to help myself. And what's most remarkable about this man isn't even his immense height, cruelly symmetrical face, or pristine head of hair. Instead, it's the two leathery bat-like wings that protrude from his spine. Talons adorning the tip of each wing glint wickedly beneath the chandelier, lethal from every imaginable angle.

The room around us is silent, and suddenly it occurs to me that this man might be the reason that upon the opening of the double doors and my arrival, the attention of the crowd was notably elsewhere. I can feel eyes on me, but most of them have moved beyond my mere presence and onto the main attraction.

"Um— yes. I'm Kairi," I hold out a hand, trying not to flinch as I look the Draconian straight in the eye and square my shoulders.

I'm terrified, but I can't let him or the rest of the Aetherial aristocracy know that, not if I want to stay.

He looks down at the hand I present, cautious for a moment before taking my palm in his.

"In Aetheria, we bow and curtsey to our superiors. I do not know what you do where you come from, but you are not there any longer. When in Rome— yes?" His words wind me as I inhale with sharp reverence, blushing deeply, and he takes a step back from the hem of my skirt. "Shall we?" he asks, bowing before me.

I falter a second, heartbeat rising so I can feel it in my throat, before dropping into a deep curtsey to match his greeting, skirt flowering around me in a cream pool of tulle.

"Lord DeLaurent, High Lord of Drakos Vale, Kindred of Hecate." He announces himself, straightening inside his jacket and nodding to me with reverence.

He doesn't smile, instead balling his hands into fists at his sides as his mouth puckers. A hand comes to rest upon my lower spine, and suddenly, I am no longer alone with him.

"Here." Aro looks between us, shoving a wine glass with wings cupping the bowl into my hand. I curl my fingers around its stem and bring it to my lips, letting my eyes wander between the two men as I drink deeply. The water tastes faintly of violets as my palms begin to sweat again, the tension in the air growing thicker by the second.

"Lord Black." The Draconian High Lord breaks the silence first, closing the space between us and holding out a hand. Aro's arm slides further around my waist, pulling me closer to his side. I feel the muscles in his arms tense, becoming acutely aware that the whole room is still watching as eyes dart subtly our way and the conversation remains at a resounding low hum.

After all, hadn't Aliandara told me it was rude to stare?

At least she and the rest of the immortals follow their own advice.

"Lord DeLaurent, how nice of you to grace us all with your presence at last," Aro's voice is snide, his face a sudden unreadable mask of cold steel contorted from what had once been soft adoration.

"Lord Black. I was surprised to receive your invitation." The two men glare at one another, one pale and one handsomely dark in features.

I'm left standing between them and their scorn, feeling hotter and more bothered than I'd like.

"I wasn't anticipating you'd actually attend; you know. I suppose that was wishful thinking on my part." Aro bites back, and I chew down on my bottom lip, watching Lord Delaurent's reaction with obvious reserve.

I take a small step back, letting myself rescind from the spotlight cast by the chandelier overhead.

"I'd gathered from the reception I received. I'd advise next time not to invite guests you don't intend on welcoming into your home— if that's what you call this enormous crystal mausoleum. Then again, perhaps this isn't your home and you're merely a lodger. You are not King of Aetheria after all," Lord DeLaurent retorts, a snake-like smile twisting those powder-soft lips into a goading invitation for retort.

I feel Aro's body heat beside me, his free hand balling into a fist to match those of his opponent. He takes a step forward, pushing me behind him and squaring up to the Draconian, his wings spreading wide in defence.

"Not yet," he hisses with feral abandon, momentarily losing his cool before straightening and relinquishing a measured exhale. Quickly composed, he continues, "I'd advise you not to go where you are neither wanted nor required, Lord DeLaurent." Aro's voice is now a slowly constricting and scrupulously controlled vice, squeezing the air from my lungs as his eyes hollow out into bottomless pits of rage. Where once I had seen galaxies, a pair of black holes float in his eye sockets instead.

I look over my shoulder, finding that the conversation has now stopped dead. Golden armoured guards stir at the edges of the room, and all eyes are undeniably fixed on the three of us standing focal to their scrutiny.

I count heartbeats in my head; one, two, three—

Then, a sound breaks the silence as a set of gilded double doors to my left sprawl wide open.

A Nephilim with jet-black hair and olive skin steps forward, looking flustered beneath the thin veil of her formally composed façade.

Navy blue skirts flutter around her swift-moving ankles as she straightens within the tiny bodice of her modest attire.

"Dinner is about to be served, so if you could all proceed to the dining room, that would be lovely."

LUCIEN

My blood cools oh so slowly as the tension between myself and the arrogant dark angel dissipates, all attention now on the promise of food rather than our ancient and far too predictable feud. It had been obvious to everyone except me apparently, and I wonder if I've grown soft in my solitude.

Genevieve had been right. They hadn't wanted me here at all. They sent the invitation out of respect for protocol, not for the Draconians.

Brooding and unable to uncurl my fists, I spin rapidly on the spot, tucking my wings in tightly like a shield and turning my back on both Lord Black and his pet mortal.

She had seemed sweet, pure, almost too innocent, and now I am wondering if this entire event is one enormous choreographed trap.

Regardless though, I cannot deny the scents wafting from the dining room have saliva rushing across my tongue. My feet carry me forward as my stomach rumbles, and I feel like slapping myself.

So? Even mouse traps offer cheese you moron. I chastise myself as I wish that only a few more mortal vices had been stripped away when I'd become a Draconian.

The crowd seems to follow suit, piling through the high archway of the doorframe and into the elongated banquet hall. It's warm in here, almost too warm, as I pull at my cravat once again, eyeing the three enormous fireplaces on each wall. I have no idea why you'd need such heat in a place with such a clement climate, and all I can seem to feel is angry that Drakos Vale doesn't contain the same kinds of facilities.

If this is not enough to put me in a permanent bad mood, I find myself dithering between the three long banquet tables that face the elevated head table. Each of the High Lords or Ladies in attendance, no matter their race, are seated promptly upon the stage, and so I'm left dancing awkwardly between the Aresian and Artemisian Equinians and the Nephilim, who are looking at me like I might bite them.

If I can't find a seat, I might be forced to. Not that it would be so terrible, they probably taste pretty fantastic. Like highly perfumed veal that's been soaked in talcum powder and pretentious entitlement.

Either way, I'm eating something rare tonight.

I'm the last one left standing in a sea of glowing skin and feathered wings, my leathery span nothing short of an eyesore among the rest.

Finally, after coughing extremely loudly several times and attempting to get the attention of the head table, a flustered and intimidated-looking waiter approaches with an extra chair, squeezing me in between two of the burliest Equinian males I've ever seen. Aro gives me a smug smile as he caresses the hand of the mortal girl beside him, a gloating maniac floating behind the serene veneer of his pupils.

It's a squeeze, no doubt, and for a moment, all eyes are on me and full of utter disgust as squish myself in between the two mountainous pegasi riders. The heat coming off their glistening gilded flesh is palpable, as though the dark swirls of their tattoos are a link to hell's very own furnace. A bead of sweat rolls slowly down the back of my neck as waiters fluster around me, providing an extra improvised place setting.

I smile up at the head table with an innocent expression once I'm settled, flashing a full set of teeth and making sure to give Aro a thumbs up from where I'm forced to look up at him.

I mean, if I'm trapped here by my utter stupidity, might as well stir the shit while I'm at it. If there's anything a Frenchman is notoriously good at, it's being an utter asshole hidden behind a fine suit and exemplary surface etiquette.

The meal passes with slow tedium.

I am elbowed every few seconds from alternating sides as the two men beside me wrestle with the fine cutlery and even more delicate courses.

The food, at least, is beautifully executed.

Even I cannot deny that Soleus has the best cuisine of anywhere in Aetheria, but then again, they should. They bullied Eclipsia and Nirvana into trade agreements and started wars so they could maintain such finery as this.

The Draconians, however, could not be bought with fine silks, gold, or even orchid tartlets topped with tight curls of edible gold.

I am pondering this as I take another, fuller than my pants are willing to allow but determined to make such social torture count for at least a decent meal.

The Equinians around me don't try to make conversation, other than the odd grunt when one of them elbows me, which I take as a blessing. Hell, the last time I held a conversation with a male Equinian I was left queasy after only two sentences. They do love their war tales heavy on detail, especially if that detail involves exactly how loudly a bone snapped in two or how violently a carotid exploded.

So, revelling in the silence, I continue to stuff as much food as I can in my mouth, taking small gulps of water and drinking nothing else during the meal.

Finally, after my third Orchid tartlet, and lucky for the seams of my waistcoat, Aro stands, taking Kairi's hand in his. He leads her from the grandiose chair in which she's sat and around the dining table to the front of the stage.

"Now we are all fed, I'd like to propose a toast. A thank you to all of our friends for travelling all this way as a personal favour to me. I think you will agree, that the young woman standing behind me is not just any mortal, but is truly destined to soar among us, perhaps even to choose who will next sit on the throne, which has sat empty for so long just upstairs." He puts particular emphasis on the word *friends* as his eyes jump to mine and then back to the general space above the heads of the crowd.

I watch as Kairi clears her throat, taking a step forward. Aro's eyes widen in surprise as if he forgot she was there and had a tongue of her own.

Typical Sephilim.

"I just wanted to say—" she stutters, flushing and bringing her hand to her lips with a self-consciousness bordering on childish. Finding herself after a few moments looking out over the faces of the crowd, she continues without ever having laid eyes on me. "I just wanted to say thank you for letting me return to your world. Even if only for this one night, it's the most incredible place I've ever seen—" She's cut off as Aro steps forward, gesturing for a waiter to ascend to the height of the stage and ending her chance at speaking. The waiter carries a silver tray, upon which stand two glasses full of red wine.

The scent hits me immediately as the couple each takes one glass, and my eyes narrow, nostrils flaring.

"To good friends and to the most magical world this young woman has ever seen, long may she continue to return," Aro announces, and the two clink glasses as he glances firmly over his shoulder at the head table full of visiting aristocrats.

Then, I'm on my feet.

"Stop!" I bellow, causing Kairi to startle, glass almost to her lips.

The two Equinians on either side of me duck as my wings flare sideways.

"Don't drink that! It's poisoned!" I exclaim in a breathless burst, my voice falling from unfeeling and cold in its deep rumble.

Aro's eyebrows pinch together, mouth falling slightly open to protest as Kairi turns to him. I await his argument, but no matter what he tries to pull, he won't convince me there's no poison in her glass. I can smell the rancid stink of it from here, even beneath the wine he's tried to mask it with.

Draconians have a nose for such things, or perhaps he had forgotten.

Then again, he had insisted he wasn't intending me to show up.

That's just too bad, Lord Black.

Too damn bad.

KAIRI

I don't want to believe it as the gold of the glass's stem goes cold between my fingers.

Turning to stare at Aro, mouth going dry, I narrow my eyes, my gaze darting between his expression and that of Lord DeLaurent, who looks mad with rage.

"Don't be so ridiculous Draconian. You're just jealous." Aro turns to me, eyes wide and shaking his head.

"Ignore him, Kairi. I'm simply trying to toast your future here." My heart is in my throat as his hand tightens on my wrist where before he was holding my hand. I look down into the depths of the bloody red glass, then up to the crowd.

Far beyond the centre point of the room, a woman with dazzling silver hair and equally shimmering wings, who I've been watching stare intensely at me throughout the length of the meal without taking a single bite, shakes her head subtly.

He's lying. That's what both her look and my gut are screaming.

You wouldn't notice it if you weren't looking, but her eyes are urgent to the point it looks like she might burst into flame, the tremor of her ringlets discernible as the rest of her body remains unnaturally stone still in her ornately carved seat.

Aro catches me staring and steps forward to follow my line of sight.

Instinctively, I snap my head back around to face him, vomit rising fast up my gullet as my heart hammers like a power tool in my chest.

His fingers loosen around my wrist for a second as he gives me a reassuring smile, but my stomach is full of lead. I take the chance and let the glass fall from my trembling fingers, watching as it tumbles to the floor in slow motion and the red of the wine stains the front of my skirt bloody.

The fairytale of whatever had been between us shatters.

I turn on my heel, gathering my sopping skirts in my shaking palms and taking flight from the room, hair bouncing around my face as my eyes fill with tears.

I hear chaos erupt behind me as my breathing becomes but fleeting wisps and my feet carry me faster and faster away from the dining room and through the winding corridors of the Solis Castra, poisoned wine dripping from my skirts and mingling with my tears, a trail of crimson salt spatters the only thing left in my wake.

DR JEKYLL AND MR HYDE

KAIRI

"KAIRI!" THE VOICE CALLS out, but it isn't who I expect. I'm turned around, lost in the labyrinth of amethyst corridors, and my heart is racing so hard I wonder if it'll ever stop.

I spin, my stained dress flaring out from my hips. I'm gasping, tears streaming down my face, lips trembling, body shaking uncontrollably. Everything about this is shocking, and not just to my body but to something deeper.

I feel fractured, betrayed— and utterly lost.

Dawn hurries toward me, closing the distance between us in rushed strides and grabbing onto my wrists tightly before yanking me around the corner. She places her finger to her lips, eyes wide and concerned. Her golden blonde hair has come loose from her updo and is plastered to her forehead. Her wings rustle, and then she pulls me into her chest, letting me bawl on her shoulder as the soft caress of her feathers cradles me.

I feel her conduct, but my eyes are screwed too tightly shut to take in the blinding fork of lightning, and the sound - like a whip being struck against steel - is lost among my sobs.

My chest heaves as she pushes me back from her, allowing my makeup to run haphazardly down my face in black salty rivers.

"Kairi, you have to leave. I didn't know— I didn't know. I swear it! Oh Goddess, what has Lord Black done— whatever was he thinking?" She sounds as breathless as I feel, and in my heart, I know that she has come to the same conclusion that I had. Without a shadow of a doubt in my mind, the wine he had presented me with was spiked with poison, and Aro knew that because he was the one who put it there.

Did he want to kill me?

I don't know how Lord DeLaurent had known, or the silver-haired Nephilim, but I had seen the tightness in Aro's face at their accusations, the way he had flushed slightly with guilt, and despite everything I've felt for him, my instincts had reared like a spooked horse and screamed at me to run.

I have felt twinges all night of that same instinct; when he took my glass from me and wouldn't allow me another drink, when he interrupted me during my speech in the banquet hall, but it wasn't until those instincts screamed that I listened.

Now, I'm terrified it might be too late.

Taking a pace back from Dawn, I realise she's brought me back to my room. My eyes dart about the space as my panic refuses to recede, paranoia clutching me ever tighter.

"It's okay, Dawn. I know you didn't know. I need to leave, to get out of here— I have to—" I am cut off by a blinding flash that guts me and the crack I don't want to hear, my breath catching in my throat as pure fear throttles me.

I turn slowly, not wanting it to be him. But it is.

"Going somewhere?" he asks, his face that of a stranger. It's as though the mask I thought I had been watching him place over those adoring eyes is his true face, and the one he's been showing to me is the lie instead.

"Aro, look. I have to leave. I don't belong here." I don't mention the wine, feeling scared of what he might do if I outright accuse him. His fists are balled at his sides. His jacket has been discarded somewhere between the dining room and here, and for the first time, I notice a dagger in the waistband of his pants.

My skin chills as he takes a step forward, looming over me.

His eyes soften, taking my hands into his own. I want to flinch away, but I'm equally scared of angering him.

"Kairi— you see. I can't let you leave. Not again. Not after losing you once already. You've been brought back to me for a reason. It is destiny. You understand that, don't you?" He smiles, his eyes empty as they had been when he squared up to the Draconian Lord what seems like a lifetime ago.

"You tried to poison me!" I yell, abandoning my tack of trying to play nice as he grabs hold of my wrists with both hands, hauling them up so I'm squirming in his grasp only inches from the end of his nose.

"I tried to end your torment so we could be together for eternity, my dear. Can't you see? I was doing you a favour," he informs me, certain of this truth. His eyes are dark but imploring now, the stars I once saw in them having long since burned themselves to dust.

I struggle against the savage friction of his fingers around the thin fragility of my wrists, panic rising through me as I realise he's far stronger than I will ever be and that there's no way I'm going to be able to beat him in a physical confrontation.

"My Lord." I hear Dawn's voice, small but defiant, stutter into life behind me.

"Get out!" Aro roars, and I feel her physically wince even though I can't see her.

I turn back, hanging from Aro's grasp and giving her a pleading look to leave us. Despite the fact I can't bear the idea of being left alone with him, I'm afraid he'll hurt her too.

She catches my glance, and then in a second of blindingly brilliant light, she's gone, leaving me and Aro alone.

"You mortals. You never know what's good for you. Can't you see I was trying to do you a favour? I offered you the goddamn supernatural world on a plate, and you want to go home to your faggot family and suffer day in and day out? What kind of a 'thank you' is that? I brought you into this world Kairi, and I will be the one who says when you can leave." He's speaking through gritted teeth, every muscle in his body wound tight and ready to snap. I inhale deeply, the scent of vanilla and violets making me nauseous.

My heart breaks at his words but even more at my stupidity.

Did I think a man like this would ever truly fall for a girl like me?

"And when will that be?" I ask him, my voice diminishing as the ache in my body begins to deepen, and I feel tears returning to my eyes.

"Well, let me put it this way. You can go home once you give me what I want," he says, putting on a fake impersonation of how his voice has always been. Something inside of me shatters at how obvious his façade now seems, hopelessness making me feel weaker than I ever have.

"And what is that?" I ask, voice rising, defiant again. He smiles, though at my resistance or his certainty of squashing it, I cannot discern.

"So glad you asked. I want you to become a Nephilim and crown me the next King of Aetheria. You see, that bitch Hera made it so only the Heirbound Nephilim could touch and bestow the crown to the next king. Thought she was being clever, I suppose," he sneers, waving a hand and letting my wrists go.

I stumble back, looking beyond the double glass doors and past the balcony railing as I catch myself, heel lodging in the crack in the marble floor. There's only cloud for miles.

My heart sinks, realising that Aro doesn't feel any concern about me escaping.

After all, where can I go?

I'm alone in a tower that's hundreds of feet off the ground with only one exit, and he's blocking it. If I want to get back to Tennessee, to Hickory Oaks, then I'll need him to take me there.

The faces of my pa and dad float to the front of my mind as I take deep breaths, trying to calm myself.

Your faggot family— His words echo around in my skull as I watch him staring at me, utterly calm and collected, it would seem.

And what's worse, he used my disease, the thing I had been trying to escape from, been made victim by, to lure me here and attempt to end my life. He was using it as a way to justify what he was doing as a mercy rather than a crime.

I lunge, senseless, hurt, and angry, right for him, scratching ferally at his face with my pristinely manicured nails, courtesy of Dawn, though I'm not sure this is what she had in mind when she shaped the French tips into points.

I manage to take a slash of his skin from beneath his eye in a shallow gouge, but too soon, he has me back in his clutches and is hoisting me off my feet, causing me to fall still in the vice of his palms.

"Let me say this again. Slowly. So your tiny mortal brain can understand what it is I'm trying to impress—" He licks his bottom lip as though he's savouring his cruelty. "You will do as I say. You will drink what I tell you to drink. You will bow when I tell you to bow. You will die when I deem it time. Or, I will just have to take a little trip back to that shithole you call home and have myself some fun with those two freaks you call parents. Are we clear?"

The thought of anything happening to my parents, the people who saved me from living a life alone, being shuffled from one place to the next, makes my blood run cold and my eyes well with tears. He has struck me squarely in my greatest weakness.

Salty trickles run silently down my face as I realise I've put the people I love at risk— and for what?

So, I could dance around in a fancy dress and feel like a princess?

I guess I am a princess now, a princess who's about to be locked in a tower for a very long time.

"Are we clear?" he repeats as he puts me back down on the floor, yanking me close to him and holding my left hand up to the light. He looks at the mark on my wrist then back down at me, tightening his grasp slowly as we stare at one another.

"Yes—" I breathe, fear paralysing me now.

All I can see as I look at him is the dark angel he truly is, standing over the charred bodies of my parents, smiling.

He gives a sweet grin, almost boyish, and then without blinking, he breaks my arm like it's a matchstick.

"That's for messing up my face, whore." He spits on me as I fall to the floor, cradling my arm with a cry of surprise, eyes streaming.

I splay out on the cool stone, the chill the only relief from the burning agony rippling up from my wrist, coming eye to eye with the crack I had noticed earlier.

Aro doesn't say goodbye. He simply exits the room on swift feet. I listen, cries wracking me silently, as I refuse to scream.

He turns the key I had willingly given back to him for safekeeping in a lock, trapping me inside.

I don't know how long I lie on the floor after he leaves, but all I can do is stay still with my cheek pressed against the marble, my ruined dress splayed out around me, tracing the cracked stone with my unbroken fingers.

There is no sound other than the slow drip of my tears falling and splashing against the floor.

How could you be so stupid?

Don't you know fairy tales only exist in books? I think, wondering exactly how desperate I must have been for change to allow myself to get in so deep, so fast, with the wrong man.

I have had the right men by my side all along, and now because of me, they're at risk of losing their lives and each other too.

Why wasn't it enough?

Why did I need to go in search of something more?

I ask myself the same questions over and over until they lose all meaning and take up the rhythm of my throbbing broken arm.

I scrunch up my eyes, trying to stop crying, but it doesn't work.

The silence is broken in but a single second as I hear smashing glass and the loud thud of rock hitting rock.

Covering my head, I feel shards pepper me and cower, wondering if Aro has returned to punish me further for my perceived crimes.

I hear footsteps, loud and heavy.

Not Aro's.

I notice because his are much lighter.

Opening my eyes, I look up, finding the face of Lord DeLaurent staring down at me, his Dragon-esque wings spread wide behind him.

"What are you doing here?" I stutter, wiping my eyes with the back of my uninjured hand and flushing, embarrassed.

"What does it look like?" he asks, bending down and examining my wrist with a quick glance and then a grimace.

"It's broken—" I explain, and he nods.

"Yes, it is." His voice is gruff, his arms encircling my body and hoisting me off the floor.

"What are you doing?!" I ask, my voice a mouse squeak as panic begins to rise in me again.

"I'm rescuing the damsel in distress. If that wasn't clear—" he mutters, adjusting me in his arms as he starts walking across the smashed glass. I see the cause of the wreckage, an amethyst geode lying heavily on its side amongst the sparkling debris. He must have thrown it clean through the glass window of the French doors so he could open it from the inside and let himself in.

His enormous foot kicks the frame open as my mind races, trying to fit everything together, and it flies back, the remaining glass tinkling onto the floor like heavy rain.

"But—" I begin as he steps out into the night.

The air is electrified, a brisk breeze whipping my hair from my tear-stained face as a light rain blankets us. I shiver, my bare skin both relieved and protesting the icy layer of water that immediately begins to pepper my chest and shoulders. Lightning crackles overhead as my rescuer extends his wings and launches upward in a single inhuman bound so he's standing on the balcony railing.

"Look, I don't have time for this, do you trust me or not?" he asks, snapping suddenly as his pure white locks are blown back from his face and his eyes are made bright beneath the moon.

A flash of lightning too close for comfort illuminates the sharp plains of his face, making every single feature intimidating.

He looks wicked in this light, phantasmal almost.

191

"Of course, I don't trust you. I don't even know you!" I retort, raising my voice over the increasingly violent wind, my eyes darting down into the abyss beyond the edge of the railing.

I cling on to him tighter as I take in the sheer drop, my arm throbbing and fingers aching as I clutch the silver fabric of his cravat in my terrified palm.

He teeters, laughing at my expression and rolling his eyes.

"Well, that's good. I've seen who you trust. For the record, your instincts suck." His light sense of humour amid the storm makes me relax, my body turning to jelly in his arms.

I don't reply, don't have time to, because by the time he drops off into the thin air beyond in a gut-wrenching free fall, I've succumbed to unconsciousness from the trauma of too much pain and heartbreak.

<u>ARO</u>

I awaken instantly to the sound of wrapping knuckles on wood.

Lolling forward from the armchair where I fell asleep after pacing myself to exhaustion, I catch sight of Ariah, who is curled up in a dark furry puddle on the floor. The enormous black lion shifts a lazy eye toward my hunched silhouette and then the door as I call, "Enter!"

My wings unfold, feathers ruffled, from where I've been resting against them all night as I stand. I cannot help but stretch them wide, enjoying the way they grow my shadow by feet on either side. The door opens a crack, and Dawn slithers through, her tread silent and eyes trained firmly on the floor.

"Good morning, Dawn." I smile at her, stretching tall with my arms and giving a slow yawn.

"Good morning, my Lord," she replies, her voice cracking like fine china that's been thrown in anger against a wall, each syllable sounding fragile and less cheery than I'm used to.

"Fine morning, isn't it?" I ask as I stride across the room, treading nimbly over the sleeping Kensari who doesn't so much as look up to see who has entered the room.

"It is, my Lord." She nods, striding across the room and drawing the curtains without pause, fumbling at the tasselled rope ties on either side with shaking hands.

"And how was the atmosphere after I departed last night?" I enquire, deciding that with her holier-than-thou sudden subservience I had better cut to the chase.

"I couldn't possibly say, my Lord. I was busy helping the Nephilim undress and ready themselves for bed. Some of them were quite intoxicated," she replies, that edge to her broken syllables cutting no matter what the volume.

"You're angry with me?" I leave it as a question and take off the crumpled white shirt I slept in before moving to the ornate wardrobe to replace it with another.

As I shrug the white cotton, that's perfectly pressed and smells of violets, over my shoulders, I look up to her and start buttoning.

"It isn't my place to say. My feelings toward you matter not. I am here to serve you." She brushes away my question, making my fingers fumble with the button that will close the fabric over my pectorals.

"Dawn, you've been my maid for centuries. If you have something to say, say it." I give this request softly, but there's an abrasive undertone to my voice that cannot be ignored.

"I like Miss Freemont, my Lord. What you did, well— it was wrong." She shuffles across the room, linen skirts swaying around her ankles as the morning sunlight bathes the floors beneath her feet. Picking up the tray of empty glasses from which I'd drunk deep last night, she makes her way once more toward the door.

"In your opinion. I don't see how giving her a life of immortality, a life free of pain, can be considered wrong." I spit back, trying to hold my temper. I had let it loose last night but with great distaste. When I become this way, the Mr Hyde to my well-received Dr Jekyll, I am left remembering how much I sound like my father and with an entirely disgusting aftertaste on my tongue.

"You didn't give her a choice, my Lord. You tried to take her life from her without a word of warning, in front of everyone." Dawn stands, statuesque and straight-backed by the door, inching closer to it as our eyes lock and I feel the burning rage behind her stare.

"And Zeus gave me a choice when he stole me into immortal life, did he? Did Hera ask you if it was alright when she strapped wings to your back and made it so you would spend your endless life bending to others?" I ask, face incredulous, and Dawn merely shakes her head.

193

"No, my Lord."

"I thought not. At least, what I intended to do came from a place of love, unlike the Gods who bind us to life for selfish purposes." I exhale, heat flushing my cheeks.

"So, you weren't trying to kill her for your own agenda? Are you sure about that?" Dawn asks, and her question takes me by surprise so completely that my head snaps up from where I'm trying to fasten my collar.

"Even if it was, that kind of question is far above your station. Now get out, and don't forget to light the fire this evening. I returned to a cold bed last night, and I don't appreciate being made to light my own hearth. I'm far too busy to be worrying with women's work!" I spit, and she nods, silenced yet again. Giving a fast but undeniably graceful curtsey, she leaves the room in silence. The door clicks behind her, leaving me alone with my thoughts once again.

Once I'm dressed, I think carefully about Dawn's words as Ariah rises and stretches, claws popping one by one from beneath the pad of his enormous paws. Maybe I should apologise, but if I hadn't taken the matter of Kairi's mortality into my own hands, I know that in leaving it up to a vote, I would have lost her forever. The Lords and Ladies of Aetheria were not likely to vote in her favour and allow her to visit, and despite the fact I had hoped otherwise, the truth was too damning to ignore. I'd seen the way Aliandara regarded her, and the fact that Lord DeLaurent had responded to my invitation was yet another valid vote that would no doubt be cast against me.

In truth, the only vote I really have in the bag was from Morpheus, and whatever the Fae voted for almost guaranteed that every single Equinian Lord or Lady would oppose.

It had been foolish, but it had also been a game.

Once she had died in front of everyone, nobody would have questioned her legitimacy as the next Heirbound. They would have known she was chosen, seen her rebirth for themselves, and also known she was truly in my grasp.

Perhaps then, it wasn't about her transformation at all but showing the Aetherial aristocracy that the next Heirbound was enraptured with me, that I truly am to be the next King, and by legitimate means no less.

So, what now?

In my blind rage last night, I had snapped Kairi's arm like a twig, insulted her family, and told her exactly what I expected of her without thought of her reaction or the consequences.

My mother used to say that you catch more flies with honey than with vinegar, so perhaps my first order of business this morning should be an apology of sorts. The girl is probably hurting, hungry, and terrified after how I lost my temper, and that is no condition in which to bend her to me willingly.

I do so want her to bend willingly, I muse, stroking my chin as I pick a jacket out of the wardrobe.

For forceful measures are so less savoury and far less convincing to prying eyes.

Conduction comes naturally to me now, but it didn't always. When I first re-awoke a Sephilim, travelling via lightning currents caused me a certain amount of disillusionment upon rematerializing. As I find myself standing once more upon the floor of the highest tower of the Solis Castra, I discover myself victim to similar disorientation followed by shock-induced vertigo.

I blink, hoping my eyes are mistaken but, upon the lifting of my lids, realise that what I'm seeing is no nightmare, but reality instead.

The crystal floor is speckled with glass, a large amethyst geode amongst the sparkling debris.

How on earth did she get that? I wonder.

I haven't noticed it before, but the maids change décor around all the time, and I've never ventured farther into the suite than the bedroom.

Perhaps she found it in the bathroom—

I tread across the glass, the jagged edges of each speck crunching beneath the heel of my boot.

It's too familiar, too terrifyingly resonant of what I had found before when—

Shaking my head, I dissipate the memory as though it's noxious gas, running my fingers back through my dark hair and exhaling heavily, heart quickening by the moment.

Making my way beyond the glass door that's been kicked wide open, probably because I'd broken her wrist, I find the gauzy curtains on either side are blown back into the room by a sudden breeze, the air cooler after the anticipated flash storm last night.

Then, looking back at the mess on the floor, I wonder.

Why did she need to break the glass at all?

I didn't lock those balcony doors, and they only open from the inside—

She could have simply opened them.

Was it rage, her need to smash and destroy that overcame her, or something else?

Or *someone* else.

Rushing forward through the door that's dangling by a single hinge, I glance down over the balustrade of the balcony, roleplaying myself a hundred years earlier in a scene exactly this fraught.

How can I be back here again?

I need to think but cannot do it here, cannot bear the scent of her hay and lavender aroma that still lingers in every corner of the suite.

Curling my hands into fists, I go where I know I will find solitude and, hopefully amongst the quiet prayer, answers.

The Temple of Zeus had been one of the only buildings that stood before the first Sephilim was reborn. Long before the Solis Castra, the city of Soleus, or any of the roads had been paved, the agenda of Zeus was definitive, carved in white marble and platinum, towering suddenly from nothing, on a lone floating island above the meagre lodgings of Prometheus' Seraphim. Myth says that one day, they awakened, and the monstrous architecture was blocking the sunrise, the shadow of it drenching their small villages in darkness and causing fear to spread like wildfire.

Of course, if the Seraphim had nothing to hide, they would not have been afraid.

As it is though, they had been toiling to resurrect their maker, and they knew that nothing good could come from the sudden presence of Zeus's magic abruptly hovering above their lands.

I cannot help but understand their fear as I rematerialize in the archway entrance, fledged on both sides by sky-high white marble Grecian pillars, the high eaves of the ceiling almost devoid of shadow as every plane of the cool stone is gilded in solid platinum.

I remember waking here, coming up for air from within the depths of the pool of Aether-rich fluid that births Sephilim, and finding myself wondering if I was in heaven; the bright lights, the luxurious marble carvings of bulls and eagles, as well as the oak saplings potted in enormous Grecian urns of platinum making it seem elysian in every regard. The saplings, I had soon learned, will climb tall fast, and soon be replaced by other younglings still in the stages before their branches explode into a glistening bloom of amethyst leaves. It's a continuous rotation of potting, uprooting, and replanting for the sake of vanity and our devotion to the god who has given us the gift of immortal life.

I wonder often if it is a gift, this life.

For we can never truly grasp control of our destinies, never truly break from the path that is paved by the whims of those very same gods who saved us from the oblivion of the Crucible's recycling process.

I feel like a pawn more than I ever had, kneeling in the confessional.

Letting the line of amethyst geodes that flank the main aisle of the temple bathe me in the purest white light, I brush my fingers along their sharp shimmering edges, catching sparks from the faceted surfaces.

The stone takes me back to the reason I'm here, and so, nearby fountains trickling in my ears and light from the diamond-tipped stained glass of the windows throwing kaleidoscopic rainbows across the floor, I stride on through the house of Zeus.

Approaching the statue of the idol that lies central to the sprawling complex housing private prayer rooms, shrines, re-birthing pools, and archives from the earlier days of Aetheria, I look up out of habit.

The sculpture is enormous, towering over me by at least twenty feet, the lifelike eyes of this predatory man gazing down at me, unseeing through cold white marble.

Do the Gods watch us?

Do they see our struggle and laugh?

I want to know the answer to these questions, and they've burned within my chest for centuries, yet the one that slips from my lips and out into the deserted hall is something else.

"Why bring her back if you were just going to take her from me? Is it not your whim for me to be King? Am I not worthy after everything I have done?" I demand, sounding violently angry as the syllables escape from between my teeth like the hissing steam of a kettle. I don't sink to my knees as many winged warriors have done before me, for I do not bow before Zeus.

Instead, I confront him as an adversary.

I didn't come to pray, but instead to demand answers from a cruel tyrant who lords his power over us as though we were insects scurrying beneath his magnifying glass.

I stand before him for minute after minute, heart pounding, ears ringing in the silence absent of answers, absent of apology. My fists slowly ball tighter, my breathing heightened as my skin grows hot and irritated with the rushing rivers of heated blood that run close beneath the surface.

Then, I realise as I stare into his face, that I'm demanding answers from the wrong tyrant.

My quarrel lies not with Zeus.

Oh no.

But with the whore Hera instead.

The atmosphere in Hera's temple is a different kind of electric from that of Zeus. The air is warm and thick with the pungent scent of white lilies, the entire structure carved from rose quartz and bathed in warm light by scattered amethyst lamps that are dimmer than the ones I've just left by far. Golden filigree forms patterns of peacocks wearing intricate diadems, cuckoo birds in lofty flight, and pomegranates spilling their speeds like drops of rain, one image flowing flawlessly into the next.

I see her, kneeling beneath Hera's rosy stone gaze, silver hair spilling over her shoulders, and the sight of her blooming opalescent skirts brings me back to last night. The way she had kept intense eye contact with Kairi as she weighed up whether to drink the wine.

I knew Silver disliked Kairi, but I had not imagined she would dare sabotage me, a High Lord.

This kind of disobedience cannot be allowed to stand.

My eyes remain trained on the back of Silver's head as I raise and wave a hand, dismissing the guards peppered around the edges of the great hall. At the sound of their gilded gold boots marching from where they were flanking the room, Silver turns to look back over one shoulder.

Finding me there, she turns away a little too quickly, remaining hunched over in prayer. As if that will save her.

"That won't help you, you know." My voice echoes around the high ceilings of the sloping temple roof, rebounding in Godly reverberations deep enough to rattle bone. The last of the guards' monotone tread dies into silence with the first word that falls from my lips.

We are utterly alone within the house of Hera.

Silver looks up from beneath thick black lashes, her metallic eyes shimmering pale pink as if blood has fallen into the pools of her irises, polluting her.

"What would you know of it? When was the last time you knelt before your God and asked forgiveness?" Silver demands, arms straightening as she rises to stand tall between myself and the statue of her Goddess.

"In fact, I just came from the temple of Zeus. I must admit though, penance was far from my priority." I brush lint from the embroidered collar of my jacket, keeping my breathing steady within the constricting confines of its cut.

"I can't imagine it would be. You feel perfectly justified in trying to kill that poor girl, don't you?" She cocks her head and takes a step closer to me, utterly unapologetic. Her eyes are fearless, but her body gives her away with the tension of her forearms where tendons stand out like taut fraying ropes of emotion. Her breathing is also far too controlled to be naturally calm.

The scent of her fear is sweet, the aroma lifting from her skin in cresting waves of iris and snowdrops.

Her breath, hot, hits my face as she comes within an inch of me.

"You don't scare me, Aro. I admire your gall and clear ruthless intent. The mortal's involvement, however, I cannot abide." She keeps her chin raised as the words come out sharp like knives, eyes locked in a battle of wills with mine.

I raise my chin, looking down the length of my nose at her.

The violent urge claws at the cold innards of my chest, pent-up rage causing me to harden in stature as I lock my jaw, teeth gritted against the infuriation her too-perfect face is known to induce.

I let my hand sweep from where it's hanging tensely at my side to poise in the belt loop of my pants, my thumb caressing the handle of the dagger that presses its edge lovingly into my thigh.

"I don't scare you?" I ask her, taking the smallest step forward so we're practically flush.

She counters, stepping back and closer to the statue of Hera while shaking her head.

Silver's metallic locks look cruel and dull then against the radiance of the temple, her features colder than any monument I could erect in stone. Her hardness, her chill, bothers me. It makes me want to crush her into dust, to make her whimper and plead.

After I take another predatory step, she repeats her previous motion, causing me to elicit a smile.

"You should have kept your mouth shut," I spit, and she laughs, a good attempt at fearlessness but far too hollow to be genuine.

"So, what? You could go off with that slip of a girl? She's not what you're looking for, Aro." Silver speaks boldly, but as she takes another step back, she meets with the sandaled feet of Hera.

Watching her, now caught between myself and the unforgiving quartz limbs of her Goddess, I smile, pulling out the dagger so it glints in the hazy rose light.

"You don't know what I'm looking for, Silver." I hiss her name, heart pounding an alluring and ragged tempo like the call of war drums has risen within my very own ribcage from somewhere ancient and cruel.

I press flush against her so the corner of the statue's base cuts into the back of her spine, raising the dagger to her cheek and letting the edge bite into the soft flawless porcelain of her face.

"I know that it won't bring you what you seek. A crown will not give you the power you desire. Only fear can do that—" Silver stutters, her breasts rising dramatically and threatening to spill over the top of her corset.

I clench my hand around the handle of the dagger, letting it slice clean down the side of her face and relishing the scent of copper as it hits the air.

"You'd do well not to give such advice to a man strongly fighting the urge to punish you," I growl, eyes narrowing into slits, nostrils flaring at the alluring river of blood falling from the high-arched bone of her cheek and into her ample cleavage.

"So, punish me." She shrugs, her face a sexual challenge.

She'd like that, me fucking her right here on the temple floor.

So how can I take her desire— and hurt her with it?

My body stiffens against her, taking the dagger in my hand, smeared with blood, and dropping it to catch the top of her corset. My wings flare out from my spine, shrouding her opalescent glow in the darkness as I cage her in on either side.

I let the blade wander down her breast, slicing effortlessly through her skin before it catches the bindings of her dress and makes short work of them in only a few moments.

The front-lacing corset falls wide, exposing her to me.

I spin her, quickly grabbing her skirts and hauling them up so I might gain access.

She will not gaze into my eyes, for this isn't for her but for me.

It will not be as she has dreamed, hot and wanton under the sheets alone.

The pale curve of her rump causes me to harden despite myself, wondering exactly how I can punish her through such a pleasurable act. I take the round of my hand and slap her legs so they're wide enough for me to inspect her, letting the dagger in my free hand cut the inside of her thigh in the process.

She's glistening for me as I had expected, and as I let my fingers wander across the plains of her buttocks, I realise that in punishing her in a traditional way, I would only be giving her what she wants.

I let my fingers slide into her, the heat immense as she whimpers like an unsated whore, before withdrawing them quickly.

No. This will not do.

The sound of my belt buckle being unfastened, followed by my pants dropping to my ankles, causes her to spread wider, giving me exactly what I want unknowingly.

I bury myself into her, the tightness of her rectum an agonizing vice fighting me every step of the way and causing me to swallow back waves of ecstasy that form in the current of her agony.

It is not about the climax that will inevitably come but about control, about refusing her everything she wants while luring her to me with the promise of exactly that.

She screams as I defile her in the driest possible manner, an abhorrently broken cry escaping her lips like that of a baby animal that's been kicked with no warning. She cusses, making me laugh.

"Fuck you! You bastard!"

Her anger spurs me on like a prize stud, and so I bury my fingers into her hips, forcing her backwards onto me and revelling only further in her cries as I dig my nails into her skin.

I look up at Hera's face as I sodomise one of her chosen Angels, a serene smile curving my lips as I climb closer and closer to climax.

As I groan louder, drowning out the cries and the pleas of Silver's bargaining prayers to the Goddess who watches over us, I grab her hair in my fist, yanking it back and dropping the dagger I've been clutching throughout. The copper-tinged weapon falls to the floor with a clang of steel on stone as I empty myself inside of her in a final and violently unhinged thrust, slapping her viciously on the vulva in a final degraded flourish.

She screams as I ebb, growing larger in the final moments and tearing her apart.

Stilling, I keep her matted hair knotted tightly in my clammy palm, pulling her straight towards me without warning. She gasps, a broken sound, the two of us separating with painful finality at the waist.

"Think about that the next time you cross me. My next punishment will not be so merciful." I lick the blood from her cheek as I gasp this warning headily into her ear, my breath still ravaged and guttural from my orgasm.

She squirms in my grasp, helpless, her wings fluttering furiously against my torso, a bird trapped in a cage.

I wipe the blood from my fingers on the white silk of her feathers, tainting the silver tips ruddy, before stepping back and pulling my pants back up with one hand.

Straightening, I fix the collar of my jacket and let go of the whimpering Nephilim in my hand before buckling my belt.

She slumps to the floor like an autumnal leaf, the crack of bone on stone echoing timelessly from the watching eyes of peacocks and cuckoos.

Her head rests against the cool of the rose quartz statue base, face and dress smeared with crimson, her silver eyes streaming, cheeks flushed.

Her mouth becomes a distorted 'O' of horror as she fails to stifle the sobs wracking her once proud form.

Saying nothing, but giving her one final look of disgust, I turn, striding from the room at an even and unfeeling pace.

As I put distance between myself and the unblinking eyes of Hera, I return to the matter that had brought me here.

The temple of Hera has not provided answers but, instead, a release from the rage that has been clouding my judgement, and so it is only now that I see things more clearly.

A solution is becoming increasingly clear to me as my heartbeat regulates, blood cooling beneath my skin.

I hear Silver's sobs reverberating high off the beauteous carvings of Hera's temple, even still down one of the seemingly endless corridors, but move only to drown it out by hurrying to invoke the blessed lightning of Zeus.

Conducting from the scene of her damning repentance, I move on from uncontrollable fury to retrace my steps and uncover the truth of Kairi's disappearance with new and bitter control.

15

IF TOMORROW COMES

KAIRI

CONSCIOUSNESS FINDS ME LOST deep amongst billowing clouds of disorientation, of an inability to place myself or reconcile reality with the truth of what I know has happened. Lashes fluttering against my cheeks like the rain-soaked wings of a butterfly, I open my heavy lids, warm and surprisingly comfortable despite the circumstances under which I'd lost consciousness.

I half expect to open my eyes to something archaic; with stone walls, heavy torches lining the walls, and even heavier wood in the door blocking my escape.

Instead though, as my heart plummets through my chest, free from the sanctuary of sleep and exposed once more to the trauma of what has happened, I take in the room around me, surprised if not shocked by the sight that greets me.

I'm lying in an enormous mahogany sleigh bed, white blankets and thick furs piled on top of me, nestled against a cocoon of extremely soft pillows. The ceiling has high wooden eaves, and the entire room is lit by an enormous chandelier holding at least thirty flickering candles, long white bodies curved with globules of wax.

I try to push myself up so I'm sitting, but I find my broken wrist bound and in a sling of thick bandages that wrap around the limb, suspending it from my neck.

I wince.

It aches, but surely not as much as it should for such a fresh break. The pungent scent of cloves and something like tea tree oil wafts up to my nostrils, causing them to flare and my eyes to water slightly as I examine the swollen fingers sticking out. I wiggle them, causing a sharp shock to stab along the length of my forearm with needle-like precision.

I close my eyes, fighting the pain, and take a deep breath, trying not to panic.

Then, the tears come.

I don't fight them, letting salty streams run fast down my face and causing my already raw eyes to burn even harder. I remember the face of Aro as we had danced that first night across the amethyst floors of the Solis Castra, the way he had held me, the way I'd trusted him as we flew up to the highest clouds and waltzed on sparkling thin air.

It was all a lie.

The words come to me, and I feel my heart break all over again, remembering the empty face of the man who had broken my arm and left me shattered on the floor of a locked high tower.

The inside of my chest feels like it's full of shattered glass, and every movement, every memory, every breath threatens to shred me to ribbons from the inside out as the fragments of recollection shift and slip, teetering dangerously close to a landslide.

I let my uninjured hand run through the fur of the blanket that's heavy on my legs, tears falling among the grey fluff, my head hanging as my breathing becomes shallow.

I want my bed.

I think and then realise it isn't my room I'm longing for at all, but rather the two men who have always and will always constitute home. I have put them at risk, opened them to a dimension that is as lethal as it is beautiful without thought of the consequences.

I have never been so ashamed.

I sit amongst the warm blankets, letting myself cry for a good five minutes. I allow myself to feel the memory of Aro's eyes adoring me, the way he had seemed to care so completely evaporate into the truth of things, into the smokescreen that I had believed hook, line, and sinker.

I fell for his beautiful lies, his act, and now I'm a whole world away from where I belong with a creature who I know to be a murderer. I saw the violence in the Draconian High Lord for myself when he threatened Aro at the ball.

His temper left no question in mind as to the kind of man he really is.

So why then did he stand up amongst the crowd? Why did he warn me of the poison that sat waiting in my wine?

Why did he rescue me?

Taking a deep breath, anxiety creeps up on me as the world threatens to close in on every side, trying to gain some semblance of calm before drying my tears and deciding that no matter what happens next, nothing is ever going to be resolved with me sitting in bed, feeling sorry for myself.

I swing my feet off the side of the mattress after pulling back the blankets, letting my feet touch down onto the dark hardwood floors of the bedroom. The floorboards are colder than I expect, the change in temperature sending a noticeable shiver tap-dancing vindictively up the backs of my legs and spine.

Catching sight of myself in the mirror directly opposite the right side of the bed, the arch of the top of the reflective glass reminding me of old castles in its medieval design. The wood around the outside is carved into a strong stand, crafted by some master carpenter to mimic tree bark.

I creep toward it as though unfamiliar with my reflection and find myself dressed, not in the white, wine-stained gown I fled in but in a pair of navy cotton pyjamas with white piping. They're enormous and smell overwhelmingly of wintergreen and peppermint just like the High Lord who rescued me.

The legs of the pyjama pants pool around my feet, so I roll them up to my mid-calf but find myself shivering as the cool air of the house nips at my ankles. The waist is drawn in tightly with a string around my hips, and I'm left blushing as I wonder who the hell changed me out of my dress.

I can only hope the High Lord has a handmaiden.

The shirt also falls off my shoulders in a shroud of dark fabric, and I wonder if the brutally masculine winged man who I met only last night really wears these. They're awfully old-fashioned and rather grandpa-ish for a vicious killer.

Regardless of the size, I'm grateful he, or whoever is responsible, has redressed me. I can only imagine how I'd feel waking in that enormous gown that's covered in tainted red wine and tear stains. My hair has also been unpinned from where it was braided against my skull, and someone has brushed it out, so it now falls in irresistibly soft caramel waves over each shoulder. I let my fingers dance through the tresses, each strand buttery soft like new sunlight.

The more I think about it, the more likely it seems that a woman had me redressed and readied for bed.

I suppose a High Lord, much like Aro, wouldn't have time for such things.

I pull an extra blanket off the end of the bed and wrap it around my shoulders, shivering despite the windows being closed, pure white drapes drawn, and the fireplace at the far end of the room crackling with hearty orange flame.

Fastening my makeshift cape with my one good hand, I creep toward the door, heartrate snowballing. With each step, I realise that my joints ache, more than they ever did in Soleus.

I guess though, I'm not in Soleus anymore.

I feel the weight of my disease potentially returning like a slap and so hold my breath as I reach out, letting the cape slip from my shoulders as I try to turn the door handle with my one working hand.

It opens with ease, the door coming toward me with more momentum than I intend.

Bending, I rewrap myself in the blanket and step through into the hallway outside.

Looking left and then right, I expect to find a guard by the door, but there's no-one. The house is silent, almost eerily so, and so I pad down the periwinkle blue hall, feet light on the floorboards and with my blanket trailing behind me like a bridal train.

There are many doors made from the same dark wood like the one I've just come through, all adorned with silver handles that are well-made yet far from ostentatious. The hallway is lined by portraits of various mountain scenes, all breathtakingly detailed, and far past where a dark wooden staircase leads to what I assume to be the ground floor of the house, there's an enormous arched window preceded by a cream-padded window seat. It looks like a wonderful place to read, but before I can think any more on that and allow my homesickness to swallow me, I'm captured by the view beyond.

I rush closer to the window with hurried, soundless steps, the source of the chill in the air increasingly obvious as I reach the glass with wide and curious eyes.

Kneeling up on the window seat, I look out beyond the heavily leaded pane to where snow is falling in an endless sheet of arctic white. The world beyond is dark, the sky seemingly endless as the golden moon hangs, smaller than I've ever seen it. The sky is peppered with dense grey clouds gilded dull by the weak gibbous orb, but in places, there are patches of emptiness that seem endless and speckled only with cold distant stars and the first touches of daylight.

Mountainous silhouettes climb, barely visible against the darkness of the early dawn, and I shudder unwillingly as the ferociously ominous landscape causes a slow drip of fear to fall into the depths of my stomach, the ripple it causes multiplying my anxiety.

Where am I?

And more importantly, *how will I ever get home?*

Turning my back on the window as tears threaten to overwhelm me, I take to the staircase, padding down every single step with absolute care so as not to emit a single sound.

At the bottom of the staircase, I allow my eyes to drift beyond the wooden ball that brings the bannister to an end and toward the front door.

I wonder if it's locked.

Then again, with the look of the snow falling outside, it doesn't matter anyway. There's no way I'm going out there with a broken arm and dressed in nothing but some strange man's pyjamas.

I pad back up the hall, turning reluctantly from what might have been an escape under different circumstances. As I ponder my fear, I begin to wonder why I had let Lord DeLaurent bring me here in the first place. I know I wouldn't have been any safer within the Solis Castra, but at least I knew the place a little better than wherever I am now.

I had Dawn and maybe Vail I could have turned to.

Here, I have no one.

As I'm thinking this, my frantic gaze comes to rest on a pair of high double doors at the end of the hall, one of them cracked open. The entrance is grander than any I've come across on the upper floor, so I wonder if what's inside might be important.

Looking over one shoulder and finding myself to be alone even still, I scurry forward, finding what I don't expect waiting for me.

The room is an enormous personal library. Warm chocolate leather armchairs are situated facing the centre of the room, fireplaces spilling warmth from the left and right walls, surrounded by floor-to-ceiling shelves.

Leather volumes are packed into every nook and cranny, the scent of it taking my breath away.

Maybe then, Lord DeLaurent and I aren't so different after all.

Feeling furtive, I pull the blanket closer around my shoulders, finding the snow even more intimidating through the enormous window opposite as it rises in a slope, leaning oppressively against the lowest pane. Then, descending two shallow wooden stairs, I step onto the middle of the room, where the floor is deepest. I'm expecting the wood underfoot to be colder with it closer to the ground, but it's surprisingly warm instead.

I find a cup of tea abandoned on a mahogany table beside the armchair closest to the window, a copy of *Draconian Sword Making – A History* put aside upon the cushion of the comfy-looking seat.

I guess Lord DeLaurent and I don't have so much in common after all.

While I'm a fan of fantasy, romance, and thrillers, he prefers more technical instruction on how to go about beheading his enemies.

Figures.

I'm staring at the thick leather cover that's embossed in silver when the clearing of a throat startles me.

I let the blanket fall from around my shoulders yet again, jumping and causing my wrist to throb as a figure peeks around the door.

"Oh, you're awake."

The man to whom the voice belongs isn't someone I know or even recognise. He's a total stranger, yet this doesn't stop me staring at his navy reptilian wings with wide eyes.

"I'm sorry— I just—" I stutter, heart racing and mouth going dry as fear threatens to overwhelm me. The man's dark eyes soften at my obvious discomfort, his broad cheekbones protruding as a small smile curves his thick lips.

"It's alright. Kairi, is it?" he asks, taking a step forward and cocking his head. I tense, wanting to step back but having nowhere to go as the armchair meets with the back of my knees.

"Y— Yes. That's me. Who are you?" I ask him, chewing feverishly on the inside of my cheek and acutely aware of the way my legs are beginning to ache beneath me.

"I'm Kaiden. Lucien had to attend to some pressing business. But he'll be back soon and then I'm sure he can answer all your questions." He takes another step forward, his foot causing one of the floorboards to squeak beneath his broad gait. I relax a little, noticing his eyes sparkling as they catch the flames from the fireplace on the left-hand wall. "It's alright. I won't hurt you," he promises, holding out a hand to me and letting it hang in the wide divide between us.

I take slow steps toward him like a nervous foal, feeling his hand claiming mine in a warm vice and pulling me behind him. Together, we exit the library.

209

"I'm sorry. It's not you. I'm a little jaded when it comes to trusting winged strangers lately—" I admit, and he chuckles.

"Lucien did mention you'd been through rather an ordeal. You're lucky he found you when he did. We all are—" he says thoughtfully as we walk together through a corridor, which cuts behind the staircase and into an enormous kitchen with wooden cabinets and granite countertops.

"Lucien— that's Lord DeLaurent?" I ask.

He nods, rolling his eyes and running his fingers back through his dark, wild curls.

"Well, that figures. Of course, he wouldn't give the girl he was rescuing his first name—I mean, why would he— not like he needed your trust or anything," he chuckles, the sound dry and patronising.

"I'm sure it just slipped his mind," I reply, my voice a listless wisp, but inside, I feel oddly defensive of the man who had saved me.

This fact terrifies me, and so I distract myself by letting the fingers of my broken arm caress the cool silver granite of the kitchen's sweeping central island.

Kaiden strides over to the fridge, an enormous wooden box that's stood silently in the corner.

I don't suppose they're short on ice. I muse, eyes surveying surrounding frosty panes of thick glass set into the walls. The glass is divided by dark lines in simple but striking patterns in what appears to be lead.

"Breakfast?" he inquires, opening the bottom door of the icebox and looking back over his shoulder at me.

"I don't know. Are you going to poison me?" I ask, unable to so much as crack a smile.

"Not my style. I'm more of a 'rip your throat out' type of killer—" he explains, smile spreading wide and wicked across his face. His dark eyes glint but still hold only shadow.

I must look startled because he cocks his head, rolling his eyes.

"Wow, Lord Black really messed you up, huh?" he probes, placing his hands into the pockets of his pants half-heartedly and letting his wings shake out behind him with casual abandon. He has left the door to the fridge wide open, and I feel the draft from inside tickle my face.

"What gave it away?" I look down at the sling, and Kaiden nods slowly with sad understanding, biting his bottom lip.

"I tell you what— I'll make you breakfast *and* promise not to poison you on one condition—" he leaves the sentence open-ended; I cock one eyebrow.

"And what's that?" I demand, leaning forward and wincing at my forgotten injury as my wrist contacts the cool granite with too much force.

"Well, you tell me about the mortal world, of course— I've got some seriously important questions. Like about baseball—" He grins, and I laugh, the breath I've been holding rushing out of me like air trapped in a balloon close to bursting.

"Deal," I reply, relief flooding my gut in a comforting wave-like warm milk.

The winged man turns back to the icebox and begins getting the ingredients together to make me breakfast, the bustle of his motion calming as I gaze at him.

However, despite the domesticated setting, I cannot help but fixate on the dangerously sharp talons that tip each of his wings.

As I carry on watching them, they glint ferocious shades in the oddly pink horizon of the early dawn that invades from beyond thick frosted windows.

GENEVIEVE

The magenta of the sky looks like pools of lake water tainted with blood have spilt from the horizon, staining the sky this odd colour as it bursts from behind the silhouettes of two rising mountain peaks. Being that we have a blue sun, you'd think the sky would boast cold shades at every hour, but that simply isn't true.

Just goes to show you that appearances can be deceiving and that assumptions are for the idiotic.

The glen's deepest glade, where I first found Algoric all those many years ago, has become a sanctuary to me over the years, and as I haven't been able to do much but incessantly worry about what kind of mess Lucien is getting himself into, I've retreated here for a little private training among the peace of the dawn.

The thick cluster of alabaster pine leaves the air that blooms with the fog of my hot breath hitting the early morning chill, pungent and pure.

My nostrils flare at the intense Aetherial sting of it.

On my left, the thick snow that layers the ground tumbles into a gentle slope, caressing the side of the river with a fluffy shawl of light powder, and then dissipates, making way for the flawless sheet of ice that blankets the frozen water. The ice cuts through the land from where I'm standing, creeping like cold claws to the opposite side of the deep valley where Lucien's little wooden house stands on the edge of the resulting lake.

He loves the solitude of that place, the way it stands defiantly on the edge of our world, but all I can see is a vulnerable wooden box with no defences and the utter naivety of the man who built it.

I love Lucien, but he is a dreamer. A dreamer with an uncontrollable temper that comes to the surface every time he realises that he cannot make the world what he wants it to be through sheer willpower alone.

The way things should be is so obvious to him, he simply doesn't understand why others don't share his vision.

My grip tightens on the sword in my palms as I realise that I'm letting my rage toward his sheer ignorance warm my hands to dangerous temperatures beneath my white leather gloves. I grit my teeth, taking a long deep breath and steadying myself as I push back the alabaster fur hood of my thick velvet cloak.

It's embroidered red along the edges and dripping with rubies like droplets of blood left over from the animal who gave its life so it might be made. I'm wearing white leather pants and a corset of the same hue atop a matching velvet tunic. The fierce look is completed by knee-high boots, porcelain in shade, and a pristine marble and steel dagger holstered at my hip. The handle of the sword in my gloved hands drips with rubies to match my cloak, and I'm momentarily transfixed as they glimmer coldly in the stark chill air.

A rustle in the leaves behind me causes my senses to prick, heightening in the way a predators surely would at the merest inkling of being surrounded by some unseen enemy.

The shuffle of feet touching down softly amongst the thick arctic pine needles scattered amongst the snowfall from the surrounding trees is unmistakable, and so before I turn, I raise my sword from where the end of its long blade is buried in snow, preparing to defend myself.

Spinning on the spot, I bare my teeth, lifting my sword, ready to strike the moron who is stupid enough to sneak up on High Lady Genevieve Thomas.

I see his face as I stiffen my posture to deliver the blow, his hand stretched out and ready.

He catches the blade in his hand, a cocky no-good smile, spoiling his otherwise pleasant features.

"With friends like these, who needs enemies?" Lucien smirks, his hand gripping the blade of the sword in a flat palm without so much as flinching.

When he releases the blade's weight back into my power, I see he's left a thin veil of frost behind, blunting my cutting edge.

"Oh good, you're alive." I snort, turning from him and readying to begin my drills again.

"Don't act like you're not happy to see me. You only come here when you can't sleep," Lucien reminds me that he knows me far too well, more than I'd like in fact.

The soft weight of his palm falls on my shoulder, causing me to glare back at him as the scarlet roots of my white hair become peppered by the starting flurries of another ebbing snowfall, each flake sizzling out of existence against my scalp.

"So, what happened? Did you have a nice time eating potpourri with our mortal enemies?" I spit at him, unable to control the obvious vehemence in my tone.

"Actually, they weren't even expecting anyone to respond to the invitation, though, as you mention it, the food *was* rather good." Lucien's eyes are teasing, trying to break past the walls of solid molten rock I keep erected against the hurt of the outside world.

"Well, I'm glad you had a lovely evening, stuffing your face." I cross my arms over my chest, the sword still heavy in my palm as it hangs cold against my thigh.

"It wasn't a lovely evening at all—I—" He looks suddenly guilty, the sharp planes of his face softening as if readying to try and implore my understanding.

"Oh, so the Sephilim turned on you? Tried to hack off your wings and mount your head on an ornate golden spike? Well— that is a shame. If only someone had warned you such a thing might happen— Oh, wait! I did." I bite, and he shakes his head, the long blonde locks that cut through the cold early morning air flawlessly kept even as he stands there, obviously dishevelled in every other regard.

I swear, if I had that man's hair, all I'd do all day is brush it.

"Not exactly— I—" he begins again, and I glare at him.

"I don't want to hear it. Whatever you did is your problem now. I warned you and you chose to ignore my advice. You fix your own blood feuds." I put a palm on his chest as he goes to move in closer, taking a noted step backwards and shaking my head. Rage is threatening to drown out my senses, to engulf me, but I cannot let it, and so I cannot let him get any closer.

The urge to burn him, to remind him of his own stupidity with a brand of my making is overwhelming, to say the least.

Turning on the ball of my foot, I let my wings spread through the slits of heavy velvet as I pull my cloak closer around me, readying to take flight.

I'm done with this conversation.

"That's the thing though— It might not be just my problem— I—" I hear his fear so snap back around, my cloak whirling in a typhoon of cold pallor as I narrow my eyes, focusing on his face.

"What. Did. You. Do?" I ask him, each word succeeded by a step, my sword raising to point directly into the centre of his chest.

"The mortal girl, Lord Black, he tried to poison her. I stood up and stopped her from drinking the wine just in time. Then, she fled— when I found her locked in that tower— he was going to kill her, or worse. Genevieve, I didn't have a choice—" His words are half babble, half relieved confession.

I bite down hard on my bottom lip, nostrils flaring as the heat in my core creeps slower and slower toward the surface of my skin.

"You didn't have a choice? A choice in what?" I ask him, lashes trembling as they catch snowflakes and dispel the resulting cold slurry down my face. It would look like tears if my cheeks weren't scalding, so instead, I produce only small wisps of steam.

"I had to save her, Genevieve. I couldn't leave her there to die," Lucien confesses as I push the sword into the fine silver fabric of his wrinkled formalwear. He doesn't stop me, stiffening against the blade as I exert pressure on the tip between his pectorals.

"Where is she?" I growl, feeling my muscles tense, winding up to release like a murderous jack in the box. The wind whips around us both, our eyes remaining locked through the thickening sheets of falling snow.

"She's at Lakeside," he says plainly, slumping as the words leave his lips like they've been weighing, glacier cold and heavy, inside him.

"You brought her here!" I exclaim, shoving the sword forward and watching him fall backwards into the snow. I stand over him, looking down into his expression as his gaze steels over, like his very soul has been flash-frozen.

"Yes, we need to protect her, Genevieve. They want to use her to—" he begins, but I've heard enough.

"I don't care if they want to string her up and use her limbs to decorate the Christmas tree. She's not our problem! How dare you put our people at risk this way! And for what? A mortal girl?! I thought I'd taught you better than this—" I feel the shock of the revelation coming through in my tone in a way I wish I could hide but am too slighted to. "You send her home, Lucien. Send her home and never speak to me of this again. I will not go to war with the Sephilim again. Not for you, and certainly not for a mortal!" I exclaim, spinning from him and letting the sword in my fist drop into the snow, the handle melted and bubbling in a twisted mess of superheated metal and cold, unchanged rubies.

"But she can't go home—" Lucien tries to explain, struggling to inch away from the molten pile which lands only inches from his feet.

"And I care? Get rid of her, Lucien. I won't ask you again." I give this final command in a feral growl, spreading my wings wide and remaining with my back toward him.

"Genevieve, wait!" he exclaims, and I hear him scrambling amongst the snow to get to his feet.

It's too late though, because by the time he's upright, my sword still smouldering at his side, I've taken off at a sprint.

Cape billowing behind me in heavy fur-lined folds, I launch myself onto the crust of ice that the once ravenous river has become, each footstep causing the substance to split deep from the heat radiating through the soles of my boots, threatening to melt the rubber.

I spread my wings as a rumble sounds underfoot, the ice fissuring downward and readying to crack wide open.

Just as the surface gives way to the heat of my fury, I'm at velocity and lifting into the air as the cold breeze catches beneath the leathery sinew of my wings.

I don't look back; I don't even think on the potential consequences of Lucien's ridiculous supposed heroism.

I can't.

For the thought of another war is simply too much to bear.

16

THE GIRL WITH THE DRAGON TATTOO

KAIRI

THE SPOON CLATTERS AGAINST the edge of the bowl, laughter filling the kitchen around us as I lick the last of breakfast from my bottom lip.

Kaiden is asking me about the mortal world, and honestly, seeing it through his eyes, the way he explains it makes me realise that I've had it easy. He comes from the mid-twentieth century with no cell phones, no home delivery for groceries or internet, only radios and black and white television, and that is only a hundred years ago. I can't imagine that it gets any easier if you go back further than that.

He informed me, as he made thick grain into a milky oatmeal-type concoction before dishing up and adding a flourish of winter berries upon the top of each portion, that he was killed trying to stop a robbery in his neighbourhood convenience store back in Chicago.

"So, you just got between the gunman and the cashier?" I ask, eyes wide as he nods.

"Of course. It was wrong, what he was doing," he expresses without question or second thought.

"Did it— you know, hurt?" I query him, flushing at my forwardness.

Kaiden makes me comfortable even though I can't stop sneaking glimpses at the wings slipping through the tailored slits in the back of his white shirt. His sleeves are rolled up as he runs his hand through the thick curls of his hair, eyeing me with interest.

He opens his mouth to answer, but a sound at the front door distracts us both, causing our eyes to dart in the direction of the hallway. The stained-glass mural of an icy blue dragon in the door's oblong leaded pane has been letting the light of early morning into the hallway, causing it to puddle in a cacophony of chill rainbow hues upon the floor. Now though, a wide shadow interrupts the light fall.

A key turns in the lock, and in he steps from the cold, shaking his black wings out and letting excess snowfall drip from the twin peaks of his talons.

"Good morning." He nods courteously at us both, and I find Kaiden on his feet beside me.

He had moved so silently from where he was sitting that I didn't even notice.

He nods his head, averting the Draconian High Lord's eyes as he says, "Good morning, my Lord," making me wonder if I should be standing and curtseying as well.

Lord DeLaurent, or Lucien as Kaiden calls him, certainly seemed hung up on etiquette when he introduced himself last night.

Was that only last night?

The conversation between Kaiden and me had taken me back to my home, however momentarily, and allowed me to become lost in nostalgia as I told him all about the state of modern baseball. Now, in the wake of seeming normality, I'm left with only a strong homesickness that churns the thick oatmeal around in my guts, the taste of sweet winter berries growing tart and acidic on my tongue.

"Good morning, Kaiden. I have a list of tasks for you, the first being acquiring the services of my seamstress. Are you fit?" he demands without looking up, unbuttoning his jacket.

Kaiden nods eagerly, looking over at me briefly and smiling.

"Oh good, your pyjamas are so very last season, Lucien." He winks at me, and Lucien rolls his eyes, producing a scroll from the inside of his rumpled jacket, the very same one he had been wearing when we had first locked eyes in The Solis Castra.

Kaiden rounds the edge of the kitchen, taking the parchment in his hand and then making his way towards the stairs.

"I'll just fetch my cloak. Nice meeting you Kairi!" He gives me a small nonchalant wave as he disappears behind Lucien, leaving only the sound of his footsteps climbing the staircase echoing in the hall behind him.

I hop from the stool, wincing at the pain in my wrist from the sudden motion.

"Oh, don't stand for me. I'm not your High Lord, and you can call me Lucien." He waves a hand as if to physically dismiss the formality, his voice gruff as he removes his damp jacket and loosens the dishevelled cravat from around his throat, flinging it down on the stool opposite me.

"Is there coffee?" he asks, eyes sweeping across the countertops as he undoes the top button of his shirt. From beneath the once-crisp collar, a myriad of tattoos peek from atop obvious and well-defined muscles.

I shrug.

"It's your kitchen, Lucien." I test his name on my tongue, but he doesn't wait to hear it, setting about searching the high cupboards for supplies. His shoulders are stiff within the wrinkled cotton of his shirt, his wings pulled in awkwardly so he doesn't swipe me. The span of them is larger than Kaiden's by far.

"Where have you been?" I ask, my voice trembling. He makes me nervous simply by being in the same space, his immense height and width intimidating in every regard.

"Well, after I tended to your wound and tucked you in, I went to seek High Lady Thomas' council about our little predicament," he explains, taking out a small woven sack of coffee beans and opening the top. I don't need to see the contents to know the scent as it wafts, overpowering me.

It's the strongest coffee I've ever smelled, and I can't help but inhale deeply, a craving undeniably ignited.

"Would you like a cup?" he offers, and I cock my head, looking around for his coffee maker.

I don't find one.

"Um, yes. Please," I reply, tentative yet intrigued.

Taking a soft-looking cloth from the drawer at his knees, he wraps a handful of beans inside and then holds the small fabric bundle between his fists, pushing hard.

I cock an eyebrow, confused as he grinds the beans by hand with little effort.

"Don't you have a coffee grinder?" I query, my lips quirking as I watch his knuckles turn white. The sound of crumbling coffee beans fills the air between us followed by the scent of it intensified.

"A what?" he asks me, frowning.

"Never mind." I shrug, watching as he takes a copper saucepan down from the hanging rail overhead. He adds the coffee to it, then cold water, followed by a pinch of salt from a nearby jar made of copper that looks as if it's been hammered into shape by hand and labelled in cursive scrawl.

Placing the pan over the stove, he lights the gas and turns to look at me.

"How is your wrist?" he demands, face unreadable.

As I'm about to answer, Kaiden comes flying down the stairs, fully dressed in a thick black cloak and heavy winter boots. I turn to address him, watching him give a passing wave before he sweeps across the threshold and out into the cold without a single word.

"Sore— but not as bad as I thought it would be. I thought I'd broken it." I express, flexing my fingers and feeling them twinge with agony. Still, I've felt worse from dislocations, so there's no way it could be broken.

"It is broken, but I've set it and applied some natural pain-relieving ointment. The sun here is weaker than in Soleus, but even as a mortal, you should heal quicker than usual," he comments, turning and stirring the pan with a copper spoon from the pot of utensils beside the stovetop.

"Are you a doctor?" I query, wondering how he knew what to do.

"I am not. I was a military medic back in France in the 19th century. I'm no surgeon, but I know what to do in a pinch," he shrugs it off like it's nothing, and I wonder what it must be like having lived so long.

Then I remember, I had wondered that same thing about Aro.

Back when I thought he was kind and sweet.

I feel my chest tighten, suddenly impatient as I slump back onto the stool.

I want to go home.

"What did Lady Thomas say? I want to go home, but Aro threatened my family. What should I do?" I ask him, feeling vulnerable as I hear the coffee mixture come to a boil behind him. I know how I sound, how pathetic, how afraid, but I can't make myself sound any braver or any less rattled by the insane circumstances I seem to have landed myself in.

Lucien stands, ankles crossed, resting on the lower quadrants of his wings against the countertop, assessing my face with an irritating stoicism I can't read while I'm left to blush under his scrutiny.

"As far as she's concerned, you aren't our problem. You got yourself into this mess, so we are under no obligation to get you out of it—" he looks aggravated, I assume at me.

Like I could have possibly known what was happening when I agreed to come here?

"Well, I think that's rich. If it weren't for you Draconians and your murderous streak, Storm would still be alive, and Aro wouldn't be trying to kill me so I could make him King or whatever!" I exclaim, standing again.

"So that's why he wanted to make you a Kindred so desperately— he really does believe you're the next Heirbound—"

His eyes widen as I ball my uninjured fist at my side.

"Apparently, I have the mark," I retort, showing him the inside of my left wrist beneath the bandages. He nods, brushing the bottom of his jawline with his index finger, thoughtful. I wonder if he had noticed it before when he was dressing the injury.

"I see. Well, I don't know what Lord Black has been telling you, but I can assure you that whatever it is isn't true. I don't even know anyone called Storm, let alone have I murdered anyone with that name. And believe me, I remember the names and faces of every single person I've killed," he insists, turning off the gas with a flick of his wrist. His eyes are cold, his face stony as the ghosts of his victims dance behind the dark pools of his irises.

I frown, confused and simultaneously intimidated by the enormous man in front of me.

"Aro told me to run if I was ever alone with one of you," I confess, narrowing my eyes, and he laughs, the sound dry and broken with unspoken bitterness.

"The door is wide open, Princess. You might want to wait for some shoes though— I'd think with a broken wrist you'd want to preserve your remaining limbs from frostbite. Especially if you're around a vicious killer such as myself." The sound of boiling water dies down as the heat dissipates from the pan. Lucien gives the contents a sideways appraisal before moving past me. "Not that you could outrun me. I'd be off the ground and swooping in like a bird of prey before you could even make the treeline," he threatens, glowering.

I flinch as he comes closer, eyes burning angry, still skittish and aching from last night.

The scent of coffee is rich in the air between us as I grit my teeth and set my jaw firm, raising my head to him and trying to show him I'm not afraid.

It's a lie, but one I need to maintain if I hope to get out of this alive.

221

"Move, I need to get coffee mugs," he explains in a blunt grumble, reaching past me for the cupboard set into the island where I've just eaten my breakfast.

He pulls out two white coffee mugs, letting the door close with an annoyed bang as he returns to the stove to set them down, reinstating the wide space between us.

"Look, I don't want to be here either. I just want to go home. If I weren't so afraid that I'd end up captured or worse, I'd be demanding you conduct me there right now," I explain, brushing a lock of caramel hair behind one of my ears with a determined stare that's far braver than I feel. The hair between my fingers is silken soft, and I wonder how it had come to be so as I gaze at Lucien's flawless white mane of poker-straight tresses.

Did *he* brush my hair?

"You don't know anything, do you? Draconians can't conduct. Only Sephilim and Nephilim can do that. They're the only Kindred in Aetheria who can physically move between dimensions." He turns from me and uses the large copper spoon to separate the coffee grounds from the brown liquid before pouring equal amounts of steaming coffee into each cup.

He passes a mug to me but I'm too busy staring at him, trying to figure out the ramifications of what it is he's just said, to take it. Placing the mug down on the table beside me and returning to his own, I feel the single exclamation slip from my lips in a wisp of hopelessness.

"*No.*"

"I'm afraid I can't take you home. Besides, even if you could go home, you'd be too vulnerable. Aro knows where you live, I mean, that's how he found you, right?" he asks and I nod, blinking slowly. "If he believes you hold the key to the Aetherial crown, which I think it's obvious from last night that he does, you're in more danger than you know."

Lucien sips his coffee and adopts a casual pose once more, like what he's saying is nothing more than a report on the state of the weather.

"So—what do I do?" I'm almost pleading, tears threatening to build behind the glassy surfaces of my eyes. I swallow them down, not wanting to appear weak or stupid to the immortal before me, turning my attention instead to the mug that's steaming at my side.

I take it in two shaking hands, blowing on the contents before taking a small sip.

Even through the heat, I can tell there's something magical about this coffee, something you won't find in any neighbourhood Starbucks.

My lashes flutter against my cheeks as I inhale the aroma deeply, steeling myself and swallowing down my fear as I look at Lucien.

"Well?" I give him a more determined look, and he sighs, fingers running back through the snowy perfection of his hair.

"Look, I can't promise anything, but I am going to try to get Genevieve, I mean High Lady Thomas, to grant you sanctuary here for a while. It's by no means a permanent solution, but sending you home would be a death sentence."

"You want me to stay here?" I conclude, incredulous as I realise that there is no easy way back to Tennessee or to the girl I was before last night. My naivety has been fractured, my ability to trust shattered, leaving behind only dark empty voids where before there was hope.

"No. But I don't want you to die either." He takes a long gulp of his coffee, and I watch the perfect curve of his Adam's apple bob beneath the arctic sheet of his skin, his eyes resting relentlessly on my face.

"Well, gee. Thanks." I roll my eyes, feeling the tears rising again and threatening to spill down my cheeks. I bury my pain in another mouthful of coffee, letting out a deep exhale.

"What can I say? I'm a real hero." He shrugs, fingers tapping against the coarse china of his mug.

"I can tell," I reply, boredom falling across my face.

It's not pretty, but at least it's not crying.

Suddenly, something occurs to me.

"How are we going to get High Lady Thomas to grant me sanctuary? I thought you said she didn't want to help me?" I recall, and he shifts uncomfortably on his feet.

"Ah, well that's why we're going to grace her with a little visit. I think she might have a change of heart once we explain to her about Lord Black's ulterior motive with regard to the throne," he reveals, finishing the coffee in his cup in one final swig.

I let my lips pucker, anxiety creeping through the darkened spaces of the unknown.

"I see. Well, is there anything I should know about her before this meeting? Should I be concerned for my safety?" I ask, heart beginning to pick up pace in my chest.

"I'd be remiss in my duties as your official hero if I lied to you at this point." Lucien moves to the sink to wash the dregs from the bottom of his mug, the early morning sunlight casting his wings slightly translucent and highlighting every violet vein within.

"Well, what would you say to me if you *were* lying?" I ask him, forehead scrunching up in concern.

"I'd tell you that you're about to meet the High Lady of Rainbows who devours the wishes of the virtuous and shits sparkles." Lucien doesn't pause in his reply or break a smile as he walks right past me and out of the kitchen.

Unable to keep a straight face, I spit coffee down my chin.

I'm sweating profusely, standing atop a small wooden box as the seamstress, a beautiful blonde woman named Aska, finishes adjusting the pre-made garments to my height. She's not overly chatty, merely frowning at the hem with a mouth full of carefully placed pins and a single French braid falling heavily over one shoulder while her icy blue wings help her balance.

The garments are beautiful, a simple baby blue gown beneath a complementary lilac cloak, both made from heavy wool. They're embroidered intricately with bluebells and snowdrops along the edges of the sleeves and neckline, the thin thread that's been used shimmering wildly silver in the clear daylight that falls through the window of the room in which I'd woken.

Finally, as I pull the high collar from around my throat with a slight glare at the still roaring fireplace across the room, Aska removes the final pin and gives a single nod, rising from where she's tucked her jade skirts beneath her knees to work upon the hardwood floor.

Removing the pins from her soft mouth and sticking them back into the pincushion tied to her wrist, she appraises me critically.

"There," is all she says, pale lips pressed together in reluctant approval as she offers me a hand.

I step down off the wooden crate, and she turns toward the heavy bag and empty garment covers she brought with her, rummaging for a few seconds before procuring several items.

She spins back to me, all business as she barely misses clipping me with the edge of her wing, handing me a pair of white, fur-lined gloves with a pair of matching earmuffs.

"Here, Lord DeLaurent also insisted you remain warm." She eyes me with a wary gaze now, her stare darting from my face and down to the broken arm that's nestled within the confines of the soft lilac cloak hanging from my shoulders. "You might also consider putting

224

your hood up while outside. I doubt you'd want anyone recognising you as mortal," she suggests hotly, making me wonder what on earth I've done to upset her.

"I will, thank you." I nod, grateful for her help, and watch as she sweeps her belongings into her arms and strides from the room as if she's fleeing some kind of monster.

She doesn't respond to my thanks, leaving the door hanging wide open.

I find Lucien standing just beyond the doorframe, wings draped over either side of his spine, leaning over the thick wood balustrade and staring after Aska as she descends the stairs.

He's changed since earlier and is now wearing all black in the form of a high-necked sweater and fitted slacks. His hair is almost blinding in contrast as it falls down his back in pristine white ribbons.

"Sorry about that," he apologises, taking several steps toward the doorway after the sound of the front door being slammed has long faded into silence.

"Did I do something?" I ask, sitting on the edge of the mattress, facing him. Putting the gloves and earmuffs Aska had given me atop the comforter, I lean down and start trying to unlace the footwear she'd left by the side of the bed. As I struggle with my broken hand, Lucien steps forward through the doorway without thought, dropping to his knees and helping me to unlace each shoe with quick fingers. They're supple cream leather, fur-lined, and feel sturdy as they come, my toes immediately warm to match the rest of me as he slips the first one over my foot.

"Nothing. She's just mad because she thinks I'm setting her against High Lady Thomas by asking her to help me. I don't think she quite understands that even Genevieve would not want you to be wandering around Drakos Vale naked." He smirks up at me.

"She couldn't refuse you?" I query, slipping on my other boot and watching him lace it tightly.

"Actually, no. I'm a High Lord, and she's beneath me on the social ladder. Also, with the amount of coin I offered her, she'd be a fool to say no," he informs me as I pucker my lips, feeling suddenly guilty.

"I'll pay you back, I promise. I just— I don't have any money with me, obviously—" I flush, feeling vulnerable at being indebted to a stranger.

225

"I don't want your money, Kairi." His reply surprises me as I slip on one of my mittens, keeping the other, for my injured hand, stored in the deep pockets of the cloak.

Placing the earmuffs over my ears, I stand, ready to leave.

Lucien, taking the hint, rises from his knees. Then, he is descending the stairs before I can even blink, his black boots heavy on each step under the immense weight of his warrior's physique.

I follow him, closing the door behind me and making my way across the landing. As I descend the stairs after him, I watch, waiting for him to put on a coat or cloak.

When he doesn't, I scowl.

"You're going to catch your death like that," I comment, and he sighs.

"I'm sure I'll survive, being immortal and all." The bluntness of his tone, the succeeding sigh, and his stoic expression make me blush, feeling stupid.

"Right," I mumble as he places a hand on the handle of the front door.

"Come, Kaiden should have prepared the sleigh before he departed," he commands, reminding me of Aro. The way he expects everyone around him to simply bend to his wishes, to obey without question. I suppose, having seen the way Aska was forced to, I shouldn't be surprised.

Then, as I swallow and step forward to make my displeasure known, I look up at him, eyes widening as I realise what he's just said.

"Wait— did you say sleigh?" I ask, excitement clutching at me despite the fact terror is making itself equally known by rooting itself deep among my ribs, a thick cluster of knotted vines.

If Aska was afraid of Genevieve's wrath and she's immortal, I guess I have every right to feel downright terrified.

"Yes, why? Were you planning on flying with wings I don't know about?" He snorts at his own joke and I scowl.

"I've just never been on a sleigh before, that's all," I retort, my cheeks hot as I pull my hood over my face, hiding my embarrassment.

Lucien's humour seems less and less funny the more it comes at my expense. It's increasingly obvious he thinks I'm a complete idiot.

I step past him without another word as he pulls the door open, a crisp chill rushing me and cooling the raging heat beneath my cheeks. My boots are heavy upon the porch as I stride out, the sounds of them too loud as I'm engulfed by the cold silence of the outside world at last.

The scent of pine, cedar, maple, and wintergreen hits me full force as I descend the two porch stairs and step out onto the snow-laden path, the entire world covered in a flawless blanket of glistening white. The only footsteps are a single pair that begin and promptly end just before the porch where Lucien had landed earlier, and even though they've been lightly covered, it's not enough to disguise his hefty tread.

I gaze across the landscape on my left, to where the world seems to end.

Here, an enormous frozen lake sprawls toward the periwinkle horizon, reflecting the small cerulean sun in its pristine frozen facet. To the right, the landscape grows teeth, the earth bursting upwards in shard-like mountains that are covered in snowy trees that cluster together to create thick and secure coverage for whatever lives beneath.

"Come on, we don't have much time before nightfall, and you don't want to be caught out here when the temperature drops. Days are annoyingly short here, by the way," he adds.

The High Lord strides past me without another word, snow kicking up in little flurries in his wake. I follow clumsily in his deep tracks, swallowing my awe at the breathtaking mountains and dreamy frozen lake, focusing instead on his silhouette, starkest black against the purity of the snow. I see his wings shudder a little in the cold and wonder what they must feel like to carry around all the time.

Are they heavy?

My question floats still in the waters of my curious mind, the surface of its endless depths freezing over as my eyes fix on the sleigh he had mentioned before and, more importantly, the majestically arctic white dogs that are harnessed to the front.

Well, I say dogs. But that implies some kind of Border Collie or Golden Retriever.

"Wow, what are those?" I ask, knowing they aren't anything from the mortal world. They could be mistaken for wolves if they didn't come up to Lucien's shoulder in height. Their thick white coats are glistening, each hair trapping the snow like tiny diamonds. I stare in awe at the five of them, their paws bigger than my head as they dig in the snow and sniff the air with eagerness. The animal leading the pack has deep silver eyes, and it doesn't take long before I realise they're trained on me.

The hulking dog growls, pacing from one plate-sized paw to the other and fogging the air with his breath, incisors dripping thick with saliva.

"Hush, Ecto!" Lucien barks, and the animal immediately drops its gaze with a puppyish whine.

"They're spectral mountain dogs. Come, let me give you a hand." He offers me a palm gloved in soft black leather and a chill runs up my arm as I take it despite the fact neither of us is offering bare skin. He helps me navigate the thick snow so I'm standing by the side of the sleigh, which I can see is made from dark, rich wood just like the house and filled with a bench padded by equally thick furs.

Without warning, as I'm still staring at the ornate carvings of cave bears on the sleigh's body, he puts both hands beneath my cloak, causing me to stiffen. He doesn't seem to notice as he lifts me off my feet, placing me down so I'm sitting on the bench of the sleigh.

My arm twinges at his sudden interference with my posture.

The step was high, but I could have made it, so why does he feel the need to manhandle me?

I must look so weak to him, so pathetic.

The stupid mortal with her broken arm and crazy fantasies that got her into a world full of trouble.

I shiver as the cold penetrates my bones despite the thick wool of my dress, wrapping my cloak tighter around my shoulders as Lucien steps up into the sleigh with graceful ease.

"Move over," he grumbles, grabbing the black leather reins from where they're draped over the front of the vehicle.

Sliding across the bench, I flush as we both try to get comfortable, his wings making this more difficult than it should be.

It makes me wonder if he usually has passengers.

He's gruff as we set off, clearly angry that he had to go to the trouble of rescuing me at all, and it makes me wonder why he bothered in the first place.

He barks commands at the five spectral mountain dogs who don't doubt his authority, their fluffy white behinds rising fast at the merest whisper from his lips. Soon, their powerful legs are pulling us into motion, and I can't help but look back to where the house I'd woken up in disappears into the distance, fear causing me to grit my teeth against the growing cold as we rush through the chill air.

The sleigh is faster than I expect, and I watch Lucien as he pulls on the reigns, barking orders and driving the animals as hard as they'll go.

He seems so angry like this, his eyes cold and pale skin glacial with sharp lines.

Despite myself, it makes me wonder if Aro was right.

What if he really did kill Storm?

And if he didn't, why would Aro lie?

Then again, he knows I think of him as a killer, so why would he bother lying either?

The problem is, I may have these thoughts, but my current predicament means I have no choice but to abide by his rules and follow the flow of the cold current into which I've been suddenly dunked.

I had chosen to come here, but now my choices are severely limited and defined by his willingness to help.

I guess, no matter what Lucien did or didn't do, he saved me when he didn't have to, and for that, I should be grateful. After all, I'd rather be in this plush sleigh being pulled toward a snow-blanketed forest than dead.

Trees rise on either side of the sleigh as we rush along the side of the river, the mountains climbing into a steep and glorious valley. As we race through the snow, the only sounds the heavy breaths of spectral mountain dogs and the harsh slam of their paws into the snow, I realise that what I had assumed were snow-covered pines are trees boasting naturally white needles.

I gawp, the flawless arctic white of the foliage magical despite the fact I'm rushing, once more, toward an uncertain fate. I can't work out whether to be blown away by the breathtaking beauty of the landscape or terrified by the vastness of an unknown world.

Either way, all I know is that I've never felt so alone, or so far from home.

I expect to see the silhouette of some grandiose palace rising above the tree line, but as the sleigh slows and Lucien talks the dogs down from their rigidly high speed, I find that we are in a clearing that looks no different than any other. The white pines rustle in the cool breeze, and Lucien lifts me down from the sleigh, turning me toward a rockface that upon arrival had been hidden.

"This is the Astrid Keep?" I ask in a diminished voice, cocking my head at the moonstone columns surrounding a simple set of double wooden doors. They seem to lead into what I can now see is the base of the tallest of all the jagged, snow-stained teeth that soar into the sky.

"It is. The most easily defendable landmark in Aetheria. It's built into the mountain itself," he explains, and I nod, understanding.

I still can't help but wonder though why they need such a defence in the first place. After all, from what I've seen of them, the Draconians are ferocious.

Looking back, I remember how frail-looking the crystal Nest of the Solis Castra had felt, despite the golden-armoured Sephilim guards hovering in the surrounding airspace. Wondering, I look up, trying to determine if there are any guards hidden by the thick cloud overhead.

I don't have time to squint into the sky to try and find them though, as Lucien walks in front of me, leaving the dogs and sleigh behind without a second thought and pressing on quickly.

"Aren't you going to tie them up?" I ask him, gesturing to the now breathless team of Spectral Mountain dogs. He laughs to himself, shaking his head.

"The guards on duty will tend to the sleigh; don't worry about that. Focus on the meeting we're heading into. That should be your only concern right now."

He looks back over his shoulder briefly as I struggle to keep up with his enormous strides and easy pace despite the snow. My boots seem to get buried into the top layer, threatening to trip me up even though I'm far lighter and nimbler than the bulky, winged immortal leading the way.

I watch him pull open one of the wooden doors without knocking as we reach the rockface façade of an entrance and find myself wishing I felt as confident in my body as he looks in his. I did once, when gliding over ice like it was air and leaping into ambitious spinning jumps without a second thought, knowing I would land on my feet. My body, though, has long lost my trust since then.

Stepping across the threshold and kicking snow off my boots, I'm greeted by two guards in black-scaled armour. With their wings, they look like erected dragon statues, and I wonder if when taking to the skies, they could fool those below into believing them to be the living breathing equivalent.

I want to take a moment to examine the protective gear closer just so I can soak in the detail of each piece, but before I can take a step toward the statuesque warriors guarding the hall, Lucien has slammed the door closed behind us and is taking off down a hallway on his left without looking back.

The corridor rises at a steep angle as it cuts through the mountain, the walls covered by opalescent moonstone that sheens dully in weak sunlight falling through stained-glass windows. The panes depict dragons, constellations, and various moon phases with the utmost attention to each gliding line, every part of the image carefully constructed to create an incredibly powerful macrocosm for the viewer. I take it all in, the rush of my steps that struggle to climb the steep incline of each corridor leaving me breathless and with protesting muscles in every part of my body.

It seems that Ehlers Danlos Syndrome is fighting to make itself known, pushing back against that mystical sunlight that, until now, has kept it at bay.

I try not to gasp, feeling weak and pitiful, ashamed of my lack of fitness.

Lucien looks over his shoulder at me as I make it to the top of yet another corridor but can no longer hide my wheezing as the walls transition into a dark blue topaz.

His eyes glimmer with irritation.

"Come here," he grunts with a sigh, and before I can protest, I am in his arms, and he's carrying me forward without breaking his even and rhythmic stride as though I weigh nothing. To him, I suppose I probably do.

I could protest, but I can't deny that I'm exhausted, and we probably haven't even made it halfway to where we need to be. I try not to blush, staying rigid in Lucien's arms as we journey deeper into the Keep, biting down hard on my bottom lip and examining our surroundings to distract myself from the humiliation of having to be carried like an infant.

It's beautiful, just as I had expected, but it's so very different from the Solis Castra, not just in construction or architecture, but it feels—cold.

The sconces aren't lit, and there are no fireplaces to be seen in any of the corridors despite the immense raging chill of the world beyond the many colourfully glazed windows. The walls are bare of art, the floors empty of rugs, and as we continue up endless ramps and inclines, I begin to feel less like I'm in someone's residence and more like I'm walking through the corridors of some kind of melancholy museum.

Shivering in Lucien's arms, I wrap my cloak tighter around my chest with my uninjured hand, and he looks at me with something like pain flashing in the backs of his eyes.

"Sorry, one more minute." The apology surprises me, but before I can answer, I find us in a final corridor that levels off, ending in an enormous set of double doors.

Double doors that I recognise.

My heart stops in my chest as Lucien places me down on both feet, the weight of my cloak pushing down unexpectedly hard on my body, making my exhaustion only more evident.

"Come on." He grabs my hand, pulling me along behind him as I try to remain on the spot, staring only at the doors that loom in front of us.

I pick up my feet as his pull grows persistent, taking a deep breath and allowing him to lead me forward.

My eyes widen, head tilting back as I gaze up at the enormous threshold, unable to believe what I'm seeing.

When we reach them, he lifts his gloved fist, knocking three times upon the wood and then waiting in silence beside me with stiff posture.

"Enter! The voice is determinedly high-pitched and dripping with jagged superiority.

Lucien looks down at me, eyes stern, and whispers, "Let me do the talking."

I nod, grateful but also stunned that he'd think I'd try to lead the conversation in any way, shape, or form.

As if I'd want to be the one saying anything in front of someone who claimed I'm not her problem?

The doors are opened by guards on the other side, both sweeping forward and revealing us to the room.

As the space comes into view fully, my stomach drops through my ass and I feel my mouth fall open.

This is the same room where I'd run from the dragon in my dream, the dream where I'd seen Morpheus for the very first time. Every detail, down to the glistening chandelier overhead and the ceiling-high, stained-glass windows flanking the entrance is identical and just as vivid as I remember.

I gawp, but then remember why I'm here as Lucien grabs my hand and squeezes it firmly in warning.

My gaze flits from the windows on either side of me and lands directly on the throne, which sits behind the enormous hematite symbol etched into a metal disc set into the floor.

She's on her feet, hands balled at her sides, white wings flared wide and teeth bared. Her hair is snowy white, but the red roots make it look like she's suffered a head injury and has forgotten to try to stop the bleeding.

Her eyes are ghostly, lashes black as sin, and her expression warped into a furious feral snarl.

"Lucien— I have to wonder. Did you fall and hit your little fucking head on the ice?" she demands, stepping down from the platform where her throne, carved from what looks like ivory, sits in understated grandeur.

I'm taken back to something Serenity said right before the ball—

"Genevieve herself slaughtered the Nephilim Queen- Pandora. I've heard that she even makes her people call her Queen now."

As I'm recalling this, her hand brushes the outside of her left hip, drawing my gaze to the sword that hangs there.

She catches my stare, and I flush bright red beneath the lilac fur of my hood, terrified as I allow myself to breathe only in shallow wisps.

"Genevieve, stop," Lucien says, his voice less assertive than I've ever heard it.

"What part of *'get rid of her'* evaded your meagre intellect? Did I use too many words for you? Or perhaps I should have made myself definitively clear—" She reaches out for me with a clawed hand, but before she can get close enough to touch even the fur lining my cloak, Lucien has put himself between us with a single swift sidestep.

"You will listen to me. Or I will be forced to leave and never return. Besides, what I have to tell you will interest you— if you do plan on keeping the Aetherial Crown firmly out of the hands of the Sephilim," he threatens her, surprising me. Genevieve doesn't seem as though she particularly cares for him, or his company, so why threaten to leave?

Then again, I know neither of them well.

Perhaps this is some kind of sick foreplay or maybe just the oddest friendship I've ever witnessed.

Perhaps in this world of Unicorns, Angels, swordfights, and magic, power is the only truly coveted resource. Perhaps Lucien's allegiance to Genevieve is precious, or perhaps he's got something over her she'd rather have kept quiet.

Either way, I'm relieved when I glimpse around his broad frame and find her face has relaxed a little, her sharp features softer— if only just.

"Speak!" she barks at me as though I'm a dog, eyes fixing on me with acute disdain as she turns her back on her audience.

"It's like this—" Lucien begins, but Genevieve only looks over her shoulder with disdain for his apparent stupidity.

"I asked the mortal, Lucien—" she purrs, her voice dripping with self-assurance as she brushes her white hair over one shoulder and returns to her throne.

Sitting down in its enormous hold, she crosses her legs, resting her chin in her palm.

"Well, girl, speak!" she exclaims, eyes bored as they hood with heavy yet pale lids.

Lucien steps aside, and I take the smallest pace forward, shaking inside my cloak.

I hate public speaking in the best of circumstances, and I don't exactly have the most forgiving audience.

I blink before raising my terrified gaze to hers, trying not to look away for even a moment once the connection between us has been made.

"My Lady, Lord Black intended to kill me because he believes me to be the next Heirbound." I pull off the mitten on my uninjured hand with the fingers poking out the side of my sling, taking several steps forward and showing her what I had always thought of as nothing more than a unique birthmark by pulling back the bandages on my other wrist. Her eyes fall a moment to my broken limb, lying there not even a minute before flicking back to my face.

"And?" she asks, uncrossing and re-crossing her legs with obvious impatience. Her alabaster wings spread wider, increasing the size of the shadow that cloaks my form as I stare up at her. "You are hardly the first girl to be marked in the name of a higher power." She lets her hand fall forward, exposing a bright red brand on the inside of her left wrist, a dragon coiling around her forearm with gaping wide jaws. "How do we know he has not branded her himself? A little fire on flesh is not so hard to come by after all—"

"I was not branded. I was born with this mark, I swear to you. He wanted to force me to crown him as the next Aetherial King. He threatened my family and said he would torture me for the rest of my immortal life if I didn't do as he asked," I confess, almost pleading.

She tilts her head, throwing her thick white locks back over one shoulder and narrowing her eyes.

I wonder momentarily if she's giving me pity as she looks at the sling around my neck, but instead, she merely says, "He did that to you?"

I nod, feeling the ache of the break I've been trying so hard to ignore.

She sits for a moment, silent, her emerald eyes moving slowly between myself and Lucien with a dull expression, almost like a mask falling over her once feral features. Without the anger, she could be a masterpiece of marble, cold— yet stunning.

"Then it would seem we have a problem. If he went to such trouble over a mere mortal such as yourself, he must believe you hold true worth," she expresses, sighing loudly as if I'm inconveniencing her greatly.

"So, you'll help me?" I ask her, and she laughs.

"I hold no allegiance to you. I owe you nothing. As Lucien well knows—" Her eyes are dangerously unhinged as she examines her long nails. Lucien steps forward, opening his mouth to speak, but before he can get a word out, she's raised one of those pointed nails to silence him.

"However. I *do* have an obligation to my people. And considering that the last Sephilim King demanded our undying allegiance and then in failing to secure it caused a war the likes of Aetheria had never seen, I am swayed to offer you temporary sanctuary if only to keep you away from his poisonous influences. I'm assuming that's why you dragged her here, Lucien? For sanctuary, am I correct?" she asks, twirling a lock of hair around one finger and eyeing us down her nose.

"You are correct." Lucien doesn't look grateful or even hopeful, and I have to give him the credit he's due for keeping his posture and face unreadable. If it was me at the tail end of her stare, I'd be crying and running for the door just as I had done with the dragon in my nightmare.

"You have one week. On the condition that there is no attempt on the Sephilim's behalf to retrieve her by force before then. I won't get in the middle of some blood bath for the sake of preventing the inevitable. Because, girl, I'll be honest with you. If the Sephilim High Lord really wants you, there's very little any of us can do to stop him. You understand that? The Sephilim are immensely powerful and ruthless, and their High Lord has all their might at his disposal."

She stands, folding her arms and taking several gentle steps down from the throne's platform, stepping so close to me I can feel an extraordinary heat radiating from her skin.

I swallow, and her face turns, not feral or cruel, but grave.

"If Lord Black really does believe you're his ticket to becoming King, I suggest you find a way back to the mortal realm, pack up your family, and run."

17

THE LIVING MOUNTAIN

KAIRI

WHILE HEADING BACK TOWARD the double doors of the throne room in a swift exit, I hear Genevieve's voice ring out behind us, chilling my guts.

"Lucien, I'd like a word in private. If you could wait outside?" She glances at me expectantly, still not referring to me by name. Lucien nods, eyes flashing a warning, and so I turn, continuing past the two guards, one stationed on either side of the doorway.

As I exit, they close the doors behind me with a firm and synchronised thud that makes me jump.

The cold of the corridor nips at my ankles through the sturdy leather of my boots, and I wiggle my single mitten back onto my uninjured hand as a shiver climbs up my spine.

I didn't realise quite how tense I had been in Genevieve's presence, but as I'm left alone in the dim shadows of the hallway, I slump against the cold blue topaz of the wall, my entire body trembling with relief and even still, anxiety.

If Genevieve is afraid to go to war with the Sephilim, then what hope do I have?

What can a mortal like me possibly do to fight back against such an indomitable force?

Am I destined to be tortured and used as a pawn in a royal game I am too young to understand and too fragile to protest?

My breath comes in wisps as I slide slowly down the wall, moving to sit on the cold floor and wrapping my cloak around me as tightly as it will go. My wrist is throbbing, my legs aching, my chest tight with fear. In the cold emptiness of the corridor, the loneliness inches in on all sides like a very real predator equipped with claws and teeth.

Tears threaten to fall as I realise that the threat to me is very real, that this is no game and there are no easy solutions. I could very well die, never see my family again, and leave them wondering what became of me. And if that isn't enough, I could be the one responsible for handing the crown of Aetheria to a complete tyrant.

How the hell did this happen?

How had things gone wrong so fast?

Suddenly, Ehlers Danlos Syndrome seems like the least of my problems, and I want nothing more than to return to two weeks ago when my worst flare day couldn't even compare to the difficulties I'm now facing. I miss my books, being an observer and not caught in the middle of two enemy nations.

"Kairi?" The low rumble of his voice interrupts my panic, and I look up through unshed tears.

"Sorry," I apologise, feeling silly as I wipe my eyes and get shakily to my feet. Lucien gives me a hand up, face unreadable as I sniffle, trying to compose myself.

"Genevieve shouldn't have tried to frighten you like that," he murmurs, clearly uncomfortable with my emotional state.

I frown.

"Was she telling the truth? Is it that bad, what I've gotten myself into?" I demand, taking full responsibility for the situation despite the fact I want nothing more than to ask— *why me?*

"She wasn't lying. I'm not sure Genevieve knows how to lie—" Pursing his lips, his face tightens, and his chest rises with a taut inhale. He shuffles from one foot to the other, clearly uncomfortable as I take the deepest, most calming breath I can manage.

"Well then, you have nothing to apologise for, and neither does she." I give Lucien a small smile, feeling my insides cracking apart under the fear of what the future might hold. I had thought my future was uncertain after my diagnosis, with the threat of organ rupture, gastroparesis, and losing my ability to walk by the time I was fifty becoming an all too real possibility.

Now that seems about as urgently pressing as what I'm having for breakfast two years from now.

Lucien is thoughtful for a moment as I straighten, drying some escaped tears and composing myself with shaky resolve.

"Come with me." He holds out a hand, his body relaxing as he does so, taking my palm in his as he turns me back to the throne room.

My chest tightens at the thought of coming face to face with Genevieve again, but instead of finding her sat upon her throne, the room is empty, the guards having presumably followed her to wherever she stalked off to.

I eye the immense chandelier overhead, the memory of it falling to the floor during my dream as vivid as though it were yesterday.

We cross the floor, my reflection seeming tiny against Lucien's in the polished stone as I catch our image from the corner of my eye.

When we reach the symbolic seal that's laid into the floor, we stop.

"Stay there," he instructs, dashing to the stage and rounding the throne before I can blink. He's so fast, and I wonder if he's been purposefully slowing down for my benefit.

Of course he has, I realise as he darts back to my side in a blur. His wings aid his deceleration, flaring out behind him, and he slows.

I stare then at what he's holding, the vicious edge of the silver and moonstone studded athame glimmering like a watchful eye beneath the lit candles of the chandelier.

He wields it quickly, exposing his palm, but as I open my mouth and let out a squeak of protest, he's already sliced clean through the skin there, leaving a neat bloody line behind. He doesn't hiss or show any signs of discomfort, simply going about his business without falter. Holding out his hand, he lets the blood drip onto the seal in the floor before shepherding me on top of it. He steps on after me, and within a few moments of the blood making contact with the ore, the entire thing is rotating and descending through the floor.

My eyes widen, and I have a million questions, but one look at Lucien's stoic face says that he's had enough of my mortal curiosity. Intuitively, I keep my mouth shut and observe as we corkscrew downward through the floor of the throne room and into what reveals itself to be deep caves below.

People are working at a forge close to where the archaic elevator comes to a grinding halt, and Lucien helps me step down from the considerable height and onto the naturally formed chambers. I stare as they rhythmically strike hot steel against cold, hypnotised as my feet touch down on the unusually warm stone.

The stalactites of the ceiling drip down around us, making me glad of my hood as Lucien dips and ducks between them, leading me away from the cacophony of metal on metal and through a labyrinth of jagged corridors lined with flaming sconces. Several workers stop to raise a hand of greeting to Lucien as we pass them toiling over leather or metalwork, but he's too distracted to notice, and I find his pace quickening the deeper into the caverns we journey.

Finally, he stops just shy of a corner that's completely veiled by a convenient outcropping of rock.

"Look, I'm not supposed to bring you down here, but I don't want you to be terrified. What Genevieve said about the Sephilim is true; they are formidable, but so are we." He places a hand on my shoulder, guiding me past him and around the corner. What greets me there isn't what I expect, my mouth turning immediately arid as I'm left gaping.

"This is Ebonara." Lucien introduces the enormous creature that's eyeing me from within the cavern ahead. The space ends in a naturally steep drop-off where suddenly the protruding ledge of rock ends and the clouds begin.

The dragon turns from me, looking back out into the fading daylight with wistful disinterest.

"But— I thought dragons— The Nephilim, they told me they died out," I say, my answer feeling lame on my tongue even to me. I can't take my eyes off the black scaled body, the enormous folded wings, the vicious talons, the horns of an elk that protrude from the dragon's skull above a long snout and enormous lilac eyes.

This is the dragon I had dreamed about— the dragon I had run from.

My stomach is a pit of terror, opening wider with each discovery in this place, threatening to swallow me whole.

"That's what the rest of Aetheria knows to be true. And if you ever tell a soul otherwise, I'll slit your throat for the pleasure of it. The only reason they've managed to survive is the extreme heat lying just under the surface of Drakos Vale. Without that sanctuary, they'd have perished centuries ago, which was the intention of the Sephilim king at the time, Midas," Lucien explains, and I nod, staying quiet and swallowing hard at the casual nature of his threat. The skin pulsing above my carotid has never seemed overly thin to me until this moment.

"Why are you showing me this?" I query, watching carefully as he steps around me and over to the dragon. At his proximity, she stirs, rising onto all fours and stretching out her wings before bringing her snout down to nuzzle the side of Lucien's face. He scratches beneath her chin with his long adept fingers, expression melting from glacial to warm at the feel of her scales against his fingertips.

"Because I think that you see me as a monster, and I want you to know that even if Aro does come for you, I will try to protect you as

240

best I can, and so will Ebonara. I won't let you die." He can't look at me when he says it, focusing instead on running his now-healed palm across the planes of Ebonara's glistening skull. Her scales are black, but as they emerge from the shadow of the cave and into the light that's filtering in from the world beyond, they tinge violet like precious black pearls.

I continue to stare, transfixed, not knowing what to say to his confession or his vow.

Do I see him as a monster?

Yes. The tiny voice inside me whispers.

But why? Because Aro had told me so, or because *I* believe it to be true?

"She wants you to come closer," he tells me, his voice bouncing in a deep echo from the ragged stone of the cavern walls.

I frown, taking down my hood and letting it land heavily on my shoulders, stomach tightening with uncertainty.

What if Lucien had brought me down here to give Ebonara a snack at Genevieve's suggestion?

"Wait— how do you know that?" I ask him, not moving even an inch. He smirks, looking sideways at the dragon and then back to me.

"What do you think, Eb? Should we tell her?" he asks, and I watch as the dragon tilts her head, appraising me with narrow eyes. She snorts, breath invisible despite the chill in the air, nostrils narrowing into snake-like slits among the dark shadows of her incredible face.

"We have a telepathic link, a bond," Lucien explains, and I take a step forward. My boots crunch on the stone underfoot, echoing in my ears, but are only just audible over the sound of my blood rushing ravenous and fearful around my body.

The closer I get, the harder my heart beats, the sound of my fear primal and impossible to ignore. I ignored my instincts with Aro, so why the hell am I doing the same thing again?

The scaled beast towers over me, maybe twenty feet tall as she sits up straight, lithe like a feline. I glimpse a lethal-looking tail that swishes gracefully behind her, talons protruding at all angles from the end which match Lucien's exactly. As I look between them, I find it's like they're two halves of one whole.

I hold my breath as I finally dare to enter her personal space, and Lucien's eyes remain firmly locked on my face with interest.

Ebonara bends down, her skull coming toward me faster than I expect and so I flinch, unable to breathe as I feel her nostrils sucking in the air from the side of my face, her curved horns glinting dangerously as they come alarmingly close.

Biting down on my lip hard, I try not to move as she lets her snout glide across the width and breadth of me, looking at me this way and that, lilac eye curiously diluting wide as she comes closer. I tremble despite my best effort to stay still for her inspection, trying to keep my breathing even and deep.

I can smell her as I inhale with tense ribs, her scales giving off the aroma not of ash or fire as I would expect, but instead of fresh water and the mildest greenery. She nudges my hand with the end of her nose, and I look to Lucien as he nods, encouraging me to touch her. Removing my mitten yet again and raising my hand, I cup a single scale on her cheek with the palm of my hand, the feel of the dragon smooth but undeniably tough as my skin chills with her proximity.

She makes a low growl, purring almost, and I feel myself relax, the first natural smile I have expressed in what feels like forever causing my lips to spread wide, my face flushing hot and exhilarated as I exhale heavily.

"She's so gentle—" I comment, and he nods, watching me as I rub my hand over several scales at once, feeling the way they lock together and observing Ebonara presenting her chin for rubs.

"She is, and it's a tragedy that these creatures have the reputation they do. I mean, they don't even eat meat; they eat crystals. They draw their life energy and power from Aether, much like Kindred do—" Lucien explains, and I cock my head, wondering why he hadn't mentioned this before I'd almost had a heart attack thinking she might eat me.

Biting down on my lower lip once more, I find myself missing Catticus Finch immensely. "It's also lucky she was with me that night I saved you. We never would have made it back through that storm without her," he explains, laying his own palm flat on her chest and stroking rhythmically.

"She was with you? Why didn't I see her?" I ask, incredulous.

I mean, I know I was out of it, but surely, I would remember a dragon—

"She can camouflage. She's actually the only dragon with that ability, and it's very useful. She was waiting for me underneath the tower balcony. After I jumped over the railing, she caught us, and we took off. You were out of it by then, which was good because I wasn't in any mood to explain all this at that particular moment—" he adds and

I nod, not letting my eyes meet his as we both focus painfully hard on Ebonara.

"Why are you doing all this? Why risk your life for me? Why risk Ebonara?" I ask, more confused than ever as to his motive but more certain that knowing it is of vital importance.

"Because this isn't your fault, Kairi. Lord Black manipulated you. You're only a mortal, and you're ignorant and naïve just like I once was. You don't deserve to die for that." He sounds tired as he speaks as if I'm a responsibility he didn't sign up for but now can't shake for the sake of his guilty conscience.

I blink fast, trying not to feel the sting of his words, instead, feeling grateful only for his aid.

Looking into Lucien's face, I find the momentary warmth I had felt for him, the hope that he didn't see me as some stupid human girl who didn't know any better is snuffed out as quickly as it came.

"Well," I say, trying to hide the hurt and utter loneliness I feel surrounded by this century-old immortal and his unimaginably majestic dragon, "this mortal thanks you."

Leaving the cavern and Ebonara behind with a noticeable wistfulness, Lucien leads me through a labyrinth of increasingly narrow tunnels lit by flickering and heavy steel sconces. We aren't heading back toward the descending hematite platform that brought us here but are, instead, heading farther from the throne room of the Astrid Keep with every step, leaving me uneasy.

"Where are we going?" I ask, breaking the long-held silence that has formed from tentative threads of awkwardness and grown stronger, weaving into a rope of thick quiet in which I focused only on Ebonara and my breathing.

I had enjoyed the lack of emotional turmoil as my fingertips traced the ridges of her crystal-cut scales, the flesh beneath chill with every rumbling breath that shuddered through her bones. Something about being close to her immense stature, looking deep into the dark abyss of her pupils and knowing she was staring right back into me, gave me more comfort than I can reasonably explain.

"We are heading out a back entrance. Then, I'll fly and retrieve the sleigh for us," he explains, voice not even slightly breathless as we climb the tight and steep stairs that wind up through solid rock, the walls closing in tighter the farther from Ebonara we roam.

"Lord DeLaurent!" An unknown call stops both of us in our tracks as Lucien pauses at a landing break between staircases. After a few moments, the sound of heavy rushed footfall grows closer before a dishevelled brunette woman rounds the top of the staircase.

"Juno, what is it?" Lucien's voice is suddenly colder than I've heard it since we stood before Genevieve, his demeanour chilling noticeably as he straightens within his sweater, wings rising slightly so his talons are pointing directly upward.

"Just that I couldn't patch your boots, my Lord. You'll need to call by the leatherwork shop in Vega before tonight if you want to participate in the race with any hope of staying upright," she explains, and Lucien laughs slightly, his tone warmer than I expect as his shoulders relax.

The girl, Juno, looks relieved as her posture slumps a little, the violet leathery folds of her wings turning translucent, peppered only by scarlet veins as they fall behind her and before one of the many lit sconces.

"Your faith in my riding abilities is flattering, Juno," Lucien retorts, causing the woman before him to flush scarlet. Her nose is peppered with brown freckles, her eyes similar in tone to the evergreen pines of an Alaskan forest.

"I'm not saying anything against you, my Lord. You just— you know how Ebonara gets when she races. She's competitive, and if winning means dumping you in the process, you and I both know you're going to finish ass up in the snow." She cocks her eyebrow, eyes glimmering with half-amused fear, half-challenge. Lucien looks at me, then back at her, fighting his amusement at the conjured visual.

"Right you are. I'll drop by Vega City on my way home. You don't mind a little detour do you, Kairi?" he asks, pulling the attention of the young winged Draconian from his amused expression and onto my mortified timidity.

"Of— of course not," I stutter and he nods, looking back to Juno.

"Thanks for catching me. I'll see you tonight?" he enquires, and she nods enthusiastically, giving me a final curious look before turning on the ball of her foot and descending the stairs out of sight.

Lucien turns to me, smiling.

"Ready to see the capital city of Drakos Vale?" he asks, and he begins to climb the stairs, overtaking me and leaving me staring after him.

I feel a little giddy with excitement before that feeling is drenched in new fear, wondering when this insanely fast fantasy whirlwind is going to slow down and let me catch my breath.

"Lead on, my Lord," I reply, setting to climbing the stairs after his broad and formidable gait.

Racing through the valley, it's clear that the days are just as short here as Lucien had suggested. The snow crunches and squeaks under the tread of the sleigh as it packs down powder in the wake of twenty plate-sized paws, my hair whipped back from my face in the growing shadows of twilight.

Lucien runs the dogs hard; I assume because the dusk is creeping up from the horizon, which is barely visible behind the multiple rising peaks that surround us on either side. Fingers of goldish moonlight crawl from where the earth meets the sky, readying to claim it in the name of the night and turning what had once been a pastel periwinkle, gilded both majestic and metallic, into a veil of matte velvet black.

We pass houses that stand in random isolation as well as clusters of stone architecture that seem far sturdier than the wooden lodge I'd woken up in, each location sleepy but growing more awake as lit gas lamps flicker into slow life like candles in the distance.

The further on we race through the dying light, the closer together these lighted clusters become, until finally, the thick foliage of trees that clutch close to us on both sides fall away, becoming sparser at first and then disappearing entirely, the valley culminating in an enormous bowl of greenery.

A waterfall, equidistant to two sharp peaks, is fully frozen as it sprawls over the farthest edge, its creamy glacial blue looking like a vein of crystal as it cuts mercilessly through the rock and greenery, carving out the frozen jugular of what is the most archaically beautiful city I've ever seen.

"Welcome to Vega City," Lucien whispers beside me, his breath refusing to condensate in the dying light despite the early evening casting a new and bitter chill like a silent spell on the air around us.

"It's beautiful," I acknowledge, nervous within the fur lining of my cloak as I welcome the shadows of my hood. They fall over my naïve and awed expression, hiding my youth and inexperience from prying immortal eyes.

Lucien doesn't reply, merely urging the dogs on along the edge of the frozen river and into the city centre, which sprawls out across the valley floor and climbs, charmingly crooked, up the bases of surrounding mountains.

The sidewalks glisten like black ice, the hematite I had seen featured inside the Astrid Keep becoming abundant as narrow walkways, snaking through the city like hungry reptilian tongues. The roads are heavily covered in snow, the stuff packed down so it forms a sleigh-friendly crust atop what I can only guess are cobbles beneath. The houses have thatched rooves, whitewashed walls and heavy dark wooden beams as common architectural features, like something straight out of Tudor-era England. Strings of fairy lights litter the space between the upper floors of houses, covering the various roads in expertly draped veils of faux starlight, the air thick with the scent of stewing meat and rich gravy. The Kindred residents are different than I expected and certainly more in number than I'd witnessed as I had ventured through Soleus with Aro.

It seems like a lifetime ago, and yet it was mere days ago I was satisfied and calm within the cage of such a dark angel's arms.

I shudder unwillingly, the thought of his touch like ice down my spine, as Lucien barks a command and the dogs suddenly lurch right, the sleigh careening wildly around a sharp corner that leads onto an even narrower street.

Where I'd expected to find weapon-toting assassins and trained killers walking proudly, winged silhouettes huddle together on the thin sidewalks, their boots heavily treaded to help them keep upright against the slippery clutches of the ice and snow underfoot. They all wear heavy woollen cloaks, their faces covered, the only distinguishing feature of each individual being that their wings vary wildly in colour, shape, and size.

Bookstores catch my eye, their glass fronts showing cosy nook-ish interiors stacked floor to ceiling with leather-bound portals to other literary worlds.

I miss my books, though if I ever see them again, I think it'll be a long time before I want to read anything in the fantasy genre again.

Next, I see stores packed with men, though what they're doing, I have no idea. They're huddled around a single desk manned by a multitude of tellers, but there don't seem to be any products in sight.

Before I can ponder this any further, we are far past the shopfront, and the street widens into a central courtyard. In the middle of it all, a fountain that weeps sabre-tooth length icicles stands proud, two Goddesses holding hands upon a pedestal in its centre. The cobbled stones are arranged beneath them, darker pieces placed as to create the shadow of the triple moon symbol – that of the maiden, mother, and crone.

Lucien calls loudly for the dogs to halt and barely waits until the sleigh has slowed to a mere slide before dismounting. He looks up at me, face concerned as he glances over his shoulder and then back to where I'm sat upon thick furs in the now standing sleigh.

"Are you going to be alright for a little while if I go in that store over there?" he asks me, and as he does, my stomach blooms with terror.

"Sure." I smile, feeling nowhere near as confident as I sound.

"Great, I'll be just inside if you need anything, alright?" he speaks hurriedly, barely pausing to catch my nod of acknowledgement before he's turned on his heel and is disappearing into the shop closest to where we've parked.

The dogs pant loudly, the sound of their breathing becoming more apparent as I tentatively step down into the slick snow. I think about moving toward one of them and giving it a rub between the ears, but after the fact I have already petted a dragon today and lived to talk about it, I decide I might be pushing my luck.

I wander across the courtyard, careful to keep my face shrouded by my cloak and painfully aware that I'm lacking the wings which would help me fit in. Draconians move fast along the sidewalks, keeping their eyes on their feet as they huddle against the cold inside their outerwear, and I'm surprised to find after a few moments that nobody has even given me a second glance.

I inhale deeply as I pass what claims to be a public house, the scent of slow-roasting joints, gravy, and sizzling potatoes making the air thick as it overwhelms the scent of the nearby pines. I salivate, my stomach empty and growling in protest.

To distract myself, I spend a few moments examining the statue in the middle of it all, finding the faces of the Goddesses carved from stone surprisingly lifelike and warm, despite their reputations. Moving along, I wander the hematite sidewalks, careful not to slip, staring into the windows of coffee shops, bakeries, bookstores, furniture stores, and an especially tiny corner shop that sells handcrafted leather journals, feeling oddly at home for the first time in what seems like forever.

It's like something out of an Austen classic whereby everyone seems to know everyone, and each individual knows exactly where they fit in within the winding crooked sprawl of the quaint mountainside city.

It seems like a microcosm of the world where problems are small and the community tight-knit.

I wonder what it must be like to live here, whether the residents become tired of the weather— but then I remember Lucien doesn't seem to mind the cold one bit.

The town is packed with people, but I'm seeing that this is mainly because it's so small in comparison to what I've witnessed in Soleus. The Sephilim city was probably four times this big, and though it was grander, shinier, and more decadent, this feels more comfortable, more familiar and somehow more real.

Taverns with their frosted windows spill red-faced and merry couples out into the street, singing songs I've never heard and probably never will again, while lanterns flicker into life inside each proprietor's abode one by one, the motion within becoming more apparent as darkness begins to fall and people start to tidy their stores for closing.

I stand, wandering as slowly as I can, trying to take it all in as I put one foot in front of the other and make a journey around the entire courtyard. Eventually, I come back to the leatherwork shop where, in the window, something extraordinary catches my eye that I hadn't noticed before.

Among sheaths, purses, belts, and boots, the centrepiece of the store's display is a pair of hand-crafted white leather ice skates with solid gold blades. The blades gleam warm in the strung lights that decorate the window's border, the white leather manipulated expertly and adorned with swirling imprints that make the simple and one-dimensional material nothing short of mesmerising. The laces are woven white and gold, the eyelets a matching metallic hue, and the toe picks on either blade have been teased into the shape of a Spectral Mountain dog's face, jaws gaping and teeth outstretched, ready to devour the ice and propel the wearer into the skies.

I stand, transfixed, knowing that these are definitely the most beautiful and unique pair of skates I've ever seen. The cold of the air becomes irrelevant, and time seems to stop as I stand on the curb, taking in every single detail of the boots and committing them to memory the best I can.

"Ready to go?" Lucien's voice causes me to startle, my heart kicking up into a sprint as I whirl around to face him. He looks at me, confused as to why I'm so surprised.

"That was fast—" I mumble, feeling silly for becoming so entranced. I don't belong here, but every time I seem to get that through my thick skull, I'm enraptured by the beauty of my surroundings, the violence and the cruelty of its residents too easy to forget as I watch them bustling about their daily lives in these sleepy, snow-blanketed streets.

"They have my measurements on file, so it was a simple re-order. Ready to head home?"

He nudges me, turning to face the sleigh that stands idle with the spectral mountain dogs lying in the snow before it, still harnessed and unaffected by the cold.

Home. The word makes me feel sick, so much so I'm afraid I might burst into tears at the thought of never seeing my family again. I quickly change the subject, trying to distract myself from the fear that refuses to stop gnawing at me.

"Did that girl say you needed the boots for a race?" I ask, pulling myself away from the window and heading back toward the sleigh without maintaining eye contact.

"Yes, Anastasia, our High Priestess, predicts quite the blizzard tonight, perfect weather for dragon racing. We can only race under the cover these kinds of storms provide, you see, so we don't get detected by the other Kindred. The dragons love it—" he sounds passionate despite himself, looking up to the skies and seeming to approve at wisps of cloud beginning to gather in the dusk.

"And you don't?" I pry, cocking my eyebrow as I step into the clutches of the sleigh and take up the seat I had been nestled in before.

"Oh, I do— it's the most exhilarating thing I've ever done in my life," he exclaims, smiling as he steps up into the vehicle behind me and palms the reins.

"Wow. That's a big claim for someone who has wings and a sleigh pulled by Spectral Monster Dogs—" I say, turning my eyes skyward and wondering exactly how fast a dragon can fly, wondering what it must be like to sit astride one and command it like a noble and malleable steed.

"It's Spectral *Mountain* dogs, and it is the absolute truth. If you don't believe me, you should come along tonight. I know a place you can observe from if you wish."

He doesn't look at me, instead, commanding the dogs to start running again as soon as they're on their feet. It's as if he hasn't offered me a kindness, or a once in a lifetime experience, but rather milk and cookies.

The sleigh pulls away as my mouth falls open and then I snap it shut again.

After a few moments wondering the true motivation of why it is he has taken me quite literally under his wing, I nod, simply replying, "I'd like that," with about as much emotion as Lucien had displayed extending the offer.

I still feel as though he's taking pity on me, as though he feels bad that I've got a mere few days before I'm hunted and killed by the Sephilim or perhaps, in his eyes, worse; that I have to return to live out my measly eighty-year lifespan before pruning up and withering into dust without ever having seen a dragon fly.

Then again, I haven't.

And I really can't deny I want to.

After all, what kind of philistine declines an invitation to watch a real-life dragon race?

18

INTO THIN AIR

LUCIEN

THE WIND WHIPS MY poker straight locks back from my face as we climb higher into the clutches of the city, winding through steep, snow-blanketed inclines that are narrowed by shops crowding both sides, our path leading back toward Lakeside. The sky is now almost fully darkened, the vast canvas transforming into matte indigo velvet scattered with fine, speckled starlight like sugar.

My nostrils flare against the freezing temperatures, relishing the strong wafting scent of pine and the way in which I can, for but a single moment, forget I am carrying a wanted fugitive of the Sephilim High Lord, Aro Black.

I glance down at her shivering silhouette from the corner of my eye as I remain steadfast in my stance, hands twisting around the reins in an effort to turn my frustration into torque-induced skin burns. At least I can be angry at that, at my own pain and misery.

Truth be told, I'm furious at her as she sits there nursing the arm which she seems to be less and less protective of as the minutes tick on, her wide innocent eyes watering against the cold, lips slack and unassuming.

The problem is that fury isn't making me the most personable, and I don't want her to hate me either. The thought of her looking at me the way she had when I had mentioned Lord Black curdles my soul, making me physically nauseous.

I've never much cared before what others thought of me, or the Draconians in general. I knew we were misunderstood, and that prejudice against our Kindred race was by far the most venomous, and the most present in all of Aetheria.

That's what happens when the new kid shows up with a bigger horse than you, I guess.

You get shit scared.

Only our horses had scales, wings spanning the lengths of roofs, and the ability to breathe any number of vile pestilences down on the unknowing populace at a single command.

As Genevieve has always told anyone who asked, and many who didn't, the first thing those afraid of us had done was try to intimidate us into breaking like a prize stallion under a jockey's riding crop. We did not, and so it had left them with no choice but to ostracise us, to make us into the enemy, and turn everyone else in this dimension against us with increasingly obvious effectiveness.

As I said, I've never much cared— but when it comes to her, to those wide blue eyes taking me in, the way they dart from my talons to my fists and back again before she completes a deliberate but automatic gulp of air as though she's suffocating in dark imaginings of what I might do to her— I can't stand it.

She's so fragile, so much bone and flesh and blood and beating heart which might one day stop that I want to shake her, to scream at her and ask her what the hell she thinks she's doing.

Does she have no sense of self-preservation? Because I wonder sometimes if I'm risking my life and those of everyone who comes into contact with her, for a girl with no sense of her mortality at all.

Watching her, I'm struck once again by her demureness.

Had nobody told her not to talk to strangers? Not to trust men upon first meeting, least of all those who look as though they've been plucked right out of *Dante's Inferno*?

We turn a corner at speed, now racing down the final street on our route out of Vega City and toward the mountainous outcrops, which will take us around the scenic edges of the valley and back to Lakeside, avoiding the obstacles on the ground such as dense trees and foliage that we had encountered on our journey here.

The motion as we swerve around the bend is a sudden jolt, and yet she barely moves upon her seat, a stone statue wrapped in wool and furs, eyes wide and furtive like a baby doe caught in a hunter's snare. Again, my fury rises within me like bile, burning the back of my throat and causing me to wring my hands even more furiously as I grit my teeth.

How could she be so careless?

When I was alive, people were struck down by hideous diseases, raging fires, revolutions for equality, and quests to give voices to the downtrodden. They fought for every breath, even if their lives consisted of little more than struggling to feed starving mouths day in and day out.

Now, I wonder; are all mortals this careless? Or perhaps she knew exactly what she was doing, perhaps the mortal world as I knew it is but a myth, and things have gotten so bad that death seems like an easy grace—

I shudder, watching her peer out over the ledge of the sleigh as the valley opens up beneath us, exposing the icy veins of the river and endless porcelain fields of white pine.

I think about what the rest of Aetheria called this place before we were banished.

The Frozen Waste.

To me, it has never seemed like a waste of anything except the potential no Kindred had stopped to try and see beneath the ice and snow.

"Have you ever skated before?" I ask her, the words escaping my lips and carrying on the cold rush of the breeze before I can stop them. She looks at me, head snapping around, her eyes wider still like she's looking at a ghost and not the man who risked his life to rescue her.

"Oh, uh—" she stutters, unsure of herself as a wave of crimson splashes across her cheeks.

"I saw you looking at the skates— in the window," I add, trying to make my inquiry seem less random.

"Oh, right. Yes. Once," she admonishes, words coming out fractured like an amateur seamstress who drops stitches more than she successfully makes them.

"You didn't like it?" I press her, finding the awkward silence that so often falls between us to be tiresome. She got herself into this situation, and it's almost as if fear has made her into a ghost like a tortoise that has retreated into its shell and now refuses to face the world.

If she's going to be staying here for a week, then she needs to at least make the effort to be a good conversationalist. I won't have some weepy mortal wandering the halls of my house and making everyone, namely me, uncomfortable.

Not only that, but as a fugitive, I need her to speak her mind, because if not, someone is going to end up dead or worse.

"Oh no, I loved it. I performed and competed all over America, actually. I used to train like fifty-something hours a week. It's kind of like what you said about dragon riding. I never found anything quite as thrilling. Well, until all this other dimension stuff anyway—" She plops her chin into her uninjured hand, elbow resting on the rim of the sleigh as she looks out over the immense sprawl of the valley.

I try to picture it, her performing— but the liveliness I'd expect to find, that I've witnessed in dancers or acrobats, simply isn't there, let alone any substance within her to indicate a competitive streak. Her form is soft, muscles long since unfurled from their athletic days, and so I'm left wondering then what happened.

"Why did you stop doing it if you loved it so much?" I ask her, pondering what it would take for me to give up climbing atop Ebonara and flying off carelessly into a storm.

The answer, unsurprisingly to me, is nothing short of death.

"I got sick," is all she says, and I turn a little, surprised as I pull my eyes from the cliffside path ahead and take in her face. I thought she'd look sad or maybe teary, but instead, a calm mask of indifference has fallen over her overly emotional features.

"You don't look sick—" I say, stiffening my shoulders and posture.

"Well, you don't look like an asshole— but here we are!" she snaps.

I'm caught utterly off guard, the shock bubbling up through my chest like helium and exploding from my lips as an uncontrolled laugh that echoes high off the mountain walls, causing several species of native bird to scatter from nearby trees.

If I'd been drinking coffee, she would surely be wearing it.

"What's so damn funny?!" If she wasn't wearing a sling, I know she'd be crossing her arms over her chest, her face riddled with indignation.

"Nothing, I just wasn't expecting such *sass*," I admit, smirking and glancing over at her as the dogs continue to pull the sleigh along the increasingly narrow ledge. I tug on the reins, urging them faster for the sake of having something to focus on that isn't her shocked expression because I probably shouldn't start laughing again.

"And why not?" She wrinkles her nose, brows nipping inward in obvious irritation as she clenches her teeth, jaw tensing noticeably.

"Well, you're usually all stutters and dropping your gaze, now that you mention it. Quite the demure damsel if I do say so myself—" I confess, and Kairi sighs, suddenly sad. Not the response I expected.

"I wasn't always this way," she relinquishes with a devastatingly melancholy exhale.

"Well, obviously not. I'd assume as a child, you were quite a lot shorter—" I try to cheer her up, not sure I'm up to a deep emotional exchange.

"Ha. Ha." She shrugs off her annoyance, tone colder than the surrounding snow, lips pushing firmly together until they turn a similar shade.

For a moment, we are lost in the unceasing rhythm of paw against snow and wind whipping mercilessly past our ears as the vehicle tilts and curves on its trajectory.

After a long pause, she speaks again, "This disease I have, it's better here, in Aetheria. But in the mortal world, my whole life has been dismantled piece by piece." I look over to her where she's no longer gazing at me but now peers over the ledge of the sleigh and down the steep drop of the mountainside again. She talks wistfully into the crisp evening air like she's saying these things to no one in particular.

Suddenly though, something makes sense.

"That's why you came back here with him even though you didn't know him—" I muse aloud, but she shakes her head.

"The first time, no. I was curious, and I really did believe he liked me. He was charming, and I can't deny that he appealed to me. But after that first visit, it was a factor, yes." She could easily have agreed with me, so at least she's honest.

"I see. Well, I'm sorry," I apologise to her, feeling guilty for a reason I can't quite fathom. I owe this girl nothing. I have already saved her life, and now I'm risking more lives for her sake. It should be enough, so why isn't it?

"There's nothing to be sorry for as you've so rightly said, and as Genevieve also pointed out, the fault is mine," she confesses, face earnest.

"Yes, but I judged you," I admit, hands tightening on the reins as the sleigh begins a gentle descent back toward the valley floor.

"And I judged you," she admits.

I feel myself taken by surprise again, turning to her with raised brows.

She continues, holding my gaze now with intensity. "I never thought you were a monster, Lucien. But I also never thought you could be a hero."

"Then, it seems we were both mistaken," I confess, feeling my cheeks flush, something which hasn't happened for at least one hundred years.

"Well then, how about this— instead of making assumptions, if I want to know something about you or you about me, why don't we just ask?" she suggests, and I nod slowly.

A simple solution but one that has clearly taken courage for her to voice.

I give her a small smile, appreciating the effort as the sleigh peters out onto level powder.

"Alright then."

KAIRI

Even though things have settled between Lucien and me, the questions don't pour out like I expect. Instead, we settle into silence once more, my eyes resting on the cold light of stars as they wink awake, the night yawning wide as the deep dark of its jaw consumes the sky. I barely notice when the lights of Lucien's house blink into existence over the horizon, the distance we cover lost on me in the light of the weak golden moon as it rises.

The temperature drops what feels like a full twenty degrees in a matter of moments, and I find myself shivering as I wrap the wool of my cloak taut around my shoulders only moments before the sleigh comes to a stop metres from the front porch of the house.

"Go on inside and get warm, I'll just settle the dogs. I'll join you in a few minutes." He jerks his chin toward the front door, eyes sparkling like steel.

"Don't I need a key?" I ask him, and he rolls his eyes.

"And what good would that do?" he asks me, and I shrug.

"I don't know. I'd think with your enemies, you'd see the value in a lock." I bite back, hating how stupid he makes me feel.

"With my enemies, a lock would do as much good as one of those hideously loud decorative beaded curtains. Go on in. You're shivering." He gives me a stern look I can't ignore as the moonlight causes the tips of his talons to glint with menacing coldness from the crux of each wing.

Without another word, but fairly exasperated nonetheless, I get down from the sleigh and trudge the small distance to the porch now shimmering with fresh frost.

I lean into the door after clambering the slick wooden steps, and the warmth of the place immediately envelopes me like a welcome hug. The scent of rich wood polish and this morning's coffee lingers, stale in the air, as I kick the snow off my boots and remove my cloak haphazardly with one hand, hanging it on the bannister.

I stand in the long hallway for a few moments, staring up at the chandelier that's crafted from many copper branches and holds multiple candles, spinning on the spot until I'm a little dizzy.

More moments pass, and I'm pulled back to the library behind me as I become bored, the large dark wooden door left ajar just as it had been the night before.

Surely, if Lucien wanted it to be kept private, he'd shut the door?

Then again, the man is opposed to locks, so who the hell knows?

After our heart-to-heart in the sleigh, I'm not as scared of him, of his obvious brute strength and seemingly cold heart. He'd rescued me, I can't deny, but talking to him still feels like fencing with an expertly chiselled ice sculpture.

I take slow steps toward the doors of the library, wondering why I'm so on edge as I listen for his approaching footsteps and come up with nothing but empty silence and the barely audible static of fast-falling snow beyond the window.

Then, straightening my shoulders and noticing the hopeful lack of twinge in my broken wrist, I stride confidently into the safety of the room that's lined on three sides by thick leather, parchment, and ink.

The scent calms my heart as I move quickly to a shelf on the left, knowing that I want to learn what kind of books Lucien keeps in here, even if he does eventually kick me out.

I trace my finger along the thick leather spines that are embossed gold in a declaration of their immortal value and wisdom, finding the titles to be more interesting than I expect.

Aetheria – Maps and Topography of the divine border dimension.

Fae Art, A visual collection of Nirvana's finest masterworks.

Interspecies romantic theory – Inter-Kindred relations and sexual pleasure.

I baulk at the last title, half-tempted to take it out and see if there are any rude diagrams. After all, what kind of twenty-first-century woman would I be if I wasn't curious about whether Draconians have scales in *other* places—

The thought of Lucien naked makes me feel suddenly hot beneath the surface of my skin despite the fact I'd been cold only moments before. His tightly packed muscle, the cold distance in his stare—

I bet he's primal in the sack.

"Interesting reading?" His voice startles me from my imaginings, causing me to jump slightly on the spot as my hand drops from the spine like it's been burned, hoping he didn't see where I was lingering.

I spin, face scalding with sudden embarrassment.

"Oh my god, you know you shouldn't just sneak up on people! Jesus Christ, Lucien—"

He smirks, his perfectly angled blond eyebrow cocking and rising fast on his forehead. He lurches forward, still dressed in only a simple sweater despite the blizzard outside, tread soft as a predatory cat. His lips spread wide and his tongue flicks over the top row of teeth, eyes lighting as he moves to bite his bottom lip.

"If I'd known that was your intention, I'd have let you into my private collection sooner. I'm mainly preferable to Fae Pornography, but I'm sure if I ask in town, someone will be able to find me something with a nice burly Sephilim in the centrefold for you—" he whispers in my ear, creeping around me with a malicious joy carved thoroughly into every line of his face.

I smack his bicep, and he laughs.

"Again, you surprise me. I didn't take you for physically unhinged—" he's teasing me, and I roll my eyes.

"Did that even hurt?" I query him, cocking my hip. The effect is somewhat diminished by the lack of curves allowed by the heavy wool of the gown I'm wearing, but I'll be damned if I don't give it a shot anyhow.

"Tickling doesn't count does it?" he asks, folding his arms and leaning back against the high wings of an armchair at his spine.

"No. It does not." I narrow my eyes, coughing quickly and stepping away from the books I'd been examining like they're radioactive.

"So, you like all books? Or just the dirty ones?" he asks, twirling around on the ball of one foot with more grace than you'd ever expect to see from someone so burly.

"I love books, actually," I retort, and as I go to cross my arms, his gaze darts to my bandaged arm.

"Come here," he orders me, and I reluctantly cooperate. He pats the leather cushion of the chocolate armchair he was leaning against, and so I sit, watching as he bends down and reaches around my shoulders to release the sling.

"I think, by the way, you're no longer protecting this, it's healed," he observes, his fingers gentler than I expect as he unwraps the bandages, revealing my bare flesh beneath with tender care. "Wiggle your fingers for me?" he asks, and I oblige, the pain barely noticeable now.

Thank the Gods for Aetherial healing— I exhale heavily, relieved that I won't have to wear the sling any longer. After all, being a mortal among immortals is bad enough, I hardly need to look any more vulnerable.

"Thank you for fixing me," I smile gently, allowing the expression to reach my eyes.

"I didn't fix you. I fixed your arm," he corrects me, brushing off the sentiment entirely. I shrug, choosing to look around at the ceiling-high shelves instead of into his eyes. He traces my gaze then says, shoulder relaxing, "You know everything in this room is available to you. Please, feel free to read as much as you'd like—" he offers, rerolling the bandage in his fingers and nodding to the shelves.

I expect him to make a dirty joke about porn again, but he doesn't, so I make a joke instead.

"Well alright, but if you suddenly tell me that you have a talking candlestick, clock, and teapot, then I'm out of here—" I smirk and he looks puzzled. I explain quickly, "You know, in Beauty and The Beast, he offers her his library as a romantic gesture—" I add, and he looks startled.

Then, as he passes me, he pats me on the shoulder and simply says, "Now Kairi, I know your hair isn't as well kept as mine, but I'd hardly call you a beast, dear," before leaving me with my mouth hanging open, surrounded by pages upon pages of magic.

Lucien makes us both dinner while I peruse his shelves, finding each title more intriguing than the last as the scents of freshly cooked salmon, greens, and garlic-buttered potatoes fill the lowest floor of the house. Once we've both eaten, me while I leaf through one of the topography books and him while watching me with half interest, he disappears upstairs, leaving me alone with maps more complicated than anything I've ever seen.

For you see, the dimension of Aetheria isn't just North, South, East, and West, but takes on a whole new third dimension. Four floating continents, each as enormous and diverse as the last, hovering at different altitudes in what appears to be, but obviously is not, a gravity-less void. I don't know how the landmasses are hanging in mid-air, but there's nothing to address the cause in anything I've read so far, leaving me wondering if I should simply accept it as *magic* and leave it at that.

As I'm turning the page from the current map of Drakos Vale I'm studying, I hear footsteps and allow my eyes to lift, however reluctantly, from the thick parchment pages to find Lucien rounding the corner of the kitchen's broadly arched entryway.

His change in attire startles me, the contrast from his earlier turtleneck and dress pants almost laughable. Though, his clothing is not what first draws my eye. No, what I notice first and what causes me to baulk is his hair.

Pristine arctic blond locks have been expertly braided so the poker straight tresses are pulled back tightly from his neck. The braid is intricate, somewhere between a fishtail and French in style and pulls his features taut, causing his cheekbones to become even more prominent than usual and his brow to seem heavier as it casts dark shadows over the masculine deep set of his eyes.

He wasn't wrong when he said my hair wasn't as well kept as his.

His eyes are covered by a scaled metal visor, his torso wrapped in leather that cuts close to his silhouette and is layered up the sleeves to give the effect of yet more scales. Buckles and thick straps wrap around his waist for no other purpose I can discern than aesthetics, and I find his long legs clad in a pair of velvet riding trousers that aren't unlike what you would expect to see on a young girl during her first dressage event. However, there's nothing feminine about the cut as the fabric clings provocatively to all his bulges, the taught muscles of his quads and calves not hidden in the slightest for anyone who dares sneak a peek. Finally, I find his feet bare on the hardwood and scowl before remembering that he hadn't commissioned new riding boots until late this afternoon. The person making them must have one hell of a turnaround for him to expect them to be ready in time for tonight's event.

Pulling on a pair of leather gloves I hadn't noticed him holding in matching onyx velvet, he gestures for me to begin getting ready to depart.

"It's a little early, but I have to drop you off before I make my way to the catacombs, so we'd better get going," he explains, and I can't help but feel fatigue slowly creeping through me at the thought of heading out into the cold again. I look wistfully at the book on the table before me, feeling as though I'd finally been getting some semblance of answers and sad to have to leave. Lucien smiles at me, his eyes glinting bright with excitement and anticipation.

"You can leave that here. I'm sure Anastasia will answer any questions you have once I drop you off," he adds, pulling up the collar of his tunic so it's angular around the pale skin of his throat.

"Anastasia? Does— does she know about me?" I stutter, wondering if I'm to expect utter disdain from yet another immortal, if I'm going to have to justify my presence and existence in a world that is far from home.

"I imagine so. Anastasia knows most things, hence why she's the perfect person to answer your questions. Now, come along. We don't want to be late."

He picks up my cloak from the bannister as I reluctantly slip from the stool and round the granite kitchen island, placing it over my shoulders without being asked.

Pulling it around me, I watch Lucien stride across the hallway, his presence practically vibrating with anticipation and energy for the night ahead. As he opens the front door, a gust of icy cold air blows into the hallway from outside, causing me to shudder. He looks back at me, jiggling on the balls of his feet and imploring me to hurry with only his gaze.

And so, without any further discussion, we head back out into the darkness of the blizzard raging outside, leaving all warmth, along with the library, behind us.

I don't know why I didn't equate watching a dragon race with having to be far above ground level, but it never even occurred to me. The sleigh has taken us up, up, up— high above the trees, high above the clouds, to the highest peak in the land, except for one other that I can glimpse standing adjacent in the distance.

The dogs pant heavily as the sleigh finally slows at the zenith of our ascent. A figure appears from the fog and stands unperturbed by the freezing temperatures in only a thin gossamer gown and floor-length cape that glitters intensely with cold light. Her eyes glow like a frozen ocean in the dark, her skin emitting an ethereal aura like it's been made from liquid starlight.

I'd thought Genevieve had looked remarkable, and even High Lady Aliandara had left me awed, but this woman is something else altogether— something— otherworldly. Someone blessed.

"Anastasia," Lucien says her name, more of a statement than a greeting, and her thin lips curve into the glowing crescent outline of a smile. I find her wings, as we grow closer and finally arrive at a halt, are a deep midnight blue and studded with crystals that make them look as if rain has frozen solid whilst still in freefall upon their leathery span.

"Kairi," Anastasia says my name, the pallor of her eyes causing her face to appear phantasmal in the dark tundra-esque snowfall. I wonder how she knows who I am as she offers me a hand, and I pause, a little too awed by her complexion to move.

"I'm alright to leave her here with you?" Lucien enquires, his voice rising louder so he can be heard against a sudden rush of wind.

"I'm here, aren't I?" she asks him, her face not unhappy nor pleased. Instead, she inhabits a realm all of her own, a place of utter knowing and calm, her voice steady as the mountain on which we stand and the stars that hang eternal overhead. Her hair captures the occasional snowflake, the left-over slurry sparkling amongst the diamonds peppering the tangled locks of her hair that sheen like liquid chocolate.

She's beautiful, unusually so even for an immortal, causing others I've met to pale in comparison.

"Come, Kairi." Anastasia takes my hand in hers, the flesh of her palm cold like marble but not chill, simply cool and remarkably smooth. I take in the details of the fingers that intertwine with mine carelessly, her nails perfect half-moons lacquered shiny, her wrists wrapped heavily in chains of silver stars. Every finger is adorned by a stack of delicate silver rings interspersed with astrological symbols, crystals, and runes. I wonder idly if they're carefully ordered or placed at random.

When I look back over my shoulder, I discover Lucien is either long gone or indiscernible against the static of the blizzard that seems to swallow everything in a raging yet silent fog.

The cold whips at the backs of my legs beneath my cloak, and I quicken my steps as the navy blue of her gown seems to acclimatise against the star-studded sky, leaving only her glowing seafoam eyes and insistent tugging to lead the way.

The snow is so thick that the building seems to appear from nowhere, bulbous in architecture and ridiculously delicate seeming for such conditions. Glass rises out of the ground and casts the slightest shadow over my face as I squint into the blur of the snow, finding a set of wooden doors with inlaid silver filigree of intertwined stars, moons, and planets. Anastasia pushes the doors open with seemingly little effort despite her willowy form, and heat rushes forth, surrounding me as I step across the hypnotically welcome threshold.

As she closes the door behind me, the sconces lining the walls reveal details of the hall in the new shadow. The floor is made not from what looks like liquid sky but deep navy goldstone, which catches the orange light of the flames. Turning increasingly fiery within the peppered gold specks of the crystal, the floor beneath my feet is suddenly a night sky of deepest matte navy, alive with hundreds of flaming meteorites. The walls themselves are grey flint, sturdy and archaic-looking in comparison to the fancy elegance underfoot.

"May I take your cloak?" Anastasia asks, and I nod, feeling the heat of the nearby flame seeping into my bones and threatening to make me sweat. I remove the thick wool from my shoulders, handing it to her and feeling all kinds of wrong about handing something so bland to someone so transcendent. She shouldn't be taking my cloak; instead, I should be offering to take hers.

Folding the lilac woollen garment neatly across her arm, she beckons me forward through the flint archway, moving with seamless grace as though she creates her own, much finer gravity. I follow her, feeling heavy on my feet as I carefully try not to step on the lengthy train of her delicate attire.

As we exit the hall, the space opens up into something remarkable, an enormous glass dome. The walls that rise to just above my head height, before becoming utterly transparent, are carved from pearlescent moonstone, but perhaps the most alarming thing of all isn't the enormity of it but how that gargantuan glass dome of a ceiling is staying entirely free of any snow or water.

I look up at it with a querying eye, straining my neck as my mouth falls open, awed. I want to ask how this can be, this spotless glass globe in the midst of a blizzard, but Anastasia simply looks back over one shoulder at me.

"Oh dear. Well, if you're impressed by this, then we're never going to get to the main observatory. Come along—" She sighs though her eyes are kind and mischievous as they glint pale in the silvery glow of the room.

"This— isn't the main observatory?" I ask, feeling rather small as I give a glance back up to the magically water-repellent ceiling.

"Not even close. Come on." She gestures again, her long, perfect fingers beckoning.

She leads me through a door to the left, which comes out at the top of an enormous spiral staircase adorned with a complex silver balustrade that spills the constellations between its railings like glistening bejewelled milk.

Anastasia's feet are featherlight upon the stone as she descends, her train continuously hypnotic on the floor behind her as I trail behind, trying to take in every single detail. I glance up to where a skylight allows pure moonlight to fall in an uninterrupted column through the centre of the spiralling stairs, the smooth moonstone walls making me feel as if I'm exploring the winding innards of a snail's shell.

After a few moments, I realise I've stopped moving entirely, staring up through the skylight, and so pick up my pace quickly to make up the distance between me and my guide, who honestly hasn't even seemed to notice I wasn't following her.

When we reach the bottom of the tightly curled spiral staircase, having descended deeper into the stone of the mountain, I find myself in a round hallway with four archways that lead off to long corridors.

Something catches my eyes in the southern archway, this not leading to a corridor at all but an abnormally long room. Within the heavy torchlight and orange glowing walls, something glows a distinct ghostly white from the floor.

Forgetting Anastasia entirely, I let my feet carry me beyond the archway so I'm standing before what looks like a small swimming pool of molten silver, only less viscous.

Stepping closer, I gaze into it, hypnotised by the metallic glow of what seems to be regular water. It doesn't give off any kind of heat, and when I look up, I find a glass panel has been inserted into the sloping ceiling overhead that allows pure golden moonlight to fall into its depths.

"This is where we're reborn, you know. Where it all began for High Lady Genevieve all those hundreds of years ago— of course, it wasn't so civilised then, just a natural spring in a mountainside cavern." Anastasia's voice, though low in volume, bounces off the walls and causes me to jump as my dreamlike connection with the silvery pool is broken. I stare back over my shoulder at her, her silhouette made slim and elegant in the doorway as she stares at me thoughtfully, hair and dress glittering even in the shadows of the thick archway.

"So— this is where Draconians are reborn?" I ask her, feeling dense as I silently long to reach out and touch the surface.

"Indeed. A blessed pool of liquid starlight. Our bodies form deep within, and when we are ready, we break the surface and take our first breath of Drakos Vale. Usually, I have guards standing watch, but seeing as the race is a highly anticipated event and almost all of my guards enjoy spending their free time gambling, I thought I'd best give them the night off, lest I spend the entirety of my evening with them gawping up through windows to check the results—" She waves a hand, shrugging.

"You don't approve of gambling?" I ask her, a smile upturning the side of my face. The fact that anything so seemingly base or human seems to cross her mind at all is amusing, to say the least.

"Well, even if I did, it would hardly be ethical. A seer gambling, can you imagine?" she asks, eyes twinkling even still.

I think on this, my lips curving into an amused half-smile.

"I suppose that rather takes the fun out of it. Unless, of course, you're looking to make a quick buck—" I express, and she cocks her head at the expression, narrowing her eyes before tilting her chin upward in eventual understanding.

"The material holds very little interest to me, and while many decide to shower me with riches, I've never been one for possessions. I suppose that's the Catholic sister remaining ingrained in me after all these years—" she sighs, and I take one final look at the pool before tearing myself away and returning to her side as she exits the space.

"You were a nun?" I ask, sceptical as I glance at her obvious cleavage and youthful pallor. She doesn't seem the habit-wearing type.

"Oh yes, in England. My father sent me away, and I was consigned to a convent for my visions. I lived a long life in service of His Holiness." She says it as her pace quickens, leading me across the circular landing and over to the northern archway. I match her steps, more purposeful now as she spills insight for me to latch onto and absorb.

Suddenly, we move from the darkness of the narrow corridor and into what I figure is the main observatory she had been referring to. It's easily triple the size of the domed room upstairs with a silver staircase that leads to a balcony running along the entirety of the room's inner curve. Up on the raised platform, I can see shelves stacked with glimmering orbs, their silvery metal catching the light leeching in through the ceiling and making them sheen. In the centre of the space, an enormous silver telescope sits on a slightly raised pedestal, lens raised to the heavens. An ornate silver chair that's designed to appear as if it's woven from crescent moons sits directly beneath the enormous bulk of the instrument, waiting for the next viewer.

"Wow," I exhale, eyes drawn to something else entirely as I journey deeper into the observatory.

On the left of the entrance archway, something remarkable sits. I step over to it, bending to look within the outermost metallic weave of constellations and into the four floating continents inside. The three-dimensional model of Aetheria takes my breath away, doing justice to the topography in a way that Lucien's book never could.

"Mortals are so distracted by shiny things, like magpies," Anastasia comments, stepping to my side and spinning the outermost globe so the stars whirl across the model sky. She pulls up an orb of lapis that slowly travels a vertical trajectory around the globe.

"The sun— it doesn't move from east to west?" I ask her, feeling resoundingly stupid.

"No— I suppose that would make it unpleasant for continents floating at a lower altitude. The Blazen Plains, they get the most heat and the longest days because they're positioned just right— whereas Nirvana—" she explains, pointing to the metal forming the intricate floating continent that's farthest away from me, "and Soleus, they receive more clement weather." I don't ask about Drakos Vale, the farthest removed in both distance and altitude from the other continents, which seem to be clustered in a way that excludes the mountainous jaws of it entirely.

The void between Soleus and Drakos Vale has never been clearer to me as I watch Anastasia spin the crystal sun between her fingers.

"Anyway, the race is about to begin, shall we get you situated so you might watch?" she suggests, and I half expect her to take me over to the telescope. I nod, curious as instead, she leads me up the small staircase and over to the centre of the enormous glass window that faces away from the mountain's peak. I find that I was not mistaken about the contents of the shelves, which cease lining the walls around the centre of the balcony, offering an unparalleled view of the night sky beyond, each one clutching multiple silver orbs.

I want to ask what they're for, but before I can, Anastasia is pointing out into the night beyond the glass.

"You see that over there—" She points directly ahead, and I squint, making out the mountain's rival peak all the way across Drakos Vale. I nod, brushing my hair behind one ear as I stare up at her delicate profile.

"It's Gemina One. This observatory is built into Gemina Two. They're the two highest peaks in Drakos Vale, like a set of dragon fangs in the continent's jaws. They're the same height, which is why they're named for the twin Astrological sign of Gemini, and they earmark the two farthest points in the dragon racing circuit." She comes finally to her point, and I realise she's enjoying herself.

"Why— why don't you hate me?" I ask her, suddenly feeling bold. She looks completely surprised as her eyes lock with mine, entrancing me entirely.

"Hate you? I barely know you— Other than what I've seen in my visions," she expresses, making my brain flood with yet more questions. I address the one I had posed first.

"I just— I'm sorry. I know that must seem odd, but ever since I got here, almost all of the immortals I've met dislike me purely for the fact I'm not one of them. I've been too afraid to ask many questions, and here you are— just laying out answers for me on a silver platter. Why?" I enquire, and she smiles.

"Because I deal with so many people who want to abuse the power of this place; it's nice to find someone who is as awed by it as I once was. Someone who wants to know the hows and whys purely for the appreciation of what is, not for how they might use it to their benefit," she confesses, face serene as she breaks the gaze we're both locked into. I flush, feeling foolish for doubting her motives.

"You had visions about me?" I ask, unwilling to let this fact slide. She nods, light dancing in the curls of her hair.

"Indeed. You are a mystery, Kairi. I see you, and yet I cannot discern if I am having a vision or a memory. Everything surrounding you is sort of— blurry. Like someone has tried to erase the writing on a chalkboard and left only smudges." She frowns, clearly troubled by this.

I begin to ponder on what it is she's trying to say, about if she even knows what this means, but before I can ask, I hear her inhale sharply.

"Here they go!" She brings her hands together in a joyful pose, and I peer out into the dark static of the blizzard, squinting to try and find what it is she's seen.

I see nothing but white noise for a few minutes, and then, suddenly— among the dark an enormous shadow sprawled across the entire panorama of the observatory window, the glint of a mint reptilian eye causes me to startle. One moment it's there, and the next— gone.

If I had blinked, I would have missed it.

After the first dragon, however, a creature of alabaster scale and immense speed, many more pass close enough to the window for me to be able to reach out and touch if it were not for the glass parting us.

"Will they come back?" I ask after the final scaly blur has definitively passed.

"It's a one hundred lap race, so I hope so. If not, they're all gravely lost—" Anastasia smiles softly, peering out of the window with what seems to be genuine interest. She's probably seen this hundreds of times before, and yet, her excitement does not seem the least bit diminished by this fact.

The dragons lap around the peak of Gemina Two multiple times during the next ten minutes, and I'm left awed by their speed, by the way their bodies seem to disregard the current climate and conditions entirely. Anastasia keeps me abreast of who holds which position, and I'm left wondering, out of the fifty dragons competing in the race, if any have been held back in the caverns underground.

How many dragons are the Draconians hiding exactly?

As I watch them soar, dipping and diving as they try to overtake and sabotage one another's flight paths, I can understand why the other Kindred had been so wary, so afraid even. They're enormous, and even though the Draconian riders seem fully in control of them, they could wipe out cities in mere minutes if they wanted to. Let alone what would happen if a Draconian with a vendetta decided to try to seek revenge on an unknowing Sephilim or Nephilim.

It makes me wonder why the Sephilim King all those years ago had gone with such an either-or approach. Either they bent to his desire, or he made an enemy of their entire species, dragons included.

Then again, nobody knows these dragons exist.

And if the other Kindred races ever found out— I shudder at the thought.

The trust Lucien has placed on my mortal shoulders suddenly occurs to me. He let me get up close to Ebonara, probably the most precious thing to him in this world, second only to his hair of course, and yet he barely knows me. He does trust me. Despite the fact that

I've convinced myself I'm a burden and a stupid girl in his eyes, he's given me more freedom and more trust than Aro ever had.

As I'm pondering this, another dragon swoops past the window so close that if the glass wasn't between us, my hair would be blown back from my face entirely. The white scales of it, the way it's so ruthless in its competitiveness, makes me immediately sure who is riding this dragon. Only High Lady Genevieve could be at the reins of such a beast.

A few seconds later, a flash of pure white glints amongst violet and onyx, and I smile to myself.

I look up to Anastasia, ready to make some comment about Lucien and pry her for further information.

What I see, though, turns my blood icy in my veins.

Anastasia's eyes are bone white, her mouth gaping in a silent scream.

I freeze on the spot as I watch veins protrude on the flesh of her arms beneath the thin veil of her gown. Every muscle in her body has gone taut, her expression terrified and ghostly.

"Anastasia?"

I speak her name in a fraught whisper, heart beginning to pound, feeling utterly helpless as the ethereal High Priestess falls to the cold star-studded stone of the floor, writhing in undiluted agony that dances mercilessly behind the deathly pallor of her unseeing gaze.

19

A ROOM WITH A VIEW

ARO

THE VAULT THAT EXISTS beneath the Temple of Zeus has always been a well-kept secret between the High Lords and Ladies of Soleus.

Upon taking your vows, you are given this most sacred information, though only the King of Aetheria himself ever has access to the key.

How did I become the bearer of such an object?

Well, it's very simple. Right before he breathed his last immortal breath, King Midas gave me the key himself. The identity of the criminal responsible for this atrocity, I might add, is still a mystery.

Or that's how the story goes anyway.

It was on that day that I transcended to become a High Lord, and on that day, I took my sacred vows before moving into the suite within the Solis Castra that His Highness had once occupied. It was off the back of King Midas' demise that I rose to my current station. It had been an extremely unlikely set of circumstances, of which no one, even I, could have guessed.

Yet here we are.

Divine intervention perhaps?

I snort at this, unable to believe the lie even as I tell it to myself, staring at that which I have coveted as long as I can remember. It sits on a pedestal in the centre of the vaults beneath the temple, which by happenstance also connect to the Solis Castra via an intricate network of tunnels, perfect for allowing items of great value to be moved with discretion. The room itself is unextraordinary with simple stone walls and a single door to enter and one other door on the opposite wall that has never been opened and probably never will be. I don't even know what's inside, and I've never been curious enough to ask.

The crown of Aetheria is a glorious thing to behold, but not by comparison to that which one gains by wearing it. Or should I say, by having it bestowed upon one's head by Hera's chosen winged whore? Gold interlaces itself with amethyst and cloudy rose quartz as it forms delicate oak trees, the symbol of this land, which will wrap around the wearer's head. A reminder of both the roots from which we are reborn, this being Zeus, and how we must now reach for the stars in our mission of defending the dimension above.

I reach out to touch it, knowing it's hopeless, and remember the melting of my fingertips as they had come into contact with the crown last time. It was no ordinary wound either and took weeks to heal even beneath the Aetherial Sun. I was forced into wearing gloves to cover my disfigured hands, something which, luckily for me, nobody looked at twice or found suspicious.

I hear an approaching set of footsteps, glad that this vault is the only location in Aetheria in which nobody can conduct in or out. No, this vault is sacred, and as such has been relegated to a simple lock and key, oh, and of course the blasted curse that Hera laid on the most precious object in the entire place.

The heavy footfall is unmistakable as the haphazard piles of golden treasure stacked from floor to ceiling around me vibrate, eliciting a tinny clatter as singular pieces slide to the floor.

The individual in question grows closer and closer.

I had left the door ajar after entering, which I now realise was my first mistake.

Around the solid gold of the door, Caleb's glistening dark face appears, features drawn taut and eyes narrow upon finding me standing, staring at the pedestal holding the cursed crown.

"Lord Black, I thought I might find you here—" he exhales in a heavy sigh, his silver feathered wings becoming jaundiced and sickly in the yellow light of the vault as he steps fully inside. I clench my fist at his tone, letting the grooves of the elaborately carved key bite into the palm of my hand.

"And why, do tell, did you assume to find me here, exactly?" I ask him, curious as to what he thinks of me after the entire debacle with the mortal girl. It had left my true colours showing in a way I'd rather have avoided.

"Only that I know you enjoy thinking while staring at this thing—" He gestures to the crown with something akin to disgust, surprising me.

"Thing? Why such disdain for the symbol of our race's power over this dimension, Lord Abara?" I use his official title, increasing the intensity of my gaze as my dark brows lift, showing my surprise.

"Too many people have died over this hunk of metal. Surely you must realise that there is no need for a King of Aetheria. We have been functioning for over a century with a certain level of Democracy between the High Lords and Ladies—" he reminds me, and I roll my eyes as he steps further into the room uninvited.

"What you are saying is blasphemy. Zeus created us to keep order here, if he had desired that every Kindred had a vote, I hardly think he'd have risked Ares, Artemis, Nemesis, or Hecate creating their own races of warriors. They're volatile. They aren't like us." I'm certain in my stance, but he doesn't look moved to agree with me.

"I note you don't consider the Fae a threat—" he adds, changing the subject as he straightens his shoulders, eyes leaving my face and resting warily on the central pedestal.

"The tree huggers and dream walkers? I have a long-standing relationship with Morpheus, and I can guarantee you he agrees with me. He has no desire to deal with trade agreements or democracy. He just wants to indulge his immortal desires. I'm surprised you hadn't noticed his utter lack of interest in anything even slightly political," I add in, bored of this conversation already as I shift casually on the balls of my feet.

"Regardless. It is not about what one wants. It is about what is best for Aetheria." The hulking Lord looks angry at my previous insinuation of Morpheus' lack of care.

It makes me want to smile, but I fight the urge.

"How can one want a council of squabbling Lords and Ladies who take centuries to agree on anything? Aetheria needs strength in its leadership, one clear vision, a clear voice and direction," I reiterate, tilting my chin and looking down my nose now at the crown. Caleb gazes between me and its amethyst detailing, cautious as he noticeably chews on the inside of his plump bottom lip.

"And that's you, is it? The visionary with a singular direction?" he asks, and I laugh a little, the sound snide.

We both begin to pace as the sound dies into nothing and his question hangs between us, two lions circling a prize kill atop a pedestal shrouded in the light of divine power, waiting for the other to pounce.

"And that surprises you? I was a cat's whisker away from receiving the title of King before Storm was kidnapped by the Draconians and killed. If anything, this is Hera's way of course correcting. Of setting things right. I have long suspected her intent for me, but I realised that if I truly wanted such a destiny, I'd have to do some of the legwork myself. The Gods and Goddesses cannot be expected to make such a title easy to attain, I suppose, or the wearer of the crown might be a total imbecile," I reason, staring at the High Lord accusingly.

Caleb nods, reluctant but seeming to agree at last.

"I suppose you are right. Anyway, I did not come here to debate theology with you," he says, pious as he stops pacing and exhales an impatient breath.

"Then why *are* you here, Lord Abara?" I challenge him, and he shrinks slightly, pleasing me immensely as I let my wingspan spread from my spine in measured increments.

"I come with a message from the head of your security. He has found something up at the high tower he wishes you to see for yourself. He couldn't locate you, so I said I would take on the task, seeing as he wouldn't know to search for you here," Caleb informs me, and everything we've been quibbling over suddenly seems inconsequential.

"Well, why didn't you say? Come, I have a kidnapper to identify," I order him and miraculously he follows quickly and without complaint, watching like a hawk as I lock the vault door behind us both with the solid gold key. Central to its design is an enormous amethyst, and on either side, a feathered metal wing extends proudly.

"Be careful, Lord Black," the High Lord warns me as we stand among the flickering sconces of the stone passageway that crosses beneath the miles that separate the vault and Solis Castra.

"I'm always careful!" I bite out at him, impatient as I slip the key into my innermost pocket and pat the place where it rests with an assured hand.

He nods at me, and as I move to conduct, he says something he thinks I won't hear. As the lightning sparks between my synapses, the current carrying my essence through the air and toward the high tower, his final words echo in my ears, almost making me laugh.

"Don't forget, Lord Black, pride always comes before a fall."

I arrive in the high tower in mere seconds but find myself alone.

If Leo found something, then where the hell is he?

I storm through the balcony doors, noticing the glass still scattered across the floor from where I'd found it, determined to leave everything as it was and refrain from destroying any evidence.

The gossamer curtains surrounding the French doors billow inward in flighty feminine ribbons.

Outside, the night air is balmy, and the sound of the rushing falls below greets my ears, the aroma of lilacs and vanilla permeating the late summer air.

I look left and then right, finding no one.

"Lord Black!" The volume of my title is tiny from this lofty height, and so with curiosity, I waste no time crossing the balcony and peering directly over the elaborate railing.

There, hanging in the night, is Leo, his red hair blazing in the golden moonlight as a wicked and triumphant smile mars his face. "Come on down!" he beckons, waving a hand carelessly as his chocolate and crimson wings beat calmly at his spine.

I don't pause, climbing quickly onto the top of the railing so I'm perched atop it in a crouch before spreading my wings and launching off into the night. The warm air catches fast under each of my onyx feathers, enveloping me as I slow my freefall, descending to the level of the commanding officer in mere seconds before my wings catch me in a single and powerful beat.

"You found something?" I enquire, getting right to the point as I raise my voice above the pulsating of my wings, out of time with Leo's calm hovering tattoo.

"Indeed. It seems that what would not reveal itself by day has become apparent beneath the moonlight instead," he explains, gesturing for me to follow him in a steep dive as his wings tuck in beside him and he lets gravity take hold.

The wind rushes through my cropped hair, causing my eyes to water slightly and my dinner jacket to flap in the air as we plummet. Shortly, we level out into a glide, swooping in concentric circles until both sets of feet touch down amongst the crystal gardens surrounding the amethyst fortress.

"You found something here?" I look at him with wide eyes but with a sharp intense gaze, incredulous.

These gardens aren't even on the same side of the building as the high tower.

"Humour me, my Lord. You'll see—" Seeing my disbelief, he hurries, leading me past several crystal fountains and beneath the weep of three or more willows weeping pear-cut emerald leaves.

Finally, I see where he is taking me as several soldiers milling about the gardens in a relaxed cluster come into view, the golden gleam of their moonlight-soaked breastplates unmissable.

Hearing our footsteps, they straighten, standing to attention and then aside to clear the path for their High Lord and Captain.

Curiosity piqued, I let Leo lead me down a twining pathway of smooth quartz slabs and close toward the Solis Castra's outermost wall. When we reach a curve in the path that leads to a set of double doors, Leo walks off the track and onto crushed quartz, which crunches underfoot, before stopping several paces in front of me.

"Look—" He gestures down to the crushed stone, and I can see exactly what he means. Where before the sunlight was too stark, now the moon has exposed an enormous footprint in half shadow. The kind which could come from only one type of creature.

My heart chills, my mouth pursing in hopeful disbelief.

"But that's— a dragon footprint. Dragons died out years ago—" I muse aloud, and Leo shrugs.

"You asked me to find you evidence of her kidnapping. This is what we have. This and some talon marks on the tower walls from where the beast clung on waiting for its rider to return— If I had to guess anyway," Leo adds, lowering his gaze as if he'd momentarily forgotten his station.

He's not wrong in his assumption.

Dragons didn't just show up in Soleus, even when they had been alive, without a rider.

And there had only been one Draconian present at the ball that night.

Lord DeLaurent.

My teeth grit together, jaw tensing and rage rising fast in me like bile.

It's like a terrible nightmare where he steals her away all over again.

No.

I cannot let this happen.

Balling my fists at my side, I back up from the footprint, knowing I must take action without hesitation. Every moment she's among those monsters is a moment I risk losing her again.

"Captain Bond, follow me," I bark, turning my back on the evidence and dismissing the other soldiers with an explicit wave of my hand.

"Don't you want to see the talon marks first?" Leo asks me, his voice wavering in uncertainty as to whether he should even be asking this question.

"No. I've seen enough. Come. We have not a moment to lose—" I quicken my strides so the man behind me is practically running to keep up, launching myself into the air in a single bound. My wings spread instinctually, letting me soar as my mind races in panicked circles. Circumnavigating the Solis Castra until I reach the balcony of my Suite, I land without breaking stride, dusting aether from my shoulders as I storm through the open double doors and into the darkened room where all but one amethyst lamp remains unlit.

"Captain, come. You will go to Drakos Vale at once," I snap, hearing his feet land on the balcony with less stealth than my own.

"Drakos Vale? But— you know that it's almost impossible to navigate the skies around that godforsaken pit. The weather alone— without the turbulence, heavy cloud, and low visibility— it's a suicide mission." He sounds astounded by my suggestion, and this irks me greatly.

Sitting down at my writing desk and whipping a piece of letter paper from the pile, I twist back on the stool, glaring at him over my shoulder.

"Why do you think I'm ordering you, my next in command? If you can't do it, then nobody can, and everything we've been training for all these years has been for nothing," I say, breathless as I roll my eyes. His mouth opens then closes fast again, eyes narrowing.

"That's why you've had us training during storms?" he asks, sounding incredulous.

"You truly are a genius," I spit, picking up my quill and dipping it into thick black ink before beginning to scrawl, each letter an angry slash, violating the virginity of the flawless white parchment.

"What do you expect me to do? Go in there and slaughter them all single-handed?" he asks, and I laugh as his brows rise high in disbelief on his freckled forehead.

"Have you ever seen a dragon, Captain?" I demand, hunching as I continue my angry letter.

"Well— no, but—" he stutters, and I raise a hand, silencing him.

"If you had, we would not be having this discussion. Your discovery has changed everything. If dragons are still alive and thriving somehow, then we are all in incredible danger. I wouldn't risk your life with this journey if it weren't important. And more than that, I need you to find us a landing site so we might locate a place to conduct without being noticed or washed out by the weather. Do you understand?" I demand, my handwriting becoming faster with every angry word that leaches into the too-sweet fragrant air between us.

"I do, but— why the letter, then?" he enquires as I sign my name with fury before reaching for my envelopes and wax sealing kit. Trying to slow my breathing, I fold the letter, stuffing it with uncouth speed into the envelope and sealing the back with a defiant slam of my stamp in the molten wax.

"This letter is a declaration of my intent to go to war with the Draconians if Kairi is not returned, because if they do not return her, I want the full support of the other Kindred nations. I am giving them a deadline of forty-eight hours from receiving this letter by which to return her and asking them to surrender High Lord DeLaurent as collateral for my suffering and as insurance that this will never happen again. You will deliver this to High Lady Thomas and then return here swiftly with a location for us to touch down. You will go directly there and come directly back, speaking to no one of what we have discussed here, am I clear?"

Spinning on the stool, I hand Leo the letter without pause. He looks down at it and then straightens, holding himself to attention.

Swallowing, the following words pass into the air between us.

"I will not fail you, my Lord."

I nod, not giving him further courtesy as he turns smartly on the spot and rushes once more for the balcony, taking flight into the starry night beyond.

"Godspeed," I mutter under my breath, unable to stop my hands from balling into fists, or my desire for vengeance, bloodshed, and all-out war to diminish by even an inch.

KAIRI

I toss and turn beneath the heavy furs that cover my shivering form back at Lucien's lakeside house.

He found me on the observatory deck with a very much uncon-scious Anastasia's head in my lap, holding her as she seized. Then, he brought me, the dogs, and the sleigh, which he had left atop the peak of Gemina Two before flying across to its twin for the races, back home with unrivalled speed. The journey had gone by in a blur of what felt like being pelted by hundreds of cold lead pellets, but I didn't feel them. Instead, I just wrapped my cloak tighter around myself and tried to fight the overwhelming desire to sleep for a very long time.

As soon as he had me safely inside and settled beneath the covers, he had left on foot, taking to the skies for a speedy return to the observatory. I had fallen asleep within moments, my body finally relaxing and my mind succumbing too easily to sleep after such a shock. Unfortunately, the deep slumber that followed hadn't lasted all that long, and so now I'm left tossing and turning in an empty house, haunted by the images of Anastasia's tormented face that have been thoroughly branded into my brain.

I understood that Anastasia, being a seer, must have visions all the time. But even so, I knew what I had witnessed was something different. She had cried unintelligibly as she writhed on the floor, unconscious. Words like *run, Sephilim,* and more terrifyingly than those, *death* pouring from her in a torrent. And if that weren't enough to unsettle me, Lucien's face upon arrival had answered any of my remaining questions about whether this was a common occurrence.

A creak on one of the stairs beyond my bedroom door, which is cracked and allows the hall light to flood in through the gap, alerts me that I might not be alone. My skin turns clammy as I sit up, jaw tremoring as the cold air of the house causes goosebumps to rise beneath the simple silk sheath I'd been wearing as an undergarment beneath my woollen dress.

"Lucien?" I call out into the silence, hairs on the back of my neck rising.

"Hey, you're awake. It's only me. I was trying to be quiet; you know, to let you sleep." He pops his head around the door, and I pull the thick furs up so they're covering my chest, self-conscious and shivering. His face is tired, but not the kind that sleep might fix. His eyes tell the story of his bone weariness in a way that dark circles under his eyes never could.

"Yeah, I, uh, couldn't sleep. Is Anastasia okay?" I ask, half scared of the answer as I lean back against the cool curve of the wooden headboard.

Lucien steps inside the door tentatively, catching me shivering and turning toward the fireplace, taking several strides and then bending to light it efficiently.

"Not really. What you saw, that's not a normal vision for her. Those types of— episodes, well, they only happen when the powers upstairs are trying to get our attention." He sighs, lighting a match and tossing it into the hearth. He stokes the growing flames with a fire poker that's stood against the left wall, a metal dragon curling around the handle like a snake.

"What— what did she see?" I ask him, swallowing down my fear that the vision might be about me.

"That's the problem. According to her, well, as much as I could get out of her, being as she was extremely tired, is that whatever the Gods are trying to show her is being— tampered with somehow. It's why they're sending her these— 'skull breakers' as she calls them." He stands from his crouch, the elegance of his motion unnatural for such a burly silhouette. His face is lit orange momentarily as he turns away from the fireplace, his midnight blue eyes sparkling with intense frustration.

"Tampered with? Who has that kind of power?" I wonder, and he looks at me darkly.

"I have a few ideas, but Anastasia thinks that whoever is doing the tampering is targeting you specifically. Like— they're trying to keep your future from becoming known to us," he expresses, and I nod, puckering my lips and letting my fingers caress the fur in my grasp. As he steps closer to me, I see that the braid he had so flawlessly put together earlier is becoming ragged at the edges where he's been flying amidst the snow outside.

He sees my nervous expression, the way the blood leaves my face as I take what he's saying. Why would the Gods and Goddesses have any reason to care about my future? I don't belong here. I'm just a stupid mortal who got carried away with her romantic notions and swept up in the middle of someone else's war.

"Hey, don't worry. I'll make sure nothing bad happens to you," Lucien promises, his posture becoming almost prim as he folds his hands in front of him.

"Thanks. I guess I just couldn't sleep because my mind is going at a hundred miles an hour. Everything is coming at me sort of full speed. These last few days— I mean it's been dragons and High Ladies and running for my life. I don't know why Anastasia is having visions about me. I'm just a mortal who got stuck in the wrong dimension." I feel myself getting worked up, the air in my chest curling into dense knots of anxiety about things far beyond my control.

"Well, The Higher Plains seem to disagree with you there. But I can see that you need something to take your mind off everything. Actually, I got you something to help with that." He gives me a bashful grin, turning and quickly striding from the room before I can query him further.

When he comes back, he's holding a black box tied with a purple ribbon, jumping up and down on the balls of his feet like a little boy on Christmas morning with flushed cheeks. The sight makes me smile because I realise then I've never seen him look so young.

"Here— I hope you like it," he says, practically vibrating as he darts forward and lays the box, which is slick with rainwater, on the bedspread.

Curious, I swallow hard, blinking slowly as I tug the slightly damp violet silk ribbon free from its elaborate bow and pull it away before removing the lid.

I inhale, tears springing to my eyes.

"*Lucien*—" I whisper as the glinting gold of the blades catches the light and shimmers wildly like some kind of molten star.

"I saw you admiring them, and then after you told me about having to stop skating because you got sick— I thought— well, it seemed silly to waste the opportunity as the sun here makes you feel better." I stare at him, mouth agape as he rubs the back of his neck with a nervous hand. He's beet red in the face.

"You didn't have to—" I begin, but he shakes his head.

"I wanted to. I wanted to do this for you. After all, I get to fly every day, so you should at least get to fly again while you're here, right? I mean, I can't let Lord Black totally ruin Aetheria for you," he says gently as I lift the boots out of the box, finding a pair of tight velvet leggings and a skin-tight fleecy tunic beneath. The fabric of both garments shimmers with the occasional splash of gold glitter, matching the boots perfectly.

Bringing the leather to my fingertips, I feel the buttery softness of it.

It is even more amazing than I had imagined staring at them in the shop window.

A single tear drops down my cheek, and I start to cry, completely overwhelmed.

"Did I do something wrong?" Lucien asks, sitting down on the side of the bed and looking at me with immediate concern.

"No, stupid! This is just— this is the most thoughtful thing anyone has done for me in a long time. And you saved my life, so you had one hell of a standard to top! I don't understand why you're so nice— not when everyone seems to think you're some kind of— some kind of—" I exclaim, smacking him on the bicep again and choking on my tears.

"Monster?" Lucien finishes my sentence, his eyes wide and frank.

I nod, sniffing and wiping my tears away with the back of my hand.

I must look like a complete mess, but I'm unable to repair the dam that's broken inside.

"People see what they want to see," Lucien adds, getting up from the side of the bed. I nod, knowing exactly how true this is. When I had first been diagnosed, people didn't want to believe I was sick with no cure. They were happier to believe I was faking it for attention. If what I claimed was true, then it meant that just anybody could suddenly find themselves living in an inhospitable body with no hope of recovery or cure. If I was making it all up, it meant they didn't have to be afraid or try and understand my new reality for themselves.

Lucien heads toward the door, looking back over one shoulder and giving me an encouraging smile.

"Well, what are you waiting for? Get dressed, and let's get you back on the ice."

Lucien moves a couple of the rocking chairs from the porch and out onto the edge of the lake while I change. Once I'm fully dressed in the black velvet leggings and tunic, I head on out wearing boots, skates in my gloved hand. The air is cool still, but the snow has stopped, thank goodness.

The moon is lowering toward the horizon, the night drawing to its inevitable close, and the frozen lake waits in a flawless reflective mirror as if the stars have fallen and are floating just beneath the surface of the ice.

As I trudge across the snow blanketing the land between the front porch and the edge of the ice, I shudder, knowing I need to get moving quickly if I don't want to freeze.

Taking a seat in one of the cushioned rocking chairs, the pale wood and white upholstery of the furniture making it blend perfectly with the snow underfoot, I pull off my boots, exposing my thick wool socks.

I watch Lucien as he paces around the ice, checking for what I think is any potential weakness, and when he's satisfied, he takes flight from standing, carrying himself on thin air back to the house before landing quickly and moving inside without breaking stride.

I don't know if he's coming back, but as I unlace the first skate and slip my foot inside, I kind of hope he is. I want him to see me strong and capable if only this once.

Then again, I haven't skated in well over a year, so he may very well see me going splat on my face.

The skates are a dream, the leather creamy and soft on the inside while remaining supple enough to fully support my ankles. I don't know what they've done to the leather to make it so comfortable to wear, but any bootmaker in the mortal world would kill for their secret. I mean, no skater wants to spend six months wearing in new skates with countless blisters and cramping, but that's usually how things go and I'm sure most of the girls I know would have paid through the nose to get around it. My boots, a pair of Graf figure skates with parabolic blades and Kevlar-enforced ankle support, had caused me 6 months of agony and then several more months of mind-numbing pain after that. I recall one time, removing a skate and a large chunk of my heel's skin coming along with it underneath my sock. I had cried out with the suddenness of the flesh tearing clean away from my foot, my entire sock turning crimson as I sat fighting back tears on the metal bleachers.

Tying the boots tightly on my feet, it's like my soles are sinking into a foam hug as I stand for the first time, stepping out from the snow and straight onto the milky smooth ice of the lake.

Most pond or lake skaters will tell you that without a Zamboni to melt and re-smooth the ice, the experience can range from uncomfortable to just plain dangerous. Most natural ice is lumpy, bumpy, and uneven at the best of times.

To my surprise, though at this point I can't help but wonder why such perfection surprises me, the ice here in Aetheria is like melted chocolate in its flawlessness. My blades glide over the surface like it were glass.

I take my first step, arms spread out wide in the way I always used to warm up, not trusting my body as I once had. Then, pushing forward on one foot, I feel the golden blade's edges cut through the glacial surface like a knife through butter.

A giggle rises through my body at the familiar rush of air against my face as I begin to pick up speed, expanding in my chest and making my heart race, the scent of wintergreen and crisp air waking my mind and dissolving my anxiety.

My existence reduces to only this moment, my feet and legs and arms working in perfect unison as if they haven't forgotten a single training session. My lips spread wide beneath the star-scattered sky as I cross over to take a corner, tracing the familiar pattern of a figure eight to get my muscles working for the first time in I don't know how long.

I feel it all come back, the rush, the burn in my legs that only makes me push on harder, the way in which I am in control of speed, of height, of rotations and direction. I turn backwards, increasing my pace with crossovers and bringing one leg up for an ambitious Biellmann spiral, arms reaching back to catch the free blade with my gloved fingers.

I form the move, but my legs are weaker than they were, and I can't hold it. Falling over forward while still travelling backwards at mid-speed, I laugh to myself as I splat onto my back. Spinning out slightly on the flawless sheen of the lake, flat like a gingerbread man, I'm left staring up at the endlessness of the sky.

"Graceful."

Lucien's head pops into my field of vision as he offers me a hand.

I take it, shaking leftover ice and powdery snow out of my hair, which is pulled up into a high ponytail, before giving him a breathless grin.

"Thanks," I blush, looking into the deep midnight blue of his irises. They capture the starlight that shines, unabated, overhead.

"I thought you said you were good at this," Lucien smirks, and I flush.

"Well, maybe I'm starting out too easy then," I retort, feeling my cheeks heat.

I burst forward, heart hammering as I grit my teeth with determination. I need to prove I'm more than just some pathetic weakling, even if I'm scared I'll fall and break something all over again.

I could do a jump, but the thought of my ankles bearing the landing makes me feel physically nauseous with how prone to dislocation they've become.

A spin then, perhaps.

I wind up, flipping around so I'm gliding backwards before beginning to circle where I intend on centring the move. Lucien comes in close to me, watching with hawk-like scrutiny that makes me only more determined to prove myself.

When I feel the forces threatening to pull me apart from the tightening fluid spiral, I exit the wind-up and burst into the spin. Twisting, I bring my foot up and cross it over my opposite knee, only making me whirl faster as I pick up rotational speed. I tuck in my arms, and the world around me becomes a surreal and rapid blur as sky and snow meld together.

It feels great, feels like it used to, but just as a huge smile is making its way across my face, I'm brought back to reality with a cold thud as I hit something rock solid.

"Hmph!" I exclaim as I knock Lucien back off his feet and fall right along with him onto the smooth singular facet of the ice.

Then, as the world rights itself and the spinning ceases, I'm locked into the endless night of his gaze. Lying upon his chest, I feel his steely muscular torso turn rigid beneath me, causing my blood to warm where I'm flush against him. His arms have wrapped around me instinctively, his wings darting to cradle me and stop me hurting myself in the fall. His blonde hair smells like peppermint as I lean up to get a better look at him, seeing his pore-less skin up close for the very first time.

I'm enraptured.

As my stomach flutters like a pack of dragons have been set loose inside, we are both breathless, noses almost touching, hearts matching beat for beat. It's then that I realise what I'm feeling isn't only enraptured, but terrified.

He's too close.

I'm too close.

This is too much.

Clearing my throat and flushing with embarrassment, I climb to my feet and then offer him a hand which he doesn't bother taking.

"If you're not falling, you're not trying hard enough—" I quote my Russian coach from my competing years, Nadia, trying to dispel some of the tension.

"That's funny coming from someone so timid," Lucien quips, moving fast into gliding around me as he shrugs off our closeness.

I look down at his feet, to the skates there that look so well worn I can't help but wonder if he does this often. I hadn't even noticed he was skating until now, which tells you exactly how seamlessly the man moves.

"As I said, I didn't used to be this way. People change. I thought an immortal would recognise that more than the average person." I narrow my eyes, and he cocks one eyebrow, spinning on the spot a full one hundred and eighty degrees and taking off in a speedy arc around where I'm stood, motionless. The moment between us has thankfully passed, and I feel my body relax a little as I swallow down fresh air and try to refocus.

I watch him go as he says, "I'll have you know, and most would agree with me, that I haven't changed at all since the day I was reborn with wings." He sounds proud of this, but a part of me feels like it's kind of sad.

"Lies," I protest.

He cocks his head, gaze confused as his pristine white locks fall across his shoulders.

"Lies?" he retorts, stopping abruptly on the front of his blades, toe-picks digging ferociously into the ice.

"You said you were French. You don't sound very French to me. Or, do tell, did all Frenchmen in the eighteenth century speak flawless English?" I ask, a smugness lifting the sides of my mouth and causing my cheeks to flush against the cold. The ice is making me bold, allowing me to remember how fearless I had once been.

"T'es rien qu'un petit connard, mademoiselle," he shoots at me, eyes narrowing with malice. I cock my hip, one eyebrow rising in amusement.

"Calling me an asshole isn't going to change the fact I'm right, Monsieur," I goad him, looking sweetly from beneath fluttering lashes.

"You speak French?" he asks me, throwing his head back in an unrestrained laugh that seems to grow only louder in the vast emptiness of the surrounding landscape.

"Just profanity mainly. My friend, Holly, was the real language whizz. Especially French. Her parents have a house in Saint Lucien there—" I say, skating off after him as I begin raising my voice to cover the distance between us.

"Ah, mon homonyme!" Lucien says, spinning so he's travelling backwards, feet crossing over to increase his pace as I take chase after him.

"Subtitles, please?" I ask, and he scowls. I copy his expression, crossing my ankles and increasing my pace to match his despite my much shorter legs. "In English, if you please, Monsieur!" I rephrase, and he rolls his eyes.

"Wasn't it you who was irritated with my lack of French only a few moments ago?" he accuses me, blonde hair glowing gold in the moonlight.

"Actually, I was just making a point to prove you wrong. But it's nice that you forgot all about the 'me being right part' of this discussion and instead turned me irritated in your mind. Such a man." I roll my eyes, stopping in my path and changing so I'm gliding forward this time instead.

"Saint Lucien is where I was born. It's where my name comes from—" he elaborates, relinquishing to my bored gaze. I nod, curious now more than ever about his past.

"Does this little nugget of gold mean you're going to tell me about your mortal life?" I tease him as we grow closer.

As the Draconian comes within inches of me, I spread my feet sideways, gliding around him gracefully in a miniature spread eagle as he whizzes past.

"Tit for tat, mademoiselle," he retorts, and I give him a look of surprise as my toes curl in my boots at his fluent use of the French Language.

"Why would you want to know about my life? It's very boring— I assure you," I inform him. He stills and then glides closer at a relaxed speed, slowing just before reaching me and looking down into my eyes.

"I want to know how someone goes from being so outgoing, so alive, as I see you now— to being— well, a damsel?" he asks as I scrunch up my face.

"I'm not a damsel!" I retort, trying very hard not to stamp my foot down on the ice. He cocks his head.

"Kairi, I literally rescued you from a tower— on dragon back. You're a damsel." His words hurt me in a way I can't describe. In my studies of Literature, I had always sneered at the female characters who longed only to be saved and not to fight for themselves. I had never understood their fear of the world— of how they would rather live some half-life in safety and comfort than bear the pain of breaking out and finding their freedom.

Has Ehlers Danlos Syndrome made me hopeless? Made me give up the fight because I don't want to face the pain of trying to live my life in spite of it?

"Ehlers Danlos Syndrome—" I reply, feeling my world tilting on its axis. Aro had manipulated me but in a way I'd wanted to be manipulated, to be taken away to some fantasy so I didn't have to deal with the truth that real life, especially for me, was going to be a long and largely painful affair.

"Um— Subtitles, please?" Lucien repeats my turn of phrase back at me.

"It's the disease I have. It means that the glue holding my body together is defective. My joints come out of place a lot, and I have pain and fatigue all the time. Like— all day every day. There's no cure. And they say my symptoms will get worse as I age," I tell him, trying not to use technical medical jargon as I don't know how modern his understanding of collagen and genes is.

"That sounds awful." He sympathises with me, but I don't want it. Instead, his damnation of me echoes in the back of my mind over and over, making me feel nauseous and pathetic despite the fact I should feel stronger than I have in years.

You're a damsel.

"It is. I don't really want to talk about it," I admit, turning from him and taking off across the ice.

He doesn't come after me, doesn't push me for more answers, and where before I was curious about his past, now I'm curious about what had become of the girl I used to be.

He leaves the ice without a word, and I skate on until dawn.

20

DEATHNOTE

GENEVIEVE

FEELING BETTER, MY LOVE? I ask Algoric with a relaxed smile as I stroke the alabaster pearl of his scales. He purrs, throat vibrating at a low rumble, lips curving up in an almost feline smile as his fangs glint with painful promise.

Much. There is no invigoration quite like flight, is there Gen? Algoric replies, his voice a warm echo against the dark cavernous walls of my skull.

His pupils dilate, head on level with mine as his long neck snakes slightly from left to right, his excitement obvious.

I rest my forehead against the raw molten heat of his scales, the temperature high enough to cause most to flinch away, but not me, not I. For this exquisite creature and I are two of a pair, our souls made from the same tatters of star-studded sky and volcanic ash swirled together endlessly over aeons.

"Uh—" The voice causes my eyes to snap open, breaking the connection between me and my dragon. My fingers pull back from the scorn of Algoric's heat as I spin to face the intruder.

Gage stands, his boyish face taut with concern. I narrow my eyes, the calm I had felt after flying through the night at the speed of light and the gentle caress of the Algroric's sated wanderlust dissipating like steam.

Running his hand back through his fauxhawk, I find his mahogany irises rich, not with their usual mischievous glint but instead a deep-rooted anxiety.

Instead of worrying about the fact he had not properly addressed me by title, I take quick strides toward him. He takes a small step back in response, only too aware of the damage my touch can cause.

288

Once upon a time, his caution would have bothered me, but now it is something I simply expect.

"What is it?" I snap, feeling Algoric's warm mass shift noticeably at my spine. The chains around his rear legs clank, the sound physically painful to me as the sound of steel on steel cuts through me more sharply and with more definiteness than any sword ever could. The air in the caverns is unseasonably warm compared to the bitter chill, which had bitten against any piece of exposed flesh it could find during flight, making me clammy. My heart picks up pace to a jovial if not slightly cautious canter beside my lungs that are struggling for air as my blood pressure climbs.

"It's— a Sephilim. He's here, and he's demanding to see you. He says Lord Black sent him." In this, the now early hours of the dawn, I feel fatigue hit me like a wave, not in a physical sense but in the fact that I must now once more enter some kind of ridiculous political dance with the people who had once banished us to die out. I mean, if they wanted us to die out, can they not at least leave us alone to get on with it rather than incessantly turning up where they aren't wanted?

"He looks— well, a little dishevelled is an understatement," Gage explains, his lips turning up in the corners in a smug smile that makes me curious without my consent.

"Where is he?" I demand, nervous as I rub my palms against the cream leather of my riding pants. The constraints of my matching leather corset are pushing against my ribs with increasing bite as I watch Gage's posture stiffen.

"He's in the hallway. I asked him to wait outside the throne room so we could close the pit," he explains, and I sigh out, relieved. I'm grateful for Gage's quick thinking. Given his age, he's easy to underestimate.

"Come, we must hurry. I don't trust the patience of Zeus' feathered mongrels." I sweep past him, my wings pulling into my spine, a part of myself silently withering with each step I put between myself and Algoric.

We pass the ever-clanging anvils and the Draconians that work all hours to see that the metalwork needs of Drakos Vale are met. I smile at them, if only slightly, as we pass toward the column of hematite waiting to take us back up into the throne room.

I step up, the flat sturdy sole of my riding boot leaving no sound behind as Gage follows after me. Slowly the column begins to rise as it senses our weight, corkscrewing through the ceiling as thick blue topaz surrounds us. It takes only moments, but it feels like an eternity as I expect to rise into the throne room and come face to face with the waiting dark angel. Instead though, and much to my relief and surprise, the room is full only of anxious-looking guards who line the walls in stiff and alert formation.

Gage and I hop off the column as fast as possible as though the metal beneath our feet forming Hecate's symbol has become molten. I take the distance between the seal and my throne in seconds, letting my wings flare wide on either side of me as I sit amongst the porcelain construct of the archaically designed chair.

Taking in a deep breath and composing myself as I push my loose hair, braided on only one side so it's tight against my skull and exposing the scarlet roots, behind one ear, I nod to the waiting Draconian.

"Show him in," I order, straightening, crossing my legs and raising my chin so I can appraise the visitor from a proper level of superiority.

Gage strides purposefully back across the room and past the guards waiting on either side of the high-arched double doors. Their eyes linger on mine as he goes, a determined sparkle assuring me of their loyalty behind their oxidised steel helmets, their faces cupped by faux reptilian jaws spread wide.

I wait, holding my breath a few seconds before the Sephilim in question appears from the shadows of the corridor beyond the room's sprawl, his appearance causing me to suppress a laugh, but unable to stop my lips curving into a smug smile.

"Comfortable trip, Sephilim?" I ask, unable to help myself as the boy's damp reddish hair turns an odd shade of brown in the cobalt light falling in through the stained-glass windows. That hair, now I mention it, couldn't be further from groomed if the boy was raised by spectral mountain dogs. His feathers are ruffled, some pushed the wrong way, with water dripping from almost every plume. His pale skin cannot hide the flush of scarlet that's taken over his cheeks from the freezing tundra skies outside as he stands, shivering in front of me like a drowned pigeon with water pooling around him in small yet satisfying puddles.

His teeth chatter as he moves to reply, reaching into his jacket and rummaging for something. Amazingly, he pulls out a letter almost identical to the invitation I had received once before, the envelope only damp at the tips.

What, was my total disregard for their last extended invite not clue enough that I want nothing to do with them?

He takes several steps forward, not bowing, nor acknowledging my title in any other way, handing me the envelope from soggy fingers and simply saying, "I've had better—" through trembling blue lips that seem further frozen by the cerulean light of the room.

I smile, taking the envelope from him in a quick snatch, feeling the edges of the parchment soggy in my fingertips.

I open the letter, scanning the angry and striking scrawl forged from ink as black as the soul of the Sephilim who wrote it, cocking an eyebrow to the still sopping Sephilim who watches me with an interested if not slightly worried expression. He clenches his jaw, straightening on the spot as I observe him, trying to seem more intimidating despite the fact he could do with a mop instead of a sword.

"So— what? I'm being accused of kidnapping some girl called—" I squint for effect, "Kairi Freemont?" I say the name, my tone displaying the same distaste for the girl as I have for the entire situation. Lucien seriously owes me.

"Yes. We know she's here. We found evidence," the boy retorts, his voice diminishing further with each syllable beneath the scorn of my expression.

"Oh, did you now?" I sharpen my gaze as I would a blade, standing and letting my wings spread as far as they'll go, my porcelain talons glinting in the early dawn light.

"Yes. We know she's here." He balls his fists at his sides, several droplets of melted snow trickling down the path of veins, just visible below his translucent skin and off one of his knuckles.

I step down from the platform on which the throne sits, predatory and tired of this already. I can only guess what kind of evidence they have to prove our involvement; all I know is that I have to shut this down once and for all.

"Well, I suggest you look at that evidence again. I have no idea who this girl is you're searching for, nor why you think you can simply fly into our territory unannounced after it was your kind who banished us here in the first place. You wanted us uninvolved with the rest of Aetheria, and that is how we have remained." I grit my teeth, seconds away from snarling.

The Sephilim's wings flare a little at my proximity, the chocolate brown and scarlet of his feathers dull and unimpressive.

"Lord Black doesn't care for your excuses, High Lady Thomas. He cares only for the retrieval of what is rightfully his. The girl he is looking for is the next Heirbound, therefore Sephilim property."

291

The Sephilim has some gall, talking of the girl as though she's a possession, as though she is the crown, a lifeless piece of cold metal.

"Well then, perhaps Lord Black shouldn't misplace his things if they're so precious to him. Why is it you insist on making the problems of the Sephilim the fault of others? Can you not take responsibility for your own failings in securing what you claim is so coveted?" I ask him, cocking an eyebrow and trying very hard to control my temper.

As much as I loathe the Sephilim, as much as I wish to maul the one standing before me to death in a rage-fuelled frenzy, I must protect what is mine. Must protect what lies beneath my well-worn soles.

"You have forty-eight hours to return the girl, Lady Thomas. If not, you can expect the Sephilim army to be landing on your doorstep for an official search. As Lord Black has already warned you in his letter, I'm sure." The boy before me doesn't blink or even flinch as I glower at him.

So at least he has some backbone.

"You had better get the hell off my continent before I stuff you and mount you on my wall, Pigeon," I hiss, narrowing my eyes and watching him flinch finally. I smile, baring my sharp incisors and feeling the heat growing beneath my skin.

"And if your Sephilim army thinks they have a chance against the Draconians, then you have another thing coming. And that thing is Sephilim blood running off the edge of Drakos Vale in an endless hot torrent. Come near my people or my lands, and you're dead. You hear me?!" I growl, lunging slightly as my wings rise defensively behind me.

The boy swallows, sighing, and shakes his head.

"We warned you. Anything that happens from now on is on your shoulders, Lizard Bitch." He turns on his heel and strides from the room, leaving a trail of ice water in his wake.

Gage, I notice only now, is standing propped against the far wall, his white and aqua wings resting against the crystal slab at his spine, scales shimmering coldly.

He's watching with seemingly casual interest though I can tell he's on edge just like me from the way his foot incessantly taps and how he feels for his metal teeth with his tongue, remembering how they were knocked out in the first place and the pain that he never wishes to relive.

"Well, that went well," he says as I turn my back on him, prowling back up to the throne where I had left the letter sitting, still damp, on the cushioned seat. I snatch it from the velvet, holding it up to the light pouring in through the window and promptly burning it to ash with only my fingertips.

"What do we do?" He looks at me now, pushing off the wall and crossing the vast space between us. His discomfort becomes increasingly evident in the way his strides are measured, his fists balled at his sides as he becomes enveloped in my white-hot rage as well.

I exhale heavily, knowing exactly who is to blame for all this, and exactly who I need to summon.

What has he done?

"Get me Lucien," I command.

It seems the time for hesitation is long dead and gone.

LUCIEN

I watch her sleep from beyond a small gap in her bedroom door. She looks so peaceful, so much less at war with herself than when she's awake. The crackling of the fireplace is audible, but other than that, all I can hear is the comforting rise and fall of her chest, her breath heavy and delicate as though each inhale might be her last.

I've never felt a mortal quite as fragile as I do her.

It's infuriating. Yet she won't hear me call her a damsel, even though in my eyes she's breakable as glass and infinitely more precious.

I get it now, though. Why she came here, longing to be the person she had once been, longing to recover her strength, the energy that made her come alive before my very eyes as she had flown over the surface of the lake, every stride seeming effortless though I know it was anything but.

I can't deny I feel like I know her, in those moments where she comes alive when her face relaxes and she smiles or a laugh erupts from her like a long-awaited firework. There's something there, some memory lost among the blizzard of my history, but as soon as I feel the static clearing, she drops her gaze or fumbles finding her words, and suddenly she's a wisp of who she had once been again and entirely unrecognisable. The life within her, that strength she's so determined to reclaim, evaporates like dew from summer parched grass, any recollection of who she had once been disappearing with it and leaving me wondering if I'm grasping at the smoke left after a blaze has long since died.

She stirs in sleep, her hand coming up to cup her cheek as she turns so her face is obscured from view, and I stare at her outline, narrowing my eyes and hoping if I just stare at her long enough that I'll remember what it is I'm forgetting.

Anastasia says that whatever forces are involved with her are obscuring the truth of her past and possibly her future. So, is it possible then that she was right, that I really did murder her?

But how would I have even met her if she was a Nephilim? I haven't been to Soleus in— maybe a hundred and fifty years— give or take.

The thought of my stealing her immortal life from her revolts me as it's tossed, heavy like wet concrete inside my gut. She's sweet and has a passionate curiosity that's hard to resist, the way she's awed by everything, which to me has long since lost its sparkle, makes me feel young again. And then— there's the fact that though her inquisitiveness is puppyish, her soul is old. She's suffered, and she is wiser than her years by far.

It's curious, and a part of me wants to remain in denial, wants to see her simply as an impermanent inconvenience.

I can't deny, though, the harder I focus on trying to remember if I've ever laid eyes on a face like hers before, the more persistently a thick fog sweeps across my consciousness. If there's nothing to remember, then why does it feel like my brain is hiding something from me? It's not a good sign, and I feel the emotions inside myself twist and contort like metal, glowing white and hot as I turn them over and over inside my mind, agitating their consistency and pulling them apart.

A knock from downstairs disturbs these thoughts, and so I close Kairi's door soundlessly, wanting her to get her rest after she'd spent so long out on the ice.

Padding down the stairs in only socks, I inhale deeply, the early morning light not pouring in through the ice dragon mural that makes up the stained-glass pane in the front door as it should be. Instead, there's a male, winged silhouette obstructing the sunlight.

I'm not expecting anyone, and so I know that this unannounced visitor can mean nothing good.

Crossing the hallway and shoving my hands into the pockets of my jeans, I pull open the front door, revealing the young High Lord I've been training for the last twelve months in the ways of Draconian aristocracy.

"Gage, to what do I owe this unexpected visit?" I ask, my eyes coming to settle on the deep chocolate irises that warm his entire face. His alabaster wings are spattered with aqua patches, and he looks fairly chill as he hops from one foot to the other on the porch, flashing me an uneasy smile and revealing several of his silver teeth.

"Genevieve requires your presence immediately." He says it with less enthusiasm than I'm used to hearing from him. In fact, he looks downright pale and morose compared to his usual lively self.

"Does she now? I'd remind her that I'm her equal, not her lapdog," I bite, feeling irritation rising in my throat. It's early, and though I don't need to sleep, it doesn't hurt my mental clarity or my mood.

"Lucien, just go. She's not kidding around, and I really can't deal with the Sephilim starting another war. I've heard stories of the last one, and it's not something I've ever desired to experience first-hand." He looks seriously anxious, hands shoved into the pockets of his high-collared trench coat, wings erected to attention behind him.

My ears prick at the word *war*, and I feel my heart grow heavy behind the shield of my ribs.

I think back to the girl sleeping peacefully upstairs, of how foolish she had sounded asking if she needed a key to enter my front door. It doesn't seem so silly now though as the thought of leaving her defenceless upstairs makes my stomach curl into thorny, tangled knots.

"If I go, will you stay here with her?" I ask, letting my eyes wander upstairs. Gage purses his lips, nostrils flaring slightly in the raw chill of the air, the light pure and brutal behind him.

"Yes. I'll stay. Just go." He steps across the threshold, furious in his speed.

"Am I detecting you're angry with me?" I demand as he unbuttons his overcoat with quick fingers.

"I am angry with you. Because of you, a secret that's been successfully kept for over one hundred years is at risk. If Algoric dies or is even discovered because of what you've done, or Aqua for that matter, I'll never forgive you, and neither will Genevieve." He shrugs out of his coat, the back of the garment parting and then slipping around his wings where it's been tailored to accommodate them.

I'm surprised at his frankness, considering he usually idolises every word that passes my lips. Then again, he has the same close bond with

Aqua, his dragon, that all of us do, and the thought of anything putting the beasts at risk is enough to anger even the gentlest of souls.

"You think I should have left the girl to be tortured and killed after all you know of pain?" I ask him, and he shrugs.

"I think you forget that your first duty is to the people of Drakos Vale, not your heart." Gage throws the words I've said to him many times back at me. He's not wrong, but I couldn't help myself.

I couldn't have left Kairi in that tower to die. Not after I suspected what Lord Black was planning to do.

No one, even someone I had thought was a foolish mortal, deserves what he had planned for her.

She didn't know any better.

I don't reply to Gage, stepping past him as he hangs his coat over the balustrade, and pulling on a pair of black leather boots.

"I'll be back soon," I inform him swiftly, not catching his eyes as I hurry through the front door and close it behind me with a soft click. I breathe out, relieved as the cold envelops me. Standing before Gage, an empath, is like being stripped bare, and in this moment, I can't stand it.

Jumping down off the porch, I channel my fury at the impossibility of the choice I had been faced with into a ferocious sprint that leaves snow flying up in my wake.

Quickly, and without any certainty of what will happen next, I take to the skies.

I don't know where I'll find Genevieve, so with my wings out-stretched and beating hard against the unbelievably cloudless morning sky, I circle the peak of Gemina One, eyes keen. Catching a wind current and banking a hard left as it gives me a boost in gliding speed, I see that Genevieve's balcony doors are wide open, a usual indicator that she's residing inside her suite.

I plummet around fifty feet in only twenty or so seconds, my long blonde tresses swept clean back off my face and left trailing behind me in the air like flawless blades of pure white. I let my wings spread as I turn myself upright, coming in to land and slowing my speed. My feet catch habitually on the edge of the twisted steel railing as usual, and I land soundlessly upon the balcony without so much as a stumble.

So at least that's not gone wrong.

"Lucien."

Genevieve is lounging on the chaise longue in front of a smouldering hearth, her long fingers wrapped, claw-like, around a glass tumbler of whiskey. Her use of my name isn't a greeting so much as it is a summons.

I let my wings relax against my spine, folding them in close to me as the chill breeze catches my hair in its fleeting clutches right before I step through the balcony doors toward her.

"You know you can't just summon me whenever you feel like it, Genevieve. Unbelievable as it may seem to you, I don't sit around waiting for you to send for me." I scowl, cocking my head and watching as she glowers at me over the rim of her crystal tumbler.

"If you don't want me to summon you, then you might think before causing Sephilim to arrive unannounced in my home," she bites back, a small hiss escaping her lips after she swallows the firewater. Her ankles uncross gingerly as she slides around to face me straight on.

"Lord Black sent a Sephilim? He made it through the storm?" I ask, disbelieving. She suppresses an amused sparkle that smoulders in the back of her eyes.

"He didn't look what you'd call put together upon arrival, but that's not the point. If Lord Black sent him here, then he's not kidding around about the girl. He says if I don't surrender her in forty-eight hours, they're sending an army. He also says that you left evidence behind when you kidnapped the girl."

She downs the rest of her drink without pause, the glass looking more tenuous within her furious grip by the second.

"An army? He couldn't—" I begin, but she raises a hand.

"That isn't the point, Lucien. You've put our secrets at risk of exposure, and I am doing what I should have done when you came to ask for sanctuary. You need to get rid of the girl. She isn't our problem, not mine or yours. People shouldn't have to die or have their dragons taken from them because of your poor judgement," she scolds me, getting to her feet.

"I won't abandon her, Genevieve. If she goes, so do I. I couldn't sleep knowing I sent her off to her death and just abandoned her. What about honour? What about doing what's right just because it's right? Isn't that why Hecate chose us? Isn't that—" The words pick up speed, like an avalanche started by a single tumbling pebble upon some precarious peak.

"Then go. You might have abandoned your people, but I haven't. Whatever the hell it is about this girl that's got you so invested, I suggest you seriously re-evaluate your loyalty. You're risking *war*, Lucien. You weren't alive back then, so you don't know. But trust me when I say that guilt over the death of one mortal is in no way comparable to the suffering the Sephilim will cause across this continent should they decide to descend upon us. You have put us all in grave danger. So, either put it right or leave. I have no use for someone so reckless." She waves her hand, and I wonder if she means it. She's awfully passionate for someone who seems so detached from the situation, but perhaps that's because she doesn't believe I'd leave. I thought we were closer than any one issue could divide, but apparently, I was wrong.

"You've made yourself clear." I nod, heading for the door without a second thought.

"Where are you going?" she asks, voice suddenly a husk of fear. Is she afraid of what I'll do or afraid that I really will leave?

Is she afraid of being alone?

I've always known that I was her only real social lifeline, the person that kept her from falling slowly into insanity, but maybe she's more aware than I thought. Though, I had certainly banked on it when I threatened to leave earlier.

However, compared to what I'm asking of her now, the odds back then weren't so obviously stacked against us.

Could we take the Sephilim in an all-out war?

Who knows, but I'm betting she's not willing to risk finding out. Not for me, and certainly not for Kairi.

If she won't go to war to protect the innocent, to protect the fragile, and the rest of Aetheria, then what will she fight for?

I turn back to her, my eyes cold.

"I'm leaving. You're right. I shouldn't put Drakos Vale at risk, I guess I just thought you'd trust my judgement and stand by my decisions, especially after everything we've been through. There's something about this girl, Genevieve— something I can't simply let go, something I refuse to surrender to that malicious shit, Lord Black over in Soleus. So, if you won't help me protect her, I'll find someone who will."

Her mouth drops open, her eyes widening, but I don't give her a chance to reply, feeling myself letting go of what I thought was a bond of mutual trust and honour between us.

She calls after me, voice ringing out as ever superior, but I don't turn back.

Instead, I head toward the pit, down many crystal winding corridors, and into the unknown, my alliances set now in cold, permanently hard stone.

21

GONE GIRL

KAIRI

THE SLEEP I HAVE within the warm clutches of Lucien's guest sleigh bed is the best I can remember having in what feels like forever. The warmth and weight of the furs press my body into a state of calm immobilisation, so when I finally do stir, it feels as though I've slept for weeks instead of mere hours.

Between the gap in the heavy velvet drapes, the day seems to be almost over or maybe just beginning, the time that's passed not surprising me as I stretch my arms over my head and toward the sloped eaves of the ceiling that capture shadows as a spider web catches flies.

I fling my legs out from beneath the heavy blankets, stiff, but nowhere near as sore as I would be if I were waking back home in Tennessee after hours on the ice.

My skates are propped by the side of the hearth, their blades glinting warm in the sepia light of the dying embers.

Slipping out of bed before treading silently toward the window, I pull open the drapes, finding the cobalt sun weak as it falls into the infinite endlessness of the horizon beyond the lake.

I've slept all day it seems, and though the balls of my feet give a slight throb against the wooden floorboards, other than that, I can say I honestly feel more put together than I have since arriving. I find the trails of white lines I had carved with Lucien into the lake's surface, tangling over themselves and knotting into intricate designs, a blatant and irrefutable map of everywhere I've been.

If only I had a map for where I'm going.

Though, despite the fact that I'm fleeing for my life and that my time here is under a strict limit of seven days, there's something about Drakos Vale that undeniably settles me.

Is it the beauty of endless snow making the world seem new and un-tarnished each morning or the utter exquisite splendour resulting from the brutality of the prior night's storm? Perhaps it's the cosiness of feeling safe in the warm caress of a crackling fireplace as the cold whips mercilessly across the landscape outside.

Or maybe, just maybe, it's the fact that despite how Aro had so utterly charmed and then betrayed me in the most violent of ways, I can't help but trust Lucien. Even when he's stoic or angry behind a thin and flimsy veil of indifference, at least he's honest about it.

I turn from the creamy pastels of dusk, treading across the room and trying not to trip over the too-long pant legs of Lucien's navy pyjamas as I head for the door. My stomach is rumbling, and even though I'm extremely tempted to get dressed and head straight onto the ice again, I know that I'm going to need food first.

I cross the landing, holding the pyjama pants up at the knees and calling out for my host.

"Lucien?" I poke my head over the side of the bannister, but the reply I receive isn't from anyone I'm familiar with.

"He's not here. He left hours ago for an urgent meeting with High Lady Genevieve. I'm Gage, by the way. It's nice to meet you." The young man's caramel fauxhawk shimmers golden as the dying light of the day pours in through the front door's stained-glass pane and illuminates his face.

"So, what, he just left me here?" I ask, feeling bold as my stomach begins to churn furiously.

An urgent meeting with Genevieve doesn't sound good.

"You were sleeping, and as a mortal, I doubt you'd have been any use. Unless you are well versed in Draconian and Sephilim politics? I mean, it's terribly boring after all, so I can't say I blame you for the ignorance," he quips, spinning on the spot and walking backwards so he can fully take me in as he gazes up at me. I frown, but he only grins, his smile exposing several shiny metal teeth.

"The Sephilim?" My ears prickle at the word as though it's a very real and sharp projectile being launched through the air.

"Yes, you are quite popular with much of the aristocracy it seems, not that I blame them. You're very pretty, for a mortal anyhow—" he flushes a little, tone suddenly losing its edge. The cream and aqua hues of his scales glimmer coolly as he turns on the spot, peering curiously through the pane inlaid into the front door.

301

"Um— thanks—" I whisper, touching my face, but he doesn't make further comment, instead looking back over one shoulder with a small but sad smile.

"Lucien has returned, and he's not alone it would seem." I feel horror drench my skin in a wave of sudden clamminess as I realise I'm standing on the landing in nothing but oversized cotton pyjamas. I look down at myself, heartrate spiking.

Gage laughs.

"Oh, don't worry about that, doll. I doubt Ebonara cares what you're wearing." He smiles salaciously, his eyes glinting with mischief and amusement. He has a boyish air to him, and I have a strong feeling that given a chance, we could be very good friends.

I swallow, wondering why on earth Lucien would bring his dragon out into the dying daylight. The panic rises inside me as the muscles beneath the thin veil of my flesh start to glow red hot with anxiety. The heat refuses to dispel, making me feel like I can't draw breath despite the fact I'm swimming in fresh air.

"Don't you worry. You've gone terribly pale. But I can tell you, it'll all work out in the end," Gage promises, launching from a standstill and letting his wings spread so they're only inches from both walls of the hall. With two enormous pumps of their full width, he's risen above the railing and almost hit the ceiling. Letting his wingspan visibly relax, he falls through the air, closing the space between us as I struggle to breathe even still.

"Thank you, that's very kind. Most Kindred seem to think I'm just some stupid mortal—" I sigh, vision going fuzzy around the edges.

"Oh, doll. You *are*. But that's not your fault, and we were all stupid mortals once, as easy as that is to forget after a few centuries. No one who ever wore a crown or held a title in this place was anything but once upon a time. Don't let them pretend otherwise." He puts a finger on my chin and nudges it, causing my eyes to rise to his. The deep chocolate depths of his thick irises are warmer than I expect beneath decadent lashes.

"Chin up, or the crown slips. Don't forget." He places a firm calloused palm on my shoulder, the warmth of his touch bringing me back down into my body and grounding me upon the wooden floorboards.

"Thank you." I exhale heavily, my body relaxing.

He nods.

"Whatever happens, just remember that pain won't kill you. Not in the big picture. We're pawns in a game too big to understand, played by creatures we cannot conceive. Don't fear the pain of playing; fear the nothingness that comes from being knocked from the board entirely."

"That's— exactly what I needed to hear. Thank you—" I breathe, brow furrowing in wonder at the uncanniness of his intuition.

"I know, I'm an empath. Most of the time, it drives me crazy, feeling everything for everyone. If there's one thing I've learned it's that indifference, the silence of not caring, is far worse than any rage or fear. If you're feeling that pain, it means you still have something to lose. But, being in this house with you, with a *mere* mortal as you say, is a relief. I haven't felt this calm in a long time despite the raging anxiety. Your awareness of your helplessness seems to be quite the tonic to the violent urges I usually feel." He smiles at me, and I no longer feel so alone.

"Thank you—" I smile back at him, totally unsure of what to say or whether to be offended. In response, he only shrugs.

"No problem. I love being a personalised fortune cookie." He smirks, lightening the mood, and I can't help but grin back, forgetting everything around me and focusing on what he has just said.

I'm afraid because I still have something to lose, and in that regard, I'm lucky.

As I'm pondering on what to say next, Lucien bursts in through the front door, looking much different than when I'd last seen him.

His hair is no longer in a thick braid but loose and flawlessly smooth as it cups both sides of his face in a sharp-edged caress. His eyes are bright, if not slightly panicked, weapons with long blades not only strapped to his thighs in thick leather sheathes but also bound to his back as a vicious-looking axe hangs down between his shoulder blades, the steel of it cast dull in the shadow of his wings.

"Kairi, we have to go. Come. I want to be air-bound by nightfall." His words aren't a request but a command. Blanching slightly where the cold air of outside sweeps in behind him through the open door, the tops of my bare feet chill as it rises through the immense height of the hall, causing a ripple of goosebumps to blaze icy across my skin.

"Why? What's going on?" I ask, unable to hide the desperate fear in my voice as it rises in pitch.

"You are no longer safe here. The Sephilim believe you to be here, and they are willing to force their way through our borders to prove it and take you back to Soleus. I'm going to take you somewhere safe," he explains, turning and shutting the door behind him. He's changed from what he was wearing before, now clad in similar attire to what I had seen him wearing the night of the race beneath a thick velvet cloak. Now though, a large bag is slung over one shoulder, and I wonder if it's full of weapons or something else entirely.

After all, how many weapons can one man need?

"Get dressed. You won't be able to take any bags, so make sure anything you bring is small enough to fit into your cloak pockets," he orders, not blinking as I begin to tremble.

"And where is this promised safe haven, Lucien?" Gage enquires, asking the question that's most nagging at me but that I can't seem to vocalise.

"It's better for you and everyone else if you don't know, Gage. Thank you for watching over Kairi." He nods, giving a gracious look from beneath the curtain of his silken locks as they fall languid across his cheek.

"I see. Well, I'll be going then," he replies.

I don't want him to leave and contemplate reaching out to take his hand to stop him. Before I can though, he turns to me, eyes kind even still.

"Go with Lucien, Kairi. Do what he says and take his warnings seriously. It might seem beautiful, but this world is more dangerous than you know." The words are more of a decree in theory, but the way he says them makes me feel like he really does care about what happens to me, so I take them on board, promising myself that I'll try to do what Lucien asks of me.

"What will you do?" I ask, insides icy at the thought of him getting injured, or worse, because of me.

"I will do what I can to keep my people safe," he looks to Lucien now, and I detect a slight animosity between them as both men stiffen in posture, and the silence that follows becomes momentarily unbearable.

Then, as they break their intense and unmistakably angry gaze, everything falls into motion very quickly.

I turn from the landing balcony, striding into my bedroom and moving to dress into the garments I'd worn yesterday that I'd hung neatly in the wardrobe opposite the bed. As I close the door behind me, the ice skates catch my eye, and I feel an overwhelming sadness that I'll never get to wear them again. After all, there's no way I can fit them in my cloak pockets.

Letting the pyjamas lie in a discarded navy puddle at my feet, I rush to put on a fresh silk slip before pulling on thick socks and then unbuttoning the wool dress from its hanger. Flapping it out in front of me, I step into its baby blue folds, bringing it up over my hips and then shoulders, fastening the buttons once more over my breasts. The weight of the fabric comforts me despite the fact everything is moving so insanely fast, reminding me to breathe in full, and letting me know that I am still physically grounded, that I'm safe here, at least for now.

In a few more moments, I've managed to pull a hairbrush from the vanity by the window through my bedraggled hair, shove my feet into my leather walking boots, and throw the lilac wool of my fur-lined cloak over my shoulder in a whirl of soft fabric and fast hands. Delving deep into the cloak's pockets, I pull out my gloves and earmuffs and wrangle them on with fumbling fingers, my breath coming all the while in mindful but undeniably panicked wisps.

I look back over my shoulder at the room, the skates and the clothes Lucien gifted me the only sign that anyone other than the house's owner had ever been here.

Giving the sleigh bed a wistful once over, I wish I could climb back beneath the furs as I head for the door.

Once I'm out in the hall, I hear Lucien's voice, hurried as everything else is quickly becoming.

"Come, Kairi." He is blunt in his command, but I don't get offended as I had done. It is just his way of dealing with stress, I think, distancing himself from all emotion by focusing purely on action.

I take the stairs two at a time, almost tripping over my own feet before Lucien grabs my hand and pulls me quickly across the threshold and onto the porch. The day I'd missed is entirely gone as the sun's last wink of light fades from the edge of the world.

The golden moon makes its debut, and I marvel at how quickly the days seem to fly in this dimension, especially in Drakos Vale, which receives so very little daylight. So much has happened, and yet it feels as though I only just got here because realistically— I did only awaken here for the first time 48 hours prior.

Lucien leads me off the porch with a gloved hand, his weapons clattering beneath his black velvet cloak that's fastened by a silver clasp shaped like a snake that's eating its own tail. It glimmers coldly, lifeless emerald eyes watching me as our steps crunch fast and hard against the snow-covered earth.

Waiting, her nostrils flaring but emitting no condensation, Ebonara is perched by the side of the lake, her shackles gone, scales gleaming like oil slick whetstone.

Her wings are fully extended but erect and at rest, the golden moonlight illuminating the amethyst shades of the veins that crawl like powerful rivers beneath the veil of flesh that webs the space between their bony architecture. Her eyes glow, lilac and eerie in the chill air, her teeth glinting with subtle malice between her jaws as they spread in a slight growl.

"Ebonara, come now. I'm taking you on a long-haul flight. It matters not that I'm bringing another rider." Lucien rolls his eyes as he mutters these words under his breath, clearly stressed as his Adam's apple bobs noticeably when he swallows his frustration.

We reach the dragon's flank, and she stirs, rising from the snow, seemingly unaffected by the cold against her scales as she stretches and extends her talons only too noticeably before me.

She shakes her head, her horned skull shedding slurry and snow.

"Come on, I'll help you." Lucien holds out a hand, and I look between his waiting palm and the dragon's immense height.

"You want me— to get on the dragon?" I ask, gulping.

I can't tell whether I'm exhilarated or terrified.

"Well, if you want to make this journey in reasonable time, then yes. It would take me days to fly us both where we're headed, nor would it be very comfortable for either one of us," he explains, blowing a loose tendril of hair from his eyes and watching me expectantly.

"Alright then—" I breathe in deep, the cold beginning to seep into my bones as I stand stationary on the spot before placing my hand in Lucien's and relinquishing myself to him.

He pulls me close to his torso, wrapping his arms around me and fully extending his wings. He launches upward, crushing me against him as his wings work powerfully to gain altitude. After several white-knuckled moments, he stills, letting us glide down so we land snugly on Ebonara's spine.

The saddle beneath us is a single long piece of smooth, supple onyx leather, almost indistinguishable against the dark surrounding scales as it wraps around the apex of the dragon's spinal vertebrae.

There's a wooden hold in front of me, so I grab on fast as Lucien lets his arms slip from where they're firmly supporting my upright posture like he's a parent helping a child to mount their first pony. His touch remains on my waist, and though it's featherlight, I can't deny I'm acutely aware of his every movement as he guides my feet to rest on metal pegs for support

"Alright?" he asks me, eyes wide with concern. I stare up at him, the scent of peppermint and wintergreen overwhelming as the sharp sculptured curve of his mouth turns up into a smile at my bewildered uncertainty.

"Yes, thank you," I reply in a whisper, scowling and trying not to seem as utterly terrified as I am.

He nods, wordlessly taking his hands from me entirely and sliding off the dragon with more grace than I could ever muster. The only way I know he's even landed is the crunch of snow, and after the several minutes of silence that follow, I wonder if he's coming back.

"Lucien?" I call, nerves tattered as my fingers tighten around the wooden hold between my spread thighs.

"Yes, *Mademoiselle*—" His voice startles me as he slides into the two-person saddle behind me from above, his wings having taken him into the air so he can mount Ebonara the correct way without my bulk messing up his trajectory. His lips are against my ear, the only thing separating skin from skin the raised hood of my cloak.

I'm glad of it, a shudder fighting to take control of my spine.

"Are you going to tell me where we're going?" I ask, deathly curious, and he laughs.

"Ah, but what fun would that be?" he chuckles, his heels gently kicking into Ebonara's scaled underbelly. He clicks his tongue like he's commanding a prize stallion to canter, and she rises on all fours. My stomach falls through my butt, and my hands clutch the handhold so tight I am sure that beneath the white of my gloves, my knuckles boast a similar shade.

The dragon lurches forward, and I clench my thighs around her spine, watching wings spread on either side of her as she gallops forward with thunderous footfall along the edge of the lake.

I can feel Lucien's racing heart pounding into my back as he clutches my waist, pulling our bodies together and holding them firmly while Ebonara hurtles toward maximum velocity.

The dragon's wings spread, and we take off into the thick aether-filled cloud of the sky, wind rushing into my face and making my eyes water, my cheeks flushing crimson with the exhilarated and fast-pumping blood being propelled by my jackhammering heart.

Fleeing into the night, we soar over the endless snowy peaks of Drakos Vale and disappear beyond their comforting immensity, leaving behind only the sound of my breathless screams.

ARO

My time at The Volaris Institute remains one of the most physically gruelling yet rewarding experiences of my life. The military school for young Sephilim warriors perches atop a floating island attached to the edge of Soleus via a single glass bridge seldom used for anything other than formal ceremonies.

The building itself is carved from un-precocious white marble inlaid with turquoise accents for protection, the floors formed from sweeping facets of citrine shot through with veins of silver that fork like lightning. The architecture is surprising, unlike any of the temples which sport the same materials and looks not unlike a grand French chateau, with a full-bodied main building flanked by multiple spiralling turrets. These, due to their alabaster stone construction, I have always mused, appear like contorted spines.

The roof is made entirely of glass, and the floating island on which the institute resides holds little other than the campus grounds and an enormous reservoir lake, used more often than not to strengthen the wings of the newly reborn.

I remember the warm clutches of the water beneath the sparkling silver overlay of the surface as though it were yesterday, my wings twitching instinctually despite the fact I'm standing on the farthest side of the campus. Next to Lord Abara, on a balcony overlooking early morning flight drills, the rich sunlight falls over us in dappled pools, warming our skin and causing the dark hue of his to glow with silver slivers that contrast his dark flesh, as mine turns a supernaturally charged gold. I've come here because ever since Leo left, I have been unable to sit still, so figured that assessing the strengths and weaknesses of the current crop of seasoned graduates would be a far worthier use of my time. The visit had alarmed Lord Abara, which is not surprising considering I haven't stepped foot on the campus in almost five years.

The newly graduated fleet is dressed in the traditional Institute uniform of dove grey tunics, white leggings, and knee-high grey leather boots with little weight and nimble soles for soft landings on loud surfaces. Their wings range in hue and shape, but the basic build of each one is fairly consistent, their enormous wingspans stretching wide from behind the silhouetted bulges of adequate biceps and torsos that narrow into petite muscle-bound waists.

These men, who I now watch soaring in a V formation in the earliest rays of the day's new sunlight, have been trained as a unit, living in barracks with no doors and therefore no barriers to prevent them forging together as one single unit with sixty wings all working in unison.

Caleb observes me watching them, trying to appraise my expression and garner whether or not I'm impressed.

Impressed, no, but pleased, yes.

It takes more than mere diligence to impress me, and though the formation and drill this squad are demonstrating is precise and well-executed, it is nonetheless unimaginative.

Still, I suppose one can never have too many obedient soldiers.

A throat clears, the ragged echo from the study at our spines causing us to turn in unison, our feathers touching at the wingtips for the briefest of moments and causing an unnatural shiver to run up my spine.

My eyes fall on the tangled auburn mess of Leo's hair, his face slick with sweat, making his freckles stand out like tiny grains of pepper across the bridge of his nose. His chest is rising and falling rapidly, his exhale coarse in his throat as it scrapes its way up his windpipe and into the air between us.

"Captain Bond," I greet him, feeling Lord Abara's eyes narrow and thinking fast on my feet.

I have not told him of the letter, nor of the traces of a living dragon I discovered. "You have returned, and it seems the experimental new drills did their job as well. Come, we will adjourn to the roof to discuss the elite training—" I beckon him to follow me as I stride across the cool confines of Caleb's turret study, heels clicking against the citrine floor. Leo's tread can be heard behind me as I pass through the threshold and onto the landing without looking back, impatient and

309

unwilling to deal with Caleb's questions or piousness as I rush down the spiral staircase leading to the main building, Leo on my heels.

We take the hall that's lined with Fae oil portraits of notorious Sephilim in flight, several of them including the Draconians as they had been before banishment, before they lost the war that Midas started, clashing blades with those who would come to be my brothers even before I was reborn.

The portraits are eye-catching in their swirling silver frames, having been designed to look like weightless clouds forged of heavy metal. I have always loved Fae art, hence why I cannot bear to part with the portrait over the fireplace, and yet I am unable to stop to appreciate them.

My heart beats a little faster in my chest like a trapped baby hummingbird desperate for its first flight.

As I take an extremely tight spiral staircase from the third floor landing up onto the rooftop with Leo directly behind me, I can't work out if I'm more nervous or excited by the prospect of violence against the Draconians again. After all, I have dreamed of war with them for years, yearning deeply for the power I would feel standing atop the cold-blooded corpse of a real gutted dragon.

At the top of the staircase, the early dawn opens up, blades of stark sunlight falling over the curved bodies of turquoise shingles and turning them cold. I slow in my pace as I shield my eyes with a hand at my brow, turning toward the staircase before looking to Leo with an expectant gaze. His auburn hair is honeyed by the sunlight, but despite the golden halo, he looks undeniably fatigued, wigs drooping ever so slightly with feathers jagged around the edge of his silhouette.

"Well?" I ask as he straightens up, ascending the final step with painful slowness.

"Well, High Lady Thomas is adamant that the girl has never set foot in Drakos Vale. I handed her the letter, and she responded as you would expect." His voice is weary, and I nod slowly at his words, considering each one with utmost care.

"I see, and the journey?" I demand, watching as he runs his fingers back through his tangled mess of locks.

"Horrendous. I almost hit a mountain peak. The visibility is terrible, the weather even more so. Honestly, I think I might have found a location to which we may conduct, but any kind of aerial assault is out in my opinion. The Draconians have years of training, not to mention hardier wings than any Sephilim. I'd say our best bet is taking them on the ground if we can." He looks grim, and I wonder why he isn't more excited. Most Sephilim I know are waiting for the day they get to draw blood again like impatient children on Christmas Eve.

"But you have a location? Something we can all visualise?" I ask, cursing the limitations of conduction. For if you cannot imagine it, cannot see the location you wish to move to clearly in your mind, the current will not take you.

"Indeed, I will put together a sketch to distribute among the soldiers if we choose to attack," Leo answers, shoulders slumping forward as he exhales heavily.

"If? I'd have thought that my decision on this matter was clear to you. They have the girl. I will take back what's mine," I snap, folding my hands behind my back and beginning to pace.

A group of three Sephilim swoop overhead, looping one of the turrets in a common beginner drill that teaches effective banking. I watch them, scrutinising every angle of their rigid air-bound bodies with a cruel sneer.

"And what if she isn't there? Are you willing to slaughter innocents on a hunch? What if someone took her back to the mortal world?" Leo calls as I put more distance between us, my eyes following the trio of training Sephilim until they're but specks in the distance.

"What makes you think that any Draconian is innocent?" I spit, turning on a knife edge and letting my wings flare out from me with displeasure.

"What makes you think that we would triumph in a battle against them? It's been years since anyone has been anywhere near Drakos Vale. We have no idea if their numbers have dramatically increased, and if the dragons are still alive and thriving, then we'd be walking into a bloodbath—" His thoughts turn my insides icy, freezing that excited fluttering of my heart and turning it heavy as stone falling through cool green water.

My mind whirs as I watch the cobalt sun blazing across the sky.

Leo is right— it would be better to be safe than sorry. But I know that neither the Equinians nor the Fae would go to war without good cause, and Kairi is not enough.

But what if— what if they were to discover, as I have, that the Draconians have been hiding dragons away from the rest of us?

Why hide such creatures unless you intend to weaponise them?

Suddenly, a trip to Drakos Vale seems not only appealing but necessary for another purpose entirely.

"I will go to the ranch, check to see if she has returned as you suggest. If not, then we shall descend upon Drakos Vale. Prepare the troops." I order Leo, watching him slump even further. He's clearly exhausted, but I have no time for his weakness.

"You don't think she simply went home?" he asks me, eyes widening in his gaunt face.

"I think if she did, after I had threatened her parents the way I did, she would be very stupid. But then again, she is mortal, so who knows just how far her idiocy will guide her unknowingly into harm's way," I retort, a smile upturning the corners of my lips.

"Very well, My Lord. I will begin the preparations," he stands to attention, visibly shrugging off his tiredness with steely resolve. I nod, dismissing him wordlessly as I become lost in fast and violent thought.

He turns, but before he can descend the staircase, I call after him with a sudden image dominating my consciousness, stilling the Captain as his hand takes to the newel of the bannister.

"And Leo, make sure you include some of the heavy nets, collars, and shackles from Midas' personal collection, will you?"

THE SECRET GARDEN

LUCIEN

AS I STEP OUT of Lumeria's open-air cathedral, I am hit by the sudden realisation that Nirvana is more overwhelming than I remember. The smells carried on sweet spring air meld into a pungent floral aroma that is nothing short of intoxicating, and the colours remain more vibrant than any I've ever seen anywhere else.

They say that Nirvana has the most fertile soil in all of Aetheria, maybe of anywhere in existence for all we lowly Kindred know, and by all accounts from the way I'd eaten at the Solis Castra, they also have the produce to back up that claim.

Wildflowers grow here exactly as Gaia intended, blowing into the breeze and extending up with petalled fingers and hungry stems toward the growing heat of the early morning sun. The flowers themselves make a poor mockery of their earthen cousins, and I let my fingers run rampant through a cresting wave of snapdragons as thick vines of vibrant lilac wisteria part like curtains around my shoulders. In this place, they are allowed to sprawl and wander through the earth with delicate tiptoeing roots without restraint or fear of being trampled. I have always admired the way Fae cities are constructed as well, their beauty having faded in my memories but now returning full force with an extravagant exquisiteness that leaves me breathless. The way they refuse to bulldoze their way into an architecturally sound space but rather work with what nature has provided makes for nothing short of utterly unique homes, stores, and communal gathering spaces.

I tread among the thick moss carpeting on feet that seem far too heavy and not nearly nimble enough for the setting, my senses soothed yet oddly sharp with paranoia from a lack of constant battling with the environment. There's no wind whipping back my hair from my high cheekbones, nor snow speckling my wings with a ghostly chill, but my gut is tied in knots with anxiety at leaving Kairi alone.

Still, though, I didn't have the heart to wake her, and I don't have time to walk her through losing her Nirvana virginity until I've secured us permission to be here. I mean, I can only imagine if she thought the endless white of Drakos Vale was enchanting that she'll be stunned speechless by this place.

Sweat beads within my high-necked riding tunic, and I swelter even though I've left Kairi sleeping beneath the thick velvet of my cloak under the protective veil of Ebonara's camouflaged wingspan.

I shouldn't be warm, but I guess I've grown especially used to the cold. Not only that, but it's easy to forget my magical affinity for ice magic leaves me feeling far too warm even in the mildest of climates.

I know where I'm headed, roughly, and yet I can't help but feel somewhat disoriented as the dense wildflower growth made up of hydrangeas, cornflower, and foxglove seems to close in, looking identical in its untamed vibrant weave on every side.

The pungent sweetness of the air should be calming, but the more seconds pass, the more it fatigues me, the blue sun beating down mercilessly through the cracks of tree branches that form the endless green canopy overhead making me feel trapped like a bird in an overly perfumed exhibit.

"Well, by Shakespeare's very disappointing beard, I'll be damned." The voice sparks relief through me even though it probably shouldn't, the tone akin to that of a harp being plucked by the most delicate of fingers.

"Lost, Draconian?" Quinn, the self-proclaimed King of Spring drops down from the crook of a nearby oak tree. His skin, just as I remember, smells so strongly of roses that the aroma asserts its dominance over the other floral blooms surrounding him without the least bit of effort. His mahogany locks are swept back from his face, peppered with the very wildflowers that surround us, his eyes glinting the emerald of dew-splattered grass. He smiles, wicked, as his butterfly-esque wings flutter, boasting delicate paper-thin shades of malachite through to the deepest honeyed amber with fragile tremors, capturing the new sunlight.

"Now that you mention it— sort of," I admit, flashing him an easy smile and holding up my empty palms to show him I mean no harm. My weapons are still heavy on my back, and I watch his eyes flit to

314

them and back again as he navigates the wildflowers before striding out into the clearing on languid long legs, his lithe body delicate and precise in its movements as a watercolour artist's nimblest brush on canvas.

"One is never lost among nature, Lord DeLaurent," Quinn says, inspecting his long and perfectly manicured nails before gesturing outward to the surrounding greenery. His nails are lacquered jewel tones and dim in comparison to the bright hues of his intricately embroidered clothes. He's wearing a jacket over a bare chest, making him look thinner and therefore weaker than I know he truly is, and lime green breeches that stop right below his knee where his bare and muddy feet protrude beneath.

As he steps forward, he leaves barely a footprint in his wake, his wings serenely floating behind him in phantasmal jewel sheets of gossamer, fluttering in the slightest breeze.

"Well, it would appear not. I was looking for you—" I explain, and he smiles. Looking at the earth as he digs in his toes, his hair falls forward, exposing the pointed curve of his ear's angular tip.

"I know, the trees told me— Poplars are, after all, such terrible gossips." He circles on the spot, and I wonder for a moment if he might not evaporate into a tornado of rose petals. Instead, though, his dreamy expression merely stops with a sudden and intense focus on my face.

"What brings you here? I know this is hardly a social visit— After all, we are but deadly enemies, are we not?" His smile is wicked, and I smirk, shaking my head.

"But of course. Deadly, deadly enemies." My voice drips with sarcasm, sickly sweet like poisoned honey, sweat dripping down the arch of my spine as I stand wary before him.

"Come then, let us have a drink together. You look thirsty, and besides— I can hardly pass up such a wonderful opportunity to poison you. I hear it's all the rage in Soleus," he quips, and I snort. Bounding forwards across the springy moss carpet, he's light as air on his feet, long raven locks fluttering out behind him in thick floral ribbons, shedding petals here and there as he goes.

I follow him as he navigates invisible paths I cannot fathom being able to understand, never so much as treading on a bud or disturbing a single bloom, the forest and him becoming one as the colours of his intricate wingspan melds with the greens and golds of the surrounding woodland.

After what seems like only moments watching him, transfixed by the dreamlike effortlessness with which he moves, he stops, looking back over the edge of his ghost-like wing and waiting for me to catch up with him.

The trees thin out as we both stand at the top of a rolling hill, giving me a view out over the impressive treetop sprawl of Lumeria, one of two capital cities in Nirvana and home predominantly to the Fae of Light, Kindred of Aphrodite. The forest where I've been wandering is home to the Fae of Light's *Ecclesia Naturis*, or *Nature's church* for those of us who don't prefer poncey Latin, and lies at the highest natural peak on this side of Nirvana, making it the best place for invisibility with regards to landing a dragon unnoticed.

I stare out across the treetop city, finding intricate wooden carved bridges joining each tree to the next and creating a macrocosm of spiderwebbing pathways between the homes of the resident Fae.

"I'd forgotten how—" I begin, wiping the sweat off my forehead as Quinn smiles at me.

"Beautiful it is? That is one thing I will say for you Draconians, you appreciate that which has been provided, seeing not what could be yours, but simply what is."

I'm left thinking on this as he flounces off down the path leading to the city, paved in nothing more than the rich verdant mosses which had led us here.

He's not wrong.

Where the Sephilim and the Equinians have moved to invade, to pillage, and take more for themselves despite the god-given riches in their own lands, the Fae and Draconians have always been contented with what they were given.

Quinn looks back to me yet again, those green eyes wicked with amusement at my presence alone. His curiosity and desire for a good tale are written plainly on his face as if he'd taken to it with quill and ink.

I close the distance between us, and he calls back, taking off ahead of me once more in a mad and wild dash down the hill.

"Hurry, Draconian. You know I don't have all day—"

Being a High Lord, Quinn has a beautifully expansive shared residence with his long-time partner Phineas, the Fae High Lord of Fall. We ascend a twisting wooden staircase, the balustrade decorated with thick pinecones and ivy and formed from raw fallen branches that have been stripped of their original leaves but have otherwise been left untouched. The entrance resides within the entirely hollowed-out trunk of a great oak tree, bigger, and I'd bet older than anything you would ever see on Earth. As we climb to the height of it, I feel my blood coursing even closer to the skin, heat threatening to strangle me.

"And how are the Sprites?" I ask, making conversation and addressing our last meeting. I don't want Quinn to forget, even for a moment, that he and Phineas are both greatly indebted to me for the medicine I created to stop the Rainbow Grove from being overtaken by a plague of thick white lichen, the stuff stinking of sulphur and the likes of which they'd never seen.

"As well as can be expected. Phineas has been out this morning, teaching the newest about different types of trees," he explains and I nod, pretending to sound interested as his expression turns besotted.

"That is wonderful. You do have such a responsibility to them, being so innocent. I don't know how you stand it in this place—" I am bitter in my words, knowing the fear that clutches at me every time Kairi is threatened.

How must it be for the Fae when it comes to the Sprites?

I can only imagine immeasurably worse.

"Aetheria is more brutal than ever, but we manage. Though I suspect you are not here to discuss my charges?" Quinn cuts to the meat of the conversation quickly, despite being a vegetarian, as we reach the top of the staircase at last.

The apartment has been structured around the tree itself, so the floor of the hallway is at first flat but then goes up a single step to accommodate the supporting branch beneath. The scent is thick with pumpkin spice, fresh wisteria, and pungent raw wood.

Quinn walks past a table that grows right out of the floor in a continuous oaken branch, a glass sheet atop it supporting a vase of flowers.

As his fingers swirl above the lilies in the vase, they shudder a second, tightening and then reblooming so the scent of them scatters quickly through the space with new intensity.

"So, what will it be? Something alcoholic?" he enquires, moving past the flowers without breaking stride and letting his wings flutter silently behind him.

I stand uncomfortably, my weight causing the floorboards beneath my feet to creak in protest.

It's true, I'm certainly no Fae though I've never thought of myself as particularly heavy.

Judgemental bastard treehouse— I cuss internally as I give a nervous glance down to the narrow planks beneath my feet.

"I'd better not. As you said, this isn't a social visit," I call through, trailing leisurely after him.

The main room has no windows, merely arches that look out over the surrounding city. The way the Fae live is undeniably communal, and even with the warm weather, I know I couldn't bear living without proper walls.

"Elderflower and cucumber tonic then?" he suggests, and I shrug, wondering why he couldn't just offer me a damn glass of water or a coffee?

I would kill for a coffee right about now.

As I'm pondering how exactly I could go about doing that without offending anyone, I hear myself reply, always the model guest.

"Yes, that would be great. I can't be long though, actually—" I stutter, sitting down in a swinging hammock chair that's blanketed in raw cotton and soft heather, the vines from which it's suspended twisted thick with yet more wisteria.

"Ice and lemon?" He pops his head around the corner of a raw branch that spears right through the floor beneath his feet, separating the open-plan kitchen and living space.

"Uh, whatever you think—"

His head pops back around the other side of the wide barked trunk, and I hear rustling from beyond the divide. "I, uh, I actually came to talk to you about—" I begin, but again the soundless protrusion of his head from thin air beyond the dividing branch causes me to pause.

"Straw? They're biodegradable of course—" he asks, cocking a perfectly plucked and entirely feminine eyebrow as if this should be a serious decision-making factor. I nod, gritting my teeth and reminding myself to stay calm. After all, I need this Fae's cooperation.

"As I was saying—" I begin, hearing the clinking of ice and watching his silhouette flourish like a snaking stem as his long fingers and willowy arms twirl intricately around the kitchen.

His head pops back around the corner so fast it catches me by surprise—

"*Sacrebleu!* I don't care if you put a freaking bridal bouquet in the damn drink! That's not why I'm here, and I don't have time for this!" I burst, getting to my feet and balling my fists at the sides. The wooden

318

planks beneath my feet creak in warning, causing my rage to rise higher in a tidal wave of icy shards.

Shut up, you stupid splinter box.

"Now, now! Temper, DeLaurent. I was just going to ask what you wanted to talk about—" he says, picking up a glass serving tray that's carved to look like the surface of a tranquil pool. The cups atop it are china waterlilies, completing the functional masterpiece.

"Sorry— It's just been a long night." I exhale, collapsing back into the hanging seat and burying my talons deep into the cotton padding.

"A long night? It's early morning if you hadn't noticed." Quinn places the tray down soundlessly upon another naturally formed table, this one lower than the one in the hall, before falling elegantly into the seat beside mine.

"I've been flying all night. You know it's a long old trek from Drakos Vale." I huff as he picks up a tall waterlily glass and passes it to me, watching the straw spinning around the inside of the rim precariously as I take it from him. The glass is sweating, and the beads of cold are a comfort as I raise the drink to my lips.

I sigh as the fluid rushes right down my gullet in a mixture of floral notes and cool cucumber, gulping it down a little too eagerly and feeling the bubbles rush straight to my nose.

"See, nice, isn't it? That's what happens when you take a little extra time, Lord DeLaurent. Though I'm not sure why I'm telling you that. Draconians never were fit for luxury living, philistines." He takes his glass to his lips, perching on the edge of the swinging seat beneath him as though he weighs less than a feather, legs crossed elegantly and eyes watchful.

"Mmm. Sorry—" I mumble, and he shakes his head.

"Brutes, the lot of you. But as you so rightfully put it, it's not why you're here. So, why don't you enlighten me?" he suggests, and suddenly the room goes very quiet around us. The weight of the request I need to make of him is hefty, and I know that I'll be asking him to put the people in his care, including the ever-innocent sprites, at risk.

"It's quite the story— to be honest—" I admit.

Quinn doesn't blink as a butterfly lands on one of the rosebuds in his hair before he simply replies, "I have no doubt. If it's caused a Draconian to seek the help of the Fae, then times must be desperate—"

It takes me a little over thirty minutes to deliver the tale to him, and he says not one word from the moment I start until I take a deep inhale at the end of my last sentence. By the time I've finished regaling him with the events of the last few days, both the water lily glasses are empty on the pond-like surface of the glass tray between us. The breeze barely stirs, the heavy curtain of wisteria and ivy that divides this room from the private bedrooms and bathrooms in the back perfectly still as if it were fake.

I stare at Quinn, letting my seat swing a little as I rock my foot from ball to heel, anxious.

He watches me closely, his expression unreadable, his seat stone still, biting on the inside of his bottom lip as he thinks on my story with intense concentration.

He opens his mouth to say something but then closes it again, and by the time he seems to be inhaling to finally speak his mind, Phineas' deep and rich tone tremors viscous through the air.

"Quinn?" he calls out, the scent of him hitting me far before his physical appearance. Pumpkin spice and dark, rich coffee with a hint of chocolate washes over me, causing my caffeine craving to return with a vengeance.

"In here, Phineas," Quinn replies in a soft melodic voice, sitting forward and lacing his fingers over his bony knees. His dark locks fall forward, casting gentle shadows over his face, but they cannot hide the way his features slacken in relief at the presence of his long-time partner.

Footsteps barely audible, Phineas rounds the corner of the open plan living room, his hair just as vibrant as I remember. It changes, he once told me, depending on the seasons and the state of the natural world around him, and today it's a deep sunset orange at the root, fading ombre into amber tips. The style is long and feathered, not unusual for the summer months of Nirvana, and will be cropped by winter and then grow long again through the following spring. His eyes are a rich light brown, the colour of freshly collected hazelnuts, and beneath the narrow cut of his burgundy velvet jacket, I can see the swirling amber, chocolate, and auburn designs that whirl across his skin as though caught in a hearty breeze, identifying him as chosen by Aphrodite.

He stills as his eyes fall on me, his tan face flushing a little as his eyes widen with surprise.

"Lord DeLaurent— what a— surprise." He picks his words carefully, but the sentiment falls flat. I nod to him, getting to my feet and offering a hand.

"Hello, Phineas, thank you for having me in your home," I greet him, and he clutches my forearm, squeezing with spindled fingers as he simply replies—

"Don't thank me. I didn't invite you in after all." He doesn't sound bitter, merely curious as he glares suspiciously at Quinn.

I nod as the situation becomes awkward once more, returning to sitting as he continues to stand. The veins running through his leaf-like wings are made stark, silhouetted as he stands with his back to the open archways, through which noon sunlight filters with increasing strength.

"What is he doing here, Quinn?" Phineas demands, whisking a strand of bright hair behind a pointed ear that's studded through four times with simple gold hoops, obviously unable to put up the same mask of pleasantry as his partner.

It has always alarmed me, the contrast between the two Fae. Where one is optimistic and brimming with hope, with positive energy, the other is the utter definition of a realist, his cynicism creeping through the air like the first bitter morning chill of autumn.

Perhaps it was the spirit of their representative seasons, or maybe they were just attracted to the fact that each was a twisted mirror image of the other.

"He needs our help. The girl who Lord Black tried to poison, she's here with him. He needs sanctuary. The Sephilim army is threatening Drakos Vale if they do not return her. Lucien here claims that Aro wants to torture the girl into crowning him the next King of Aetheria." He summarises my story so concisely that it makes me wonder why exactly I've had to come through a million conflicting emotions to get here. The way he puts it, there seems to be no reason for doubt, no complexity. You either hand the girl over and resign to His Highness, King Aro Black, or you don't.

"Ah yes, the poisoning. I do remember there being some gossip going around in Aramis about that. Morpheus himself said it was quite a distasteful spectacle. Said he felt sorry for the poor girl." I am not surprised that Morpheus has spread his opinion because he's simply a walking tabloid with a mouthpiece and distinctive hair. Heaven forbid you piss off him or the muses when it comes to your historical reputation.

I mean, just look at what they've done to Lucifer.

"Well, I'm beginning to wonder if that's all he thinks of the situation. Lucien has mentioned that the Draconian High Priestess is having her visions tampered with and, she believes, her memories as well. Sound like anyone's modus operandi we know to you?" Quinn crosses his legs, leaning back against the soft heather cupping his fragile wings. Phineas rolls his eyes.

"Why would Morpheus want to mess with memories surrounding a random mortal?" he asks, incredulous. His eyes become glassy, his stare crackling with the fire of deep impatience.

"I couldn't possibly guess," Quinn replies, watching as the butterfly in his hair departs soundlessly, its flight path aimlessly beautiful.

"Morpheus?" I ask, butting in.

The two men turn, Phineas' wings rustling like falling autumnal leaves as he pivots to face me, both seeming to have forgotten I am here.

"He has the power to wander The Nether. Memories can be trapped there if you believe the mythology. Though I've never heard of anyone doing it." Phineas is sceptical, but Quinn only laughs, the sound irritating and over the top in its untameable high tenor.

"It's not as though, had it been done before, any of us would remember," he adds.

Phineas scowls, seeing his partner's point despite not wanting to.

"Regardless, Quinn. This isn't a Fae matter. It's between the Draconians and the Sephilim." He juts out a bony hip, folding his long, angular arms across his chest.

I rub my forehead with tired, rough fingertips, sick of arguing about whose problem this innocent and unknowing mortal is.

"It is a Fae matter if Aro Black is made King of Aetheria. I'd say that's almost wholly a Fae matter considering what happened the last time a Sephilim King was crowned. And that's why, Lucien, I'm agreeing to your request. Kairi may stay here as long as she needs. And you might think of visiting Aramis while you're here and seeing if Morpheus might be able to explain your little memory problem as well—" Quinn adds. I get to my feet, almost falling on my knees before him in a bow from sheer relief.

"Oh, thank you, Quinn! That's an enormous help. It won't be permanent of course, just until I can get her safely home and out of his clutches."

Phineas cocks his head, eyebrow arching into a flawless burgundy peak.

"Quinn, you can't just—" He begins, but Quinn merely smiles serenely, letting the chair swing beneath him.

"Oh, but I can. And— I did." He bares his teeth, the incisors sharper than any vegetarian might ever have use for. "Now, Lord DeLaurent, you will want to be going and retrieving the girl, wherever you might have stashed her for safekeeping. No need to stay and watch Phineas and me argue. I do not doubt, by the way his eyes are doing that rather unattractive squint, his fury will be coming my way full force in just a few minutes. Not only that, but he likes to get physical in his anger, and I doubt you want to witness his climax face when he's throwing a temper tantrum. Such wind he summons, he practically strips the chandeliers— it is most undignified."

He's saying it to embarrass Phineas, but the tight-lipped High Born Fae beside me doesn't look phased, merely irritated as his once warm brown irises turn dull in his skull as if their contents are rotting.

"Well, uh, I'll be going then. Thank you again." I tiptoe past the two, the warring scents of rich pumpkin spice and sickly-sweet roses battling for dominance in the air.

"I'll have accommodations arranged," Quinn calls sweetly and with exaggerated enthusiasm, only seconds before I hear Phineas' low rumbling tones explode in fury.

I take the steps of the spiral staircase down to the base of the tree trunk two at a time, wishing for only a moment that I could stop running and catch my breath.

KAIRI

The light is so rich as it hits my closed eyelids that for a moment, I think I'm back home in my own bed.

It isn't until my other senses awaken that I know I'm anywhere but.

My lids flutter open, and I find myself veiled by an enormous sinuous wing; veins silhouetted by the sunlight beyond. What I had taken for a soft pillow beneath my cheek is a thick patch of emerald moss, and the air is rich with the smell of greenery and rainfall recently hitting thirsty earth.

I stretch, feeling Ebonara shift beside me, her wing relinquishing its protective shield over my sleeping form. As she tucks the appendage back in beside her, I watch it ripple from obviously scaled to invisible, stealing the light and shapes of the outside world as the camouflage takes her presence with it.

I blink once, then twice, making sure I can still hear her sleepy breathing being forced lazily through slit nostrils, even though I can't see her.

Then, I go about shedding the black velvet shroud of Lucien's cloak and revealing the lilac wool of my own.

Reaching up, I run my hand through my windswept curls, finding an unruly tangle that's been backcombed by the fingers of the night air that had swept over us as we soared above endless miles of cloud and aether. My cheeks still feel raw from the sting of it, my eyes watery from the cold, and yet my skin is warm. I scan my surroundings, finding myself in an alien grove, the entire place covered by a thick verdant canopy with a single beam of light falling, a precise hot ray, through a naturally formed skylight.

I stretch, letting my head fall back and the sunlight wash over me, warming my bones that ache from sleeping on the floor, my neck stiff from where I'd fallen unconscious against Lucien's hard chill as rejected sleep entirely, steering us with steadfast effortlessness through the night.

It takes me a few minutes to realise that where I might have Ebonara for company, Lucien is gone.

Wondering if he's nearby, I set out, sweating beneath the thick wool of my dress and cloak, eyes bleary from the depth of the sleep which had claimed me after hours of fighting to stay awake for every moment of flight.

I hadn't wanted to miss it, not a single beat of Ebonara's mighty wings, nor the passing of even one cloud.

I had flown— on a dragon.

I know as long as I live, I'll never be able to claim I've done something as utterly incredible as that.

The fact it's over makes me feel deflated, the fear of what's to come rearing its head as the shadows of the grove grow long and thick.

I hurry from the circle of trees, looking back only to find a thick pool of moss that sprawls across the entire space. There's no dragon and no sign that a Sephilim fugitive had ever taken refuge there except for the pooled black velvet of the cloak I've left behind among the lush green.

Beyond the grove, I find only more greenery, wildflowers sprawling and invading every nook and cranny of forest floor they can find. The smell is overwhelming, my feet tripping over the hem of my cloak as I fight my way through the grasses, Queen Anne's lace, and bushels of ranunculi.

It occurs to me, stupidly and after I've been walking for maybe half an hour, that maybe I shouldn't have wandered off, but by this time, I'm utterly turned around, not finding a single pathway or sign of civilised life anywhere. That is until I come to a sight that simultaneously awes me and sparks a brand-new dam of questions to unceremoniously burst.

There, in the middle of the forest, a large wooden structure stands, obviously not naturally formed but as close to it as you can get.

It's made from hawthorn trees; their branches and trunks have been intricately picked and plucked for their specific size and shape. They create an enormous archway, or what could be the ribcage of an enormous sleeping wooden giant. However, when I see the inside of the space, I realise the truth of what it is I'm seeing.

A second before I can take another step, a twig snaps close by, causing the hairs on the back of my neck to stand on edge. I pull my cloak tighter around me despite being far too warm, my skin slick with perspiration.

My eyes dart from left to right and then tentatively back over my shoulder. I find no one and feel nothing but a chill nip around my ankles.

Shrugging off my paranoia, I step forward towards the building, moving to sit in one of the raw wooden pews, awed as the trees rustle around me restlessly.

You see, it isn't a wooden giant's ribcage but the barest most natural cathedral I have ever seen. There's no roof, no walls, no glass. Only thick wooden tree trunks that stand in two parallel uniform lines, their branches leaning inward to create the great airy eaves of the sacred architecture.

As I look at the trees making up the cathedral's skeleton, it occurs to me suddenly that these hawthorn trunks are actually rooted to the ground, the tendrils of them sprawling over the floor and turning it uneven.

Is it possible they grew like this? That this cathedral was formed not by the residents, not by immortal hands, but instead by the Aetherial earth itself.

I stare up and around the ceiling, realising that this place could compare with any of the greats.

Notre Dame. Lincoln. York. Westminster Abbey.

So many years of struggle and toil put to shame by the natural world in an effortless sprawl of branches and roots.

Another twig snapping causes me to turn on the spot, but this time, I do catch something out of the corner of my eye, a comforting sign that I am not going mad.

I wait, tracking the luscious emerald hues of the floor beneath the felled pews, for whatever it is that's skulking around to return.

It doesn't take long, the chill around my ankles, which before had seemed somehow natural despite the heat catching my attention and causing me to focus harder on the clutter of natural debris, trying to pick out anything untoward.

Furtive at first, something like a ghost, made from swirling white light, pops up, its head suddenly staring out from behind the pillar in front of me.

The narrow face, the whiskers, the pert ears and narrow eyes give away its fox identity, and yet it isn't like any fox I've ever seen.

I watch it as it leaps between the pews, leaving a trail of what appears to be thin ice behind it.

Every few moments, it stops, looking back at me as though urging me to follow.

My heartbeat accelerates.

I guess all this trauma and running must have broken something inside my brain if I think a ghost fox is trying to send me messages.

Sure enough though, the creature, or spirit, or ghost, stops when it reaches the end of the long central aisle, scampering back to me and bringing the chill back right along with it.

It whines, making small sounds halfway between a cat's yowl and a puppy's whimper.

I get to my feet, shoulders hunching with stiffness from the night before, watching as it leads me up the length of the cathedral and out between two of the rising hawthorn trunks that make up the furthest wall. The trot of the ghostly fox is proud, its feet making tiny but definitive thumps as they hit the earth and leave it sparkling with frost. It keeps looking back at me, waving its white plume of a tail provocatively as if daring me to keep trailing after it. So, unable to think of a better way to find my way out of the forest, I do.

Where we end up is more startlingly divine, the air more holy than even the inside of the hawthorn-constructed cathedral had been, and a sudden whiff of lavender, baby's breath, and lilies washes over me in a wave so intense I stop still in my tracks as though unknowingly, I've stepped into another world entirely.

The fox urges me on, yapping with snappy little teeth around my ankles and causing icy chills to run rampant up the backs of my legs as my eyes widen, feet carrying me forward again in a sudden jerk of unrestrained forward motion.

I'm not sure I could have stopped even if I had wanted to.

It's another grove— but this one is different, to say the least. The air shimmers thick with aether, the sparkling powder more prevalent here than anywhere else I've ever been.

Hawthorn trees, hundreds of them, ring the space, but other than their distinctive shape, they are unrecognisable compared to the trees forming the cathedral. Rainbow-coloured veins run from deep within the roots, thickening as if someone has melted hundreds of children's wax colouring crayons and poured the mixture into the essence of the tree itself. My ears prickle as the sound of nearby running water enters the assaulting barrage on my senses, tiny laughs and whispers catching the air and making me wonder if I haven't entirely lost my mind.

I tip-toe forward, the air electric with the power of the fact that the place merely exists, my fingers hungry and longing to trace the rainbow veins of the trees.

If I can touch it, maybe I'll finally believe it's real.

I reach out, extending my fingers with painful slowness, the fox chattering around my ankles.

Suddenly though, the yips and yaps of the creature's excited form stop dead. I turn around, watching as the fox runs with purpose back to a figure shrouded in the darkness of the edge of the tree line.

The air around me freezes, my arms erupting in goosebumps and my breathing becoming shallow as it condenses before my eyes.

Her voice rings out, cutting as an ice-sharpened razor, while fear drips down into my stomach like runoff from a melting icicle.

"And what, little girl, do you think you're doing trespassing in this holy place?"

I freeze on the spot as she emerges from the shadow, her silhouette widening as the thin sheets of her wings appear and ingest the light like frosted glass. They look like they're made of ice, and I'd honestly believe that to be true if it were not for the milky paleness of the veins running through them like glacial rivers. She paces like a hungry snow leopard, her gown a thin web of duck egg blue gossamer that trails behind her in a river of glossy sparkle, coating the floor of the grove with the chill of her bare soles. Her black hair sheens blueish in the bright light pouring down, a small circlet nestled among the thick glossy braids that circle her head, snowflakes picked out amongst the shimmering silver band in darkest sapphire and pale aquamarine.

"Well?" she demands, her cheekbones sharp as her head snaps toward me it's as though she's fastened razors just below her skin. My tongue trembles behind the sealed gate of my lips, unable to be coaxed even by my desperation to explain.

My heart hammers unwillingly as the ghostly fox walks timidly in the wake of the woman who appears to be its mistress, eyes enraptured by the train of her gown that reflects the sky with glassy clarity.

"I— I—" I stutter, unable to catch my breath. My eyes dart, furtive, from left to right, like an animal caught in a trap.

"This is The Rainbow Grove, rebirthing place of lost innocence in wait. How dare you step within its confines. How dare you breathe this air— *mortal.*" Her face turns disgusted, the corners of her eyes sharpening into knife tips as her gaze intensifies and the deep cerulean of her irises vanishes as her pupils dilate, dominating her features with terrifyingly inescapable darkness. Expression stony yet somehow feral, her lashes are frosted with ice, her lips a pale lilac from the chill that runs through her veins. All I can do is try to catch my breath, frozen upon the spot as if she's fixing me there with merely a gaze, staring.

My bottom lip begins to tremble, palms slick with cold sweat as they ball within the fur lining of my cloak. I swallow hard, trying to force my brain into some kind of action, but I can't stop staring at her, can't stop forcing myself to take the next breath, to even contemplate forming a coherent sentence under such potent scrutiny.

I blink, and by the time my eyes are open once again, I'm enveloped in a ferocious cold that reaches deep into my marrow, making the very essence within me ache and shudder. The ice woman's fingers are clasped tight around the delicate skin of my wrist, which only a few days ago had been freshly broken, and I watch as slowly the veins that run closest to the surface of the skin begin to turn an icy blue.

It feels like someone is running acid through my veins, the icy sting of it, the utter and complete abyss now in place of the heat that once ran through my blood, devouring, cancerous, and paralysing. All I can do as my mouth falls open and my eyes roll back inside my skull, the very surfaces freezing into vast salty spheres of ice, is stand. I gaze up helplessly into the eyes of the arctic-faced woman who refuses to relinquish her glacial clutch, sure that hers is the very last face I will see before dying in her arms right here, surrounded by what she had aptly called The Rainbow Grove.

"Stop!" The familiar voice comes like a bullet-shattering glass, my eyes managing only the merest flicker toward the winged and vicious silhouette of my rescuer.

I feel the air chill another few degrees, but before I can wonder why I'm slumping to the ground, warmth flooding through me like precious oxygen to a drowning man, I pull my cloak around my shoulders tighter, body wracked with trembling muscles and sparking nerves as the heat spreads too slowly.

Inhaling the air and letting my legs remain jellied beneath me, I gaze up from beneath the rim of my fur-lined hood, which is now shrouding my face, finding Lucien with his palms outstretched, challenging the woman who had very almost frozen me solid.

"Kairi, get back!" Lucien's voice is urgent as the woman straightens, baring her teeth which are almost vampiric in their sudden sharpness though match the rest of her features perfectly.

"Lizard man—" she growls, bringing her arms up into the air as tense as though they were made from steel. I feel the wind whip around me, causing me to lower my head once more as rainbow-coloured leaves of every hue are flung up into the air as exquisite shrapnel.

"That's enough!"

When I next peek up, Lucien's eyes are dead, their enormous depths the darkest shade of black I've ever seen them. His biceps bulge, straining against the leather seams of his cropped tunic sleeves before he throws them out in front of him in fury.

Then, something amazing happens.

A slick stream of crystal-clear ice materialises from nothing in front of him, the substance forming like a frozen skin knitting together rapidly through the space between him and his enemy.

She throws up her hand without bravado, erecting a snow globe of blue-ish ice around her, and only her, protecting herself without second thought with a shield that has come from nothing. The shield is thick, causing Lucien's icy projectile to make a single fracture right before her eyes and then shatter, falling to the floor as little more than rain.

I watch him raise his arms to take another shot, but before he can, the defensive icy bauble explodes in a shower of hot mist. It coats my face, spattering my skin with a warmth I desperately need.

"Enough." The voice of a third party interrupts the dangerous ice duel, her voice rich as treacle and with a warmth I can't help but be magnetised by. The tension in the atmosphere melts at her presence alone, and my eyes dart to her as she emerges from the trees, closing the space between us and offering me a hand.

The woman, who had just moments ago been trying to kill me, glances back over her shoulder, veiled by a shimmering gossamer cape and her frosty wings, as though she'd forgotten I was there.

"Thank you—" I mutter, shaking off the last stiffness remaining deep in my bones. The woman before me smiles, radiant, and about a full foot taller than me, the wings of some kind of golden dragonfly spreading out behind her in an effortless sweep of glimmering veined flesh.

Her bone structure is a piece of art, every inch of it blanketed by intensely dark skin. The sunlight makes her shimmer as if her body has been lacquered in a heady coat of gold flakes before she got dressed this morning, the dual tone of her burgundy and gold gown complimenting her in both shape and hue. Her legs seem to go on for miles, and one protrudes from the high slit in her floor-length skirt as she steps with ease over the thick rainbow-veined roots that scatter the floor.

At her heels, a flaming orange fox trots, head held high, superior as it fans the flames of its bushy tail with a rhythmic swish from left to right. It looks like it's made of pure sunlight, the glow from its tail catching in the many-layered bangles around the woman's ankles and setting them ablaze.

It peeks around the edges of her glimmering skirt, growling at its alabaster twin, the ghost that had led me into this mess.

The woman who had intervened looks down at the two creatures as their growls of warning deepen, wasting no time before snapping, "Winter's Rage, Summer's Scorn! If you're going to scrap, do it elsewhere! This is sacred ground. No place for duelling— or death for that matter."

As if they were never there, the two foxes disappear into thin air at her command.

After they depart, her golden eyes intensify to laser precision as she glares at the pale woman, but the rigid steel of the dark-haired Fae's spine doesn't whimper nor bend beneath the scrutiny. Instead, she turns to her, composed as sculptor's stone yet more defiant and unyielding to any chisel that might attempt to change her. Permanent.

"You're right, Ember. This is no place for fighting— or mortals for that matter. I was merely protecting what belongs to the Fae." She glances back at me with a stare brazen enough to wither the sun, and I shrivel back inside the depths of my cloak, wishing I could disappear.

Lucien watches the two women with half amusement, half irritation as he folds his arm tightly across his pectorals, face a mask of defiant reserve.

"Neve, do not be so utterly pious. What threat is a mortal girl going to pose here? You almost killed the poor girl. You could at least apologise, or look sorry." The one called Neve shakes her head like a stubborn horse, eyes still dead as she stares blankly at me.

"Sorry." She rolls her eyes, voice deadpan.

For a moment, I almost laugh. She looks like an overly powerful teenager.

The final ebb of cold leaves my body, and I look up as Ember smiles, running long golden fingernails back through closely shorn hair. They catch on the back of a golden choker that climbs the length of her long neck before wandering to touch the garnet dangling from her left ear on a long gold chain as she looks from Lucien to me and back again with interest.

"You two had better come with me before you cause any more trouble."

I smile at all six foot three of her as Lucien visibly relaxes, Neve still pouting at her lowly five foot two, but inside I can't help but know the instinctual and undeniable truth of the matter.

The trouble for them is only just beginning because we brought it with us.

23

THE WIND AND THE WILLOWS

ARO

THE WILLOW TREE'S LEAVES flutter around the delicate onyx tips of my wings as I conduct back into the mortal world. Inhaling, I am, as always, underwhelmed by the air here, the scents nowhere near as powerful as in Soleus, the moon's almost sepia glow overhead comparatively pitiful.

The weeping branches rustle as I part the naturally formed curtain blocking my view, looking out over the ranch that's veiled thinly by the night.

The last time I was here, everything was different, and it had seemed to me that nothing could have possibly gone so terribly wrong as it has. I suppose then that just shows what being overly confident gets you.

My mother had told me once, when I was small enough to be bounced up and down upon her skirt-laden knee, not to count my chickens before they'd hatched. Perhaps I should have listened more carefully.

The suddenness of night overhead is flimsy, unnerving me.

The difference between Aetherial time and Earthen time makes moving between one dimension and the other disorienting, inducing in me an odd sense of mortality. The temporariness of even my immortal existence settles heavily over my shoulders, the independent rotation of this world reminding me I belong to no one place but flit between all without anchor or tether to root me. Regardless of where I roam, no matter where I reside, travelling like this makes the truth of it known: the universe will continue to tick by, with or without me.

With that harrowing thought firmly lodged in the forefront of my mind, I swallow the thin air that's lightly coated in the musk of hay and heather, cicadas loudly chirping as I step out so I'm positioned by the edge of the pond. I had seen Kairi for the first time from this very spot, found her reading in the hanging chair that's bolted to the wooden beams constructing the gazebo's thick eaves. She had taken my breath away then, but now the vision of her only brings my blood to a steady boil.

I have no time to lament her stubbornness, so instead pass along the water's edge like a ghost, my wings camouflaged against the night, heather and lavender swaying carefree in the early summer night's breeze on all sides.

The converted barn stands, lights blazing from the substantial windows like a jack o' lantern's wide-eyed and toothy grin, a car with spiralling crimson and cobalt glass bulbs on the roof painting the entire landscape in an intermittent cacophony of red chasing blue.

Feeling the light hitting my face as I grow closer to the porch, I bend my knees, my weight pushing me into the dry earth underfoot as I spread my wings and lift silently into the air.

I touch down on the brick red shingles that speckle the roof in orderly and obedient rows, ears prickling as I try to home in on the voices that are sending delicate vibrations through my soles. Her fathers and the law enforcement officer, who had arrived with his dualistic lights blazing, can be heard as soon as I'm able to drown out the sounds of awakening wild nightlife.

"So, you say she's been missing how long, Mr Freemont?" The voice has a real American twang to it that I recognise from Kairi herself.

Crouching down, I feel my fingers gripping onto the roof's pointed tip, and I bite down hard on my bottom lip, steeling my muscles to prevent giving myself away.

"Four days." The cracked voice of a broken father creeps out of the bedroom's open window and up into the night.

I lean further forward.

"Do you think she might have run away? I mean, she is an adult. We're not dealing with a minor here." The officer's tone grows louder and more serious as I note his weight shift from one foot to the other. One of Kairi's parents sighs loudly. Though, which one I can't be sure.

"Her truck is still here, so we know she hasn't gone far. We're just concerned because— well, she hasn't had an easy time of it. This last few years, what with her health and all—" The tinnier voice of one of the two mortal parents trails off, my wings adjusting slightly to help me balance as the breeze picks up a little.

"Ah yes, you said she suffers from something called—" I hear the rustle of pages in a notebook being turned. "EDS?"

"Yes, Ehlers Danlos Syndrome," the cracked, deeper voice replies this time.

"Never heard of it." The officer mumbles, and I can feel even from here that both the men who raised Kairi tense in synchrony.

"And that's the problem. She feels utterly alone. She's been depressed for months, and we're worried sick that she might have decided she couldn't take it anymore—" The deep voice becomes volatile as though molten fury is threatening to ooze out of the fast-forming cracks in his composure, consuming everything in its path.

"I think then, the best place to begin is the outlying lands of Hickory Oaks. I will call in a few floaters to conduct a sweep of the area. Alright?" The policeman uses the most patronising voice I've ever heard. Neither man responds, and I wonder if they're nodding, too exhausted and anxious to use words any longer.

Either way, it's time for me to go.

The last thing I need is a run-in with law enforcement.

You see, we have this little agreement; the Sephilim and the mortal privatised military force. After several of the more volatile newly reborn Kindred had decided to conduct back to earth and electrocute those they felt had wronged them, the unit was left to clean up and then cover up our messes.

That didn't go down well, to cut a long story short.

It had taken a while along with a lot of tense meetings as well as several casualties and one planned assassination, but in the end, it was resolved with the mutual understanding that if we stay out of their way, they'll stay out of ours.

Regardless though, I'm out of here.

I have a blazing conflict to spark.

I reappear in the throne room this time, the amethyst walls and floors capturing my reflection without flaw, dark and intimidating, once the lightning recedes.

Leo is waiting, exactly where I ordered him to be, looking bored as he leans against the farthest wall of the enormous octagonal space.

"And?" he asks, pushing off the slick purple stone and erecting himself, chocolate and burgundy feathers looking far more well-kept than the last time I'd seen him. He's quite clearly showered as well, his auburn hair now dull brown and damp.

"She's not there. Not that I expected her to be. I can't imagine any Sephilim or Nephilim aiding her escape back to the mortal realm, not with the consequence of treason being death," I muse, thinking about how many beheadings I've attended over the last few years. Considerably fewer than when I had first ascended to the rank of High Lord, so I suppose that's some indication of my effectiveness at least.

Leo's calloused palm grazes the top of his sword, the handle carved to boast the open roaring jaws of his namesake.

"It's true, I couldn't see anyone openly defying you in such a way. Besides, it would have been pointless. She's too easy for us to locate now. Unless of course, she has protection of the immortal kind—" Leo muses, cocking his hip and lifting the ball of his foot from the floor, resting all his weight on his heels.

"She's here, in Aetheria. As I have known since the moment she was taken. I can feel her. And she's with *him*." The final word comes like a spit of oil from a scalding hot skillet. My fists ball at my sides, and Leo nods, swallowing hard and tensing as if he's worried I might attack him.

"How long is it going to take us to be ready to begin the search and seize?" I demand, my eyes narrowing as I turn from him, chest tightening within the vice grip of agitation. I should never have been put in this situation, especially considering how I had warned Kairi of the Draconians.

Stupid girl should have listened. Because now she's going to get herself killed, one way or another.

I pace, watching Leo out of the corner of my eye as his golden armour glints with dull defiance against the damage it has previously taken. He bites down on the inside of his bottom lip, clearly trying to come up with an answer that will please me.

"Maybe twelve hours. Maybe more. We need to make it to our designated landing point, then get everyone briefed, and make sure nobody gets lost. Scoping out the lay of the land beforehand will be difficult, but with any luck, the skies will be in our favour with poor visibility. If we were attempting this anywhere but Drakos Vale, we wouldn't be able to pull it off," he says.

I smile.

"Luckily for us, the rest of Aetheria knows what's best for them when it comes to defying The Sephilim. Then again, they have had longer, far longer, to see what becomes of those who resist." As I spill these words, I think back to the way The Sephilim had begun, to how they had come to Aetheria for the sole purpose of destroying Promethean Seraphim.

Our history alone should have been enough to put High Lady Thomas in line with the rest, but for some reason, the bitch just wouldn't come to heel.

"Indeed, My Lord. I will order our troops to head out and send word for you when we are ready for you to join us." Leo stands more alert now, wings tucked in sharply at his spine, hand moving to clench in a fist as he brings it to rest over his heart in the ultimate sign of respect.

"I'll be waiting," I say simply, watching him nod with a sudden jerk of his chiselled jawline and then turn on his heel.

In a flash of bright lightning that cracks against the air of the throne room like a whip, he's gone.

KAIRI

The shower within the treehouse suite that I'm given to stay in is unique, to say the least. High above the main tree canopies, the entirety of the building is formed from the same oak that is hollowed out to house the entryway staircase. The spiralling steps lead not only to the open plan suite I've been offered but also to the one that Lucien has been assigned beneath.

It had taken me a few moments to work out how to use the shower with a glass wet room that holds no obvious metal faucet or taps as you would expect. Instead, there is only the thick vine of a plant that blossoms into a showerhead. After a few tenuously executed experiments, it turns out that you turn it on by stroking the stem with gentle fingers.

The petals open suddenly, letting droplets loose from the inside of the bloom gentle as rainwater but twice as fresh. It's warm, neither hot nor cold, which is lucky because there's no way I can see to change the temperature.

I wash quickly, unsure of how long the plant will continue to spill the torrent, reaching for several large bars of fragrant floral soaps that are held by stiff palm leaves that climb the highly lacquered oak of the panelled rear wall on thin vines.

The air is full of the scent of roses, bluebells, and violets, a hint of vanilla toning the strength of each flower to be just below what's over-whelming as I finish bathing, the perfumed soaps melding together with an organic seamlessness nothing short of aromatherapy magic.

As I step out of the wide glass door, the shower stops without me stroking it once more, either because it's run out of water or because it's sensed I'm no longer standing beneath.

The towels are jersey cotton that's thin but luxuriously soft to touch in a sage green, hung on an oak towel ring that seems to grow effortlessly from the wall. I wrap it around myself, turning in a half circle atop a spongy moss-like rug that's damp between my toes, and gaze at my long, wet tresses in the mirror as they dangle down over my shoulders.

I barely recognise myself in this world, surrounded by such fantasy. My mortal skin is underwhelming and sickly in comparison to the rich tones of flowering buds and raw wood, my pallor only exaggerated by eyes rimmed with black circles from poor sleep. My silhouette is lacking, no wings, no pointed ears, nor extraordinary tattoos.

I have never felt more self-conscious, and yet, I cannot help but yearn to belong here, to become more than human so that I might fit in and revel in the majesty of it all. Ironically, I'm also more homesick than ever at the sight of myself in such a usual pose amongst the foreign and undeniably magical. My stomach ties itself in knots as I turn my back on my face, partly a stranger and partly someone I wish I could escape entirely because I know her only too well, shedding my skin to become— *more.*

It terrifies me, the idea that I might have once been immortal, that I might take up that chalice once more.

I don't think I want to live forever. It's too overwhelming, too much responsibility.

Not that I have a death wish, but I don't think I would want to shoulder the burdens placed on the Kindred of Aetheria either.

I pad across the shiny wooden floorboards and into the open-plan apartment beyond the bathroom door. Vines of wisteria climb a high-set, four-poster bed that's made from the same wood as the rest of the structure, the sheets green jersey with a comforter that seems to be weaved finely from raw cotton and interspersed with tiny glass beads. They catch the light pouring in through the glassless windows that stretch from floor to ceiling as I look out over the lush horizon beyond, my eyes glistening right along with them.

Breathing out in a heavy and overwhelmed breath, I move over to the armoire that I had been informed would contain some basic clothing that should suit my needs. I am grateful for the gesture, having sweated profusely beneath the heavy wool of my dress on the journey here.

Pulling open the drawer, I find a silk dress accompanied by a thin lace thong. There's no bra, even though I make sure to double-check as I pull out the pear-coloured mini-dress and let the silk run cool through my fingers.

I shed the towel, uncomfortable at the fact there's no glass or even drapes between me and the surrounding treehouses that are also wide open to external viewers.

It seems the Fae certainly aren't shy, and I'm left wondering how any of them can be intimate with one another when there's so little privacy to be had.

Taking a deep breath, I slip quickly into the underwear and then let the slinky dress fall over my damp head. The fit is loose and airy as it falls to just above my knees. Blood still rushes close to the surface of my skin from the shower, warmth flooding every inch of my pale flesh mapped with silver stretch marks. I'm self-conscious, having so much skin on show, but I can't deny the pattern of the dress is exquisite. The delicate silk is unstructured and free-flowing, its ripe pear hue embroidered with poisoned ivy in a golden shimmering thread so fine it may well be spider spun. Thin straps cross between my shoulder blades, presumably to accommodate wings, and are woven from something so soft I wonder if it's heather.

There are no shoes provided that I can see, and with the sun so warm from beyond the edge of the floorboards that simply fall away into thin air, I decide to descend the spiralling staircase within the oak's trunk and venture outside to allow my hair to dry while I take in some of the city's alternate views. My feet are quick upon the wood floors, my curiosity for this incredible floral Fae world mounting as the sun kisses my back and I leave my rooms.

I take the staircase in a rhythmic and quick stride, coming upon a landing that leads to not another apartment but that lets out into the sprawling interconnected system of bridges that link one tree to those surrounding it.

Stepping out into the warm late morning air of Lumeria, I find Lucien standing, wearing only sage green breeches. He has bare feet and no shirt on, exposing the massive network of tattoos that wind around the bulk of his chiselled torso, the archaic symbol of Hecate etched right over his heart in a defiant and bottomless black ink that seems abyssal in its intensity. His blonde hair lies down the length of his back in a pure white waterfall of poker-straight strands between the high-rising outlines of his wings, and even without the intrusion of his lustrous mane, I can tell the tattoos cover more skin than not.

"Kairi—" he turns to me, eyes widening as they fall over my form, my name more of a question than a statement. It's like he doesn't recognise me, or maybe he has suddenly remembered knowing me in another life— which, though, I can't tell.

I cross my arms over my chest as he scrutinises every inch of my skin, self-consciousness rearing its head once again, particularly because I'm not wearing a bra.

"Hey," I breathe in the floral aromas of the Nirvana air, my eyes struggling to take in the masses of detailed carpentry that have gone into the construction of the bridge we're both standing on. The balustrades on either side dip along with the hanging angle of the bridge's construction, each rail wound tight with vines and plants blooming into a spectrum of radiant colours.

"You alright? You were quiet on the walk here—" Lucien asks as I take several steps toward him, turning so we are side by side, elbows propped on the sloping of the railing.

"Yes. Just tired," I reply, eyelids suddenly heavy as if the admission itself is a kind of sleeping curse. He nods, not carrying on the conversation as we both hang over the corkscrewing oak vines of the railing, looking at the intricate wings of different Fae as they flit from tree to tree or hover just above the forest floor, their motion so fast they blur into nothing more than the vibrant hues of their clothing.

"Thank you," I say, my tone as sincere as I can make it. A shudder runs through me at the memory of Neve's icy clutch, my skin rippling with goosebumps despite the fact only moments ago I was feeling warm. Honestly, among the calls of nature and the silent but rapid motion of the Fae, I've been feeling more relaxed than I have since waking back in the lakeside lodge after skating until dawn.

Perhaps it's the floral perfume or the vibrant lusciousness of the surroundings, but either way, I am soothed and cast out the memory of Neve's icy assault.

Lucien looks sideways at me.

"You shouldn't have wandered off, Kairi. I know this world is enough to intrigue even the most cynical of hearts, but it's equally as vicious." He sighs, running gentle fingers back through his hair.

"I know. I'm sorry." I pause, looking at his fingers as he brings them back to rest on the railing. "How did you—" My lips twist, and his eyebrows lift, surprised.

"What? Cryomancy?" he enquires, and I nod. Guessing that his ability to knit ice out of thin air is what he's referring to.

"Yeah, the whole— freezing thing. I didn't know you could—" I say, but he shrugs.

"I guess I forgot to mention it. It's pretty common knowledge among the Drakos Vale residents— Lord Black knows too— so I thought he would have told you while warning you about what a horrendous psychopath I am, I suppose—" He shrugs, as though his magical ability is nothing more than a party trick.

"That's why your breath doesn't condense— when it's cold," I surmise.

"Yup. Most useless power ever when you live in the frozen wasteland that is Drakos Vale." He sounds disappointed, but all I can feel is awe.

"Well, thanks for saving me, and sorry for the trouble. I guess I'm just the stupid mortal getting herself in trouble again. I should really do something about that—" I admit, deflating despite the fact the sun is warming me through.

"Self-pity doesn't suit you. Knock it off," Lucien adds, nudging me and giving me a small smile from beneath the shadowy curtain of his thick tresses. His entire face lights up a moment, contrasting his usual stoicism with alarming potency.

"So why here, why Nirvana? I thought the High Lord here, Morpheus, was in tight with Aro—" I ask, recalling the way the two High Lords had mingled the last time I'd seen them.

"Morpheus isn't the only High Lord in Nirvana. Lumeria is home to four, and they rule Lumeria in seasonal shifts. You met two this morning actually, Neve and Ember. Morpheus and his partner Hypnos rule the other Fae Capital, Aramis, but they have little clout here," he explains, and I nod, feeling like I'm drowning in a sea of places, titles, and races. There's so much here, far too much for my brain to absorb after so little time.

"I see. So, you're friends with Neve?" I ask him, smirking at the thought of them becoming pals. He grins, white teeth noticeably carnivorous as his incisors glint in the too-bright sun, matching his talons with their gleam.

"Pfft. You don't become friends with Neve. You sort of achieve a status of disdainful tolerance, and that's as good as it gets. Ember however is lovely, and the only person I know who has a chance in hell of wrangling Neve when she's in a rage," Lucien adds.

"So, it was Ember?" I ask him, feeling that knowing who had decided to shelter me is oddly crucial. I am still unsure of who to trust, even when it comes to Lucien, so it would be nice to know if I have a shot with another High Lord or Lady.

"No. Quinn, actually. He's the Fae High Lord of Light for Spring. And he owed me a huge favour, otherwise we wouldn't be here. The Fae, by and large, are pacifists down to their very core. They won't get involved in a conflict unless it's absolutely necessary," he explains, mouth twisting in distaste.

"You disapprove of pacifism?" I ask, watching his face turn thoughtful as my brows rise in surprise.

"I'm against doing nothing while good people die. We are immortals. We should have nothing to fear— and yet, we live beneath a veil of cruelty. We live like we were mortals, knowing no better. Those of us who want change, who are willing to rebel and are caught trying to do so, are punished by death at the hands of The Sephilim and The Aresian Equinians." My brows kiss on my forehead as I frown. The subject clearly bothers him greatly, and I really want to know why.

"And they call you Draconian," I mumble, trying to make him smile. He looks at me for a moment, his eyes lingering hard on my face as if he's trying to remember something of vital importance.

"You know that the Sephilim have so few prisoners that they converted the dungeons beneath the Solis Castra into servant's quarters? That isn't because they don't have enemies, Kairi. It's because they won't compromise on getting the power they desire. They'd rather be murderers than democrats," he explains. I purse my lips, hair kissing my shoulders in loose, almost dry waves.

"And that's why Aro wants the crown so badly. Because, right now, everything has to go to a vote—" I realise. Lucien nods in agreement, jaw tensing hard.

"He will have the power to overrule everyone and everything, even the Senate if he gets his hands on that crown. The other Kindred will

342

become slaves to his whim— some more willingly than others, I'll grant you, but still powerless whatever way you slice it." He breathes out, causing me to frown.

"That scares you?" I ask, trying to be unafraid as I stand at his side, anxiety heavily coiling silently in my stomach like a serpent waiting to strike.

"Lord Black has never liked me— in fact, loathe is more of an apt description. He has a great hatred toward the Draconians but me in particular. If he comes into power, I'm as good as dead, regardless of whether I've broken any laws or not. He'll find something to make me guilty of— His intense and unprovoked hatred of me is why I was so interested to see why he had invited me to the ball that night. You have to understand, him extending such an invite, even out of propriety and regard for the laws of our people— well, it's like a lion and a lamb becoming fast friends."

"And you're the lamb?" I ask, cocking an eyebrow as the wind tickles my knees.

"What do you think?" He gives me a mischievous smirk, and I feel my heart constrict a little, blood rushing warm around my limbs in a sudden energised burst.

"So, what do we do now? Do I stand any chance of getting out of this alive?" I ask, watching his face tensing as his wings flare out, casting his angular features in shadow as they block out the sun.

"Now, we rest. For today at least. I'm extending feelers to try and get us an invitation to Aramis. According to Quinn and Phineas, his partner, Morpheus would be the one to know if our memories have been tampered with," he surmises, shoulders lifting a little as he shifts his weight from one foot to the other.

"You didn't answer my question." I retort in a flat and blunt mumble, refusing to let go of the query that is hanging over my head like a razor-sharp guillotine.

"I can't promise you a happy ending, Kairi. But I can promise you I'll do everything in my power to give you the best chance of getting one."

He sighs, cocking his head and staring at me with an intensity I have never seen from him before. Then, he smiles, his gaze softening wistfully over my features as though he's committing them to his memory now, searching for any hint of familiarity.

"Come on," he says, placing a chill hand on my shoulder as he stands up straight, eyes suddenly bright, "I have something to show you—"

The thing that had most stunned me upon first setting eyes on the city of Lumeria was the scale.

When I describe the oak trees here, even referring to them as the same species as the earthen trees I know seems ridiculous. The trunks tower over the ground at almost one hundred feet, the roots alone bigger than a small beluga whale with width enough to hold a small house.

The city is home to what must be thousands of these enormous wooden beasts, each one supporting several spacious wooden buildings within its thick but gnarled clutches. The buildings that hover over the ground flaunt the physical law of gravity, their precariousness among the branches nothing short of effortless.

The leaves are enormous too, some of the greenest bigger than my head, with veins running through them thicker than the ones which run closest to the surface of my wrists. They scatter the floor, peppering the thick carpet of cloudlike mosses that surround the pebbled pathways flanked with wildflowers, the entire city growing out from the single central vein of the river.

It throbs with life, the water's surface glistening silver and then a milky shade of duck egg blue as it slides through the land without harshness or brutality but instead as a natural caress. Along its banks colour explodes; waterlilies, crocuses, tulips, and daffodils flourishing beneath the protective weep of hundreds of willow trees, their branches stirring incrementally in the light fragrant breeze.

The trunks of each tree are veined through with precious metal, just like in Soleus, but unlike Soleus, I can't find a single indicator that any of the trees have been cut down or scaled back, and the flowers grow where they will instead of where they are wanted.

The Fae of Light have high regard for the natural world around them, and a part of me feels ashamed of how humans have so completely decimated the planet we call home.

"What are you thinking about?" Lucien asks as we stroll from the exit of the tree's trunk, bare feet whispering sighs as the soft moss underfoot cradles my weight like moist velvet.

"I was just thinking about how the Fae have such respect for their environment. Humans could learn a thing or two— I mean, Neve was willing to kill to protect the grove I stumbled into," I remember, eyes taking in every detail of the surrounding world, my gaze daring to linger too long on the ostentatious and scanty wild attire of some of the passing Fae.

"The Rainbow Grove— it's sacred. More so than anywhere else in Nirvana." Lucien acknowledges, his eyes serious and intense. He keeps his gaze trained on his bare feet as we take a leisurely pace along the riverside path.

"What makes it so special?" I ask, my questions surfacing after being submerged in the fear of freezing to death.

"The Rainbow Grove— it's where the souls of children or babies taken before their time wait for their parents to pass and join them. I guess when a child dies before they are matured, the energy of their souls has not cleaved entirely from the souls that made them. So, the trees give them form here, and they wait for their makers to lead them back to the crucible—"

My mouth is dry as I swallow, hanging off his every word, my eyes wet with tears and throat full of emotion.

"That's the most beautiful thing I've ever heard—" I breathe, and he stares into my face, scrutinising every inch of me.

I flush, dropping my gaze.

"I forget— how this must seem to an outsider. How idyllic—" he mutters, voice no more than a bitter sigh.

"It is idyllic, Lucien. Look around us," I turn on the spot, the balls of my feet cool with freshly squeezed dew.

"Those sprites represent the most innocent souls— you have no idea the lengths to which the Fae must go to keep them safe, how many Fae have died for them over the years. This place isn't idyllic, Kairi. It's dangerous and cruel. What kind of a world is it where you have to guard a grove that pure night and day? Nothing here is sacred." His face is taut with passion that's swirling into dark clouds of rage behind the rich blue surface of his eyes, his hands balling into fists as the tattoos marring his chest ripple atop bulging muscles.

"I'm sorry—" I whisper, reaching out to touch his arm. He flinches away, straightening and releasing a strained breath.

"You have nothing to be sorry for. It is my own stupid dreams that cause me such pain at the reality of Aetheria. Genevieve often tells me I am a fool to stick to such beliefs about justice and honour when the reality is so far from it," he expresses as we pass by a bend in the river, our feet mindlessly following the pebbled outlines of the pathway that curves with it.

"Dreams?" I pry, curious now more than ever. I have never thought of Lucien as an emotional person, but right now I'm seeing a side of him and a depth he's been hiding behind layers of what is now fast-melting frost.

"All the history books say the same thing. Aetheria didn't used to be four floating continents, Kairi. It used to be one. It was only when the Equinians were created that the island fractured apart at the hands of the Gods because the power they gave us made us murderers. We were never supposed to hate each other like this, to kill each other without second thought. This place was supposed to be a paradise, just as you think it to be." He sighs, and I look up at him, biting the inside of my lip.

"So why don't you do something about it? There's always a way—" I implore him, knowing I sound foolish and naïve, knowing I sound young but seeing the desire in his face and saying it anyway.

"Paradise lies just beyond the horizon of our greatest suffering. That's what my father used to say. The people of Aetheria would rather be comfortable and oppressed than risk it all for a chance at freedom and true democracy. Most of them spent their lives fighting and don't want to give up their immortal years as well. I'm only one man, and the system is so old, so ingrained, that people don't even question it anymore." He twirls a lock of his long blond hair around his index finger, smiling at a Fae clad in little more than bloody crimson petals and dark vines of ivy that climb her languid form in thick emerald tendrils. Her dark eyes are curious as she gives us a stiff smile in passing, the crimson veins that run through her glassy transparent wings the only evidence that they're there at all.

"Where are you taking me, anyway?" I enquire, feeling the Fae's curious eyes roaming my spine for wings and coming up empty.

"Patience. I don't want to ruin the surprise— but I will tell you that I'm taking you to my favourite place in Aetheria." He has a wicked glint in his eye, and I feel myself becoming excited. What could be incredible enough to rank at number one for a man who is surrounded by the fantastical and sees only the cruelty behind the beautiful veil of it?

Comfortable silence falls between us again as we continue to trace the bulbous curves and swirling edges of the river. The further along we journey, the larger the spaces between the trunks of trees become, leaving me to believe that we're reaching closer to the outskirts of the settlement's cluster with each step.

346

Eventually, Lucien grabs my hand without thought, pulling me off the main road and down a smaller branch that breaks into a subtle fork. The trees become sparser still, and I can't help but gawp, overwhelmed by the luscious curtains of green that close in on every side.

"Almost there," Lucien promises, tugging me a little harder behind him as we reach something almost as odd in this wildly unregimented landscape as the hawthorn-formed cathedral I had sat in earlier.

A narrow column of space is created by two regimented lines of thick trees, the path formed by them creating a precise and unfaltering entranceway that leads directly toward an enormous wooden building.

This isn't like the other wooden constructs in Lumeria though, and where usually the wooden architecture is left wild and raw beneath your fingers, I can see the lacquered sheen on the pristine roof from here as it gleams madly warm in the sun. This wood has been manipulated and carved, patterns that are unmistakably Renaissance-inspired, following every plane of the building's outer shell.

It's huge, standing steady on the solid earth beneath my feet instead of in the clutch of a tree, towering at least five stories and seeming to reach back through the forest forever as I try to get a glimpse of what's behind it.

"What is this?" I ask, cocking my head and trying to work it out.

Lucien laughs, narrowing his eyes as an amused smirk tugs at his lips.

"I forget how impatient mortals can be. Come on, let's go inside—" At the notion that we will be entering this incredible place, I straighten within my dress, wondering how many High Born Fae I'll be presented to for scrutiny. Lucien said this is his favourite place in Aetheria though, so the thought of someone so seemingly introverted wanting to make a house call is a little odd.

Lucien pulls me down the narrow pathway, the flickering dark shadows of trees blinking in and out of existence across our faces. When we finally reach the end of the road, I'm left staring up at the building's double wooden doors, their surfaces mahogany polished to within an inch of its life. The door handles, two simple golden rings, glint, taunting me.

Lucien nudges me, the glee in his face almost piqued as his lips twist and his eyes watch my every motion, causing the hairs on the back of my neck to stand at uniform attention. Suddenly, I realise I'm shaking, adrenaline making my heart thunder wildly beneath my rib cage.

Tired of the anticipation, I take a few steps forward, gripping the golden ring in my hand and pulling the door open.

Then, without pause, I step inside.

What awaits within is so beautiful I want to cry.

The scent of it hits me full-force as my eyes widen and my head falls back, craning up at the ceiling and trying to take it all in.

Lucien laughs, the sound pure joy.

"I knew you'd like it," he whispers, stepping past me. I can't move to follow him though; I'm frozen on the spot.

It must go on for miles, but it begins right beneath my feet, a single corridor that cuts through every floor, capturing the dark airy light of the entirely warm wooden interior. On both sides of me, perfectly symmetrical, they sit. Thousands, if not hundreds of thousands of leather-bound spines, perfectly tucked away in hundreds upon hundreds of shelves.

The scent of books fills my head, making my anxiety dissolve. No matter what dimension I'm in, that fact always remains.

"Welcome to The Library." Lucien grins wider than I've ever seen, wider than when he presented me with the ice skates, wider than when I'd watched him race Ebonara through the blistering cold night.

"The Library— seems a little underwhelming a title for something so—" I begin, but he chuckles.

"Oh no, you misunderstand. This is the origin. The very first Library, Kairi. It houses every book ever written." His words shouldn't surprise me. After all, the place seems endless, and yet they do.

"Eh— Every book?" I stutter.

"Well, technically every mortal or Aetherial book ever written. After all, most of their inspiration originated within these walls. The Muses have worked here for longer than most of the Fae can remember— and before that, they worked in The Higher Plains. Their books weren't available like this though. It is said that information is more valuable than Ambrosia up there, if you believe Hypnos' drunk stories," he adds, the story going in but not registering with my brain as my eyes endlessly roam the surrounding stacks.

The sound of a rolling ladder catches in the high eaves of the building, and a Fae appears like something out of a musical.

Dust motes glitter golden in the dry air, her honeyed blonde locks turning a similar shade as she leaps off the ladder with more elegance than any mortal. Her wings look like withered paper, crackling as she moves, when she turns toward us and settles a pair of periwinkle irises on my form.

Her eyebrows rise on her brow, the heart shape of her face dimpling at each one of her blushing, apple-round cheeks.

"Lord DeLaurent, this is a surprise. Long time, no see," she breathes, the crumpled golden silk of her flighty gown fluttering around her knees.

Her body is covered in words, every inch of her skin telling its own story.

"Everly, you're looking as radiant as ever." Lucien compliments her, bowing his head as the corners of his mouth lift in the slightest smile.

The silence that falls thickens around us as Everly's gaze turns back to me, the soundlessness becoming malleable like glistening golden syrup.

"This is Kairi. She is quite the bookworm—" Lucien introduces me, and I step forward lamely, holding out a hand. Everly looks down at my palm, smiling as her entire face relaxes.

"I can tell, there are stories written all over her aura. Come, Kairi. Would you like a tour?" she asks, and I feel myself shaking my head with an automatic vigour I don't sanction nor can stop.

My lips spread in a grin I can't contain, wondering exactly which stories have left their mark on me.

"I'll leave you both to it. I have to go and check on our travel arrangements for tomorrow. Will you be alright here, Kairi? I can return to make sure you find your way back if you'd like?" he offers, but the pause in his voice tells me he'd rather not make the return journey.

Everly steps in, looking at me with far more kindness than I expect.

"I'll help her find her way back, Lucien. No need to worry." She takes my hand in hers, leading me with quiet but energetic steps down the immense corridor that lies at the heart of the library. I gawp around, but all the while, I can't let my eyes stray too far from Lucien as Everly leads me away from the man who has saved my life now for the second time.

"Now what's your favourite genre?" I hear her ask, my eyes leaving Lucien and moving to her excited and elegant face for only a moment.

I consider this, looking back automatically, but my answer gets lost as I turn to find Lucien is already gone.

LUCIEN

Her words echo within the cold chamber of my skull.

So why don't you do something about it? There's always a way—

She's so naïve, but I can't help but love her for it. She has a beautiful soul, and an enchanting way of seeing the colour, the light within even the darkest of shadows.

The city of Lumeria teems around me, the effortless and endless barrage of Fae tending to nearby plants, grasses, and herb gardens as I pass back through the city. My mind wanders slowly, keeping pace with my feet as I stay snug against the riverbank. Letting my fingers tickle through thick curtains of weeping willow branches, I enjoy the tepid glow cast across my bare skin by the sun lazily reaching its zenith. I let my wings stretch, each plane of webbed leathery skin tautening, my lungs expanding as my face tilts up to the sky, blond locks tumbling warm down my spine. I had left the library as soon as she had been far enough away for me to break free of the intoxicating way she sees and loves everything about the world I've only ever been able to make real in my visions and dreams. Her reactions make it seem almost close enough to touch.

I remember the feel of her racing pulse beneath my palms as I had steered Ebonara through the night, the scent of her skin the most alluring warm concoction of lavender and heather— a specific kind of musk that I know I'll never find anywhere else.

Her excitement, her wonder has been infectious, and I feel as if I have a hangover from the way she makes me want to mould this world into something far more than it has ever been. It's as though where I have always known I'm standing on a lump of coal, she has shown me the incredible shimmer of the diamond it could become, making me lustful and wanton for a future which is entirely impossible.

I'm happy when she's beside me, overjoyed at even the chance to see the world I've come to detest in a way that isn't as ruthless as reality.

"One would think you've been stuck in a blizzard for one hundred years, Lord DeLaurent—" The call of Phineas' rich tone startles me, causing me to raise a hand, shielding my eyes from the sun.

"Where are you?" I call, swinging around with wings still extended at full span as my eyes scan the pathway. Several Fae glance up from their busywork, eyes curious if not slightly disturbed by the presence of a foreigner in their midst.

A breeze tickles the back of my neck, causing me to spin once again, facing an enormous willow tree with a weep that sprawls halfway onto the moss of the path, tendrils stroking the ground lovingly. The other half of the tree spreads over the steady sloshing of the river, this fact revealed as the breeze I have no doubt is the responsibility of The Fae High Lord of Light for Fall parts the curtain of greenery closest to me, exposing the pair of lovers hidden within.

"Good afternoon, Phineas. Quinn," I acknowledge them with the respect they're due.

"So lovely to see you appreciating Lumeria, and how is our lovely fugitive?" Quinn asks.

I step within the shroud of the tree; aware I might look not entirely sane as I appear to be talking to myself in the middle of the city.

The leaves drop behind me as I enter, the golden light of the day turning a rich sage as it falls over the pair of High Lords that lounge on the floor, Phineas leaning against the trunk with Quinn's head in his lap, mahogany locks spread out over his thigh. Phineas strokes the silken strands, twining flowers into the braids of his lover, the sense of utter calm pulled over the pair of them nothing short of enviable.

"She's in The Library with Everly. She loves books so I thought it would be a shame for her to miss it," I admit, cocking my hip and feeling the leaves behind me as featherlight wisps across my wings, making them itch. I use the sensation as a distraction to stop myself seeming too attached.

"How very sweet of you— I would assume from this gesture that you had affections for the child. But even you aren't so foolish as to get involved with a Mortal— let alone one who is fleeing the extremely ruthless Lord Black—" Quinn quips, one eyebrow arched provocatively. I watch as his fingers trace alluring circles across his bare abdomen, the velvet of his jacket tossed asunder, revealing the garden of floral tattoos budding across his stomach and chest.

351

The glistening silver ribbons of light that dance off the surface of the river's smooth flow leap up onto his face, playing with the soft lines of his feminine features.

"Of course not, I was just wanting to get her out of the way so I might come and discuss the suggested trip to Aramis with you. You have transportation to the city I assume? I cannot fly there with Kairi. There is no cover here, and I do not fancy broadcasting her location to the skies, as I'm sure you understand," I explain, interrupting the intense gaze of Phineas as he looks down into the emerald pastures of Quinn's eyes.

My throat constricts at their obvious intimacy.

"Huh—" Quinn replies, as though he hadn't heard me, before breaking eye contact with Phineas and turning to look up, propping himself up on one elbow. "Oh yes, transportation. I can get you a carriage. I'm going to be joining you. I haven't attended a full moon celebration in a few cycles, I'm becoming restless—" Phineas' gaze blazes as Quinn's declaration hits the fragrant air trapped beneath the willow. I feel the breeze stir, becoming chill and crisp within seconds as the aroma turns stale and brackish.

"Restless? Am I not satisfying you, sweetheart?" The endearment is tender, but the tone is sharp as a razor blade.

I understand his concern because even I have heard the wild rumours about what goes on during Morpheus' full moon celebrations.

"Oh Phineas, darling. You know that is simply not who I am. We agreed on an open relationship—" Quinn is direct, cupping Phineas' cheek.

I become hot just under the skin as I feel as though I'm intruding on an ancient argument, a source of conflict between them that runs to their core.

"Doesn't mean I have to like it and act as though I'm happy about you going to one of those— orgies." Phineas' eyes become full of warmth, of longing, but then dart to me.

Clearing his throat, he removes Quinn's fingers from the line of his cheekbone, nodding to me.

They will continue their battle of hearts later.

"We will leave tomorrow morning, early. It's several hours by carriage, and we need to arrive in time to get ready for the night's festivities." Quinn's eyes glimmer wildly, vibrant as the world humming around us, in tune with his excited heartbeat.

"I wonder what Kairi will make of Aramis. She is extremely enamoured with Lumeria. She's like a newborn, fascinated with everything!" I exclaim, an unwanted and revealing smile taking hold of my face.

"Ah, Lucien, smitten looks odd on you—" Quinn grins wickedly. "If she loves Lumeria, you wait until she sees what happens when it begins to rain tomorrow night in the jungles of Aramis. If I were you and were vying for a kiss— or to steal the heart of a fugitive mortal— that's when I'd make my move." Quinn laughs melodically, but I can only scowl.

"Don't be so ridiculous!" I exclaim, turning my back on the pair of them and storming from beneath the shadow of the willow tree.

"See you and your lady tomorrow, Lucien—" he calls, cackling madly from behind the leafy veil.

As I burst onto the path, leaves catch on my talons and rip free like confetti.

The sun hits me again, though this time it aggravates me as I'm already hot and undeniably bothered beneath the thin shroud of my skin.

I shake my head, the floral aroma and sound of Quinn's tinny laughter causing my heart to accelerate in an annoyingly predictable and telling manner.

Then, hurrying on down the path, I flee from The King of Spring and his ridiculously emotional notions.

24

ALICE IN WONDERLAND

KAIRI

THE SUN DRIPS IN through the panes, turning from a bright and youthful lemon to a rich and weathered amber as hours pass. Here, among the stacks of the library, time succumbs as effortlessly to the onslaught of the next moment as sand slipping through the waist of an hourglass succumbs to gravity.

"I think it's almost closing time. I should get you back to Lucien—" Everly says, her blue eyes wistful.

We've talked like we've known one another for years, in the way only two women who have spent exceedingly large times in worlds made of little more than ink and imagination can. Her wings, light on her spine as crumpled old parchment, flutter, casting long shadows on the floor. Setting down the pile of tomes she's been showing me, she flicks through the pages of a particularly thick volume with excited yet careful fingers.

Glancing over her shoulder at me, she places them on a mahogany table by one of the large arched windows with more care than if she was handling a newborn.

"I guess— how long have I been here?" I ask timidly, the bottoms of my feet throbbing from pounding up and down spiral staircases after rare volumes, spine stiff from craning my neck up at the sheer magnitude of the towering bookcases.

"A little over six hours—" she says, checking an enormous golden sundial that hangs from the ceiling like a chandelier. My mouth pops open, stomach dropping.

"How is that possible? I feel like I only just got here!" I frown, feeling my brows knit together on my forehead in frustrated disbelief. For the first time since I arrived, I feel like throwing a bit of a temper tantrum. I don't want to leave, and even though I've apparently been here for hours, it isn't enough.

I wonder how long would be, how many years one might spend wandering the endless labyrinth of words long since scrawled.

"Come on, Kairi— I don't want Lucien angry at me."

She looks unnerved, and though my shoulders slump in defeat, I nod reluctantly, giving her a small smile.

"Is that because he's a Draconian?" I ask her, and she puckers her lips, eyes narrowing as she leads me back down the gargantuan central corridor.

"Why else?" she asks simply, her slippers soundless against the polished floorboards underfoot.

"So, you don't have a personal grudge against Lord DeLaurent then?" I ask her, and she shakes her head.

"Of course not. It's just— his kind, they're— well. You must have heard the stories," she says, waving her hand as we reach the oval, light-drenched foyer. Even though it feels only moments since I was first standing here agape, I can see the evidence of the lost hours by the way the shadows of the stacks grow long, darkening the wood of the floor. Everly disappears for a few moments, returning with a wicker basket slung over her forearm, its handle twined with rosebuds.

"The night guard will be here momentarily to take over," she explains as I follow her outside when she leans hard on the immense double doors. Looking over my shoulder with obvious scepticism, we leave the place unattended and veiled in noble silence.

"Not really. Which stories about the Draconians are you referring to specifically?" I ask her, knowing full well their reputation but wanting to hear a Fae opinion nonetheless.

"Oh just— you know— stories—" Everly flushes, and I cock my head at her, feeling suddenly irritated.

"If you hold enough stock in these stories to hold grudges based on them, you should have no problem sharing them. You obviously believe them to be true," I remind her with a bitter boldness, and her pupils dilate, face becoming lined with seriousness before her eyes sharpen on my features, her pointed Fae ears twitching a little beneath the thick fall of her hair.

"They say that the loss of their dragons made them mad with rage, that they became monsters in grief—" she whispers the story almost as if she's afraid Lucien will pop out from behind a tree and attack us both.

355

"Lucien saved my life. Twice. How do you explain that if he's crazy and violent?" I ask her, but she only frowns.

"Perhaps he has more stake in keeping the crown from Lord Black than you realise," she responds, startling me with the acuteness of her observation as her eyes dart to the mark on my wrist and back to my face so fast I barely notice.

I think on this for a few moments, wondering whether she has a point.

I had thought Lord Black honourable, and look how accurate my judgement on that turned out to be.

"Kairi," Everly clutches my shoulders, "I know you love stories; I do too. But this is no fairy tale, and you are no damsel who can rely on rescue simply because she is mortal and innocent. There's a reason I stay firmly locked in the library with my books, and that's because even in a place this beautiful, reality isn't kind, or just. Don't forget that everyone you meet is stuck in the same reality— and we all have our motives." Her nails are gripping me so hard I resist the urge to cry out as their points threaten to pierce the skin.

"So, what's yours?" I ask her, tilting my chin and gritting my teeth.

"Me? Oh, well, I'm an extraordinarily simple creature, I just want to be left alone with my books," she explains, and I chew on my bottom lip, thoughtful.

What she's saying sounds wonderful, and once she would have had my full empathy. But the longer I'm here beneath the cobalt sun the more I realise that her dream seems an awful lot like resignation to the cruelty and pain suffered by others.

I'd been her, not a week ago, content to lose myself in another world less tangible than smoke while the rest of my life wilted around me, my precious mortal time seeming worthless and with the potential to give only more pain.

Silence engulfs us, and so I let myself become lost in the extraordinary surroundings and my sudden epiphany as we make our way back to Lucien.

"Hey, Everly!" The voice is male, and it breaks the trance I'm in, every step back along the mossy path so far having gone unnoticed as I ponder on my own life back home in Tennessee.

"Jace, hey," Everly sounds suddenly weary as the male Fae makes himself visible from behind the trunk of one of the enormous oak trees flanking the path's wide border of Queen Anne's lace.

His chest is tanned, hair a similar shade to Everly's and swept side-ward from his forehead in a sandy blonde wave of a fringe that cuts close to his eyebrows. He has unusual wings like those of a bejewelled gold dragonfly, the veins running through the thin and slightly cloudy veil of them intricate and gnarled like the roots of trees.

"And who's this?" he asks, cocking his head and taking me in with a mischievously boyish grin.

"This is Kairi. She's visiting for a while," is all she says.

A knowing look passes between the pair of them, and nothing more is said on the topic.

"Nice to meet you, Kairi!" Jace bounds forward with elegant enthusiasm, offering me a hand.

I take it, the roughness and heavy callouses peppering his youthful skin taking me by surprise.

"I just wanted to let you know your order is ready," Jace explains, looking away from my enraptured face, that's suddenly overcome by the oceanic blue of his irises and their intensity, and toward Everly.

I wonder if I'll ever get used to being surrounded by such transcendently beautiful creatures and whether I'll ever stop feeling like a gawky teenager all over again.

"It's done already?! Oh, great! Can I see it?" Everly asks, giving a little hop on the spot, her wings vibrating with the excitement which dances across her lips and up into the depths of her eyes.

"Of course, it's inside if you have a moment—" He gestures back to the wide tree trunk at his spine, and I feel a small knot form in my stomach.

What if it's a trap and they're both up to something sinister?

Paranoid, I stand still for a moment, pausing as Everly follows Jace through the thick bunches of Queen Anne's lace and toward the tree trunk.

"You coming, Kairi?" she calls back over her shoulder, basket swinging from the crook of her elbow. I nod, looking left and then right, knowing I don't want to be left without a Lumerian resident to accompany me back to my suite in the current situation.

The flowers tickle my knees as I traipse after the Fae pair, my bare feet unused to the sudden rough stones underfoot.

By the time I reach the entrance of our destination, my soles are tender, and I'm too busy being relieved to find more moss to ease the burn of forest floor debris to fully take in my surroundings. I hurry just inside the natural archway and relish cool dew on my feet once more.

It takes me a moment, but once the ebb has subsided, I look up, not finding the staircase I'd been anticipating but instead a workshop that extends upwards. A single shelf filled with seemingly random wooden knick-knacks spirals up the tree trunk's hollow inner tube with an abrupt verticality, small glowing balls popping in and out between the many levels.

I frown, confused at what I'm seeing.

Fireflies perhaps?

"Here it is." Jace's voice can be heard now I'm inside. Curiosity piqued; I move across the large circular area of the floor to join them.

"Oh Jace, it's perfect—" Everly breathes.

Craning my neck so I can see over her shoulder, I find what she's staring at and smile.

It's a quote I'm familiar with carved onto a wooden plaque in beautifully calligraphic font.

"All we have to decide is what to do with the time that is given us."
-J.R.R. Tolkien.

"You made this?" I ask him, enchanted by the attention to detail, by the way each of the carved letters is uniform beside its fellows.

"I did, I'm a carpenter," Jace beams proudly, and my heart flutters at the humble beauty of this trade. He lives in a world of magic, a world of endless possibility, and yet he is content to sit here with the raw fruit of the earth, taking his hands to task day in and out, making it more beautiful than it had been before.

"You're too modest, Jace. He's more than a carpenter. He's a protector—" Everly strokes her fingers over the surface of the plaque, a faint smile making itself known on her face as she looks at me, eyes wide and awed as I imagine mine have been ever since I arrived.

"Can I show her?" she asks his permission, and he blushes, eyes darting to my face and then back to Everly's within but a split second.

He nods gently as though afraid to move too vigorously.

She turns, taking my hand and pulling me over to the farthest wall where the spiralling shelf finds its origin by the edge of the doorway.

Here, the lights I had noticed earlier become large as I grow closer, squinting slightly as what I'm seeing becomes clear, leaving my heart pounding in my throat.

The shelf isn't home to a bunch of wooden objects at all but instead the tiniest architecture I've ever seen. Miniature houses have been carved from oak, acacia, and hawthorn; the most minuscule pieces of river-worn glass inserted into spindle-framed windows.

Jace moves silently into the space behind me, unlatching the front of the very first house like a doll's house. In doing so, he exposes the smallest slivers of the finest silk blanketing a tiny four-poster bed, bowls made from acorn cups piled haphazardly in a tiny wooden basin in the kitchen, walls wrapped in delicate daisy chains like bunting. Cerulean capped mushrooms crowd a tiny wooden table, a small hearth smoking where the resident has recently departed, the carpeting emerald moss that looks as lush as any I've seen outside. Jace moves to close the front of the house again, drawing my attention to the jasmine climbing over the tiny pebbled roof like a fully-grown tree.

"The Sprites?" I ask, dipping my head lower so I might peer closer at the tiny lights flickering from behind the frosty glass of the windows.

"Yes, though Paisley, my very first charge, isn't at home right now. Let me see if I can find her—" He looks around the room, narrowing his eyes and biting his bottom lip, his wings remaining still. His face relaxes suddenly, and with an excited wave, he beckons me to the farthest point of the circular room.

Here, further along the same winding shelf that I've just been staring at, a hand mirror sits like a flawless miniature glass pond.

Upon its surface, the tiniest, most beautiful creature I've ever seen is dancing. She wears a white and black spotted dress, the skirt made from the petals of white roses patterned black with hand-adorned ink. Her tiny waist is cinched with a red silk ribbon too small for any other purpose, an amber butterfly watching her performance from the far side of the glassy surface, antennae twitching excitedly.

Her feet leave traces across the mirror as she dances on to music nobody else can hear, a precious trail of lost memories, of touches that could have been but were stolen, left in her wake as she spins and twirls effortlessly and with unrestrained joy in the tiniest red shoes. Her cheeks are dimpled, mouth wide and beaming with the kind of innocence that can only be found in a child who has never had it tainted or diminished, chipped nor worn. Wholly, she laughs as Jace approaches, looking up at him and giving a small bow as he claps, causing her white blonde hair to flutter back from her face in the breeze created by his meeting palms.

Twirling once more, she sticks a single leg out, making her skirt flair. The skin of her tiny body glows the purest white as if her very form is radiating that unshattered and eternal childlike wonder which runs playfully rampant as magic through her veins.

Wings spread from her spine, no bigger than rose petals, red to match her shoes with black polka dots, like a ladybug. Without faltering, she lifts into the air, spinning and giggling until she lands in Jace's warm and waiting palm.

A tear runs down my cheek without my consent as if the scene is too much, too precious for any mortal to witness.

"Hi Paisley," I breathe, my voice barely above a whisper.

The Sprite, placing her hands demurely in front of her and becoming suddenly shy, pulls one of Jace's fingers up, ducking behind the digit before peeking out around his knuckle at me with sparkling blue eyes clear as tiny aquamarines. She waves for Jace to bend, and he obliges, his hair falling over his eyes in a hay-hued sweep. I hear something then, like the chirping of a hummingbird crossed with the buzzing of a bumble bee, and Jace smiles.

"She likes your dress," he informs me, and I smile at her, eyes watery.

"And I love yours," I tell her, tone hushed to be as gentle as possible.

She gives me a spin, stepping out from behind Jace's index finger and letting the petals flare around her pinhead-sized knees.

I could stay here all day, watching the tiny child's spirit create pure whimsical magic by only turning pirouettes and attempting arabesques alone, but as soon as she stops twirling, the tiny creature's eyes fall hazy with sleep, lids drooping.

Her mouth opens wide in a yawn, and Jace walks her back over to the house I'd just been examining, placing her into the four-poster bed and tucking her beneath scraps of rose-pink silk.

"We'd better be going. It's getting late. Lucien will be expecting you," Everly prompts me, her voice coming in close as a whisper. She leads me across the circular room, letting a hand rest gently on Jace's shoulder as he smothers the smouldering hearth completely with a thimble before turning out the lights.

"I'll be back tomorrow with the payment," she informs him before tugging me through the archway.

I feel listless as I leave, humbled almost, having just met the tiniest girl, owner of a spirit larger and more vibrant than life itself.

Everly drops me back by the tree trunk where Lucien and I will be spending the night, her departure little more than a subtle wave and a knowing look as she moves on soundlessly down the moss-laden pathway. Basket slung over her elbow even still, the dying light of the day turns her wings the colours of fall leaves pressed between old pages, and I watch her become small against the great magnitude of the surrounding trees, disappearing slowly into the white beams of sunlight stealing through the thick canopies overhead. When she's turned a corner and out of sight, I take a deep breath and head inside, climbing the curling wooden staircase like an inverted helter-skelter, drawing closer and closer to the centre of its concentricity with aching thighs.

There's a spell cast over me in this moment, the kind that speech will shatter, the kind caused by a moment suspended in the thick sweet honey of purest wonder and awe. As I take one step and then the next, I let myself bathe in its fragile optimism, a smile dancing on my face at the memory of Paisley's mirror-top ballet.

Lucien opens the door to his suite as I reach his landing, and the moment is gone like a bubble popping. His face is relieved as our eyes lock, and he gives me a bashful smile, disarming me entirely.

"You were gone longer than I thought—" he blusters, pulling in the wide leathery span of his wings so he can move through the door and toward me.

"Yes, well, you know— leaving a bibliophile in *The* Library wasn't an entirely sensible decision— You're lucky I came back at all." I smile, coy as my eyelids fall and rise again, leaving my irises hooded by a fan of thick lashes as I look at him, teasing.

"I knew you'd love it; I couldn't let you miss it," he confesses, voice becoming an emotive husk as his eyes drop from me as though he wants to say more but can't find the words.

I reach up on my tiptoes, heart swollen by the magic I've found today, knowing that the fact I'm alive to experience even my next breath is almost entirely thanks to him. I place a soft kiss on his cheek and inhale the scent of mint and wintergreen, taken momentarily back to Drakos Vale by the aroma as the silken curtain of his blonde hair brushes the shell of my ear.

Lucien actually blushes, the pallor of him becoming shockingly pink for someone so pale even if anyone else would find it so faint as to be barely noticeable.

As he stares at me, furtive and disarmed by the warmth of my lips on his marble cool cheek, Everly's words come back to me, the echo of her most melancholy truth desolate in my too-quiet mind.

This is no fairytale, and you are no damsel.

Everyone has a motive.

My stomach coils into knots, and I take a step back, suddenly terrified by his proximity.

"I had better get to bed, I'm exhausted— it's been a long day— a long week in fact," I admit, stifling a yawn as a veil of exhaustion falls over me like the final curtain of a Shakespearian tragedy.

"There's fruit, cheese, and fresh bread upstairs in your suite. Quinn had it sent up a while ago. I think there's wine too," he informs me, stepping back and straightening.

"Oh good, I'm starving—" I'd grabbed a bunch of grapes from the fruit bowl in my suite before showering earlier as an afterthought, but before that, the last thing I'd eaten was a chunk of bread Lucien had given me as we walked to the city with Ember and Neve, and before even that was the meal Lucien had made me in Drakos Vale.

Neve's icy touch had killed my hunger, it seems, as it feels like days since I've had a decent meal, but my appetite has only just awakened at the mention of this early evening offering.

"Goodnight, I'll knock for you in the morning. We're leaving just after dawn. Aramis is quite a distance, and we need even more time if we want to reach Morpheus' by nightfall. It's on the very farthest outskirts of the city, of course." Lucien rolls his eyes as though I should understand why this is typical of the Fae High Lord, but I don't. I've only met the man once, and it was an odd interaction to say the least.

"I'll see you tomorrow." I turn from him, taking the first two steps of the next part of the spiral staircase, stopping and looking back over my shoulder, wanting to say something more.

By the time I've figured out what that is though, Lucien's door has closed behind him with a definite click.

I wake with the sun, wrapped tightly in the cotton bedsheets as soft light creeps in through the glassless windows. Stretching, I swing my legs off the side of the mattress, my soles greeted by floorboards lacquered warm in the dawn.

I dress quickly in yesterday's slinky green silk dress, having brought nothing with me worth taking and leaving only my cloak and Drakos Vale attire behind. This bed was only mine for one night, and yet I am sad to leave it behind, pondering whether to leave the boots that are tucked just beneath the bedframe or take them with me.

Nobody here wears shoes, but what if Aramis is different?

It occurs to me now as I stand, biting down hard on my bottom lip and anxious with indecision, that no matter how at home I might feel here, I'm still a foreigner, and this still isn't where I belong.

I grab a fistful of left-over purple grapes and a chunk of uneaten bread thick with rosemary and thyme as I decide quickly on leaving my boots right where they are. After all, I feel like the bulk of the leather soles would only hinder me navigating such an uneven and delicate landscape. As I'm affirming my own decision, a knock on the raw wood of the door makes me jump a little, though I don't know why because I've been expecting Lucien.

I pace across the airy wooden room, making my way to the door and pulling it open to reveal Lucien dressed in only breeches again but, this time, with thick leather straps winding around his waist and torso. The swords he brought press their cold steel visibly against his spine, impossible to ignore.

"Morning." He smiles, looking impatient as he fidgets on the spot.

"Hey, I'm ready—" I say, tearing off a chunk of the herby bread with my teeth and swallowing. My throat is dry from the thick crust, so I shove a few grapes in for good measure, the tart juices soon slicking my throat.

"Great. Quinn is downstairs," he adds, and I nod, my eyebrows knitting together in a frown.

"What about Ebonara?" I ask him, lowering my voice to a whisper.

I know he's friends with Quinn and some of the other Fae aristocrats, but I somehow doubt that means they're aware of his other more scaled half.

"She will follow us, but she is taking a slower route as to remain hidden and will travel mainly after nightfall," he informs me, and I wonder how it is she knows where to go.

Then I remember their telepathic bond so don't bother asking the question.

"You don't have anything more?" He looks at me, at my empty arms and bare back, glancing back into the empty room I'm leaving behind.

"Nothing. I can't wear the clothes from Drakos Vale here, it's far too hot. I'm assuming Aramis is a similar temperature?" I ask him as he nods, stepping back on the landing so I might move over the threshold, closing the door behind me without looking back.

"It's warmer actually. Tropical almost. I've only ever visited once, and all I can remember is how muggy it was. Quinn has also sent a messenger ahead of us. He left yesterday evening. Hopefully, Morpheus will have accommodations ready when we arrive," Lucien explains, and I swallow hard at the prospect of coming face to face with the erratic and vibrant Fae High Lord once again.

Come to mention it though, I have another High Lord to greet first, and as we descend the spiralling wooden staircase, I realise that this one is far more pressing as he's waiting just outside.

As we wander out of the archway at the very base of the oak tree, I find the verdant road before us flanked with activity. Central to it all is a Fae with long, thick, mahogany hair, braided and threaded through with flowers of every hue. His pointed ears stick out under two low-hanging plaits that encircle the crown of his head, which turns as he senses our presence.

His eyes lock on mine, making my breath come in a short and sudden wisp, the intense emerald green of his irises stunning me silent as his pale lips twist into a charismatic and flawless smile.

"You must be Kairi!" He hops slightly, feet too fast to follow, as his wings billow and glisten like freshly woven silk. Butterfly-esque in shape, they force my gaze to follow the transitioning ombre from the exact colour of his eyes to a bright and unignorable sunflower yellow at the very tips.

He holds out a hand to me, his arm and torso jacketed in gold velvet, the buttons of its double breast made from some kind of forest green crystal, maybe apatite, that are shaped into leaves. Taking it, I follow the design of the remarkable garment as the cuffs and collar swirl with the shimmer of embroidered sea-green vines. His fingers are heavy with more greenery, the bright tattoos swirling up his wrists before disappearing beneath his sleeves, budding next onto his chest and blooming across his pectorals. The scent of roses intoxicates me as I grip his soft palm in mine.

"Does she always stare quite this much? Or should I be flattered?" Quinn asks, a sweet rumble emitting as he laughs, causing his long, flower-laden locks to bounce jovially against his shoulders.

"No, she usually gawps like that." Lucien laughs as I whip my head back to glare at him.

"Well, when it comes to Lucien, it's sort of like staring at one of those specimens in a jar— you know. But you— you're just so

364

beautiful—" I blush deep crimson as I turn back to Quinn, my smile sweet as belladonna.

The Fae High Lord of Spring throws back his head and cackles, the sound melodious and full of hope, just like his representative season.

"I like her, Lucien. In fact, I'd say you should consider keeping her around. If for no other reason than she might be the one prophesied to keep your ego in check." He snorts, and Lucien rolls his eyes, walking past the both of us and toward the waiting carriage.

Following his brooding tread, I find the vehicle being prepared, chests of yet more raw oak being fasted onto the top of the carriage with ropes by the quick fingers of low-born Fae. They're just as beautiful as the High Born, in my opinion, wings stretching out in veils of jewelled shine like spiderwebs catching late fall rain. However, there's something about them that is lacking in spirit. Whether that's magic, or that the High Lords have been blessed differently, I suppose I'll never know.

"Do you really need three chests of clothes for a weekend?" I hear Lucien ask Quinn, but the Fae merely shakes his head, grinning at me.

"I need options, Lord DeLaurent!" He rolls his eyes again, the green of his irises making a full and sarcastic orbit. "I've got two more chests to be brought out yet—" he whispers to me with a wink as he leans in close over my shoulder.

I smile despite myself.

He strides off like a peacock, leaving the wafting delicacy of his pungent aroma in a thick cloud behind him. Distracted, my attention is captured suddenly by the animals who will be driving the carriage that's made of solid wood, the wheel spokes twined with flowers.

"Are those—" I begin, and Lucien nods.

"Lynxes. Yes. Fast as anything. Their paws make them rapid over the forest floor," he explains quickly and without falter, pulling open the carriage door by pushing down hard on a solid gold handle designed to look like a rolling wave.

Glancing at the pointed ear tufts of the enormous feral cats chained to the front of the carriage by leather bridles twined in yet more floral blooms, I take a deep breath and step up into the vehicle, finding benches padded with velvet waiting inside.

Lucien follows me, and as I take my seat, I find him struggling to wrangle his wings inside.

It takes him a few moments, but finally we are settled, his right wing pressing into my upper arm with leathery chill as he pulls a curtain across the window on his side.

"Shut the drape," he commands.

This is not a request. His midnight blue gaze suddenly absent of any star-like glimmer.

I give him a confused look, and he sighs, obviously tired of my questions despite the fact the day has only just begun.

"Please. Aramis has a militant Sephilim presence to help them with the ongoing Equinian conflict. We can't be seen," he warns.

I draw the purple velvet across the glassless space and feel my heart sink. I had hoped to pass the journey by staring out over Nirvana and taking in as much scenery as I could.

"Equinian conflict?" I ask, hearing the door on my side of the vehicle open suddenly.

Quinn steps in, making himself comfortable on the opposite side of the carriage before commandeering the conversation.

"Yes, brutes. They hunt on Aramis soil as it's close to Eclipsia's southernmost point. Their home continent is mainly barren desert you see. The Sephilim have been helping protect the most vulnerable lands ever since Lord Black and Morpheus brokered a deal over a century and a half ago—" he adds.

My eyes widen at the mention of Aro's official title, stomach becoming an icy vortex of anxiety and fear despite the proximity of two other warm bodies.

Something niggles at me as the carriage suddenly jerks into motion, but as the wheels begin to spin faster and faster, I'm overtaken by the rhythmic drumming of enormous feline paw pads on soft moss.

Lucien sits back, and he and Quinn begin to talk about Aramis and its latest rumours, about the Lunar Celebration— whatever that is.

I try to keep up, but the momentum of the carriage and lack of view, paired with the endless travel, fleeing from the man who would kill me if it meant he could be King, makes my lids feel heavy, heart and mind tired of running, craving only to be still.

Slumping against Lucien's shoulder and blanketed by the heat of the carriage, I fall into a deep and sudden sleep.

"Kairi."

The next thing I know, I'm being poked awake very gingerly by Lucien, his voice a gentle hush against my ear.

366

I stir, the air sticky and thick, my skin clammy and throat horribly dry.

"Hmm—" I let my eyelids flutter open, the wooden build of the carriage making it more like a sauna than a vehicle with the drapes closed.

"We just passed through the city walls; Morpheus received the message, and we're expected. We've been directed to his villa where we'll be staying, so I thought you'd want a chance to wake up before we arrive. We can open the drapes now, and you can look out the window if you wish. No Sephilim are permitted within the city."

I nod, happily yanking the tiny drape away from the glassless window and letting fresh tropical air flow in through the space. Lucien opens the drape on the other side, allowing late afternoon sunlight to filter in from both sides, turning his silhouette jagged and vicious in its darkness. I shield my eyes against the glare, and once I'm used to the brightness, I allow myself to peer out through the window and into the city beyond.

Aramis isn't like Lumeria, not even slightly, and where Lumeria had been the pinnacle of naturalism and the bare necessities, Aramis is over the top and artistically vibrant with Fae-made sculptures, the architecture alone enough to drive an art enthusiast to their knees.

The city is flush with tropical plant life, the decadently coloured flowers enormous with petals as big as small saucers, as they climb up the edges of Grecian-style buildings, clinging to golden trellises that glint in the ageing afternoon light. The immediate buildings flanking the street are flawless white in façade, but I find more buildings behind them that are painted in a rainbow array of bright and precocious colours.

"They say that Morpheus had this place designed around visions of Olympolis for his beloved. She missed the architecture back home—" Quinn explains, catching my awed expression as the white marble pillars of museums, restaurants, and theatres fail to obscure the detailed carvings on the front of each.

The air is filled with the scent of honeysuckle and hibiscus, aloe vera, and coconut. The fanning branches of ylang-ylang and eucalyptus trees reach higher than any mortal mockery could attempt, casting the mosaic-lined walkways in rich jewelled shadow, gifting them a precious glisten.

"Olympolis?" I ask, voice faint as I try to concentrate on what he's saying despite the onslaught of fine detail and artistic flare that lies just beyond the next street corner.

"It's the capital city of Olympus in The Higher Plains. Legend has it that Morpheus seduced his lover Hypnos so completely through her dreams that she sacrificed her place among the Gods to descend to this dimension and be with him—" Quinn adds, and I blink, turning to find his face trained on my silhouette as he scrutinises my reaction.

"She's— here? A Goddess?" I ask, feeling entirely underdressed.

"In body yes, in mind— most of the time. She and Morpheus wander between here and The Nether, the land of dreams and things forgotten—"

"That's how Morpheus came to me, how Aro— I mean Lord Black, how he knew where I was. How he knew where to find me." The idea of getting close to the man who had lured me into Aro's clutches makes me tense, every instinct in my body telling me to get out of the carriage and run in the opposite direction.

Lucien senses my worry, placing his hand atop mine where it rests lazily on my knee.

"I won't let anything happen to you, Kairi. Don't worry. Morpheus is— he's tricky. Things aren't always as they seem with him." His gaze is reassuring, but my heart is still stuttering as I force myself to relax, slumping back against the seat.

Quinn nods, agreeing with Lucien's assessment.

"Indeed, I can never tell what he's thinking or what he'll do next, and I wager there aren't many who can claim any different. Of all the Fae High Born, he is by far the most powerful and the most mysterious."

The Fae opposite me crosses his long legs as the carriage suddenly tilts over a change in the road, brushing a lock of loose hair from his pore-less brow.

Glancing outside, I find the source of the discomfort is that the lynxes have pulled us through the heart of the urban jungle and are now taking to a far less travelled path, the road rocky and rough.

Ascending the side of a cliff, which both borders and overlooks the artistically decadent sprawl of the city below, I am stunned by the pure scale of it. The pathways are natural and wild in outline, more so than any mortal city I've ever seen on a map, the veins of the place veering left and right in whimsical defiance of the traditional blocks and symmetry I'm so used to. Everything shimmers, the air rich, not only with the scent of the place and its undeniably radiant hues captured in the floating glisten of aether but with a relentless hum from the surrounding jungle, making it feel every inch a thriving tangle of life just waiting to be captured by the minds of resident artists.

"Polytechnic Pastures lies to the west of here along with The Fountain of Youth, where Fae of Night are reborn as Kindred of Apollo," Quinn explains, and I scowl a little, feeling my mind racing.

"But— The Fountain of Youth— that's just a story." I smile with self-conscious heat rising up my neck, feeling foolish as Quinn cocks an eyebrow at my disbelief.

"And so, as art informs life does life not also inform art, Kairi? The Muses live here among us, do not forget, so why should they not place images of their reality into the imaginations of waiting mortals?"

"So, you're saying that many of the stories I know were inspired by Aetheria?" I ask, astounded, and he nods, mouth quirking up on the left side.

"It feels like home despite the extraordinary magic, doesn't it?" he enquires, but before I can answer, my attention is caught by a cliff-top villa.

I assume it belongs to Morpheus, unable to imagine anyone else living in such an oddly decadent construction.

Made from slabs of white marble and glass, the villa is enormous as it creeps close to the absolute edge of the cliff on which it's perched. Vines and multicoloured flowers twist across the roof, forming a delicate natural veil of lacey colour over the otherwise stark architecture. The windows sprawl from floor to ceiling as they stare out over the city below, infinity pools of deep teal waters sprawling from definite barriers of the glass windows.

Gardens of tropical plants come into focus as the carriage turns a corner, and we begin the final part of our journey toward the entrance with whimsically large parrots with violet, emerald, and cyan feathers cawing in greeting as we approach from atop a myriad of kaleidoscopic glass statues. These look like impossible rainbow-hued ice sculptures, somehow resisting the sun and the heat, every facet pristine and expertly cut as diamond.

"You're right, she does gawp," Quinn comments, and I hear him and Lucien burst into amused laughter, but I don't care.

Everything here is too beautiful for words, not like Soleus, which was stunningly cold, or Drakos Vale which was breathtakingly sublime, but instead its own recipe, the key ingredient being heaping spoonfuls of diverse life, immortal inspiration, and fearless use of the brightest most vibrant colours in the universe.

They can laugh, but I'll be damned if I miss it.

The Lynxes slow, their panting almost silent as the thud of their velveteen paw pads diminishes into a light pat upon the soft moist earth of the villa's entranceway. Lucien's hand tightens on mine as he opens the carriage door on his side, pulling me through the opening after him. The sudden sheet of rich sunlight that hits me causes me to shield my eyes as I stare up into the cloudless sky, the cobalt sun scrutinising all of us like a giant sky-bound eye.

Quinn follows after me, though if I hadn't turned to see him, I never would have known, his feet soundless despite the white gravel beneath the now stationary carriage. His wings ripple rhythmically like the most delicate handwoven fabric in the heavy sticky breeze, his face contorting into a smile as he basks in the heat.

"Come, I don't like the idea of us standing out here in the middle of the day. Even if the Sephilim aren't supposed to be within city limits—" Lucien warns, his voice a low purr as we take hurried strides across the gravel. I should be wincing in pain from the stone against bare feet, but instead, my soles are met by river-worn smoothness, the heat of them more of an irritant than the texture.

The glass door is circular, surrounded on either side by towering tropical trees in urn-like clay pots, their curves dotted with neon mandala designs. Something is hanging from the fanning width of the branches, but I'm not close enough to see what.

I squint into the bleary mix of sun and shadow cast by the roof's overhang, vines hanging from the ledge like tangled tresses of hair.

While I'm staring, Lucien doesn't knock on the glass, instead leaning forward against it. I turn to watch, attention recaptured by him, as the entire pane swings inward on a central axis, the part of the door closest to me sweeping out so I have no choice but to step inside.

Another rotation of the glass passes before Quinn enters after us, stepping onto the floors of polished teak sprawling endlessly from the entrance of the open-plan Villa in which we stand. The ceiling is high, the space airy, walls flanked by balconies belonging to the two upper floors with railings stylishly carved from bamboo.

"I thought I smelled Lizard—" The voice is terribly familiar, and I can claim to have heard nothing like it since our first meeting.

Morpheus strides across the living space, bare feet quick on the floorboards as an unreadable mask of sharp scrutiny falls over his unforgettable face.

"Morpheus," Lucien steps forward to meet him, letting my fingers fall from his.

I watch, alarmed as the two men embrace fondly with a mutual and synchronised clap on the back.

What?

Their alliance doesn't make sense, and I'm suddenly left with an uneasy feeling in my chest.

"But—" I say, watching as Quinn walks forward from where he's been waiting behind me, nodding respectfully to Morpheus in passing.

I'm left alone as the three men stare back at me, faces gentle, though not enough to ease my panicked breathing.

"Relax, sweet girl." Morpheus moves from beside the two watching immortals, coming close to me and placing my cheek in his hand.

"You do look so like her—" he sighs, and I flinch at the luxuriously creamy hint of his touch.

"You— you told him, Lord Black. You told him where to find me—" I stutter, and he shakes his head.

"And you came. You returned as I knew you would. It was time, and now it is time for you to leave. I cannot be a part of the violence he is causing to regain your heart. Had I known his true intent, I would never have found you in the first place." He cocks his head, eyes glassy with something fragile like hope.

"Morpheus, what are you talking about? He has never wanted her heart. He tried to kill her." Lucien sounds as suspicious as I feel, and Morpheus turns in a whirl of viridian hair and shimmering wing.

"Do not assume to know of Lord Black's true intentions. You here can have no opinion, and besides this is all your fault," Morpheus spits, eyes wild and suddenly wide with prejudice and disdain.

"I beg your pardon?" Lucien says, balling his fists at his sides.

"Enough, Draconian. All will be revealed in due time, but for now, all you need to know is that Kairi will return home where she belongs tomorrow. Then, if she has any sense, she will flee, and this ridiculousness will be over."

His face settles, his certainty in my compliance frustrating. "But first, we must tend to the full moon. All will become clear to you both in the morning."

He gives an artistic flourish of one hand.

"No. I want to know now! I've been threatened and kidnapped and tormented. You can't just drop me back home like nothing happened. He will kill my family!" The words burst from my lips in a sudden and angry explosion, leaving Lucien and Quinn looking at me with wide eyes.

"Young Lady, I was born in the year 1387, and still, the rage of an immortal woman is the one thing that holds the potential to terrify me more than anything else. Your mortal rage, however, though sweet and well-intended, is akin to the fart of a hedgehog in a hurricane at this point. Now, I will not harm you, but neither can I bend to your request as my power doesn't and has never extended to protecting mortals. My best advice is that you run with your family and don't look back. I will not help Lord Black find you again. Though, for heaven's sake, if another winged stranger offers you a date, and you have no intention of dying, turn the man down!" He pats me on the shoulder with a pitying stare that makes me want to slap him.

Still not offering any real solution, he spins next to face Quinn.

"Quinn, I was hoping while you were here, you might take a look at the botanicals, I fear I might be overwatering again—" Morpheus says with great sadness in his voice as if the conversation between us never happened. Quinn nods, but I only see red. The Fae High Lord of Night is wearing an indigo velvet morning coat and teal leggings, his chameleonic irises changing from magenta through to darkest violet as he surveys me as my fists ball to match Lucien's.

"Your accommodations are upstairs. Third floor, first door on the left for you Lucien, and on the right for you, Kairi," Morpheus explains, linking his arm with Quinn's in a single fluid motion as the two of them depart, wings fluttering in a cacophony of greens and blues behind them as they speak in rushed yet hushed bursts between themselves.

"A hedgehog fart in a hurricane?"

I turn to Lucien, cocking an eyebrow and pursing my lips as I try to steady my temper.

Lucien lets out a small sputter of laughter before pursing his lips shut and fighting the urge to continue, the unrestrained expression fighting for dominance beneath his usual mask of chill reserve.

"I would offer to beat him up for you, but I don't think it would do much good. Whatever game Morpheus is playing— I do trust him even if he doesn't like me. So, I'd say it wouldn't be a bad idea to play along— just for now."

"My hero—" I mutter, and his face sharpens into something contorted between anger and sadness.

"I'm sorry. I am trying my best," he bites out, and I watch as the veins on his pale biceps make themselves known, the icy blue tinge of them a reminder of how he had defended me against Neve.

I want to apologise, but then I realise there's no real point. Tomorrow, I will be back home with my fathers, and I'll never see him again.

Shaking his head at my continued silence and falling expression, he takes my hand in his, like it's second nature, and leads me through what I can only describe as being somewhere between an art gallery and a home.

The infinity pools I had witnessed outside carry on as motionless deep teal canvases reaching out into the room, the only visible clue that the hue is comprised of water being the fluid tongues lapping against the surrounding teak. A crystal piano stands off to one side, and as we wander through the open airy space, I am brought face to face with a life-sized satire of *The Creation of Adam* by Michelangelo. The likeness to the original, from the pictures I've seen anyway, is remarkable. However, where before God and Man were lying sprawled upon clouds, fingers outreached to touch, now the familiar wicked grin of Morpheus is sprawled, naked, reaching out to a God I don't personally recognise.

"Is that—"

I cock my head, trying to break the tension between us.

Lucien nods and rolls his eyes, choosing his words carefully as he looks back over one shoulder, searching for our host.

"Apollo. Ghastly, isn't it?" He scrutinises the painting with a tired expression, and I wonder then what exactly The Lunar Celebration will involve.

Will I be expected to attend?

Being as it's my last night in this insanely magical dimension, I can't imagine sitting up in some stranger's guest bedroom while the very last chance I get to experience Nirvana evaporates.

As if hearing the question said aloud, Lucien moves toward an enamelled spiral staircase leading to the upper floors, each step a different vibrant hue, before beckoning for me to follow with only a look over the sharp, angular rise of his left wing.

"Come, you'll want to rest before the festivities begin," he beckons in a soft tone.

I bite on my bottom lip, more exhausted than I want to admit despite the fact I slept all the way here.

"I will?" I ask, making him stop in his ascent. His head pops over the edge of the staircase as he looks down on me from above, eyes somehow more distant now than they had been when we'd arrived.

"You will. It's going to be a long night."

25

A Midsummer Night's Dream

ARO

THE WHITE TARPAULIN, CHOSEN for its easy assimilation against the greyish alabaster of the sky teeming vicious and bulbous above Drakos Vale, flaps wildly in the brutal winds.

Despite wearing my thickest cloak that flutters as it clings tightly to my form, and despite the fact I'm inside the only tent upon the Eagle's Perch, I shiver. Kicking a loose dark stone trapped beneath the sole of my shoe aside with undiluted rage at the low temperature and unacceptable conditions, I grit my teeth against my discomfort.

Leo stands opposite me across the table, a quick assembly piece that holds a map of mostly guesswork topography for the continent that floats several hundred miles below where we are currently standing, each corner held fast by a heavy piece of stone.

"How on earth did you find this place?" I demand, my voice rising over the insistent slapping of the plastic tarpaulin against the metal tent poles.

Leo glances up from where he's leaning over the weathered parchment of the map, the feathering of his red hair slick against his forehead from the pounding rain that had greeted him zealously on arrival.

"Some of the older texts on the Draconian-Sephilim conflict refer to an aerial vantage point free floating above Drakos Vale, just above their vertical border. I got lucky in finding it though I knew it was here somewhere from the records," my Captain explains, his thumb and index finger cupping the fine point of his chin and tenderizing the skin beneath as he ponders over the only maps we have of the Draconian's home continent.

"I see, well very good work indeed. And the men? Are they prepared?" I snap, pushing the conversation forward as fast as I can. The Captain nods, his gaze not rising from the latitudinal curves of the map, focus unwavering as he pores over each tumultuous cross-section.

"And what of the equipment I asked you to retrieve from Midas' personal vault?" I enquire, insistent in my haste even still as my body stiffens in the cold beneath the ionized steel of my chest plate. I have never favoured the golden jaundice of Midas' choice in military uniform and so had my own armour commissioned the second I became High Lord upon his death. The gold makes me look sickly pale and is hardly inconspicuous, though I suppose Midas never worried about that.

"Sorry, what?" Leo regards me, and I narrow my eyes, impatient.

"Captain, please pay attention. The equipment from Midas' personal vault—what did you find?" My hopes are high as I feel my heart trapped like a wild woodpecker within my chest, beak razor sharp and ready to disembowel as it struggles in the darkness behind my ribcage.

"Sorry, my Lord. I did actually find quite a few things that I think will be of use. Come, let me show you." He straightens behind the table, treading sideways beneath the awning that continues to be pounded with sleet and wind on all sides. His tread is heavy upon the bare frosted stone underfoot, our shadows turning the space increasingly chill as he leads me toward a pile of wooden crates stacked uniformly against the opposite side of the temporary war chamber.

Using his left hand gloved tightly in a thick black leather hide, he pulls off the lid of the first crate, causing splinters and nails to fly haphazardly through the air and onto the hard-frozen ground with a tinny echo.

I do not flinch.

"This— is what I was most intrigued with." He reaches into the crate, the wood noticeably damp from the journey here, pulling out a vial of what looks very close to a poison I am intimately familiar with. It glows cyan within the bulbous glass container, casting cold light up onto Leo's freckled face, the entire bottle wrapped in a design of swirling black ink that forms a dragon cupping the length of it in a continuous reptilian spiral.

He passes it to me, and I swill the viscous glowing fluid inside from left to right, feeling my excitement race hot through my blood, sparks dancing between my synapses.

I know what this is. I just didn't think it really existed.

I had thought it was a myth. In this land of myth made real.

How foolish of me.

"You found this among the weapons specifically forged to take down dragons?" I enquire, making sure, and he nods enthusiastically, pulling an enormous crossbow from the depths of the crate along with a bunch of coral-tipped arrows, the substance beautifully porous as it hardens in a matte point just waiting to be tainted.

"Yes, sir. Along with this. We could only find the one full vial though; the rest were empty except for a tiny amount of glowing residue," Leo adds, and my heart falters in its sudden optimism. I stare into the glow of the bottle in my palm once again.

"We best not miss then," I mutter, and Leo looks at me with curiosity.

"This, Captain, is a Draconian-made tranquillizer made specifically to render a Dragon unconscious." I smile, and Leo's brow furrows.

"Draconian made?" he asks, and I nod.

"A last-ditch effort by some of the High Lords of the time to resist High Lady Thomas' preposition of war. Those who wished to make an alliance and avoid violence conceived of it in secret. Genevieve was not aware of its creation, seeing as it uses parts of Dragons in its synthesis. As you can imagine, something that potent— that large, it can only be rendered unconscious under a power of its own making. They would rather have tamed the beasts than seen them extinct, but Genevieve thought it was blasphemous, that wanting to control such enormous killing machines was against the will of Nemesis and Hecate. Stupid woman." I shake my head, remembering the history I had learned from the mouth of Midas himself.

"I had no idea." Leo straightens, handing me the enormous quiver of arrows and crossbow. I place the vial of tranquillizer inside my cloak pocket before taking them in my hands. The arrows are enormous, the wooden body as thick and long as my forearm, the coral tips dully matte yet unforgivably sharp.

I look to my captain, thoughtful, seeing the soft youthfulness in his face, the gentle sparkle in his eyes as he watches me with interest.

I pass the bow back to him, thinking carefully before handing over the vial of poison to him as well. An intense glare passes between us as I do.

"You want me to use this? What, are you expecting us to come up against dragons?" Leo asks, his eyes alarmed at the mere thought of coming face to face with something so large and deadly.

"Oh no, the Draconians would never willingly risk their precious dragons in open battle, at least not without us striking the first blow," I muse, confident as I shove the now empty crate onto the floor before opening the next one myself.

Within it, shackles lined with smooth curved pieces of kyanite lie, the steel and crystal contrasting and making the other definite in outline. Beneath them, the sharp kyanite-tipped wing hooks glimmer a deadly azure with a beauty that can only come from such a violent promise.

"Then why would we need Dragon tranquillizer?" Leo presses me, and I smile as I pull out a shackle, thinking of how much Genevieve's white monstrosity had terrified Midas, who had vowed uncertain death to the very creature who had stolen his queen from him. The kyanite was used to absorb the heat magics of this one dragon in particular, stopping it from melting the metal shackles. These weapons suit my purposes perfectly, and for a moment, I'm grateful that the old man who had last possessed the crown had been so singular in his obsessions.

"Because, my young Captain, we are going to strategically lure one into a primed and waiting trap."

KAIRI

I stand in front of the floor-length mirror, examining myself with wide eyes. My hair falls over my bare shoulders in silken waves, but even the lengthy style cannot cover how revealing the dress Morpheus has provided is.

I know it's warm, the fact my windows are flung open as wide as they'll go, revealing the front gardens now glittering with strung lights beyond, not lost on me as ironic. The muggy fragrant air wafts in as an alluring cologne of Mother Nature on every whisper of breeze as I turn this way and that, feeling more self-conscious than I can remember, even when I'd been presented with Lumeria's scanty attire.

The gown is, as you would expect, heartbreakingly beautiful. Indigo silk falls over my form in effortless streams, puddling upon my curves and capturing the exquisite light of nightfall in a network of glass beading that weaves itself into a lacey veil of falling stars. Hoisting itself up around my neck in a halter style, the back of the gown, or what there is of it, plunges so that the fabric of the skirt begins only inches above the start of my ass crack, exposing the silvery stretch marks between my shoulder blades. The front offers little in the way of coverage either, the fabric being allowed to do as it wills sans much, if any, tailoring, the neckline plunging so low it comes to a fine point at the apex of my cleavage, revealing what I now feel to be my extremely underwhelming bust in the most overt way possible.

I run my hands over my stomach, over the curves of my hips, over the round of my backside, appraising myself with a critical eye.

I can't wear this.

Can I?

I cover my mouth with the palm of my hand, shaking my head and taking a deep breath, glancing back at the discarded green garment I had taken off before enjoying a long soak in a clawfoot tub. The air of the suite I've been provided is still rich with the scent of jasmine from the bath oils, my hair and skin causing it to waft in my wake as I pace aimlessly.

My skin rises in goosepimples as I take another deep breath, steeling myself for exiting the room.

I know I have to wear this because it would be rude not to.

I place a pair of indigo slippers on my feet, the shoes more comfortable than anything I've worn in days, as a knock at the door causes me to jump, my anxiety spiking as the banal sound makes the butterflies in my chest flutter wildly, panicked.

My feet are anxious scuffles upon the teak floorboards as I cross the room, passing by the circular bed that's suspended from the ceiling and veiled in gossamer netting. I want to crawl back beneath the silken sheets, my nap having been like floating upon a cloud as every toss or turn made the entire structure effortlessly swing. It had soothed me.

I open the door, the knob an Aztec-style golden sun beneath my clammy fingers, and Lucien is revealed in the hallway beyond.

His brow furrows, like he's in great pain as I am unveiled, making me feel even more self-conscious than I had before. I take him in during the silence that is him just staring at me as I glare back, moments passing as eternity.

He's wearing purple velvet leggings, a teal and gold belt slung low across his hips, and his chest is bare, revealing those endlessly dark swirling tattoos that map his pectorals and then abdominals in turn. My eyes trace the contorting shadows, lashes fluttering and eyes jerking up nervously to meet his gaze as he clears his throat.

"Tell me— is it— is it terrible?" he asks, and I cock my head, wondering what exactly it is he's talking about.

"I don't—" I begin, giving him curious eyes.

He grimaces.

"Kairi, I am wearing violet velvet leggings so indecently tight I could practically tattoo my endowment on my forehead and it would be less obvious," he exhales, skin flushing a deeper pink than I've ever seen.

At the mention of this most private part of himself, my eyes drop, unable to restrain their curiosity.

"Hey, eyes up here!" He grips my shoulders with quick rising palms, eyebrows jumping so high on his forehead that I fear they might take off skyward, never to be seen again.

The darkness of his pupils grows wide, his lips tightly pursed, a twinkle of embarrassment alight in the back of his eyes.

"And I was worried I was underdressed—" I whisper, unable to control my laughter as it rumbles through my chest, playing a tickling melody upon my ribs before escaping into the tense air between us.

"You're uncomfortable?" he asks, looking down at my body, hands still firm on my shoulders.

I flush.

"Seems only fair now—" I give him a playful glance, moving to walk past him. "Oh," I add as I pass, "and you have nothing to worry about with regards to your endowment—" I wonder what's come over me as I hear Lucien inhale a little too sharply. It must be the dress making me bold.

I blush furiously, giving him a full view of my bare back as I walk along the hall toward the balcony overlooking the main room, the narrow walkway leading on smoothly toward the spiralling staircase.

I place my warm fingertips upon the cool art nouveau curve of the bamboo balustrade, looking down over the giant room with an assumed elegance I usually lack.

Apparently, boldness isn't the only thing the dress brings out in me.

"Hey, come on down! The body painters are here!" Morpheus calls, his viridian hair starkly visible from a sofa on the opposite side of the house.

I look back over my shoulder to Lucien with a confused gaze.

Body painters?

He shrugs, lips wavering as they press tightly into an expression that appears just as oblivious as I feel.

Going with it, I take the tight curve of the spiral staircase step by step, the puddle of indigo silk slipping over each one like water as I descend.

Reaching the bottom floor, I feel infinitely more relaxed as I find Morpheus, Quinn, and a woman I can only imagine as the Goddess made Fae, Hypnos, scattered between casual furniture designed for lounging. Each High Born Fae is wearing the same, if not even less fabric than Lucien and myself.

So, I guess at least I won't stick out.

Hypnos is breath-taking, as I knew she would be, her entire body glistening a silverfish grey, her hair floor length and soft looking like cotton wool, each lock adorned with crystal butterflies, dragonflies, and flowers. Her floor-length gown is gauzy white, almost see-through in parts, as panels of shimmering opalescent lace twine around her waiflike body, tall as a reed and seemingly just as fragile, though I very much doubt that's the case.

A man with a long nose and intense dark eyes is tending to her bare spine with a paintbrush, his beard braided and tied at the bottom with a golden cord. She watches me as I examine her, her face serene as scudding clouds in the spring sky.

The scene itself is odd, and as the enormous golden orb of the moon is birthed over the tree canopies that obscure the horizon, light falls upon the flawless skin of each of the Fae, working painters brushing something sticky and pungent smelling across their skin in artful swirls. I look at the artists, a shimmer of recognition rolling over me at the face of the man who is making new art of Quinn's already exquisitely decorated skin. The brush strokes follow the lines and edges of the High Lord's tattoos as he looks at me with a wicked glint in his eyes, the silently working man adding an original flourish here or there.

"Vincent, you can do Lucien and his mortal friend. Angelo here does like to take his time—" Morpheus instructs the man, who looks back over his shoulder, blue eyes of infinite emotive depth catching mine.

I inhale, looking at Lucien, who gives me a questioning look.

"You're— you're Vincent Van Gogh—" I breathe, looking into the now stormy blues of the Fae artist's irises as he finishes his rapid brushwork upon the backs of Quinn's ankles.

He cocks his head, thin lips spreading wide over his white and pristinely straight teeth. I feel my eyes wander to his ears.

Pointed at the tip, both sit exactly where they should.

"See, Vincent, I told you, these young ones— you're all the rage." Hypnos' voice is like a lullaby, the tone of her words caressing my mind like a lavender-infused incoming tide.

"You know my work?" Vincent asks, getting to his feet from where before he was down on his knees, the patchwork colours of well-worn trousers an oddly fitting sky blue and sunflower yellow.

"Know? You— your paintings— Starry Night over the Rhone—" My mind falters, unable to equate the flesh and blood man before me with the paintings that have always captured my heart.

"I told you she always stares—" Lucien says, resting a palm on my shoulder.

"Lucien— do you have any idea— that's *Vincent Van Gogh!*" I hop on the spot, unable to contain my excitement, and Vincent blushes, his eyes becoming warm as he offers me a paint-stained hand. The others laugh, cocking their eyebrows and rolling their eyes at my starstruck expression, but I don't care.

"It is a pleasure, Kairi. But you should know I'm a little after most of the Aristocracy's time. My mortal work didn't become well known until The Muses— well, until after I had crossed over to this realm." I take his hand, feeling his flesh calloused from years of holding a brush.

It makes me wonder— is this why so many artists receive no recognition until after their deaths? Is it the work of The Muses putting them in the spotlight after meeting their Kindred selves instead of unfortunate timing?

"Come, we are already late, and Vincent needs to tend to you both," Quinn beckons me forward, and I stand where he was only seconds before, letting the moonlight bathe me.

Vincent walks around me in a slow curve, appraising my body, his eyes seeing potential where I see only flaws and the loss of who I had once been.

"Starry night over the Rhone? That's your favourite?" he asks me, his reddish honeyed hair wild across his forehead as he bends down to the vat of sticky clear paint he'd been using on Quinn.

"Yes. For as long as I can remember—" I breathe.

Vincent smiles before taking his brush, a deep breath, and getting to work.

When Vincent has done both Lucien and me, his work rapid, the paint dries clear, his artistry invisible. I want to ask why this is so, but I also don't want to know, loving the way that Aetheria manages to surprise me just when I think I can no longer be awed.

Lucien glances over at me, Hypnos watching us both with heavily hooded eyes as she steps down off the pedestal she had been hiding beneath her skirts. The man they called Angelo, who I have a sneaking suspicion is *The* Michelangelo responsible for the Sistine Chapel, gives her a final appraisal and then nods, satisfied as she walks with a dreamlike slowness over to Morpheus' side.

Vincent packs up his brushes, fingers working just as fast as they had when the paint had slashed against and caressed my bare skin beneath the natural light of the rising moon. It filters in through the floor-to-ceiling glass window, uninterrupted now, and I can't help but smile as I realise the truth of his existence. The sadness, the madness of his mortal life hadn't led him to an end but a beginning. Here, he will paint for years to come, and something about that makes me feel unexplainably at peace. Here, he will be adored and appreciated for the one-of-a-kind spirit he is, and so I smile.

"Thank you both. We are privileged to be your canvases on this night, and I hope for many to come." Morpheus gives them a small bow before taking Hypnos by the waist, his eyes wandering softly across her skin, as gentle as the stroke of a butterfly's wings in his adoration. "You have made my beloved, if possible, even more beautiful, I am sure." He lays a soft kiss on her cheek, looking over her silhouette as though she may evaporate into smoke before his eyes.

I wonder then if anyone will ever look at me like that. So certain, so entirely enraptured that they would gamble forever on the very notion of us.

"Come, we are late. I must conduct the opening ceremony so the party can begin." Morpheus winks at Quinn, who is looking between Hypnos and the Fae High Lord of Night with fascination.

The five of us stroll from the house and into the muggy hold of the night, the air rich with the scent of jasmine, and as I grow close to Lucien, aloe vera. I suspect now that this is part of the paint that was used to cover us all in translucent patterns and swirls, but cannot tear my eyes from the moon and it's larger than I've ever seen it before.

"Aramis is on the western side of Nirvana. The view of the moon here is the best you will see in Aetheria, except for in Eclipsia," Quinn explains, following my gaze. I soon see, as I carry on staring, that the sky is full of dense clouds, and after a few moments, the moon is obscured, casting the party in darkness only moments before we enter the thick jungle at the rear of Morpheus' villa.

The air becomes denser as enormous leaves and towering palm trees surround us. We follow a path lined only in large white pebbles through the greenery, vanilla and hibiscus catching in my nostrils as Lucien gazes around right along with me.

Perhaps then, this is all new for him too.

We trail the silvery glow of Hypnos' silhouette, made only paler by the vivacity of Morpheus as he guides her seemingly fragile steps over roots and around dips in the moss-blanketed path, treating her as if she is made of glass.

I envy them then, the way in which he is so devoted, so willing to bend for her. I had lost any chance of that kind of love when I became sick because I was no longer a prize to be won but a burden to be shouldered instead.

Who would willingly choose that?

As I'm wondering this, I suddenly notice vibrations becoming stronger with each step, the tremor of nearby music growing as it rises through the soles of my slippers, a gradual and building oscillation of the peace.

Up ahead, the light that has been guiding us is suddenly and un-apologetically swallowed by a thick curtain of green vines that twine and interlock like desperate lovers. Morpheus, leading the way, parts them with a gentle but certain hand, utterly at home within the teeming shadow of the jungle.

On the other side of the natural drape, a deafening cheer rises as Morpheus steps beyond the threshold, the music becoming so loud I can barely hear myself think.

Lucien looks at me nervously, passing beneath the veil of leaves before me as he glances back over his shoulder, warning me to stay put.

When he doesn't return within a few moments, I follow him, Quinn pressing eagerly into my spine and urging me forward.

The leafy greenery serves as a kind of gateway, and beyond it, the jungle opens up into a gargantuan clearing, the interior dark but filled with hundreds of pairs of glittering jewelled eyes and wings alike.

They don't track me, however, the waiting crowds of Fae too busy parting to allow Hypnos, arm looped with Morpheus, to pass through the centre of the gathering.

They don't bow to him, nor her, as I might expect with a High Lord and a once-Goddess. Instead, Morpheus visibly high-fives the male Fae and kisses the ladies quickly on the cheek, making some of them overtly swoon.

Lucien grabs my hand in the darkness, the only illumination tiny pinpricks of moonlight that manage to pierce through the dense, aromatic overhead canopy of wily branches, luscious water lilies, passionflower, and heliconia draped like bunting.

It's beautiful, but the dark crowding of jungle trees makes it too dark for me to truly appreciate. I see the clearing is veiled off from the rest of the jungle with more of the same natural drapery, the space teeming with florally scented bodies clad in revealing silks, or in some cases, petals, leaves and nothing else.

"Welcome, welcome!" Morpheus' voice booms within the confines of the inner ring of trees, hundreds of pairs of glittering irises turning to him as the crowd stills completely, and the musicians at the farthest end of the gathering let their melody fade out with natural abandon.

The jungle stirs around us, the sound of cuckoos echoing out through the trees in a majestic drumroll preceding the Fae High Lord of Night and his speech. Hypnos watches the crowd with detached reverence, her eyes resting on me for longer than they should.

"Welcome, beautiful Kindred, to our latest Lunar celebration. When we can be sure that the veil between worlds thins just a little, and so we will dance and flit between dreaming and wakefulness with whispers and secret kisses. Are you ready?" He sounds like a DJ as he grins wickedly, loving the attention of the crowd who raise their voices in a roar of ascent that ripples from east to west in an excited wave.

"As you may have noticed, I have two esteemed and rather unusual guests with me this evening. I ask for your discretion in this matter. You can be sure that any of you who chooses to put either me or them in a difficult situation with the Sephilim will be certainly disembowelled by Hypnos and myself by the morning. And Hypnos does love a good disembowelling, don't you darling?" His face never falters as the threat falls from his lips.

A few Fae turn back to gaze in our direction.

I blush under their unwanted scrutiny, squirming as Morpheus kisses the back of Hypnos' hand. Her smile is serene as usual, but even from this distance, I can see the feral lightning forking behind the glass of her cloudy irises.

"Now that's out of the way, I would like to thank you all for coming and for your offerings! The cornucopia is looking fabulous, I might add!" He gestures to the enormous golden horn on his left, which I have only just noticed, taking a few steps back so I can get a better view of the spilling pile of fruits and floral wreaths.

The band at his spine are all Fae, their instruments beautiful and odd all at once with panpipes and drums mixed in with modern electric guitars and portable amps, electric violins, and bass.

I wonder how they got the more modern equipment here from the mortal world, and then realise that after what I've learned of the muses, I may be thinking about this backwards.

Perhaps the ideas for such objects had not originated in the mind of Thomas Edison, or any mortal in fact, but instead in the hearts of muses, having been passed down to humans as a gift left for them in dreams, only to be discovered later as divine inspiration— or genius.

The thought hangs in my mind for a moment, like overly ripe fruit ready to burst, until I'm distracted by Morpheus once again.

"Enough from me, you all know by now that this is not a night for words, but a night for presence, for being, and living in the now, as the now is all we might ever and will ever truly possess. The clouds are fit to burst my fellow Fae. So, dance, drink, eat, and love as if it were your last night. For you know as well as I that we are promised no tomorrows." He takes a small bow and gestures back to the band, which immediately starts to drum up another tune. This song is slower and more hypnotic than what they had been playing upon our arrival, and the crowd roars as their High Lord slips forward

386

into a mass of outreaching hands and hungry fingers, a celebrity of the night.

As the music begins to rise in volume, Lucien looks over at me. The Fae gathered begin to break into pairs, dancing in the darkness as the world around them hums with vibrancy and life that cannot be tamed.

"It would be best to occupy ourselves, lest we become targets for questions and small talk. Would you like to dance?" Lucien whispers in my ear, his breath a minty wisp of cool air against the bare skin of my shoulder.

"I don't understand— the celebration— it's just a party? I thought it would be more— religious," I admit, bending close so I might make myself heard.

"It is exactly that. A celebration of life by simply living. From what I understand of Fae culture anyway—" Lucien replies, pressing close to me as a Fae edges past him and disappears behind another leafy curtain.

"So, dance?" Lucien steps forward, turning to face me, his blonde hair starkly white as a trickle of moonlight catches the crown of his head. With his sharp features, the way his body is cut into thick slabs of muscles, and the tips of his wings glinting, he looks like a marble statue come to life for a moment.

He extends a hand to me as he slips back and into the crowd of dancers, trying to pull me with him.

I let out a sigh, my heart hammering and heavy at the thought of his proximity.

I suppose I can't just stand here, but the thought of being close to him makes me nervous, makes my stomach flip in a way I can't help but desperately want to ignore.

I decide not to answer him with words; instead, stepping forward and slipping my fingers into his palm, I let him tug me into the writhing mass of dancers.

He pulls me flush to his bare chest, his hands sliding down to rest appropriately on my waist as my fingers lace naturally behind his neck, arms resting on his shoulders.

I stare up at him, and in the darkness, I feel the chill coming off his bare chest, causing my skin to ripple into gooseflesh beneath the intensity of his sharply focused gaze.

The music is loud, but not loud enough to even stifle the sudden roll of thunder, which erupts from overhead, bringing welcome distraction.

Lucien looks up to the canopy overhead, to the enormous black clouds obscuring the stars, as enormous drops of hot rain start to plink down onto the earth of Aramis.

It happens slowly, like a slow weep of gradual magic that rises into a torrential sobbing downpour, but suddenly, though I'm still in Lucien's arms, my entire body comes alive with wonder, the hairs on the back of my neck stood to complete attention.

Where the rain hits, bioluminescent neon follows. It starts in spots like someone is flicking paint off the end of a brush, but eventually, as the rain begins to soak through my hair and slick my skin, the jungle comes alive with light.

I look at Lucien, a smile I cannot contain splitting my heart wide open with the unbelievable nature of what I'm seeing. Laughing, my chest feels like it's full of helium, my breath coming only in short wisps.

I wonder then if I might not fly without wings.

Lucien's face glows as he watches me, unable to restrain his smile, his torso revealing the artwork of Vincent Van Gogh beneath the hardening weep of the sky.

"Look—" Lucien gestures down to my own body, and where the translucent paint had dried, I find A Starry Night reawakened on my flesh. The swirling brushstrokes and the vividness of the original is not lost, the greenish-blue glow enchanting as it whirls, dances down my arms and up my neck in an endless awesome tattoo.

The flowers overhead come alive too, in hues of neon magenta, vivid violet, and bright orange, their petals beacons among the intricate canopy veined a luminescent cyan.

Fireflies join us, attracted to the newly awakened jungle light, a swarm of fast-moving glowing specks above the dancing crowd. The Fae cheer as the rain pours down, each and every one revealed in neon hues similar to my own, but nowhere near as expertly applied.

I could stay here forever where there's no pain.

A sudden and desperate sadness falls over me, tangled within a knot of guilt, knowing that this is the last night I'll stand, dancing beneath these stars without fearing my legs will collapse beneath me. This is the last time I'll ever feel this untainted sense of wonder, believe in the fact that dreams can come alive and that pure magic is possible. Because how in the mortal world can anything compare to this?

Suddenly, I'm too warm, even in Lucien's cool grip.

My eyes fill with unexpected tears.

Stepping backwards, I stumble over the train of my gown, raising my hands in apology to an alarmed Lucien whose hands have slipped from me only too easily.

He didn't want to possess me, already adept at letting me go, not like Aro.

And yet, I still don't trust him. I can't, not after how sure I was about Lord Black.

Though, my trust in Lucien is not the only faith missing from me, as I can't seem to trust myself either.

I turn from the dancing Fae, lit in a rainbow of glowing hues that writhe and spin to the beat of the drums and the rapid squeal of an electric violin, and run.

I don't get far, my hand parting a curtain of vines, only to find a pile of multiple naked Fae lost in one another on the jungle floor. The small grove in which they lay with one another is filled with a thick pungent scent of some kind of hallucinogen, the pupils of each creature dilated to black holes among the vivid glow of the surrounding plants, confirming my suspicions almost instantly.

The light casts the rising and falling of hips primally rhythmic, the curve of tensing buttocks and the mouths widened in untainted pleasure into stark detail as I stand, heart suddenly breaking into a full-out racing pound.

My mouth falls open as I find a familiar face, or more accurately a familiar tattoo design, among the orgy.

Quinn smiles at me, biting down on the nipple of a female Fae with her head hung back, long black hair falling and tracing the glowing swirls decorating her spine as another male Fae takes him from behind.

I turn, trying to wipe the horrified look off my face as I rush from the entryway, my cheeks flushing crimson.

Desperate for air, I push past dancing forms, becoming lost in a scalding riptide of glowing flowers, overwhelming bass, and pungent floral aromas mixed with perspiration and the tepid sweetness of drugs that linger in thick smoky clouds.

I'm too hot, surrounded by too many bodies, and I can't find Lucien even though I know looking for him is only a sign that I'm reliant on his strength in a way that simply cannot become acceptable.

Hoisting my skirt from around my ankles, I run through the original drapery of vines from which we entered, purely because I know I won't find an orgy beyond.

My feet pound hard against the wet forest floor, the trees and flowers alive with light that causes me to become disoriented as my attention is drawn in a million different directions.

I can't breathe and so bring my trembling hands up around my throat, which seems to be constricting as the trees around me loom overhead in a collection of suffocating shadows.

My feet refuse to stop moving until, suddenly, I break free of the line of trees, cool night air and hot rain pounding my skin.

I stare up at the clouded sky, a sob choking me as I feel myself tearing apart.

"Kairi?!" I hear Lucien calling for me, but I can't answer him, can't breathe. I hear his heavy and deliberate tread growing nearer, and take a shuddering deep breath, looking up to find myself on the edge of a small pool of glowing aqua water that lies at the foot of an enormous luminescent waterfall. Flowers spill over the cliff edge, waterlilies boasting bright neon indigo petals amongst the luminescent spray.

I don't respond to Lucien's call, but after a few moments, I hear him emerge from the line of trees behind me.

I stand, staring out over the water's gentle ebbing light flow, tears rolling down my face even still.

"There you are— I—"

I turn back to face him now, and his words become lost in a vast and howling silence I can feel expanding between us in my bones. When he sees my tears, each one reflecting the bioluminescent magic of our surroundings in its salty bulbous curve, he strides forward, closing the distance between us without hesitation.

Getting down on his knees before me, he wipes a tear from my cheek, cocking his head and trying to read the expression on my face.

His wings draw back like he's physically opening himself to me.

"What's wrong?" he asks, his voice small, as though he's afraid speaking in his usual deep tone will panic me further.

"Everything, Lucien. Everything is wrong—" I sigh, wiping my tears on the back of my wrist and watching as the skin comes away glowing with paint. The fact I'm smudging Vincent's work makes me want to cry even more, but I don't, allowing the emotion to fill my chest like a water balloon, stifling my breath.

"Did I do something wrong?" he pleads for an explanation and for a way to fix it, the pain in his eyes at the mere thought of hurting me enough to scare me silent.

I take a deep shuddering breath, my knees weak beneath the weight of being torn between this world and my home, between trust and paranoia.

"No. That's the problem, Lucien. You haven't done anything wrong. Nothing at all. You're perfect. Too perfect. And I just— I can't trust you. Not because of anything you've done but because of everything Aro did. It's not fair, but whenever I feel myself opening up to you, getting close to trusting you, everything inside of me is screaming for me to run."

I know I must sound like an overly emotional and pathetic mortal, and half expect Lucien to tell me that I have no reason to be afraid of us getting in any way intimate because everything I've been suspecting has been slowly growing between us is only a figment of my imagination.

"I understand. Why would you trust someone again after what he did to you? You thought— you thought he was the one," Lucien breathes, speaking the truth I don't want to hear.

"I don't want to go home tomorrow. I know, after everything, that's insane. But— I'll never see this place again, never see you again. And that's a best-case scenario. What if he finds me and my family? What if—" I begin to breathe rapidly again, tears brimming in the corners of my eyes and threatening to spill.

"Kairi, I told you. I won't let anything happen to you. I vow it, right now." Lucien is firm; his eyes steeled over with determination as he takes my hand and places it over his heart.

"Lucien, that's very sweet, but once I leave this place, you won't have any part in what happens." I speak the truth that's splitting me in two, between the life I had, the people I love, and the possibility of Aetheria's magic and Lucien's stoic loyalty.

"I'm coming with you, Kairi. If you'll have me," he says, face emblazoned with honour and pride. I cock my head, eyebrows lifting, lips parting slightly in a small 'o' of surprise.

"But— you can't," I whisper, feeling his heart begin to hum beneath my fingertips.

"Why not? Of course, I won't be going to the theatre and out to the local men's clubs, but I see no reason why I can't keep watch over you and your family until the threat has passed. You shouldn't have to run."

The thought of him watching over me, over my parents, fills me with sudden relief and a sense of ease, my chest expanding and drawing in the fragrant night air like a drug.

"And what about when this is all over? What then? You return here, and I never get to see you again? You saved my life, Lucien. I don't want to let you simply disappear. I don't want to forget." I'm crying, voice broken and desperate, and his eyes fall, my heart turning leaden at his obvious conviction and the sadness it brings.

"Kairi. We aren't of the same world, you and I— Maybe one day, if Aro is right and you are the next Heirbound, we will see one another again. But even so, you must understand, Nephilim and Draconians— they simply don't end up together. I am doing what I can for you. Giving you everything I have to offer. Please know, if you trust nothing else that, truly, I am sorry it isn't more." His head hangs, and I see his true face for just a moment as he glances back up at me, the eyes of a dreamer wide and wild with possibilities as he gazes into my face.

I stare back, the happily ever after at the end of every fairytale on his knees before me. The true white knight, who came not on a steed but on dragon back.

The only problem is he's not *my* happily ever after.

I place soft fingertips on the razor edge of his jawline, pulling him up to stand with the gentlest of gestures, before stepping forward and wrapping my arms around his neck and resting my cheek against his pectoral. The smell of aloe mixes with wintergreen and peppermint, the blazing anxiety in my mind cooling to mere embers at the scent of him. His heart thuds, a hypnotic drumbeat beneath my ear.

"I must confess, before I met you, I felt like I was crazy. Being optimistic for a future in Aetheria with no conflict, without fear ruling us. But you— you made me remember what it means to be alive, whether immortal or mortal, and that suffering is inevitable. We get to decide only what we suffer for. You risked everything for a better life, a life without your pain, your disease, and you lost the gamble. But now I look at you, I see not the foolishness, but the courage. I see the risk I should be taking to make this world, my world, what I have always dreamed it could be for my people. The problem is, I fear I would stand alone. With you, it feels like I have somebody who would fight for that vision too." Lucien's confession leaves me breathless, his words a hoarse whisper against my ear.

I smile into his skin, pressing my body flush against him. His wings wrap around me, and for a moment, the shadow that blankets us becomes the most comforting darkness I've ever known.

"Lucien, tell me your dreams— your vision for Aetheria. I want to know it all," I implore.

He cocks an eyebrow, running a hand through his silken white locks before bringing it to rest on my hip.

"Why? Tomorrow you will leave this place behind, and I don't want you to get lost in this fantasy. It will only make leaving harder. Besides, this place is no fairytale, death and fear rule here. The idea that it could be— it's just a story," he reminds me.

I let my hands fan out on the back of his neck, pulling his head so his gaze is locked on mine.

"Please Lucien, tell me a story."

26

ONE FLEW OVER THE CUCKOO'S NEST

GENEVIEVE

THE DREAM IS THE same, always. ▨

Mould covers the brick walls, damp creeping in beyond the single glass pane of the attic window perched between the eaves of the sloping roof. A single bed shrouded in the shadow of a lone corner, sheets fetid and moist with sweat.

Footsteps ascend the attic stairs, their tread heavy and undeniably masculine.

My body aches as I sit on the solitary wooden chair. It exists as a skeletal form, without forgiveness or the slightest hint of comfort. My joints are broken glass in the cold as the bones of my bare buttocks grate against the woodgrain, hair a matte tangle of damp chill, sweat-slick at the tips as it hangs down my spine.

The only silver lining I can find is the warmth they bring. The desolate scalding flesh that ripples and heaves as they take from me the only thing I have to trade, the only part of me worth more than a stale crust of bread or a sliver of cheese. Even now, as each day passes, my flesh value decreases steadily but surely like the slow descent into my inevitable grave.

The smell of sweet alcohol wafts up through the wide gaps in the barren floorboards, toxic as it is pungent, the wooden surface worn smooth. Smoke clouds from a very specific kind of patron lost to opium rises like steam through the cracks as well, giving the illusion that the red-walled lower floor might be more hell than anything else.

I wouldn't say that's wrong, not that I've ever known anywhere else, or have anything to compare to.

My father says we are the lucky ones, that the streets of Paris are colder and more brutal than you can imagine.

As if to prove the point, he no longer allows me to wear clothes, though whether this is for ease of access for his friends or to remind me what awaits beyond my working years, I am yet to discern. He says he chooses my visitors with the utmost care, that out on the streets I would be at the mercy of anyone with a knife to press against my throat.

He says he will always protect me because he loves me as any father should love his daughter.

As the tread of my next master grows closer, I feel something change in this familiar charade.

Building within my muscles, it's merely an ache at first, but as the pounding of the footfall turns to war drums in my ears, I cannot help but cry out, my body contorting in unfamiliar agony.

My limbs splay wildly jerking, as though I am no more than a puppet.

Though, in this life, I was little more than a flesh dummy. Certainly, upon my father's unforgiving knee, throwing his voice as my own, but this doesn't seem quite right.

As I fall from the chair, naked, onto the floor, I jolt awake with a start.

Staring down at me are two abyssal dark eyes, glinting with malice, white teeth luminous in the early light of the dawn.

"Good morning, Lady Thomas—" Lord Black's voice is delicate as fine china, but I know that within an instant, it could easily shatter, become jagged, and threaten to meet with my carotid in no civilised terms.

I stiffen beneath the silk of the sheets covering my helpless body, heart breaking out into a feral sprint beneath his intrusive dark gaze. The smell of lilacs permeates my personal space, causing a wave of nausea to rise in the back of my throat, my jaw clenching as I swallow back the bile of his presence.

My limbs twitch, electricity still coursing through the muscle fibres where he has left his index finger hovering over the flesh of my bare shoulder, sparks fizzling noticeably between his fingertips.

Of course, he wouldn't touch me because his skin would become little more than molten flesh and raw nerves.

I stare out then into my suite, knowing he can't possibly be alone, and find no less than a dozen fully armed Sephilim men staring down at what had been my sleeping form only moments ago.

So, I cannot help but wonder, *why am I not dead?*

Surely if the intent was the murder me, it would have been done already—

The scarlet light of dawn filters in through my open balcony doors, gossamer drapes blowing into the room like spectres of warning, and I wonder how they managed to get past the wall— past the airborne fleet of guards I have stationed in case of such an unexpected visit.

The dark feathers of Lord Black's men catch the light, turning each one ablaze, and I take in each face of my attackers as I sit up, my white silk nightgown clinging to my skin beneath the sheets.

"And why, Lord Black, are you in my suite?" I practically snarl, despite the fact I know he has me at a disadvantage. I can't help it, the ferality of my spirit untamed by fear even in the face of such unfavourable odds.

"Where is she, Genevieve?" Lord Black spits, my name a curse as it escapes his lips in a mess of sharp syllables.

"She's not here. As I told him—"

I know he'll be here, the carrier pigeon, and so narrow my eyes, scrutinising the crowd as the red-headed Sephilim with chocolate and burgundy wings stares at me from behind a glinting gold helmet. His eyes, dead in his skull despite their richness of hue, give him away.

I nod in his direction.

Aro shakes his head, not taking his eyes off me for a second.

"Liar. I know she's here. Your High Lord Lucien DeLaurent left behind traces of what can only be dragon tracks."

My heart falters in its beat now, my blood rising to boiling point beneath my skin.

I swallow hard, fists balling in the sheets despite my desire to appear calm.

"That's ridiculous. Dragons died out over a century ago, no thanks to your dead king," I retort, my laugh a hollow sound. Edging across the mattress and away from his lingering fingertips, I watch them shake, waiting not so patiently to unleash his next barrage of electric shocks like an addict itching for their next fix.

I let my wings spread from where they've been cocooning me during sleep, their leathery span more comforting than any security blanket. The talons glint, catching bloody red light and reminding me of my power as Lord Black takes a small but noticeable step back out of instinct.

"Interesting. Would you bet your life on proving that fact?" Lord Black asks, placing a black glove on his bare hand before reaching forward and grabbing my forearm within his thick leather-clad fingers, closing the distance between us with confidence.

I smile, lips drawing back to reveal my satisfaction at his underestimation.

Stupid boy, I was riding dragons before you were weaned from your mother's tit.

I let my core temperature rise without the restraint I usually maintain, not caring if the entire room bursts into flame around me.

I need to get out of here.

"Ah, no use trying that. These are rare antique welders' gloves. Dragonhide lined with Kevlar and an aluminized fabric. You could be a corpse for all I can tell— who knows, perhaps you will be soon." He jerks me off the mattress, causing me to stumble as my wing catches against one of the four posts that surround the mattress. My talon rips clean through the drapes in a jagged slash as the Sephilim High Lord drags me to my feet and then across the room toward the balcony. My stomach plummets as I realise he hasn't underestimated me at all, but instead, I have underestimated him.

"Cuff her!" he barks, and Leo comes forward, placing crystal and iron manacles around my slender wrists. Something in his eyes implores my compliance, making me want to spit in his face all the more.

I immediately try to melt the iron, but nothing happens.

Aro smiles.

"You see Genevieve, I have this little theory. And my theory goes that if dragons really do exist, that if, as I suspect, Kairi really is here and Lord DeLaurent kidnapped her using such a creature, that by putting you in mortal danger, I might just be able to bring out your little lizard friend to prove it. After all, Sephilim have a psychic link with their Kensari— so perhaps the Draconians are linked to their dragons in the same way. Or perhaps your people will rally and bring their dragons to your defence instead—" He grins like a lion stalking a wounded gazelle.

"Neat theory, huh?" He implores my compliance in his attempt at stoking the fires of his ego, chin raised high above the tall metal collar of his black armour turned copper by the odd early sun.

Out on the balcony, I find lightning forks rippling through the sky. Gold glints that could be mistaken for falling stars clash with dark-winged shadows, silhouetted far off in the distance against the sanguine dawn.

The Sephilim are gaining aerial ground from what I can tell, their numbers greater than ours even with dragons at our disposal, making it an uneven fight at full force, let alone when they resort to guerrilla tactics.

Where did they come from?

The walls were never breached. Someone would have sounded the alarm.

It must have been from above— they must have finally found a way to infiltrate the tumultuous skies that have protected us for so long.

Goddess help us.

Wind tears around my body like desperate clawed fingers, begging me to take flight and never look back as the gravity of the situation punches me hard in the stomach.

I can't though, because the sky is full of lightning forks and enemy steel.

Why hadn't Anastasia seen this coming?

I have always counted on her for early warning, and she has never failed me.

Not once.

So how, now, could she have been so blind?

The electric current causes every single muscle in my body to tense.

I know it's not usually like this, but resisting the conduction of my captor turns the experience painful, making him laugh.

The soles of my feet recoil as they hit the solid ice of the lake now beneath us, Aro's clutch still tight around my forearm, each and every scale of his glove imprinting itself on my skin and making me sick with the thought of it.

The wind sweeps across the open landscape that cocoons the lake like a jewel in the setting of an unforgiving crown, the home Lucien built for himself, the man whose reckless actions have led me here, becoming an architectural reminder of his betrayal as I glimpse it out of the corner of my eye.

The freezing rush of air is furious as it batters my aching and bony form, the white of my hair flying out from my face as my eyes narrow in the face of nature's fury. My nipples harden into star-like points, my breath a shudder as it fogs in front of my eyes.

We are alone for only moments, forks of light piercing the air around us and leaving behind only smouldering pinpricks upon the lake's glacial surface from the jaundiced tread of the Sephilim entourage's golden boots.

"Come." Aro yanks me by my forearm so hard I fear my shoulder may come loose from its socket, my wings spreading out behind me to help me balance.

I could fly away right now, headbutt him in the face and take my chances in the sky. After all, I know this airspace better than any one of them can claim.

If only they didn't harness that pesky ability to shoot bolts of lightning at whim.

Fucking Zeus.

The dark angel stands beside me as the heat of my skin begins to turn the ice beneath my feet into a slippery wet mirror. Then, he looks to one of his men, pointing at something on the shore wordlessly.

The soldiers follow his silent order without question or complaint, their heads hung low against the brutal wind, bodies leaning all the weight they can muster into forward momentum as multiple pairs of wings try to help them maintain their footing on the increasingly unstable ice.

He pulls me out onto the centre of the lake, turning me to face him while maintaining his vice-like grip on me.

"What the hell are you doing?" I demand, my heart hammering as my blood continues to boil beneath my skin.

"I'm setting a trap, see. If I can't make you cooperate with me, can't make you give me Kairi, then perhaps taking something you love will force your hand. You're lucky. If I had no further use for you, if for example, I cannot lure a dragon into the skies, I will be killing you instead. Perhaps then, your people will see more sense than you did. You cannot harbour a fugitive of the Sephilim, I will not be disrespected this way, least of all by a Draconian whore."

He pulls something out of his cloak, another manacle, lined with blue stone.

"This here is Kyanite. See, it'll absorb any heat that you decide to put near it. No escaping for you." His eyes glint like black flint as two of his men return to him, boulder hanging between them from tense arms.

Aro bends, and I *let* him lock the manacle around my ankle, gritting my teeth as his gloved hand pinches the leg beneath the skirt of my nightgown, his touch bringing back memories I'd rather remain long dead and buried.

My fury is great, but as of this moment, my fear is greater, and so I stand stone still, willing my emotions to turn to stone and sink to the depths of my logical mind so I might comply.

Then, he proceeds to stand, watching with only too obvious pleasure as the long chain he attaches to the manacle around my ankle is wrapped like yarn at a hundred different angles around the boulder in question, binding us together.

"You're going to drown me? You know Kindred don't need air to survive," I bite out, feeling my superiority crest as his enormous gloved hands press down hard on my shoulders.

I shake him away, causing him to chuckle.

"I don't want you dead, Genevieve. At least, not yet. I want you to suffer, and I want the rest of Aetheria to want it too. For what I have in mind I need you out of the way, and as you sink to the bottom of the lake, ice melting under your feet, the only one who will be able to find you is a creature psychically linked to you. You see where I'm going with this— I'm sure. I'm betting you're just as curious as I am to find out what leaving someone with an affinity for heat in the depths of a frozen lake will do. I think it's going to be fascinating—" He really looks as though he believes this, giving a nod to his inferiors.

I let my arms tense, the crystal of the inner manacles biting into my wrists as I feel heat course through me, a missile waiting to detonate just beneath my skin.

"Careful now, you're on rather thin ice, remember?" Aro grins, glancing down to where I now feel the water lapping at my toes as the top layer of frost melts in contact with my skin.

He and his men walk away, watching from afar at the edge of the lake as I stand, braced against both the elements and rising heat within.

I wonder now if I could have been more prepared, have ordered the men among us who were not equipped to be soldiers or guards to fight anyway rather than becoming farmers, shop keepers, or teachers. I stand, the ice around me audibly cracking underfoot as the boulder sits, dead weight beside me, questioning my decisions as a High Lady.

For that fact, if no other, Lord Black will pay.

The best decision, the most proper would have been to have tackled Lucien to the ground at the slightest notion of him attending that damn party in Soleus, but maybe even before that, I should have ordered a dome built over this land, turning the entirety of Drakos Vale into a snow-globe of fortitude and silent strength.

I think of the dragons beneath the earth, of the riders who love them, of the eggs lying warm in the nursery, waiting to be hatched.

Will they fall into Sephilim hands now?

Be made into the killing machines that Zeus' Kindred have always claimed that they are, that they have always been, since the very beginning.

Gen. You're frightened. What's happening?

Algoric's throaty rumble echoes inside of my skull, the relief of his sudden presence diminished immediately by the fear that follows like a tsunami dousing a volcanic spill.

Algoric, I have been captured. They're using me to lure you here. Don't move. It will be alright—

I unwillingly try not to send him any mental images of my location, but I don't know how effective this will be at staving him off. After all, even in another dimension, Algoric could still find me.

I feel his fury through the bond that links us, twisting the metallic links in our chain and grinding them against one another as he does his enormous teeth.

Genevieve. No.

Algoric's message becomes clear, his rage building.

The image of his mighty wingspan flexing and spreading makes my eyes fill with simmering tears.

I said no. I repeat.

The ice beneath my feet gives an audible crack then, the sheet beneath my scalding soles now paper thin. Water laps at my ankles, a tremor running up my spine like a fissure breaking the earth apart from deep within and threatening the very foundations of my being.

From the shore, I watch golden armoured forms load an enormous crossbow with what is more like a javelin than an arrow.

My heart wilts, the fire that usually powers the furnaces of each chamber sputtering as the water rises to my knees, flooding across the ice as cracks radiate out from beneath me, water escaping and then cascading over the frosty surface.

Next, the cracks radiate toward the enormous boulder as I sink, teeth beginning to chatter as the water beneath me opens up into abyssal jaws.

Gen. I am coming for you.

Water laps at my belly as the ice groans, I let out a sob I can't stifle.

No. Don't you dare!

The emotion in Algoric's reply makes the tear fall, scalding down my cheek.

I cannot live without you. Will not. I would rather die.

I grit my teeth.

You will die if you come here.

I warn him with all the strength I have left, the surge of my power causing the ice beneath the boulder to disintegrate. I have only moments before it drags me down to the bottom of the lake with it.

The cold lake waters will not kill me. He says wisely.

But what about the Sephilim? They will murder you.

His next response makes me want to scream, my power having never seemed so far out of reach, not even when I had been a naked girl waiting upon a bare wooden chair in a Parisian attic for her next caller.

Then so it will be.

Algoric's reply is like my worst nightmare coming to life, the point of the enormous spear-arrow harsh in the early morning dawn as the boulder begins to sink. Its weight pulls insistently at my ankle as the last of the ice I'm trying to balance on dissolves into nothingness.

ALGORIC NO! I scream in a psychic burst, wanting to tell him that it won't be me who dies but him. Unfortunately, water continues to cover me like a cold and heavy blanket, smothering my voice as I thrash.

I am your protector, Genevieve Thomas. My divine duty here was never to be a pet but a warrior. Your people need you as I have needed you. Now you need me.

I hear his roar, a mere vibration beneath the surface as all sound is eclipsed and my head fully submerged, but I know it's him nonetheless. I feel the bond between us shudder and contort as he flexes the magical muscles within him that have slumbered for almost two hundred years.

His chains, his bondage, stand no chance.

It makes me almost laugh that I ever thought they did.

I sink through the water as I feel his soul soar, wings spreading and scaled body taking to the skies, his fury terrifying even to me, the one who knows him inside and out.

I love you, Genevieve.

We have been through so much together, but war was never like this. Never with such dishonour, never so underhanded, so personal.

My tears dissolve into the icy clutches of the surrounding lake as I struggle, fighting, beating my wings, flailing to no avail.

Stilling, I look up to the surface, squinting as the boulder clashes with the bottom of the lake. The cold ebbs around me like a thing alive, stealing my energy, my will to carry on fighting.

I feel him as the world around me floats and stills, my white hair dancing in front of my face like frozen seaweed as I find my place on the lake floor; the cold catching within the leathery span of his wings, his body banking left with more grace and precision than any Kindred could ever muster. He tilts right next, curving around the tip of Gemina One's peak, barrelling toward the lake, toward his end.

The first arrow misses him, just barely, and I feel my lungs fill with icy water as I let out the breath I had been fighting to hold onto, heart rising in my throat as my pulse roars in my ears, a dragon in its own right.

I can't save him, can't stop him.

This is his choice, his reckless sacrifice.

As the arrow heads toward him, piercing through the air effortlessly and with deadly precision, I send out one last message into the void.

I love you, Algoric.

The bond between us shatters as one end of the line goes dead, the weight of him landing upon the earth overhead with a crash so great the water vibrates, thrumming dully in front of my frozen, unblinking eyes.

I'm left then, tied down, trapped and floating in an endless cold silence, alone

KAIRI

The dreamcatchers tinkle in the barely existent breeze. The crystals, twined within the glistening cords webbing their hanging discs, catching the ethereal glow emitting from the water nearby.

One hangs, a bloody white feather-tipped violet twirling like a dandelion seed in the air, the very sight of it stirring something deep within my gut far heavier than the object in question. The water is still, not much of a fountain

at all as the source of the pool is merely a trickle, and yet, somehow, I know I've found myself walking the banks of The Fountain of Youth.

The trees surrounding the edge of the small reservoir grow tall and broad in stature, their leaves luscious and dense as they crowd out the moonlight falling from the sky like liquid gold.

I don't know how I got here, whether this is a dream or reality, but all I do know is that I have been summoned, not by any one person but by a single object strung high above the foliage, winking at me with eyes made of amethyst.

It's white, this dreamcatcher, and I can't tear my gaze from it. If there weren't the glowing water between us, I think I'd have already climbed the tree in which it's hung and claimed it as my own.

Or perhaps, despite me never having seen it before, it has been mine all along.

"You shouldn't be here." Morpheus' voice gives me an overwhelming sense of relief as it reaches me, and I turn, feeling torn between facing him and the object that had brought me here.

"This is my dream. I'd say it was you who was trespassing," I comment offhandedly, wondering if you can die in dreams, wondering if Morpheus can hurt me here.

Should I be scared?

He has sheltered me thus far, provided sanctuary and experience beyond what I had expected, and yet— so had Aro.

"Kairi, something has happened. You need to wake up." Morpheus' face is more serious than I've ever seen it, the silly putty of his flawless flesh suddenly tight and cold over his features. The enormous grin, the vibrancy that shines in chameleonic hues from his irises are dulled, if not almost extinct on his face.

My stomach curls in on itself, knotting tightly like a writhing serpent trying to devour its own tail.

Whatever it is that's happened, it can't be good.

"Wake up. We don't have much time." Morpheus' words ring out long after the form of him, hanging from the lowest, thickest branch of a tree directly at my spine, is gone.

The urgency in his sentiment tickles my ear, and so letting out a sigh riddled with anxiety, I leave The Nether and return to Lucien and my body.

His femoral artery leaves a steady thrum in the ear pressed closely against his thigh; my long hair strewn out over his lap. He is watching me as my eyes snap open, his expression turning to one of surprise as his acutely angled brows jump up a notch on his forehead.

"You're awake."

He says it not as a question but as a kind of shocked statement, as though I've intruded on him watching me slumber.

"What time is it?" I ask, sitting up and feeling my spine creak. I'm still covered in paint, whorls and stars faintly glowing from where I've been laid down on the damp mossy ground.

"Just before dawn." Lucien smiles at me, but I can't bask in it.

Instead, I'm on edge. A sensation that is jarring when contrasted with how I had felt only hours ago.

Last night was arguably one of the most intimate of my existence, not physically but on a level so deep and personal I don't even know how to describe it in any other way than being profound.

Lucien and I had talked for hours, mapping out and expanding on his vision for a united Aetheria, for a governing body that didn't hate one another and wasn't in constant competition, for open sharing of resources between continents and more equal distribution of the finer things.

After all, in Lucien's mind, the soldiers, farmers, blacksmiths, and other low-level workers toiled harder than any of the High Lords with much less power. They deserved, in his mind, to be compensated for it.

I added how I thought that the mental health of the newly turned should become a priority because it seems to me that many of the immortals I've met have some kind of post-traumatic stress, unsurprising really when you think about how many of them died.

Maybe if that were the case, there would be less egomaniacal psychopaths like Aro with the power of Zeus behind him.

It was all sky-high dreaming, but it was also perhaps the most connected I've ever felt to anybody.

Lucien understands something inside of me that I had forgotten was there, and that I'm beginning to realise might be able to make a return despite everything that comes with going home.

He says I make him remember what it feels like to know that your death is inevitable, and that time is precious, but the truth is that he's reminded me that I still have a voice. That despite being sick, I still have a life to live, and even though I might be in pain, it can still be a gift if I see it as one.

405

I am not powerless unless I choose to be, and even if I can't heal my body, I can still fight to make my mind somewhere I want to be.

But it's over now, and as much as I want to claw back those dusky hours when we'd dreamed freely under the stars among the glowing jungle and pungent tropical perfume, I can't.

The sun is rising, and a new dawn is about to break.

I hear his tread, spritely though it might be, before I see him, his viridian hair shocking in the soft light.

He emerges fully onto the bank of the small waterfall-fed pool, and that's when I notice he isn't alone.

"Vail?" I ask, frowning and confused as I get shakily to my feet. Her blonde hair is coiffed, the exaggerated layers of her peach gown bursting from her hips like one of twilight's softest clouds.

She gives me a small but tense smile, waving to me with a gloved hand as her wings become ruffled ever so slightly in the muggy breeze.

"Hello, Kairi." She smiles at me with the demure grace I remember, flawless skin bathed in the dawn's soft terracotta.

"What is she doing here?" Lucien tenses as he rises to his feet behind me, wings flaring out defensively and widening his shadow as it falls long upon the ground.

"She's here to take me home," I answer his question before Vail can open her mouth, my heart sinking. I don't turn back to face him, to see his reaction, because I know it will break my heart.

Morpheus' eyes are worried, and I cock my head at him, taking a small step forward and setting my shoulders firmly for his news.

"What happened?" I ask, not waiting for Lucien to catch up to what I already know. He said we don't have much time, and I get the impression that Morpheus very rarely rushes anything.

"Aro has summoned Hypnos and me to Soleus. He has captured a dragon while searching for you in the mountains of Drakos Vale. I believe it is the same beast who killed Queen Pandora all those years ago, or so he claims," Morpheus explains, and I hear Lucien's sharp inhale behind me.

I turn, hesitant but knowing I can't keep my focus on Vail and Morpheus any longer.

"Is that— Genevieve's dragon?" I ask him, scared that deep down I already know the answer. His eyes are wide, his face deathly pale, and his pectorals rise and fall dramatically as the rustling of surrounding jungle foliage drowns out his ragged breathing.

"Yes. Algoric. I have to go. I have to go to her. I'm sorry—"

He's frantic as he paces, looking between me and Morpheus, clearly torn between duty and his promise to protect me and my family.

Morpheus watches us with interest, something behind his eyes lighting with realisation or perhaps recognition.

"Why are you sorry, might I ask, Lord DeLaurent?" he demands, cocking his head and narrowing his gaze, dreamcatcher earring twirling as it dangles precariously from his left earlobe.

"I was going to accompany Kairi home with Vail, to ensure her family was safe until Lord Black had relinquished his search—" Lucien stands a little straighter as he explains his plan.

Vail blinks once then twice, seeming confused.

"But that's— unorthodox to say the least," Vail states, distaste in her gaze.

Morpheus nods right alongside her, making it apparent that he shares her surprise if not disapproval of Lucien's diligence to me.

My spine stiffens, feeling their prejudice weigh heavy, but I try not to let it poison my mindset.

"It doesn't matter now. It's alright Lucien. I understand. Your people need you. Genevieve needs you." I give him a firm glance and nod, the midnight blue silk of last night's party dress twisting loosely around my ankles as I take a step toward him. I close the distance between us, very aware of the fact we're being closely watched but also not wanting to waste my chance to say goodbye and to thank him properly for everything he's done for me.

Staring up into his eyes, I give him the widest smile I can manage.

"Thank you for saving my life, Lord DeLaurent." I reach up and lay a soft kiss on his sharp cheekbone, the scent of peppermint and wintergreen lodging itself firmly in the forefront of my mind, an aromatic snapshot of the moment I know I won't be able to forget.

"Thank you for changing mine, Kairi Freemont." Lucien smiles sadly, his eyes overwhelmingly cold and desolate within the artistically perfect planes of his face. He places a hand on my shoulder, then another cups my cheek, the ice of his panic momentarily melting to show his deep concern.

My heart stutters like it's made of glass and his touch might rock the pedestal on which it balances.

"Take care of yourself, won't you?" he asks me, gaze serious as he forces another small smile.

I take in his appearance, the skin-tight velvet leggings even more absurd in the stark contrast of morning, trying to ingrain his tattoos, his build, the way his wings expand and contract like a beating heart, in my memory.

"Of course, and don't worry. The next winged stranger I meet, I'll run in the other direction," I joke, but the sentiment falls flat as he inhales deeply as though in pain at a bone-deep level just thinking about me being in danger.

Crouching, his wings spread on either side of his body, and I note the concentration on his face which can only mean he is reaching out for Ebonara across the space that separates them. Then, in an enormous upward thrust of muscular power, he's airborne.

I watch the jagged familiarity of his silhouette until it's but a speck in the distance, frozen to the spot as if moving in any direction is inconceivable.

"Come, Kairi. We don't have much time. Morpheus should have left for Soleus by now—" Vail clears her throat, taking a delicate step forward and looping her arm through mine.

"Why are you doing this?" I ask her, trying to distract myself from the emptiness of the tree trunk where Lucien and I had spent the night talking.

"I'm in love with Leo, and what Aro is doing to you is tearing him up inside. He would never come out and oppose his High Lord publicly; it would cost him his life. But I can help get you home, so I am," Vail explains and I nod, realising now that what I had seen in the nest that day wasn't in my imagination. She and Leo really do have chemistry.

"I see. Well, thank you. And thank you Morpheus." Things still feel uncomfortable between me and the Fae High Lord, as though we both know he's keeping something from me but that there's no way he'll relinquish it even if it does both of us good.

I shuffle on the spot, feeling ridiculously self-conscious in the scanty dress under the morning's stark glare, every bare part of my flesh illuminated and exposed for anyone to see.

"You know where you're going, sweetness?" Morpheus asks Vail, and she nods.

"Yes, I remember the dream you showed me in The Nether. Don't worry. It'll be a simple drop-off, and then I'll be back. You need to get going, or Lord Black will start asking questions."

Vail's gaze betrays her anxiety as she blinks more than is necessary, her wings trembling ever so slightly against her skirt.

She grabs my hand in hers, twining our fingers together as she glimpses the Heirbound mark on my inner wrist.

I brace myself for the return journey, something inside of me clinging to every moment my feet touch Aetherial soil with a furious determination that I won't forget the scents, the sounds, and the sights.

Sadness engulfs me, and tears threaten to build and then spill without restraint as I take one last look around the incredible jungle of Aramis.

I can't help but wonder then, as everything dissolves in a familiar and blinding flash, why I feel so entirely empty, so very bereft.

After all, I should be happy.

I am finally going home.

ARO

The beast slumbers, restless under my watchful eye, fighting the tranquillizer as my soldiers finish working quickly to secure both its wings with Pandora's parasols, my new favourite toys.

"Lord Black, what is the meaning of this?!" Lord Abara's voice is angry, more furious than I've ever heard it. Though whether it's because I have gone against what is considered to be morally justifiable, or because I went behind in back his doing so, I can't discern. Nor, really, do I care.

I turn from where I'm standing on the white marble steps leading into the Temple of Zeus; the stage I have so carefully chosen to set this tragedy upon, cocking one eyebrow, my gaze smug and stance confident beneath the tumbling velvet of my cloak.

"I don't know what you mean. Why, this is the exposure of the deception of the century, Lord Abara. The Draconians have been coveting these monsters in secret, pretending they do not hold immensely powerful, living, breathing weapons right beneath our noses. I am unable to imagine what might have happened if I had not stumbled upon their existence in my search for Kairi. We might all have been slaughtered in our sleep."

It startles me that he is opposing this, especially considering he personally fought in the war against the Draconians the first time around.

"They've had them all this time and nobody has ever been attacked, Lord Black. You're scaremongering," he accuses, ascending the steps in his tailored silver suit, his wings catching the blue light overhead and turning it metallic in sheen. His dark skin glistens, the muscles of his face tightening and his fingers twitching as he fights the urge to ball them into fists. His discomfort, his opposition and sudden development of a spine, pleases me immensely.

Finally. He awakens to his own power.

Now to coax that power in the direction I desire.

"If they intend us no harm, then why hide them? Why steal away the girl who might have crowned me the next king? They're planning something. You cannot deny how this looks. And besides, the first stone was cast by Lord DeLaurent, not I," I say, lips curving upward in a smile as the hostage finally stirs. Its cry causes the golden chandeliers holding multiple sconces to clatter in their fixings far behind me, the ground vibrating with its disoriented fury.

"I heard rumours that you captured not just any dragon but the creature responsible for the fall of Queen Pandora." Caleb's curiosity overtakes his rage, and I raise my eyebrows, posture relaxing slightly as I find myself undeniably amused by his lack of resolution.

"Take a look for yourself—" I gesture into the temple gardens where I have had the dragon contained, taking the two steps down to the luscious green grass peppered with citrine dandelions and sapphire bluebells without thought.

I have wondered how terrified I would feel in the presence of one of these legendary winged lizards for my entire immortal life. Impressively though, even to me, I am underwhelmed.

Caleb follows me as I walk directly towards where the creature is being held captive.

"And what, pray tell, is stopping it simply flying away? You're restraining it with manacles alone?" Caleb asks, noticing the obvious lack of men surrounding the creature. There are maybe thirty of them, the rest having been ordered to watch the skies for any kind of rescue mission.

"Look closer—" I relish the mystery as it sizzles on my tongue, hot and delicious.

The Sephilim High Lord cocks his head, examining the porcelain pallor of the white dragon that towers before us, its jaws locked shut in a crystal vice, its wings pinned down to the earth, neck and limbs manacled to the ground. It's a majestic beast, even in its current state of complete helplessness.

"What are those?" Caleb asks, suddenly finding the secret to my smug certainty as he steps closer. The creature's nostrils flair at his proximity, its hide recoiling backwards as far as its bindings will allow.

"Those, Caleb, were a stroke of genius conceived by our late King. He named them Pandora's Parasol, in honour of avenging his wife and the monster who ended her immortal life.

"How do they work?" he asks, taking a cautious step around the dragon's writhing form, its jaws fighting the muzzle with a roar that becomes stuck as a deep vibrating rumble in its throat. Scalding hot air pours forth from its nostrils, but other than the slight ruffle of my hair, I remain proudly unaffected.

I step after him, finding the spread spokes of the umbrella-esque device and pointing to them.

"The parasol is inserted closed, like an arrow, and shot through at high velocity. Once the wing has been punctured clean through, it fans out wide on the farthest side blocking the entry and exit wound. Then the side closest to the shooter is tethered to the earth, stopping the beast from becoming airborne. More brilliantly, if you ask me, each spoke is tipped with razors, so if the creature should try to pull free, it will be rendered unable to fly regardless by an enormous gaping wound in each wing, should it survive the blood loss that is—" The way the parasol blooms into this kind of lethal flower appeals to my sense of poetic masochism no end.

"That's— barbaric." Lord Abara looks at me with wide eyes, and I cock my head.

"Oh, you think so. That's convenient, especially when you of all people fought these creatures first-hand and watched the chaos they wrought. You risked your immortality to rid the world of them. You're not saving anyone by acting like some kind of life-loving liberal now, Caleb. Not only that, but opposing me for the sake of it makes you look like a petulant child." His mouth pops open at my frank speech, at the way I no longer care for treading on eggshells around him.

I've done my bending, my conceding, and my waiting.

"I've already summoned the Senate and anyone else I think might be of use in the course of this campaign, so get on board, or get out of my way. I won't hesitate to have you killed. High Lord or not."

"You cannot kill me, Lord Black. The only person who would have the authority to get away with such a crime would be The Aetherial King, which thank Zeus, you are not."

I watch as Caleb's fingers finally twist back into a fist, the static in the air between us crackling as his wings spread wide and sparks jump between his fingertips.

"And what better leverage to convince the other High Lords to join my campaign in tracking down Kairi, the future Heirbound, than a murderous fire-breathing dragon that we had been assured was long dead and buried? You think the Equinians, the Fae, won't fear these beasts after everything that's happened? They hold the power to wipe us off the face of the continent."

I'm serious now, remembering the stories about how dragons had killed legions of Sephilim soldiers in only a few minutes.

"You think they'll be scared into helping you track down that poor girl so you can kill her and torture her into crowning you king?" Caleb snorts, his expression disgusted and immensely satisfying to me.

I simply smile as the dragon slumps within its manacles, the majestic creature crushed under the weight of its own suffering, its own helplessness to my whim.

Power courses through me, the visual image of such pure magic caged by my hand intoxicating.

As it groans out, the kyanite sapping its firepower and the parasols carving crimson mandalas upon its pale scaled flesh, I am filled with joy – the sky suddenly seeming the most luscious purple, the air around me sweet as sugar and twice as tempting as I take a deep inhale.

"Oh no, dear Caleb. I think they'll help me gladly and with a smile on their faces as the streets of Soleus run red with the Draconian blood long since owed to our people."

27

THROUGH THE LOOKING GLASS

KAIRI

THE INSTANT THAT MY feet touch down on mortal soil, I know that the weight of the gravity here, and even the sunlight, are invisible enemies I have foolishly forgotten.

It hits me like a wall of blunt-force trauma, and I hear Vail's concerned voice as but an echo like I'm stuck inside a vacuum and she's calling out from behind a thick glass wall.

The heather sways around me as I collapse to the ground, darkness inevitably waiting as my head smashes into the cold soil of the early Tennessee evening.

"Well, that was faster than I expected." Morpheus' surprised tone is accompanied by a cocked viridian eyebrow. Relief erupts from within my chest like a water balloon, the contents spilling from my lips in an uncontrollable and high-pitched laugh.

"I thought you were supposed to be in Soleus?" I say cautiously.

"I am in Soleus. I just arrived, I just— I've seen what Aro has done with the dragon he captured and realised we needed to talk. Luckily for me, you sleep more than most people."

I roll my eyes, feeling oddly relaxed as I face his pristine figure.

"Yes, lucky for you." I feel bitter at the mere thought of the painful flare I'll face upon waking, the dread building.

"What, thought you'd seen the last of me?" he asks, sitting upon the tree branch on which he had been perched in my earlier dream.

I'm back by The Fountain of Youth, surrounded by slow-turning dreamcatchers that tinkle and chime in the slow dreamy breeze.

"Actually, yes. Seeing you again so soon is— I don't know, a relief, I suppose," I explain, and he nods, a sad smile crossing his face.

413

"Would you like to know why?" he asks, hopping down from the branch with an enviable spritely energy and landing silently upon the balls of his violet velvet slippers. I look at him with a questioning expression, my body stiffening. He returns my gaze, seeing the worry plastered across my face, and then strides past me and around the edge of the water before calling back over his shoulder. "I owe you an apology you know—" he says wistfully, running his elegant fingers back through the feathered tips of his hair.

"An Apology? But why?" I ask, sure he must be confused. He offered me sanctuary when he didn't have to, protected me at risk to himself.

"Because I have long believed something to be true, and I now know it to be a lie deep in my soul," he says, taking to the trunk of a tree and climbing up its bark in a flurry of practised exact movements. I wonder why he doesn't fly, the beautiful film of his wings glistening with teal and indigo veins.

I watch as he reaches a high branch, turning and working to free something from a lower twig with quick fingers.

"And what is that?" I demand, tired of the games, of the waiting for some looming threat to emerge from the shadows and devour me whole.

As he moves to answer, he removes what I see now is the dreamcatcher which had called to me before from where it was hanging, taking it in his hands and turning it over. The amethyst chunks glisten with lustrous promise among the silver webbing holding them captive.

"I was told, and believed until this afternoon, that Lucien DeLaurent had stolen you away from your betrothed all those years ago with malicious intent. Lord Black fed me the lie, and I had no reason to believe otherwise. Now though, after seeing the two of you together, I realise I owe you both an apology. He didn't steal Storm away. I believe she ran away with him of her own accord." Morpheus sighs, and I frown, confused.

"So— you're telling me that— what? Storm chose Lucien over Aro?" I demand, wondering now if this is why I had taken Lucien's hand and let him rescue me.

Had the Storm left in me reached out for him across dimensions?

Was that how I came to be here?

"I'm saying that Aro had me steal your memories, and everyone else's, for that matter, surrounding the event of your disappearance from the Solis Castra because he told me that he didn't want to cause another war. He knew, as did I, that a Draconian High Lord kidnapping the Heirbound, and next Queen, was going to be the catalyst in causing that war. I'm saying that this in itself was a lie, that Storm made her choice, and she chose Lucien. I'm saying that— I have it all, right here, Kairi. Her memories— Storm." He looks down at the dreamcatcher in his hands, the bloody feathers tethered to the bottom of the frame taking on an eerie new chill.

"You stole my memories?" I whisper, feeling somehow violated even though they were never really my memories in the first place.

"I kept the memories of your past life from you so even coming here could not prompt them to return. And, not that it matters, but I did it to try to save lives. Can you understand that? I trusted the wrong man, and I traded my services in stealing your memories for protection from The Equinians. I didn't want any more of our animals slaughtered in their barbarous hunting practices," he explains, looking mightily ashamed of himself.

I swallow, momentarily distracted by a monarch butterfly passing me with vibrating and vivacious wings of midnight blue.

"You did what you thought was right with the information you had. I understand that. I trusted Aro too, remember?" I remind him and he hops down from the tree, his wings breaking the fall. He sighs, fingering the marble of the dreamcatcher thoughtfully before handing it to me.

"Here. These belong to you, or to her, and they always will." I take the dreamcatcher in my fingers, the stone cold and the feathers disturbingly crimson.

"How do I—" I begin, but before I can ask the question, my fingers are wandering across the web of silver threads and toward the place where the weave is tethered.

Placing my fingers around the knot, I untie it slowly, and everything comes, at last, into focus.

The memories unravel like I'm watching a movie, but I'm hovering only feet away from the actors as some kind of ghostly apparition. I twiddle my partially transparent fingers and wave them in front of Aro's face tentatively, my gut coiling in disgust at the reminder of his too-perfect face and his unexpected proximity.

He doesn't blink or even flinch, so I guess I'm just a bystander then.

Lucky me.

It's then, as I'm pondering trying to ghost kick him in the balls, that I notice he's staring at me, except— it isn't me. It's her.

Storm.

I'm taken aback by the likeness of the woman facing him; despite the fact everyone has been telling me how similar we look.

We could be twins.

Perhaps the only difference is that her hair is much longer than mine, hanging right below her waist in flawlessly groomed liquid caramel curls, and her irises are a deep lilac where mine are periwinkle blue.

I'm standing watching them for only moments, a crowd of Sephilim and Nephilim gathering on all sides, none of whom I recognise.

Aro, his pristine sculptured chin raised, drops to one knee, presenting a purple velvet box like the one he had given me at dinner during our first date, only this one is smaller and deeper in shape. He reaches up, gripping her gloved hand in his fingers like she might slip away in the slightest breeze.

"Storm, will you marry me?" he asks.

She stills entirely, her feathers becoming statuesque as the fabric of her long white skirt freezes like marble around her slim frame. I scrutinise her face closely as I realise the moment I'm bearing witness to.

The moment she had said yes.

The moment he had secured his place on the throne.

Did he know what she was?

Or was it only after the fact that he discovered what his proposal truly entailed?

The Nephilim wear gloves to stop the Sephilim knowing if they are Heir-bound, so in theory, Aro didn't have any clue the woman he wanted to marry came with the crown attached.

In theory—

So, was it simply that Storm and Aro were pulled together by the force of their mortal connection, or was there something more sinister, more purposeful in his act, I wonder?

Was Storm betrayed by someone who knew the truth about her, about the fact that Hera had chosen her to decide the fate of the Aetherial Crown?

Did Aro manoeuvre her just as he did me?

When I see Storm's reaction, it isn't what I expect. For me, the thought of being reunited with my long-dead mortal betrothed would make me ecstatic. His proposal should not have come as a shock, and yet her eyes are wide and glassy as his question rings silent in the fragrant air of the ballroom.

The crowd murmurs, and her cheeks noticeably flush, she blinks several times, taking a deep breath and straightening within the fine embroidery of her ivory corset.

"Yes." Is her reply. No squealing, nor jumping up and down, nor embracing Aro or moving to kiss him.

Instead, she removes her glove, allowing him to place the enormous egg-shaped diamond engagement solitaire onto her ring finger as the silver filigree of the Heirbound mark on her inner wrist is exposed.

The crowd gasps as Aro presents her to the applauding crowd like a trophy he's won.

As Storm moves to the Nephilim who rush at her, wanting to see the ring, the winged men in the audience dart straight past her and begin to congratulate Aro. They tell him he will be a fine King, be a great ruler.

The memory disperses like ink droplets dissolving in water, the image of Storm's bewildered stony expression the only thing that lingers.

The next image materialises, swirls of rainbow hues crystallising into the petals of various shimmering flowers lining the Solis Castra entryway. Beside the large double doors, Storm waits upon a golden bench, the legs of which formed from solid fleur-de-lis. Her ankles are crossed beneath voluminous layers of gossamer and taffeta, her violet gown accented with insanely detailed gold vines of ivy which wrap around the corset's high neck.

In her hand, a hardback is slung open, her lilac eyes scanning the page voraciously. I catch a glimpse of the cover, the title Pride and Prejudice *making me smile to myself unwillingly.*

The peace of her reading is broken, shattered unceremoniously as Aro strides, confident and with gusto, from between the opening double doors of the Solis Castra. He's followed by a few familiar faces this time, one of which being Lady Aliandara, Morpheus, and then, to my surprise, Lucien.

Aro finds his bride-to-be sitting and clears his throat, demanding her attention. Storm looks up, slowly and with little alarm, her hair curled pristinely as it falls before her ears in calculated ringlets that barely move, her posture poised and unruffled despite Aro's expectant expression.

"Yes, Lord Black?" she asks, closing the book soundlessly and getting to her feet, skirts billowing in a floral cloud.

I watch the scene unfold, keeping my attention most raptly upon Lucien and no one else. As Storm rises from her seat, I see his eyes widen. Taking in her face, his Adam's apple bobs in exaggerated rhythm as her wings flutter delicately.

Aro presents his hand in a demand for hers, and as she reluctantly gives it, I watch Lucien's cheeks flush undeniably red with a fury he quickly and silently swallows.

Is this the first time he has ever seen the future Queen of Aetheria I wonder?

"I apologise for my fiancée's rudeness. This is Lady Shaw." He yanks the girl who looks just like me forward, and I watch as the hardback book tumbles from her grip and onto the floor. She exclaims as though she's been slapped, but Aro glares at her.

However, Lucien is there, picking it up and returning it before I can blink, the deep navy blue of his formal attire making his skin milky pale and silken in the early morning light of the Sephilim capital. His hair is thickly braided down his spine, each lock appearing like liquid moonlight as his hand brushes against the bare skin of Storm's fingertips.

He flinches back, and Storm inhales sharply.

"Oh, I'm sorry— I'm not used to being out without my gloves on—" she explains, blushing and furiously timid as Lucien rubs the place where he had touched her, clearly having been shocked.

"Quite alright, Lady Shaw. It was an accident. I see you're reading Pride and Prejudice; you have good taste," he compliments, changing the subject to try and put her at ease.

Storm's eyes widen.

"You— you've read it?" she looks surprised, which in itself makes sense to me. The initial reception of the novel was shaky at best, and a man reading such a novel was practically unheard of.

"I have. I am not ashamed of my sensibilities. The description alone is enough to bring even me to tears, though Mr Darcy is an indecisive shit." Storm bursts out laughing, and Aliandara quirks an eyebrow, gazing nervously at Morpheus, the two of them suddenly outsiders.

Aro laughs, his tone becoming high-pitched and cruel.

"I should have known someone such as you would read such garbage. I don't understand why she feels the need to indulge this fantasy. After all, what could she possibly find in a book that she does not have by the wagon load right before her very eyes?" Aliandara nods in agreement, but Morpheus remains impassive and shuffles from foot to foot like he's got an itch somewhere inappropriate.

"I think you misunderstand, Lord Black. For these kinds of novels, they are perhaps only paper and ink, worth very little materially. The worth of a book is not in gold or silver, but something more precious by far. Feeling." He doesn't look at Aro as he says this, but instead at Storm, who is as enraptured by his words as she was by the words of Austen only moments ago.

I watch, feeling my stomach tighten at the obvious connection between them.

"I'd keep that opinion to yourself, Lord DeLaurent, lest you want to be perceived as a pansy by the rest of the Senate." Aro's face is deadpan as he yanks Storm closer to him, causing her ringlets to tremble.

Aro might dismiss Lucien, but it's clear to me that he had stirred something inside of Storm with this small first meeting. Something passionate and something which I'm growing surer and surer is what led to her ultimate demise.

As the next scene forms from swirling mist into solid clouds, the skyscape gives me nostalgia for my very first date with Aro. I couldn't have predicted how differently I would feel floating here, partially existent, and yet I can't help but look at the memory of us dancing among the very same clouds with an undeniably illogical fondness.

"You managed to get away—" Lucien's voice is a relieved whisper as I see Storm's silhouette rise before his eyes. He's sitting, cross-legged on an aether-thick cloud, waiting in a meditative pose, wings relaxed and hanging loose behind him.

The moon is high above them, a gilded golden bauble, dangling precariously among a hundred scattered diamond stars.

"Barely, but yes— The Nephilim are harder to shake than Aro, that's for sure," Storm admits, rolling her purple eyes and letting out a sigh as she hovers, wings beating gently behind her.

Twirling in the air, she crosses her legs beneath her and lets herself drop down so she's sitting beside Lucien, her skirt pluming around her like smoke.

"They're really that bad?" Lucien cocks his head, pulling a gleaming carmine apple from the inside of his cloak and quickly polishing it against the black velvet falling over her breast before taking a large bite.

"Ever since the engagement, it's like they're the jailers of my very own personal bird cage—" Storm admits, snatching the apple from Lucien's grasp and taking a bite of her own.

"Drakos Vale produce is—" she begins, but The Draconian High Lord cuts her off, his tone gruff.

"Bland, bitter, sour?" he substitutes different words, voice turning sharp, but she only shakes her head, rolling her eyes.

"I was going to say refreshing and sweet." She gives him a gentle smile, and his icy expression melts slightly.

"You're full of surprises, Lady Shaw." He rewards her kindness with a crooked smile, tearing his gaze from her face and looking out over the star-scattered sky instead.

"I could say the same for you, Lord DeLaurent. After all, you're the big bad wolf, and I'm little red. Isn't that right?" She throws the apple back to him, and he catches it, his hand becoming a blur of supernatural speed as he snatches the fruit from the air.

"Actually, I think I'm the dragon, and you're the damsel in distress—" he jokes, and I smile to myself then, thinking of how ridiculous that fairytale stereotype seems now.

"Who knew it would be the white knight holding me hostage in a tower—" Storm sighs, and I marvel at how similarly we had felt about Aro across two different lifetimes.

Perhaps we truly are the same soul.

"Sounds like you need a rescuer—" Lucien jokes, tilting his head toward Storm as her face turns thoughtful.

Then, as the silence swallows them both, Lucien brings a hand to her cheek.

"Let me save you—" he whispers, and then the two of them are kissing.

My heart is in my throat, wishing I was Storm, wishing it was me being kissed by Lucien.

The two of them break apart after a few moments, breathless beneath the stars.

"We've never— done that before." Storm is breathing hard, but after a moment, she shakes her head and regains her composure, eyes sparkling. "No, Lucien. I have to be the one to do this. I won't have you implicated. But— You can help me save myself—" She looks down into her lap, his hand clutching hers just as he had clutched mine.

"I should never have said yes to his proposal— but, he changed so completely. Everything changed once I had this stupid ring on my finger. It's like a tiny shackle." She stretches out her hand, glaring at the diamond as hatred laces her stare. Lucien places a hand on her shoulder, empathy rife in the gesture.

"I don't know how he fooled me so completely," Storm adds, looking to Lucien now for justification, for redemption.

"He fooled everyone. From what I understand, he has the other High Lords and Ladies utterly smitten with the idea of his upcoming reign." Lucien admits. "I was almost convinced before myself, but I saw how he treated you. You can tell a lot about a man that way— by how he treats his woman." Lucien is pensive then, his face cast half dark in the golden light.

"Run away with me," he says then, the suggestion a sudden exhalation of caged desire, set free upon the night.

"I can't. Wherever I go, he'll find me, Lucien." She's close to tears now, my own heart hammering at the desperate situation that they find themselves in.

"What about— if I could protect you?" Lucien asks, his eyes full of hope.

"He has an army," Storm reminds him, shoulders slumping forward as she leans her full weight into the cloud below.

"Stay here—" He gets to his feet then, taking off at a running jump and diving from the cloud into the thin air below.

Storm follows his lead, standing and then peering over the edge after him, face taut with anxiety for the few moments he's gone.

After a few seconds, he reappears, but this time he is on dragon back, Ebonara's enormous wings rippling in a dark silhouette against the moon.

I crave his touch then, seeing him rise in all his glory, wishing I could go back to the night before, to when he had been within touching distance and I could have so easily kissed him myself.

I had found more comfort there, in his arms, than I can ever remember having.

Storm's face turns flabbergasted and then scared as she takes a step back.

"They're real. I thought— You lied—" She's stammering as he kicks off Ebonara's back, the dragon hovering among the heavy cloud coverage, camouflaging herself after a few moments so the surrounding sky is mirrored back at the viewer. Lucien touches down on the cloud-top beside Storm, taking her hands in his.

"We had to. To protect them. They aren't monsters, Storm— just like I'm not a monster," Lucien confesses, and Storm's eyes glisten as they gaze at Ebonara's flickering outline.

"If I can protect a dragon, I can protect you. I promise. I— I love you." He kisses her again. Her hair blows back from her face as the world spins, my vision tinging emerald around the edges. Her eyes brim with more tears, and soon they begin spilling down her cheeks.

"Do you trust me?" he whispers, the sound of his low tone leaving the hairs on the back of my neck standing on end.

He had asked me the very same question, and as I'm thinking about my own response, the memory fades into swirling aether clouds and stardust.

The next memory I witness is far more frantic and much less emotional. I watch Storm rushing around the tower in which I had stayed as Aro's guest, her hands working fast to shove a few essential novels and fine silk garments into a white leather satchel with gold buckles.

She knocks over a bottle of perfume, and it smashes, glass breaking and falling onto the floor, tinkling. She looks down at it with an exasperated sigh, but merely kicks the crystal-encrusted lid aside with her shoe, stepping over the spilt fragrant puddle and hurrying to snap the satchel shut before slinging it over her shoulder.

Looking back over one feathered wing, it's as if something has caught her attention that I can't hear or see, perhaps because her senses are more finely tuned than mine. Either way, she stills, furtive, eyes wide like a doe caught in a hunter's sights.

"Hello?" she calls out, but the only response is the sound of her voice echoing back at her.

Taking one final glance back, she goes to the balcony door, but rather than moving toward the handle, instead, she thrusts a closed fist through the glass, twisting the lock from the outside and letting herself out. Glass tinkles to the floor yet again like jagged rain in her wake, and I watch as in the darkness of the early evening, Storm makes her escape.

She takes off from standing, enormous wings beating a frantic but defiant swan song as she rises off the top of the tower and disappears into the night.

I stand, ghostly in the empty tower suite, until after a moment I realise that I'm not alone.

Silver creeps from around the archway leading to the bathroom, a small smile tugging reluctantly at the corners of her lips, eyes glistening with malice in the shadow.

Then, in a blinding flash, she's gone.

The night is silent as I rematerialize, still a ghost atop a large expanse of aether dense cloud.

Lucien is standing, wearing a simple black suit tailored to cater for his enormous wingspan and tiny waist. His silhouette is crisp against the night sky, his hair loose around his shoulders and flawlessly straight as he waits for her, jiggling nervously on the balls of his feet.

She appears, flying in from the east with more grace than any of the male Sephilim I've ever seen. She's wearing the same dress I had watched her leave in moments before, confirming this is the same night, the white satchel still slung over her shoulder.

Her delicate soles touch down on the cloud, causing puffs of aether to spray up into the air, her wings dispersing it with their final beat, hair sweeping forward over her pale shoulders and crowding her flushed expression.

"Are we really going to do this?" she breathes.

Lucien nods.

"So long as you haven't been followed, we are all clear," he adds, glancing around into the surrounding empty sky. I wonder then how they intend to get beyond Aro's clutches. Where are they planning on going?

"And they won't find us at the Academy of Arcane Arts?" Storm asks, biting down on her bottom lip, obviously nervous.

"No. Nobody will know you are there. My suite is entirely private, and there is no trace to link you and me. Aro has no evidence that can implicate me, so anything he suggests will be questioned thoroughly. Nobody wants another war," he reminds her, placing a hand on the small of her back just below where her hair and wings cease, guiding her to the edge of the cloudscape.

"Ebonara is waiting in denser cloud cover, I thought it best to keep her hidden until you arrived. I'll call her now, and we can get out of here," Lucien explains and Storm nods, her lashes tremoring in seismic waves as her eyes dart toward a flash of light in the distance, and then another.

"Lucien, wait—" she places a hand on his wrist, stalling the psychic command as his eyebrows begin to knit together in concentration.

"What is it?" His eyes narrow, and I watch his gaze turn glacial as golden glints like catastrophic meteorites begin to appear on all sides.

"Storm— I can call Ebonara right now. We can still make it." He knows that it won't be easy, but as he grabs both her wrists in his hands, I see the fear in both sets of eyes, the magnetic pull between them becoming molten with desperation to cling onto what could have been.

"Lucien— they can't know about her. They'll kill her— and when that's done, they won't stop until every single dragon is dead—" Storm's voice trembles as Lucien's gaze turns feral.

"I won't leave you here. He'll kill you," Lucien says forcefully, swallowing hard and trying to pull Storm with him, eyes darkening above his razor-sharp cheekbones and blunt jawline.

"No. He won't. He won't kill me. Not if I still vow to make him King. Lucien you need to go! I won't have Ebonara's death on my conscience, let alone the extinction of her species that will no doubt follow. I can't— it would rip you apart, and that would rip me apart too. I do love you. I know I never said it before— but I do. Let me do this. Please— let me be the hero in our story." Storm's gaze flits from his face to the slowly closing golden ring of soldiers that surround them.

At this point, they're around a mile away, but soon they'll be close enough to recognise Lucien, and the war they've been trying so hard to prevent will be ignited in a single striking of Draconian flint against Sephilim gold.

"Storm I— I won't leave you." Lucien grips on harder, but she yanks her hands from his, her wings beating hard and causing a blast of warm air to fly into his face, blowing back his hair.

"If you ever loved me Lucien, if you have any kind of feeling for me, you'll go. Don't make me into a murderer. Please—" She pleads with him now, tears welling up in her eyes, but before a single one can fall, Lucien takes a step forward, mouth open to retort.

"GO!" she screams at him, lightning flying wild from her fingers.

It travels through the cloud, up into the soles of his feet, so he is rendered unconscious where he stands. He falls back, the unhindered weight and momentum of him causing the surface supporting him to smash apart. He plummets through the air like a stone, shocked into the darkness of unconsciousness.

She stands there, still as a too-beautiful statue, tears running in salty rivers down her face. A silent prayer crosses her lips then, pleading with whatever Goddess is listening that Ebonara catches him and keeps him safe from all this.

The clouds around her begin to plume and bulge then, the electrical charge of the Sephilim soldiers causing them to form and dissipate at will, static flying in all directions.

Then, Storm straightens, and a single bolt of lightning strikes so close to her I fear for a moment she's been hit.

When the flash recedes, Aro is standing there, his eyes two abyssal black holes that are all too familiar. They are the same eyes that gazed into my soul and whispered that I would die alone as he broke my wrist and threatened my family.

His fingers curl around her wrist just as they had mine once, where only moments before Lucien's desperate touch had clutched the same flesh, causing me to shudder involuntarily.

Lucien's desperation had been for the love of the woman in front of him though, not the love of the power she could bestow upon him.

Aro's chilling voice echoes off the surrounding cloud as he lifts a single hand and locks a set of glistening crystal manacles around her fragile wrists in one swift and practised motion, halting the increasingly close-knit circle of approaching soldiers with a single raised finger.

They stop, hovering, wings beating in time as they watch the capture unfold.

The Sephilim High Lord looks down at her, long black hair falling across his shoulder and casting half his face in shadow, piercing Storm with a gaze I can only describe as murderous.

424

"Hello, Storm, darling," he says through gritted teeth, his fingernails visibly digging into her and breaking the fragile porcelain of her skin. She looks up into his eyes, trying to hide the fear embedded deep beneath her tear-stained expression.

"I think it's time we rehearsed our wedding vows." Aro smiles. "Don't you?"

I brace myself for the next memory, hoping beyond hope that this wild emotional montage of my past life will be over as quickly as possible.

I had thought maybe I wouldn't identify with her, that I would see her as an entirely different person, but I couldn't have been more wrong. Every harsh word, every kiss, I feel as an echo of her experience, rebounding from one hollow chamber of my heart to the next in a symphony of longing and lost chances. It's making me sick as I am held hostage by the chain of memories, forced from link to link, watching forged an inevitable fate I cannot change.

The scene forms from clouds of suspended rose pink ink and plumes of ivory smoke, the two of them reappearing upon the scene of Storm's earlier escape, glass still shattered across the floor. The moonlight drips in a rich molten veil across the otherwise dark suite through the shattered panes of the balcony doors, casting them both centre stage.

He releases her as a flash of blinding light and a sound like a whip hitting wet marble cleaves the space in two, parting the still calm of before definitely from the now terrified grunts of Storm's form.

She flies forward onto the ground, hands bound in front of her even still.

Aro laughs as she hits the quartz and curls into a ball on one side, tears streaming down her face. He kicks her mercilessly in the stomach, making me physically wince as I spectate the atrocities he seemingly perceives as sport.

"You stupid bitch. Did you really think I wouldn't find out? Did you really think you could ever run and I wouldn't find you? You belong to me now. You are MINE." He delivers another kick, square in the face this time. She takes it, not raising her hands in defence, but simply whimpering as her lip splits wide open and her eyes squeeze shut against the agony.

I watch Aro pull something out of the inside of his dark jacket then, the tip of it curving the light as it is captured and made lethal. It winks at me, malicious and insidious like the sparkle in a predator's eye right before a long-awaited kill.

Stepping forward, he yanks her up onto her knees by her hair, but still she remains silent, pressing her lips together in an attempt to resist his punishment.

425

"I didn't want to do this, Storm. You made me do this—" He holds the curved dagger to her throat, and she swallows, her flesh undulating delicately beneath the edge of the blade.

I find myself holding my breath, knowing with too much certainty what happens next.

And yet— it doesn't.

He doesn't kill her, instead, he pushes her forward onto all fours, standing on the delicate bones of her fingers to keep her manacled hands pinned to the floor.

He kicks her arms from beneath her, so she's forced to lie on her stomach, and then it is he who drops to his knees, knuckles white around the hilt of the dagger.

I feel my eyes fill with tears as he frees the corset's twin bindings from around her torso by cutting the cords with two effortless swoops of the blade's flashing edge, hands busying themselves with exposing the bare skin of her back.

The light casts them both in a richness that could be said to be almost divine, creating a visual oxymoron as she dares to glance back over her shoulder, her eyes illuminated as hollow in their utter terror.

At first, I think he might rape her, but then again, I am not only mistaken but horrified by the fact that what he's doing is seemingly even worse.

As his intent clicks for her too, she wails out.

"No. Please. Aro. Don't do this—" she is begging as his lips twist into a smile, tears flowing freely down her cheeks and onto the unforgiving stone.

"It's far too late for that now, Storm. Far too late—" he mutters, sitting astride her backside so she's pinned down by his weight.

"No. Please— NO!" Her screams grow into animalistic wails as he begins to hack at her shoulder blades with the knife, easing her left wing from her and cleaving the divinity from her physical form with each purposeful slash.

Blood flies out across the floor and walls in splashes and spatters like crimson stars, and I watch as she pushes her hands out so they're high above her head, smashing them into the floor and trying to get the manacles binding her to give. It doesn't work, and as she realises the futility of it all, and goes silent, her left wing is ripped clean from her spine in a spray of bloody feathers and dangling mutilated flesh.

I watch her succumb, her hands ceasing their banging against the marble floor, suddenly realising the origin of the crack I had noticed in the stone what feels like several lifetimes ago.

It had been from her.

A message.

A warning.

One I hadn't understood or heeded.

But how could I, when I had thought the man who is raping her of the ability to soar loved me?

His hands are full of ivory feathers with lilac tips stained carmine.

Storm is crying, one wing fluttering from her spine like a twin that's just watched its other half brutally murdered, shoulders shuddering and weeping red tears down her bare back.

She brings her hands back to her forehead, resting her face atop the cool crystal of the manacles as he finishes his work, silent sobs wracking her. The fight has left her, or so it seems, the sound of blade against bone enough to make me want to vomit all over the floor despite the fact I'm not really here.

The feathers flutter like broken dreams around them, tinged scarlet as he finishes hacking off her right wing and throws it asunder. As it lands with a cold and hollow thump, he gets to his feet and wipes a bloodstained hand across his cheek. Then, picking up a handful of feathers in each fist, he laughs, letting them fall over her freely like brutal rain.

She doesn't cry any longer though, her newfound silence perhaps more painful than her sobs.

As the white feathers fall into the pool of blood that's growing from her waist, she simply stares at them, eyes vacant as if nobody is home.

"I'll see you tomorrow for the ceremony. You can explain how that Draconian monster took your wings from you. And then, you will crown me King so I have the power to destroy him and the rest of his mongrel Kindred."

Aro's face is cold as stone, the crimson of Storm's blood sheening sticky on his cheek.

I watch her then as she closes her eyes, lashes fluttering damp against her cheeks.

She places her bound hands beneath her, letting her pain fuel her in getting to her feet. Feathers fall from where they've been caked to her naked spine and flutter onto the floor, the two gaping holes in her shoulder blades still weeping red tears onto the purity of her skirts.

She takes a shaky step, breath a shudder that rattles her ribcage, before raising her chin to him, and looking him right in the eye.

"I will NEVER crown you King." She spits in his face, blood mingled with saliva hitting him on his clean cheek.

Gritting his teeth, he pulls his hand back, unleashing a slap so hard that Storm is whirled back onto the floor, the sound of his palm upon her face like the sound the ocean floor makes when splitting into a gaping chasm.

He stands over her then, giving a single final kick to her spine before conducting from the tower.

She lies there, and outside the sound of rain falling is all that can be heard.

I want so badly then to reach out, to take her hand, to tell her that we will be okay.

That I won't let her sacrifice be in vain.

That all this was for something.

But then I realise I had walked right back into Aro's clutches and handed him what she had suffered so fiercely to protect.

He was going to kill the dragons. He was going to murder their riders.

All because of me.

One stupid mortal girl who wanted to run away into a fairytale.

She stirs slightly after a few moments, her hands trembling and still bound. She's speaking under her breath, but I don't know why or who to. She glances up at something which isn't there on the far side of the room, her eyes wide like saucers as she staggers to her feet yet again, breasts spilling over the top of her ruined corset.

She nods to no one. Silently, and with utter decisive power.

I step back, stunned by her strength, as she turns from the bloodied floor of the room, squaring her shoulders and taking a deep breath, tears running continuously down her face without pause.

Then, torso heaving with grief, she takes off into a powerful run, skirts flying out behind her, before bursting through the balcony doors. Her soles, peppered with shattered glass leave the balcony floor, and she leaps without fear or pause, flying, wingless, over the gilded railing.

Rushing after her, the rain doesn't touch my ghostly form as I skid to a halt, invisible amid the sudden downpour.

Then, peering over the edge, I feel my heart thunder in my throat, the eye of this emotional storm that is changing the landscape of who I am more powerful than I could have ever imagined.

I watch as she— as I— fall into the abyss of cloud below, perfectly calm, face serene as silk, plummeting toward the end of it all.

CRIME AND PUNISHMENT

KAIRI

MY EYES FLUTTER OPEN, the golden light of the living room comforting as dust motes twirl in the gilded beams of light pouring in and
dappling amongst the familiar high beams of the barn's eaves.

There's a heavy warmth bearing down on my chest, and as I raise
a hand to investigate, I discover that Catticus Finch has decided to
watch over me, albeit closer than is necessary, as I sleep.

In fact, I'll be honest, the cat's butt is in my face.

"She's awake—" I hear my dad's voice, the familiar tenor of it
relaxing me so much that I sink deeper into the sofa cushions beneath
the blanket that's been pulled up over my shoulders.

Momentarily, as the ache of my body washes over me in overwhelming waves that crest hard against my bones, I wonder if I didn't dream
it all. Aetheria. Aro. Lucien.

Had I been pulled into some kind of coma by Ehlers Danlos Syndrome?

Was it a dream?

I panic at that, the feeling like something precious is being stolen
from me making me feel suddenly vulnerable and off balance despite
the fact I'm lying down.

"Woah, woah—" Pa brings a hand to rest on my shoulder as I try to
sit up, ribcage creaking. Catticus yowls at the upheaval and jumps off
me with a disgruntled glare shot at me from the rug.

Then my eyes settle on her, where she's propped on the arm of the
chair closest to the fireplace, watching me with a pallor that speaks
to her concern.

I breathe a sigh of relief, gaze resting on the otherworldly glow
of her skin. I hadn't noticed it in Aetheria because everything was

aglow with the intensity of the cobalt sun's purer brand of light. Here though, she looks like a ghost, her skin shimmering.

"Vail. You're here." I breathe, slumping back against the arm of the sofa.

"I couldn't exactly leave you. You passed out— and then I had to explain—" She looks at my parents, who despite her incredible beauty, haven't been able to tear their eyes from me.

"We've been so worried," is all my dad says, leaning forward and embracing me in a bone-crushing hug. I whimper slightly, my limbs throbbing beneath the pressure of his desperation to hold me, to assure himself that I really am here. Then, as he releases me, my pa comes and performs the same act, the scent of him bringing me almost to tears as I, at last, find the home I've been running toward ever since that night I had discovered Aro's true intentions.

"I'm sorry— I don't know what else to say. I just— I didn't want to be in pain anymore," I whisper to my Pa, closing my eyes as a single tear is released from beneath the fan of my lashes.

"It's alright, it's alright—" he vows, stroking the back of my head with his enormous hand. I slump into his torso then, the tension of everything momentarily lifted as I'm once again a child with a father who can fix anything with a kind word.

And I cry.

I'm left like this for a few moments before Vail clears her throat, getting elegantly to her feet from where she has been balancing with pristine poise.

"I should go—" she says loudly, causing both my fathers and me to stop in our reunion. Turning to stare at her glowing silhouette, the extraordinary suddenly among the ordinary, I watch her wings brush the edge of the coffee table as her feathers rustle against the steep bustle of her skirt, and I take a deep breath.

"Wait— I— I remember. I know what happened to Storm," I admit, and she looks at me with curiosity.

"So, you really are her." Vail brings a gloved hand to her lips, eyes widening as I feel a throbbing in my ankle make itself heard above the din of the rest of my pain.

"I am— or I was— I don't know how that works," I confess, running my fingers back through my tangled and paint-matted hair. I realise then that I'm no longer in my gown from the Fae's Lunar celebration but instead in a pair of fuzzy, coffee-coloured pyjama pants and a matching shirt that reads - 'Bearly Awake—'

"Kairi, what's going on?" My Pa asks, swallowing hard.

I turn to him then, taking the pain of every motion not as punishment but simply as fact.

"You found me in a basket on a beach all those years ago— but didn't you ever wonder where I came from?" I ask, realising that the question itself has, for me at least, been answered. I was never given up by a desperate unwed teenage mother or abandoned by a woman who had decided not to be a mother. Instead, I was reborn from another form entirely.

I don't remember it, and perhaps I never will, but I know now that I was never born into this life, that instead I fell into it from the heavens.

Storm had leapt into the abyss, and somehow, I had ended up a baby being cradled by the waves over a century later.

It doesn't make any sense. But maybe it isn't supposed to make sense to me. Perhaps it was the doing of a Goddess with far more knowledge and power than I will ever have access to.

Hera.

"Of course we did. But we also accepted a long time ago that we will never know. We never cared where you came from, only that you were ours," my dad explains, his face tired and sagging from the stress of my disappearance.

"I still am, and I always will be. You saved my life—" I speak the words, knowing I've said them before but really hearing them for the first time.

"Kairi, why did you run away? You didn't even leave us a note." Pa doesn't seem angry, he seems sad.

Vail watches us, stone still and statuesque among the boho chic of the living room décor.

"I wish I could tell you I had a good reason, but honestly, I was convinced to go by a man who promised me a pain-free existence. I was just— so tired. I wanted to run away from this disease, from what my life has become," I confess, and they nod slowly with synchronised sighs. "I didn't realise I would be gone so long. I thought I would be back before you noticed," I add, and Vail glances at me with sympathetic eyes.

"It seems that your return to Aetheria was inevitable. I explained everything best as I could to your fathers, but I know it's still a heck of a lot to get your noodle 'round. I mean, I barely understand it." She frowns, crossing her arms over her corseted breasts. I see my Pa taking in the details of her gown, his eyes glistening with a silent appreciation for the intricate peach embroidery.

I want to tell him to stop staring, and then find myself smiling, remembering how Quinn and Lucien had both teased me for exactly the same behaviour.

"You can say that again. I mean, you left us for another dimension. There's a winged woman with glowing skin standing in my living room. But— is it true that you don't have pain in Aetheria?" My dad asks, his face seeming fragile as it tiptoes a narrow crevasse between relief that I'm safe and sadness that I'm once again trapped in a body that feels more like a cage.

I nod, sitting up straighter and trying not to wince as I move my ankle. I recognise now that I've tried to move it that I probably dislocated it when I passed out.

"Can you help me with this?" I ask them both, Vail's face becoming confused. The two men know exactly what it is I'm asking though and assume practised positions I wish we'd never had to learn.

My dad moves to the end of the sofa supporting my head, pressing down hard on my shoulders as I grit my teeth. My Pa takes his own role at the opposite end of my body, gently pulling up my pant leg and revealing my swollen ankle beneath.

Vail watches us, her distaste mingled with curiosity shifting uncomfortably on her face at the spectacle.

"Ready? On three—" My Pa promises, but I know it's a lie. He never actually relocates my joints on three, for fear I'll tense up and make the dislocation worse.

"One—" he doesn't even make it to two, pushing my ankle up in a sudden jerk. A loud snap rattles through the air and up through my femur in an agonising tremor edged with slight relief as I grunt in pain, closing my eyes and willing it to pass.

Vail's face becomes sadder as I exhale, her fingers rubbing circles on the outermost layer of her silky skirt, trying to distract herself from my too-obvious mortality. Pity is written plainly in her expression and on the faces of the two men who care about me more than anyone else I've ever known.

My ankle continues to throb despite being put back into place.
Fantastic.
Especially for what I have to do next.

"So, I've spent the last week or so running for my life. From the man who promised me a new life. A second chance." My fathers look at each other as I prepare to get to my feet, face screwing up as the pain sears red hot through my lower calf and into the nerves riddling my left foot. My dad lifts his hands gently from my shoulders.

"You're going back, aren't you?" He is the one brave enough to ask as he steps around the side of the couch, and I feel close to breaking down in tears as I answer him with my eyes only.

He helps me to my feet, and I hop towards him, hissing through my teeth as I get reacquainted with the pain of a recent dislocation.

"I don't want to leave you— you're my family," I whisper to him, closing my eyes as I wrap my fingers around his neck and inhale the scent of bay leaves and hay.

"And I don't want you to leave. But not as much as I don't want you to suffer. No matter where you are in the universe, we will always be family."

He pushes me back a little, kissing me on the cheek, and I plop down on the couch again. Then, he takes his husband's hand in his, the two of them interlocking fingers, united for me.

"We adopted you to give you a better life, Kairi. Standing in the way of that now, even if it means you're no longer here with us, wouldn't make us very good parents. Don't you think?" Pa's tone gets higher, his eyes filling with tears this time.

"We've been so worried. We thought you were in pain, maybe even dead. We want the best for you even if that means stepping aside now. Besides, it seems like it's out of our hands. You're destined for something bigger than all this— we always knew you were special, so I guess this just proves us right," my dad says, his eyes watering as his lips spread into a forced smile.

The emotional confessions leave me speechless, making me want to break down and cry, to curl into a ball and never leave. It would be too easy to stay here, to let them care for me, too easy to turn my back on everything I've so recently come to know and love.

I stare at them, the silence threatening to drown me in indecision until Catticus breaks it with a single yowl, as if he's annoyed at being anything less than the centre of attention.

"Kairi, what are you thinking? You know I cannot just take you back to Aetheria. Lord Black will kill you." Vail doesn't condemn me but is rather patient, her eyes curious and burning with silent rebellious encouragement.

"I know what happened to Storm. I also know why nobody else can remember. If I can bring back those memories, I think it could expose

433

Aro's true nature. Maybe then we will have some chance of convincing the other Kindred to support the Draconians. Maybe then we could save the dragons," I muse, the words feeling right as they leave my lips, echoing deep, not only in the air but in my essence.

It's as though Storm is smiling, nodding, saying *yes. Finish what I started.*

I don't know what I'm doing, but I do know I can't let her— our, sacrifice be in vain.

"Again, that's a great plan, darlin'. But you're only mortal. Lord Black will kill you before you can so much as draw breath." Vail comes forward now, taking a seat beside me on the couch and glancing down at my still-swollen ankle.

"Not only that, but you can't even walk right now, honey," she reminds me. "You'd be hopping into your execution in this state."

"Vail— you don't understand. I watched Storm die. I watched her clutch freedom with both hands despite Aro trying to rip it from her. I used to think freedom was the ability to run free without pain, but it's now I know that isn't it at all. Freedom is being able to choose what to suffer for. And I want to suffer for this. I want to save the dragons, to save Lucien as he was willing to save me. I started this. Let me end it."

It's the most concise, truthful thing I've ever said. The bravery in my voice shocks me, and I feel my heart swell inside my chest as I realise, I've fallen in love, not with any one person but with an entire world.

My truth echoes over and over.

Pain is inevitable, but I can choose what to suffer for.

And I choose him. I choose them. I choose Aetheria.

"Well, in that case, you'll be needing this." My father disappears momentarily and then returns, presenting my wheelchair to me.

I no longer see it as an enemy but as an aid in my cause.

It matters not how I get there, only that I do.

Even if I am wearing pyjamas.

LUCIEN

The cold air of Drakos Vale is like the tongue of a whip against my bare skin. I hadn't had the forethought, or time, to change, so here I am, flying through a sea of swirling snowflakes in nothing more than some purple velvet leggings.

In any other situation, it would be laughable, but not today.

Today it's desperate, and with the weight of the anxiety in my stomach, I think it's a miracle I'm airborne at all.

I part from Ebonara in a sudden upsurge of speed as I leap from her spine, commanding her to circle the land mass in case of leftover Sephilim hunters, hiding herself within the clouds and calming my tattered nerves.

My hair lies in a thick braid down my spine, the plait growing damper and colder by the second, the drop in temperature a comfort rather than a hindrance for me as I plummet toward the ground.

The twin Gemina Peaks come into view fast below, piercing through the thick grey blanket of morose cloud that hovers over the land like a veil of mourning, the wind hissing in my ears as my wings fight against it moment by moment.

I bank a sharp left, the cold rivulets of melting snow sticking to my pectorals as I burst through the lowest layers of cloud, dropping altitude as fast as I can.

My ears pop violently with the drastic pressure change, but I grit my teeth through the discomfort and keep moving forward, everything else merely a distraction or irritation compared to my real problem.

I start to see traces of it the closer I get to the white-dusted ground of the floating continent. Draconian bodies lie like broken dolls beneath me, wings broken or twisted at painful angles, red blood seeping into the snow and staining it crimson under their black steel armour.

There's more wounded than I expect, and I wonder then just how many Sephilim it took to take down so many. I know they're more than us in number, but I've never believed any one of their warriors to be any stronger than one of ours. After all, Draconian soldiers are forged in the icy skies over soaring jagged peaks, their wings strengthened by flight alongside dragons, their hearts hardened by the prejudice against us and our own.

We are blessed by the fury of two women scorned, and that should be enough to terrify anyone.

And yet, I am the one who is terrified now.

At first, I think of heading directly for the Astrid Keep, but something deep inside me, call it survival instinct, puts me off this idea. If there are any remaining Sephilim, that's where they'll be, and I don't even have a sword with me.

I think then of landing dressed in only purple velvet, realising that before I attempt to storm and reclaim any kind of fortress alone, I need to stop by the lakeside house for supplies.

I yank my body around, defying the air currents that have been propelling me forward and fighting them as I turn back on myself, flying instead for the farthest southern point of the floating island below.

When I can finally see the silhouette of my lodge appearing in the distance, something else strikes me as off, but it takes me a few moments, and a drop of another hundred feet or so to realise what it is.

Below, the usually flawless silver gleam of the frozen lake is shattered by a sharp jagged hole, right in the centre. I swoop in lower, wondering what the hell happened here and why it happened here instead of somewhere more focal to Draconian settlements.

I hurry to the ground, wings billowing behind me and catching the air to slow my descent as I land, bare soles not even flinching as they touch down on the solid ice beside the enormous central puncture.

I pace around it for a few moments, cocking my head this way and that, and then see it, barely. The sun is high overhead, and for just a moment what looks like white bloody seaweed can be glimpsed floating innocuously far beneath the surface.

It takes me a moment, but then it hits me with the force of an arrow piercing the core of an apple.

Genevieve.

It's her hair, pale and eerily sanguine, floating beneath my feet.

So that's how they captured Algoric without her melting them into fleshy puddles, I muse, realising now that I should have guessed she had been incapacitated somehow. Genevieve would have never let them leave with Algoric if she had the power to fight, even if it meant sacrificing her life.

With a strained beat of my leathery wingspan, I rise from the ice, taking two enormous pulsating strokes upward before letting myself plunge through the lake's surface.

The chill of the water isn't unwelcome, the mugginess of Nirvana having been riding on my last nerve for the last twenty-four hours, and yet I feel an abstract horror for Genevieve's suffering. This kind of cold would certainly render her powerless, if not kill her.

The thought is abhorrent, making my wings work harder as they propel me deeper and deeper below the surface with desperate and unpractised motion. I find her there, on the bed of the lake, floating and chained to a boulder, helpless.

I don't need air to survive, and neither does she, but the presence of it means staying underwater for this long is hard on my wings as they're fighting my body's desire to float to the surface.

Genevieve's eyes are wide open as they meet mine, but rather than relief, all I see is her fury.

Her ankle is chained to a boulder with several fissures running across the surface, and instead of trying to communicate my regret to her, my apology for putting these events into motion, I focus only on freeing her.

I freeze the water that's lying within the boulder's deepest fractures, watching as the rock shatters apart as the icy fluid freezes and expands. I watch as the iron loop screwed into the stone comes free as the boulder disintegrates into smaller and smaller fragments, my power freezing and refreezing any new cracks made by my first attempt. When the rock is finally a scattering of stones and nothing more, I spin, creating a whirlwind of glacially pale bubbles as I take her delicate frame in my arms.

Together, and with several furiously synchronised wingbeats, we rise to the surface.

As soon as we break into the icy noon air, Genevieve is heaving up cold water all over the nearby ice, turning it translucent as she purges her system.

She hoists herself up onto the ice sheet covering the lake, allowing herself to rest with her cheek flat to the glacial facet for a moment and her eyes squeezed shut, her hair slicked back against her scalp in a phantasmal and bloody skull cap.

I pull myself up out of the water to stand beside her, velvet leggings heavy and threatening to fall down under the water weight as I drip onto the solid ground beside her, the metronomic intensity of each droplet hitting the ice like a gong in the furious silence I feel building.

Slowly, dripping with icy lake water, she gets to her feet, hands bound in front of her see-through nightgown by crystal-lined manacles. I've never seen anything like them, but you don't have to be a genius to work out they've stopped her melting the iron and getting free under her own power.

She balls her fists still bound in front of her, lips bloody crimson as they pull back over her perfect porcelain teeth in a snarl.

I brace myself, standing strong and preparing for her to hit me, to slash and bite and claw until I'm standing bloodied.

It's what I deserve, and she sees that I know it as I look down at her with a pity I know full well she can't stand.

I brace for the slap, the scratch, the punishment, the vengeance, but nothing ever comes.

Instead, she merely screams at me.

Opening her mouth wide and letting out an angry half sob, half scream right into my face as her wings flare out from her spine, icy water dripping from her talons as it finds her flesh too hot to freeze.

"YOU DID THIS. YOU DID THIS!" She screams at me and then begins to pound against my bare chest with her tiny furious fists. I take it as her voice reverberates in the air around us over and over, only making the absence of Algoric even more obvious to us both.

When she finally looks up at me, her expression taut with loathing, I swallow hard.

"I know. I know I did. And I'm sorry. We will get Algoric back. We will go right now. If you are willing—" I test the waters, whispering in her ear as I hold her steadfast to my torso, letting her rage within the safety of my arms. I wonder what she will say now, knowing all along she's been opposed to the idea of conflict with the Sephilim.

Things are different now though. Everything is different, and the look on her face tells me this without a shadow of a doubt.

"Assemble the troops. We leave in one hour!" she spits at me, shivering as she takes off across the ice now, moving with determined fury toward the lakeside house, tremors of her rage visibly wreaking havoc along her spine. She adds, hatefully, "I hope you're happy, Lucien. You've sacrificed a lot of lives for a mortal girl who will never repay the favour."

Her words sting, but I expected worse.

I deserve worse.

And yet, what was the alternative?

Allow Kairi to be murdered, or tortured into crowning that psychopath King?

What would have stopped him from doing this exact same thing once he had a crown on his head?

I know the answer, and the answer is nothing.

This war has been coming for a while. So perhaps then, we should simply get on with it.

The revelation makes something within me snap, hardening my resolution and making me grit my teeth.

"What about the dragons?" I call after her, stiffening on the spot as I realise now that what I've done, what I've sacrificed for Kairi is more than I ever realised and that it wasn't mine to bargain with in the first place.

She doesn't flinch, or pause, or even turn back.

She simply gives the order.

"Ready them for war!" she barks, ruthless. "All of them."

ARO

"Here, my Lord, as requested." The nameless soldier passes me the object I ordered him to retrieve over an hour ago, eyes anxious as he presents it to me with an open, dark-skinned palm.

"At last." I snatch the hilt of the sword from his unworthy grip, unsheathing the amethyst blade to ensure he hasn't brought me the wrong weapon.

It might seem silly, the symbolic attachment I have assigned to an object that was once held by Midas, but the dragon in question had slain his queen, and I know that his intention for this sword was to end the beast's life with its brutal crystal edge. To have his revenge at last.

I cannot help but appreciate the poetry of the fact it will finally fulfil its long-awaited destiny this night at my hand.

The sun is high overhead still, and a bead of perspiration forms beneath my high steel collar as I see Leo approaching from within the temple.

It seems my wait is over.

"The High Lords and Ladies are assembled and waiting inside as you instructed, my Lord," Leo announces from behind the golden-tinted visor of his metallically feathered helmet, red locks of his hair set ablaze beneath and pressed flat against his broad forehead.

His eyes are dark, steeled even, and I wonder if he too is as excited as I am at the prospect of what's about to happen.

My skin prickles, heart racing slightly beneath the steel of my breastplate, wings fluttering impatiently against my spine as I nod to him, making my way quickly up the white marble steps of The Temple of Zeus. I hold myself back from sprinting across the entrance hall, knowing I need to appear not overjoyed or excited, but anxious and sombre. I must channel my energy into the definiteness of my intention, into an intensity that cannot be ignored by the others.

Celebration can come later in my private quarters with fine wine and one of the newer Nephilim who have not yet become acquainted with me on a more intimate level.

I will make my selection from the crowd of the show I must choreograph now, making sure to pay attention to the widest, most enraptured pair of eyes in the flock.

"Lord Black. I do not appreciate being summoned whilst I am in the middle of lunch." Aliandara's face is pursed as I grow closer to where she and the other High Lords and Ladies are clustered. They are grouped in the main corridor of the larger chamber, watched by the enormous statue of Zeus, which looms over them.

Her irritating voice echoes off the high walls with a tinny nothing short of blade clashing against shield, the pitch of her disapproval grating on my nerves.

As I grow closer, I find her not in a gown but in loose silk harem pants and a simple midnight blue bikini top. Her fellow High Lady, Evangeline, is at her side, clutching her hand and shadowing her every movement with furtive golden eyes and luscious, ivory-feathered wings.

Ember and Neve, the two Fae High Ladies of Light stand, statuesque and disinterested, watching me with dead twin gazes. Beside them, Hypnos is standing, looking off into the air around her like she's watching ghosts do the waltz, while Morpheus, who remains at her side, seems just as much, if not more, distracted.

I wonder then if the two of them are having a conversation invisible to the rest of us, and my eyes narrow on the blank innocence of their misleading faces.

"Yes, Aro. We are not dogs to be whistled for on a whim." Asher, one of the many Equinian hoard Chieftains frowns, his black Arabic brows and tanned skin crinkling and curving like sun-crisp paper with undeniable scrutiny. His onyx hair is braided to his waist in an archaically basic style, each strand so thick it's better described as rope than actual hair, a symbol of his undefeated status in battle.

If it's supposed to intimidate, it doesn't. If anything, it gives an opponent something to grab onto during battle in my opinion.

"Well, perhaps if you'd stop acting like a little bitch, then the rest of us would treat you like a man—" Aliandara quips, causing a small smile to pull at the corners of my lips.

"Where are the other Chieftains of Ares?" I demand, tactically changing the subject as Asher's carotid begins to throb noticeably beneath the thick tanned skin of his neck, looking to Leo who was sent to retrieve these most valuable allies personally.

My commander pales slightly beneath my scrutiny, causing me to hold my breath.

Asher speaks for him, voice a booming declaration of his supposed masculine dominance.

"The other Chieftains are on the move. I know, in particular, Landon John has gone off on some treasure hunt and could not be located by your methods of conduction." He straightens, and I freeze slightly, concerned. "As I said, we are a nomadic race. And no one's to beckon at whim. You could not possibly harness our power, so I suggest you stop trying to." He sounds angry, so I think carefully about my next words.

I need the full support of all the High Lords, Chieftains, or whatever they want to be called if I'm going to have the kind of numbers I require, harnessed or not. I cannot risk that the Draconians might get their claws into any of them, and I know for a fact that the missing man in question is arguably the softest of them all when it comes to the idea of mass murder.

"I would not have brought you here if it weren't for a matter of great urgency and one that puts all of our people in immediate danger. I am sure that as this is the case, you can speak for the rest of the Chieftains. We do not have time to lose on the democratic process today." I let my voice become clipped and sharp, jabbing the importance and urgency of my cause into each of the onlooking Aristocrats with the potency of salt in an open wound.

"This is ridiculous. I cannot possibly see what could be so urgent that you had to send your Sephilim soldiers to escort us here so suddenly." A Fae High Lord of Light, Quinn, says.

I notice his eyes are sunken deep into his beautiful skull and dressed in dark circles.

"Well, of course, you wouldn't. You are obviously quite hungover," I spit back at him, causing his shoulders to sag. I watch his partner, Phineas, place a hand protectively on his lover's shoulder before scowling at me.

"Get on with it, Lord Black. I don't have all goddamn day for your theatrics," the redheaded Fae retorts, and so I spin on the ball of my foot, black feathered wingspan flaring out behind me as I clutch the golden sheath of the requested amethyst sword in my fist.

"Gladly. Follow me." I command, authoritative as I take off at a brisk pace, my shoes echoing out with a dominant purposefulness as I lead them from the inside of the temple and down the shallow front steps.

The clicking of Aliandara's heels grows louder as the beast I've chained to the holy ground beneath our feet comes into view.

"It cannot be—" she gasps, voice but a wisp of its usual gale force intensity.

"But it is," I confirm, sounding almost bored as I watch the dragon slumbering, head resting upon its enormous front feet and still groggy from the tranquillizer. It gives a sudden shift, exhaling a cloud of thick steam and causing the growing crowd of Nephilim, who had been summoned to give more weight to the occasion, to gasp right on cue. Several of the women even swoon despite the placidity of the simple snort, but not Silver, who I see watching me with a sullen face from the shadows of the farthest cluster of oak trees, the dull sheen of her hair unmistakable as it had been that day in The Temple of Hera when I had shamed her insolence.

Asher takes a few steps forward, coming level with Aliandara who is now right beside me, staring straight across and past her elegant profile with dark wide eyes, their depth immeasurable.

"What did you do?" he asks, blinking slowly as the golden caramel of his enormous wings spread from his shoulders defensively.

I turn, ignoring him and facing the small cluster of bodies as more Nephilim land quietly on the outskirts of the crowd, joining the wall of winged bodies encircling the enslaved dragon.

Straightening, I prepare to begin the most important performance of my immortal life so far.

"I did nothing. After the ball, Kairi and I reconciled once she realised that all I wanted was to give her immortal life. I was, of course, foolish not to tell her my intentions, but I only wished to free her from the pain of her mortal existence and was worried her survival instinct would implore her to run. Lord DeLaurent, however, had a different idea about her fate. He kidnapped her right from the Solis Castra and, in doing so, ignited the suspicions of myself and my men to the continued existence of what he had long been assured was dead. Just as he did all those years ago, he planned to kill my beloved. I could not let him succeed again." I pause, taking a deep breath.

"And why on earth would Lord DeLaurent want to kill a mortal girl?" Morpheus speaks up now, his eyes becoming clearer as he focuses in on my face, taking a step from deep within the crowd where, up until now, he's been unusually quiet.

"Perhaps for the same reason he killed Storm. He doesn't want me to be the next King of Aetheria," I say, putting blunt emphasis on the title.

"And why, do explain, would one High Lord have any reason to get involved in such a lofty affair? The Draconians have been banished for over a century. Surely it matters very little to them who sits on the throne?" Hypnos adds in, coming to Morpheus' side. The other High Lords and Ladies turn at the sound of her dreamy tone, all of them compelled to revere her as the Goddess she once was. They somehow think she is more than us, even though she sacrificed her station for a stupid little thing called love.

I, however, feel differently.

I think she's a fool.

"As you might remember, The Draconians have a seer as one of their High Ladies. Lady Dragos. Who knows what she has seen? Who knows whose destiny they are trying to destroy? After all, why hide the dragons if they are not intending to launch an attack?" I ask them, and it causes the crowd to pause for a moment.

Morpheus speaks up once again, making me wonder why he all of a sudden has an infatuation with the Draconians. After all, he was the one who helped me falsely incriminate them in Storm's unfortunate suicide-named-murder in the first place.

"The Draconians might have been keeping dragons a secret. But what makes you think that they intend to cause us harm?" He sounds foolish, and Aliandara and Asher both turn to him now, eyebrows raised.

"You cannot deny that hiding such powerful destructive creatures is nothing short of suspicious." Asher growls, balling his fists as the idea of conflict begins to arouse him. Quinn steps forward then, his undulating ombre wings floating pathetically behind him.

"And what if they were protecting them? Just as we have been forced to protect our precious creatures from your insatiable hunter's instinct?" he asks, eyes blazing the bright green of envy. The flowers in his hair tremor as his fury causes a few petals to come loose, falling in elegant spirals onto the ground at his feet.

I watch as the three Fae High Lords and three present Fae High Ladies begin to band together, causing Asher and Aliandara's fellow High Lady, Evangeline, to step in on her side.

This isn't how it was supposed to go. They are supposed to be backing me, not fighting one another.

I need something to unite them, to make them see my side.

I have one tool at my disposal that will never and has never failed me.

Fear.

So, I turn, moving toward the beast without caution and letting myself taste the static in the air. A storm is building, perfect for what I intend to do next.

The world around us has darkened during the time the High Lords and Ladies have been fighting, and so I reach out into the air that grows slowly chill and damp. Taking a deep breath, I see the beast's broken soul as it lies, wings tucked against its spine, eyes half open.

I reach out with my empty hand, sending a fork of electricity sparking wildly through the air with a crack, fingers taut and extended before me. The strike hits the beast on the side of its skull like the sudden agonising kiss of whiplash, causing it to rise to its feet with a heinous roar of agony.

Watching Nephilim scatter as the pale scales of the dragon bulge, it inhales, trying to breathe fire within its kyanite-lined steel muzzle.

Jaws clamped, only steam escapes, followed by a few embers that float from between its gritted teeth, escaping from its pale thick lips and into the air like a vision of the ominous blood-soaked sky full of falling carmine stars that will soon come to pass. Only they will not be stars but flaming dragon corpses and their riders, hurtling toward the growing scarlet rivers that will stain the snow of Drakos Vale a permanent crimson.

This vision makes me smile.

As the beast spreads its wings, I watch the parasol blades do their job, causing it to let out an ear-shattering screech as the razors dig their teeth into the leathery flesh of its wingspan. The monster scrapes its claws against the ground, thrashing left and then right, metal clanging louder than rolling thunder.

The ground underfoot shakes with its fury.

The world around us cools, the icy promise of fear-induced violence settling over us as the long tresses of the High Born Kindred are blown back from their faces in a single stunted beat of the dragon's scaly alabaster wings.

Aliandara and Asher turn, Evangeline's face rocked with the shock of seeing such power manacled to a speck of land that has so utterly lost its sublimity by comparison.

Morpheus looks up from the faces of the others, a sad melancholy in his eyes that I've never seen before.

Then I realise it as the group stand awed by the pure steely destructive power of the flesh and blood creature before them, the same myth they had thought long dead brought back to life from the depths of their oldest nightmares.

Morpheus knows the truth about Storm and Lucien.

I swallow this, satisfied with the reactions of the others as the dragon before us continues to flail, its wings leaking silver blood where it strains, trying to escape.

Turning to them, I find their pupils dilated, hair ruffled, shoulders stiff, postures closed and defensive.

I know then I have been successful.

"Any questions?" I ask, smiling with genteel composure.

29

THE ART OF WAR

<u>KAIRI</u>

LEAVING MY PARENTS IS brutal, and as Vail conducts both me and my wheelchair from the porch of the converted barn, I see the tears sparkling in their steeled yet affectionate gazes.

It takes everything inside of me not to open my mouth and confess that I can't bear to leave, to relinquish this idea I have of being able to fill Storm's extremely sparkly and high-heeled Aetherial shoes and go back to finish the work of keeping the crown firmly out of Aro's hands.

I do go though. Choking on my own strength, my own ridiculous courage, I leave them standing in the doorway, unsure I'll ever return.

It turns out, even when you fully believe what you're doing is right, when the cause you're willing to die for is the noblest you might ever find, that fear doesn't merely dissipate. Instead, it grows larger, the stakes inflate, and the knowledge that what I'm sacrificing is enormous looms only larger. Only in this realisation do I find myself fighting my own decision and reminding myself of why it needs to be done and why I need to be the one to do it.

I'm battling between leaving and staying, and this friction is what confirms that I'm doing the right thing, not the easy one. My uncertainty births my resolve, amazing even me as the Fae continent of Nirvana suddenly surrounds me once more.

Overhead, the sun is higher than when I'd left, the air pregnant with untapped humidity. Vail pushes my wheelchair forward, allowing me a few moments to take in the place I've never actually been but know intimately.

"This is the Fountain of Youth," I name it, awed. Vail sounds impatient.

"Well, this is where you asked me to bring you, Darlin'." Her southern twang is masked by the anxiety in her tone now. I turn to her, apologetic.

"You're right— I'm so—" I begin, but before I can get out another word, I'm interrupted by an unmistakably familiar yowl.

I twist in the wheelchair, the thin fleece of my pyjama pants causing me to perspire already. My ankle throbs, but I ignore it, watching Vail turn a full circle behind me atop a thick layer of moss, the train of her gown barely visible to her beyond her wings.

"Well, butter my butt and call me a biscuit—" Vail's southern drawl returns full force as she bends, picking up a sheepish Catticus with both hands, hoisting him beneath his front paws and into mid-air, Simba-style. "We got ourselves a stow-away!" she shakes her head as she removes his back claws from the silk of her skirt, rolling her eyes and looking stressed as she passes me the ginger tom.

Catticus isn't content to stay in my arms though, giving a loud meow and slithering from my grasp before I can even begin to wonder if I should send Vail back to return him.

"Well, he can't stay here. Y'all need to catch him!" She looks at me with further impatience, and I cock my head, allowing my eyes to drop down to my ankle.

"Yeah, you might have to do the catching. My ankle is still throbbing," I admit, feeling useless as the sound of nearby dreamcatchers tinkling in the sudden yet slight breeze reaches my ears.

It's then I remember, staring after Catticus as he heads toward the edge of the glowing water that is The Fountain, that I'm here with a very specific purpose and that I don't have time to waste.

"If you just—" I begin to instruct her on how to lure Catticus back to her so she can make a quick return trip to Hickory Oaks, but before I can, she's stepping past me, her face marred with the tension of curiosity.

"Look at that—" She points, her index finger as elegant as the rest of her as I gaze beyond it. Catticus, never one for even a light rain, is straying from the bank and wading into the deepening luminous aqua glow of the water.

I scowl, confused.

"Catticus hates water—" I whisper, a chill running back up my spine, though why I have no idea.

I watch as the silhouette of the tiny ginger tomcat gradually disappears beneath the glowing surface until he is merely a head in the centre of its shallow depths.

Then, he completely disappears, popping beneath the surface and remaining submerged for far too long.

My heart stops, leaping up into my throat as my stomach plummets. I get to my feet, forgetting about my ankle and paying dearly for it. The ankle dislocates again, tendons and ligaments still loose from where they've been stretched too far already, causing my balance to falter as half of my weight loses its column of support.

I fall to the floor, hands catching me and nails digging into the thick emerald carpet, the scent of moist damp earth and lush tropical greenery pluming in an aromatic cloud around my flushed face.

My vision is obscured by my hair, which falls fast in a thick curtain around me. When I finally manage to prop myself up on my elbows and shake it from my eyes, what I see is odd enough to make me wonder if I've knocked myself unconscious.

"Cat— Catticus?" I breathe, watching as the Kensari, fully grown and purest white, emerges from the fountain's waters where my adopted ginger stray had entered.

He raises his head, his intensely cobalt eyes meeting mine as he opens his enormous jaws before confirming his realness with a spine-tingling roar.

"Holy wombat on a wagon—" Vail breathes, moving forward slowly and helping me to my feet.

I limp, transferring my weight to my good foot, ankle still throbbing and probably twice as swollen now, but unable to take my eyes from the purity of the Lion's enormous fur-covered silhouette.

Treading closer to me, each step splays his paws wide atop the moss, exposing the lethal claws hiding between his toes. His majestic weight is suddenly a too-noticeable underfoot vibration as he approaches, causing my heart to race along in time.

As the lusciously arctic mane crowning his regal head is slightly ruffled by the breeze that twirls lazy pirouettes in the stagnant humidity, the sound of crystals hitting one another gently rises in a weak lullaby, and I gawp, open-mouthed, awed.

"Did you know about this?" Vail asks me, her enormous lilac eyes wide as she tears her gaze from what Catticus has become.

I cock my head at her, mystified as to how she thinks I would have had the slightest idea.

"You mean did I know that my ginger tom cat that I recently adopted was actually a winged lion?" I ask her, and she purses her lips.

"I see your point. Though, you know I've heard things about a white Kensari with striking blue eyes before— just gossip of course," she adds.

"Let me guess, he belonged to Storm?" I ask and she nods.

"He disappeared as do many bonded animal partners, after her death— or according to Trinity anyway—" she explains, looking back to the lion who is now stretching its wings as though it's waking from a hundred-year slumber. Stretching back onto its hind legs and yawning, the lion's jaws splay wide, exposing the feral incisors inside.

"Do you have a Kensari?" I ask her, and she nods.

"Yes, Peaches. My lioness. She's golden in colour. Most of the Nephilim have female companion animals," she explains, and I cannot help but smile at the name.

As if we're being extremely rude in talking amongst ourselves, the now enormous Catticus roars, stealing our attention from one another and focusing it solely on himself. His eyes are intense as they lock with mine, and where I expect to hear his voice among my thoughts, only silence follows.

His intent, however, could not be clearer as he lays down on the ground in front of me.

"I think he wants you to get on—" Vail translates, and I feel my stomach churn.

"Me? Ride on that—" I begin, and Catticus roars again. "Sorry, him—" I correct myself beneath my breath in an anxious addendum as the hairs on my arms rise.

"It's a sign Kairi. A sign that you're exactly where you are supposed to be. He will protect you. You have nothing to fear."

She steps forward, pulling my frozen form with her before helping me to mount the lion. Situating myself between the mountainous peaks of the Kensari's shoulder blades and enormous white feathered wings, I let my fingers twist into the mane of the animal, feeling the hair softer than any house cat, hips aching as they spread the full width of his enormous spine.

Just as I feel myself getting some semblance of stability, Catticus gets to his feet, causing me to rock forward and then back, feet leaving the ground as he stands, his head rising to the height of Vail's shoulder. I tighten my grip on his fur, worrying about hurting him.

He nuzzles her a little, and she scratches him behind the ear.

"Vail—" I call, gripping hard onto the lion's fur as my heart begins to race.

"Yes?" she enquires, hurrying toward me over the lush ground with her skirts fluttering around her ankles.

"I need you to do something for me—" I ask timidly.

It's then that I see it.

As she looks up at me, her face becomes adoring, almost as if she's seeing some deity, some goddess on lion-back in my place. The intensity of her respect startles me, but I don't have time to contemplate it as she simply says, "Anything, darlin'."

The journey is unlike anything I've ever experienced.

Flying on a dragon was almost seamless, the enormity of the scaled beast making the flight exhilarating but fairly consistent in speed and altitude. The entire experience had a feeling of safety and security attached that I had clearly taken for granted.

Flying on the back of a Kensari, however, is rougher and far more turbulent, and as Catticus pounces from solid cloud to solid cloud, my stomach finds itself in a constant sickening somersault. Aether is stirred up around me, clinging to my hair and pyjamas, the pain in my ankle dulling considerably as we rise higher and higher above a grim and thick layer of cloud that has formed like a looming shadow over the floating islands below. Whether it's because I'm alone now, where before I had Lucien to stabilise me, or that Kensari flight is just rougher, I don't know, but either way, I know I'll be glad when the journey is over. I guess all the Nephilim and Sephilim who have their own Kensari have wings of their own too, so if they tumble from the animal, they're not risking a certain and painful death.

Leaving my wheelchair behind was the right thing to do as this makes my journey to confront Aro so much faster, and yet I know I'll never take the gentle ebb of the rotating wheels for granted again.

We begin to sink from the open airy light of the space above the layer of cloud, and with it, my spirits fall too. Fear eats at me, nibbling away at my certainty that I am exactly where I'm supposed to be moment by moment. As I finally see Soleus come into view, a kind of sour nausea lodges itself in the back of my throat at the immense beauty that had captured me in the first place.

I think, as the air chills and my hair is whipped back from my face in a sudden gust of wind, that we're going to end up at the Solis

Castra, right where this all began. But, again, I find myself mistaken as Catticus heads not for Oblivion Falls but instead for a smaller floating rock mass that I hadn't seen during my carriage ride to the amethyst palace what seems like several lifetimes ago.

Upon the floating mass of crystal and Aetherial dirt, I see the outline of a building and realise that I actually know what it is.

The Temple of Zeus.

As though Storm is reaching out across the time separating us, I pull on the knowledge stored in her memories without knowing it, naming the destination that approaches too fast with a kind of mystic effortlessness. I wonder then if I can get a true name for the creature carrying me— as Catticus seems somehow unfitting for such an incredible feline, but only silence comes back.

As we bank left, circling, Catticus dives through clouds, instinctively taking a longer route to avoid a heavy armoured Sephilim presence in the skies, their gold-plated torsos and thighs dull in shadows of heavy storm clouds forming around us.

The proximity with which he banks around their sprawling formation makes me stiffen on his back, my breath but a wisp yet still seeming far too loud.

Finally, after what seems like an eternity, Catticus drops dramatically into our final descent. As we fall through the air and toward the ground, the scene in front of us becomes clearer and increasingly nightmarish with each passing vertical mile.

I see him, chained to the earth, alabaster scales dull and dim in the stormy half-light of the oncoming dusk, his cries shattering a part of me ingrained so deep it is only too easy to forget it is there.

It's the fundamental understanding that no living creature should suffer like that at the hands of another.

It makes my jaw tense and causes adrenaline to spike through me as Catticus makes a final drop in altitude and his paws meet with solid earth. We land between where Algoric is chained and a watching crowd of assorted immortals stands, their faces a woven tapestry of expression ranging from disgust to arousal and boasting every emotion in between.

At the sight of me, of Catticus, a collective inhale that's almost a gasp but not quite can be felt as the air around me thins.

I see him then as he turns, his broad silhouette causing a steady stream of undiluted hatred to mix in with the blood that flies hot through my veins.

If I thought I had hated him for how he used me before, it's nothing compared to how I feel now I know what he did to Storm.

He smiles, those dark indigo voids of his irises staring at me with a kind of cold joy that can only be described by saying that it's the same look a leopard gets when it sees a limping baby gazelle all alone in the middle of the savannah.

He smells my blood, my weakness, but he doesn't see my spirit or my strength. And that, I pray, will be the thing that undoes him. Because honestly, there's no way I can take him in a fight, even without a seriously fucked up ankle.

I dismount Catticus, who stands at my side, loyal, between the Sephilim High Lord who had shattered my world and that of Storm so completely, and the innocent dragon he has captured in the name of my return.

He wanted it. Now he will have to deal with me and everything I bring that can expose him and his desolate heart.

"You came back, Kairi." His words are uncertain and bordering on that sweet tone he had used with me once upon a time, unsure of my intent.

Perhaps he is hoping I have come to tell the tale of my capture and torture at the hands of the only man in the whole damn place who seems to see me for who I am, and not who he wants me to be.

Perhaps he thinks I am coming back to him as a damsel in need of rescue.

He'd be damn wrong on both counts. Because my only intention is to destroy his reputation once and for all.

It turns out that even my physical disease never robbed me of my real power. Because, I know now, that power is to be found in the uniqueness of my voice and the courage I have summoned in making it heard now above the din.

"I came back to stop this. To tell everyone the truth!" I announce, my voice echoing loudly from the emerald facets of leafy oaks.

The agonised struggle of the dragon behind me goes silent as do the murmurs of the crowd.

Aro stiffens on the spot, wings spreading wide as I limp several paces forward, feeling the first specks of rain hitting my scalp in icy plops.

I watch him as he observes me, taking in my *Bearly awake* fleece pyjamas and smiling at the limp in my step as I close the distance between us a little more. I ignore his gaze, looking beyond him now and to the crowd of High Lords and Ladies he has summoned here like he's holding some kind of despicable performance.

My focus then becomes steel as the next words leave my lips, sharp like razors in their sincerity.

"He lied to you. To all of you. The Draconians never kidnapped and killed Storm. He did. He hacked off her wings. Just as he tried to kill me. Lord DeLaurent saved me, or at least he tried. Twice. The Draconians are innocent, and so are their dragons." The statements come out as clearly and concisely as I can make them, wincing through the lessened pain of my re-dislocated ankle and carrying on as the rain grows more insistent, soaking into my hair and wetting my eyelashes, the ground beneath me becoming slick under the soles of my slippers.

"You're only a mortal. You know nothing of our affairs!" Aro spits at me, and then in retort, Catticus roars, bounding forward in warning.

I watch as Aliandara and a large, dark-haired, male Equinian I've never met cock their heads, eyes becoming intrigued by the scene unfolding.

"I am Storm reborn, and I have her Kensari's allegiance to prove it!" I retort, standing tall as rain runs down the back of my neck, causing me to shudder against my will.

"Wasn't it you, Lord Black, who insisted she was Storm reincarnated, to begin with?" Aliandara asks, her voice serrated with suspicion.

The tension between myself and Aro thickens as several members of the watching crowd push forward to get a better look at the unfolding drama. I see Morpheus' hair flash Viridian among them and allow myself a covert look to the stormy sky overhead, hoping Vail arrives soon.

Aro takes what seems to be a measured but deep breath, controlling his response as Aliandara looks now to him and him alone.

"The Draconians are monsters, Kairi. Just because you swoon at the sight of any winged immortal doesn't make that untrue. We have all seen first-hand or learned from history what they're capable of. Many of us were there during the war which we thought would surely tear this world apart." He says it with curt formality, but I can tell beneath the shiny veneer of his armour he's more of a monster than any Draconian.

"The Draconians have been ostracised and segregated out of fear, Lord Black. Because King Midas couldn't possibly tolerate what he couldn't fully understand or control." I accuse, watching the heads of Aliandara and the Arabic Equinian male beside her snap around harshly.

"And what would you know of it? You weren't even there." Aro smirks, sure of himself now.

"Neither were you," Asher interjects, face deadpan.

I seize the opportunity.

"The Draconians never wanted that war. They were backed into a corner by three races with more power and greater numbers and then given no choice but to fight their way out. They aren't warmongers. Why can't you see that?" I implore not Aro but the crowd now, my eyes wide as Catticus bares his teeth beside me.

Suddenly, just as I'm feeling confident that I might be able to convince the High Lords and Ladies what I'm saying is true, Ariah lands beside Aro with a light thud, his black fur and orange eyes the polar opposite of the creature beside me.

He growls, and so does Catticus in retort. Aro smiles.

"I suggest you look behind you," he gestures to the skies, and I turn as the crowd raises their heads.

What I find makes my heart fall and then soar as a full fleet of dragons, not seen since days long lost, fly once more over Soleus.

GENEVIEVE

My wings physically throb with the psychic pain being sent down the bond that is tenuously bridging the enormous distance between me and Algoric. I may be getting closer, Ebonara leading the pack of dragons with the directness and focus I have come to expect from Lucien and his dragon partner, but with every mile that closes between us, his pain becomes more my own.

Digging my fingers into the bare skin of Lucien's torso, I bite down hard on my bottom lip, drawing blood and relishing the salty metallic taste as it rolls across my tongue, distracting me from the fact it feels more and more like my wings are being dismantled, each leathery panel sawed mercilessly from its neighbour.

What on earth are they doing to him?

The too-hot breeze, thick with static and the humid weight of un-shed rain, causes my skin to prickle as my heart races, every moment spanning an eternity.

Soleus passes beneath us now, the edge of Oblivion Falls spraying frothed rainbow mist up into the air, offering only a momentary respite from the heat I've been divorced from entirely for over one hundred and fifty years.

The place has not changed, still the same arrogant high turrets built from precarious crystal, as though no one in Aetheria would ever have the strength nor audacity to topple them easier than a stack of cards caught in a hurricane.

I am that hurricane, and today they will fall.

"Are you sure you want to do this? You know once we reveal the truth about the dragons, there's no going back—" Lucien yells over the rushing air that sweeps by us in fluid streams. Rain begins to fall, a single drop hitting the back of my neck and evaporating in a sizzling of steam.

"We are here. I will not turn back now," I respond, the reply more of a bark as it flies out from between my teeth, gritted against the psychic pain that rocks through my bones with increasing intensity.

"I want them dead, Lucien. All of them. Are you ready to defend your people, even if it costs you your life?" I whisper to him as I lean in close to his air, assured by his unfaltering nod and the way his fists tighten on one of the spikes protruding from Ebonara's spine.

"I am ready, and I vow I will do all in my power to avenge Algoric," he promises me.

Leaning around Lucien's shoulder then, I see what he does, and re-alise why he asked the question about me being certain in my decision. Algoric is being held outside The Temple of Zeus on the independent floating island on which it had long ago first materialised, and he is not alone.

There are obvious crowds of people watching on, waiting to see what will become of him, of how their winged angelic heroes will save them from the monsters of their nightmares. The nightmares they had thought long since dead and buried beneath mountains and snow.

I should have known Lord Black would be putting on a show.

"Very well, here we go—" I see his head turn left and then right, scanning the skies and then peering back at the fleet of dragons silhouetted against the dense storm clouds growing only thicker in our wake. On all sides, tiny golden shimmers alert both of us to the presence of Sephilim guards, watching and waiting for the order to put an end to us once and for all.

The rain begins to fall properly then, each drop making a tiny sibilant protest as it hits my scalding skin.

"Land near The Temple, on the edge of the floating isle. I won't be cornered," I hiss against the shell of his ear.

"Genevieve, you're giving me heat rash—" Lucien retorts in a low growl, and I suddenly realise that where my palms are pushing themselves flat into his pectorals, I'm sending an immense burst of heat into the muscle beneath.

"Oh— sorry." I apologise without a second thought, too distracted by the fact that the closer we get to the floating island, the more apparent it is that Algoric is not only captive but in great pain.

We make our final descent, the island becoming more fragile seeming as Ebonara's camouflage retreats entirely and the full scale of her form is revealed against the surrounding trees.

The crowd backs away from the landing dragon, their eyes wide, mouths either open or gnawing on lower lips with anxious fear, lines marring their otherwise perfect faces. Feathers tremble as Ebonara's wings give a final cool beat, the rain coming down harder with each passing second as I feel my hair, which had been still damp from the lake, slicked now fully back against my skull.

I waste no time in dismounting, but as Lucien and I hit the ground with both feet, I feel the presence of guards closing in tighter and tighter, the hairs on the back of my neck prickling to attention.

I ball my fists at my side, unafraid, only desperate to save the one being in this universe who has never failed me.

Algoric—

I say his name in my head, a psychic plea for him to come back to me with something, anything, to prove he's still in there.

Lucien flanks me, wings drawn erect against his spine, shielding me from the rain as I dash around Ebonara's wide gait and over to where my other half has been rendered unable to fly.

I see then the thing of my nightmares and realise that my wings feel like they're being ripped apart because Algoric's wings are in shreds. I want to wail then at the sight of his gentle eyes barred behind a thick crystal-lined muzzle, razors cutting into the delicate span of his wings and drawing thick blood which runs down to the ground in a molten silver that refuses to lose its potent shimmer despite mixing with hot rain.

Lucien is beside me, and then he isn't anymore.

He's turned his back on me and is staring at something else instead.

My instincts whisper, the truth of his distraction a deep knowing in the back of my brain.

The mortal.

I know it's her before I even lay eyes on her sodden and pathetic silhouette, the way that he's enraptured by her without fault every time she is near. She stands between Aro and Lucien now, her spine straight as an iron rod, a purely white Kensari at her side.

But what is she doing here?

This is all because of her.

So why won't she just leave us the hell alone?

Hasn't she done enough?

"Put down your weapons—" Lucien commands, voice ice and steel as it slices clean through the din of the downpour, cutting me deeper than any flesh wound.

I blink once then twice, watching as the man I had always thought of as my brother betrays me in but a moment.

"We don't want a war. Put down your weapons and let Algoric go and we'll be on our way!" he repeats, voice heavy with authority even still. As I take furious steps to close the distance between us, I see that Lord Black, who has not changed at all in the last hundred years except for a haircut, is unmoved.

We don't want a war— That's what Lucien had said, and yet he had brought me and our army here.

He had vowed. He had promised.

"I vow I will do all in my power to avenge Algoric."

Liar.

If it was Ebonara in those chains, he wouldn't be saying that we didn't want a war.

If it was Ebonara in those chains, Lord Aro Black would already be dead.

Steam rises around me as the heat of my rage seeps out of the soles of my shoes and causes the puddle I'm standing in to evaporate with a vicious hiss. I look back over my shoulder to Algoric, to where his eyes, those beautiful mint green pastures in which I have so often sought comfort and sanctuary, tell me the truth.

Even if he does get out of here, he will never fly again.

And a dragon who cannot fly is no longer a dragon. At least not in spirit.

Algoric would rather die than live a life grounded—
But I can't let him go.
Won't let him go.

"Genevieve—" Lucien is staring at me now as is the rest of the crowd. His eyes flash a warning, but I'm beyond caring about what he has to say. He says we don't want a war, but I say that war has never been more inevitable. In fact, I've never been hungrier for anything in my immortal life.

And so, with the Aetherial world watching, I draw my sword— and I charge.

ARO

The events of this afternoon could not have unfolded any more perfectly if I had written the script myself.

High Lady Genevieve Thomas is just as incensed as I had hoped, and if that isn't enough, Lucien's feelings for Kairi could not be more obvious as his motivation for trying to keep the peace. Bringing their entire fleet of dragons was a surprising move, even to me, but I think I had underestimated just how enraged capturing Algoric would make Genevieve.

Apparently, the Draconians have a stronger bond with their companions than even I had anticipated.

High Lady Thomas rushes forward, dressed all in black leather, eyes turning ferally violent as she draws her sword from its sheath and rain flies up as steam beneath her steel toecaps.

Lucien tries to stop her but fails as the sheer fury powering her momentum forces him backwards, his wings spreading wide in jagged leathery parachutes to catch him.

Kairi steps back just in time, but before Genevieve can so much as begin to swing for me, I click my fingers, and several Sephilim guards conduct in beside me, crossing swords before my torso as I pull my own hands behind my spine, watching as Genevieve is restrained and forced to her knees on the damp ground.

I stare down my nose at her, a smile curling the left corner of my lips, smug as I let my wings spread, my shadow growing to loom over her.

"You're making yourself look very foolish, Genevieve," I warn her as Aliandara and Asher step forward to look down at the Draconian High Lady along with me.

"High Lady Thomas, what do you think you are doing?" Aliandara demands, giving me a thrill.

"I think she's attempting to wage war on the Sephilim capital. After all, why turn up armed to the hilt and with a hundred dragons that you had professed were long since dead if you, as Lord DeLaurent claims, *don't want a war—?*" I mock his French accent, hating him more than perhaps I've ever hated anyone.

"We came to retrieve what belongs to us. That's all," Lord DeLaurent speaks now, his fists balling at his side as he steps closer to where Genevieve is held down, albeit not without a fight, by four Sephilim guards. Genevieve struggles against the golden gloves that lie heavy on her shoulders as they begin to bubble at contact with her flesh. Still, the soldiers do as they were trained to do, baring the agony of their armour turning against them and pinning her down without so much as a pained expression. Her submission causes the dragon behind her to rile.

The scaled monster rises on muscular hind legs, causing the razors of each Pandora's Parasol to bite deeper into its wings, blood spurting into the rain.

"And what about what belongs to me? What about how you kidnapped Kairi?" I ask, reminding the two Equinians at my side of the reason why I was drawn to Drakos Vale, to begin with.

Kairi watches us all with wide eyes, her panic so obvious I can practically hear her little racing heart from here.

It makes me want to throttle her now, that innocence I had once found endearing making me unnerved by her misleading fragility, her desire to risk what most mortals see as more precious than anything having caught me off guard completely.

"I chose to leave with Lord DeLaurent. I don't belong to you, and I never did."

She's a loose cannon and far more reckless than I had ever guessed for a mortal without the perk of immortal life as a safety net.

It seems that even after all this time, I can still be surprised.

But I am not one for leaving things to chance, and so I will act now to bring this spectacle to a close in the way I had intended.

"Guards. Kill the dragon." I spit the order, done with the theatrics as the beast lets out a roar thunderous enough to cause the crowd at my spine to visibly flinch.

The dynamic between the woman on her knees in front of me and her companion in chains is practically perfect for my purposes, one feeding off the other and vice versa.

"No," Kairi says as Genevieve continues to struggle harder, her lips pulling back in a snarl that is not in the least bit attractive.

A fresh unit of guards conduct in on either side of me, the clunk of their metal armour relinquishing to gravity ringing in my ears as Kairi steps forward, blocking their path.

If she was an immortal, they would have cut her down without a second thought, but with her obvious vulnerability, her shuddering, limping body, and ragged breath— she's turned her weakness into strength.

I watch her standing, defiant in the rain, her pyjamas sodden, hair ratty and wet, limping, realising I really, truly, underestimated her.

"I won't let you do this. Storm died to stop you from becoming King. To stop you from killing innocent Draconians and their dragons. I won't let her sacrifice be in vain!" she yells, her stand pathetic.

And yet— Aliandara steps forward, and then Asher follows her.

I see Caleb emerge finally from the crowd of Nephilim on my left, the sky crackling with lightning as more of Zeus and Hera's Kindred come to witness the event I've waited a lifetime to initiate.

Hypnos takes her place among the other High Born, facing Kairi as she stands on the spot frozen and shaking, and not looking at all as if they intend to attack her.

Enough.

I let out a sigh, realising that I'm going to have to deal with both my problems myself.

Lucien sees what I'm about to do before I do it, raising a hand and summoning the lightning that's so potent in the surrounding air I can practically swallow it.

"KAIRI, NO!" he bellows, his composed façade shattering. However, it is too late as the bolt of lightning flies from my palm and into the rain-formed rivers mapping the ground between me and the girl who had started all the trouble.

It takes a moment, nothing more, nothing less, to end her protest. To finish the stand which she had bet her fragile mortal state on so completely.

I watch, unphased, as she crumples to the ground, the life gone from her eyes before she reaches the damp stone in a pale blue-ish heap of flesh and bone. The spark within her is snuffed out before it had even begun to burn, as though it were no more than a single match in the great airless void of space.

The guards spring forward then, but I'm faster, and before they can even get within range of Algoric with their long-range crossbows, I've conducted the distance and am straddling the beast's neck and unsheathing the amethyst sword which has been lying in a vault, waiting for this very moment for over one hundred and fifty years.

The muzzled, chained creature doesn't rear now. Instead, it merely sits stone still beneath my weight, waiting for the end to come.

The fight in it has gone, and with it, I feel a little of my joy stolen.

"NO!" Genevieve screams, her pain reigniting my passion.

Soon though, her voice is lost to me as I act with as much haste as I can manage. I waste no time, determinedly raising Midas' amethyst sword and plunging the crystal blade between the dragon's horns and directly down into its skull. I feel the crunch of the bone giving way and the fleshy softness of its brain as the blade sinks into it like fresh souffle.

Something runs up my arms, a shuddering fire that threatens to consume me and then birth me once more from its ashes.

In that moment, I feel like something more powerful and closer to god than Kindred.

My hands cling to the hilt of the sword with all my mustered grit, but the flow of power between myself and the dragon is unbearably intense, so much so that I begin to feel my eyeballs vibrate inside my skull.

After what seems like forever but is more than likely only thirty or so seconds, I'm let go by the clutch of whatever had taken me over.

I hide the limpness of my muscles, the sweat on my brow, using my legs to balance and maintain my majestic posture as I straddle the dying creature.

I look around as I'm left shocked and shaken, but nobody seems to have noticed.

Genevieve's pain-wracked form can be seen sinking to the ground beneath the grips restraining her before falling limp onto the

461

drenched cobbles as the dragon gives a final deep sigh and relinquishes its last breath with an agonised shudder.

The satisfaction I feel is immense, but just as I'm getting to my feet so I can stand atop the corpse of the beast I've dreamed of slaying ever since I knew they existed, my victory is cut short.

A viridian-haired figure walks slowly and carefully from the mass of the crowd, coming to a standstill beside Hypnos.

Even through the rain, I can see what he's holding in his hands, and it fills me with a sense of sudden urgency sharpened by the slightest hint of fear.

He wouldn't?

Would he?

30

TO KILL A MOCKINGBIRD

LUCIEN

THE WORLD AROUND ME erupts into chaos, but all I can see is her.

She's crumpled on the floor, eyes glassy and lifeless, hair strewn back from her like the haphazard roots of a tree that's been felled. At her side, a large white Kensari I've never seen before curls around her body protectively.

I hear a gasp, and before I can process the development, before I can so much as act to stop him, Lord Black is straddling the helpless Algoric, sword raised, eyes desolate as any starless night I've ever seen.

My eyes dart to Genevieve, her struggling form ferally violent as it takes four Sephilim guards to hold her down.

I want to take them out, to free her, but by the time I've worked out how exactly to disarm so many combat-ready assailants, it's already too late.

The rain is hot on my skin, and for a moment, I wish I had the ability to freeze time and not water, the society I have known unravelling fast in every direction like runaway spools of tenuously thin thread, ready to snap clean through.

"NO!" Genevieve's cry is a guttural shattering of the soul made tangible for the rest of us to hear, the dragon who has been her companion for the best part of half a millennium taking a final exhale among the onslaught of the raging storm.

His enormous white head falls to the ground, blood spurting from the head wound and cloaking his face in a fluid silver death shroud made quickly dilute by the falling rain as Aro withdraws the blade.

Starlight spatter peppers the creature's alabaster horns, the purity of his magic tainted by the violence of fear in a way that all can see.

The Draconians wait for my command, hovering far off somewhere beyond the storm clouds, yet I still cannot make a move.

Genevieve slumps onto the ground, forehead pressed against the slick cobbles beneath her, defeated and broken in a way deeper than any of us have ever known.

I drop to my knees too, the vision before me carving my soul hollow in every sense of the word.

In that moment, I cannot help but see the horrendous future that waits for not only Ebonara but every other dragon, echoed in the image of Algoric's stone-cold corpse, his fire finally extinguished, body chilling amongst the weep of the sky and cold steel shackles that had bound his final moments.

I had said we didn't want a war— I had backed away from the thought of standing by Genevieve as she wrought bloodshed and death for not only her dragon but for them all.

Now though, I see that we either fight, or we die. She had been right, and I hadn't listened.

She may never forgive me, and I know deep down that even if she can find it in her to do so, I absolutely and unequivocally do not deserve it.

Amid the stillness that follows the final exhale of the very first dragon, the rain is all that can be heard.

Aro is still, chest rising and falling, face slack and shocked as though he cannot believe what he's just done.

His seeming lack of conviction, his shock at the consequence of his violence, makes me even more furious. Especially when I realise how easily he had snuffed out someone who had seemed so strong, despite her mortality.

Kairi lies dead and cold before me.

I reach out for her, flinching back a little as the Kensari emits a low growl, not knowing what else to do. I meet the cobalt gaze of the lion as I check for a pulse with all the automation of a machine, the stillness of her telling me everything I need to know as the scent of hay and lavender fades slowly, the rain washing her away so easily and leaving me numb as hell.

The Kensari, its wings slick with rain as it tries to cover the body, relinquishes its position begrudgingly, getting to its feet and giving me more space, watching even still as it sits close by.

I lift her then, resting her head against my stomach as I bend, cradling her fragile frame in my arms and rocking back and forth, wishing more than anything I could apologise for not being able to save her.

The fight leaves my body then.

The corpses of two of the most incredible souls I've ever met lie cold on the stone slabs of the courtyard, the onlooking crowd so quiet you could hear a pin drop.

I'm overcome, for what feels like an eternity, by a wave of bottomless nothing, but suddenly the soft steps of Morpheus approaching make me look up, breaking grief's vice grip on my heart.

I see him then, not just his body but what he's feeling, his face sad beyond what I've ever seen it.

In his hands, he holds an enormous white marble dreamcatcher, the gold thread of it glistening dully.

"Lucien—" Aliandara uses my first name, alarming me immensely, but when my gaze moves to hers, I find her eyes are filled with a melancholy brass.

"Do not let her sacrifice be in vain," she whispers, dropping to her knees beside me and loosening my grip from Kairi's shoulders.

She takes her from me, a broken ragdoll of a thing, flesh and bone made limp and lifeless by the simple wave of one man's hand.

I get to my feet, the rain dripping down every plane of my taut frozen muscles before falling in icy rivulets from my bare chest. I clench my fists, straightening, and allow my wings to flare out behind me, the icy white of my poker-straight locks blowing back from my face as a rumble of thunder cracks like a whip on cloud.

I turn to Aro, focusing on his face, narrowing my eyes and setting my sights on the man who seems to hate me for no reason that I can discern.

Enough is enough.

Ebonara. Go! I command her, and she obeys without pause, taking off in the skies to rejoin the others.

Aro rises from the spine of the dead Algoric, facing me with a satisfied smile spreading, feline, across his face. He holds the amethyst sword, slick with dragon blood, and then darts forward.

I meet him in mid-air, finding his eyes not on mine at all as I shoot an ice missile right for his left wing.

Curious, I allow myself to twist back, finding his gaze travelling far beyond my silhouette and toward Morpheus and the dreamcatcher in his hands instead.

What is it I see in his eyes? Is it fear?

The ice missile contacts his feathers, increasing their density, but has little effect other than throwing him slightly off-balance as his sword begins to slice the air, swinging for my throat.

I twist, reaching back for my blade and pulling it high from the sheath strapped between my wings, my steel meeting his crystal in an odd disproportionate clang.

"Does it hurt, Draconian? Losing her twice?" he hisses in my ear as we pass within inches of one another, twisting in a whirlwind of feather and scale in what feels like slow motion.

I scowl, tired of not being in on the secret he so clearly knows and holds close to him as precious treasure as we are blown apart by the force of our disentangling blades.

I see it then as Aro's gaze jumps suddenly back to Morpheus. He's holding the dreamcatcher high to the sky, locating the origin knot, and untying it with a single motion of his elegant fingers.

Aro blanches as though he's physically pained, but quickly recovers, his jaw tensing as he grits his teeth and prepares to strike another blow, this time at my abdomen.

The central weave of the dreamcatcher unravels, moment by moment, passing like scrutinised sand granules through the intensely tiny waist of an hourglass, the string becoming a singular linear golden thread in his fingers.

As it falls away from the white marble frame, the black and white feathers hanging from its lowest curve ruffle as though a large, desperate breath being held has been let loose.

Suddenly, as a warm breeze rushes over my limbs and through my hair, bringing with it the scent of a stormy summer's eve long ago— I know.

"*I can protect you. I promise. I— I love you.*" My own words echo through me like an earthquake, my heart captured in palpitations of seismic proportion.

It rocks me, the memory of Storm's face, of how she had believed in me, of how we had hoped for a better life together. The sparkle in her eyes so like Kairi's that it's hard to believe they are not the same person.

Then I remember how it ended— her final words to me—

"*If you ever loved me, Lucien. If you have any kind of feeling for me, you'll go. Don't make me into a murderer. Please—*"

The force of this stuns me further, causing me to falter and pause at just the wrong critical moment.

The handle of Lord Black's amethyst sword comes up then, smashing into my jaw as he pulls a dagger from the inside of his boot.

In a single swipe and the moment that follows it, I realise he's cut me diagonally and deeply across my torso.

The pain in my body is sharp and complete as muscle is torn and sinew snapped, but nothing compares to the returning memories.

I fall through the sky as I watch the way in which Storm had been ripped from me all those years ago.

I expect Aro to end it all as I hit the hard, wet cobblestones, finding myself half wishing he would hurry up and get it over with as the wind is entirely knocked from my lungs. The pain of everything happening overwhelms my survival instinct entirely with a wave of fatigue deep enough to drown in.

Instead though, as I wait for the final blow and death to come with eyes squeezed shut, I am greeted by a flash of light from beyond the thin pale veils of my closed eyelids.

Blinking, I look up to the sky, into the dark billowing depths of the still-raging storm, seeing only the Heirbound Nephilim's desperation as she had chosen to save Ebonara at the cost of losing her own life, her own freedom. She had died for her beliefs, for her cause, in a way that mirrors the way I had lost my own mortal life.

Again, history has repeated itself, and again, she lies dead after standing for a cause not her own.

Lord Black is gone, and in his wake the High Lords and Ladies of Aetheria stand stone still, silent among the dead, seeing light among the darkness for what feels like the first time in years.

The surrounding crowd watches on, the magic of Morpheus washed clean from them like a terrible baptism.

The mood of the collective becomes obviously sombre and empty as they simply look at one another, eyes filling with tears, mouths falling open, and friends placing arms around one another for comfort.

The truth of this, of all of this, is finally set free, leaving me empty as a cage with the door flung asunder, blowing desolately in the winds of change.

"Is he dead?" The voice comes in a low rumble, echoing out in the darkness of my unconscious mind as I stir reluctantly toward waking.

"I doubt it." I feel myself return to my physical body then as someone delivers a swift kick to my side. My eyes shoot open at the dull yet sizable pain, the rain but a drizzle now as I remain where I had passed out, staring up into the sky.

"Do you mind?" I croak, finding High Lady Aliandara, Morpheus, and the brutish Equinian High Lord, Asher, staring down at me with bored expressions plastered across their pristine faces.

"Actually, yes. Not exactly the ideal moment for a nap is it, Lord DeLaurent?" Aliandara asks, cocking an eyebrow and offering me a hand, her features sharp despite the obvious concern behind the glass of her eyes.

I take the damp palm offered, rising to my feet with a cringe I can't quite hide.

"Such a drama queen, 'tis but a scratch!" Morpheus chuckles though the sound is hollow and uncomfortable as they come.

"I'm reminded why we erected walls now—" I make the joke, trying to join his effort to lighten the mood but feeling my abdomen tearing open as I straighten. Blood trickles down in thick rivers from the gash across my torso, but I am relieved to see it's at least beginning to heal already.

Still stings like a bitch though.

Lord Pidgeon definitely needs to be taken down more than a peg or two.

"Yes, well, despite that, it seems I owe you an apology. And you owe us an explanation, Morpheus." Aliandara gives him a wicked side-eye, the dark locks of her hair crowning her regally as they sit, heavy with rain and braided close around the peak of her skull.

"Me, an apology? From you? Excuse me while I scan the skies for signs of soaring bacon—" I say in a low mumble.

The woman who comes now to Aliandara's side, who I've never seen before, laughs, but Aliandara merely snorts as the laughing woman intertwines their fingers possessively.

"Oh, do shut up, lizard. I mean only that I see now you have been framed for a crime you didn't commit. Though as to why I know this I'm still waiting for Morpheus to explain." She raises her chin, shoulders squaring as she spins on the spot to shoot a haughty expression at the Fae High Lord.

Hypnos wanders now to her mate's side, the both of them straightening their spines beneath the scrutiny of the others. Neve and Ember join them shortly after, their stark contrast lost by the identical sorrow lacing their stares.

The crowd around is still silent, but their attention has wandered from the two corpses and settles instead on the circle of High Born.

As we stand, each of us coiling tighter and tighter together with each passing moment, a ripple of whispered guesses as to what we're saying begins to hum like low-grade static in the background.

"I made a bargain with Lord Black many years ago. I would remove all memories of Storm's disappearance from the general population, and in exchange, he would provide me with the man-power to stop the scourge of barbarian Equinians hunting and slaughtering sacred animals on our land," he retorts, eyes narrowing as their chameleonic depths morph to an aggressively dark gunmetal grey, the spark now dancing within his pupils teasing the ignition of his infamous temper.

"That is highly unethical, to say the least," Aliandara retorts, and I watch Asher's hands ball into fists at his sides. The tattoos of past battles he has won pulsate as his veins bulge close to the surface of his rain-slick skin.

"And the mass slaughter of innocent animals is saint's work I suppose then, is it?" Morpheus counters, his voice rising in pitch so it's almost melodic in its disdain.

I watch the age-old conflict between the two sides predictably build, my jaw tensing as the ebbing of my slashed nerves begins to wear my stamina thin.

I feel her before I see her, Ebonara returning from where she had been circling overhead at my command that she keep her distance. Her landing blows back a scattering of crystal leaves and ripples the puddle by my feet, silencing the crowd and causing the fighting Aristocrats to jump as she lets out an enormous, bone-shaking wail.

Algoric. My brother— What have they done to you?

Her wide eyes are glassy with pain as she moves toward the corpse of the once-mighty dragon, shielding him with her wings.

Her grief hits me then as she feels his cheek with her maw, the cold of him wrong in every way. Her pain makes my own rise in a high wave, once more hitting me upside the head in a way I don't anticipate. As she wails out repeatedly, circling the body, I see soldiers looking uneasily up at her, hands moving toward their weapons.

She senses my unease, and before they can so much as move, she's let out an enormous glacial exhale, turning the water pooling on the ground around the fallen Algoric into vicious blades of ice.

They rise high in a wall of thorny fractal threat, the chill of her rage making even my skin pebble with goosebumps.

"Lord DeLaurent, control that thing—" The other Sephilim High Lord steps forward now, and I wonder why he hasn't stepped up before.

He should have been the first one trying to reign in Lord Black.

"And you are?" I ask, unimpressed by his lack of courage.

His dark eyes sparkle among the shadows of his equally dark skin, but I can see it's not from malice but from anxiety instead.

"High Lord Caleb Abara," he answers, the name not quite carrying the same weight as it should.

His inaction reveals his shame.

"If you want my dragon to behave, then I suggest you control your men," I counter, my eyes finding Genevieve lying motionless on the floor in the rain, surrounded even still by guards. "All of them," I add, nodding toward the cluster of golden bodies that fence in her defeated form, though why they continue to bother is unclear.

She barely seems conscious, let alone a threat.

"Stand down," Lord Abara barks, his silver-tipped wings rising slightly as though this might give him more authority over his soldiers.

I want to shake my head at the ridiculousness of his attempt at superiority, but I steel myself instead, realising now why Lord Black has managed to get away with so much right under his nose.

As the soldiers re-sheath their swords and step back, their poses visibly relax.

However, their comfort is obviously physical alone, as all eyes turn to the frozen wall that's been built between them and the closest threat to their immortality, anxiety palpable.

As everything comes to an abrupt cease-fire, an empty yet terrifying place of limbo among immortal enemies, Genevieve begins to stir.

GENEVIEVE

I can feel their eyes on me as I lay face down on the wet cobblestone. My insides have become incinerated by the sheer fact that the bond between myself and Algoric has been brutally uprooted and set ablaze by his sacrifice, decimating everything we had once shared.

I don't care that they're watching, only that they might perceive me as weak in my grief. I am not weak, but now stronger than I have ever been, my fury more absolute, my resolve more obsidian and steel than ever before as I realise the truth.

Nothing in this world is sacred. Nothing is just. Nothing is fair.

No goddess or god cares what happens to their so-called chosen Kindred. Nor does the universe care about them.

Are we blessed?

Cursed more like.

Existence seems merely to be one long drawn-out torture session with small glimpses of light to be viewed from behind a barred window by the starving, abused, and desperate.

I can't help but wonder, forehead pressed against the chill stone: What's the point?

I sense Lucien's approach, the absolute rage I feel toward him born not only from the fact that I have loved him like a brother but because I know he loves me like a sister too, and yet still, he has betrayed me with his hesitancy.

"Genevieve—" His voice is there, right beside me, but I am not home.

Not that girl he knows any longer.

Instead, I have become merely a sum of several parts designed to bring order and death to a world with respect for neither.

I am no High Lady but have been forged into a harbinger instead.

Growling, I bring my hands to my breasts and push up off the cobbles, rain sizzling against my spine. I glower, feral, from beneath the crimson-stained veil of my white hair, baring my teeth at the guards who had held me down while my soul was ripped in half.

They back away, gloves misshapen and melted from my resistance, and as I turn, I feel my body cooled slightly by a sudden pulse of wind so familiar I could have made it myself.

High Lord Gage Lee lands with his dragon, Aqua, just beyond the edge of the ice wall separating me from the lifeless body of my soulmate.

"Lucien, stay back—" Gage calls as he leaps from Aqua's spine, diving through the air toward us.

He can sense my rage, my violent urges about to be made real by the blood coursing molten, and too close to the surface, through my veins.

He lands between Lucien and me, the precision of his descent enviable even for a seasoned aerialist, let alone someone who is new to the skies.

"Genevieve, it's alright—" Gage promises, but his words fall on deaf ears.

"No, it isn't. How can you say that?" I snap at him, tearing my eyes from Lucien's pathetic expression and lasering in on the empathetic lines marring Gage's forehead as he frowns, literally feeling my pain.

"Alright. It isn't. Nothing is. Nothing is alright. But you need to say goodbye." He offers me an outstretched hand, and I feel the eyes of the other High Born burning into me like white-hot irons as they brand me with their labels.

Monster.

Beast.

Murderer.

Perhaps then they will become the authors of their very own self-fulfilling prophecies.

Ask and you shall receive.

"Genevieve, don't allow this to become about them. Let it be about Algoric, let it be about honouring his sacrifice." Gage is forceful as he catches my gaze with his warm brown eyes, his hand outstretched even still, a lifeline amid the storm.

Something inside of me breaks then, like the single remaining chain between Algoric and me, the one I've been refusing to sever by accepting he's gone, snaps as though it were no more than a single thread.

Emotional hell is unleashed from beyond.

I begin to tremble, the violent urges in me dissipating like steam as my temper cools and all I'm left with is cold nothingness.

I take Gage's hand, and though I know my skin is burning his, he doesn't flinch.

Eyes continue to scrutinise as he leads me forward, the chill coming off Ebonara's towering ice shards coating me like a thick glacial syrup as it seeps through the air. High Lord Lee doesn't falter in his step. He only supports me, not walking too fast or too slow, and lets me set the pace.

I come face to face with my reflection in the pristine facets of ice, but the spark of recognition isn't findable within the cavernous darkness of my eyes, nor do I care to see the lifelessness in my face.

Having had enough, I raise my hand, placing it on the ice and letting my natural heat do the rest.

After only a few minutes, there's a passage wide enough to slip through, giving us some semblance of privacy for what comes next.

Ebonara is curled beside Algoric's still corpse like a mother cat caging in her kittens protectively. His face is still confined by the enormous metal muzzle lined in the same crystal that they'd used to contain my powers.

My heart breaks at the sight of his eyes, closed as though he's asleep, his wings battered and bloody, limp at his sides.

Ebonara whines as I approach, the sound guttural and chilling, but nothing chills me quite as much as the fact that Algoric's body is cold, a state he had never even been close to while breathing.

I take my hands to the metal binding his jaws shut, careful not to touch the crystal and focusing solely on the weakest parts.

I work furiously, pouring grief into each action as I single-handedly dismantle the muzzle.

Gage watches on, silent, his face twisted to be practically unrecognisable by the intensity of the emotions I am feeling but refuse to process.

With the high-pitched ring of steel hitting stone, the muzzle falls slowly away from Algoric's face, each piece having to be melted by my touch in exactly the right place to allow it to come free without the kyanite interfering.

The sound is more than I can bear, and as I slip down from his neck, I see now his lifeless face in unobscured clarity for the first time.

A tear leaks down my face, sizzling on my skin as a chill runs gracelessly up my spine.

I'm sorry I couldn't save you, I think, closing my eyes and placing a warm hand on the scale of his cheek.

You were more than any of us deserved.

I have never felt so powerless, not even as a mortal whore who was beaten and broken more times than she knew how to count.

Gage lets me mourn, lets me cry, and stands taking all the emotion I cannot bear. Lucien keeps his distance, and nobody breaches the wall of ice forged by Ebonara.

I don't want to leave, but when the night starts to fall and the rain ceases hitting the ground entirely, Gage lifts me up in his arms, my body limp and defeated.

I don't have any fight left in me to protest.

Without a word, he cleaves me from the corpse of my other half, sweeping over the wall of ice with silent air-bound grace, soaring over Lucien and the dead body of the mortal he had destroyed me for.

I don't feel rage anymore, don't feel pain. Instead, I feel nothing, curling into myself and turning my back on the sky.

Silently, gravely, Gage mounts Aqua with me still in his arms and then sends the signal that the rest of the Draconians should follow us home.

I let myself fall into nothingness, now indifferent and unreachable to all, before we even break the clouds.

31

GENESIS

LUCIEN

I WATCH, STUNNED, AS Gage carries Genevieve off into the dusk. Ebonara looks wistfully after the others of her kind as their silhouettes fade like smoke, but stays, diligent as ever. The gust created by her immense wingspan ruffles feather and coiffed hair as she lands on the outside of the ice wall, keeping a close eye on me.

"It seems you have bridges to repair with your fellow High Born," Asher states gravely, eyes serious beneath his heavy brow.

I don't respond, hating him for stating something so obvious, falling to my knees where Kairi's body lies now among the full skirts of the woman who had returned her home. The white-winged lion is lying at her side, chin resting on its enormous paws, cobalt eyes sad.

"It is time for us to be on our way—" Aliandara's voice is cold at my spine even to my frozen disposition.

I don't turn to face her, eyes fixed on the glassy emptiness of Kairi's once sparkling periwinkle irises, anger at the unjust way she had been ripped from her life rising in my throat like heavy bile.

"So, what— you just leave now? She died to stop that lunatic becoming King and lording power over all of you, and now you walk away and leave her dead body here? What, is it just over now? Bam, sorry you're dead. Too bad? Thanks for your sacrifice. Aren't you even going to see her buried? Don't you owe her that much basic respect at least?" The fury is immediately hot in my veins at the casual way in which the other High Lords and Ladies simply sweep her under the rug, an unfortunate mortal casualty in a war for the benefit of those far more important, far more superior.

I can't bear to turn, to look at them, for fear I'll freeze every single one of them solid, matching their flesh to the consistency of their souls.

I have never wanted to be one of them less. Never felt less blessed.

It feels, instead of a possession of power, a lack. That we had lost, along with our human bodies, our humanity as well.

That was why I loved her. Still love her.

Because she was everything wonderful about what it meant to be human, and despite the pain and the struggle she met in every waking hour, she shone.

She shone not in spite of it but because of it, and it made her even more beautiful.

"Vail, thank you for bringing me the dream catcher. You changed the tide on the direction this thing was heading," Morpheus admits, breaking the awkward silence that has left me swimming in the tumultuous depths of my own thoughts.

Vail looks up at the Fae High Lord, eyes narrowing. She looks at me, too, and then sighs, staring down at Kairi and stroking her hair with gentle fingertips.

"I didn't do it for you, Morpheus. I did it for her," she says bluntly, her eyes not leaving Kairi's face for a second.

Aliandara speaks up then, changing the subject.

"Lord DeLaurent, you forget yourself. This is not our business. Her fate, and the responsibility of what happens next, lies solely with the Nephilim. It would not be appropriate for the rest of us to become involved," she declares, not waiting for my reply as she turns, lacing her arm with her fellow High Lady's and beginning to stride back toward the white marble eaves of the temple.

It wouldn't be appropriate to act as if you give a damn about the girl who has saved your arrogant ass? Really Aliandara?

The words infuriate me, but I can't bring myself to run after her, not as Vail gestures for a group of whispering Nephilim on the edge of the crowd to come forward.

"We need to take her to the Temple of Hera— to the baths," she says to a woman with tanned skin and sharp features. The accent that falls from her lips as she replies is Spanish, I believe.

"Vail, you have never performed rebirthing rites before— are you sure?" she queries, but Vail only gives her a steely glare.

"I want to do this, Trinity," she insists, all softness in her petite and genteel features vanishing as if they were no more than a façade all along. Her pink-tipped feathers vibrate, damp from the rain, shaking with the weight of the situation she's been presented with.

"Very well, we will prepare the waters," one of the other more curvaceous Nephilim promises, touching the sharp edge of Trinity's shoulder with gentle fingers.

The huddle of winged women turn promptly on the balls of their high heels and, within a few moments and several blinding flashes of light, are gone.

Vail looks at me, lips twisting into an uncomfortable grimace.

"If you're thinking about telling me to leave, you have another thing coming," I bite out, jaw tensing.

Ebonara rises behind me, straightening and making her full height known, sensing my defensiveness and shifting from one clawed foot to another.

Vail's eyes lift to the dragon watching us with intense suspicion.

She swallows, eyes catching mine and ensnaring them with the blunt seriousness of her gaze.

"You can come and wait outside. But you can't bring—" She gestures up to Ebonara.

"Her," I finish for her, and she nods.

"It's a delicate process, and I can assure you a— dragon has no reason to be anywhere near it. I shouldn't even be letting a Draconian into the temple. I'm not exactly a High Lady," she reminds me, making me wonder.

Why aren't there any High Ladies?

Storm had been the last— but surely, there was more than one.

"Come on. Let's get her indoors," Vail says with insistence, passing the dead weight of her fragile skull into my hands and getting to her feet as she brushes down the pale silk of her skirts.

Hoisting Kairi fully into my arms, I look at the disappearing figures of the other High Born as they make their exit on the far end of the courtyard, my hatred for them intensifying.

Vail takes my arm, but before I can ask her where I'm flying, the lightning has struck and receded, blinding me and leaving a heavy ringing in my ears.

The courtyard of The Temple of Zeus has disappeared quicker than I'm able to process, the world around me turning rose-hued, the air thick, warm, and fragrant with lilies.

Beside me, an enormous statue of the Goddess to whom the temple belongs looms, staring down at me with a powerful stone gaze that lacks any and all feminine softness.

I shiver, knowing instinctually that I do not belong here.

"Follow me," Vail instructs, wasting no time as she storms off ahead, her heels clicking sharply against the rose quartz underfoot.

I do as she asks, Kairi's skull dangling precariously over my arm, her sodden hair leaving a trail of chill rain droplets in our wake.

Vail leads me down a set of shallow steps and into a labyrinth of rose quartz corridors that feel increasingly claustrophobic as the scent of lilies becomes unbearably concentrated. Golden filigree coats the walls, swirling into peacocks, lionesses, and feathers interspersed with pomegranates and water lilies upon their leafy pads. The metalwork is exquisite, and I'm grateful I have something to look at that isn't the corpse of the girl I've spent the last week trying to keep alive.

Finally, Vail comes to a halt, opening a pale wooden door.

From within, a flock of Nephilim rushes forward toward us. Warm air like that of a sauna rushes at me from behind them, settling over my skin and making me uncomfortable at the stark difference between the heat in the air and the cold of Kairi's skin. They take her from my arms despite my reluctance to let her go, my hesitancy causing several of them to give me sympathetic glances.

"You can come no further," Vail announces without pause, blocking the doorway with the large circumference of her skirt.

"What—what do I do now?" I ask her, and with that, her eyes glisten slightly with the soft light of kindness.

"You may wait out in the main entrance if you would like—" She pauses then, looking at me thoughtfully and with a certain measure of sadness. "I can come and get you once we're finished if you would like to see her. To say goodbye—" she adds, her tone definite and painful in its connotations.

She's not wrong, and I cannot expect her to bend centuries of tradition. She has not the power, nor the influence to make such a decision.

So, it settles over me then, the truth of what Kairi returning to her Kindred state will mean.

No matter what happens here, whether Kairi is reborn a Nephilim or not, I will not be included in her future.

Draconians and Nephilim just don't end up together. So, she will be within touching distance, but not mine to possess.

She will marry a Sephilim if Lord Black can ever be disposed of, and if she returns as she did before, her husband will be the new King of Aetheria.

Still, though, I cannot bring myself to walk away. Not after everything.

I might not be able to possess her entirely, but I know she will always own my heart.

"Very well—" I reply, placing my hands in my riding pants pockets. "I will
wait."

KAIRI

For a long time, there is nothing, and I am left floating in shock and darkness.

I had been alive, and then in a single minute motion of Aro's wrist, I had felt the chains binding me to my mortal coil snap without warning, my heart faltering to a standstill within the cage of my ribs.

For a long time, there is nothing.

But then, suddenly, out of the darkness, like a star born from a void, there is something.

A speck of light that grows larger and larger, causing me to hold a ghostly hand to my brow, shielding my face from the pure unbridled glare.

Dying is nothing like I expect— over and above anything, it's so damn quiet.

The world forms around me like plumes of ink suspended in water, curling and coiling in on itself in a spectrum of indescribably otherworldly colour and light as it had done as I watched Storm's memories return. Beneath my phantasmal soles, clouds materialise, the sky overhead bleeding into existence as though someone has spilt star-speckled paint over the blank canvas of this world.

Mist chills my ankles, the air around me aromatic in a way so complex I can discern no individual scent.

The light is undeniably stark, grainy even, and everything is bright, vital— everything is beautiful.

"Kairi, I thought you'd never arrive." The dreamlike tone startles me, causing me to turn radically on the spot, face falling slack.

Hypnos stands, the cotton softness of her hair falling in smoke-like wisps down over her shoulders.

"I died. I'm dead, right?" I stutter, my voice feeling foreign in my mouth, the taste of my words too sweet and too bitter all at once. They form an oxymoronic elixir of hope and despair as I hang between one life that I love and another I have long since been destined to return to.

"I wish I could say no," Hypnos replies, words hypnotic as they travel through the shimmering air between us in spirals and whirls of genteel sound.

The sky overhead soars on endlessly, the world below falling away.

Hypnos holds out an elegant hand, her nails lacquered the baby blue of a too-delicate eggshell.

"It's alright. It's going to be alright—" I whisper to myself, bringing a hand to rest over my heart. It lies, still, in my chest beneath.

"Come on. They're waiting." Hypnos prompts me, the opalescent shimmer of her pure white gown falling through the colours of the rainbow effortlessly as water falls through thirsty cupped hands.

"They?" I ask her, taking her hand in mine and feeling the softness of her skin. It shocks me, the scent of lavender and white musk dancing around her form and capturing me in its calming balletic allure.

"Indeed. Quite unprecedented you should know." She doesn't give any more detail or information, merely leading me to the edge of the heavily misted platform on which we stand.

With a wave of her hand, a staircase of fluffy, white, sparkling cloud forms. She steps aside, gesturing for me to climb to the lofty heights obscured by a thick blanket of cloud that has materialised overhead in a spectrum spanning from deep indigo to brightest magenta.

"Go on— I can't follow you any further. I just thought you might like to see a friendly face." She encourages me with a sad smile, and so I reluctantly drop her hand and begin my ascent.

On the third step up, I look back over my shoulder to thank her, but she's already gone.

I look back up at the steep incline of the staircase, an exhale escaping my lips in something like a sigh as I begin my journey toward the top.

I feel no pain as I climb, no burning calves, nor throbbing ankles, so I simply enjoy the view until I'm so high above where I began that the thick blanket of cloud swallows me completely.

I break through the other side in a few moments, trusting my feet to feel and guide me up the remaining stairs.

When the cloud recedes, I'm left breathless by the sight that greets me.

An endless pristine blanket of purple and pink cloud beneath the now bright lemon of the star-peppered sky. The sun isn't blue but an ever-shifting prism of rainbow hues, kind of like an opal, overhead.

Silhouetted by its insane beauty and pure light, four feminine figures stand staring at me with silent beckoning, compelling me forward toward their lusciously curvaceous outlines.

I tread, looking down at myself with all the self-consciousness of someone who was until very recently mortal. My body is covered by a simple Grecian gown in ivory silk, golden clasps that look like the sun cinching the fabric upon my shoulder and then hip in an asymmetrical style. I can't help but find it flattering.

"Kairi. You made it."

Her voice is like the embrace of a mother I never knew. She steps forward, the light's rainbow fractals revealing her incandescence in a moment of divine yet deeply personal revelation.

Caramel locks glisten with a pinkish rose gold hue, her enormous lilac eyes evidence of a depth of character that has seen millennia of pain, if not more. Her shoulders are rounded by a lavender silk cloak that joins around her throat with a rose gold lily clasp, the gown beneath a waterfall sheath of the same fluid silk until it pools discreetly around her ankles.

"Hera—" I breathe, knowing her immediately. She's no stranger, but instead an old friend it feels like I've been missing forever.

"I wish we had time for long reunions, Hera, but as it is, our time is short. Zeus will discover our absence soon." The sharp voice of a pale-faced woman hits me before I fully see her. The pinkish hue of her eyes, the determined tilt of her mouth, and the pink spattering of sugary freckles across her nose all come to give a kind of fragility to the woman's appearance. Though, as so many of the women I've met recently, beneath the layers of silver silk and pink sapphires shrouding her, I doubt she's as helpless as she seems.

"Yes, Hecate is right."

As Hera nods in agreement, her face becomes determined in its pristine and definite structure. Then, the other two women step forward to stand beside her, looking at me with interest.

"This is Aphrodite and Nemesis," Hera introduces them, and I frown.

What are they doing here?

"Hello." I wave, shy as I push my hair back behind my ear and fidget gawkily on the clouds of this otherworldly and elegant setting. I feel far too conspicuous as they stare at me.

"Again, no time for introductions. Hera—" Nemesis warns her this time, the galaxies behind her irises glinting dangerously. Her dark hair shimmers as the diamonds threaded through each lock catch the light like fallen stars, her head shaking with brusque impatience.

"I don't understand. I exposed Aro. Did I do something wrong?" I ask, wondering suddenly if they're angry at me. Did I ruin their plans?

"No child. You did everything— perfectly. Fortunately, this is the easy part—" Hera sighs, and the goddess Aphrodite places a hand on the woman's shoulder. Her irises tinge pink as she gazes at me, the white gold of her hair gleaming wildly as her tea-length beige skirt flounces around her calves.

"Hera, you're scaring the mortal. Speak plainly," Nemesis warns her again, the undertone of her voice a siren of impending disaster in itself.

"Kairi. War is coming. And not between the Aetherial Kindred. A recent meeting with a certain God of The Underworld has revealed that ancient pieces of a game, much bigger than any of us can comprehend, have been once again put into motion. You know why the Aetherial Kindred exist, don't you?" Hera asks me, her brows arching. The tiny motion causes shivers to run up my spine.

"Um— I think so." I blush deep crimson, feeling like a child even still.

"You are there to protect the border of The Higher Plains from succumbing to outside threats." Aphrodite's voice is harp-like in its endlessly harmonic rhythm, her lips curling into a small smile.

Hecate speaks again, her face harsh now as she brushes her hair behind one shoulder and looks down her nose at me.

Goddess she's tall, Is all she can think.

"The shape of the Aetherial army is currently divided and weak. We need something to bridge the gaps between the Kindred races. We need them to come together as we always intended. To fight for us and for the order of the Universe that we help maintain." Hecate explains, and I raise my head now, tightening my lips.

"You want the Draconians and Sephilim to work together? Are you insane?" I ask them, being franker than I probably should be.

"No. No, Kairi. We want you to kill them. All of them. No alliance can exist while the Sephilim still roam the Aetherial skies," Hera expresses, the wicked glint in her eye undeniable.

So, I guess the myths about her marriage really are true.

"So— what do you expect me to do? I'm just one person," I ask, never having felt more inadequate. Though, they only collectively smile in a way that honestly makes me uneasy as all hell.

"You're not just anybody, Kairi. We have, and will continue to make sure of this," Hera assures me, reaching out and brushing my bare shoulder with her fingertips.

I open my mouth, my eyes narrowing and my heart becoming heavy in its stillness as something suddenly occurs to me.

"Did you— did you make me sick?" I accuse her, unable to believe the words are even coming out of my mouth.

"What do you do if you want to make a diamond?" Hera asks, and Aphrodite interrupts.

"Other than pinching a Mermaid and making them cry—" she adds, but I don't get the joke.

"Yes, other than that." Hera rolls her eyes a little.

I shrug, biting down on my bottom lip.

"You apply extreme pressure to the ordinary. Your disease is what made you empathetic enough and gave you an open enough mind to give the Draconians a chance," Hera explains, and suddenly I'm furious.

"So, you did that to me? You made me suffer like that? For your own ends?" I ball my fists at my side, straightening my spine.

"No. Not directly. The universe decided on your physical form, on your genetic defects, I just specified what I needed you to be when I directed your soul to a suitable new home. When I plucked Storm's soul from The Nether after her death, I used potent magics to return her to Earth with the intention of preparing you for this moment. She needed to be strong— you needed to be strong— to survive what is to come in me giving you both a second chance. I needed you to

483

find a lifetime's worth of strength in a handful of years and with no memories of who you had been. But I didn't know how the magics would achieve that. You'll need everything inside of you if you hope to win the challenges ahead of you, Kairi. I know what I'm asking isn't easy, but I believe you are the only one who has a chance at succeeding."

I suppose a mortal's suffering matters little to her in the scale of the universe she keeps talking about, but it doesn't negate the fact I've lived years in agony. She sees the look on my face and bends at the knee.

Taking my hands, the goddess Hera falls before me and looks up into my face.

"Kairi, you would not be the remarkable person you are without the pain you have suffered. No matter your feeling concerning how it came about, the circumstances made you who you are, and who you are is one of a kind. Extraordinary, even to a Goddess like me." She's complimenting me, and I feel for a moment just as I had when Aro was speaking to me.

Is she just as two-faced as he was, or is the cause she's sacrificed my comfort for even greater than the suffering of any one person?

"So, what? I just do this for you, and then what— you have your army— but what do I have? I lost my family— and Lucien. I can never be with him. Not now," I exclaim, unable to keep the bitterness from my voice.

"The mortal in you is showing, girl—" Nemesis growls slightly, and I feel my knees quake.

"I cannot deny you are right to feel used. But if you were not the person for the job, you would not be questioning the likes of us, even in the face of death. You're the one, Kairi. The one to save Aetheria. If you won't do it for us, or the universe, then find your own reason." Her words echo in my head then, and I realise that I have a better reason than I think to change the way Aetheria runs.

Lucien.

Hadn't we dreamed of this exactly that night beneath the glow of Nirvana?

I clench my jaw, nodding then.

"You're right. Lucien is my reason. I want to improve things for him. I love him." I say it to them before I've ever said it to him, realising that regardless of the bigger picture, I had wanted to change things in Aetheria before I knew there was a greater agenda. The task has always called to something deep in me, even before I knew why.

I have breathed the air and seen the sights, embraced the culture and met the people.

And I know they deserve better than the oppression of Sephilim rule. They deserve more.

"You aren't alone in this either, we are going to give you a few gifts to help you along the way," Aphrodite assures me.

"Time is running out, and we must return to The Higher Plains. Are you ready to be reborn?" Hera asks me, and I nod, feeling my heart, heavy and motionless in my ribcage.

"I am," I breathe in deep, ready to get my wings. Ready to soar. To bring change and to breathe life into the vision Lucien and I had shared for the realm I'd so fallen in love with.

"Come then. Let us embrace you— let us bless you."

Hera places a kiss on my cheek, and the other Goddesses encircle me, joining hands.

As their arms close around me and I feel a power I've long since been missing coursing into my skin, the world goes dark.

Not, however, before Hera whispers one last thing in my ear.

Her demand sends chills up my spine.

"Never forget, Kairi, who you are."

32

THE UNBEARABLE LIGHTNESS OF BEING

KAIRI

MY LASHES QUAKE UPON my cheeks, my spine flexing beneath me as unfamiliar feathers caress my bare skin and cup my shoulders, an Aetherial embrace I feel as though I've been waiting for my entire life.

I stir, the scent of lilies overwhelming, opening my eyes to find the world in a new and spectacular glory overhead.

I see the aether that swirls in each of the individual wind currents, as slight as they may be, each grain of the magical glitter turning from scarlet through to indigo and back again in mere seconds. I take it all in, my lips spreading wide into a smile of delight at how everything suddenly has a crystal clarity I never could have imagined.

"Oh, thank the Goddess—" I hear Vail's voice, but it's somehow different, more nuanced, not as though her voice has changed at all, but my hearing perceives more layers to her tone and pitch. I sit up slowly, expecting pain, the wings beneath me tugging as I realise my lower body is pinning their tips to the rose quartz altar.

Vail looks at me, her eyes filling fast with tears. Each one catches the light like a crystal prism as it falls delicately from her lashes, this simple movement more beautiful than anything my mortal eyes could have perceived.

"I thought I'd gone and killed you!" She claps her hands over her silken rosy lips in shock, the twang of her southern accent having never sounded more welcome or akin to a banjo than in this moment.

"I'm—" My voice sounds unfamiliar too, now a mix of the classic American I'm used to with an undertone of proper nineteenth-century English that I seem to have somehow adopted from Storm.

"You're beautiful as a southern sunset," Vail breathes, pacing now around the altar and examining me on all sides.

My hair has gotten longer, matching what I assume is the length that all Nephilim are reborn with, falling in caramel silken waves over my breasts and down to my waist.

I'm wearing the same white silk gown I had been when talking to the Goddesses, and as I twist, feeling each and every feather crushed painlessly beneath the weight of my body, I fling my legs off the side of the altar, finding my feet bare beneath the skirt.

Vail takes my hand, helping me down from the cool stone, her eyes still leaking tears.

"I'd never done a rebirthing ritual before, not ever. I thought I'd gone and screwed it up— you took so long— longer than anyone I've ever known. I thought you were lost to us." She hiccups, choking slightly on her own words.

The ease with which I'm standing has my body relaxing in a way utterly foreign. My heart pounds again at last, and I pull her toward me, crushing her in a painless hug that feels like flying.

"You saved me, Vail. Thank you—" I breathe, able only to raise my voice above a whisper.

"No— you— you went and exposed Lord Black. After all this time. We owe you everything, you hear?" She pushes me back from her, looking down at me with the sincerest eyes I've ever seen.

Well— almost ever.

Lucien.

His name is like a siren call inside me, and Vail senses my urgency as I search for the door, my wings dropping from the table so I feel their full weight for the first time.

I expect them to hurt me as everything has done for so long, but instead, I merely feel the strength of the newly woven muscle that connects them to my shoulder blades, supporting them, strong.

"Where is he?" I demand, stepping down several shallow steps leading to a walkway that separates two steaming pools of perfumed water, the hot mist rising and filling the room with its aromatic lull. Waterlilies bob on the crystal-clear pools, undulating gently as my steps cause ripples to quake across the water's thin reflective surfaces.

"He's been waiting outside for three days. He wouldn't leave—" she admits, and I grin to myself then, my body feeling my own in a way it hasn't for longer than I can remember. Even as a mortal in Aetheria, I hadn't felt like this— so indestructible— so free.

With the ease of a creature that is featherlight and nothing more, I take off across the quartz floor, tearing open the door and finding myself in a corridor made entirely of the same pinkish stone.

"Kairi— wait!" Vail calls after me, but I'm not listening, letting my feet carry me along with my brand new wings as though I'd never been anything but Nephilim.

The corridors all look the same, but somehow, I feel like I've been here before, and make no wrong turns on my journey back to him.

I burst into the main hall of, I assume, The Temple of Hera, finding the goddess I had been speaking with what could have been only moments ago before me in a larger-than-life sculpture. At her feet, propped by the end of her left foot, Lucien stands, snoozing upright in crumpled trousers, his chest bare and scarred by an enormous diagonal slash.

His face is everything I've been searching for, even sleeping not so peacefully, and so I let my wings spread behind me as I run, sprinting faster and faster, my feet slapping painlessly against the stone underfoot.

The distance between us closes more quickly than I ever could have attempted before, and before he's even opened his eyes, I've thrown my arms around his neck and am crushing him in the largest hug I can manage. The scent of mint and wintergreen overwhelms me, and I feel him startle awake as my scent reaches him too. I realise now that he must have had similar heightened senses all this time and wonder how I must have looked to him before— how I must have smelled.

"Is this real?" he whispers into my hair, his voice cracking as he inhales me deeply and wraps his arms around me.

"Yes. I'm here. I remember it all. I remember, Lucien! Everything. You— and me— what we did. I remember—" I'm breathless as the words rush from my lips and into his ear, my clutch on him only tightening with each passing second.

"You're so beautiful—" he says, pushing me away from him so I can look into his eyes.

I stare into them, their sky-like depth and the endless possibilities dancing beneath the surface, transfixed by the soul I have crossed both centuries and dimensions to find once more, my emotion swelling so intensely I wonder if I might explode.

"And so are you—" I cock my head, looking at his face with my new eyes, hearing his voice for the first time, and touching his skin with an angel's hands.

He's stunning.

More so than I could have ever appreciated before, the lines and symmetry of his face are nothing if not divine. His eyes, the depth of them more than I could have perceived, his hair flawlessly straight and luminously bright as it falls over his shoulders in bedraggled strands.

I feel his heart racing wildly against my palm as I press it to his pectoral, feel the slightest shudder of his wings and notice the slight pulsations of the veins running through each leathery panel.

"I'll just— give you two a minute then—" I hear Vail's uncomfortable confession as she finally catches up to me, panting as she rounds the corner and finds us wrapped up in one another, but I don't care.

She couldn't pull me from Lucien if she tried.

Not after everything we've been through to get here.

"You have her eyes again—" Lucien comments, and I frown a little at that, realising I haven't yet seen myself.

How different am I now? Does he think me beautiful because I'm more Storm than Kairi?

More her than who I have so recently become?

"Is that— is that why you think I'm beautiful? Because I look like Storm?" I ask him, swallowing my fear and leaning into the unknown territory of his truth.

"No— No, Kairi. You have her eyes, but you're *you*. She never had your—your—" He traces my cheek with his finger, staring at me with wide eyes like I'm the world's most incredible work of art.

"Shhh." I place my finger to his lips, seeing his slight blush as he flounders to put words to his feelings.

I tear my gaze from his then, feeling attention on my back that isn't wanted skirting around the edges of our imagined intimacy.

Turning, I find several guards stiffening along the walls of the temple, their hands lingering over their swords, watching him with suspicious eyes.

Really? It was a Sephilim who ended my life. Idiots.

I cuss them internally, grabbing Lucien's hand in mine and pulling him after me as I lead us down the enormous length of the main hall toward the grandiose arch leading outside. Weak sunshine beckons ahead, but I can't help but look back over my shoulder and beyond the unfamiliar curve of my wing, catching Lucien's elated expression as I lead him into the light.

The details of the temple are intricate on all sides as we pass, and in any other circumstance, I'd be mesmerised, especially with my new clarity of sight, but now— with him, the only thing I want to stare at is his face, and no architecture, even Aetherial, could possibly compare.

White peacocks roam the grounds of the temple isle, their silver and gold embellished tail feathers quivering as they take cocky steps across the courtyard while I look out over the horizon, finding Oblivion Falls and The Solis Castra silhouetted ominously to the east.

At the very end of the aisle where the land beneath my feet falls away and an intricate golden balustrade has been erected to segregate the steep drop-off from the rest of the pristinely kept landscaping, an enormous rectangular reflecting pool sits, sunken into the floor. Swans with silver beaks glide effortlessly upon its unwrinkled surface as Lucien and I approach, hand in hand, the sun of dawn baptising us both in a violet glow.

I step forward gingerly, letting Lucien's hand fall from mine, approaching the edge with my breath held captive in my lungs. Reaching the pool's periphery, I peer over into the surface and find my reflection.

It takes my breath away.

My skin is poreless now, lashes longer than humanly possible framing my vivid lilac irises. My hair glows slightly as does my face, the rounds of my cheeks perfectly symmetrical as they're brought into contrast with my darker hair. Lucien steps up behind me, taking in every inch of me as he lays a comforting hand on my lower back, his fingers falling casually through my silken locks.

"What do you think?" he asks me, a small smile playing on his lips.

"I think— I can't believe that's me," I breathe, nervous as he stares now at my reflection too.

I lean self-consciously on an old mortal behaviour, pushing my hair behind my ear.

Lucien looks at me with an odd expression then, turning my head gently with his fingers so he can examine my profile.

"Did you know about this?" he asks me, biting his bottom lip.

"Know about what?" I demand, wondering if there's something wrong with me.

"Your ears— look—" he turns my head, sweeping my long hair back from the nape of my neck and directing me to lean over the reflecting pool.

As I do, I startle a little, my hands jumping up to the shell of my ears, which now sport Fae points.

"But— I don't understand. I'm a Nephilim, not a Fae," I exclaim, anxiety immediately churning in my stomach.

"Did you see her when you died?" he asks me in a low whisper, pulling me straight to look at him and brushing my hair forward so it covers my odd new feature.

"Well yes. I saw Hera, and Aphrodite, and Nemesis, and Hecate—" I list them off, and Lucien's eyes widen.

"Kairi— that's— not normal," he admits, looking concerned. I blink a few times, my mouth becoming arid.

As my mind is beginning to fill up with more questions, Vail's unwelcome voice breaks the thick silence between us as she appears at the top of the temple's rose quartz stairs.

"Kairi. I have to take you to the Fledgling Finishing School. They're expecting us—" she warns me, looking truly sad as she does.

"Two more minutes?" I plead with her, and she shakes her head but relinquishes, turning to go back inside.

"Kairi, don't tell anyone about this— not if you don't have to. Okay?" Lucien says, and I frown but nod. He's right. I am new here and having the body parts of other Kindred isn't going to make assimilating any easier.

"Okay— I guess I can hide it with my hair." I shrug, and suddenly I feel like bursting into tears because I know what comes next.

"Kairi— I'm sorry I couldn't save you—" Lucien apologises, taking my hands in his and looking down at his feet.

"But Lucien, you did save me. You reminded me of who I am and helped me discover who I was. I owe you everything—" I confess, and he nods, eyes desolate as they search my face.

"When I saw you with her, with Storm— all I wanted was for it to be me. For it to be me kissing you," I confess in a rush of emotion I can no longer hold back.

He moves forward then, pulling me into his chest, his hand swooping along my jawline. The chill of his body makes the flush heat of mine grow only warmer. Looking down into my eyes, he lifts my lips to his, and at long last— I'm his.

He kisses me with all the longing of the man who had lost Storm as well as with the loving desperation of the man who is about to let me walk away into a brand new life where he cannot follow.

My body explodes with the sensation of him, the taste of mint tantalising me and fogging my thoughts. I push myself as close to him as I can, kissing him back ferociously, my heart pounding so hard I fear it might fly out of my chest as the world around us dissolves on a heady tide of long lost and unrequited love, finally brought out into the light.

The kiss ends, his touch setting me on fire and leaving every inch of my newly sensitized skin aching for more.

"Was it everything you hoped it would be?" he whispers in my ear, kissing me on the cheek and stepping back.

My eyes brim with tears, my heart still thudding so loudly my blood is roaring in my ears.

"More—" I say the only word I can think of, not only because it was truly more than I'd ever thought anyone could make me feel, but also because more is all I truly want.

"I don't think I can walk away from you—" I whisper to him, tears falling down my cheeks.

"Then I will do it, for both of us. Just know— you're breaking my heart, Kairi Freemont, but only because it is yours to break."

He kisses me on the forehead, and I close my eyes, inhaling the scent of him for the last time.

Then, he's gone, and when I open my eyes, still sobbing silently, the last glimpse I get of the man who has stolen my heart is the shadow of his jagged beautiful wingspan disappearing over the horizon.

33

THE STAND

GENEVIEVE

THE COLD DOESN'T TOUCH me, for I am not at home within this skin any longer.

Instead, as I soar the skies trying to escape my own barren emptiness at the loss of Algoric, I feel an undeniable and inescapable scalding heat running rampant beneath my flesh, fuelled purely by rage.

I keep going through the same repetitive thought cycle, each completed journey only stoking the flames of my outrage so they lick to greater heights, so they reach further for something fitting to consume. Something with feathers and fine embroidered suits.

But there is nothing here, only snow that falls too gently in the chill air that follows its own currents on every side, the clouds seeming empty and frail just like everything else. The moonlight illuminates the truth of it all, the seeming impermanence of even immortality.

They had killed Algoric.

Algoric.

The sheer concept of such a seemingly immovable and immortal beast simply ceasing to exist shatters me entirely, seeming utterly unnatural, if not impossible.

And yet it is so because of Lord Aro Black, because he is afraid, and scared little men cannot help but destroy everything they touch.

Maybe he finally feels safe now.

I hope so.

It'll be all the more delicious when I tear him to shreds with my bare hands and burn the arrogance right out of him starting with his smug smile.

I see it then, the clearing where Algoric and I had begun, all those years ago as I had been flying over a far more primitive Drakos Vale, hunting for my next meal. I had seen him fall, sheltered by a molten crust as he tumbled through the skies like a falling star.

I thought he was. A gift from the heavens, from Hecate.

How could I have known that his very existence would be the one thing the other Kindred could not make peace with, could not swallow?

Because they are weak, because they are mortals trapped in immortal bodies, because everything they touch must be tamed.

I begin my descent through the swirling columns of puffed snowflakes, my heart lodging itself firmly in my throat like a stone as I remember taking this same plummeting path toward what I had thought was a celestial gift from the Goddess.

Maybe it was— but then, why bring them into a world like this?

I land amid the silence of the clearing, the trees dressed in pristine white robes of snow, each leaf crystallised in ice. The snow beneath my bare feet sizzles, and the simple white nightgown Gage had helped me into before leaving me to rest presses flush against my skin, the breeze catching it so it clings to all my jagged edges.

The trees watch me as I take a step, my foot sinking through the blanket of fast-melting snow beneath the sole of my foot and finding the frozen earth below, eyes fixed on the place where the dragon's egg had crash-landed into my life almost half a millennium ago.

Has it been that long?

The scalding white marble of the shell had cracked right before my eyes then, the veins of mint green running through the stone a preview of the majesty that was to burst from deep within its molten core.

Draconians now, younger Draconians will never understand the fear I had felt knowing that the tiny vulnerable creature inside depended entirely on me, and I had no idea about how to care for it. I had learned everything by trial and error, catching meat as I assumed that the dragon would be a carnivore, only to discover it gnawing on the remains of its own eggshell. It was only then that I knew I had to start searching for sustenance underground, and that was what led me to the underground labyrinth of caves that run the length of the continent at varying depths.

The people of Drakos Vale owe more to Algoric than they realise. Because of him, I had found the strength to survive alone. Because

494

of him, I discovered the caves that allowed the dragons to thrive in secret after their banishment.

Because of him, future Draconians had known how to care for their dragons, how to raise them.

Because of him, they had someone to learn how to ride from, someone to look to for answers to the hundreds of questions dragon rearing naturally produced.

And yet, Lucien—

My fists ball without conscious thought, teeth gritting and lips pulling back in a vicious snarl. The water beneath my feet hisses as it reaches boiling point along with my temper.

We don't want a war—

His confession echoes out through my mind, stabbing me in the heart a million times over, each syllable a slash at the tether of our friendship.

I had thought of him as family, as the closest thing I would ever have to a brother, and he had traded my happiness for her.

My thoughts are interrupted as the silence is broken. A flash of lightning causes me to lunge into a defensive stance, my wings flaring out behind me.

Good. I could use a fair fight. I think, expecting to see Lord Aro Black appear right before my eyes.

But then, as the lightning recedes. I see it isn't him at all.

It's someone far less important, and yet no less malignant.

"You better get off my continent before I rip your throat out, boy—" I growl at the redheaded soldier still dressed in his sickly gold armour, sans helmet. His red hair blows across his forehead, peppered by falling snowflakes that catch in his feathered locks. My eyes narrow.

"High Lady Thomas." He falls to one knee, bowing his head.

I take several strides forward, tired of Sephilim insolence, bending so I might wrap my fingers around his windpipe.

Tightening my grip, I lift him from the ground with one arm, allowing my skin to burn his, the scent of chargrilled flesh making me salivate as his feet dangle precariously in front of my knees.

He looks down at me, his wings stone still, wincing in pain, gasping for air, but he doesn't struggle.

Instead, he lets me brand him as I stare into his eyes and wish him dead over and over.

As I see he's about to lose consciousness, I release him, unsure why.

He slumps to the snow, clutching his throat and allowing the icy blanket beneath him to cool the burn I'd made.

I hope it scars.

"You'd better have one hell of a good reason for being here. In fact, I'd quite like to kill you, so you'd better give me one now before I decide to finish what I've started and throttle you to death," I bark, turning from him and taking a few measured steps, trying to clear my thoughts and look at the situation objectively.

He chokes, coughing, the skin around his throat bubbling and burning in the shape of a handprint closing, vicelike, over his Adam's apple.

I look at him; my eyes dead as he struggles to resume his position on one knee, body shaking with pain.

"I came to vow my service to you," he says, voice barely a croak. I throw my head back then and laugh, the sound hollow and terrifying even to me as it bounces from the skeletal white of the surrounding trees. The absurdity of his claim tickles something deep inside me, which, though entirely changed, I'd thought had died along with Algoric.

"I'm serious," he continues, coughing again, "What we did to you— what he did to you— it was barbaric," he confesses, looking up into my eyes now.

They're sparkling with tears, a nice touch indeed.

"So nice of you to notice," I say, debating on kicking him in the balls as he kneels with them dangling in his armoured cup, vulnerable, above the snow.

"I want to help you. To serve you. I want to atone for what I've done," he explains, swallowing with a wince.

I give him a disgusted look, eyes still unfeeling to his cause.

"You can never atone for what you've done. Never make up for what you've taken from me, Sephilim. If you feel the guilt of your own innate violence, then it is no problem of mine. I hope you choke on it!" I spit at him, and it takes everything inside of me not to kill him where he's kneeling, to take all the grief and violence and pain, and end him with it.

"What about if I could help you? Lord Black trusts me, I could give you information— I could help you put an end to him, to this, once and for all."

The presented notion intrigues me then, the face of Lord Black's smug smile as he buried the amethyst sword deep into Algoric's brain branded into me and smouldering even still.

"And how can I possibly trust you— what's your name?" I click my fingers, tired suddenly and wanting to do nothing more than fly back to my bed and curl up in my silk sheets alone.

"Leo. Leo Stephen Bond," he says, getting to his feet now.

I glare at his face and then at the still-fresh burn on his throat.

Even I cannot deny the kid's got balls.

"Well Leo, why should I trust you?" I ask him again, blinking coldly as snowflakes settle on my lashes and my gown stirs around my thighs.

"I know you probably know nothing of this— but I was killed in a war to stop a man very similar to Lord Black. He gave big speeches and grew fear towards a particular religion that people considered to be 'other' from themselves. I've seen what comes of that kind of hate, and it is death and pain and loss. Nothing is so black and white in this life, and anyone who tries to make it so is dangerous. This place— Aetheria, it's supposed to be a reward for a life well-lived. But I see it quickly becoming an oppressive hell, no different than the camps that mass executed millions of people back in the mortal world. Lord Black wants to exterminate the Draconians because he fears you, and he believes that fear will unite the rest of us behind him. That is all." He sighs loudly, watching me with utter and undiluted scrutiny as he draws breath to speak again. "I cannot see you have done anything to deserve this, and as someone who has died once fighting off a dictatorship, I'm hesitant to let myself fall into another." His plea isn't what I expect. It isn't based on some morally ambiguous sense of right and wrong.

He's seen this before, and he isn't fooled.

Interesting.

I let my posture relax as he stands before me, a little breathless, a little afraid, but standing nonetheless, and nod slowly without diminishing the intensity of my gaze.

"Very well. You will bring me information you think I can use. But I will not be meeting you anywhere within secure Draconian premises. I will meet you here, and I will bring an accompanying guard. You will come alone. Do not be mistaken, Leo; I do not trust you. But my hatred for Lord Black goes beyond my disdain for you. And to be clear, I do hate you, and I have not forgiven you," I say, the finality of my decision feeling oddly right in my chest as I make it. It does not fill the hole

Algoric has left behind, but it opens a channel for me to utilise in my revenge.

He looks thoughtful then, holding out a hand for me to shake.

I pause and then move forward, taking his fingers in mine. I crush them with all the strength I can muster, letting the heat of my skin burn into him once more, watching as he looks me in the eye and takes it.

LUCIEN

As I step over the threshold of my lakeside house, I deflate almost entirely.

I hadn't wanted to come straight home, I had wanted to apologise to Genevieve, but when I got there, Gage had told me she didn't want to see anyone. He then proceeded to personally advise me to back off for a while. My heart, already broken from leaving Kairi after seeing her made immortal, is bruised further by the absence of my fellow Draconian High Born, but I can't say I blame her.

I stand in the hallway for a little while, dripping melted snow onto the wooden floor, unsure of what to do with myself.

Do I just— what, return to everyday life now? After everything that has happened in the last week?

It feels impossible, but nonetheless, I find my wary footsteps sounding out in an echo as they trudge up the stairs, my eyes darting immediately to the cracked door of Kairi's room.

Kairi's room.

That's what it has become, and she'd only stayed in it for a matter of days.

I shrug off the memory of her looking at me from beyond the doorway, pushing my bedroom door open with haste and stepping inside.

My bedroom has a glass turret, which while not the most practical for keeping the heat in, not that this has never been an issue for me, allows me the pleasure of stargazing from my bed. The snow isn't entirely covering the apex right now though it will be soon, and so a single shard of light falls from the moon overhead, bathing the room in a ghostly glow.

Usually, Kaiden comes by and cleans it off daily, but with the recent summons to all our warriors for the charge on Soleus, I guess he hasn't gotten around to it. Not that I mind. The stars would only remind me of her awestruck face anyway.

The memories are unbearable now, more so than they had been as they first hit me, my brain marinating in a concoction of unrequited desire, grief, and the new pain of walking away from her yet again. I see how I had once fantasised about bringing her back here, to my bed, about giving myself to her in a way I have never before managed with anyone else. I had thought we could look at the stars, curled up together among dull candlelight, my fingers trailing through the luscious caramel curls of her hair while I inhaled the scent of lavender and fresh hay.

I break then, taking a few slow steps and sinking onto my mattress as I lean over the edge of the bed, putting my head in my hands and letting out a stifled sob that's been waiting to break like a heavy raincloud.

I cry, as un-masculine and as pathetic as it might seem, everything suddenly so overwhelming I want to hit something.

Perching on the edge of my bed, I let the tears fall for everything I've lost and for everything I've found again but is just ever so slightly out of reach.

I sit for a good long time, bathed in the cold moonlight, alone in the shadows of my turreted sleeping quarters, eyes closed as I allow myself to feel the pure scale of everything that's happened hit me like a freight train.

Then, though, I see it.

On the nightstand, a worn hard copy of Pride and Prejudice, by Jane Austen, sits.

I see the scene unfold then. The first time I had seen her enraptured, and the first time I had been enraptured in turn, coming to me with a painful and devastating crystalline quality I can't escape.

I recall her jumping to her feet, embarrassed by her uniqueness, and dropping the book with shame. The way it had tumbled, pages fluttering like butterfly wings against her enormous violet skirt before hitting the floor. That book falling was a small event, tiny, but the effects of it, of our first touch, had rippled outwards, the fluttering of creased pages causing a storm over one hundred and fifty years later.

I remember the way Lord Black looked at her with utter disdain, mocking her gentle heart and hungry imagination.

I remember the feeling I had as he put his arm around her, claiming her as his.

And then I know.

I can't do it.

Can't let her belong to another man.

She is mine, and I will die before I let her go.

34

THE SHINING

ARO

THE GOLDEN SANDS OF The Blazen Plains stir, endlessly shifting in the chill of the desert night beneath a golden half-moon larger than you'll find anywhere else in Aetheria. The sound of heavy breathing Pegasi, paired with the low mumble of Equinian soldiers exchanging war stories, is all that can be heard above the crackling flame of the camp's enormous central hearth as it spits embers into the surrounding dark.

As I perch on the piece of sun-bleached driftwood, sand worming its way stealthily into every nook and cranny of my armour, I stare at the orange-tinted amethyst of the sword, holding it up to the firelight and wondering, silent as I feel the undeniable thrum of new power flowing through my veins.

I flex my fingers, passing the golden hilt of the weapon from one palm to another, still missing some vital link.

Then, out of the darkness surrounding Chief Archard's camp like a shroud, a bulky figure appears, face obscured by flimsy muslin that is elaborately draped over him. The profile of the figure isn't familiar but is well muscled and, more noticeably, hasn't got wings.

"You've seen better days—" the familiar voice calls from beneath the veil of shadow obscuring his face, and I pause, heart pounding.

Is it a sign?

That after such an eventful day, a true son of Zeus suddenly appears.

I can't believe it isn't at least a coincidence.

"Hercules," I bow my head in respect for the Demi-God as he moves into the tent made of animal hides and constructed from similar driftwood to that on which I've been sitting, pulling back his hood to reveal a halo of golden feathered locks.

By contrast, inky black strands of hair fall loose across my broad forehead, my body tightening as I straighten to my full height.

His face is divine without a doubt as he steps closer and I reacquaint myself with his features, the symmetry of his cheekbones and jawline, the striking blue of his eyes and the incredible muscles that rope around his arms and legs. I wonder how he's not married by now because I honestly can't imagine what kind of woman wouldn't want him and, of course, the privilege that comes with him.

"How are you feeling? You've been rather busy, haven't you?" he asks me with a small smirk, gesturing for me to sit back down as he eyes the sword in my palm.

"I suppose you could say that," I mutter, returning to perch on the thick bleached log behind me as I look into the face of Zeus's son with rapt attention.

"You made quite the show today. One might say you were almost dragon-esque in your speed towards the end there—" Hercules delivers the compliment, and I blush a little, tearing my gaze from his now and looking into the curling tongues of flame, trying not to seem too pleased. Then, as I'm looking down at the sword still lying cold and still in my hand, something clicks.

"Dragon-esque?" I say it, half in thought, and Hercules merely titters, shaking his head as if I'm nothing more than a child.

I suppose to him I probably am.

"Are you saying that surge I felt— are you saying I absorbed the dragon's power when I killed him?" I demand, staring in wonder at the sword.

Hercules gives a slow clap, sitting down on the ground and crossing his legs beneath him, his skin made fiery by the light of the hearth.

"That's the funny thing about light magic. Whereas dark magic seeks to divide as many times as possible, light magic is the opposite. It seeks its own kind to make it stronger. Interesting that—" he muses, examining his knuckles as he cracks them with a brutish yet casual jerk of his hand.

"But— other dragons have been killed before. This never happened to any of those soldiers— we would have known." I frown, utterly perplexed by what he's telling me.

He rolls his eyes, gesturing to my hands.

No, not my hands, *the blade within them.*

"The amethyst—" I say, holding up the blade and examining it with a new appreciation.

"Indeed. Midas was thinking along the right lines before he died. He had realised that different crystals can be used to either store or transfer magic. I believe it was around the final years of his reign that the Sephilim began using amethysts to light their rooms?" He's smug as if I'm dumb and he's smart, and he is thoroughly enjoying proving it.

Son of Zeus or not, his cockiness irks me, and yet I cull my urge to hit him, wanting to know more.

"So that's how he discovered kyanite would hold the heat magics of High Lady Thomas?" I add and Hercules nods, his luscious blonde hair shimmering a warm gold like the sand that surrounds us endlessly on all sides.

"So— what if I could make more swords like this? I could take more power?" I ask him, and he smiles, again, smugly.

"I suppose. You and your army," he adds, hammering the point home with a subtle toss of his fringe.

I think then about sourcing the material, about the way in which the Sephilim could not have been more perfectly situated if they had tried. Is it fate? That Soleus is so completely rich in natural crystal and ore?

I doubt it.

"That's why he gave us Soleus, isn't it? He knew— he knew one day we'd have to fight for our natural place as rulers of the rest— Zeus knew." I say it, completely convinced of my theory as Hercules gives only the slightest of non-committal nods as if he's breaking some kind of rule by even speaking with me.

My mind is whirring, the sword being passed from hand to hand with new and frantic energy.

I focus then, looking at it with intensity, finding the metal warming considerably beneath my touch.

Perhaps with more practice, the power that had once belonged to the very first dragon might be mine instead.

I look up, only to find Hercules on his feet and exiting the tent, returning into the darkness of the shifting dunes from when he came.

"Hey, where are you going?" I call, wanting to ask him more questions even still.

"None of your concern, Lord Black. I have family business to attend," he replies, and then his silhouette is swallowed by the darkness beyond the fireplace that shrouds the sky even more completely after his Conduction cleaves the shadow momentarily in two.

I stare into it long after he's gone, feeling for the Draconian fire running wild and new in my veins.

EPILOGUE

<u>KAIRI</u>

THE INSIDE OF THE Finishing School for Fledgling Ladies is exactly what you would expect. High domed ceilings of rose quartz and its matching clear equivalent tower overhead, running parallel to the wide-open corridors filled with the scent of a million and one floral blooms melding together. The immediate sound which greets you as you enter through the high silver doors is of stiletto heels ringing out in a jarring pitch against the crystal floors, and the next thing that strikes you is the way in which the ladies within its high walls move with almost no other sound.

I am given my uniform, a simple white corseted gown with silver feathers embroidered on a short, but still undeniably over the top, puddle train, by a Nephilim who cannot stop staring at me and looks as though she wants to ask me a million questions but won't let herself. The long hallways we walk as she leads me to my dormitory, which she informs me are currently empty but that I will be sharing with two other girls, are filled with silver bird cages overflowing with flowers. I find this an oddly morose image for an academy of winged women.

The Nephilim, who cannot stop staring at me, doesn't give up even as she opens the door and tells me that I will be expected to get an early night in preparation for my first lessons in proper flight techniques tomorrow morning. She hands me an elaborately embossed class schedule, her fingers trembling as they brush mine like I may very well eat her face off or something.

Maybe it's the fact that I had spent time with the Draconians or maybe that my sudden appearance had been so closely tied to the reappearance of the dragons.

Either way, her staring is making me uncomfortable, so as I close the doors to my dormitory, I breathe a quick sigh of relief before turning to face the room where I'll be staying.

Dormitory is not the word I'd use to describe the place.

Not even close.

Dormitory has me thinking of wooden bunk beds and matching footlockers crammed end to end in a long narrow room, but what I'm faced with is a room shaped like a three-leafed clover and made entirely from rose quartz to match the rest of the building. Each bulge of the clover shape holds a queen-sized four-poster with thick velvet drapes for privacy, a similar drape having been provided to separate each section from the central part of the room. Here, white couches with gilded golden feet sit surrounding an angel aura crystal coffee table scattered with a few books that look nothing short of instructional manuals of Nephilim etiquette, and a vase holding a bunch of amethyst violets.

In fact, when I check, that's exactly what they are, and from the spines, I find that all three volumes on the tabletop are the same book, a copy for each resident I suppose.

Striding past the couches, I take the bed furthest to the left as my own, not wanting to be directly opposite the door. Drawing the white velvet partition across the golden rail on which it hangs, I segregate myself from the rest of the room, suddenly feeling more overwhelmed than I can handle.

I sit down on the edge of the bed with its lilac silk sheets, wings ruffling in an unsightly fashion as I sit on them, unused to having such enormous limbs attached to my shoulder blades. Their weight becomes more evident to me as I look around the space that is now mine with my flawless new vision, everything too beautiful to bear.

A tear falls from my cheek then, not for Lucien as so many before, but for the mortal girl I had shed to become who I am now.

I miss my family, but I cannot go back.

On the far side of the bed, a white vanity sits holding make-up, hairbrushes, and perfumes.

I swing my legs up onto the mattress and climb over.

Hopping down off the opposite side of the mattress, I sit down on the stool of the vanity, beside which is a glass door that probably leads to a small balcony or terrace.

I stare into the mirror, into an exact and unwavering reflection of my new face, turning my head sideways and brushing my hair back so I might peak at the Fae points of my ears.

What on earth— I wonder but simply sigh, shaking my head and letting the tears fall freely as I try to recognise the face in front of me.

Looking down at my wrist, I see it now. The Heirbound mark made real. But this time— this time, it's different. Where before there was merely a three-spoked, tentacled star, this time the icon has a swirling filigree design topping it. The lines whirl across my skin, and I trace them, seeing the new outline of the crown for the very first time.

What does that mean? I wonder, swallowing back more tears.

Whatever it is, it can't be good.

I had wanted this, wanted this world, this life— and now, it feels little more than a beautiful cage.

I know I'm just overwhelmed, just freaking out because of so much radical change, but at this moment, everything feels like it's in free fall, and I have no idea how to fly yet.

As I'm tracing the outline of the divine mark on my wrist over and over with my index finger, a sudden high-pitched bang causes me to jump from the stool, my skirts and wings ruffling loudly in alarm.

I wait a few seconds, wondering if I'm imagining things, and then there's another acute bang.

This time, however, I catch the source.

Someone is throwing rocks against my window.

Heart pounding, I take a step forward gingerly, pushing down on the silver handle of the glass door and stepping out into the warm summer night air. The doorway leads onto a balcony, and I wonder momentarily if I'm about to be kidnapped or killed.

Looking around, nerves in tatters, I hear it then, the laugh that fills me with stronger emotion than I can describe.

He ripples into existence, in mid-air, Ebonara's camouflage receding and exposing him. He's wearing a navy-blue suit that's embroidered with silver stars and moons, the same one he had been wearing the first night he kissed Storm.

I blink once then twice.

Maybe I'm dreaming.

I take a few steps toward the silver railing of the small private balcony, and he edges his partner forward with gentle half-beats of her wings. She comes close, and I reach out, touching her scaled cheek with all the tenderness I can't help but feel when looking into her enormous soulful eyes.

"Lucien— what are you doing here?" I breathe, lips still plump from his kiss.

"I came to take you on a real date, *Madame*." He bows a little from behind Ebonara's neck, still straddling her effortlessly despite his change in balance.

"But— but that's not allowed. It's against the rules. It's not— It's not—" I stutter, and he rolls his eyes.

"I've decided, as of late, I don't much care for rules," he admits, lips pulling back in a wide and heart-stopping smile. Ebonara sidles up to the balcony railing, and he holds out a hand.

I clamber up the silver metal vines of the railing without thought, but as I top them and stand there in bare feet, my balance newly superhuman, I stop.

"Lucien— what about—" I begin, but he shakes his head, reaching sideways and gesturing for me to give him my hand.

As I stand atop the balcony, my wings help me with a natural instinct I'm grateful for, the summer breeze tickling my ankles as I teeter.

"Kairi, do you trust me?" he asks, reminding me so much of the night he had swept me from the Solis Castra that I feel my knees physically weaken with the answer I know now is true without a doubt.

"Never—" I tease, blushing and giving him a sly smile.

He rises then from the back of his dragon mistress, taking my hand while hovering with gentle wing beats and helping me atop her by taking me into his arms, lifting me off the balcony railing and holding me close to him as though I'm more precious than anything.

The smell of wintergreen and mint envelopes me, and then, I'm truly home.

"Well good," he smiles as he sits me upright on Ebonara's dark scaled back, his hands winding around my waist and pulling my wings and spine flush to his chest.

He kisses the back of my neck then, pushing my warm locks aside, and whispers, "You never had very good judgement anyway."

I laugh as he nuzzles me, and I feel his smile pressing into my spine.

Then, under a sinking Aetherial moon, as we rush dangerously fast towards the cusp of a new and violet dawn, he sweeps me off into the sky and into a fantasy.

ACKNOWLEDGEMENTS

When I first put together the premise for this book, it seemed pretty simple. Having a main character with the very condition that I myself suffer from should have been one of the easiest writes of my career.

Wrong.

This book has been the most challenging novel I've written so far, without a doubt. This book, while being a story of a journey in its own right, also represents my own journey in coming fully to terms with *my* diagnosis and has shown me things about myself and my character that I never expected.

This book is personal in other ways too, like in the way that it embodies so many children who have both inspired me, and made me smile. One character in particular, Paisley, was inspired by Paisley Rae Vanek who was tragically taken from us back in 2018, at the age of only 3 years old. It is my hope that by bringing her to life in Aetheria, I might give her family, and her new little sister, a picture of her that will live on forever. I also want to shout out to my nephew Leo, Everly, Kaiden, Gage Lee, Landon John, Holden Matthew, Vail, and Jace, who are amazing kids that I have enjoyed knowing via social media through their incredible parents. The mischief of a child is pure magic, and as you all know, I love magic.

Anyway, that's it from me. A huge thanks to my tribe as always, Mark, Leeah, Jenna, Dawn, Winters, Katherine, my family and my unbeatably awesome editor Jaimie Cordall.

I hope you find the magic and the strength I did within these pages! Happy reading!

ALSO BY

QUEENS OF FANTASY SHORTS AND NOVELLAS

TIDAL KISS SHORTS AND NOVELLAS
Beyond The Shallows
Waiting For Gideon
Vexed

ASHEN TOUCH SHORTS AND NOVELLAS
Death Blooms
A Touch Of Smoke And Snow

AETHERIAL EMBRACE SHORTS AND NOVELLAS
Ambrosia Nights

EXTRAS
Infiniflash Fiction Volume One

OTHER GENRES FROM KRISTY NICOLLE

DYSTOPIAN ROMANCE:
Something Blue- A Dystopian Romance Standalone

POETRY:
I Am Arcana- A Tarot Inspired Poetry Collection
Starsong- A Zodiac Inspired Poetry Collection

To keep up to date with the latest release dates, spin offs, and exclusive content, head on over to kristynicolle.com

ABOUT THE AUTHOR

30-Year-Old British Author of Award-Winning Indie Fantasy Romance, Kristy Nicolle is escaping the pain of Ehlers Danlos Syndrome by crafting intricate and immersive worlds for her readers. She lives in Norwich, Norfolk, with her long-time life partner Mark, and can often be found writing in her local coffee shop - *Botany and Beans*, with a peppermint mocha, surrounded by beloved witchy paraphernalia and plants she knows only too well she'd kill at home.

FOLLOW KRISTY NICOLLE ON SOCIAL MEDIA OR FIND HER AT KRISTYNICOLLE.COM

www.ingramcontent.com/pod-product-compliance
Lightning Source LLC
Chambersburg PA
CBHW021836010726
47493CB00005B/1425